New, unabridged edition

ASAIL ON A SILVER SEA ...

"How can such beauty be treacherous?" Kit asked, his voice as liquid as the element upon which they sailed.

Miranda wheeled, aware of a rarer phenomenon at her back than any that worried her over the water. Each distant wave crested into the night in glittering silver spray as the phenomenon seeped across the horizon. The moonlight and the sea magic that matched it made him ghostly.

Their mutual resolves were suddenly beaten thin, perhaps because they had always been a false facade, like sheet metal over lead. Like silver plating. It was a moment for melting; she ran into his instantly encircling arms like molten metal. He tilted up her moon-white face and burnished it with his lips. The phosphorescence painted her silver-cool, but her flesh was paradoxically warm, like his own, and he reminted her features to the shape of his mouth as he traced a lover's infinite variety of routes across them.

It was cool passion they forged between them, it would dissipate in lingering kisses that did not demand satisfaction, it would lock words within lips and fold hearts away in secret velvet boxes. It would be a phenomenon as easy to deny in daylight as the mysterious silver sea.

Miranda suddenly slid away from him. "Kit, listen," she breathed, no endearment, no intimacy on her mind. "Mortal danger awaits out there. Heed it."

"deftly illuminates the intricacies of relationships and a young woman's rite of passage."
—Jennifer Roberson, author, LADY OF THE FOREST

CATNAP and PUSSYFOOT:
Midnight Louie Mysteries

The tomcat detective introduced in the Las Vegas romances,
CRYSTAL DAYS and CRYSTAL NIGHTS,
returns!

"glitters and snaps like the town that inspired it."

—Nora Roberts,
NY Times bestselling author of
DIVINE EVIL

"Midnight Louie . . . captured my imagination
from the first page . . . sure to be a hit."

—Sandra Brown,
NY Times bestselling author of
FRENCH SILK

All now available from Tor Books

Tor books by Carole Nelson Douglas

MYSTERY

Irene Adler Adventures:
Good Night, Mr. Holmes
Good Morning, Irene
Irene at Large
Irene's Last Waltz

Midnight Louie Mysteries:
Catnap
Pussyfoot

HISTORICAL ROMANCE

Amberleigh*
Lady Rogue*

SCIENCE FICTION

Probe*
Counterprobe*

FANTASY

Taliswoman:
Cup of Clay
Seed Upon the Wind

Sword and Circlet:
Keepers of Edanvant
Heir of Rengarth
Seven of Swords

*also mystery

FAIR WIND, FIERY STAR

FIERY STAR

CAROLE
NELSON
DOUGLAS

TOR

A TOM DOHERTY ASSOCIATES BOOK
NEW YORK

FAIR WIND, FIERY STAR

Cover art by Deborah Chabrian

A Tor Book
Published by Tom Doherty Associates, Inc.
175 Fifth Avenue
New York, N.Y. 10010

Tor® is a registered trademark of Tom Doherty Associates, Inc.

ISBN: 0-812-52266-4

First edition: November 1993

Printed in the United States of America

0 9 8 7 6 5 4 3 2 1

For the original Iron Maiden,
and all those who came before and after her

SONG

Give me more love, or more disdain;
The torrid or the frozen zone
Bring equal ease unto my pain;
The temperate affords me none:
Either extreme, of love or hate,
Is sweeter than a calm estate.

Give me a storm; if it be love,
Like Danae in that golden shower,
I swim in pleasure, if it prove
Disdain, that torrent will devour
My vulture hopes; and he's possessed
Of heaven that's but from hell released.
Then crown my joys or cure my pain;
Give me more love or more disdain.

—Thomas Carew, 1640

FAIR WIND, FIERY STAR

BOOK ONE:

The Salamander

Though I am young, and cannot tell
Either what Death or Love is well
Yet I have heard they both bear darts,
And both do aim at human hearts.
                    —Ben Jonson, 1641

Chapter One

*I*t was a bonnie blue sky the British merchant ship speared with her tall, white-sheeted masts. Meg MacTavish, dour Scotswoman that she was, stood on deck for the first time in days, her narrow face still a tinge green.

Home. London-bound. 'Twas but a few days' sail now—no more tossing on tumultuous waves that even on fine days rose as high as the half-timbering on a London town house. Her hazel eyes slipped from dizzying contemplation of the masts swaying above to "her lass" along the rail.

The breeze whipped back Miranda's long yellow curls, and her smooth young face bloomed like an Aberdeen rose above her starched white-lace collar. An ember of satisfaction warmed Meg MacTavish's flinty Highland heart. A struggle she'd had getting the girl into her stiff traveling gown. James Hathaway had been a willful man, Lord help him; he had ever let his lass run wild . . . and his lad.

Hathaway's death, hard as the thought was, had come in the very slice of time. A Barbados plantation was no place to rear a boy and girl from a family rich in good name and worldly wealth, merely because their father was a misanthrope who distrusted all but sophisticated virtues.

Meg MacTavish's stern eyes paused on the boy at the gunwale, a stripling of fifteen still slightly shorter than his willowy seventeen-year-old sister. A pretty pair they made, their fair heads bent over the rail to watch the froth thrown up by the bow. More often than not, Hathaway had let the lass scamper about the island in breeches and shirt like young Harry . . . trailing after that sly Spanish "tutor" of the lad's, Francisco. Meg MacTavish's face curdled like sour milk.

She could still picture the man's sleek olive face. Smooth, that one, like an oiled rapier, and handsome, Meg MacTavish could give the Devil his due. Best he had been left behind to settle plantation affairs.

Och, but now she had her lass well dressed and bound away from such wildness. James Hathaway had always been a bookish man, curled up in his library like the worms that burrowed into his soulless pagan writings. Had 'em both reading and writing by the time they were ten, though a good set of ears was as much as a body needed to get through this wicked world and mayhap too much already.

He had even named the girl after some heathen heroine in a faded folio of stage plays as are done by jades and tarts on the Paris stages, to hear tell. Devil's work. Too much Devil's work when the world had enjoyed 1,647 years since Our Lord to grow better. The Scotswoman's lips folded. Headed home just in time.

"Miranda! Dinna ye lean so far over the rail, lass. Ye'll be showin' yer petticoats to the world."

The girl straightened and blushed. Since Mistress MacTavish had assumed control and stuffed her into ladylike garb, blushes came all too easily. Rebellion flared in Miranda's gray-green gaze, but she exchanged a glance with her like-eyed brother and kept silent.

A flutter aloft made the pair glance up just as a seaman came slithering down a rope faster than a monkey on a Barbados vine.

"Look, Harry!" Miranda cried, delighted.

Meg MacTavish's long face dropped further as the man sprang lightly to deck and ducked into the captain's cabin. The trio of passengers watched the doorway for a moment, struck by a certain tension.

After a muffled bustle, Captain Coyle strode on deck.

"Ma'am, get your nurslings below," he barked, his face set, white lines creasing the ruddy folds of flesh along his mouth. Coyle was a long-serving merchant master. A voyage too smooth was a voyage not yet done, and his lookout hadn't liked the cut of the sail that sliced the horizon in the glass.

Meg MacTavish bolted for the safety of the cramped cabin she had called home for four long weeks. Her charges lagged behind to hear a thrilling word bounced between captain and first mate as they traded gazes through the glass.

"Pirates," hissed Harry, his fair-skinned face warming with enthusiasm. Miranda bit her lower lip until it was so startlingly red she seemed to be wearing paint.

"I don't want to go below, Harry! It'll be much more rousing here."

"Not for you now." Harry scornfully eyed her lady's garb.

Miranda's impatient hands worked at the heavy skirt. She could have torn it off, and the hoops that held it out in the ridiculous fashion fancied by the Spanish Infanta. She didn't want to be a Spanish Infanta, though old MacMutton thought she should.

Here the woman was now, prodding Miranda below and not caring that Harry, the beast, lingered to see the excitement.

"Ye'll be safe in the cabin, lass," Mistress MacTavish promised. "D'ye want to be prey to some horrible pirate? I've nae words enough to say what such girls as ye are to the likes of them."

Miranda paled. She'd heard of pirates; pirates who swept and burned and raped. She didn't quite know what rape was, though she'd seen the quick mating of the island wildlife in her rambles, but she knew enough to know she wouldn't like it.

"Here, lass, and be quick about it!"

Stunned, Miranda watched the steely chaperon, who on Barbados had deplored Miranda's going about dressed as a boy, now urge on her the breeches, belt and shirt from Harry's sea chest.

"Mayhap they'll nae take an interest in ye dressed so. Be quick!" the old woman begged as the *Merlin* tacked suddenly and the pair nearly lost their footing. "Oooh, I'm sick," wailed Mistress MacTavish, tamed by motion though no man.

A violent pitch hurled her onto the cot, where she found it easy to sink into misery and oblivion while Miranda changed her clothes. A frantic seaman thrust Harry into the cabin soon after. The boy's lashes flicked over his sister's new attire, but he asked no questions.

"What's happening, Harry?" Miranda said breathlessly, tying her long blond hair back like her brother's. They seemed twins there in the dim-lit cabin—she slim enough to pass for boy, he in that vague sexless stage between boy and man.

"A ship coming up fast," he answered. "Thirty guns, and we're so laden down by sugar—! Come over, Miranda, I've a dagger here. My best Spanish steel. From Barcelona. Francisco gave it to me before we left, so don't lose it. But use it."

The girl nodded her fair head, slipping the knife into its sheath and both into her belt with a cautionary glance at the Scotswoman's still figure. Meg MacTavish had finally met her match in a sea that tipped and tilted her into insensibility.

The first cannon struck with a dull thud and a sudden shivering of the ship.

"This ancient casket couldn't defend herself against an armada of ducklings," Harry fretted contemptuously as he rooted through his chest for something. "They're still trying to move their three puny twenty-pounders forward."

"Harry, don't go out!" More shots tossed the pair about the cabin, then scuffles sounded above. "It's dangerous."

Harry grinned recklessly and brandished his smallsword. "Stay here."

He lurched out the door. For undecided minutes, Miranda's teeth tore at her lower lip; finally she drew her dagger and followed her brother.

Light, a shock after the whispered consultations in the dark cabin, dazzled her eyes. Tripping on something, she glanced down. A seaman's arm was flung across her path and a trickle of blood angled toward her on the slanting deck. Men—seamen—lay still, very still, on the boards. No, not quite still.

One groaned and a hand changed grip on a pistol it still clutched. A black boot from nowhere pinioned the hand. Out of sight around a bulkhead came an indrawn gasp, then a gurgle. Another stream of red meandered thickly across the salt-swollen boards.

Miranda shrank against the stairway's shelter. Seconds later, two beefy hands had plucked her up by the armpits from the quarterdeck above. She was dangling above the deck and the trail of living and dead lining its length.

"Another likely lad," crowed a voice in English.

Phrases in French and Spanish and languages unknown flew from every side. Bright breeches and shirts and strange dusky faces, heads swathed in colored scarves, surrounded her. She felt as if she had intruded at a council of Barbados macaws, their harsh voices chattering in a language of their own and their colorful plumage rich and barbaric.

Harry was there, she saw with mixed relief and alarm, his arms held behind his back by a bearded man with a ring through one nostril. Miranda's feet in Harry's old shoes flailed at the cabin side, but her captor, an enormous black man with eyes brown as a coconut in yellowed whites, merely overleapt the upper rail and swung her down again to the deck.

"Another likely lad." His rich baritone rang across the boards and brought every alien eye to her.

She looked down and recognized a dead face, the eyes staring vacantly into the sun skewered on the masts above. Captain Coyle. She stepped carefully over the body when her guard dragged her to Harry by the gunwale. A circle of tall, grinning men surrounded them.

A lad, another likely lad, Miranda thought. Then likely

they'd not penetrate her disguise and molest her. Perhaps they'd make her and Harry serve as cabin boys—that would be an adventure . . .

"A very likely lad." A man stepped forward and pulled Harry's head back by the hair until his throat was extended as for the executioner's axe. This man, too, spoke English. Miranda read hope in his comparative youth and not unhandsome face. "This merits an extra ration of rum tonight, lads."

He pushed Harry's head aside to wink at the circle, then swaggered toward Miranda. Once before her, he tilted her chin up at the sun, the bright light bringing tears to her eyes.

"Philistines!" came a hoarse challenge from behind them. "The little foxes, the dogs shall eat thy entrails—"

On came Meg MacTavish, half-mad with seasickness and the sight of her charges in enemy hands. The doughty Scotswoman lurched up from the shadows below like an avenging Calvinistic angel, telling the only words of power she knew, the grand rolling words of the Bible.

Those words brought pause to the savage circle of men. Then a pistol discharged. Meg MacTavish rolled to deck and into the lifeless arms of a common seaman to whom she would not have even nodded in life.

Miranda smelled the lingering powder; she thought that she could smell the blood pooling maroon on the old woman's sober bodice. Miranda screamed, a long, denying—betraying—scream.

The circle closed on her.

"Likely you say, Johnny? A very *un*likely lad." The man whose hand cupped Miranda's chin jerked her jaw down so quickly that her head swam.

"Let's 'ave 'er over the side, then, for I've no taste to 'ave 'er over a cannon," said another.

The world slipped away again, crazily. For the first time Miranda noticed the other ship swaying at sea anchor next to the *Merlin*, and the long dark plunge between the nudging hulls to deep water below. She clutched her captor's jersey while he dangled her there, half over the side.

"Or does some lad want tender female flesh tonight—she's almost as pretty as the boy here. What . . . nay? Then over she goes—" He lifted her again, her head thudding against the gunwale.

"Mercy!" she cried into the maelstrom of movement that had

her half-mad with hanging somewhere tilted between life and death.

"Mercy?" A quiet, accented-English voice spoke behind her.

Miranda twisted her neck to see a face floating upside down, a face whose reversed features seemed to be smiling.

"Leave her go," the face said.

The deck lurched and righted itself. Miranda confronted a tall, cadaverous man with a visage so weary that it exhausted her to regard him.

"You've done your work well, lads," he told the crew. "We've a fat cargo to sell, another ship's ration of rum to ease the time and none to contest us for 'em."

He gazed around the body-littered deck as if he were viewing a garden party. His eyes, half-lidded in their elegantly exhausted setting, reluctantly came to rest on Miranda.

"But leave the lady to me." He extended his hand that a moment before had rested on the sword pommel at his side.

Miranda moved toward him like a sleepwalker. Harry whimpered once, but the gray-eyed pirate held the boy's shoulder fast.

"You'll not be askin' us to give up this one, Captain?" the man inquired hoarsely.

The captain gauged the eyes around him, squinting now in the late afternoon sun, circling around the English boy and girl. He shook his head. "I know better than that, me lads."

His hand rested almost paternally on Miranda's shoulder as he piloted her across the deck. She paused by Meg MacTavish's still figure and looked down. For a moment one could have sworn she was a boy, after all—something hard and purposeful formed in her face. The captain pulled her on, with a final look at the circling crewmen.

"I'll take her to my cabin," he said, as if challenging them to contest him.

"Aye, Captain." The gray-eyed sailor smiled at Miranda. "Take her."

Chapter Two

Calm and quiet occupied the captain's quarters. The late captain's quarters. The new captain showed Miranda to a corner. She huddled there while he riffled through the bills of lading. It was quiet and almost sane there.

"Sir," Miranda said after a long while. Her voice sounded infantile, piping, and she shook her head in frustration. "Sir," she tried again, bolder.

"Quiet, child."

She subsided.

Once the gray-eyed man knocked and entered. "What of the rum, then?" he demanded.

"If your battening down's done, let your revels begin."

A smile slashed the man's handsome face, making it ugly. He eyed Miranda in her corner. "You'll not be joining us?"

"That's correct." The captain's impassive eyes never abandoned the closely penned pages in dead Captain Coyle's hand.

The mate left, grinning.

Was it night, then? The new captain read on a while, then sighed and searched out a decanter filled with something ruby red—probably port wine, but Miranda thought of blood.

"Sir," she ventured again. "My brother—they wouldn't kill him? He's too young to harm them, younger than I."

"You should inquire rather whether you are safe."

"Am I?" Miranda spoke levelly, but her hands shook on her trousered knees.

"How old are you?" The captain leaned intently toward her.

"Fourteen," she lied in the wavering lantern light. He regarded her yet; for a moment she was afraid he knew that she had lied.

"Safe enough," he said finally, leaning back in the heavy captain's chair. "It's your brother they wanted." His eyes anchored once more on the black-and-cream pages.

"My brother? I thought, we . . . all . . . thought—"

Miranda's confused eyes skimmed her male raiment, then struck the captain's impassive face full on. A likely lad, a very likely lad. She listened then, for the faint sounds of revelry and ruin drifting from somewhere above. Rum, a full ration, and her brother, a likely lad.

She was at the door, thinking of Barcelona steel lying abandoned on deck and it a fine way to cut someone, something, herself. The captain was there before her and threw her back.

"Fool!" he said icily. "And whether you or I the more, I cannot say. I've never meddled in their lust before, be it flesh or blood. Go out there now and you'll swim with the porpoises and the late crew."

Miranda fell to her knees on the hard floor. All was beyond curing; she could hear that in the light lewd laughter floating down the hatchway. "Will they kill him?"

The captain laughed. "Not likely, though he might wish it."

"Harry's so . . . so proud. Better that I— Then he'd have something to avenge, like a brother, like a man. How can he avenge himself? His own honor?"

"I was a fine, honorable man once," the captain said with bitter nostalgia, "for young ladies like yourself to admire. Very gentlemanly, very . . . good. A captain in the Dutch fleet that threaded the West Indies and made every uncharted island a pearl on its string."

"Then how—?"

The Hollander laughed again. "Honor is an empty word. If I let you on deck you'd see that in a moment."

He drained another glass of wine, and she realized that he was slightly drunk. One so lean had thin blood for liquor to warm quickly. He threw himself on the cot, reaching out once to stroke her hair even as she shrank from his hand.

"You are the pearl of my old age now, my one good deed in a naughty world, as some countryman of yours once said. Rest easy, I will not let them have you—should they want you. One does not cast one's pearls before swine."

He laughed softly and drifted into sleep, his even breath sighing around the little cabin.

After a long while, Miranda unwound her cramped legs and edged to the door, cracking it open. She heard only the rhythmic snap and buckle of a ship riding a calm sea, the steady heavy wheezes of—swine—at rest after their revels.

"Where do you think you go?" the captain's chill whisper asked behind her.

"To collect my Barcelona steel," she replied with a defiant glare. "And my brother."

"Go then, but he'll curse you for it." The captain shut his eyes again.

Miranda paused. She was safer here, no doubt, but safety itself seemed a dubious condition. She crept onto deck, cleared now of its dead. Other forms slumbered there in the moonlight. She crawled past each prone figure, wanting to tear it to pieces.

Pulses pounded in her throat and temple, but she had played games like this before through Barbados' tropical gardens. She. And Francisco. And Harry. She finally found him, as unconscious as the rest, rum scenting his shirtfront.

"Harry." She slapped him until his head lolled loosely on his shoulders. "Come with me." Dazed, he finally scuffed after her.

Miranda's hand groped the deck as they went. Once she fingered a knife and thrust it into her belt. Snores drifted across the boards. Miranda's searching fingers brushed a sleeping head propped against the hatchway before she could withdraw it. A groan. Had anyone heard?

No one woke. New World rum was new also to Old World heads: raw, strong stuff—enough to drown a pirate's thirst in stupor. The pair edged across the dark deck with its geography of slumbering human islands.

Perhaps they could hide aboard ship, Miranda speculated. The thought of being towed meekly into port unbeknownst to their captors pleased her, but what if the pirates burned the *Merlin* after transferring its cargo? Hidden belowdecks, Miranda and Harry could become so much more tinder.

No, they must take a boat and row for port. Land, Spain, was nearby. That much Captain Coyle had imparted to his passengers before the lookout had swung down from the heavens in such haste, and the merchant ship's passengers and crew had been plunged into hell.

The moon cut loose from a bank of clouds and spilled pale light on the boards. Miranda crouched below the gunwale's shadow, dragging the compliant Harry down with her. Sleeping forms kept still.

Then a black and bulky shadow, like a trained bear at a roadside Gypsy circus, reared above the belowdecks passageway and lumbered forward.

Miranda shrank against the gunwale, her hand digging warning into Harry's arm. Surely the dark hid them, surely that oncoming figure was merely a half-drunk sailor lurching about before he settled into a second stupor. No one could know that they cowered here, halfway to freedom . . . The shape converged on the pair, almost as if expecting to find them. Now the soft shuffle of shoes rasped over the deck, as rhythmic as the waves that lapped the ship's side with their own muffled drumbeat.

Miranda unsheathed the blade she'd found and waited. The shape, modeled by moonlight into the likeness of a man at last, loomed over the two fugitives for one awful instant.

"So you found him," it remarked softly, matter-of-factly.

Miranda had already forgotten the captain, perhaps the only man aboard not too drunk to ignore untoward sounds. He reached down and dredged brother and sister up from the deck with a hand at each of their shirtfronts.

"Fools are ever fond of fools." He shook them lightly. "Very well." He sighed.

In that soft, weary sound, Miranda saw a spark of hope for herself and Harry strike off the Dutchman's steely self-contempt.

"Put the boy in the boat. I'll lower you away. Then scramble aboard, my pearl, and try the open sea."

"Oh, thank you, sir! Thank you." Miranda prodded Harry over the side.

"Water's aboard, and sea rations, and a compass—you know about compasses? Keep her heading southwest, the winds should favor you. And perhaps, perhaps you'll live to tell of the day you escaped the Dutchman's prize. None live to make that boast now. So keep your thanks. I don't expect to see you in any witness box of mine. At least the sea doesn't preserve the prey she takes for play. Southwest, you hear, Pearl?"

The last sound from deck that Miranda heard as she joined Harry in the rocking boat below was the Dutch captain's mocking laughter drifting over the gunwale like a farewell.

Dawn split the dull black veil that was sea and sky with a cutting edge of faint pink light, like fire reflecting on a blade . . . her own blade of Barcelona steel that her hand had happened on in the dark as if guided by some ironic fate.

Miranda, drifting away from the *Merlin* and the pirate ship that held it fast as a spider binds a fly, watched with a kind of weary wonder. They had floated into the southwest current the captain had foretold. Miranda's fingertips barely spanned the space between the oars, set wide apart and meant for the muscle of hardy seamen. She would have to wait for Harry to emerge from the half-world of rum and ravishment that held him unconscious.

The mated ships were now mere flyspecks on the horizon. She

had watched all night under fragile shafts of moonlight and now with the growing glow of dawn: watched and hoped that their little boat would be beyond retrieval when the sun danced across the water and woke all those men. Those ill-tempered men—bleary from drink and their night games with her brother, bereft suddenly of their toy . . .

She glanced at Harry in the brightening light, his face rosy as a cupid's in an Italian fresco. What to do? He had passed beyond their common experience; a cruel chasm had opened between them. At the bottom of that chasm lay guilt. Miranda felt that by rights *she* should have been the victim . . . wasn't that what they'd always heard whispered about pirates, their insatiable lust for women after months at sea, their rampaging manhood?

Perhaps all those months had only taught them . . . invention. Oh, she would have known how to be comforted, had she lain senseless in the little boat drifting softly away from last night's infamy, but how to comfort? She feared the Dutchman had been right: Harry would not thank his witnesses.

A brighter glow haloed the hazy world outside Miranda's mind; day was growing. She turned anxious eyes back to the twin ships. While she watched, a red-orange rose blossomed on the horizon. For a moment Miranda thought she saw the rising sun showing his fiery bald pate to the world.

Then she realized that she had been right; the *Merlin* would see no port either side of the Atlantic again. Stripped of crew and cargo, the ship was now a burning island that would rage to the waterline before breaking into flotsam and jetsam . . . like Harry and Miranda, bobbing mindlessly on a bright salt sea.

A black ship was silhouetted against the dual glow of a sun rising and a fiery wreck sinking. The pirates were making for the nearest free port to trade Barbados sugar for Spanish gold. And was that port in a southwest direction? If so, not even the cynical Dutchman could save them. Miranda wobbled an oar in its lock. A ponderous thing. Even with her and Harry at each oar, their progress would be sea-turtle slow.

No, nothing to do but watch that black smear on the horizon for signs of growth. Watch and pray. To whom? Father? He'd been a scholar, a bookman. He would have known about winds and compasses, Miranda thought, examining the contents of the tin box tied on board. Compass. Direction. Ah, here: this dial with the hand like a German clock's that veered and glided. Or Francisco. Were Francisco here she wouldn't be so afraid. With

Father's head and Francisco's hand aboard, the little boat would be wily prey for even the most sagacious of pirates . . .

The compass needle pointed to the "W." West. Yet the departing ship had been *between* Miranda and the rising sun. Land was *east*ward. Her body turned to ice in the warming light.

The Dutchman had lied. He'd saved Harry from his crew, but he had sent his witnesses fleeing toward the endless watery gulf between Europe and the New World. No wonder the pirate ship had sped away in the opposite direction. It was bound for land.

Miranda pulled on the northward oar. The boat turned slowly against the waves until the needle read between the elaborately scripted "S" and "E." Southeast. Land. If she was right.

What lay between here and that promised land? Only hope. Hope is the only true compass for a boat adrift in the sunny seas of the eastern Atlantic with only a girl and a boy from Barbados half a world away for crew.

And only a question mark for a port.

Chapter Three

M iranda clung to whatever piece of the boat her arms could circle. Salt water burned her screwed-shut eyes. She gasped. The world was a water bucket dipping roughly into a well and she only a fly upon its sloshing surface.

Harry. What had he to cling to? The boat had driven prow-first on the shoreline rocks, spitting itself into splinters and its passengers into flotsam to be flung back at the sea. A horrible death that would be, dashing against those rocks until finally she succumbed to that brutal drumming and washed limply against her executioner. Miranda's fingers almost slipped from their slimy purchase on the rough board. Save that she always hoped for some chance, some gentle wave . . .

In the end, her body drove into cold, shifting sand. Crawling forward like a blind white worm, Miranda finally felt the sea foam wash only her ankles.

She was racked with burning. Her eyes, shut, streamed her own salt tears trying to purge the sea salt. Lips ragged from her own teeth seemed to ooze salt from the wounds. Drawing herself along by hummocks of rock, she inched farther ashore, scraping her hands raw.

"Harry." Her voice rasped across the beach, hardly audible. His soft groan drew her like an umbilical cord. "Harry, thank God!"

Miranda crawled over to wipe the salty sand from Harry's face and pull him farther from the murderous ruffle of ocean foaming at his knees. He resisted, limply; he was waterlogged and luke-willed, still a burden to her.

A predawn haze of sunlight warmed the rocky inland hills. Above, the gulls wheeled with their betraying calls, shrieks of shrill warning. Miranda's palm sank into the sand as she drew herself up and rested on something slick and clammy—round white eyes staring blankly into sunlight. A less fortunate refugee from the sea, a dead fish.

Miranda rinsed her hand in the weedy foam at her feet. Leaving Harry to rest, she ranged inland. From the rocks of a nearby rise she saw the distant golden glimmer of a city stretching along the bay's blue curve.

Cádiz! She was not so bad a compass-reader, after all. And she knew Spanish enough to speak their way into that enticing slice of civilization already baking white-hot under the infant morning sun.

From a rock she surveyed their situation. Cádiz Bay was sheltered by a crescent moon of yellow land. Miranda and Harry had run aground on its jutting chin. They had only to make their way to where the nose flattened into the face—there, and they would be within reach of food, water, some kind of human help.

A distant, droning shout brought Miranda to her belly on the rocks. Fool, to stand so openly on Spanish soil! A seabird arced above her; she cringed beneath even its indifferent eyes. She rolled beneath the crest, suddenly, retchingly weak. Shouts ricocheted off the rocks and echoed in her waterlogged ears. She shook her head, repulsed by the fat lank cord of wet hair that brushed her cheek and the hollow gurgle in her ears.

Someone coming. Harry on the beach. And she, sinking into some inland sea that sapped her strength and lapped at her consciousness. A voice calling. She must reach it, reach Harry, civilization, a place where something besides a sea gull called to her in a teasing, dim shriek . . .

"Oye, niño! Vaya."
Fat Juana clapped a heavy tray across Miranda's arms and launched her across the crowded tavern with a brutal pinch.

Miranda spared one resentful look full into those black eyes set like cinders into a mass of suet, then wove her way through the tables, mindful of worse pinches from other quarters.

Sweat streaked the sides of her face, tracing white rivulets along the smoke-stained skin that almost made her pass for a native now. But there was no mistaking her yellow hair. That hair had made Pepe pause when he had found Fat Juana kicking Miranda from the alley behind the Taberna de la Bicha Roja a fortnight earlier.

Had fortune or misfortune directed her that far and no farther after she had awakened on the beach to find Harry gone? Miranda knew only that she had dragged herself as far as she could into the Cádiz outskirts, finally sinking against a thick-timbered door like a runaway chick collapsing under the wing of a mother hen.

Fat Juana was no mother hen. Yet she was opportunist enough to pause in the business of shoving Miranda into the byway when Pepe had said, *"Inglés, uno niño rubio inglés, no?"* A crooked smile across his half-toothed mouth spawned a twin on Juana's greedy lips. A blond English lad, yes. To all appearances.

So Miranda was hurled inward to La Bicha Roja—the Red Snake—instead of outward to join Cádiz's eternal pack of scavenging urchins and mongrel dogs.

Miranda reached her table and set down the heavy tins of stew, accepting the customers' Spanish grumblings with a rough humor of her own that usually kept them docile. She scuttled back before Fat Juana could see her and dove into a low niche near the last table. The place was crowded tonight; from her floor-side seat on the damp stones she saw a veritable forest of variously booted legs.

There, the four narrow matching boots of Spanish leather—soldiers and easy enough to serve. A few rounds of raw wine, some threats to conscript the tavern lad, and they would be gone to sleep off their indulgences. Many more feet sprawled from beyond the benches, feet in ill-made shoes. Sailors, sailors of all lands and leanings, anchored at La Bicha Roja long enough to down its greasy food, swill sour wine from goatskins as rank and kick her from table to table.

And there, in the corner. Wide Boots. The man who had ordered dry sack from nearby Jerez de la Frontera. Miranda had brought it solitary on a tray, the house's best and seldom-served stock.

She kept her eyes from the face of the man who had requested it. She had last served a drink so fine to a soulful Catalonian who had left her a coin and a significant look in change. Had she not evaded him, Fat Juana would have forced her into more than earning that coin with him—and into revealing her true sex. Instead, the silver circle lined the sole of her dilapidated shoe, a passport to something someday.

"Niño!" Fat Juana's bellow. Miranda sighed and slipped to the woman's well-padded side. *"El greco."*

Juana weighed her down with another tray and nodded to a far table occupied by a pair too swarthy even for Spaniards.

The Greek was a massive man, his face pockmarked behind a fence of wiry black hair. He watched Miranda set down the goblets and murmured something Greek to his slighter companion.

"Gracias, gracias." He grinned then, stupidly, in the way of foreigners who speak but a phrase or two and think that the passkey to everything.

Miranda ducked away, but a hand netted her shoulder and jerked her back. The Greek's face loomed against hers on a wave of garlic-laden breath. Elusive as an eel, Miranda slid away, but just as slickly the Greek inserted his heavy thigh between her and escape.

"Niño," he murmured, *"niño,"* the sick grin and something else still on his face. This was as close as her boy's guise had brought her in a fortnight. She writhed while he pawed her.

No eyes saw her own dart around the tavern seeking aid. The soldiers hunched over their guttering candle, deep in drunken argument. Voices rose to a pitch that would drown any call for help. Fat Juana would only seal the bargain . . .

Miranda pushed off the man's encroaching body, but his strength hauled her closer. His hand slid up her thigh like a snake a vine. Then she had steel in her hand, Barcelona steel, native steel, and she struck the snake a slice along its scaly back—

The room dropped a few feet. She was on the floor, the Greek was looming over her in the smoke, sucking the blood from his hand with a howl that quieted even the tavern. Then he had a knife as well, a long thick blade that scribed a vicious circle in the air, cutting it like a curse.

Miranda scrambled away until she backed into a table, then stood and brandished her dagger. Harry's Barcelona blade, like a toy, fit for a child. The Greek charged, propelled by curses in his thick native tongue, and overshot her to plunge into the table behind her.

The tavern patrons circled as for a cockfight, sealing escape. She would charge him, she resolved, force the fatal blow, rather than face anything less. He still wove like a dancing bear in the circle's center, passing the knife from hand to hand and eyeing her like a roast he intended to carve.

She started her fatal rush, but a leg shot into her path. She sprawled on the floor again, twisting to see who had caused her downfall. Wide Boots.

"This young cock," his voice announced in English-accented Spanish, "needs a longer tail to face off such a rooster as yourself, friend."

The Greek stood puzzled at the intrusion, then lunged. A long and silver tongue like a lizard's hissed into the murky air and licked at the Greek's throat. The man came on despite it. Wide Boots leapt Miranda's crouching form and engaged her attacker.

From her floor-side post, their booted feet moved in the patterns of a dance, heels striking wood with the same frantic rhythm as Pasquela's, the Gypsy girl who came nightly to dance on the tables and then retired upstairs for a parade of clients.

Then a ring of steel and a loud curse. Miranda saw the circle break. The Greek and his companion were gone. Wide Boots was tabling his rapier. Miranda was about to slip away when a heavy hand collared and shook her: Fat Juana, streaming sweat and Spanish curses: her house should not be dishonored by an ingrate, to mouth the customers, take a knife to them . . . she'd beat the boy around the harbor.

Fat Juana's blows rained down on Miranda amid the crowd's unruffled laughter.

"What? Haven't you had entertainment enough, you rogues?" Something stronger than banter ran beneath Wide Boots's tone. "I told you this lad needed a longer tail, and you, fair hostess, I'll show you the proper way to beat a boy. Soldier! Your blade."

A rapier hurled over the surrounding heads into Wide Boots's hand. He tossed the weapon to Miranda and her palm went around the pommel like a tongue around a familiar name. Wide Boots assumed a mock dueling position and circled his rapier to the crowd's approving stomps. But Miranda's blade wove through the air like a flying fish through water and knocked his teasing sliver of steel aside.

"*Jesús!*" someone in the crowd breathed at her insolence.

Wide Boots dropped his guard for a split second in surprise. Miranda beat inward on an arc of gleaming steel.

Then he was gone; she whirled to find him to the side, his own blade lacing the air with fine-drawn feints. This was mock fencing. Exhibition fencing, the kind Francisco had taught her between bouts with Harry. But Francisco had taught her the cat's play as well as the mouse's. The two blades courted each other like long-parted lovers—advancing, then retreating, weaving and kissing in a clash of steel.

Wide Boots struck suddenly to spin Miranda's blade away. She was supple enough to slide off his stronger blow. He came on again, ready to end it, but Miranda's reflexes recalled a trick of Francisco's. She danced sideways and forward, her blade passing close enough to slit his jacket an inch or two. The crowd drew in its breath.

Wide Boots stopped and laughed, throwing back his head and carelessly resting his hands on his sword pommel as if it were a walking stick. Miranda lowered her rapier, puzzled by her opponent's willingness to impale his own on the floor instead of in her.

"By San Felipe, 'tis a *Spanish* fencing master you've had," the man said, "for I've only known a Spaniard to try that feint and he was a rogue at that. Now that I know at whose breast you were weaned—"

He was at her again, the rapier lazily rising from the floor to loop and lash as if it breathed St. Elmo's fire. Miranda parried, twisted, feinted—for naught. The stranger had mastered her repertoire with a stroke and balanced her on the edge of defeat only for the sake of a show. A short show, for their blades suddenly closed at the hilt. He plucked her sword away as if it had been straw, while his foot sent her sprawling to the filthy floor.

"Here, soldier, your blade back. This rooster can grow his own tail soon enough. Up," he instructed, finishing the exhibition by slapping the figure on the floor across its backside with the flat of his blade. "Fetch me some sack, lad, for you've worked up a thirst and had better quench it."

Onlookers laughed and scattered, their mood for punishment slaked. Miranda got a fresh goblet of liquor, unwatered this round, despite Fat Juana's watching shrunken-olive eye, and placed it before him.

Chapter Four

"What is your name, boy?" the man asked in English, his eyes slitted into a narrow net to catch lies.

"Hathaway, sir. Richard Hathaway." Miranda borrowed a boy's name borne by no one she knew; it became her own that way.

"Too English a name to rot in a Spanish port. How'd you get here?"

"Ship, sir."

For a moment the man looked annoyed by her apparent impudence. Then he shrugged. "Do you get seasick?"

"No, sir."

Wide Boots leaned back against the tavern wall. His chosen corner commanded the entire room, should any Greeks bearing gifts in the form of steel return.

"I've not had the luxury of a cabin boy, and one Englishman can always find room for another. How'd you like to ship with me, Richard?"

"Yes, sir!" Out. Away from the noisy men-thick tavern where she was always a target and paid only in Fat Juana's grudgingly given scraps of greasy food. "Where are you bound?"

"First duty of a cabin boy aboard my ship"—he leaned forward until his shadowed face was so close that she feared detection—"is discretion. You know what that word means?"

Miranda nodded.

"Then whatever ship brought you to Cádiz must have had more books than the log aboard, my—discreet—lad." The man extended his hand so suddenly Miranda flinched, expecting a slap; but he was only offering his hand on their bargain. "Christopher Steele, captain of the *Salamander*."

Miranda's handclasp was as hard as Harry would have extended had he met someone as exalted as a ship's captain. In a moment, they had shrugged their way through the inn's encroaching clientele to the door.

"Innkeeper owe you any coppers?" Steele asked, pausing to sheath his sword.

Miranda snorted. "He owes me gold," she explained tersely, "more than any will ever find in his coffers."

Steele's eyes swept the dim-lit room and ended on the pale, dirty face before him. He nodded grimly, urging her into the street.

"Aye, 'tis best to steer clear of this stinkhole. Cádiz is the canker sore of Spain. I'll be glad to pull anchor and sail free of her."

He pulled Miranda over to the cobblestoned byway's side and inspected her in the bright white Spanish sun. "How old are you? Thirteen?"

She nodded. Confirming his guess would establish what seemed reasonable for her assumed sex.

Steele thumbed a streak of kitchen grease from her face. "You've a skin we could send to court. A few days on the high seas will put some color on you, Richard. 'Tis not healthy in these wharfside pestholes; no place for free men . . . or honest women," he added, as two highly colored señoritas, their dark eyes boldly assessing him from under patched mantillas, ambled past.

Miranda hadn't realized under what a burden she had lived recently until she strode the Cádiz byways beside Christopher Steele, her Barcelona dagger at her side. At her other side she had Steele and his accomplished sword. She secretly studied him as she stumbled breathlessly along. Perhaps he was merely another Greek in captain's clothing. Once aboard his ship, perhaps he would turn on her, more like those unnatural sailors than she believed.

Yet he had a good, well-cut English face, though bronzed by the sea and wind. He appeared to be a man of some education. Uneducated men did not play as lightly with words as they did rapiers. Could he be more than ship's captain?

She marked his fair hair, shoulder-length and uncurled, tied back in the way of seamen, sun-streaked in places to as light a flaxen as her own. Miranda's imagination clothed him in finery and placed him against a marbled hall as a courtier. Yes and no, like seeing a hunting falcon in parrot's dress. Yet the most vital question remained: did he take any interest in her that should encourage a dive into the nearest alley?

She remembered the two easy ladies who had strolled by. His blue eyes had casually inventoried their charms before his words had dismissed them. Perhaps that spoke best of all for her safety in her current guise.

They broke onto the open area before the docks, where a small ship's boat bobbled six feet below on a lively sea.

"I've a new seaman for you, Muffin," said Steele, impatiently waiting for Miranda to drop into the boat below. She paused, then hurled herself at the tossing surface. She landed aboard, but atop the wiry figure addressed as Muffin.

"Good thing you're a half-weight, lad. Old Muffin can't take many of yer misjumps, so mind yerself," the man grumbled.

Humiliated, Miranda settled at the boat's bottom as the oarsmen began stroking from shore. She glanced once at Steele, to see how he was taking his protégé's ineptitude, but the eyes as blue as the white-capped water around them peered intently beyond the boat. She followed their gaze to a ship anchored and riding roughly in Cádiz Bay.

The *Salamander*, he'd said, and she was indeed a long, lean whip of a ship compared to the high-waisted galleons that tossed alongside her. Excitement stirred Miranda's stomach, the first positive emotion she'd felt since losing Harry on the Cádiz beach.

Harry. The name entwined her heart. She felt suddenly queasy, with more than grief—perhaps from the close-quartered pitching of this little boat through the choppy water. She glanced at the man Muffin. An odd name for a sailor. If he was a muffin, he was a lean, underbaked one—all sinew in his seaman's jersey and wide trousers, yet with a merry, polished brown face, like an island nut.

The wind shifted, bringing something upon it, some new smell besides the wharves' wet, fishy odor. Miranda disliked that smell, but it so defied description that she inhaled deeply and it became a stench.

"Galleys." Steele's face hardened. She followed his nod to a pair of high dark ships riding heavily in the waves. From their hunch-shouldered sides protruded three delicate banks of oars.

Like strange, long-legged water bugs the galleys looked—sea spiders rocking at their web's wet center, ready to glide swiftly out and after their prey. The stench drifted closer and washed over her, every loathsome smell of the tavern, digested and then vomited up . . . Miranda leapt for the side and threw up into the tossing waves herself. A hand, she didn't know whose, held her aboard by her belt.

When she sat up after wiping her mouth with a handful of seawater, every eye was upon her. The monkey-faced man's gnarled hand was still hooked onto her belt.

"I thought you didn't get seasick," said Steele.

" 'Tis not seasick I am, sir," she answered, "it's Spanish-sick."
Steele laughed then, as a chuckle ran amongst the rowers.

"There are likely to be Englishmen aboard that Devil's dread-
nought even sicker than you," he added. The laughter died.
"Live long enough to grow older and you might do battle against
such sea vermin."

Miranda suddenly understood. An English captain in a Spanish
port, half-renegade, half-pirate perhaps. Perhaps also half-
privateer. She hadn't heard of renewed war with Spain, but Father had said that was ever a threat. Spain wanted all the New
World's gold for the coffers of Seville. English footholds in the
Indies, like her own Barbados, were insecure stepping-stones for
Britain's sea-flung empire as long as Spain plied her galleys and
warships, despite the great battle of 1588.

Miranda wanted to muse upon it, but they were at the ship's
side and she had to clamber up it. No boarding ramp for a planter's daughter swathed in stiff skirts and accompanied by a stiff
and sober Scottish chaperon now. Miranda and Harry had scaled
Barbados' wide, wind-twisted cedars since toddler days. She was
up and over the gunwale briskly enough to earn a wink from
Muffin.

She stood patiently by while Steele stared aloft and discussed
several mysterious things about the sail with the first mate. Then
he nodded her into his cabin.

"Glad I am to get the stink of Cádiz off my feet," he said, sitting on the built-in bed and extending a booted foot.

Belatedly she rushed to remove first one boot—an easy
enough task; she had christened him Wide Boots for good
reason—and the other.

Steele moved to a basin, where—stripping off jacket and
shirt—he threw water upon his face and chest. Miranda was fascinated. She had not seen a man so much as flick a drop of water
upon himself for so long that she had forgotten that one could do
so. For herself, dirt had been a masculine overlay that had helped
her survive.

"Well, go on, no sense wasting fresh water," gestured Steele,
drying his face with a cloth.

Miranda balked: too dangerous for her to go about in her girl's
face, naked of the grime that helped hide her.

Reluctance must have been plain upon even her filthy face.
Steele collared her without warning and dragged her to the basin.
Her heels dug into the floor, but she'd seen enough of his naked

shoulders to know the result was inevitable. Her face dipped toward the basin and then she was sputtering in the cloudy water.

"Now wash. I won't have a blackamoor for a cabin boy."

Miranda rubbed the water over her features and straightened to face a small shaving mirror set into the cabin wall. Amazed, she saw herself for the first time in weeks. Dirt still smudged her skin, and her hair, always a light, bright yellow, was as dull and brown as a wren's wing.

"Here," said Steele. "I've seen too many swarthy Spanish faces to tolerate another one." He rubbed her features with the wet cloth until her skin felt raw. "Now, there's an English face for you. By God, you're a pretty fellow, though! I can see why you were the belle of the taverns."

Miranda pulled her shoulder from his resting hand. Inwardly a sick fear curled. She had been wrong, he was like the others . . .

Steele laughed. "Let loose that steel, Richard. You'll not have to fight me for your virtue. I've no time for sailors more interested in each other than their duties."

Her fingers uncurled from the hilt at her belt. Then she was fairly safe here, if what he said was true, and she thought that it was. He was a likable man. Likely likable men would sail under him. Miranda auditioned the first smile she had mustered in weeks. It felt odd, especially across a new-scrubbed face.

"That's better." Steele clapped her shoulder. "Now tell Muffin to get you stowed away below."

Steele had picked the perfect mentor.

Muffin—his true name was Moffat but no one had used it for years—was a wiry burr of a man with a heart as wide as he was narrow. If anyone could champion an untried boy aboard the *Salamander*, that man was Muffin.

Still, those first days, as the ship let out her sail and wafted south from Cádiz, were hard for a new boy aboard, much less one whose credentials were falsified. The problem wasn't sexual harassment; if so, it was a different sort from the tavern's. They wanted to make a man of her, these hardy sailors, and they set about it with a certain sadism.

Her duties with Steele became the pinnacle of her days. She served him the meals that the cook, Griswold, prepared in the steamy, brick-paved galley, fetched what he called for and even acted as casual listening post.

The *Salamander* was bound for Africa, she learned, on an errand Steele despised but found necessary. For some "Spanish don." They would return to Cádiz soon, and then off, to the wide Atlantic to "resume the game." He would never say what game. Miranda began to understand the isolation of command: his men must ever be kept in their places. As long as she remained less than a man, she might serve him in some special way.

She liked the life, despite the daily menu of dry sea biscuits dusted with weevils, the pasty puddings and occasional beef jerky. She even pictured herself aboard all her days—wriggling through the *Salamander*'s 'tween decks, riding her bowsprit to watch the waves ruffle from her prow, standing in the captain's cabin while snatches of glorious plans unfolded . . .

She came to earth, or deck rather, one fair day of sunshine and westerly winds, when the ship ran herself along the waves and the crew was almost idle. Steele was closeted with his charts; landfall was near and this coast of Africa was relatively unknown. And Muffin, well, Muffin couldn't be there every moment.

At first Miranda didn't notice the sailors gathering until they formed a loose knot around her on the main deck. There was Brown, a leader when mischief was on the menu, and Smeach, the clever one who organized the games below when Steele wasn't looking too hard. And Weatherbee, only seventeen and jealous of Miranda's entree to the captain. Perhaps Weatherbee had hoped to serve in a way for which Steele had no use.

Miranda had been whittling a whistle for Muffin with her Spanish dagger when she looked up to see the sailors arrayed around her. Apprehension unpacked itself for the first time since her first day aboard, but she knew enough not to show it.

"Weeeell. Richard. Me lad." Brown gave her a long look. "We've been thinkin', there's little ye know about the ship aloft. Time you ran up a riggin' or two."

"Aye," seconded Smeach. "Today's a fine wind a-blowin', there'll be a good rock to the riggin'. As good a day as any to test yer skill on the ropes." He licked his lips then, as he did when he had a gaming opponent on the run.

Miranda stopped whittling to eye the vast network of rope swaying above. Sailors she'd seen scuttling aloft made it look so easy, as if they'd had a monkey's tail to help them.

"Richard's not man enough to do it, boys, so leave the little lady alone." That was Weatherbee, malice drawing out every demeaning word.

Miranda felt pricked in the pride. She didn't know if it was masculine pride, but it was pride, and it pinched to be so ridiculed. She stood to brush the wood shavings from her trousers. Her moist palms held the wood curls to them. She dusted them together and thought what Harry would do: meet their challenge or forever be flotsam to them. They had all been initiated as rudely on some distant day; it was their privilege to pass the ignominy along.

She gazed up at the rigging, growing small as it arrowed upward. A smart wind snapped aloft; they'd not picked an easy day for it.

"I'll hold your weapon. You might fall and cut yourself," Weatherbee offered.

"There's only one way you'll ever hold my knife, Tom Weatherbee," she said significantly.

A chuckle ran round the men. They liked brave talk, but brave deeds better. She jumped lightly to the gunwale and put her feet in the first hempen rung, already a fall away from deck.

Smeach was whispering round the circle—"Three shillin's on no further than the halfway."

Miranda curled her bare toes around the rough ropes, hardened by sea salt and warm in the sun. They were jungle vines and she was a light little monkey with a leopard behind her.

She began upward, going lightly. 'Twas more tiring than she'd thought! She paused for breath and to rest her reddened hands when a wind gust shook the rigging until it trembled like a cobweb. She stared aloft, expecting to see some huge insect of prey come stalking out from under the shrouds.

She saw only the mast top, still distant, still a sky-piercing speck above her. She looked down, a dizzying mistake. The men were far away and featureless. She saw excitement shiver around the group as they nudged one another and speculated on her. She even thought she heard someone urge her on.

Turning, Miranda shut her eyes against the height and struck upward again. The squares narrowed now. Her feet sometimes slipped a rung to catch in the one below. Her hands were rope-raw, and the wind threatened to tear her from her hempen cradle. When a gust blew up, she would sway sickeningly from side to side until the breeze died down. Then she would climb again.

At last she could climb no farther; she paused under the thick-timbered yardarm. The yardarm was wide, but she was glad no one had challenged her to walk it. Miranda forced herself to look around. The world was a billow of sail, of canvas filling and slacking around her like clouds—puffing out there, caving in here, until she was uncertain which way was north or south or up or down.

Her glance plummeted to deck for orientation and betrayed her ... only a yawning passage downward to flat hard board where a few flyspecks of a crew looked up at her. Miranda clung to her perch. She would never descend. She would hang for eternity amid the topsails' heaving white bosoms. The seas beyond were so perfect, so blue. They, too, were topped by ridges of topsail, white foothills of froth across the blue-green plain.

If at that moment she could have plunged into that sea, she would have. It would have been more welcoming than the deck, than crashing down at Weatherbee's feet. Even that hateful thought couldn't budge her. She was afraid. She had reached the top and she was paralyzed.

Fear kept her eyes fastened on the deck below. She saw a new figure inch its way over to the conclave directly below. An arm detached itself from the mass to wave at her. Steele. It was Steele from the way the circle separated and drew back. A wisp of wind wafted his bellowed words up to her.

"Richard, come down. Immediately!"

Miranda wished desperately that there really were a Richard up here to obey him. Her eyes swept the horizon again. The figure below moved toward the rigging, and Miranda made herself loosen her grip from the ropes. Steele had brought her aboard. She wouldn't have him climbing aloft after her like a nurse after a treed kitten.

Carelessly she plunged down the ropes, her feet and hands sliding from one level to the next until she was falling more than descending. Breathless, she finally glanced down to find the sailors' heads but a few feet below. A cheer went up; she could tell who had wagered on her success. Weatherbee's face was a sullen mask. Steele's face, when he caught her by the waist and swung her to deck, was simply a mask.

"Since you've spare time aplenty, we'll work on maneuvers this afternoon," he said shortly to the men.

They vanished, leaving Miranda as alone on deck as when she had been whittling. She picked up and almost dropped the nearly completed whistle.

"Quite an agile monkey," commented Steele, perusing her open palms with the skin hanging in white tatters. They began to burn like tropical ant bites. "Griswold will grease your hands. You're not sea-hardened enough for the rigging."

"Aye, Captain." She turned to go, but his voice stopped her.

"Were you merely enjoying the view up there, or were you afraid?"

"Afraid, Captain?" She debated giving him the brave answer, the boyish answer, the braggart's answer. "Aye, Captain," she said, meeting his eyes.

"Good." He smiled. "I've no room for utter fools on my ship."

Chapter Five

"Why didn't Griswold give you bandages?" Steele asked with a frown the next morning when she brought his breakfast and nearly dropped the heavy tin tray. The evil-smelling lard Griswold had smeared on Miranda's hands soothed the pulsing but made them slick. "You'll wear the skin off as fast as it grows back."

Miranda studied the tops of her hands. She didn't want bandages because there was always a sailor passing through the galley. To sit there and have her hands tended would be too much like a—girl was the word that passed through her mind, though the irony didn't register.

"Come here." Steele fished a length of linen from the desk. "A well-ordered captain's cabin always has bandages for the victims of war—of one sort or another."

He sat on the desk edge and methodically wound the long linen strips around Miranda's lacerated palms. She watched the top of his head intently, reflecting that no one had so tended her since the late Mistress MacTavish had dogged her footsteps with ointments for scratches and herbal applications for bites and bruises on Barbados. Harry—for Miranda had become more like him—cracked away. She had the odd sensation of feeling her own self for once, but fresh, as if she had become different somehow.

"There, better, isn't it?" Steele tied off the last wrist and glanced up at her as if he knew it was more painful to hide hurt than to have it.

A tear readied itself to leap to her eye.

"Aye, Captain," she said, steadying the impulse.

His blue eyes grew amused. " 'Captain,' " he mocked. "I tire of being 'Captain' all the time."

"Yes, sir," she said.

"Between us, you may call me Kit. I call you Richard, don't I?"

"Y-yes, sir. I mean, Kit."

Call him Kit! She'd only heard Old Muffin call him that. Only Old Muffin and now her. The eldest and the youngest. It meant he trusted her. It meant he liked her. Or Richard rather, Miranda remembered, coming to herself. Yet it was something few else in the crew could claim, even though it was doled out as a sweet is to a hurt child.

"That feels quite right now," Miranda said gruffly, flexing her fingers.

"Good," said Steele. "Now run along. I won't need you till supper."

He was already pulling the charts from their container when the door swung shut behind her and Miranda stood blinking in the sunlight with her new importance radiating from her. She dove below to find Muffin.

"Here comes the monkey," shouted Black Ned as Miranda made her way along the low 'tween-decks passageway. A cluster of off-duty seamen gathered around Smeach, engrossed in one of his games of dies. Calling her "monkey" now was a form of acceptance, even admiration, and she didn't mind. Brown had told her yesterday—after the grinding afternoon of maneuvers through which Steele had put the crew—that she had gone up and down the rigging faster than any "green 'un" he had ever seen.

Muffin was not so impressed. She'd given him the finished whistle that morning. The old man merely narrowed his hard brown eyes and commented, "So this is the whistle Old Muffin almost didn't get. Let's see if it makes a pretty tune."

And he blew a mournful melody upon it, a death march. So of them all, only Muffin knew that she'd nearly killed herself with her reckless dive down the rigging. And only—Kit—knew that she'd been afraid.

Brown pulled her down beside the squatting men. "Our Monkey's gettin' to be quite a little man; you care to toss the dies wi' us? 'Tis a glorious game we've got goin'."

"I used up all my luck yesterday," Miranda demurred.

"Say you." Weatherbee's face was pale with venom in the lantern light. "Mayhap it's more than luck. It does no harm when the captain comes to pull yer bloody arse outa the fire. Mayhap he has a personal interest in it."

Miranda felt the flush rinse her face, but calmed the urge to hurl herself across the circle of sailors at Weatherbee. Now she could afford to reach not for her dagger, but her tongue.

"A man," she said slowly, and there was no question what she meant by the words, "can answer his own accusers. I'm in," she instructed Brown, "though I've naught but Spanish steel to wager. But if I lose and I don't seem to have it on me any longer, I will wager that you'll find it on Weatherbee. Or *in* 'im."

The men laughed as Miranda threw the dies, a lucky toss. She kept her steel but decided to quit the game once the lad across from her had slunk away.

"A bad 'un," Black Ned whispered at her elbow. "You may need yer Spanish pigsticker yet."

"Aye," said Solitary Smith, a long, lanky seaman whose words often stood as singly as his social habits.

"Our Monkey here will soon be strappin' enough for the likes o' Weatherbee." Smeach cuffed Miranda lightly along the head in the roughhouse manner that passed for affection among them. "I even believe I spy the bristle of a hair along these downy cheeks," he added, squinting fiercely at Miranda's embarrassed face. "What think you, Muffin? You've got eyes'd put a crow's-nester to shame."

Muffin leaned forward in the dim light to drill Miranda's features with a gaze so undiluted that she anticipated being found out in the next second. Black Ned plucked suddenly at her cheek and held an invisible hair triumphantly up against the lantern light.

"Aye, here 'tis, lads. A true hair, it is. What d'ye know? Our little manny here is turnin' into a veritable ape, or I'm damned."

With which pronouncement he drew his wicked thick knife and split the air between his fingers solemnly as if he were cleaving a hair.

Utter nonsense; for a moment Miranda almost denounced it as such. Hair would no more sprout from her cheek than roses from snow, but that wasn't proper thinking for her current role.

"A hair?" She let the smallest sliver of hope intrude into her dubious accents. "D'you really think so? You wouldn't be leadin' me on——?" She rubbed a doubtful hand over her velvet chin.

"Leadin' you on? Why, me good lad, there's nary a man aboard the *Salamander* but's as honest as a church is tall." That was Smeach, looking tolerably wicked. "No, truth is, yer startin' a man's growth. So much so, I think we should have it off. What say you, me lads?" His glance around the circle ended with a broad wink. "Muffin, hav'ee any of that soap for señoritas from Lisbon? For so tender a lad a touch of lavender, I think, to take away the sting."

Miranda wriggled forward to freedom but Black Ned's hammy hand, as grimy as his name, held her back.

"Don't tell me the bucko's afraid of a wee knife?" He brandished his clumsy blade before her nose.

Muffin soon returned with the soap, a thick oily bar that smelled rancid, but a shipboard treasure nevertheless.

"We'd better have our lad abovedecks, where there's light aplenty. We wouldn't want to slit the urchin's throat 'fore he's had time to become a man full grown."

Muffin's voice of moderation won nods all round. The men had Miranda sandwiched between them and into the bright sunlight in a twinkling. Muffin reappeared with a water basin and a cracked bit of mirror, a towel from the galley flapping ludicrously across his arm.

"Here we are, milord," he announced. "Now lather up good or the blade's liable to slip an' dance a jig upon yer jugular."

Black Ned offered the soap. Miranda wordlessly immersed her face in the basin and rubbed the bar over it until a bubbly slime covered her cheeks and chin.

"Don't be forgettin' the throat, mate. You must learn to do a proper job upon yer own 'fore you take the edge to a Frenchy or a Dutchy."

Miranda mustered a quieting glance at Smeach, who barely restrained his gleeful giggles, and accepted Black Ned's extended blade. First she washed it and wiped it on the towel—God only knew how many gullets it had been run into, not merely over.

"What nicety," Black Ned noted with a guffaw. "Mayhap we have found ourselves a ship's barber, mates!"

The variously haired faces around Miranda nodded solemnly, bending close as she scraped the blade along her tender cheek. Too hard, for she drew a bit of blood in the paltry piece of mirror Muffin's unsteady hands held up.

"Hold the bloody bauble still," Miranda was startled to hear herself growl, sounding almost like Black Ned. The crew crowed.

For the first time Miranda understood that profanity was rooted as much in pride and pain as in irreligiosity. She tried again, but the cumbersome blade skipped across her face like a stone across water. Finally she swept a wide enough swath across her skin to satisfy the vastly amused crew members, who let her wash her raw face with little more heckling.

"A tiresome process," commented Miranda ill-temperedly. "I'd rather be a Red Man from the New World, for they have no hair upon their faces to shave, I've heard tell."

"That's because they pluck 'em out—one by one." Black Ned leaned close, looking ready to demonstrate the ordeal.

"Keep your distance, Black Ned, or I'll pluck out your nose hairs one by one and that would be a task to occupy the better part of a day."

The hirsute sailor threw back his head, revealing even more of his nostrils well endowed with black fur, and laughed. These sailors liked to have their tails tweaked, Miranda had discovered. It all meant nothing—unless an overample ration of rum had addled their brains and then men would die over trifles.

Life at sea bred boredom. Unwise captains used rum as an antidote, but liquor only redirected idleness, it never released it. And so they had their games, usually harmless, occasionally fatal.

She shrugged away from the circle and crawled out along the bowsprit that lanced beyond the prow, a place they seldom troubled her. She watched the green waves curve from the prow below her in comparative peace until Griswold passed the word for her to collect the captain's supper.

Steele had no time for dining that evening. He had her set the tray on his desk so offhandedly that she knew she'd find the food dishes cold and almost full when she retrieved it. Rolls of parchment cluttered the cabin like scattered bones. The *Salamander* would be anchoring soon to pick up cargo for the Spanish don in Cádiz.

Land. The idea was welcome. Used as Miranda was to the constant sway under her feet, to pitch and roll, a steady horizon would be a comfort. She nimbly made her way to the below-decks hammock, lowest of the low, assigned her.

Thoughts of making port thronged her mind when something sharp, hard and burning flashed by her ribs from the darkness.

She fell, striking the ship's hard side with a sound that echoed off the timbers. Her own knife was in her hand and dissecting the darkness around her. Something squealed near her foot and scuttled away.

The thought of rats lurched her upright. No more sounds came but labored breathing—her own or another's—and the creak of the timbers supporting the ship's wooden sides.

A dark figure rose suddenly against the distant passage light and lurched toward her. It withdrew with a shriek as her blade pierced some part of it. And now here was Smeach rounding the corner and collaring something that sought to scuttle away, like the rat.

"Here! I'd not called any game meets down here tonight. Come along, lads, there's something queer here."

Miranda, still breathless against the ship's broad ribs, held her own and welcomed Muffin's face among the gathering sailors. Things always went better with Muffin there.

Rough hands hauled her into the light. The shadow that had engulfed her surfaced also, revealing the sullen and wincing face of Weatherbee, who clutched his arm while blood trickled from his white-knuckled fingers.

"Cut me, the bloody little wharf rat did," whined Weatherbee, anxiously reading the faces around him.

"Be that true, Monkey?" Muffin sounded stern.

"Aye," Miranda admitted. Strange, her voice was hoarse and every breath seemed to evoke a wave of fire that lapped against her side. When she didn't speak again, hands hauled her closer into the light. Miranda followed the sailors' gaze to the narrow ring of red that pooled on her shirtfront.

"Oh," she said, surprised. The seamen nodded grimly, and the hands supporting Weatherbee became custodial.

Someone tossed Miranda a half-mended jersey she tied tightly around her ribs. Feet echoed along the hatch ladder; she realized that Brown had been gone awhile. His anxious face reappeared with the captain's set features directly behind.

"All right, what's this?"

Neither combatant answered. The wavering lantern light in Muffin's hand painted Steele's face into a Mephistophelian mask.

"Hathaway. Explain yourself."

"I—I was coming below, Captain . . . something hit me. It—it was dark. I struck at it. Then someone screamed and the crew came." A pause brought no comment. "That's all, sir," she added lamely.

"Weatherbee?" snapped Steele, only his eyes turning to the boy slumped between the sailors holding him.

"Captain, sir, I—I didn't do it. I was just passing. I heard what he heard. It was a mistake . . ."

Weatherbee's tongue darted through his thin lips and then retreated. As he swallowed, his prominent Adam's apple bobbed like a longboat in a sea trough and went under. Silence held in the semidark passage.

"Yes, you made a mistake, Weatherbee," said Steele finally.

Quiet held for a moment longer, while every eye but Weatherbee's held the captain's face. Steele had absolute rule on the high seas. He could hang a man for fighting, and no one would contest it; no one would rebel, as long as the offense was clear.

"I'll give you a choice and I'll give it now only," Steele went on, keeping his eyes somewhere to the side of the young sailor's face.

Weatherbee's head lifted with hope. Choice. Few captains offered seamen choice. Miranda felt sorry for him, for anyone whose gaze Kit would not meet head-on. She knew Steele had made a decision even he did not like.

"You can either take twenty lashes at the rigging, or I'll put you ashore in Africa and be done with it."

Africa—an alien, frightening land, populated by savages and as savage wildlife, but it was choice, a chance. Twenty lashes along the back before the entire crew was infinitely worse, Miranda knew instantly. She saw how the word "lashes" had licked across the sailors' faces. A public whipping was the heat of hell and hot humiliation, forever the mark of dishonor engraved upon one's flesh. Her own shrank at the thought.

Weatherbee's face had flattened until it seemed but a painting of a man, and a poor one at that. He struggled once in his captors' hands as his mouth ground in indecision. The look he turned on Steele was calm finally.

"The lashes, Captain," he said to the eyes that did not quite regard him. Steele stiffened. He would have preferred the other course.

"Very well," Steele said. "Put him in irons until eight bells tomorrow. Bracegirdle will administer the sentence."

Miranda would have gladly crossed a thousand Africas than

have submitted to the cat-o'-nine-tails. Weatherbee's pathetic choice was so servile it sickened her. She couldn't fathom that kind of twisted devotion, nor the jealousy that had spurred it. Weatherbee couldn't kill any favor Steele held for her in his heart, even if his knife had stilled Miranda's heart forever. Foolish, that kind of doting was foolish.

The sailors dragged off an unprotesting Weatherbee. He would have an early appointment with the leather, Miranda had noticed. Steele had shown that much mercy. She turned to join the sailors melting away when a hand stopped her.

"You'd better see Griswold again," Steele said flatly, his eyes flashing to her jersey-swathed side. Miranda jerked away, though it pained her.

"No," she said. "I'll be all right if I'm left alone."

She felt as if Death had reached out to brush by her. She wanted no solicitude from a captain who could assign his crew such hells as the rigging and the whip. Any fear or anger that the attempt on her life had startled up like a hare from the long grasses had soon rinsed away at news of the violence to be done Weatherbee.

Steele was a more constant danger than any jealous crewman, she realized. He was utter lord of every board and sheet of the *Salamander*. If she brought his dinner too cold, she could swing by her heels for it. Such power was evil, it was dangerous and she hated anyone who held it. Miranda slithered away through the low passage, finding her hammock and swinging until her head stopped aching and even the close rancid smell of the underdecks couldn't keep her from sleeping.

Muffin woke her barely in time to collect the captain's breakfast. He handed her a clean shirt without comment and Miranda donned it. Her side ached and burned, but the scratch would heal faster than the whip welts Weatherbee would nurse.

Griswold, even his dumpling face flat with anxious anticipation, handed her the tray. She rushed up the stairs to Steele's cabin. Outside his door she gathered herself, then knocked. Steele was at the desk, still elbow-deep in parchment. His bed, she noticed, looked unrumpled from the night behind him, but his face did not.

"A fair day, is it?" he asked, looking up. The frank blue gaze troubled her; she'd expected his eyes to flash fire as they had seemed to in the previous night's lantern light.

"F-fair, I didn't notice, C-Captain," stammered Miranda. In

her dash across deck, under strain of Weatherbee's sentence as every crew member must be until the deed was done, she had not observed so frivolous a thing as whether the sun shone.

Steele's elbows suddenly pinned the parchments to the desk as he leaned his face on his fists.

"You don't think it's 'fair' at all today, do you, Richard?"

He said the word "fair" with a difference; Miranda's throat went dry. "No, Captain, I—I—"

"You wish mercy for your attacker. You will deal with Weatherbee yourself and let fate ride the dies, isn't that right?"

"Yes, Captain, I don't see—"

"—why, as the one offended against, you should not be able to defer judgment. You would be magnanimous, wouldn't you, Richard? After all, you survived with only some dirty laundry for your trouble." His voice was becoming light and cutting, with the edge of anger driving it.

Christopher Steele stood, instinctively keeping his fair head bowed to the low cabin ceiling. He looked a bit like a charging blond bull, Miranda realized—tenacious, powerful and bewilderingly infuriated, as if gnats were driving him to distraction even as he charged. She could guess why.

Steele didn't care to have fools like Weatherbee among his crew—fools who were fuel for above- and belowdecks contention. He didn't like to stand on a good hardwood deck under a clean sky to watch the whip do its leather fandango across human leather. He didn't like to do his duty and he didn't want wraithlike cabin boys with lily-white faces reminding him of the fact.

"You like the *Salamander*?" he demanded.

The pale face flickered before him, startled by his tone.

"Aye, Captain."

"And you don't get seasick, though we've not had to put about and face off a gale as yet?"

"N-no, Captain."

"And if the *Salamander* were yours, and she could at any moment be overrun by seas, scurvy, mutiny, French frigates, Spanish galleys or Dutch men-o'-war, would you pause at giving twenty lashes where deserved if they were the glue that held all this creaking timber together?"

Miranda considered. She glanced up once to see his eyes still fixed upon her. She pulled all his "ifs" together and weighed the fragile survival of a ship manned by a half-willing, half-wild crew on hostile waters against Weatherbee. In the face of that, Weatherbee's eternal whine wound away into the wind.

All she heard was the dull roar of the seas pounding the *Salamander*'s pitched sides, all she felt was the steady rock of the floor beneath her feet. It was mere driftwood—gloriously gilded and carved driftwood, to be sure, from the prow's figurehead to the Jacob's ladder that dangled from the stern. Soon-to-be driftwood, merely a matter of time and chance. Against that had Weatherbee made his choice.

"No, Captain."

Steele had watched the inevitable answer forming on her face. He looked as if he felt inordinately pleased with himself, as if he had won a war of wills. Had she read his thoughts, she would have been even more surprised, for Steele was reassessing her.

"What ship brought you to Cádiz?" he asked casually, coming round to sit upon the desk. "Where does a cast-off boy come by such grand sentiments as forgiving one's enemies? Such notions are only to be learned in books, not in life."

Miranda edged away. " 'Twas no ship, sir, 'twas a small boat and almost dashed us on the rocks at the jaws of the bay."

"Us?" A gentle inquiry, a very careful inquiry.

"My brother and I. My brother was—lost, going ashore. I haven't seen him since. Harry." Some feminine impulse would have betrayed her by a tear but the lantern swung softly and dimmed any glisten in her eye.

"And how did you get your small boat, Richard?"

"Stole it," she answered honestly. Steele laughed until his teeth glittered as white as a Barbados beach, or as white as bleached bone.

"We were taken by pirates—we were!" Miranda protested into his disbelieving amusement. "Off the coast of Spain. Bound for England from Barbados—"

"Why?"

Should she say it—that they were pampered children of a wealthy planter sent "home" to England? Then he would send her there, too. "We were—indentured, Kit. Our families sent us there." Lies, but true enough of the many servant-children Miranda had known.

Servants indentured to the Indies islands found the settlers drunken and roistering, found mosquitoes that bit one bloody, found chiggers and cockroaches that crawled the bed and table legs at night. The island was a hot, humid place, with the fierce flesh-eating Caribs often over the next jungle rise. These bondsmen longed for premature release. And sometimes found it . . . in death or disembarking. It hurt her to tell Steele the ugly side of her beloved Barbados and not of its stained-glass colors and wild jungle calls, but it was all true enough.

"Harry and I, we hid away on a merchantman bound for England, but the pirates took it. Burned her to the bowline, too, until she was only a far, faint match on the horizon."

Steele could almost see that small red glow in the greens of the eyes before him. Could watch a good ship and true sink to her last in the emerald waters off Spain.

"So you slipped bond, not a very honorable thing to do, Richard."

"Honor. He told me honor was a sentiment from books, that Dutch pirate captain, only I disbelieved him then—"

"The Dutchman!" Steele rose, his hands on Miranda's arms as if he wanted to shake the words from her faster. "You've seen the Dutchman, been in his hands and escaped? By God—tell me about the Dutchman! Here—a dash of rum will unravel the remembering. They say there is no set of eyes that have seen the Dutchman that is not bedecking the stomach of a sea creature at this moment."

Stunned, Miranda accepted the cold tin cup filled with hot-tasting rum and sat upon the desk-side stool. "He said he left no witnesses, he said . . . but then he *did* set us wrong, adrift, out toward the edge of things. I thought it was a mistake. All this time. But had he pointed us aright, after all, to his purpose, you see—?"

"No, I don't see. Slow down."

Miranda sipped the rum—no new flavor. Father had always seen her goblet filled when any liquor was served. His girl had more need for a hard head in this world, he'd told the clucking Mistress MacTavish, than his boy. This was rough rum, not the silken topaz-gold stuff her father had refined in his sugar mill. She coughed slightly, then continued.

"After the pirates came, I—hid myself. The Dutchman found me and took me to his cabin. He was very odd; he told me he had no mercy in him, for anyone. He said that I was a fool and he as well . . ."

"What of your brother during all this?"

"Harry. Harry was—" Miranda set the cup on the desk, for it was starting to tremble in her hand. She put her palms on her knees and decided to face the truth in her tale. "They'd taken him. The crew, the pirates. For themselves. He was the only one aboard left living. Save me."

Steele finally broke the silence. "And you were in the cabin with the Dutchman. It's luck you weren't born female, for I've heard the Dutchman may not share his crew's tastes, but he has a formidable set of his own to the opposite. No woman would have left that cabin with her virtue or her life. He is said to like his lovers dead."

Miranda poured a dose of rum down her quivering throat; Steele couldn't know what he had just told her. She felt as if she had risen from a rest in a burial ground and some of its mold and dust still clung. He had let her go; he had been a fool. The Dutchman.

"Who is he, Kit?" she asked softly, almost expecting to learn the Dutchman was a spirit, after all.

He sighed. "Perhaps the finest sailor in all the wide Atlantic. The Dutchman seems to have charted in his head places that no quill has yet set to parchment. Many have sworn to seeing his ship sail into certain sinking, only to find it riding in port a month later as snug at anchor as a gull in a cliffside nest. They say he's half-fish, or half-Devil, though none be saint enough to survive an encounter and testify to it." Steele's cobalt eyes fell significantly on Miranda. "Not till you, Richard. You're an enchanting fellow to enthrall the Dutchman, no wonder you found me easy prey," he teased.

"Kit, I—" she protested, but he waved her silent.

"What is it about you—? You're fresh steel, foreign in some way, like your precious Barcelona blade there—yes, I've seen how you hang on to it. You believe in some things that few but poets ever have."

" 'The quality of mercy,' " Miranda interjected for some reason, remembering another crabbed line from her father's rapidly decaying folios.

Steele paused, caught by the phrase.

She saw his mind seek the source and find it.

"And did they have court interludes and such on Barbados, too? You make that vermin-ridden pesthole you fled sound habitable."

"I—worked as clerk, Kit, for a very well read man, though his folios were falling into a sad state from the climate and the insects."

Steele nodded, his curiosity still adrift on the Dutchman's mystery. "He's never left a single survivor. Not one man, woman or child who could point any but a bony finger at him. By St. George, I'd like to ship him to London and a hanging on Execution Dock before a bayful of ships."

"Is that the 'game' you play?"

Steele looked puzzled, then smiled. "No, that's not my game, but if the king of the board ever fell into my hands I'd be a fool not to make checkmate of it. I'm ever an opportunist; that you will learn, Richard." His eyes left her again. "The Dutchman. He had been a great explorer once, I hear, as sure at navigating uncharted waters as a bat is of his foul cave. Then he turned pirate—why no man knows—and not a country but its ships have disappeared into bubbles on the surface and rumors of the Dutchman in the breeze. I sometimes doubted him, like a heretic his God. I'll keep better faith now, if I have your word on seeing him, Richard."

"Aye, Kit, I saw him. Spoke with him. He seemed a very weary man to me. That is all. Too weary to be evil."

"You still think that evil is perpetrated from strength, don't you? Evil breeds in weakness, remember that. Your weary Dutchman has ever been so and will go on doing evil until the world wearies of him and destroys him."

"He let us go."

"Facing west into the wide, wild ocean that would have racked you well before it let you drown."

"He let us go."

"Stubborn."

"So they said on Barbados."

Steele collected the cup from Miranda's hand. "Enough for a babe of thirteen. You've had a lively life thus far, Richard; if you hang on to it, I predict great things for you."

Chapter Six

The coast of Africa slipped over the horizon like a pool of liquid butter—so hot that it shone: the Spanish Sahara, sprawling for rippled golden mile after mile.

Miranda hung over the gunwale watching it. The instant Steele had left in the longboat for shore, she had wheedled the glass from Muffin and kept that elongated eye fixed on the exotic shore party.

Beasts with silly harelipped heads and stiltlike legs abounded—camels, confirmed Muffin, beasts of burden like the mule, but odder. The robed figures that moved slowly among the grotesque mounts were as much a mystery.

Miranda swung the glass to the longboat. The *Salamander*'s crew seemed calm enough, rowing onto that astonishing shore. And Steele—there, sitting in the prow with the oaken strongbox in his hands—Steele looked a bit grim but unsurprised.

Miranda had to surrender the glass when the first cargo-loaded boat returned. It would not do to gawk. Yet gawk she did as the *Salamander*'s block and tackle came swinging over the gunwale to drop scores of bales, baskets and barrels to deck. One bale's wrapping tore away—a slice of magenta tissue worked in gold shone through like an alien sun.

When a barrel broke a foot above deck, the tinkling of brass riveted every ear as a golden harvest of ewers, lamps and lengths of small chiming bells cascaded across the boards.

The last of the new cargo climbed over the side with the sailors: four veiled women draped in dull blue-black stuff from their heads to their hidden feet. They resembled blind old crones—and blind they probably were; Miranda couldn't imagine how they saw through the face veiling. Yet, when they moved, a random jangle bespoke richer stuff beneath the black. An abrupt silence hung over the deck; Miranda glanced back to the gunwale.

The last passenger stood on deck as if materializing precisely there. He was just beyond boy, his bare feet planted wide on the heaving planks and his head thrown back to survey the *Salamander*'s furled sails. His skin was the shade of the drink made from Grenada's cocoa beans; it flowed like a mocha river from his curly black hair, across his well-modeled face, down his bare and hairless chest and even to the dusty feet visible beneath his robe. His hands were the same fascinating shade, and bound by a leather strap.

The Arab boy—for there was something clear and untarnished about him though he was likely older than Miranda—watched impassively while the rowers leapt over the gunwale alongside him.

Steele came last, nodding to the quartermaster. The women were shepherded to the passenger cabins below. The boy's eyes, hot black with resentment, swept once around the deck, passing

Miranda and then paging back to her in an instant. A frown shattered the aloof control of his brow. His brown eyes fixed on her intently, like a finger pointing.

Miranda's heart raced so wildly her arms seemed to throb. Discovery. He knew! She felt as she had on hide-and-catch-me expeditions with Harry, as though she waited silent behind a thick tropical screen and then, in a space between two leaves, a space as narrow as a snake, his finding eye was focused on her and the game was over.

All these countrymen of hers, these well-traveled sailors, this well-read captain, they saw nothing beyond her boyish façade. Yet this one knew, as if it were his nature to so know.

His lips parted slightly, not to speak but to mouth surprise in his mind. Solitary Smith came up and yanked on the leather cord. The boy's eyes left Miranda to flare at the sailor, but he followed docilely enough, like a tethered horse that knows he must serve whoever pulls his lead.

Miranda looked quickly to Steele, leaning against the gunwale with his arms crossed tightly on his chest as if holding something in. Steele was looking after the Arab boy with a frown. Then he wheeled and ordered the longboat drawn up.

No, Steele had not noticed the glance between the two "boys" on deck, for the *Salamander*'s new cargo seemed to have put new weight on its captain as well—a cargo of the conscience.

Steele was brusque and unapproachable all the way back to Cádiz. Miranda brought his meals and took away only a mechanical "Thank you." His charts were back in their containers and so were his confidences.

Miranda's duties now revolved around the passenger cabins. Each day a black-swathed woman would pad silently to Griswold's galley with a package. By the time Miranda was called, its contents had been transformed into strangely scented food on several trays that she would bear back to the cabin. Of the boy she saw no sign. And she was glad, though conscience cried not to be.

Not until Cádiz Bay rose on the horizon like a half-moon did Steele break his mood. They had arrived on the evening tide. The stars were pale beacons in a still-blue sky and the city was lighting itself up slowly to match. Steele leaned back in his cabin chair and eyed Miranda, the glimmer of a tease in his eyes.

"Richard." He laced his fingers together behind his head. "You've been naught but loblolly boy these last days, trundling trays from galley to guest—how would you like to go ashore with me tomorrow?"

Cádiz was no treat to her. He saw it in her immobile face.

"Not the port side, boy! The pinnacle. Don Ricardo's hillside palace. I go to collect my wages for serving as pack mule to a Spaniard: gold enough to make it worthwhile. The don's palace—you've seen naught like it. Nor I. Cool and hot at the same time, like rum. The gardens alone . . . you can come with me Richard. If you clean yourself."

His eyes flicked across Miranda almost as sharply as the Arab boy's had. She quailed inwardly, but Steele was nearsighted by now. She fit perfectly into the mental niche labeled "Richard."

"You're as filthy as the taverns again," he complained.

Miranda nodded meekly, eyeing the basin in which he had christened her when she first came aboard. Clean up? Aye, but where, with a sailor liable to lurch around every corner and discover her?

"One thing more, lad. You recall Cádiz. Yonder don may dance to the same desires as that Greek of yours, but there's no danger if you come with me," he added as her eyes hardened.

In the end Miranda was driven to stealing Muffin's bar of rancid soap and slipping over the *Salamander*'s side into the night-cool water during the midnight watch. She stroked away from the ship so the lapping waves wouldn't bruise her against the hull, and began lathering herself while treading water. Another island talent turned handy.

How shocked Mistress MacTavish had been that the Hathaway children could swim like fish. Such bathing was unhealthful, likely to upset the humors, produce vapors—Miranda laughed to herself, enjoying the long-withheld buoyancy of being waterborne, like a ship herself. She slid the soap over her breasts; a pleasure to have them unbound, the first she'd ever found in her own body. She soaped her hair, then sank below the waves to rinse it and rose smiling vengefully.

What would the Greek have thought if he had gotten her to himself? Or the don of whom Kit had warned her? How startled they would be to find how her outward appearance had deceived them. How amusing to think of them lusting after that which could never exist, a form of revenge, perhaps. For Harry. For the Dutchman's sailors who had lusted and been satisfied. She would like to match each one of his ravishers with one of her would-be ravishers frustrated.

Miranda's motions halted. The splash of a muffled oar, then another, came from the ship's landward side. Enough toilette. She climbed the side and peered over the gunwale. Cargo was being lifted off deck for shuttle ashore; now, in the dead of night, when no Spanish eye would see the Moslem hoard parading up to the don's hillside villa.

Miranda slithered across the deck, feeling like a snake without its skin, and dove below while her heart pounded against the clot of wet clothing she clutched to her breasts. Perhaps Mistress MacTavish had been right: sea-bathing was a most dangerous sport.

"By St. George, you *are* a towhead," Steele said the next morning when Miranda appeared at his cabin with her newly minted gilt hair tied back into a neat tail.

She had found a clean shirt of decent linen in the forecastle community clothing chest, and breeches as well. Only a rope drew the waist taut, but she had knotted it into a cradle to hold her dagger.

"You may need your fang," Steele noted. "The don is a dark-favored fellow with a yen for more that is yellow than New World gold, I've heard. Well, he's a formalist, too, so it's good you've tidied your timbers before sailing into his waters. Only look and listen, Richard—we two are not that pleased with each other beyond commerce. I wouldn't take you if I thought you'd tip the balance."

Miranda nodded. In fact, she was up to little more than listening and looking from the moment the don's lumbering carriage collected the pair on the Cádiz wharf to when they descended onto a paved and terraced hillside wild with fruit trees.

Within the walls of the sprawling stone palace cut into the incline was an open courtyard, with rows of cypress trees stretching down shaded walks. Birds darted overhead from bush to tiled rooftop niche, chirping welcome. A manservant led them up an exterior staircase and along a second-story balcony laden with fragrant flowering vines.

Their guide swung open a heavily timbered door. Kit and Miranda stepped into shadow so deep that they almost sank into it. The room was vast, shuttered and somber, its furnishings stiff and heavily carved. Flagged stone floors echoed their footsteps like a rock the drip of water. They paused at the room's center when a narrow door at one end split.

Something slender sheathed in black was in the room. It padded to them on velvet-shod feet: a slight man of middle years, no greater in height than Miranda herself. His jet hair and the slender strips of beard and moustache that intricately patterned his lower face were liberally woven with gray. Dark eyes of exceptional size and long-lashed grace floated in his neat olive face. All in sable velvet despite the Spanish heat, his body was tightly clad in breeches and doublet, like a snake's. He dressed in the fashions of Good Queen Bess's day, now long since vanished from France and England. He reminded Miranda of one of her father's woodcuts, a dapper narrow creature who should live in a portrait and nowhere else.

"Ah, my good Captain," he said, seeing only Steele. "So you found my mission possible, after all. I've a boy coming with your pay." His speech was deep and sibilant. Miranda thought of the Castillian-accented English that slid off Francisco's tongue . . . Francisco far away in Barbados, unaware of what had become of her and Harry. Ah, Harry, time to begin looking for him again, perhaps Kit would help—

"Don Ricardo," he was saying, "you didn't tell me of the passengers. The women will serve here as they would have in Morocco and do not concern me. But you did not tell me of the boy." Steele's mouth was a moving shadow in the shadowed chamber.

"Ah, the boy. Of course, you saw him. You have done more than I, then. I hear he is—beautiful, yes?"

"I am but a simple sailor, Don; I cannot speak to that."

Miranda recognized a certain distaste in Steele's tone; the same tang on the tongue that had afflicted Mistress MacTavish when she spoke of London theatricals. She glanced at Steele to ensure that he had not turned Roundhead in the last seconds.

"Ah, Captain." The don was amused. "So . . . English. No wonder our kinds war. But enough; I hear your gold coming. You can use it for your cause, and that will cool your conscience—"

The door behind the don swung open again. A boy in a richly embroidered India robe entered, bearing a heavy purse upon a silver tray. The don's ring-gilded hand wafted toward Steele as the boy came on, into the room's only pool of light—a pale shaft from an unfastened shutter.

His face was purely carved and pale, his eyes wide-set and calm, his hair beneath the elaborate turban that topped it quite, quite fair.

He was Harry.

Chapter Seven

She lunged for her brother—so long lost, so unexpectedly restored—she stepped into the light to intercept his gaze. His eyes flicked to her motion, then impassively returned to Steele, offering him the tray.

Harry, her mind screamed, it is Harry! Harry who went out on deck merely a moment ago, although she'd implored him not to, Harry who'd been at the riffling breakers' edge only a minute before she fell into blackness . . .

She lunged forward, but Christopher Steele's arm caught her up short. His vivid blue eyes silenced her, his message clear: he didn't want to ruffle the don and he intended to study this remarkable resemblance between the bootless cabin boy he had found and the pampered pet of a perverse Spaniard. They could have been twins; was this the supposedly drowned brother?

"Ah." The don had noticed the supposed Richard at last. "Sell me yours," he suggested smoothly. "Then I shall have a pretty pair of—bookends."

Miranda struggled silently, hearing nothing, hurling herself against Steele's restraining arm like a wave admonishing a rocky shore.

Christopher Steele was not unaware of her attempts. As she dashed herself upon his arm, he felt for the first time the swell of breasts against the tight jersey she wore beneath the loose shirt. He suddenly collared her by that shirt, almost jerking her off her feet.

"I'm sorry, Don Ricardo, but I must decline. This—lad—is far too valuable a member of my crew." Steele's polite words barely managed to squeeze between his clenched teeth.

Miranda darted her head to the one person who had not occupied her attention for the last few moments. Kit Steele was furious. She saw it in the way his sea-tanned face looked flat and masklike, in the tiny lines of warning edging narrowed, ice-blue eyes. She stopped flailing. This phenomenon was momentarily more arresting than finding her brother. Whatever could have caused this shift in him?

During her speculations, Steele seized the purse and made his adieus, forcing Miranda bodily from the room that held her brother.

"Not a syllable," he hissed, hastening her down the stairs and out into the quiet courtyard. "I'll not have the don's swordsmen on me with only a girl for a rapier mate."

A resident monk strolled there in the well-tended quiet. Steele bowed as the cowled figure passed like a shadow.

"How—?" began Miranda.

"Be silent, or I'll knock you so." Steele paused by a stone fountain with a flotilla of goldfish in its murky green waters. Miranda finally shrugged in silence and Steele loosened his grip on her shirt collar. "And come back to the ship quietly," he ordered less harshly.

The walk to the harbor was not long. Despite the impressive gesture of Don Ricardo's carriage, a short plummet down steep cobblestoned streets soon brought the visitor back to the glittering blue bay and dockside, were that his desire.

It was Kit Steele's desire; Miranda could barely keep pace with him. He lifted her into the waiting longboat and sharply ordered Muffin and his men to pull for the *Salamander*. Muffin's quizzical gray brows interrogated Miranda. She could only shrug.

Steele goaded her up the rope on board ahead of him.

"Kit—" she began once, turning to question him with her sea-troubled eyes. The old familiarity only struck blue sparks from the gaze behind her, and she subsided.

He shoved her into his small cabin and slammed the door. She had been alone with him there many times, but had never been afraid before. She was frightened beyond thinking about her brother for once. She'd thought she had gauged this man's moods, run the gamut of his possibilities. She hadn't.

"Damn," he said finally, throwing himself down at the desk and pulling a bottle of rum from the chest behind him. He had never done more than sip with the crew on the rare occasions he used liquor as reward or prod. Now he uncorked the neck and swigged from the bottle in the greedy manner of a pirate.

Miranda edged quietly toward the door. Muffin and a sunlit deck were infinitely preferable to her present location.

"Don't. You've caused enough trouble. I should turn you over to the crew; you'd soon find this is no Dutchman's ship. If the men knew they'd been sailing mates with a female these last weeks, they'd—"

He shook his sun-streaked head, scattering some of his anger with the gesture. "You've risked my command with the crew and you've made a proper fool of me," he went on more calmly, but still with something cold running through his voice like a needle through cambric.

Steele regarded her for a moment, then went to crouch beside his sea chest. He pulled out a cloak and breeches, shirt, stockings, laying the lot on the desk and weighting it with a jingling purse from the drawer.

Miranda felt suddenly marooned, like a ship cut loose of its moorings. "What are you doing?"

He wordlessly tied the bundle together, settled onto the chair and took another long pull from the thick green glass bottle of rum. Cheap rum, fit for sailors.

"What is your true name?" he asked presently.

"Hathaway." She had never lied about that.

"Your name," he repeated, leaning across the heavy desk like an Inquisitor.

Her given name, her first name, he wanted. Somehow she couldn't give it to him, cornered like this in his cabin. Her name was hers, her talisman, a link to what had been. She would not spend it cheaply.

"Richard, sir," she said coldly. Cross-grained . . . and stubborn, James Hathaway had always said of his daughter. Stubborn even when it was folly.

Steele slammed the bottle onto the desk so hard the amber fire within tilted and sizzled along the rim.

"Well, Richard," he said carefully, each syllable clear as a ship's bell. "I'm going to put you ashore here, Richard. A bright lad like yourself should have no trouble scavenging some simple soul, some lackwit like myself, to give you guidance in this wicked world."

He collared her again and shook her by the shirtfront until her head wobbled on her shoulders. "Damn! It's easier to acquire you than be rid of you."

His angry worrying had loosened the shirt from her wide-waisted trousers. His eyes fell to the evidence of breasts under the shrunken jersey now revealed. "Damn," he intoned again, as if expecting the word to show him the way. "You're doubtless virgin, too, despite the Dutchman?"

Miranda bit her lower lip, afraid even to discuss herself in such terms. Steele shook her again.

"Yes," she admitted, her teeth snapping down on her tongue.

"A downy-cheeked virgin—loose in Cádiz, barefoot and in breeches." He snorted in self-disgust. "Damned if I can do it."

He sank back at the desk and cradled his jaw morosely in his hand, watching her. His quandary would have been amusing had Miranda been frivolous enough to seek humor while her maidenhead was under discussion.

Christopher Steele considered the matter. He'd sailed many seas, made many ports. Innocence was a rare commodity in such places, soon put in its improper place. On the Mediterranean, a virgin was a prize as rich as Indies sugar, China silk or New World gold. Those who bought and sold such wares would scent out the girl before him more rapidly than his own rather guileless nature had—and those who bought virtue were least likely to display it. Her brother would have a softer life as the plaything of a doting don.

His eyes, blurred by indecision and bolts of rum, considered the figure before him. He reached out to undo the tie at the back of her neck, releasing the yellow furls across her shoulders.

Miranda turned her face from his hand as if expecting a cuff. His gesture had reminded her of the weary, nameless Dutch captain: he whom the man before her admired in his way . . . and longed to destroy. The Dutchman. Pearl, he had called her, that reputed devourer of maidens, the Dutchman. Then he had set her and Harry free. She believed that he had given her that chance, no matter how narrow.

Now she wanted to escape from another captain and another cabin; she craved freedom from the tight little room and the man who sat at the captain's desk and held her fixed like a compass point in his wounded blue eyes.

He studied her for so long and so soberly that she began to wish for a greedy circle of eyes, anything but this cool, blue summing-up.

But Kit Steele was realigning her, reassembling the familiar figure into its new feminine terms. She'd always looked delicate for a lad; perhaps that was why he had bothered to pluck her from the dockside tavern and the evil-smelling Greek who'd lusted so mistakenly after her boyish thighs. The clothing was over-large; it had hidden her.

Now he saw the slender waist and shoulders as well, and the pale lashes that thickly shaded those curiously colored eyes.

Eyes like a bottle-green sea waiting to spew bad weather at one, that still, sweet green before the gale.

Now they were dark, an ebony-green anxiety caught in a serious kitten face. She had been deceptively spirited for one of her sex. He remembered the tavern brawl—quick and competent with the rapier. Like a boy. Ready to trail her dagger in the Greek's ample entrails if need be. Yes, she might survive awhile by her wits and her confidence. Awhile . . . if she no longer had the intrinsic value of innocence.

He had risen and advanced on her without thinking.

Miranda retreated silently before him. She had thought many things about him—in the tavern that he was a fine swordsman who could slice her throat as neatly and unimpassionedly as any surgeon; on shipboard that he was an essentially reasoned man with heart enough to protect those more helpless than himself.

She had never thought of him as a male animal. But then, she'd never been a female animal to him.

He reached to undo the rope around her waist effortlessly—a sailor would know about knots. The breeches fell to her ankles with her dagger. The next step backward tripped her, but he caught her before she fell and scooped her up, her naked legs dangling over the crook of his arm.

Her limbs were mother-of-pearl white, he noticed, though her face was golden tan. She could have been a fine whey-faced lady, had her voyage not been detoured.

"What—?" she asked the place where the shirt collar fell away from his collarbone; she couldn't lift her eyes to those of the man who held her. The arm against her back was hard and supple as leather. His fingers dug a little into the tender edge of her breast.

"Please," she said to the neck level with her eyes—at least it wasn't a grimy neck, like most she'd seen since Barbados.

"I'm doing you a service, Madam Stowaway," he said, unloading her on the narrow bed like a bag of Barbados cotton ready for transport. "Though you may not receive it as such," he added, dropping down atop her then, not bothering to remove his breeches. "I won't have a virgin loose in Cádiz on my conscience, so I shall have to be on yours."

Too late Miranda understood and thought escape. His weight was above her, balanced on two arms that hemmed her in on either side. She lashed her head from side to side, the cabin furnishings reeling around her in an arc.

"Kit—" she said once, putting her hands up to his chest. Something might have flashed in his eyes—regret?—but the reflection was gone and he was heavy upon her, his legs between hers now, parting them. She bucked silently against him, saving all her strength for struggle. Not this, not-this-cold-taking ... better the Greek, better seaweed knotting her throat and chill, chill depths that froze memory ...

Something hard and hot and hateful drilled between her legs; her thighs tightened as a long hot knife plunged into her center. A moment before, she would have died rather than cry out, but now she did—a searing, soft indrawn cry as the veil of virginity gave before the male machine that breached her. And on that long agonizing breath he caught her to the length of his body.

"Shhhh," he whispered into the masses of tangled hair at her ear.

Miranda went limp. It was over. So quick and so much dead to her. She lay death-still on the bed as he withdrew and returned to the desk, as if her deflowering were a mere distraction from shipboard routine.

"Shhhh," he had said, and her mind hissed inwardly, over and over. She ached to make that "shhh" tangible and wind it around his throat, to strangle him with it. No undue noise at her rape, no. No undue tears. Such a casual matter. As casual as sliding a blade into a waiting back, a back like the one he so arrogantly, so carelessly, showed her now.

"You can clean up at the basin," he said without turning.

Miranda realized that her inner thighs clung to each other with something warm and sticky, like honey on a biscuit.

"And tie back your hair," he added as she started for the ewer.

She reached the water and trailed her fingers in its tepid little slosh. A sob raced round and round in her stomach, climbed impetuously to her throat and threatened to break into the open. Miranda jammed a fist between her teeth, but the wild thing in her throat broke out, half-strangled.

"Oh, God," said the man behind her whom she used to know, on a sigh.

Was that how one became weary like the Dutchman, too many maidens devoured too many times? Another sob exploded into sound, and another, until she was only a shaking thing huddled over a basin in a tiny cabin on a large ship rocking softly at anchor outside Cádiz, the roughest port in Europe.

"Sweet Jesus," swore the man behind her softly. "Your Spanish steel is on the floor. Take it—"

"And use it on myself?" she managed to pronounce between the strange noises that possessed her.

"Use it on whomever you like." A blaze of blue eyes over a white-shirted shoulder. "Muffin will take you ashore when you're ready."

The man she had thought was Christopher Steele shouldered his way into the—how strange—hot daylight outside the dark cabin and left silence behind him. Except for an odd hiccoughing that escaped from Miranda's mouth despite the hand she clapped over it.

She finally did as he had said. She washed the tender spot between her legs with a cloth, then wrung it out and brought it folded to the makeshift knapsack. She would leave no trace of her taking for him to gloat over. It was Harry's dagger she picked up from the floor, Barcelona steel retrieved from the *Merlin*'s deck, and now her only companion to exile. She almost left the careless bundle he had assembled.

Such solicitude, she thought, weighing the perfectly balanced dagger and dreaming of cutting his manhood off with it. Then the score would be even. Then he would be humiliated and half what he was.

But she needed to survive. For she would do that. Survive until Harry was safe again. What was one offhand rape compared to what poor Harry had endured? Was still enduring likely, made mindless in that slimy Spaniard's hands? Practical, she picked up the bundle after she had tied on her trousers. A better knot this time. *I learn, Christopher Steele, credit me with that much,* she thought.

It was good the little mirror was across the cabin; Miranda's face was not kittenish now. She had been so brave, surviving at the tavern. Something that had made it easy for her to be brave then was gone. He'd taken it away with him, a part of herself as bright and innocent and unafraid as a shield. He had taken her shield and left her only a knife.

She caught the blade in its sheath—and wasn't that what she had been, a mere human sheath for his blade, his dripping red blade? Someday she'd have it back of him. Some day. Now she wanted to lose herself among the street urchins who thronged Cádiz like a plague. Thank God Francisco had taught them Spanish flavored with street patois.

She counted the gold first. Small coins, unsuspicious in the possession of one so young if doled out slowly enough. How thoughtful he was. How eager to be rid of her. Down to the price in flesh and gold. But he had been generous; stingily dealt out, there was gold enough to get her to England.

She bent and laid the coins out along the soles of her shoes, covering them with cloth hacked from the cloak collar. If she had to swim for her life, the gold might serve as her anchor. If she had to run for her virtue—or had she none now?—it might serve as her hobble. But it was less likely to be stolen.

She went out onto the blazing deck. Muffin and two able-bodied rowers loafed by the gunwale and the quarter boat. Waiting for her on *his* orders. She walked over to them, to Muffin's questioning face.

"You'll take me ashore, then, Muffin?" she asked calmly, lowering her voice slightly and becoming Richard.

"Aye, lad." Muffin knit his brows, but the old seaman asked no questions.

Miranda jostled alongside the *Salamander* for the final time as the boat lowered bumpily into the sea. She had seen the last of Christopher Steele. Until Someday.

BOOK TWO:

The Forced Man

Sure there was wine
Before my sighs did dry it;
There was corn
Before my tears did drown it.
—George Herbert, 1633

Chapter Eight

*L*ondon lay limp and sluggish under the rolling gray sky of an impending summer storm. The heavy air was slightly warm with the promise of chill to come in an outpouring of wind and hail.

The Hathaway house stood on Old Broad Street behind the Strand—one of a sturdy-built row of bourgeoisie domiciles behind the gentry's grander mansions popping up along the waterway like cut-stone mushroom clusters.

The Hathaways were longtime Londoners—merchants who needed the nearby Thames with its harvest of docked ships, who required a center-city seat to weave their commercial webs. But gentry, gentry who for generations had been content to wax fat in the provinces, were now hieing to London to erect town houses.

With taxes, tariffs and tribute escalating so arbitrarily from the throne these troubled days, with Parliaments likely to dissolve and create on a whim, it was better to camp solidly on City ground and remind Londoners that England's great families were there to reckon with.

So the once-lordly Hathaway house was dwarfed these days by towering palaces competing for each aristocratic inch of Strand frontage. Inside its dark brick walls, Helena Hathaway sat at her tapestry, working the rich blues and golds into the fancied Flemish style, when the servant brought news of an intruder on the stoop.

"A street boy? In my kitchen? Why on earth did you admit him? What in heaven's name can the creature want? I'd think Silas could have seen him well out no matter how the urchin insisted. Oh, very well, I'll deal with it."

Having invoked both empyrean and natural worlds, Helena knit her placid brows and followed her bemused maid down the winding dark back stairs. "Her kitchen" it might be in concept; in fact, Helena's inclinations kept her well out of the running of it.

Such a smoky, low-ceilinged place! A grimy kitchen wench sat back on her heels and let the gray water puddle on the flagstones while her wide eyes fixed on Helena Hathaway's seldom-glimpsed figure.

They saw a lightly faded woman of five and thirty, clad in a Delft-blue gown with a broad white lace collar spreading over her sloping shoulders like melting snow. The girl's slack jaw closed with a snap as the bustling cook rustled by and aimed a discreet kick. The brush resumed its circular shuffle across the stone and the maid's eyes fell.

What Helena Hathaway saw was only steam and smoke and bustle . . . and a still figure in the midst of it, as disreputable and besmirched an urchin as she'd ever viewed running alongside the family carriage pleading for coppers near Highgate.

Helena's pale eyes darted instinctively to the nearest male for protection—only Old Silas, groveling with the air of a servant who knows he's in the wrong.

"I did what I could, mistress. Got 'im away from the front gate and 'e's in at the hind gate. Beggin' yer pardon, but I'll 'eave the lad again, though I be all over black-and-blue from the trouble 'e give me fore this—"

Helena bit her bloodless lip. The pressure made it paler. At times like these she truly regretted the husband fate had kept from her, regretted her brother James far-off and now quite dead on some foreign island, regretted—

"Aunt Helena?"

The urchin had spoken, and in precise, quite clear tones, not the street boys' mewling whine. Helena started forward, catching a high heel in a crack and tottering for a moment. The tight knot of worry bound to her for the past two months cracked open like a walnut.

"H-Harry?"

An unreadable expression darted across the dusty face before her. Then the urchin swept off the ragged scarf that bound the dingy yellow curls to its skull.

"Miranda? Miranda!" Helena regarded her never-before-seen niece, then swept forward, her plump white hands resting heedlessly on the dusty shoulders. "Oh, you've James's eyes, but child, where—?"

Helena's waxen nature melted and ran into an embrace. For a moment Miranda wilted against her aunt's stiff bodice, letting her filthy face sink upon Helena's immaculate collar like a footstep on snow. She drew back, surprised to see the woman rippling in her vision. Helena retreated and straightened her gown front as well as her ambushed emotions.

"And Harry? What of Harry? Oh, Miranda! I was so fretted. I feared we would never learn what had become of you two. I had only the one letter that you were bound here and no word since."

"Harry is—gone, Aunt."

"Gone?" The older woman's glance fell to the floor and met the startled stare of the scullery maid near her feet. "But you're tired, and so much to tell . . . we'll talk later. Come. It's quite all right, niece. You're home."

And was it home? Miranda had called everything from packet ship hold to country lane to dray wagon home during the weeks that she had spun out Steele's gold into a path to England.

Her eyes silently tallied the shape and substance of the Hathaway house as her aunt escorted her through it: dark wainscoted winding stairs, sober halls, cold stone floors, haughty high-backed chairs in dull flame stitchery, like dampened fires. Even the candles that lit the place's daylight recesses seemed fat and complacent.

Miranda trailed her aunt down a dim passageway and paused at the threshold of a solemnly hung bedchamber smelling of damp brocade and water-swollen wood. The windows opposite her were glazed, but clouded with river fog curling against the panes. For a moment the woman across the threshold looked like a pale ghost of Mistress MacTavish, urging her into the cabin, and safety.

"Come, child; don't be gawkish. My Lord, with James and Harry gone, it's yours, though what you'll do with it . . . Come, Miranda, we'll clean you up and forget the rest, whatever. Come, it's your home, your inheritance now."

Miranda lifted a shabby shoe, watching her foot as she would a puppet's, and stepped stiffly through the doorway into the Hathaway inheritance, all the while something pulling at her spirit like a wave withdrawing from shore.

Chapter Nine

*L*ondon was as much a cage for Christopher Steele when he brought the *Salamander* to berth some weeks later in the Thames's rapidly overcrowding docks below London Bridge.

The city seemed to grow so fast it smothered itself. Carriages clogged narrow thoroughfares never meant to accommodate more than a pair of horses and a few hand-hauled country wagons. England was no longer the insular oasis it had been. French fashions were as likely to find themselves befreckled by mud spatters as their more solemn English counterparts. Fashions!

Steele smiled to himself and straightened the well-laced linen cuffs on his new landsman's jacket. He seemed positively peacockish among the dark-jacketed and cloaked figures that shouldered him along Fleet Street.

Here and there passed dour pairs of Roundheads, looking like poultry well plucked with their stingy collars and close-cropped hair! And the mood was spreading, a plague of grimness—not fatal, only mortal dull. Steele sighed and pushed his way more forcefully through the crowds.

The house was behind the Strand, the Royalist informant at the Golden Bottle in Cheapside had said, but no more of the mission than that. Of brick. With a veritable Sherwood of chimneys growing on its gabled roofline. Perhaps the Steeles should have joined the tide of titles flooding the old city with new construction. Without a London base, doughty Sir Charles was likely to fall victim to the latest tiff between Royalist and Roundhead.

Steele paused before the narrow rear courtyard door of the only dwelling fitting the informant's description. A solid residence, but Steele wondered briefly if all places that housed Royalist intrigue might not be houses of cards, ready to topple at a touch of Cromwell's finger.

With King Charles in custody, it was foolish to hazard one's fortune on the crown rising triumphant from the current civil strife. Steele smiled again; after all, he had no fortune to wager—that was the first advantage to being the second son.

The door opened protestingly to his knock. A squinty eye peered around its edge, then it swung wide.

"Aye, sir, come in, sir. Yer expected, but not by the 'ole 'ouse so keeps yerself quietlike. Old Silas'll guide you."

The rheumy eye winked. Steele dusted his cuffs with his gloves before crossing the stoop into a steamy kitchen well supplied with plucked chickens hanging from hooks and a set of as scrawny kitchen maids to stare at him. He doffed his extravagantly wide-brimmed beaver and smoothed his uncurled hair.

The maids stood openmouthed, as taken by this performance as Steele would have been by a court masque. He nodded warily around the room, ducked through a low door and followed his gamey guide up the service stairs. Worse and worse. Seabound assignments had a certain dignity that let a man breathe free. Landlubbing espionage was definitely not his cup of punch.

Old Silas led him into a deserted upper room, then vanished beyond the coffered door. Steele toured the premises, his spurs ringing lightly with each step. A library, he noted with pleasure; a sober, civilized man's library. His blue eyes paged the titles on the thick-crowded shelves—Romans and Greeks, Livy to Caesar, Fox's *Book of Martyrs*—an unfrivolous choice. The dark-hued oil paintings hanging above the unvarnished wainscoting were predominantly portraits—a series of smoke-dimmed brooding eyes after the Dutch fashion watched him.

Steele grinned; this room was flavored like a Roundhead recipe. His host must be an odd fellow to espouse the royal cause. He did not so much hear the door slide open again as sense that it had—and some moments before.

He whirled, then froze, while his short cape curved around him like a cat's tail before settling into lines as static as his own.

She crossed wordlessly in front of him, her passage stirring his hat plume so subtly that his eyes fell to make sure that she had not set it in motion with her touch. She was already at the broad oak table with its bulbous legs and stood behind it.

Her hair was neatly knotted at her neck and capped with something starched and white. Her gown was plum linen; its plain white collar cut sharply across her collarbones and separated the cameo of her face and neck from the dark gown below, so she seemed to be a disembodied presence, floating . . . Steele suddenly realized how dim, how silent, the room was.

A log cracked. He walked to the head-high mantel, striking his fist softly along the polished wood before bending his gaze on the malingering fire in the grate. Idly he picked up a poker and stirred the charred logs into a rising shower of red-gold sparks that lit a brief like-glow in his features.

"I did not summon you here to tend to household chores, Captain."

Her natural voice was older than he remembered, ironic. He replaced the poker.

"No, I would think not."

"Come; sit down, Captain. You do not need an entire room between us, we who have shared so much."

Irony braided through her voice like a whip. Steele skirted the room, pacing restlessly along the burdened bookshelves with their dark bindings glinting with flickers of gold printing, like winks from silent evil eyes. He made his speechless round, a wary animal about to enter the ring where the tamer waited.

Then, suddenly, he crossed to the single farthingale chair set at a deferential angle to the table and sat. His hat he tossed carelessly on the table, where the plume wavered for a while like a dark blue question mark impaled in the wood.

"So," he said. "You found your way to England."

He did not remind her that his gold had made that possible; now was no time to extract thorns from the lion's paw.

"Yes. I found my way ... home. And found this house, my Aunt Hathaway and a fortune with none to claim it."

Restless, she wandered to a cedarwood chest and opened it, her eyes sliding over her snowy shoulder to watch him like a gilded wink from the row of books behind him.

Steele stirred uneasily—his sword clattered briefly against the chair's turned leg before he settled into waiting silence again on its red brocade upholstery.

Just as his guard relaxed, something came hurling across the table to land with a metallic challenge. He was on his feet, his palm curling around his sword pommel.

"For shame, Captain!" she chided him. "This is a civilized land for civil folk. This is England. Here one does not turn upon one's ... guests and do them harm. I have only repaid your loan in kind." She gestured to the small purse that lay lumpily on the table's shining surface.

Steele drew the cords apart and peered into a shimmer of coins. English gold, not Spanish.

"I believe that you'll find the ledgers well balanced, Captain. Pence for pence, pound for pound."

He glanced from the glimmer in his palm to her eyes—dark,

corroded with an emotion that swelled her pupils to blackened coins of no currency he cared to claim. Revenge was her denomination; pure-minted revenge, with weight enough to match any other emotional coin of the realm.

Steele upended the purse so the small gold circles spun away into a trail of glitter across the table. "I have no time to weigh balances—" He searched for some title to give her and found none. "No time to weigh anything but anchors, so—"

"But how fortunate. That is precisely what I hoped you would do. Weigh anchor."

He understood then that gold for gold was not enough.

"Where?"

"To Cádiz. To fetch Harry. You did not tarry long enough in Cádiz, Captain. A charming city, especially when one has seen it from the ground up, as I have. You did not give me gold enough to free Harry, only enough to take me back to England. You owe me more. Gold for gold. A brother for a sister. You took me; now give me back Harry."

She had come to stand opposite him behind the high-backed chair, so its fretwork latticed her like a prison grate, her small white hands turning on the chair finials.

"Took you! God's Life, girl, you have no idea." Steele spun away and bit off his words at the same time. Of course she had no idea of the fate that he had spared her, no idea of anything but reclaiming her brother. "You don't know what you're asking," he said more calmly.

"At least I *ask*." Her eyes flared to fiery life like tapers in an empty room. "But you mistake me. I am not *asking* you, Captain. I am *telling* you what I expect from you."

"You shall have less than you expect, Mistress Hathaway," he vowed, catching up his hat.

"I would it had always been so, Captain." The taunt on her lips was pure, purring London.

He was surprised that she had learned so much of civilization in so short a time. Well-laced phrases and tidily tricked-out tongues had made him yearn to leave the capital; he had liked her better when she spit like an overhot teakettle. But he had seen that only in the tavern, when she was mortal threatened.

In his cabin, when the threat became reality, she had only sputtered like a waterlogged kitten at the end. Damn . . . why had he bothered to relieve her of her virtue? He should have left the dubious pleasure to some Cádiz flesh-peddler. Now he would bear the weight of it until whatever archaic notion of honor she harbored was satisfied.

Steele looked at her face, startled to find a shadow of Richard lurking there behind the heavy chair. She seemed such a child, a child eyeing an ominous adult from a safe distance. Steele felt a dry clutch in the throat he would label regret.

"Forget it." His eyes urged her with a mixture of advice and order. "You've life enough before you to make a few moments off Cádiz a mere footnote to the whole. Didn't your Barbados 'master,' whoever he really be, teach you that?"

"He was my father! And what he taught me shall suffice. And Harry is my brother. That is the Hathaway lesson, Captain. Have you no brothers, no sisters, no father, mother, kin? I can credit it. You're a lone, cruel man and you shall go back and bring my brother to me."

Her hands were wringing the finials now. Steele sighed and dropped his hat to his side, almost obscuring the sheathed sword that swung there. Her eyes fell to that weapon as if it reminded her that he was always an armed and dangerous man to her. Then she stepped around the chair.

"You shall go. Or I will go to Parliament and tell them what this particular son of England is about on his Royalist missions. With the King under guard at Westminster, they would be happy enough to send you there, too, or to Fleet Prison."

"You have no proof."

"And you do have father, mother, sister, brothers. I made certain to discover that when I returned. Would they rest so secure in Dorsetshire if the Steeles were suspect? I wager the Puritans have wondered at your absences, Captain. Shall I add certainty to their speculations?"

He took one long stride toward her, the spur still ringing gaily in the silence as he paused. Her chin lifted and the ice-green eyes across the table stared into his flatly and fully for the first time that evening.

"You will find it very hard indeed to be rid of me, Captain, save you bring back Harry."

Steele abruptly shrugged, like a man stepping wide of an obstacle. He sat again and crossed his arms on his chest, the hat and its ultramarine plume trailing from one hand.

His pose was so much like that of a Cavalier painted at tavern-ease that for a moment words deserted her.

"Well?" he demanded calmly. "When would you have me go?

And in what? Other than the leaky barrel in which you'd truly like to see me well adrift."

Miranda spun the parchments from the table's other end between them. " 'Tis all here . . . the ship's new-built—a merchant, but you can outfit her with guns in Amsterdam. She should hold twenty-four." Steele's pale eyebrows rose. "Twenty-four should suffice for a man as adept at overpowering Spaniards . . . and girls . . . as you, Captain."

"Do you want me to recover your brother or stay here and listen to your recriminations?" Steele smiled slightly, turning the dark hat around slowly in his square sailor's hands until Miranda's eyes fixed on it as though it were something coiling to strike.

"We are beyond ordinary mediums of exchange, I think," she said finally, tearing her eyes from his hands to his face.

He was offering the same steady, true-blue gaze he had given her aboard the *Salamander* when he had bandaged her rope-ravaged hands, as if he knew that she was nursing hurt, not healing.

"Sign!" Miranda insisted between the wave of fear from the past and panic for the future that washed her. Her finger pinned the parchment to the table just below the Articles of Sail.

Steele uncrossed his arms, then spread his hands—one hat-bearing, one empty—wide. Miranda looked wildly about for his silent meaning, finally fetching an inkwell and quill from a tray table. The black ink spilled slightly as she set it down, leaving an undiscovered chain of islands across the pacific page.

Steele most meticulously raised his writing arm so his immaculate Antwerp linen cuff should not trail in her new-drawn geography.

"I gather ink will suffice," he noted as the quill scratched roughly over the paper. "You make an odd Mephistopheles to my Faust, mistress." He scratched a flourish below his surname and shot a glance like a blue cannonball at her pale face.

She only swept back the inkpot and pen, as if he could somehow write himself out of his bond in an instant.

"How long?" she asked.

"Six weeks. I've got to sign on a crew willing to whistle into the Spanish dragon's teeth."

"No trickery. You will fetch him? You won't simply sail off—?"

"—to leave my family to your mercies? Nay, I think not, now

that I've seen you in your true guise. You had better have been born boy, mistress: there are no fine edges of the female to you."

"You found me female enough, Captain."

Her eyes turned blacker than the ink she clutched. India ink; he had always thought there had been a foreign flavor to her.

"If there's any female virtue that stands peculiar to the breed, it's the ability to forgive . . . a divine attribute, I think."

"Then you shall have to look to God for it, Christopher Steele, for I would forget sooner than forgive, and my memory is very long."

He spun the document around to face her in answer. The jet of his signature engraved itself on her memory before she nodded and spoke again.

"You'll deal with Thomas Bowbridge; he's handled my father's finances long enough to know the dispersal of every farthing. I will spare no expense to recover my brother, or anything that belongs to me. You can deal with Bowbridge in the Ramsden Street offices. You need not see me again."

"It seems that you do have your share of mercy, mistress," Steele said ironically, rising to go.

"Wait," she said sharply, her fingers stretching across the table toward him for a moment.

The gesture ended with them falling heavily on the Articles of Sail he had just signed. She pulled the parchment to her and lifted it to inspect his name upon it one last time. She pouted her pale lips and blew once softly across the script, as if to ensure it was not a chimera for her breath to banish.

Steele found himself caught by the femininity of the gesture, as dainty as his sister Marjory at nine puffing steam from her mutton soup. He felt another wrench of regret.

He had thought her as rough-hewn as the boyish urchin she'd pretended to be. Now, with her angry eyes cast down, she was a pretty pointed face with a tender fringe of eyelash brushing each high cheekbone. He had tilted at that vulnerability, she whirling to present her shield to him only after his blow had landed.

She was a young woman; no confusion about that now. She should be bending her eyes to tapestry and rouging pots—not extorted signatures from captive captains.

"Have you no man, no male relation to deal with this?" he inquired abruptly.

"No. Only Harry. But forgive me, Captain Steele. You remind me that I am not ending our business on the proper note. It is traditional to toast the success of such ventures, is it not? Come then, I've some of father's fine Barbados brewed rum—hot and cold at the same time, I think you described it once . . . yes, my memory is excellent. Have a goblet, then, Barbados rum in Venetian glass to toast a fair English landing in a Spanish port."

She filled two glasses with liquid amber from a decanter and brought one to him, careful that, as their hands exchanged the narrow stem, their fingertips should not so much as graze. Drawing back to her command post behind the heavy oak draw-table, she raised her glass, where it flashed like a topaz in the taper-lit room.

Steele regarded his own crystal bowl; at least she'd not chosen blood-red wine for her leave-taking. His throat, wrung with regret among other emotions, could use a fiery quenching. He lifted the rim to his lips and drank deeply.

This was rough rum, fit for savaging not soothing the throat. The elegance of its container had misled him. Steele set the glass sharply on the table.

"For shame, Captain," she said. "Do you not know the proper way to seal a bargain?"

Her voice was pitched for mockery the way a lute is tuned to its purest note. Her green eyes never set above the amber in her glass as she drained it all in a series of neat swallows. For a moment Steele suspected her of drinking another, milder brew. Then he looked into those unwavering green eyes and knew.

He toyed momentarily with quaffing his own glass in just such a fashion. Indeed, he raised it for a split second, then anchored it roughly on the wood, leaving only a look behind him.

He was gone and the rum tilted rhythmically from side to side within the crystal bowl. Miranda's eyes followed that hypnotic swing, remembering suddenly rum in a crude green bottle that had swayed to that same rhythm, remembering only the rhythm then . . . her head swam from the rum bolt she'd just drunk.

She sank onto the high-backed chair and, with her last lazy gesture, stretched out an arm. One finger overturned Steele's abandoned glass by its lacy Venetian stem. The golden liquid pooled before her eyes as her head sank on the table.

It became a spreading honey sea. Her head became a golden sun that set upon it. She wept.

Chapter Ten

*H*e named her the *Forced Man*, that broad-beamed, narrow-keeled ship after the Dutch fashion he found awaiting him at Portsmouth harbor.

It was a piratical term. When a God-fearing, sober-sailing merchant was captured, some among her crew would be offered a choice of setting adrift, sinking or joining the pirate to fill in the vessel's battle-depleted crew.

Such a recruit was called a forced man, and such a crewman might become a Hanged Man, should he be caught at his unwilling occupation. All forced men had no man's word on it but their own that this was the way of things.

Steele doubted that word of his parting shot would ever filter back to Mistress Hathaway, but the ironic gesture gave him a spark of satisfaction that lit the bleak corridors of his thralldom.

He was wrong about her there, but by now that would not have surprised him. All the papers regarding the ship's outfitting found their way from Thomas Bowbridge's harried clerk's hand to the Hathaway house behind the Strand.

Miranda read every word, every boring list of the larder, every name on the crew. She searched for treachery, only finding barrels of salted meats and citrus fruits, crates of hens and one sacrificial lamb. She suspected the lamb.

She also found Muffin's name among the crew. P. Moffat, second mate. It gave her a pang to remember the wiry seaman who had ushered her ashore in Cádiz with such a quizzical look. What had Steele ever told Muffin of her? Oh, but it did not matter! Only recovering Harry mattered. Other crew surnames were familiar, though none was listed by the name she recalled—no Black Ned, no Solitary Smith. And no Smeach. Perhaps the men had shipped elsewhere. Or perhaps Steele had wanted more than gamesters with him on this voyage.

He would need a gamester's luck on it; she knew that also. It was one thing to flirt about the open mouth of a Spanish port; another to dart into it and wrest away its eyetooth.

This was as difficult a quest as lord ever set out to win for lady, task enough to send a Hercules fleeing back to loll among the ladies and their fancywork. A thoroughly satisfactory form of revenge, she thought, the day her white-kid-gloved hands gripped the windowsill of the hired carriage that had brought her to the docks to watch Steele, ship and crew slip out on the afternoon tide.

The vessel anchored close enough to shore for her to read its newly painted name. Miranda smiled. Anyone growing up in Barbados knew of forced men. She began to feel a weight lifting, as if a scale somewhere were slowly tilting level again. He had forced her, now he was forced. Only justice. And once Harry was returned, perhaps she could forget . . .

There, the sails were unfurling, unrolling like giant bolts of pale silk in the softening light. She leaned toward the window, caught as always by the ship's shifting poetry of motion.

Christopher Steele's eyes watched that white unfurling as sharply as hers, his neck straining upward from the *Forced Man*'s deck. The deck crew anchored the sheets in a trice; sails flapped noisily full.

Steele breathed deeply then, drawing sea air and fish stench into his lungs at once. He paced the small square of deck not teeming with busy sailors under the first mate's brisk orders.

He was not entirely sorry to weigh anchor; a twinge of excitement tugged at his self-discipline like a wayward bit of wind teasing a sluggish sail. This would be a mission worth winning, could he manage it. Never mind what circumstances or what Circe had set him unwilling on this trail, it was a challenge, and better than serving as ferry between England's Royalists and the exiled royal family in France, as he had done of late. He would much prefer plucking the don's prize English captive from that aristocratic anomaly than pursefuls of Spanish gold.

No, if she cared to fritter away the Hathaway fortune on costly expeditions to reclaim her brother, then, by God, he would damn well get the whelp back for her, perhaps then he'd be done with her tugging at his conscience like . . . Steele frowned, his eyes staring at the topgallants but seeing only the cabin on the *Salamander* and her through a green glass, darkly.

He had not been wholly rational about it, if he admitted the truth. No, something in her deception had truly stung him; until, tormented, he had stung back. Was it that he had felt a fool? And fooled by no deploy of feminine strategies—that would have been forgivable: what man had not been temptation-tripped by some Eve or other? No, she had not been what he believed her to be, after all, and there was the rub.

He had felt deceived by the very things in her that could be the result of no deception at all. He had been caught off balance and in flailing to restore it, had sought to make her the counterweight to his confusion, to put her firmly into place in the nature of things. And it had been too heavy a burden for her to bear. His palms firmly struck the gunwale; he finally began to see the way of it . . .

"Looks like we have a well-wisher, Kit, to see us off."

"What?" Steele turned from his reverie to find Muffin at his elbow with a sharp eye to the glass.

Kit took it wordlessly and trained it along the docks.

Nothing but bustle and piled barrels and—a carriage. And if one's eyes were very good, two white hands perched like doves upon its windowsill. Doves! Talons, more like.

"We'll need more than landlubbing well-wishers on this voyage," Steele said sharply. "And haven't you better to do than gawk at the shoreline?"

Steele slapped the glass into Muffin's waiting hand so sharply the older man frowned.

"Kit—" he began.

"Yes, what is it?" The captain had resumed his pacing, the clasped hands behind his back showing his impatience.

"Kit, I've a matter I been wantin' to mention. A change in the crew—"

"Change?" Steele lanced the man with a look and that one word.

"Aye, Captain," Muffin resumed, off balance. "An addition of sorts, ye might say. Sir. Why, Kit, 'tis nothing but a wretched boy I found sleeping in an empty barrel dockside. He's Yorkshire bred, like meself, an' I thought we'd make a cabin boy o' him—"

Steele wheeled, his gaze slipping past Muffin to the silent shadow of tattered clothing and solemn eyes standing across deck.

"He's not myself seawise, Kit, but I thought we'd have him climbin' the riggin' by the time we make Cádiz."

"No. I want no cabin boy this voyage."

"But, Kit, you've shown mercy yerself on some wretched urchin. I thought—"

" 'Tis clear that what you thought was wrong. I'll not have

him. If you wish to keep him aboard, you must find him work to earn his keep. Otherwise, I'll put him off though we be halfway to the New World."

Steele turned and strode to his cabin, Muffin's bewildered "Aye, Captain" trailing him like a small clap of thunder does a very fierce lightning bolt.

The boy had stayed. Somewhere about the ship, though Steele rarely saw him. He noted Muffin's diplomatic concealment of his new protégé with a certain sheepishness. They had never discussed "Richard's" sudden defection.

Things had always been aboveboard between him and Muffin—now he had somehow driven the forthright sailor into subterfuge. Steele didn't care for the trait in Muffin and he didn't care for whatever in himself had nourished this new reticence.

So the edge was off the venture. Once the ship had weighed anchor and drifted southward with the Gulf Stream current and westerly wind, once it was no longer a defiant monument in Portsmouth harbor to its owner's stubbornness and its captain's unwillingness, Steele found a certain flatness to the enterprise.

Muffin and his sharp eyes glassward found the don's galley. Well off Cádiz it floated like a great, lumpish wooden whale wallowing in sluggish seas. Steele recognized the don's elaborate arms gilded on the prow—trust the Spanish to heap more gilded gingerbread on a simple sailing ship than a Dutch baker. *Gato de Nueve*, she was called in bright red letters.

Steele laughed once to himself. "Cat-o'-Nine-Tails." Named for the whips that propelled her. And all nine of those tails would lash into fury on English backs below once the galley was under attack and sought to maneuver.

Steele eyed the innocent Hanseatic emblem billowing at the top of the *Forced Man*'s mainmast. Their four and twenty guns, brass polished to gold, stood gleaming and ready behind the gunports' blank square mouths. Soon they'd be spitting ninepounders at the galley sides, ramming iron balls that could take off a man's arm or head into the crowded rowing decks, into Englishmen likely . . .

Steele felt a cold pall of apprehension cloak him. Was he losing his stomach for the war games that had occupied Europe for as long as this century had unwound its five decades from a spool of holy wars, unholy civil uprisings, pestilence, famine and death? England at the center of it seemed to draw the most enemies—Dutch, French, Spanish, even Englishman against Englishman.

The major foes still spoke a foreign tongue. Steele's unsanctioned foray to Cádiz would win no Parliamentary censure. Of course the House of Commons would soothe the Spanish ambassador with protestations, quite true, that it had no knowledge of the affair. Once the petting was done, the same hands would pat the back of any Englishman who sank Spaniards into their own azure bays.

Sinking. That was the one thing to avoid. The galley must be surprised, overcome and taken without leveling the many English slaves in her underdecks, without suddenly saturating all who sailed on her in an instant pickling of salt—including Harry Hathaway, if his sister's information was correct.

That achievement would require a certain deftness. Steele eyed the heavily weaponed threescore of men that huddled out of sight under the gunwale and at the *Forced Man*'s hatchways. The plan was to drift slowly toward the prey like a lumbering German merchant out of her depth, then tack swiftly, draw alongside and board her *en masse*, when it would be blade-to-blade, barrel-to-barrel and bludgeon-to-bludgeon.

The wind was not quite doing its work, a glance at the mainsails told him—damn, but blow a little longer, blow a bit sweeter, and the day would be a surety. Slack—and the *Forced Man* could trip into the galley like a buffoon caught in his own wooden sword.

A few flutters aboard the nearing galley betokened a rising suspicion amongst her crew. Steele motioned Muffin to let a topgallant falter above, as if a clumsy seaman were at the rigging.

The day was ending with an inexorable withdrawal of light. The galley's great torchlights already glimmered against a deepening blue sky. The wind that had favored him seemed to be shifting offstage with the slowly sinking sun. God's Life, it would be his ill luck for the fickle winds to falter just when he needed to ride their jacket-tails most ... Steele drove a fist into his palm so violently the gesture cleared his head.

The *Forced Man* was committed, the plan the best that a lone English "merchantman" with four and twenty guns could attempt. If only he weren't shackled by concern for those faceless fellows putting their backs into it below the galley decks, if only he could smash the Spanish slave ship at the waterline with a volley of good English iron—or Dutch iron, rather, that would warm to the task as willingly, if not more so.

Captured Hollanders toiled below, too, unaware of taking Amsterdam iron in their midst. An iron sort of irony indeed. The galley likely housed only a handful of soldiers by custom. She needed too many rowers to leave much room for passengers. So. They'd have some bucklered soldiers to disarm, perhaps a few of the don's personal retinue. Then Harry Hathaway'd be theirs to whisk home to his icy-veined sister. And Christopher Steele could start afresh with no New World thorns in his flesh . . .

A glittering movement aboard the galley told Steele his merchant's mask had dropped. Cuirassed soldiers rushed to their stations with musket abovedecks and cannon below.

Steele dropped his raised hand; the German pennant aloft dipped while the lion and the unicorn leapt to its place—the unicorn of Scotland, imported southward to London by thistly James Stuart when he took the throne his son Charles had such a tussle retaining. Steele might only be a messenger in a private squabble, but he never exchanged arms or fire without it being a Royalist cause as well. The Steeles could teach even the Hathaways something of stubbornness.

The two ships closed swiftly, the galley firing a round that caught the English ship's stern. Some deft maneuvering with the sail brought the *Forced Man* athwart the Spaniard's bow.

Then her longboats were launched at the galley's broad stern and sixty-some English seamen armed to the daggers caught between their teeth began swarming over the galley's high sides, their bare feet sure upon the ropes.

The first wave took the musketeers' initial volley in their midst; some attackers ebbed behind to plunge into the sea. Clearing smoke showed only another wave of Englishmen to the musketmen awkwardly cleaning their long, death-dealing barrels.

The crest of that wave washed over the musketeers before they could prime their firearms for another round. Steele's pistol-equipped crewmen were not sterling shots. Their first firing produced more smoke and powder smell than fallen Spaniards. So they cast away their spent pistols to pull their ever-ready cutlasses against the increasing tide of gilded Spanish soldiers pouring abovedecks from the hatchways.

Steele had sent one ball through the belly of a musketeer. His second from its companion pistol fruitlessly chased a ducking Spanish captain and spent itself in the mainmast.

He drew his cutlass to direct a squad toward the infernal hatches and the spate of Spaniards running onto deck like liquid gold—no wonder the Spanish fancied their gilt braid and gleaming breastplates still: battling them was like trying to duel a looking glass.

Wind had failed Steele once already, forcing his boarding party before time; now time itself was taking its toll. The sun reddened its face on the horizon as if to rival the bloodstained deck and hovered slowly out of sight. Its desertion brought dark and only the galley torchlights to do battle by.

Steele had hoped to find the Spanish ship at its ease, its sailors taking supper in the forecastle, its soldiers lounging below. He had been right, save that the *Gato de Nueve* housed more of both than he had anticipated. But then, the don was hardly predictable, was he, and what did it matter to question such facts when he was ringed with the clash of battle all round and having hard work to keep two soldiers spinning like doubloons on the tip of his sword?

Steele slashed brutally. One soldier's face collapsed in the shadow of his gold-lipped helmet. The mouth split and the face sank below Steele's vision like an anchor into water. But the Englishman had already compensated and was facing off the second soldier.

Something burned across his back and shoulder, like an attenuated beesting. Wheel. Strike. A Spanish sailor dropping down from the rigging, his steel stinger raised again. Spin. Push. A Spanish sailor propelled into a Spanish soldier and the dangerous hacking edge of Spanish steel he carried.

Steele straightened, aware of a distant buzz of pain somewhere behind him. Spanish soldiers were still bubbling out of the galley's belly, as if she were some bloated sea monster with a serpent's nest in her bowels—metallic golden offspring armored in plate and equipped with lethal stingers.

Too many of his sailors had been tempted into pursuit in the rigging, Steele saw by glancing above. Chasing their own kind left the soldiers the deck and the smaller part of Steele's crew to defend it. And there were more, many more, than there should have been. Twice-threescore soldiers slicing and hacking, their boots rapping retreat to Steele's men upon the boards.

It was no moment for emotion. Whether Christopher Steele felt dismay, the foreshadow of defeat, a sudden comet of new anger, it didn't matter. He was merely a pair of eyes, narrowed at the scene, a mind calculating chances with a cold sort of rapid fire, a mass of reflexes waiting for an attack at which to strike.

His square of deck was cleared; he suddenly made up his mind and leapt onto the lower deck into a nest of tangling figures.

Sweat stung his eyes, but he kept his silver slice of steel dueling with the gold still flashing at him. At his back, a man cried out; Steele felt a desperate grip upon his arm. A glance to deck showed only a familiar face still as death upon it. One of his. Gone.

Steele leapt the man's body, no more than barrier now, shook his yellow head to clear the rattle and groans of battle all around and sliced once more into the swords around him shattering like broken glass off his blade only to re-form and shatter once more. Clash and shatter. Advance. Retreat. Defend. Retreat. Advance, advance. No, overextended. Retreat. Circle. Turn. "Alvays the back, vatch alvays the back, young Englishman, else you vill be a fine feather in some duelist's beaver, eh?" Gerhardt of Antwerp. Parry, feint. Beyond fine points now. Hack, slash, slip—no, not that. Balance again. Counter—now!

A blade sliced so close to Steele's face that he thought his hearing had failed, for the clatter that had fueled his rapid-paced thoughts, his quick turns and thrusts, had suddenly hushed.

He took one risky glance away from his circle of contention and across the broader perspective of the entire galley.

Chapter Eleven

Down the decks, swords were drooping in surrender.
Like hornets, the gold-and-black-liveried soldiers of Don Ricardo Esteban Diego de la Fontana y Monteverde swarmed around Kit's men, their steel stingers gilded in the flicker of the galley's great torchlights.

The ring of cutlass on sword lost its reassuring echo—now he heard only *his* steel, clanging off a narrowing circle of vipers' tongues that ringed him on the afterdeck.

Christopher Steele struck with renewed force at his Spanish attackers, his fine fencing degenerated to heavy strokes meant to sever enemy steel from enemy arm. Always they rose again, those thin lines of fatality. That metal margin fenced in only him now, and bowed before his blows like waves below a prow.

His own movements were ponderous, exhausted ... he retreated again, against the gunwale now and no salvation upward in the sheets—just that one glance away had brought the metal tongues licking at his throat.

He struck out in an arc, clearing a small circle forward. Then the steel noose tightened on him and his arm was too heavy to cut through the knot of soldiers pressing him. A thick silver stinger licked at his throat. His own cutlass dropped to deck at its prodding.

His surrender signaled a babble of Spanish. The sword point that held him at bay pricked him without warning, like a finger spearing a chest to make a point in a verbal argument. There was no arguing with the thin trickle of blood he felt meandering down his chest—warm and lazy, welling from the sharp edge of prodding pain at his throat.

That gratuitous cruelty sank into his soul like a thorn. Steele felt invaded, exposed—this was losing, this humiliation of standing helpless on ground that had once been confidently one's own ... Swarthy faces hurled toward him out of the confusion like cannonballs, exploding into laughter and Spanish taunts.

"El primero," they guffawed. The first. Steele was confused. Then grimy fingers swarmed over his jacket buttons like flies—in an instant the garment was wrenched away. He was thrown to deck and pinned while others wrestled off his boots—fine, doeskin-lined bucket-tops of French leather, worked with narrow stitches. Someone shook a buff-booted hand before his face. Disembodied Spanish promised that he would have no need of such fine footwear where he was bound ...

Then he *was* bound, crudely with cable, pulled to his bootless feet and pushed down the deck. Steele searched for familiar faces to find only Spanish scowls, Spanish sneers. He finally saw his remaining men, herded like Iberian sheep and sheared of their arms and better clothing.

Steele was forced away from that distasteful scene to the poop. The door leading to the galley's Great Cabin was slit open now, almost like a wound. The warm light behind it oozed onto deck thick as blood.

The don himself swung the door wider so that Steele could see the slim shadow behind him, a fair-skinned face flushed in the cabin light, an older edition of the Richard he had known on the *Salamander*. Steele recalled the sister in her cold London town house, her will a thing of iron. This boy was molten, a precious metal gone liquid to run where gravity would pull it.

"My pet fascinates you, Captain. Yes, he is a handsome boy. And you would wrest him from me. That is why you returned, is it not?" The don took almost physical pleasure in the precise way his deep voice intoned the English words.

Steele only nodded, dully.

"No wonder you would not sell me yours," the man continued silkily. "Now you wish to acquire mine as well."

Steele struggled in his bonds at that insinuation, knowing it was useless.

The don smiled. "Yes, I thought you still had feathers to ruffle. You will find yourself molting in the galley, my friend. There are always vacancies for fresh men to fill. I understand you English have no such ships as these. The galley will be an—education. I expect you to serve a full term, Captain. My boatswain estimates two years' service, at best. I hope you will not disappoint me."

The don lifted a square of white linen to the corner of his mouth to press his smile into place. A napkin. The man had been dining. Steele set his teeth. Two years was all a man ever wanted to live in any galley—Spanish, Moslem or French.

"There was a boy among your crew," resumed the don, his dark eyes unreadable against the light. Harry behind him shifted restively. "At least so my lookout tells me."

Steele groaned inwardly. Muffin's urchin. He should have had the lad hauled off in Portsmouth and damn mercy.

"But I cannot find him, Captain. Either dead or slipped overboard."

The don steepled his hands as if in prayer and rested his goateed chin upon them. "You cause me yet more losses, Captain. That Arab boy you procured for me—ah, it does no good to thrash so. You were somewhat concerned for him, I recall. No worry. He did not turn out well; I made a bad investment.

"You are fortunate that I have no worse hospitality than that of the galleys to offer you. We are told to return good for ill; indeed, the Church promises reward to the meek, the cheek-turner. Yet I am a frail, fallible man, Captain, and I must confess an actual delight at the idea of you belowdecks, helping to propel my fine galley. No doubt this shall cost me an additional year or two in Purgatory, and I will regret it deeply. However that may be—I hope you find your two years below pure hell, Captain."

The don's face had hardened into a mask of almost Oriental fury.

Steele said nothing, merely watched the man through cautious eyes, while the reality behind the cruelly brandished words branded itself upon him. Truly; the galleys were hell and few escaped them save by a careless toss overboard in a burlap sack when bone could break and blood could run no more.

"So good night to you, Captain Steele." The don rested a white, boneless hand on the shoulder of the boy behind him. "Say good night to Captain Steele, *pequito*, and then you shall come say good night to me."

"Good night, Captain Steele," mouthed Harry softly, his shockingly English voice falling across Steele like the shadow of the whip.

The don slowly drew the door shut. Then the deck was utterly dark, for Steele's eyes were light-dazzled, and he was pulled to the hatchway.

He was thrust below, then nearly wafted upward again by a wave of stench that washed over him and soaked him to his soul. Darkness ruled the galleys, but slowly his eyes etched in methodical rows of benches, the emptiness filled with a geography of naked human limbs resting every which way on the great, fifteen-foot poles that propelled the Spanish ship. Only two soldiers pinioned him now. Perhaps the mob had lost their stomach for their revel's last act.

Steele was pushed down the slimy aisle to an apparent vacancy on one of the benches. No, not vacant; the spot's shackled occupant had merely slid to the floor. The soldiers unchained Steele's predecessor as the boatswain came to drag away the inert form. Steele glimpsed rotted flesh beneath the wrist and ankle irons, like bracelets of blue and red enamel. No face. He was glad he had seen no face.

Then he was shoved roughly into place, and those irons—still bearing shreds of their former prisoner's flesh—were pressed shut about his own wrists and ankles. Despair circled him. He looked up to dark eyes of Spanish satisfaction and around to dull stares from his oarmates.

"*El primero,*" boomed the Spanish soldier. Some instinct from the world eons away abovedecks told Steele that this was the man who had pricked him. "*El primero,*" the man laughed, holding up a forefinger for the number "one" and then shaking it at

Steele as if admonishing a wayward child. *"Y el segundo, el tercero—"*

Steele looked beyond the pointing finger to see Muffin being hauled down the narrow stairs. And Baline. And Davy Llewellyn. Plenty of fresh English bone and blood to keep the oars well greased now.

He trailed a hand in the slimy water bucket under the bench and wiped his sweat-blinded face. For the first time he heard the dull jangle of chains that would accompany his every move from now on as familiarly as the rustle of clothing had before.

He shook the leaden metal until it made music, then suddenly jerked his wrists upward to their limit. The metal cuffs cut inexorably into his flesh, branding the notion "this far and no farther" into his existence.

Steele dropped his hands and the chains contentedly coiled into rest at his feet while the stench steamed up like mist and crept into his nostrils, coursed down his throat. He suddenly leaned over the oar and retched, as if discharging the putrification back at its source.

The spell over, Steele hung exhausted across the oar, as if he were merely an overdone carouser and the oar an old friend already. An odd emotion tickled his leaden brain: the normal, dim relief that the sickness was done, and beyond that, regret for his late, lamented last supper aboard the *Forced Man*. He could have used its sustenance a bit longer.

If Don Ricardo had hoped that the ironic ramifications of Steele's situation would increase his discomfort, the don knew less of the galleys' realities than his English prisoner.

Steele had no luxury to lament the fact that above his head the don toyed with his English boy. From almost the first moment of his fettering, he knew only the stench and steam of all those crowded half-human bodies, the few fevered eyes about him that were rational and the many glazed stares that circled and imprisoned him as surely as his chains.

This was a polyglot crew: a smattering of Moriscos—tough, half-Moor, half-Spanish brigands turned to putty by a turn at the oars ... many Englishmen, most common sailors ... dusky-skinned Arabs, laboring at their oars like lean, plucked hawks with their high-bridged, desert-vulture noses all broken-looking ... a few pale, half-dead Hollanders, remnants of the late wars

between their homeland and Spain. Holland had won her independence. These men would win theirs only by death.

Of course Steele thought escape at first. He thought it even as he
retched his miserable allotment of moldy biscuit back at the boards,
as his deepest sensibilities rejected the filthy realities of the rowing
decks. But he ate. He ate his twenty-eight ounces of biscuit thrice
weekly, occasionally slavered with a spoonful of anonymous over-
cooked greens atop a dubious heap of rice. He drank the putrid water in the under-bench buckets. He soon fell into immediate sleep
on his narrow slat of bench when the rowing day of ten, twelve or
even twenty hours ended.

And he rowed, by God, how he rowed. This was not the
dainty thrust upon a slender oar that pushed a longboat through
the shallow waves. It took every muscle in all three hundred galley slaves' bodies to thrust the *Gato de Nueve* through the leaden
waters, to plunge her mammoth paddles deep into the ocean
belly and lever her forward.

It took six slaves to a fifteen-foot-long oar, leaping forward,
their arms extended and their backs bowed like a cathedral arch,
stretching over a similar line of ridged and bowed backs on the
bank ahead, then springing back to the bench, legs desperately
braced, only to lunge forward again. And again, until sweat
seemed to be blood, streaming freely.

Often it was, for the boatswains strutted the raised bridge between either bank of oars, their indiscriminate whips circling to
prod reluctant flesh. When flesh dulled to even the whip, the
boatswains persisted until the skin quivered no more and the unlucky one—or lucky?—was tossed overboard and a fresh victim
chained in his place.

So Steele thought of escape, as if the word were a key to
something more important he should remember. Escape. The
word whispered to him on the sudden nearing hiss of the
bastinado—an evil sharp stick like a Spanish tongue. It reflected
off the gold braid lacing the boatswain's dandified clothes—
formal enough for a man en route to a festivity rather than a stint
at flaying his fellow humans half-alive. Never mind that the rowers soon had what remained of their clothing whipped off of
them; it was cooler that way.

No, only one chance offered, Kit often thought while wolfing
down his biscuit ration. Engagement. Should the galley fight another ship—a Frenchman or, better, a Dutchman—should the
Gato be taken . . . He sighed and measured time by the length of

dirty brown beard protruding from the chin usually clean-shaven and invisible to his downcast eyes, the beard of a castaway—untended, ragged.

Muffin four men down looked like an Old Testament prophet, his emaciated features lost in a dirty halo of beard and wispy white hair. Job in his misery. Or Jonah in his whale belly. If only she would fight, this ponderous, perfidious galley! But the don seemed content to flutter about in his bay, as if three hundred nearly breaking backs should provide a breeze for his floating pleasure pavilion . . .

And if the ship did sally onto open sea to engage some foreign ship, galley slaves could do little to tip the scales of that contention. For then the whip would truly dig itself into the sluggard, the dallier, expecting just such malingering. And it was still better to perform acrobatics on the oar than to bleed to death in narrower and narrower ribbons on the benches.

Besides, Cádiz was no longer Spain's official port. Seville, despite her high-breasted sandbar that made landing a dangerous venture, now counted herself home port for Spain and all the New World's Spanish gold. Enough ships still put into Cádiz to keep the ancient port city thriving, but any challenge to Spain's sea-flung empire would come at Seville now. No English armada would come blowing south to rescue Christopher Steele. One had broached Cádiz—unsuccessfully—in 1625, he recalled. Kit had been a babe of one year then. And now . . .

This much he thought clearly at some times. At others, he was a mechanical leaping monkey on a stick, like every man beside him. No better, no different, no stronger . . . save that yet he had not taken that last senseless dive over the side into the salt water that would wash wounds that could never feel it.

Chapter Twelve

"Oh!"

Miranda stared down at her finger and the cabochon of blood bejeweling it. She jabbed her silver needle into the thick embroidery and sucked her injury. Helena looked up from her tapestry table across the room, one fair eyebrow raised in silent question.

" 'Tis quite impossible, Aunt. I will never master it!"

Miranda's embroidered slippers thrust the needlework stool away from her feet; she impatiently swung those dainty house slippers under her voluminous skirt. Her thumb was red from forcing needle through heavy fabric. Miranda stared at the intricate floral pattern in her lap and the thin silver line transfixing it like a thorn. A steel needle. Steel and Steele.

Two months and no word. Not a syllable. Was the man halfway to Virginia by now? And Harry ... Harry still gone. Steele still gone. And Miranda sitting here in a thick-boned corset with her hair falling into her eyes in silly tendrils, Miranda learning niceties and needlework, French and fripperies.

"Miranda." Her aunt's genteel voice quieted Miranda's rebellious feet tapping warning against the carved chair-leg.

It did not quiet the tapping in her soul, the ticking like a clock. Miranda looked up from green eyes gone gray with exasperation, her tongue ready to prick her innocent aunt as sharply as the needle had her own finger, but a maid entered and delayed the storm.

"A gentleman, mistress. He asked for Harry Hathaway." The maid's bemusement died in the bewildered expressions that crossed both women's faces.

They rose simultaneously, Miranda's fancywork fallen heedless to the Turkey carpet. Then the gentleman was at the door. A tall man, though not so tall as Christopher Steele. A narrow man of a certain coiled grace, dressed more soberly than an Englishman, with a slim sable moustache and a small tuft of goatee under his full lower lip. He was a watchful, one might even say a worried man, but as he swept off his wide black felt hat to reveal a chin-length bob of dark hair, he smiled.

"Francisco!" Miranda fairly screeched the name and then her restless slippers were flying across the floor; she launched herself directly at the stranger's leather-sashed chest.

"Beware my blade, *niña*," he laughed, swinging it aside from catching in her circling skirts. "*Madre de Dios*, is this Mirandita?"

He held her away from him and shook her slightly, as if she were a fashion doll he had uncovered in a convent. The man's bemused smile lit his narrow features with a sort of crooked charm, the kind of which mothers warn their daughters.

"Miranda!" Helena's voice was pure reproval.

" 'Tis only Francisco, Aunt. Oh, Francisco, I'm so glad that you've come—" Miranda pulled the stranger toward her aunt, but he hung back.

"Your lady aunt has not been properly introduced to me, *niña*. Sheath your foil and begin with the verbal exchanges, as you were taught."

Miranda glanced at herself, at her furling petticoats, at the ends of her new, curled lovelocks, then at the newcomer. Of course.

"Forgive me, Aunt. This is Señor Francisco de Salazar, my— Harry's—tutor and fencing master, and our friend from Barbados. He had stayed on to salvage Father's affairs after his death."

"Ah." Helena's hand, anchored nervously at the base of her throat, fluttered finally to her side.

"Charmed, mistress." Francisco made a courtly bow, his dark eyes and flashing teeth rising from his subservient posture to pinion Helena Hathaway so suavely that her fingers ventured throatward again, this time with pleasure.

"You are welcome, sir . . . *señor*. 'Twas only that your arrival was so unlooked-for—"

"But where is Harry?" Francisco smiled eagerly as he turned once more to a suddenly subdued Miranda.

"Harry is—Harry is . . . Please, Aunt, I must speak to Francisco alone."

"Absolutely not. 'Tis grievous news, but I cannot allow—"

"Grievous, Mistress Hathaway? Miranda—?"

"This is a matter of Barbados, Aunt, not of here and now. The same rules do not apply. Trust me, please."

Helena regarded her niece's pleading features for a long moment. Then she picked up her tapestry chest and, back rigid in disapproval, silently eased herself from the room.

Francisco's smile had frozen, leaving his brown eyes wary in his narrow face. "What is it, Miranda?" he asked in a voice as smooth and serious as steel.

Steele, she thought, preparing her answer. Where was Steele? "I've told her that Harry was dead but—"

"Dead?"

"But he's not. Come by the fire, Francisco; my hands are so sudden cold. We were taken by pirates off Spain; we were nearly here, nearly home. Pirates, Hollanders mostly—and something else."

"*Pequita* . . ." Francisco's sympathetic eyes surveyed her, looking for something new in her. His frown caressed her with concern.

"Not *I*, Francisco! Harry. They did not want me, were not made to want me, do you understand?" she said between her teeth, distressed to put her meaning into words.

Something flashed across Francisco's olive-skinned Spanish face. Comprehension. And something more.

"What say you, Mirandita? You must not let me guess wrongly. You have donned a certain mainland modesty with your skirts. England is but another island, only larger than Barbados, and the English are as savage here as there, if one poor Spaniard's opinion be given. So tell me straight. You never used to flinch from any blow, be it spoken or sung in steel."

"All right." Miranda wiped her palms fiercely on her skirt of cornflower-blue silk. With the gesture, she seemed to scrape away an invisible skin that had been forming over her, a helpless attitude that webbed her like a silent spider's spinning.

"We were eight and twenty days out, Francisco. A full four weeks, and never made the fifth of that voyage. The pirates caught the ship like buccaneers an Indies cow. They stripped and devoured her crew and cargo as quickly. Their captain was a Hollander—the Dutchman, I called him; so, it seems, have others. I donned breeches to deceive them, Mistress MacTavish's doing—" Here Francisco laughed shortly. "Aye, 'twas hard for her to turn tables. The pirates had something other in mind. Harry. I . . . I was with the Dutchman. He did not harm me. But Harry—I found Harry on deck later and took him off in a boat. We were separated in Cádiz. Then—even later, I found him in the company of a Spanish don who shared the tastes of those sailors. He ignored me, Francisco. He looked fully at me and then past! 'Twas as if . . . I fear he had been drugged—some Oriental potion, for that don had a taste for the cargo that crosses inland and sandy seas."

"So. Harry. Where is he now?"

"With that Spaniard," Miranda hissed, as if she invoked the Devil. "Oh, I did not mean to slander your origins, Francisco, but if you had seen that man, knowing his vile inclinations—"

Francisco leaned back in the fireside settle, his lean face lost in its high-shouldered shadows. "How did you return to England, Mirandita?"

" 'Twas a rough road, but no more rugged than some on Barbados. It is of no consequence."

"Odd that you, the lass, as Mistress MacTavish would say, should win free and the lad should be— And what became of the Scots burr of Barbados? She figures no more in your tale."

"Nor in any other's. Dead of a pirate ball. But you say true. By rights, it should have been I. Instead of making a woman of me they have unmade a man of him. I did not ask for deliverance at his cost, and it was an evil day I gained it, for Harry has been lost to me ever since."

"Do not mourn your untaken maidenhead, Miranda," Francisco counseled.

She flinched, but his eyes were on the fire and not her face, and she did not correct him.

"Harry may not be as lost as you think." The Spaniard's long fingers teased the tuft of hair beneath his lower lip, an old gesture of his for deep thought.

"Yes." Miranda leaned forward eagerly, her skirts rustling with an almost avid crispness. "We can get him back. I sent a ship to fetch him, but it is two months sent and no word. I fear—"

"You sent a ship—by Juan de la Cruz, you are a merchant princess now! How did you find a crew? And captain?"

"English. I found English to man it," said Miranda, settling back in stiff dignity on her fireside chair.

"Forgive me. I forgot the Hathaway hardheadedness. You never plied the foil so fiercely as when your ground was lost. So your English rescuers are unheard from. Well, it means a bit of subtle prying about the Spanish taverns, I suppose. I have countrymen who will suit for it, if you have gold."

"Gold?" Miranda was on her feet. " 'Tis all I do possess at the moment, Francisco. If gold will buy my brother back, you may have it."

At her beckoning, he lazily slipped after her through dim hall and up wainscoted staircase. The library was unlit, but Miranda did not call for a servant. She struck flint herself and warmed her fingers at the flicker until the candlewicks caught in a bright burst of light.

Francisco watched her narrowly, free to inventory the girl he had known from rough-cut Barbados days in her new polished setting.

She seemed foreign to him, with her porcelain portrait profile framed by trailing lovelocks, half of her yellow English hair caught atop her head, with her pearl-circled throat and wrists. Her hands lighting the tapers were graceful; he expected her to turn at any moment and reveal a lapdog tucked under one arm, a fashionable stutter upon her girlish lips.

"I'll have him back, Francisco, though I have to go to the Spanish Main to get enough gold for it." Her voice cut the room's dimness like a new blade through silk.

Francisco exchanged an appraising glance with the grim Hathaway ancestors grouped above the wainscoting—all men and sobersides at that—and faced the girl below them.

She had fetched a small purse from a chest and held it balanced on her palm. She rolled it contemplatively into her other palm, the coins clicking like rosary beads from his long-forgotten past. After weighing the purse from palm to palm for a few moments, she suddenly tossed it at him. He caught the projectile against his bandoliered chest like a cat encompassing a mouse.

"I see that tending my father's affairs in our absence has not yet made an accountant of you, Francisco." He found the trace of challenge in her voice odd, as if she now numbered all men her adversaries.

Francisco spilled the gold onto his own palm. "No doubloons, Mirandita, but they will do."

She regarded him for a moment. "Do you still play with that?" She pointed to his sword.

"When I've a willing partner, or someone to whom to teach a Spanish lesson. London brims with fools ready to taste Spanish steel for the sake of a paltry bit of Iberian-baiting. They love teasing Spaniards more than bulls or cocks."

"London is no place for Papists, nor any with a Castillian accent. I love it not myself. When Harry's home, I'll wait till I'm of age and sail for Barbados again."

Francisco smiled. "London suits you, Mistress Miranda, I'll credit the English with that."

Her face hardened. "Nothing suits me, but to have things as they were before—"

She walked away, her fair head so solemnly bowed upon her steepled fingers that Francisco involuntarily thought of a nun. She spoke again.

"In your travels, before you came to Father on Barbados, did you exchange feints with many Englishmen?"

"A few."

"One named Steele?" Her back was to him, straight as a laced shield.

"Steele? No—ah, but of course, an agile lad! Five years past, at Master Gerhardt Thibault's Antwerp fencing school. Now, there was a fencing master who could spin one's spurs and unlace one's breeches with a mere twist of the wrist. He was but a boy then ... the English Steele, I mean. Gerhardt Thibault was never a lad. Steele, yes; one of the few Englishmen besides your father I liked. Kit, they called him—and fencer enough to fret one or two of Thibault's undermasters—including myself. What of him?"

"Very little, Francisco. 'Tis only that I've met this fencing partner of yours, and wondered at the connection."

"No connection, mistress, save at the tip of a blade and the toast of a tankard. The English are prodigious ale-drinkers, eh? I vow it makes them quarrelsome. Look at how they treat their King. Wine makes for better relations between sovereign and subject. King Philip will never have to fear for his curled head."

"Fear for his head? Why say you that? 'Tis true Charles's contention with Parliament has shown the King only the surrender side of a parley table, but it will not come to killing. Besides, what will it matter to me when I'm back in Barbados? Oh, do what you can, Francisco. I mean to send another ship after Harry. And another. And yet another. If I have to empty Portsmouth shipyard I'll have him back."

"Peacefully, Mirandita. I am used to weighing your words heavily, you needn't coin so many for me."

Francisco's tapered hands fanned the air at her, as though he thought a breeze might cool her convictions. Miranda suddenly laughed.

"Oh, Francisco, 'tis a relief to see one who understands me. But come, if Aunt finds us plotting in corners she will certainly refuse to invite you to dine. And there is much of Barbados—and your travels—I would know."

Chapter Thirteen

Within a fortnight Miranda knew more than even she wished. The Spaniard was back in her father's long-forsaken library under the conspiratorial candlelight, bringing her baleful news.

"The talk of Cádiz? Are you certain?"

"*Sí,*" confirmed Francisco, fresh from consultations with his countrymen and lost in his native language again. "*Sí.*"

He watched Miranda roam along the well-filled shelves, the books' gilt binding reflecting on her polished hair. Like most Mediterranean-reared men, he found the fairness fascinating. Then she whirled to face him, and the light reflected off her pale face and hair as off a shield in the sun.

"He's laughing at me, that miserable, statureless snake of a man! At Englishmen levering his ship through the water below and he leading Harry around on a leash above. I only knew his Christian name—Christian, the very expression is too fine for him!—but I vow I'd like to know some surname on which to anchor a curse or two."

Francisco struck his palm upon the pommel of Toledo scrollery at his side. "I am merely messenger, dear lady, not maker of these tidings. You must confess that to send an English ship to take a galley in the curve of Cádiz Bay is an impertinency that would attract some comment. If you had spirited Harry away, think you not the English should have laughed heartily at it?"

" 'Tis not the laughing, Francisco, it's the stretching out of Harry's servitude. How long ago did it happen?"

"A month or more. Word travels fast in such times, and each nation has an ample network of spies."

"And the—entire—crew captured?"

"Those who still lived. An oar is not the most lighthearted travel companion, but your English sailors are fortunate."

"Fortunate?"

Miranda's disbelief was wafted on a vision she had once had of two high dark ships slapping water rhythmically in Cádiz Bay. Two high dark ships that left a train of stench behind them like a long, invisible tail . . . The smell had made her ill, and the sight had set Christopher Steele's face into a lean, leathered mask of dislike. But that had been before . . . She wondered how he liked the galleys now. If he lived.

And Muffin. P. Moffat of the *Forced Man*'s crew list. Where was he? The angular black list of names rolled before her memory, Joneses and Smiths abounding, as well as O'Learys and Llewellyns. She'd not thought of that. Of failure. For some odd reason she'd never considered Christopher Steele's coming back empty-handed. Or coming back not at all.

She looked up to find Francisco facing her across the drawtable and her hands wringing the high-backed chair's finials. She dropped the gesture like a live coal.

"You say the crew was fortunate," she resumed calmly, coming round to sit upon the leather seat, her skirts billowing up around her waist like sails collapsing back on the masts.

Francisco paused before answering. He found Miranda's skirted self foreign, almost fey. He still expected the ardent, childish person of Barbados to pop out from beneath the swathing silk, like a court fool from behind the arras. He had been aware of her approaching womanhood on the island, but it had been a ghost-thing, easily dispelled by the rigors of Barbados life.

"The crew," he said finally. "Yes, I call them fortunate, fortunate that the don had reasons to conceal them from his Church and country. Otherwise, he would have led your English sailors off to the Inquisition and the wooing of the iron pincers and the rack. Better to pull at the oars than to be pulled."

"Of course. No public trial, no outcry for the men who had come to relieve His Serpentine Majesty of one more victim in his coils. Well. I shall send another ship, Francisco, and have Harry back. Have them all back, all that still live. Will you aid me in this, even though it's against a countryman?"

"Harry is more my countryman than any Cádiz don," responded Francisco with a level eye and a certain veiled message upon his look that teased at Miranda like a fencing blade lacing her throat.

"I do realize your great and true affection for Harry . . . and myself. You're all that's left, Francisco, of those far, fragrant days in Barbados. I long to be back there. Life was so simple then, everything was what it seemed. Not like here, not like— We will fetch Harry back and then he can claim it all: London town, the Strand, Whitehall and waiting for the King or Cromwell to win the day, but I'm for Barbados then. Where would you go, could you go anywhere at this instant, Francisco?"

"Spain, Mirandita," he said softly. "I would go to Spain."

"And so we shall." Miranda leaned her chin upon her fisted hands and smiled significantly across the dark wood table. "And so we shall."

Helena Hathaway was not nearly so certain. She stormed at her niece in a flurry of short bursts of command and despairing sleets of persuasion. Neither element worked. The one will met the other and melted through what little metal there was in Helena, reshaping her to a transmuted purpose.

Soon Miranda was almost daily in solitary consultation with Francisco, despite her aunt's misgivings. They'd found the ship and a veteran Cornish captain with one-eye-less reason enough to fight Spaniards. This time the gold flowed less freely from Master Bowbridge's coffers. A second wager did not win the faith of the first throw.

So two scowling faces confronted Miranda across the oaken draw-table. Francisco's—lean and intent, all business now—and the stout Cornishman's, whose single eye and thick dialect did not serve to soften his message: yet more money.

"Forty guns! Captain Pentreath, how on earth do you expect me to pay for forty new cannon when Master Bowbridge is deluging me with foolscap complaining still about the last four and twenty sunk somewhere off Cádiz?"

"If ye don't want us all sunk off Cádiz, mistress, ye'll give me the guns wi' no grumblin'. I've had enough sailin' on funeral barges tricked out as fightin' ships, by Harry an' St. Ives, an' beggin' yer pardon, mistress, but them's me last words on it. An' liable to be wi' only four and twenty guns.

"Ye'd be a fool to venture near the wake of a full-rigged Spanish galley wi' less than forty cannon, an' them good solid stuff that'll not burst into yer face an' leave ye wi' a leather patch for an eyeball.

"But I'll say no more about it; that's me final word upon it. 'Tis yer money and our lives only at stake. Why should an old sailor expect more sense from a lass than from the whole damn British Admiralty? That's my final syllable upon it—"

"Peace, Captain Pentreath. You'll have forty guns if I have to melt the family plate for it. And that's *my* final word on it."

The Cornish captain nodded once, donned his battered beaver and stalked out as if she had sentenced him instead of satisfied him. Miranda blew a tendril from her forehead and shrugged her white-collared shoulders at Francisco.

"He's a good captain, Mirandita, what you English call an old sea dog, but one with bite beneath his bark. To hear him talk of Spaniards over two mugs of bitter ale is enough to curl my hair without benefit of barber. One would think he had fought the Armada in fifteen eighty and eight, though even he's a trifle young for that. He takes me for a Portuguese—and since he thinks them 'damn fine sailors all' and that's his last word upon it, we travel together tolerably well."

Miranda laughed and sat heavily upon the chair. "Fetch me

some wine, Francisco; I've no desire to have servile ears at our planning sessions. Aunt is all too ready to put her foot down at these ventures. I'd not have her learn yet that I planned to sail with you."

"And still do?" Francisco asked over the carafe of sherry winking like amber in his hand. "No rum, Mirandita? I'd have thought this house would be well stocked with island nectar."

"Oh, there's rum in the cellar, but few favor it." Miranda smiled to herself. "And few can stomach it."

"You look a lady with a secret, Mirandita," noted Francisco, handing her the glass. "You always had that look about you, but I hadn't seen it since Barbados."

"I? A secret? It was you and Harry were always off about your men's business and I only one to come trailing after."

"You wouldn't have even seen the tail of us had Mistress MacTavish had her way."

"Mistress MacTavish." Miranda's face froze into faraway lines. "Meg. Her given name was Meg. Or Margaret."

"You make her sound almost human, that well-starched old virago."

"She was human, human enough to leave that condition."

The sherry glass sparkled to Miranda's lips and then her face was lost in tilting back to swallow. She took a long draught, as if she needed it. Francisco watched her through narrow dark eyes sharp with sudden sympathy.

"Little one."

Miranda found Francisco leaning across the table toward her, a smile stalking his eyes and lips.

"I promised your father when you were young that I should take great care with you. He feared leaving you adrift on the wild island he had chosen for his own, but you were his own before any exile was. When I came to the Hathaways, he made me swear on my Catholic cross to protect you, if you can imagine such an act from a good Anglican. I am not certain that voyages to Spain meet that requirement."

"Voyages to England do not offer much certitude either, Francisco. So Father feared dying even then; perhaps that was why he drilled the reading into us so early, but reading stood me in little stead on the Dutchman's prize, or on the—the other ship. No, it was your good parries and feints that gave me passage; you can't deny that; you taught me."

Francisco sighed. "That was a game, Mirandita, an amusement. This is more than game, this venture; this is true hazard. 'Tis your ship, I cannot gainsay you passage. I would I could guarantee your return. I would I could delve into the thing that goads you—"

Miranda had stopped heeding him. Her fingers spun the glass stem around as her eyes watched the sherry oil the crystal cup.

"Captain Pentreath's forty guns. Does that mean the first ship was underarmed? The *Merlin* had but three cannon, four and twenty seemed a great plenty . . . most of our merchants consider themselves well girded with such. An entire crew. Did I let them sail into certain loss for lack of cannon? He said nothing about the guns being too few."

"He?" Francisco's raised raven eyebrows served as question mark to his monosyllable.

"The—other—English captain. The first. He did not argue the outfitting. He argued nothing."

"The he was a fool, Mirandita, for everyone knows that taking a galley requires a galleon's worth of shot."

" 'Was' is a word that may well describe him by now, and the crew. We must find and free them, Francisco, for if we don't, I fear you'll not have to search for what troubles me. I'll not have an entire crew on my conscience. I never thought—"

"Ah, well, Mirandita, I am not prepared to argue either. We'll sail soon and then all your questions will be answered, no?"

"I hope all my questions will be answered, 'Yes.' "

Miranda's preliminary "yeses" came soon enough. The ship's papers were cleared, a crew gathered and her Aunt Helena tidily gagged on the subject by Miranda's obdurate will.

Captain Pentreath had his forty guns and Miranda had her passage uncontested. She also had a hand in naming the vessel. The *Winning Way*.

"Harumppph," barked the captain when he heard the choice. "I've sailed on the *Celtic Cross*—an unlucky vessel if ever there was one—and on enough *Katharine Mary*s and *Elizabeth Margaret*s to people all of Red Bull Wharf, if not a good-sized graveyard—but never a *Winning Way*. Be it taken after the *Willing Mind*? Now, there's a fine ship and right battle-worthy. 'Tis not what ye might call a simple name for a ship, but I'll not say another word on it. Why, there be too many who turn their hands to such chores as namin' vessels nowadays and less to sailing, but it's not worth my words an' I'll—"

"And I'll be mortal glad if you don't say another word on it, Captain," Miranda interrupted. "I named her for my own reason."

"And if ye had any reason, mistress, ye would not be signing on for this voyage." Unburdening himself of his opinion and his spit in the same breath, he left her.

Soon the *Winning Way* won her way out of the Thames's wide mouth, then spent three idle weeks becalmed in the sluggish Downs—a watery net for every southbound ship when the winds refused to blow, and more than mere net. The Downs were also a devouring maw ready to swallow ships in one great saltwater gulp on the treacherous coastal rocks unless they could beat their way far enough out to sea.

After the aggravating delay, the *Winning Way* billowed south again eagerly—her sheets snapping in a brisk breeze and her bowsprit dipping deep into the waves with dolphinlike exuberance.

Miranda had soon taken to wearing men's clothing aboard, though she kept off the open decks. The change levitated one of Francisco's eyebrows and drew a glaring squint from Captain Pentreath's remaining eye. Only good sense kept Miranda from climbing the *Winning Way*'s bowsprit to strain toward their goal. These sailors would never countenance it; they knew her true sex and gave it short shrift.

Captain Pentreath paused only to give his complement of forty nine-pounders some practice rounds on a Dutch trader off Brest. The cannonballs that didn't dent the enemy's pitched sides fell harmless to the waves at her waterline, raising spouts of lacy spray that Miranda watched as if they were a show of fireworks.

How good to be seabound again! A slightly green Francisco turned greener still at her deckside adaptability, but she had missed the toss and tilt, the sudden sprays . . . and only clear sailing between her and Harry. At last. Harry back. The thought propelled her, as wind drove the *Winning Way*.

When the don's galley was in reach, Miranda could hardly contain herself while Francisco dallied ashore to spy out the lay of the land. Or sea, rather. He returned to find Miranda in her cramped cabin, intent upon priming the pair of pistols acquired from her aunt's house.

"If you plan on laying the don flat on his own deck, I should tell you he's sequestered in his villa with the Archbishop of

Málaga," Francisco noted calmly, sitting on the narrow bunk to watch her struggle with the ramrod.

"We've got to carry the galley, Francisco, before we can even contemplate settling with the don. You needn't look disapproving—we need every pistol we have. And Harry?"

"Aboard, well out of the archbishop's purview—that's why the galley lies so far out of port. There would be no mistaking him for an altar boy."

Miranda's pistol clanked to the tabletop. "Don't speak so lightly. You make Harry's fate sound an escapade at times." Miranda brought a level gaze to the Spaniard's shadowed face and was surprised to find it sheepish.

"I forget myself, Mirandita," he said softly.

Miranda stared at him. His words had implied more than was plain, but his private language was a little-spoken one, for she could not read below his surface speech.

"Does it bother you, Francisco, to fight your own people?" she asked abruptly.

"I am a fighter, not a philosopher, and ever have been. As for my people, I feel more kinship with the man at my dagger's end than the fellow shouldering me in the tavern. You are of the same stripe, Mirandita—do not protest, 'tis an honorable livery we wear. We are our own people—Francisco and Miranda. The de Salazars and Hathaways are only so much chaff for the winds."

"Then why do I care so about Harry, if I am as you say?"

Francisco stood, bending his head to evade the low beams, and leaned to whisper in Miranda's ear. "Perhaps because you know that Harry is merely a portion of you and no more."

She sucked in her breath with a pained hiss that sent Francisco to the door.

"Think on it, Mirandita. I am not a fool, and I do not think that you are. It is good to know why one goes a-hunting before one faces the fangs, eh?"

Francisco's dark-garbed figure was another shadow sifting through the door. Miranda picked up the pistol and let out her breath on a long, soft sigh. Was Francisco right; had Harry become merely a flag for her to do battle under?

She thought too late of the right retort: Francisco de Salazar, who called no one his own, had come to parry with his countrymen for the sake of Harry Hathaway. Or for that of Miranda Hathaway. Or even of James Hathaway. Francisco . . . he could not even remain faithful to his own faithlessness. She smiled and found the pistol barrel clearing easily in her hands, as if things that had been awry were now righted. Would that their venture hit no more snags.

The only snag on the *Winning Way*'s horizon was a flat meadow of sea-green water and one far-off deadly hummock upon it—six hundred tons of high-hipped, long-legged Iberian sea spider, with poison enough in her bloated belly to sting the English ship into a thousand toothpicks.

Captain Pentreath's one visible eyebrow knit to meet the leather patch over his bad eye when Miranda joined the crew on deck.

"I thought I'd seen everything 'tween Land's End on my own Cornwall coast and Ti-er-ra del Fu-e-go on the New World's chin, but this is a new sight and enough to set my last eye a-winkin'. 'Tis bad enough to set sail with a female aboard, but one rigged out with a proper sword and a brace o' pistols be a good deal more than the Lord, Nature or the Law intended."

"You had better worry more about pistols at your front than at your rear, Captain Pentreath," Miranda observed calmly. "A ball doesn't know who fired it; it merely does its duty as directed. And so, I think, do good sea captains."

"I've never seen the like, by St. George and Mistress Carmarthen's suet pudding, but a man who's beyond surprise is likely beyond breath, so I'll say no more about it."

For once, he was true to his word.

Chapter Fourteen

The *Gato de Nueve*'s boatswain paused to take a pinch of snuff, his gold-laced cuff flashing toward his face like a vigil light in the galley's dim underbelly. No one noticed the incongruity of the gesture.

All backs were bent to their rhythmic task. The rowers knew only the timekeeper's steady drumming and the whip's hiss. Some raved with fever—broken phrases of Dutch, Arabic or English echoed briefly off the galley's timbered sides. Then there was only the sea's dull roar against her hull, the scrape of massive oarlocks, the chatter of the chains and the constant drumming. A musical rhythm underlay it all, including the motion, and many a fever victim danced to the sickness in his head.

The boatswain strolled to the forward bridge, his whip coiled under his arm and trailing behind him like a limp tail. He inhaled the snuff that drove the galley stench from his nostrils, the bent heads lifting slightly as he passed.

One head surfaced longer than the rest.

"Careful, man, he'll have his leather dance a jig upon yer back if he sees you're not layin' on the oar," warned a benchmate.

The head turned a bleary pair of blue eyes on the speaker. " 'Tis Muffin. The fever. I can't see him on the bench any longer. He's only four down—"

"Forget him, man! For sure, the Almighty Lord has, an' forgotten us all. By St. Pat, He's gone over for a Spaniard, I vow. Take care, me lad, or we'll both get a pet from the whip."

Steele bowed his shaggy head to the pole between his shackled hands and lay into its motion with sudden fatigue. Even talking took its toll. Soon a clatter came that raised more heads than his: a second boatswain plummeting down the narrow stairs.

The two lavishly attired whipmasters conferred, a sinister sparkle surrounding their slightly shifting forms. Then the timekeeper let a drumstick fall on his great sounding board with a quicker beat. The rowers' hearts leapt to that sudden upswing. Each man's hands wrung the wooden oar that his own skin had polished to satin. Jaws clenched, nerves tautened and the *Gato de Nueve* bolted forward in the waves as if catapulted.

Despite the intensified drumbeats, the oarlocks' quicker grinding, the slaves' hard gasps, the galley rowing decks appeared strangely static. The repetitive motion had a lulling effect, like watching some great mechanical contrivance—the perpetual-motion machine all inventors sought and none mastered. The rowers' backs glistened with sweat, the boatswains strutted and poked a human gear—here, there—and then moved on.

"Engagement," Steele exulted to his Irish benchmate as their oar swiveled on its backward stroke. "Engagement, by God."

Both men lunged forward, their muscles corded into ropes to haul the huge pole back.

"Aye, 'tis likely, but naught we can do—"

The six men manning the oar plunged forward again and effort gagged conversation.

Now the strain under which the rowers worked began to show. A man slipped from the bench; the boatswain's whip circled him like a kind of curling black script in the murky underdecks air. Its message was plain: work or bleed. The rower resumed his place, his blood-etched back a testament to his conversion.

Engagement! To that idea Steele clung as fiercely as to his oar. A long word to echo in so numbed a brain. En-gage-ment. The word lashed his mind like a mental whip as he lunged forward, then back and over.

Another ship, an enemy, drove the *Gato* to double-time strokes. Now, now was the time for their plan—their skimpy plotting hatched over scummed water-cup brims and passed in stifled snatches down the oars. A childish plan, puny, even hopeless, but with a certain zany mathematical appeal.

The scheme was simply this: should the galley ever ply her oars for battle, each oar would by turn feign some problem. Its men would droop, its rhythm break. The boatswains' whips would soon slash the laggards into action again. But . . . at the farthest possible oar across the bridge, another breakdown would occur. The boatswain would rush there and quell it only to find another, opposite oar in difficulty.

The plan's price was a whip slice out of each man's back, but the whips were applied assiduously during battle anyway. The trick was to keep the delays random enough so that the harried boatswains did not see through the scheme.

The plan offered merely a hesitation in the galley's great heartbeat, enough of an irregular rhythm to set her faltering for her enemies to overtake. Such a lean bit of hope, the plan, and every man knew it. Steele, galley-fresh and freedom-eager, had conceived it during an idle lull at the oars, when engagement had seemed an impossibility. Now the appointed hour was here. Would the rest of the rowers be willing to risk their skins for a chance at release?

Steele's head snapped up again, his thoughts instantly scattered. There, far ahead—was there the slightest shudder of a hesitation? The oars were tuned to turn in harmony; one off-stroke and the other rowers sensed it. So did the whipmasters.

The boatswains' boots tapped forward, random curses and meticulously aimed whip strokes exploding before them. Then all was quiet, save for the strain of wood and flesh against water and air. Another clatter. The gilded boatswains flashed by like unlucky falling stars. A few cries and the rear oar across the bridge was working again.

Now the forward opposite oar stalled—Steele's eyes strained

to follow the boatswains' headlong rush, then noticed that his own oar was short a man. Muffin drooped hopelessly over the shaft, acting more as burden than workmate.

Steele's oar faltered—out of turn—and brought the boatswains over, gaudy crows seeking carrion. They etched their commands into every exposed back. When Muffin did not revive, they called upon the rank vinegar-water that sufficed for galley smelling salts.

Muffin's unkempt white head reared back from the potion over which it bowed. The boatswains forced a swallow down the old sailor's mouth and propped him up again on the bench. The bastinado prodded, the whip drew its message on the oarsmen's backs and the great wooden pole resumed its clumsy orbit once more.

The other five oarsmen carried Muffin; he lay upon the oar all but unconscious despite his dousing. The Irishman next to Steele growled a Gaelic curse that needed no translation.

Soon more men were fainting on the oars in an epidemic of unfeigned exhaustion that taxed even the fast-moving boatswains. These whipmasters glittered in the ill-lit lower decks, drawn like flies to the sweating flesh of any rower who dallied over his oar. They spared no one. Muffin's spare, semiconscious form carried new crimson tracery; the Irishman leaned into his work with a desperate power but wore new stripes despite his dedication. Steele felt a sharp cut from time to time and gave it the numbed wince that was a seasoned slave's only reaction to the whip.

The oars' pathetic pattern of disruption continued, but the reason had drained from it. More rowers were drawn into the sheer effort of matching the drumbeats with their own ceaseless action. Forward, down, under, around and back. Lean, push, pull; pull, bend, break.

They sweated their spirit out, their resolve ran off their flesh in rivers. Ultimately they heeded the siren song of their own motion, a wrenching, numbing, weary plodding. They bowed their shaggy heads into their labor to a man, and, as the docile oxen pull the plow through ridges of untilled earth, the slaves of the *Gato de Nueve* pressed her clumsy wooden prow through gentle hills of virgin water.

The *Winning Way* sped lightly after the galley driving ahead of her in a ruffle of foam. No one aboard save Captain Pentreath had seen a Spanish galley in full flight, an awesome spectacle. Perfectly tuned rows of oars seemingly picked up the galley to lever her through the waves. It was impossible to believe that flesh and blood and not some monstrous mechanism propelled that implacable rhythm.

Miranda stood by the gunwale, her hands curled into fists. Francisco slid beside her, eased an elbow onto the rail, and said something the flapping sails shouted down.

"What?" Miranda reluctantly tore her eyes from the fleeing galley.

"I wondered what thoughts ran behind that fierce face of yours." Francisco mouthed his question into her ear, like an exaggerated secret.

"I—I thought how beautiful it was, how fast, how sleek. How it—she—that enemy ahead of us—was meant to fly on waves and wind. I thought how I should hate to see it splintered, broken. Is that secret enough for you?" Miranda had shouted her confession, but the rush of wind made it still a very private admission.

Francisco nodded and smiled. "So feels the matador for the bull before he thrusts in the sword, so. Why think you men love war, were there not some pity in it?"

Miranda shook her yellow head, the wind combing free tendrils that teased her face. "You only confuse me, Francisco. I do not know what we should think when we go to war, but we must catch her, that flying fish ahead of us."

"We will. Even Spaniards can't keep galley slaves moving at such a pace . . . look! She faltered there, a little. I'll ready our boarding parties, for I swear Pentreath has turned our sails to wings."

Francisco vanished, and Miranda glanced up to see the *Winning Way*'s canvas pregnant with gusts. She looked ahead. True, the galley was closer, with a peculiar stutter, an almost undetectable roughness to her oars . . . almost as if . . . Miranda frowned.

Soon the two ships were near enough for an exchange of broadsides, but they still kept in procession one behind the other, so none but the few feeble stern and prow cannon could be discharged.

They hung at this position until the galley oars slowed, suddenly lifted out of the water and were still. Francisco's party of boarding boats slipped from the *Winning Way*'s stern like an armada of goslings deserting the high, winged shadow of their mother.

Miranda, ordered to remain aboard by both Cornishman and Spaniard, had lost any debate between one's garrulousness and the other's terseness. She struck her fists once more on the gunwale. Behind her, Captain Pentreath barked out a series of commands strange even to one who had spent weeks on shipboard.

The *Winning Way* lurched as if agreeing with Miranda's thoughts as the wind caught the ship square on the sails and blew her swiftly toward the stalled galley. In moments the two vessels lay parallel, the English ship greatly overmatched by the galley's dark, swollen length.

Then the deck thundered below Miranda's feet. She clung to the rail, watching the Spanish ship and seeing a mast here, a sail there, falter, alter somehow. Was this it, then? Battle? It seemed so measured, the two ships like distant partners in a court masque, the whole wide ocean a piece of azure and white Italian marble they danced upon.

The *Winning Way* tacked swiftly, drawing away. Miranda saw the galley's red-lettered name clarify and then fade as fast.

"Gato de N-n . . . nada?" Nothing. Cat of Nothing? At a sharp answering burst from the galley, Miranda saw the full, awesome fury of three rows of cannon barking down one's throat. First came a veiled flash of fire behind the galley gunports, then smoke billowed out, making it seem that the Spanish ship had coughed.

And still the *Winning Way* slid away. No! Had Pentreath answered with his own cannon again? For a shudder hiccoughed through the ship, and she spun suddenly, as if cut loose from an invisible leash. Then the *Gato* was catapulting a score of fire bombs into the *Winning Way*'s flapping sails. Like shooting stars they arced deckward. Miranda watched, frozen, aware that any step might take her into that fiery shower.

Yet it was still remote, battle. Still unreal. A hand suddenly wrenched Miranda around to face the bustling deck.

"Off! Take the quarter boat. I've a pair of hands for ye. Now! Off wi' ye."

Miranda stared dumbly into Captain Pentreath's powder-stained face, lined as if a laugh had frozen upon it and become something else.

"Off my ship!" he bellowed, shaking her arm so roughly that

the pistols in her belt clattered like bells. " 'Tis battle yer tricked out for, mistress, and, by God, ye shall have it."

Miranda still stared into the man's face as if he had taken leave of his Cornish good sense.

"I did not want ye aboard me ship afore, and I want ye less now. They need ye yonder, I vow, so go. Trip some Spanish sailors with yer rapier, mistress. I need me Englishmen on their feet."

His last incivility propelled Miranda to the small boat and two grimy seamen who lowered it rapidly at her approach. She turned back once, but Pentreath aimed a biblical finger of dismissal at her.

"Go. An' it be me last word," he thundered, the shot-peppered sails flapping mightily above him and seamen running frantically to repair riggings that hung tattered to the deck.

Miranda shrugged and slipped over the side, no easy task with a rapier waiting to twine itself in one's legs. Perhaps the man was right, perhaps she was only nuisance . . . and she wanted to see the galley, to find her brother.

The galley ahead rocked slightly in the smoke wreathing her waterline as the clang of hand-to-hand combat drifted over her carved and gilded gunwale. The sound mimicked cutlery, like an entire hallful of eager diners, only victory was the meat for all those men contending above. She would aid in that. She was as able with the sword as Harry. And she was not afraid. Puzzled, perhaps, by the strangeness, but not afraid. Of course not.

Miranda clambered up the high side ahead of the sailors, this time keeping her long-tongued rapier from licking at her own heels. 'Twas not so different from managing a skirt.

She bounded onto the poop to survey the lower decks teeming with figures seemingly dashing hither and yon for the sport of it. Not a face, a manner of dress, was familiar. The moving men never ceased milling long enough for her to place them. She stood above the galley's Great Cabin as the fighting men washed back and forth below like waves scrubbing the foot of a coastline prominence, remembering another skirmish, another bloody deck.

How odd to feel so removed when so much was happening . . . A face rose over the edge of Miranda's perch, then its owner's shoulders labored into view: a man, clad in black and gold and waving something quite like a— Miranda drew her long-barreled pistol and discharged it.

The man and his drawn sword fell back into the sea of contending humanity on the lower deck. Miranda's palm stung as if slapped by the pistol's recoil. She had only shot for Barbados target play before; now it seemed her pistol always had been aimed at something gilded sweeping toward her on the deck of a Spanish ship.

The two English sailors bounded over the side and hurled themselves toward the fray. Miranda would have joined them, but she was uncertain about what precisely to do. She could draw her other pistol and shoot someone else, she supposed, but what if it was the wrong someone? The man who had scaled the edge and descended again so precipitously had no doubt that she was a right and proper target.

Why should she be so uncertain about friend and foe? Her eyes narrowed at the struggling masses below. She began to see a pattern, a checkerboard of dark against light. Englishmen fair versus swarthy Spaniards. She drew her rapier and walked down to the lower deck.

Hardly had her borrowed boots touched planking than a Spanish seaman charged her, his sword held high for a quick and deadly blow. Miranda's blade met his, like a bar slipping closed across a door. His charge carried her back against the Great Cabin side. She slipped away and under, turning to find him pinched between her and the wall. He lunged again but she parried easily—this man relied on force, not skill.

Again he lunged, driving her back a yard. Her heel caught on the deck edge and she teetered for a moment before she steadied herself against the rail. An eight-foot plunge into a nest of squirming figures would have been her welcome below. Her attacker bulled forward again, his sword arrowing straight for her. Miranda sidestepped, then slipped under his guard and drove her Sheffield blade into his belly like a table knife through cheese.

What came trickling out of his doublet front was not cheese. The man collapsed against the cabin wall. Dying . . . dead.

Miranda pulled on her sword pommel, something unpleasant rising in her throat. The blade remained impaled in its victim, a good half foot of steel thirsty for blood and wanting more—she tugged desperately. To let the blade drink its fill one moment longer would be an obscenity beyond bearing . . . This wasn't battle, this was nightmare. A dead man skewered on her sword point and dragging her down into a morass. Now—it must come free now—!

A hand closed over hers and pulled sharply, once. The blade slid free, only a bit of red still clinging to its point.

Miranda turned startled eyes to her unknown assistant.

"That I did not teach you, Mirandita," Francisco said. "It is easier to kill than to have killed, no? And what perversity brings you aboard? We've more battling to do before the galley's ours."

Miranda looked around. She and Francisco were islanded in quiet amidst the scuffle, as if suspended at the eye of a Barbados hurricane.

On the lower decks, black-and-gold-clothed Spaniards clotted near the gunwale, ringed in by English sailors. A pile of surrendered swords and pistols flung to deck rang with new arrivals as each soldier was disarmed. The men who had come spitting up at Miranda had been mere refugees from a battle already lost below. The two dead men.

"We've won?"

Francisco laughed sharply. "Here at least. I've sent a party below, but the *Gato* still has her claws. Listen."

A thunderous clap began rumbling at the galley's prow and steadily belched its way aft, until Miranda felt the ship shudder beneath her feet.

"We must secure the gun decks, or the *Winning Way* will— But why are you here, Mirandita? You agreed to remain aboard our ship."

Francisco's angled eyebrows produced a matching frown on Miranda's face.

"I don't know, Francisco. I fear that Captain Pentreath has shot off his good sense with his cannon. He simply became most insulting and ordered me off the ship . . . so I left."

"Ordered you off? That sounds not like our firm-minded English—ah, pardon, Cornish—captain. Why change purpose so suddenly?"

Francisco wheeled seaward, to where the *Winning Way* was waging the spit-and-cough warfare of the cannon.

"*Madre de Dios!*" Francisco's whispered profanity misted the air like pistol smoke. Miranda stared seaward with him, frozen into equal disbelief.

" 'Tis not possible. When I left she was ragged in the sails, she was earning her share of battle scars, but—"

Miranda stared in silence at what the wind and water chose to waft about their surfaces, what once had been called a ship. She was a jagged skeleton now, her blackened, broken masts bare of all but strips of sail, and these few tatters trailed into the wind like a disintegrating shroud.

A great, gaping wound in the *Winning Way*'s prow looked like an open mouth screaming for help. The ship listed as they watched, as if shrugging her wooden shoulders to fate before slipping away. She was riding low and her guns were silent.

"But how, Francisco—?"

"I see it, there. The rudder's gone, doubtless from an early shot. A lucky shot. Without a rudder, all the wind in the world would not blow her into battle. She was—a target, that is all. A sieve for the seawater, and nothing more her pumps could do for her. See the last boat rowing galleyward? Poor devils. I'd better ensure they have a berth to fly to. If we lose this galley, we've naught but our skins to sail home in."

Francisco darted below, leaving Miranda to impale her sword point in the planking and lean upon the pommel. She felt need of an anchor, for her mind was adrift on speculation. The *Winning Way*'s condition was odder still than what Francisco had said. She remembered the swift, shuddering spin the ship had made just after its first pass with the cannon. The *Gato*'s lucky shot, as Francisco had said.

Then, shortly after, Captain Pentreath had so cavalierly driven her off the ship . . . because he had known his vessel was doomed! No time for explanations, just moments to order her to safety and then take the iron buffeting that was his lot. The dear man. The foolish man. His last word upon it, indeed. He should hear a few more words from her for his well-intentioned deceit once the galley was secure.

Miranda watched the *Winning Way*'s last boat row thickly through the waves toward her. The men were tired from manning the pumps; their rowing had no heart, but no galley fire prevented their approach. Francisco's squad had undoubtedly subdued the gunners by now, subdued even the rowing decks—though few would challenge them there.

Where was Pentreath? He should be among the men scrambling up the *Gato*'s sides now. No ruddy, seamed face that answered to Pentreath appeared. Miranda leapt down to the lower decks and heedlessly passed knots of rounded-up Spaniards. She found Francisco squirting up a hatch, his brow streaming from the battle heat below.

"She's ours," he said with a grin. The smile snuffed like a candle when he saw her face. "What is it, *lindita*? Have you seen a ghost, is Harry—?"

Harry. The word exploded in Miranda's mind like a forgotten password. Harry, of course. But now—

" 'Tis Captain Pentreath. He's not left the *Winning Way*. I fear—"

They pivoted simultaneously to view the English ship's hulk sinking slowly into the bright blue sea. The yawning hole in her side had swallowed enough salt water to disappear beneath the weight of it. She listed badly now, beyond hope of righting.

Her bare and jagged masts tilted crazily seaward, like a dowager's hair comb impaled at the wrong angle. In an hour, the *Winning Way* had aged into a doddering remnant of her formerly sprightly self.

"*Diablo!*" Francisco glanced at Miranda, then retrieved the *Gato*'s spyglass rolling aimlessly upon the boards to train it on the *Winning Way*'s angled deck.

"There's our captain! By the Holy Virgin, I thought I saw a movement. He's not drowned—yet."

"Why didn't he leave, then? There's no cargo to save, no reason— Give me the glass."

Francisco surrendered his artificial eye and Miranda pressed the cold brass to her face, remembering the last occasion she'd used such far-seeing: off the African coast, when that strange Arab boy had come aboard the *Salamander* . . . before she had visited the don and found Harry. Before Kit Steele had discovered what she was, before she had lost forever what she was . . .

No long-profiled camels, no sheets of shimmering sand greeted Miranda's eye now, only timber soaking up water like a sponge, only the masts lurching toward the waves like a lover for a kiss—and there, Pentreath's scuffed leather buckler, his well-salted head of dark hair.

He was moving about the listing deck, tripping more than moving really, clearing away splintered mast pieces, as if he expected the *Winning Way* to sail again. Odd, how soundlessly the ship wallowed into the waves . . . only a random snap, a wrenching creak, announced her imminent destruction.

"Pentreath!" The Cornish name came awkwardly to Francisco's Spanish lips, but he bellowed it loudly enough to carry to the doomed vessel. "Come over."

Pentreath did not answer or turn to look, though he paused in his motions.

"Captain Pentreath!" Miranda lowered her voice enough to carry. "You've only moments—" Her eye through the glass saw the man freeze, his back as set as a stone.

"Captain Pentreath!" Her cry's intensity would have made an observer think that she, and not Pentreath, stood in mortal danger. "Captain!"

The dark figure that she held coiled in the tube in her hands turned slowly and lurched to the ship's gunwale, clinging there as the prow levered inexorably upward into a pure blue sky. Pentreath's face was white, as drained as a frosted goblet, his features but black spots, so the whole seemed a mask of light and dark. He stared directly at the galley, at Miranda holding him in the palm of her hand.

"What is he about, Francisco?" she asked without taking her gaze from Pentreath. "Why doesn't he answer?"

The small figure wavered slightly in a flaw in the glass and then Miranda saw his hand. It was white and splayed, out of focus, but it was clutched to Pentreath's throat.

Another kind of clutch choked her own throat, as when her sword would not withdraw from the lumpish, leaden form collapsed upon it.

Then Pentreath withdrew his hand, and her breath drew in as if they were in physical contact. She felt the hand slide away, felt the slow, oozing withdrawal of steel from flesh, flesh from steel.

Where Pentreath's throat should have been was only a dark, oozing hole. The glass spared her nothing—Pentreath lifted his hand high, a greeting or a farewell. She saw dark red clotting upon the palm, she traced its rivulets down his buckler front. A musket ball, directly in the throat. Not enough to kill instantly. Merely enough.

The *Winning Way*'s prow suddenly shot perpendicular to the water and sank, hurling Pentreath out of sight and stirring up a ring of white froth around her painted wooden sides.

"Pentreath!" Miranda's last invocation was to the waves. Her only answer was to see the *Winning Way*'s foremast slip underwater, one tattered bit of sail still waving from it like a white and bloodless hand.

Something, someone, slid the spyglass from Miranda's hand; she was startled to find her palms slick with sweat. Miranda watched the last of the *Winning Way* slither beneath all the clean blue shifting water.

"His last word upon it . . ." Francisco mused. "A fitting epitaph, I warrant. And this could serve as epitaph for us. We have no captain to steer us back to England. No navigator."

Miranda still stared toward the gently rolling surface where the *Winning Way*'s bowsprit had been sucked below a tightening white rope of foam. Then the froth whirled together and dissipated. She turned to Francisco.

"No captain? I am sick of losing captains, Francisco. That man Coyle—dead on the deck. Now Pentreath. I believe that I am bad luck for captains, I will have no more of them. I will be my own captain." Francisco was silent. "It is my ship."

He nodded a face as unconvinced as a wall of slate.

"And sailors?" she asked then. "Have we sailors enough left to steer this barge home?"

"We lost some in boarding, but can put the don's soldiers to the oars. If those below be in any shape for it, they are seamen all, no? And well pleased to sail for us."

"To sail for you, perhaps. But not—for me. Women are water-cursed to English sailors."

"Then we needn't tell them of you."

"No. I have earned my right to be what I am. I will command this vessel. And do not fret: I believe that I can produce a navigator, a 'captain' in name only, for you."

Captain Fifteen

Miranda quite deliberately let down her hair despite the protest of Francisco's raised eyebrow. If the seamen would accept her at all as a shipboard superior, it would be with full knowledge of what she was.

Francisco trailed her unbidden to the rowing decks.

The stench surging upward in the small stairwell almost knocked her backward, but, with Francisco behind her, Miranda entered the time-drummer's end of the captured Spanish galley.

Three hundred pair of half-human eyes stared from three hundred ragged bodies wallowing in a stench that equaled nothing of which Miranda had even dreamed. They were mere animals now—wily, wary beaten beasts that knew the wind was shifting, but was it their way?

Despite their straits, they were still sailors enough to protest the woman in their midst. A low murmur ran from bench to bench, oar to oar; chains began a clatter that echoed against the wooden hull.

Miranda picked up a drumstick sacrificed by the timekeeper in his flight. She threw it on the great primitive drum that had been the soundboard of their slavery. The reverberation quieted them by reflex, reduced rebellion to a quiver.

"My good English ship," she began clearly, "stopped your oars. Many of you, I think, set sail for me once to Cádiz. Your voyage was not smooth sailing, though the Spanish thought you might do smoothly enough at their oars. You can be free, but first you must swear fealty to me. I am not captain of this ship, nor any other, but I am—commander." She smiled. "My good English frigate sinks alongside this galley, so it's the *Gato de Nueve* I'll take back to England. Accept my right to rule here and you can man the decks above. Refuse me and you continue to ply these oars below. Perhaps you have grown attached to your present situation—"

Here, a rough chuckle broke from several of the more lively rowers.

"In either instance," Miranda continued, "you're free when we reach England. 'Tis merely a matter of how you prefer to travel."

A thin thread of laughter unrolled like a ball of renegade yarn to her feet. They appreciated a choice as clear as hers.

"Are you with me, then?" she asked formally.

"Aye," came the answer. Only a fool would let superstition and custom chain him a day longer than necessary.

Miranda drew the pistol at her belt and waited until utter silence circled the place. She uncocked it slowly and visibly.

"Release them," she ordered Francisco, "and send the Spaniard scum below in their place."

A cheer echoed off the benches slick with slime and blood.

Francisco turned, a Belgian handkerchief to his long Spanish nose the moment his back was to them, and clattered up the stairs, leaving the mates to strike off the chains. Miranda followed him, leaning against the stairwell with a white face.

"One thing more, Francisco." She laid a hand upon his arm. "I believe you'll find an old acquaintance below, and a new captain for us. Fetch him to me."

Francisco groaned faintly and raised a curious eyebrow, but smiled and bowed before diving once more into the human flotsam the Spanish made of galley slaves.

Miranda found a fine captain's cabin awaiting her—wood-paneled, outfitted in silk curtains, with a wide, inset bed of mahogany at one wall, a bay of windows at the other.

She sat at the well-tooled chair and shuffled through the Moroccan-leather-bound logbook. Then she reached to the belt at her waist and pulled something out—a fine steel dagger. The blade from Barcelona.

She smiled, once and briefly, before laying its slim silver length on the desk, beneath a chart. It disappeared except for the scrollwork handle.

A knock startled her, though it was faint and she expected it.

"Enter," she said, and a shadow of a man stepped through the low Spanish portal. Against the outer light, his form was a puzzle. Miranda struck flint and lit the two wrought-iron lamps that dangled above the desk.

Had Francisco found his man? For a tense moment she wasn't certain. This man brought the stench of the slaughterhouse with him. What remained of a shirt, whipped to rags upon his shoulders, hung like torn sails from a frame stripped to bone and sinew.

For a moment she could not bring her eyes to his face, but she thought back to another day on another ship and raised her lids. Bearded, a dirty brown beard against a sickly white face, a face that had not felt the sun for several cycles of the moon. And eyes, were there eyes in this pathetic creature? Miranda met dull blue, faint blue in which recognition was a memory.

"Captain Steele," she said then, her voice a lash. He blinked once, as she saw that the sudden light and darkness in turn had briefly blinded him.

"Are you fit, Captain Steele? Fit enough to steer a ship across the wide sea? I'd not have disturbed you in your—lair. I'd have left you to your hard-won solitude, but I lost my captain to a twelve-pounder. I need another. I will do you a 'service.' I will let you be my navigator."

Despite his still-dull gaze, she could see his mind turning the mental pages of memory, see it shuffling through time to place her words in their proper context. She had chosen them almost as an incantation and saw them eat at the core of his memory even now.

"You do remember me, Captain Steele?" She leaned toward him. If the galleys had blasted memory from him, her revenge would forever taste like dregs. "Have some brandy. I am a generous host, and it may revive your memories."

She had the odd sensation that she was assuming another's role as she dashed the Spanish captain's liquor into a goblet and extended it, her hand shaking with some emotion she would rather not name. He must be whole enough to feel her revenge!

He had been swaying slightly on his feet in rhythm to the ship's soft rock, a sailor still. Now he downed the cup at one draught, without spilling a drop, and the eyes that came over its empty rim to regard her were suddenly clearer, as if a veil had been washed away.

But still he said nothing, so she boldly walked around the desk to confront him. "Do you remember me?"

"Yes," was all he said. And it conceded nothing.

"I have been remembering you, Captain Steele." His name came so cleanly to the tongue, it had such a cutting edge; she liked to curl her lips around it and draw it slowly across his lacerated pride. "I have been wondering how you fared all these months. I have been wondering if perhaps the Spanish have taken from you what you stole from me."

She circled him, aware suddenly of something vile and predatory about her movements. She paused behind him, laid her hand lightly on his shoulder. "I was wondering if you have found a way to get it back, if you can tell me how to get it back? Or are the scales even now, have the Spanish balanced the ledger for me?"

She ripped what little remained of the shirt from his back, laying the whip welts—some fresh and others puckered to hard tissue—plain. Suddenly distasteful of herself, of the Spaniards, of the man she used to know, Miranda dropped the filthy rags to the floor and returned to the desk.

"You'll sail this ship to England for me, no trickery."

A pause, an infinitesimal pause. "Yes." Blue anger; good, she didn't want a sleepwalker at the charts and sails of her way home.

"Call Francisco. He will give you fresh water from the stores for cleaning yourself. You are filthy, but I fear you would find a saltwater bath a bit too seasoned just now. And I will keep the log. I did the chore on the voyage out, but you must give me the proper figures, as your predecessor did."

She looked down to the Moroccan-leather book that would now tell its tale in English, and penned in the date. "This day have made Christopher Steele captain," she wrote in the neat, firm hand her father had taught her.

"What of the men?"

Miranda was startled to hear him initiate speech. "We haven't enough water to bathe them all," she answered. "Find a fresh-water island and I'll give them all a day's leave."

He moved to go.

"Oh, by the by, Captain," she purred to his departing bare back.

He turned as she took the Barcelona dagger and slammed it hard onto the inlaid wood desk before her—a lucky stroke that stuck and vibrated there, like a striking snake.

"Shave yourself; a beard does not become you."

He took the knife without protest. "You call me 'Captain,' " he noted, sounding more like someone she had once known. "What shall I call you?"

For a moment Miranda faltered. She felt as if she were falling and becoming a very young girl again. *What is your name? Miranda,* she thought. *I am Miranda.*

"You may call me—" "Mistress," the customary form of address, had another, too intimate meaning. " 'Madam,' " she said, her voice steady.

Miranda sat back after the door had swung shut behind him, wishing the dagger back. It made a scathing, razor-sharp gesture, but she wasn't sure gestures pacified her. Harry had given her that knife. That slender piece of steel had swung at her hip across half of Europe, as threat, but as talisman, too. She wasn't sure she wanted it to play barber across Christopher Steele's throat unless it were in earnest. Perhaps he would think about that.

Harry. She hadn't seen him yet. Francisco had found him aboard, as the expensive information had promised, then left him in his cabin. Miranda started up, now restlessly intent upon the mission that had ridden her life for many months. Her brother. Back. Back as he was. Safe. Free. Ready to have the nightmare wiped from his memory.

The bright light abovedecks dazzled her for a moment. As she strode to the quarterdeck for Francisco, she saw Steele emerging from the galley waist below.

"I thought I told you—"

For answer he slung the burden that lagged behind him into the bright daylight—a man more ragged than he, with joints so sharp and skin so stretched that he seemed to be a mere shell doubling back upon itself. He brought fresh stench to the com panionway, this remnant of starved and shriveled flesh, and Miranda finally took a confused half-step backward.

"Are there others this—?" Her voice had become a whisper.

"He's old," Steele said.

Miranda's eyes went to the creature's face—a bony, monkey face on a scrawny neck, a face lost in the bushy gray eyebrows that canopied its sunken eyes.

"My God . . . Muffin!"

The name rolled memory back into those pale, watering eyes.

"Aye, Muffin, 'tis," came the unexpected reply. "Who be you? An angel of mercy likely. I see all gold around yer head . . ."

The eyes stared at her, weakly blinking. Miranda had forgotten her loosened hair. She drew it back and leaned close to the face she barely recognized.

" 'Tis me, Muffin. Richard Hathaway, who was cabin boy on the *Salamander*."

"Aye," the man nodded. "Left us without a word, didn't ye, Richard?" His head lolled onto Steele's shoulder. "Wee Richard. I be rememberin' now. The Monkey. Have ye grown, lad, be ye shavin' like a sailor yet?"

A shadow of a smile teased at his thin gray lips. "Hard seas since I saw ye last, lad," he confided then. "Hard sailin'. Months pullin' in the longboats, ye know." Muffin's voice turned querulous and his head bobbed toward Steele's. "Hav'ee got another bit of biscuit for me, Captain? You always been a good mate, Kit . . . just a bit more—"

Miranda stepped back, horrified by Muffin's raving. He had been old before, but spry and cheerful as a ground squirrel.

"It won't be long," said Steele over Muffin's wobbling head.

Her eyes, flashing to his face, found him looking remarkably fit compared to this flotsam of a man washed up on the Spanish galley's deck.

Spaniards. They'd done this. Starved Old Muffin and whipped him and made him row with his tough wiry arms until every last ounce of anything left in him squeezed out through some pore. He would have been dead soon; rescue merely eased the last of it.

Her eyes snared Francisco's elegant form on the afterdeck. "Frisco!" She'd never before needed to abbreviate his name. Francisco recognized her urgency and ended his amble to leap lithely over the rail to the deck below.

"Aye, aye, sir," he mocked in his soft-accented English.

Miranda frowned. He was a mocking sort of man and had long since lost allegiance to any flag. Nevertheless, the faint Castillian lisp on the "sir" irritated her.

"Are the Spanish crew in chains and ready for the galleys?" she asked, her voice harder than the toughest tropical wood on Barbados.

"I'll have the scum flushed below and put Staffleridge on the drum," Francisco flashed eagerly between his teeth. Staffleridge was a great hulking Yorkshireman, with the mean streak that only dim-wittedness can refine to a precise point. "That ought to skin the sweat out of them."

"No." Miranda turned her back to the gunwale and faced Francisco. "Hold the prisoners. Flood out the rowing deck until it's habitable again. And put our sailors on duty with the rowers."

Francisco's dark eyes narrowed in disbelief.

"I want to reach England quickly, Francisco. We'll get more from them this way. Even Spaniards tire, do they not?" Her voice was dull, flat.

Mercy was the dregs of the emotional well, with none of the searing bite of revenge, no righteous sweetening. It tasted as flat as defeat. Mercy was giving up all one's cherished pictures of vengeance, even of justice; but she could not create another Muffin, no matter his breed. She saw Steele watching her as narrowly as Francisco and gestured both men away.

Miranda turned back to the rail to contemplate her failed nerve. She'd lost respect in Francisco's cynical eyes by this. He was a man of the rapier, of quick and subtle commitment, rapacious even. She'd always known that, even as she had admired him for it. Now he would find her weak, not worth serving so docilely, perhaps. Few men liked to dance to a woman's tune, no matter how many pistols and trousers she tied at her waist. She'd always wondered why Francisco had been so eager to join the *Winning Way*'s rescue mission to his homeland. Now he had even less reason to remain with her.

And Steele: she must not forget that Steele was virtually her prisoner, a humiliated captive made to do her will. The warm glow the thought brought her must bring him an equally intense and corresponding cold anger. He had no reason not to wrest command from her if the occasion came.

She touched the still-loaded pistol in her belt. A pistol was surer protection than a sword for a woman in her position. She could lay a man flat on the deck in a second, with no need to pit strength against strength. Still, a pistol gave her but one chance. A knife could go on cutting forever. Like the desire for revenge, a knife had a doubly deadly blade.

Double. The word started another thought in her weary brain. She needed rest, peace. The wide Spanish bed in her cabin. But first she must see Harry. At last . . .

"Harry." Miranda's voice was slightly hoarse with weariness when she knocked on the door of the cabin that housed him. It opened slowly in answer. She stared into the shadows and tried to piece in the figure of the boy—man—who stood there.

"Harry . . ." He had grown half a head taller than she—that was the first sign of the time—months—that had rent them apart. Her dark-adjusting pupils patched the rest of him together—taller and more muscular, with somehow resentful eyes under slightly frowning brows.

"I've found you," she said a bit breathlessly. It had been a hoped-for, a have-to thing for so long. Now it was done.

"So it seems." Harry turned his back on her inspection. She moved to confront him. She was becoming expert at forcing the issue.

"Harry, I never meant to leave you that day in Cádiz." That day rewound itself rapidly on the spindle of her memory with all it contained. "I wasn't able to help you, but now I've got you back. We can return home, as we would have if—" Falling again from above a wildly veering deck, falling between two ships. "—we can go on to England," Miranda finished harshly.

"Yes." Harry's sea-green eyes slid over Miranda's slightly piratical seaman's dress. "As we were."

"Harry. I've sent men into the galleys to get you back. Why does it seem as though . . . as though—?" She caught his arms as he prepared to turn away, a sullen, handsome boy who was somehow contemptuous of her. "We were so close in Barbados. We did everything together."

His mirror eyes flashed irony at her but she ignored it. "No one in the world is closer to me than you, Harry."

"Then I pity you," said the boy, his eyes green-glass-hard in the cabin lamps.

Her face must have made some major change—inwardly it was merely as if her heart had been teetering on a precipice and he had brushed it over with his fingertip—but her face must have crumpled, collapsed somehow, for Harry's mouth softened.

"We were never alike, Miranda," he went on more reasonably. "Never. You always wanted to change things, to make things happen. I wanted to ride at anchor."

"And did you like the anchorage the Spanish grandee gave you, Harry, is that it? Did you like being his kept thing, his bauble? Is that the Hathaway legacy?"

Harry snorted and sat on the bed, a richly brocaded contrivance that reminded Miranda of Spanish sherry in the hand of a decadent don.

"Hathaway. Now you invoke Father's name, Miranda. You were ever his favorite. His—bauble—if you like. 'Twas why he let you grow up so unnaturally, so unwomanly. Is it any wonder that I, too, am . . . different?"

"Am? You are what you always were. I, too, have had hardship and deprivation these last months, but I do not fear to redeem what was, to ask for it back, bring it back! We must forget the horrible things that happened to us."

The boy's lips—had they always been so full, so sensuous?—smiled. He laid his arms across his knees, and the narrow aristocratic hands that were the Hathaway inheritance drooped as gracefully as the hands in a court portrait.

"Horrible." Harry's eyebrow rose cynically, so like Francisco's that for a moment Miranda was confused. "See what passion, what exaggeration to which you bend yourself, Miranda. Father would agree with you. 'Tis fortunate he's not survived to see his son unmanned—"

Miranda's interruption was silenced with one wave of the Hathaway hand.

"Such fury, Miranda; face the truth. Passion runs like sands in a glass if one doesn't keep it all bottled up. Nothing but soft silken sands drifting across time. One doesn't have to make a raging storm out of it. No Saharas for me, Miranda."

This was not the boy who had strained for engagement with pirates. Not the one who'd sailed from Barbados anxious for new sights, eager to test the world with his buoyant spirit. He was like a new-made blade from old steel.

The pirates had forged him in the furnace of their desires and he had been quenched in the cool, elegant decadencies of a Spanish nobleman. He was new steel, cold steel, now. And he was no longer her brother.

Chapter Sixteen

So the sea became Miranda's sister; it was odd how one determined to belong somewhere.

She took her duties as the *Gato*'s commander seriously, demanding that Steele report their daily latitude and speed, which she recorded in her own spidery hand.

Steele chafed under such accounting, but kept his opinions to himself. He had shaved the ragged beard. The face that emerged from behind it was still veiled somehow, and galley-lean.

Steele set a southern course, the better to mislead any Spanish pursuit anticipating an immediate homeward flight north. So the *Gato*, her oars moving almost gaily, blew south to bounce gently among the Canaries off the African coast.

"Ah, Mirandita—here's an island to drop anchor on," Francisco rhapsodized at the rail two days after the battle, when all that lay before the galley was a sparkling spot of rock in the even blue. "Here is brewed the wine of paradise. A Spanish ship floats ever so much more gently with her belly full of Canary nectar, no? Let us row ashore. I am sufficiently Spanish to cause no suspicion were I to order a tun or two of spice-tinged wine."

"Ki—Captain Steele said we would lie off one of the smaller, uninhabited islands. Fresh water was the brew he intended for the crew, and I agree."

"Ah, I thought you were more disagreeable than agreeable when it came to Captain Steele. He is the same, Mirandita."

"The same?" Miranda's unrippling green eyes met Francisco's amused brown ones as coolly as a blade engaging a cudgel.

"I have seen your English captain before, as you thought. At Gerhardt's Antwerp fencing academy. We've crossed many a younger blade when we both were more wont to use it for dancing practice than for something mortal. Why did you not tell me he captained your first ship?"

"As you say, you knew him, Francisco; I would not have you anticipate reunion to find him dead." The polished irony in her voice reflected a slight smile off the Spaniard's own ironic façade.

"You may fight like a man, Mirandita," he answered softly, "but you lie like a woman."

Yet when Steele dropped anchor off a barren spittle of rock that seemed home to none but long-winged gulls and sudden waves of the flashing yellow birds that named the islands, it was Francisco she found and made the depository of an intimate request.

"I wish to go ashore, in one of the small boats. Just you and I. The men are loose with Steele on this side of the island. We could go round that cove over there and—"

"—and?"

Miranda dampened Francisco's amused grin with a look that rained pure dignity.

"—and I wish a bath. I can't haul fresh water from below with so many thirsty souls aboard. If you'll stand guard I'll have a swim, as—we . . . used to on Barbados."

"And Harry?"

"Harry can stay where he seems to prefer to stay. In the don's cabin. I wager he's dabbled in enough of the don's Arabic jasmine perfumes to forgo something as simple as clean water."

"Bitterness is a fruit that will grow from any water you give it," Francisco warned her.

"Damn me, Francisco, I don't know what to do about Harry!" She closed her mouth upon her fist and turned to the sea view.

The man beside her was silent for so long that she spun to see if he had left.

"Ah, Mirandita, little Miranda, you have learned to swear like a sailor, and an English sailor at that. You must learn more of life than that if you are to get on in this world."

Francisco sighed and turned his contemplative pout inside out. It surfaced as a smile. "Very well. Francisco will stand guard over a Hathaway on an island once again. But, *chica*, I do not think I can prevent your being seen by that—" He gestured upward where a gull arced against the *Gato*'s furled sails, then his eyes dropped back to Miranda with a certain uncustomary warmth, as if he knew what any gull would see and liked it.

"Simply see that you ward off two-legged spies; I won't fret about winged ones," Miranda rejoined quickly.

"Aye, aye," Francisco mocked so solemnly that Miranda laughed and forgot that he had made her feel the slightest bit odd but a moment before.

Miranda waded into the cool blue pool until it lapped her shoulders. She splashed and gamboled like a dolphin as the waters soothed the last month's hardships away and rinsed her hair to honey color again. She had been no galley slave, but she relished her time in the water as fiercely as the bedraggled men on the island's opposite side. It felt good to be solitary, free of ship, sailors and sea for a time. She thought of faithful Francisco on guard beyond the rocks and walked unhurriedly out of the water, like Eve out of Eden.

Real reluctance held her fingers back as she shrugged on the clean but rough man's shirt. She lay on a rock to let the sun dry her hair to match its solar sheen, fanning it behind her. Eyes closed, Miranda heard the distant chirp of exotic island birds, so like Barbados. Canaries. Slight lemon-colored birds with voices as sweet as their coloration was tart. Would they have canaries at home? In England? Heading home, no—not to that damp dull island, England. Home was the wide, wild forest of Barbados and the bright chatter of its birds and monkeys.

Something slipped between her and the sun—a cloud, a wisp that couldn't endure. But it did. Her eyes flew open into two blazing pools in a slightly bronzed face.

"*Diablo!*" she swore, sounding exactly like Francisco when something went awry. She caught the shirt together. "How the Devil did you get past Francisco?"

"You're beginning to sound like a pirate as well as dress like one," noted Christopher Steele. "The day I couldn't pass one man on a beach as wide as a galleon . . ." His shoulders shrugged in the borrowed shirt that reminded her of how she'd found him but days before.

He was still lean, though sun and the ship's stores had begun to restore him. She turned her head to call Francisco, but he anticipated her and dropped down atop her, his hard, callused palm covering her mouth. She tasted salt.

"I've no wish to exchange steel with an old friend," he said softly. Her mouth fought against the salt of his palm, but he kept his grip and she gave up suddenly.

"That's better," he said, grinning. It may have been design or chance, but as he shifted his weight to rise, his hand brushed her breast.

Miranda reached under the arch of her back for the knife she had lain there, for the blade she always kept at hand. If he had mistaken her arch for agreement, the misconception was remedied when she slipped the dagger between them.

His hand dropped away in surprise as he felt the steel press into his throat. His muscles were still taut. She could see in his narrowed eyes a debate whether to try disarming her or not.

"Keep on and I'll slit you from gullet to Gehenna," she spat between bared white teeth. "I always did prefer my baths warm."

Her own eyes narrowed; she meant him to believe every syllable of that unsheathed threat. It occurred to her that he might be more forward because of his long fast from female companionship.

"So come lie with me, Captain," she taunted slowly with a certain sensuous undertone that made his muscles tense again, "and see how much better you like it than the lash."

Steele shrugged suddenly. His eyes turned lazy and light again. He rolled over cautiously as she followed his motion with the knife point, until she hung above him, half-sitting. The movement brought a lock of her damp hair to brush his face and the shirt fell open again to reveal the cool white curve of her breast.

She saw her motion soften something in his eyes, she saw the quick male speculation rise in him, so she ran the steel point lightly down his chest. Something in the gesture was too tentative, too caressing, but she put fury into her expression, and whatever was emerging in his mind relaxed into a grin. He cradled his head in his hands and lay harmlessly on the rocks, like a snake that had spent its venom.

She rose quickly and snatched up the rest of her raiment. The dagger she slipped between her teeth, a solution that only widened his grin as he watched her struggle to dress with some privacy while still nailing him to the rock with her eyes.

She knotted the belt around her middle with a vicious pull, as if she had his throat in a noose.

"I'd not mistake you for a boy now, madam," he commented somewhat academically. She whirled, finally dressed and free to lash him with her words.

"Then you had better make that error, Captain, for if you give me trouble I'll have you chained to the benches again where you can rot with the filthy Spaniards. And they would not be cordial to an English oarmate, you can credit that."

"If you didn't need me, you would send me back to that hole, wouldn't you?" he asked.

"Of course," she said fiercely, thinking of the horrendous fates her mind had prepared for him while she had waited in England and dreamed of revenge. "You have a choice, Captain, as you once gave someone else a choice. A choice of steering this ship safely to England or molesting mè. It may have been a while for you," she said more softly, "but if you really prefer rape to rapiers, you'll rot in the ship's belly for it now and in hell for it later, if I have anything to say about it."

"Thank God you don't," he responded ungallantly. "Very well, madam. I only came to see how long you wished to remain here. As you say, it has been a long time; but not too long for me to lose all discrimination."

The insult reassured her. "We'll leave tomorrow as the tide runs."

While she thrust the knife through her belt, he waited for her to precede him on the path. They collected a somewhat surprised Francisco and returned to the *Gato*.

Chapter Seventeen

*T*he poolside bath had cleansed Miranda of the voyage's grime, but she still hungered for another kind of cleansing.

So conscience brought her to Steele's cabin and the shadowed dusk that occupied it even while the sun stood hot and high above the decks.

Miranda's rescued captain was absent, acquainting himself topside with the galley whose belly had housed him so long. Like Jonah from the whale, he had been delivered from a devouring servitude. Unlike him, Steele then had taken a curiously intent interest in the workings of what had enslaved him.

He could be found clambering over the ship's side to inspect the galley gunports and oarlocks with the simplest sailor, or climbing the heavy rigging to see how her shrouds held. It was as if, his universe having been limited for so long to an oaken bench, a bucket and an iron bracelet, he must test the outer limits of his new, expanded world.

His fellow oarsmen—even the sour Arabs left behind on the Canaries to find a way home to Africa—had all behaved that way at first: breathing the open air more deliberately, in stages, as if it were a rare vintage worth savoring; caressing gunwales as if the wood were silk; twining cable in their hands like a living golden serpent they petted . . .

It was odd to sail with such bewitched beings; it made

Miranda nervous. Francisco, as well, frowned his handsome scowl as he paced the decks like a man eager to leap off onto the wharf. He felt it, too, the mood. Not ugly, only ... not routine. Too calm.

The sailors' eyes followed Miranda about her easy deckside rambles, until she always paused to measure her audience before stepping upon the planking. Her hair was tied back now, her manner of ambiguous gender. She reflected in all the sailors' pupils as she passed—a tiny mirror image upon pools of wary admiration.

If she spoke to one, which was seldom, he would invariably stammer answer in his coarse Welch, Irish or Devonshire dialect.

And when she had passed, they would murmur amongst themselves and swear she was a witch-woman who had gone ashore to wade into the island's freshwater pool where she had floated like a petal, as a witch was said to do. Aye, but if witch she was—and she had no proper fear in her, as women should—then it was a good 'un she was, for there be iron enough aboard this Spanish galley to hex a cartful of witches. Leg irons. Wrist irons. And all knew that iron and steel be enough to banish witch-women ... Mayhap more than one kind of steel, the gossips would wink.

Miranda was unaware of the sailor's superstitious speculations; she was as she had been on the *Salamander*, why should they not accept her?

But, standing in the low entrance of the guest cabin assigned Steele as the vessel's substitute master, Miranda became painfully certain that the *Salamander* was forever gone.

That day the air was hot, heavy and humid below. Her linen shirt clung to wet streaks down her spine and between her breasts; her hair weighed damp across her neck. The cabin shutters were closed. She focused first on the empty built-in bed before seeing the crude hammock nearby. She felt somehow surreptitious, though—Lord knows—it was to all intents and purposes her ship, and she had every right ...

> *Chests full of silver an' chests full o' gold,*
> *An' a tun of wine casks dooooown in the hold ...*

The quavery voice emanated from the hammock, swaying as gently as the canvas sling itself.

"Muffin? Is that you, Muffin?"

"Aye. 'Course 'tis. I be wantin' sumthin'. Silver? Gold? No, water. 'Tis awful dry I am. Hav'ee some water?"

Miranda spied a vessel on a table and brought a pewter cup to his lips before the last word had faded. He was bright and dry with fever, and swung in the hammock like a clock pendulum, looking like a babe somehow, his limbs all drawn up, as if his body's sick warmth fed upon the fever. He was so thin his head seemed infant-large. It lolled upon his stringy neck while his eyes rolled fitfully and his slender voice piped ancient shanties into the close, hot, cabin air.

"Muffin."

Miranda shook him gently, hoping for some focus from him, long enough for him to say—what? To give her some—benediction, the Papists called it. Some ceremonial blessing. Why had he signed on for such a mission? He was not forced. He did not have to take ship as Steele did.

It wasn't fair, now Muffin was rocking away his life aboard *her* ship and she couldn't save him! She couldn't shepherd him as he had her on the *Salamander*. Could never stand between him and the great winged thing that hovered above and beckoned the old sailor with more chests of silver and gold than he had ever dreamed of.

"Muffin. There's silver and gold enough for you; we found much in the don's cabin. We'll share with you. Muffin. I'm sorry you're so—ill. I would never have sent you into this, had I known . . . Muffin. Remember me. 'Twas better then, for us both. Don't stay here now, don't—die here. Come back with me."

Miranda wrung out a cloth in the basin's tepid water, watching Muffin from across the cabin. Old, an old man now. No denying. No more riggings for him. No more far-seeing through a perspective glass. She pattted his face with the damp cloth.

"Smeach's not aboard this trip, Muffin, so we can't have a game of dies. But there are other games—we could make a cat's cradle of hemp; you were always so clever at ropes. I need to learn more knots. You must get better, then we'll go above deck. Into the sunshine. But I'll not climb another rigging, not that. Muffin? You do know me?"

"Know you?" His teeth suddenly began chattering. "Wh-why, aye, lass. I saw ye under the lamps of Darkhouse Street . . . shinin', in yer y-yellow hair. 'Twas many years ago, I was a y-young tar then wi' more capers to 'im than a little pagan monkey." His wheezes paused. "N-n-no, I don't know you. Why, what ye be doin' here in Portsmouth, lad? Richard? 'Twas Cádiz ... nay, Calais, I last seen the tail o' ye ... Or be ye the other? Kit will have none of ye this trip, lad. I'm sorry. He's changed, Kit."

Miranda brought the cup up again, her eyes as brimful as the pewter circle she offered him. He would never know her, because what she had been aboard the *Salamander* was as dead as he would be when the last breath hushed from his mouth and dissipated on air.

Muffin's teeth danced a fit upon the cup lip, an almost musical percussion of ivory on metal, bone on pewter. His weakly clenched hands pushed the tankard away even as she offered it.

"What are you doing here?" Steele was an almost anonymous shadow in the open doorway.

Miranda clutched the cup to her shirtfront and turned to face him, feeling like a trespasser and uncertain why.

"I merely came to see him. I was giving him water. He'd asked for it."

"Men ask for many things when they're dying, but in the galleys, it's always water," Steele said after a pause.

He crossed the cabin in such long strides that he was at Muffin's hammock before Miranda could edge a wiser distance away.

"Haven't you some penmanship you should be tracing in your Moroccan fancy-book?" he asked. "Put down the winds and waves, lady. Scribble down the latitude. But Muffin here will never fit into your logbook. Or any other. Leave him be."

Retort teetered on Miranda's lips; instead, she flung down the cup to storm past Steele and out the cabin door. She came onto deck in bright sunlight and in tears. Muffin was lost to her. How could she defend her right to him now that he lay dying? When he had been alive she had only sent him into danger, into this. She was responsible. There was no nay-saying it.

Miranda stood at the gunwale, her back to everything the *Gato de Nueve* contained. All she saw was shimmering cobalt sky and sea—a shaky scene, painted in her eyes' watercolor mistiness. Her fists boxed the wetness from her lashes and cheeks. She stalked across deck to the captain's cabin and the milky daylight that streamed through its cloudy, glazed windows.

And she did play with her logbook, that record of shipboard life bound in etched Moroccan leather. Etched, deeply scribed, like the flesh of all who had served to pull the *Gato* through the waves. Miranda opened it at the beginning and slowly read the tightly scrawled Spanish for a history of where the ship had been.

Francisco found her there, paging through the heavy vellum and adrift on someone else's memories. She noted his presence, then dropped her eyes again to the expressionless page. In a moment something white shimmered across the letters. Miranda glanced up, mystified, to find Francisco's face a mask of controlled amusement.

"Plunder for the pirate princess!" He laughed at her amazement. "I've raided Don Ricardo's most well packed chests, his finest trunks. The don has been generous in his absence. Most generous." Francisco lifted a handful of the limp white fabric. "Even to, one might say, the shirts off his back."

Miranda abruptly swept the logbook clear of the filmy stuff. Her hands sank into silk to the wrists and she shook them free of its feel.

"Take it away, Francisco! I want nothing that slimy creature has touched."

"And you, who used to capture colonies of Barbados cockroaches when you were a tiny thing," Francisco chided lightly, gathering up his booty. "These are fine silks, Mirandita, worth their weight in doubloons. I'll not stick at wearing a grandee's castoffs." His black-olive eyes slid to her face. "Nor Harry."

"Enough. Take the filthy things away. You've naught to occupy you now that our mission's done, Francisco, that's your trouble. I've—reading to do."

"Methinks you have little to do now that you've extracted your brother from the don. And that will be *your* trouble."

"Out!" ordered Miranda, letting the massive book fall shut like a clap of hands.

"Very well. 'Tis certain I can hawk my goods elsewhere. Our new navigator, perhaps, will not shirk from the don's generosity. His raiment, I vow, could use a bit of freshening."

"No, I wager that our new captain will not be too particular to don such flotsam. I wish you all joy of your silks and satins, Francisco, if that be all that you hold dear."

Francisco arched an eyebrow, a silent retort of his since Barbados days. Once it had silenced Miranda. Now she only found it a cheap way to evade an honest answer. She sat again after the Spaniard had left, her hands cradling her head.

Was this to what it had come? Finding petty fault with her youth's adored teacher? Talking to Harry across an invisible veil of estrangement? To seeing Muffin only as a living—dying—monument to her single-minded will? And Christopher Steele, the man she'd known aboard the *Salamander*, the man who'd known her in the biblical sense, as the parsons so modestly put it—even he was a stranger she had lost the lust to punish . . .

Something had begun aboard the Dutchman's captured prize, the poor *Merlin*, a ship that had held none of the magic that its name should have lent it, but only misery as a cargo. Miranda brought her eyes back to the Spanish-strewn page. She read. It was the one form of forgetting that her father had taught her.

She read until the daylight dimmed and she could hardly make out the writing, something for which Father would have taxed her well. That thought and a knock brought her head up sharply.

"Enter."

No new light came from the passage, but she knew it was Steele the instant she sensed a présence in the room. "Yes?"

For answer he advanced and struck flint to light the lamps swinging from the hand-carved rafters above.

"What do you want?"

"The King James Version. Or something like. A Bible!" he demanded impatiently into her incomprehension. "I'd not disturb you, but I wish to refresh my memory—well, have you one?"

Miranda rummaged through the desk until she dredged up a thick red-velvet-covered volume, elaborately embroidered in gold-threaded crucifixes.

"This might be the Popish version, but—"

Steele spun the book to face him and skimmed the Spanish text with knit brows.

"Why do you wish it? 'Tis no use to us . . ."

"It will do," he said brusquely.

"Do? For what?"

His eyes lanced into hers over the lavishly illustrated pages. "The services for the dead."

"Dead?" she repeated. Steele said nothing. "When?"

"A half hour past. We'll send him to his Maker at eight bells."

"Eight bells. Yes, we shouldn't tarry . . ." Steele reached for the Spanish Bible, but Miranda's fanned hand appropriated its embroidered surface. "No, Captain. I shall read the passage." His hands had frozen but not retreated. "It is *my* ship, at least you grant me that."

Steele straightened into icy disapproval, his light-bronzed hair brushing the cabin's beaming. He turned on his heel and left, marooning Miranda on a sea of squirming black Spanish characters in a somehow ghoulishly gilded book. She paged through it in the relentless lamplight until she found the passage she sought.

She marked the place with her finger and sat, waiting, until the great ship's bell rang out. Once for Father, once for Mother, once for Meg MacTavish, and once for Muffin ... Once again for Pentreath, for Coyle, again for Meg MacTavish and lastly, again for Muffin. Seaborne deaths, most of them. For a moment after the final summons she sat still, then rose and carried the volume out on the crook of her arm, like a friend.

A deck as dark as the Dutchman's had been months before awaited Miranda. Not quite so dark, for the crew was already lighting the galley's great lanterns in their iron cages, as well as strings of smaller ones along the masts. Sailors who had known Muffin from their common servitude in the galley belly arrayed themselves around the forward gunwale. A board was balanced on it by the informal pallbearers, and that board's burden was a canvas-sewn bundle of pathetic flatness.

Miranda advanced to the pallet's foot—or was it the head? She split her Spanish Bible to the place she had chosen and heard someone settle beside her as her eye translated the writing.

"And Jonah remained in the belly of the great fish for three days and three nights. 'Out of my distress I cried to Yahweh and He answered me: from the belly of Sheol I cried and You have heard my voice. You cast me into the abyss, into the heart of the sea and the flood surrounded me. All Your waves, Your billows, washed over me. The waters surrounded me to my throat, the abyss was all around me. The seaweed was wrapped around my head at the roots of mountains. I went down into the countries underneath the earth, to the peoples of the past. But You lifted my life from the pit, Yahweh, my God. But I, with a song of praise, will sacrifice to You. The vow I have made, I will fulfill. Salvation comes from Yahweh.' "

And perhaps salvation also comes from silence. For that was what marked the end of Miranda's reading: a long, eyes-cast-down silence. She closed the book with a soft clap that played period to the unspoken sentences lingering in the evening air.

A motion at the corner of her eye: Steele's hand descended. Then an extended scrape of wood on wood, the board grating across the gunwale. It tilted and Muffin was gone, plummeting seaward in the lantern light with a sudden white flash like an albatross wing.

Only all of Miranda's will kept her from dashing to the gunwale and leaning over to watch Muffin sink into the galley's white-water wake.

The sailors thinned away like smoke. She went to the rail, then lifted the velvet-bound tome over the water. It dropped like an anchor, a sober-sheathed square that gave one gilded wink in the torchlight before the darkness below swallowed it.

Miranda turned to find Steele standing there still, like Conscience on a monument. No, that was Patience on a monument, that line . . . Full fathom five thy father lies . . . Lies. All lies. As if she were responsible for every evil in the world. She had done it, hadn't she? Fetched Harry back?

Miranda stalked toward the poop, Steele still an impassive obstacle in her path. She moved to pass him, then stopped and faced him instead. Steele uncrossed his arms while Miranda concentrated her gaze directly ahead in the vicinity of his breastbone and crossed hers.

" 'Twas an odd selection, the reading," he commented quietly from the twilight of a night deck.

"Was it?"

"You never did care for the look of a galley from the first time you sighted one. How do you like riding one now?"

"As well as you liked rowing one, Captain. But when we're home—Harry and I—all this will be forgotten."

"Will it?"

Miranda shrugged, a useless gesture in such dim light. She considered walking around him, but was too stubborn to alter her course. It was her ship.

"Where are you going?" he asked then.

"To see Harry," she answered before she had even thought of it. "Now, will you get out of my way or—"

"It seems our ways are ever wont to cross, madam," he mocked, his hands closing round her arms.

He lifted her and set her down to the side, so they each faced their different directions no longer on a collision course.

"There. Now you can go your way, madam, and I can go mine without either of us taking a backward step."

Miranda stamped her heel into the planking at his impudence.

"I thought the solution would appeal to you. Good night. And my regards to your bonnie brother."

He became more smoke for the empty deck.

Miranda moved on, torn between fury and the emptiness of

mourning. They were her emotional poles now, she realized: mourning what was past and fury with the present. The thought was bitter. She had not meant it to come to this. And the nearer her triumph, the more bitter its dregs.

She had Harry back, a Harry who barely spoke to her and whose even green eyes watched her with an alien curiosity. She had Steele humbled—for he had failed, he had lost and paid the price, and somehow that didn't matter anymore.

No, what mattered most was Muffin, plunging from the bowed side of a ship into nothingness. Plunging . . . she had almost plunged so once. Her fingers remembered the pull of the pirate jersey that had been her lifeline until the Dutchman had extended her the rope of his authority.

She had paid a terrible price for surviving. The Miranda who could have fallen from the *Merlin*'s gunwale was a far more contented creature than the one who walked the boards of a captured Spanish galley like a commander. Muffin had made it simple, Muffin seemed to know things without saying. And now Muffin was gone . . . so many were gone.

Her booted feet clattered up the ladder to the Great Cabin deck. Something pale and round materialized before her eyes on the boards. A face. Captain Coyle floating on a moonlit deck. Or Captain Pentreath, his patched eye a broad wink in the dark? Another step and she seemed to crush a huge white mushroom that bloomed underfoot—a dour Scottish face this time. Quite, quite still.

Miranda ran on, to the well-carved cabin door behind which Harry had entertained the Spanish don, where Harry still waited, perhaps remorseful, perhaps ready to be her friend again. Harry, only Harry could anchor her now, give her a place and a compass point . . . Harry.

She flung the door wide without knocking, as if the moon had unleashed bone-pale slivers of light to stalk her. She exploded through the opening on a lunge and paused frozen, strung between the door's edge and it's jamb like a pearl balanced on a length of string. Like a pearl she vibrated there for a long moment.

The cabin light was white, like the moonlight, an effect engineered by the cloudy chimneys covering the many beeswax candles hanging from the rafters like vigil lights before a Papist saint.

White light pooled on the great draped bed commanding the

cabin's center ... on the billowy albino sheen of silk shirts. Shirts like the don wore. Shirts Francisco had dredged from a leather trunk and then passed well round. Two shirts, transfixed by her sudden entrance. And those shirts wore faces, both staring at her with the aloof dignity of wild things interrupted at a woodland pool, who look up from their drinking and gaze solemnly at the intruder.

Harry, eyes level, face slightly flushed above the swath of white silk that slid off his shoulders like a wave off a prow. And Francisco, fierce and frozen in expression, his face bent toward Harry's ... they were both reclining upon the opulent bed, Francisco's arm draped around Harry's shoulder. Harry's hand— the elegant, limpid Hathaway hand—lying unmistakably along Francisco's long, lean thigh.

Miranda's breathless cry was already too formed to throttle. It came out like an afterthought and lay clumsily between them.

"Harry—!"

Francisco stood, Harry's hand sliding off him like some limp white flightless dove ... Francisco's Castillian face, as long and shadowed as an untruth, half-hid in the tester drapery.

"Miranda," he began.

"No!" she found herself shouting hoarsely. "Not ever!"

She spun off the door frame, propelled across the short deck and down another ladder by a sense of flight almost, as if her feet were winged. Her own cabin door clapped shut upon her but a moment after the dull thud of the door above. She pressed against the door, her heartbeats holding it closed, and waited— nothing.

Nothing but the certain drumming in her head, which told her that even before the pirates had descended on the *Merlin*, before the Spanish don had wooed and won. There. Back where it had always seemed safe and simple. On the sands, through the forests, upon the hills overlooking Carlisle Bay. Behind the broad cedar trunks, beneath the wide, verdant tropical leaves, came the soft, certain murmur of what had gone on. She trailing them.

Of course she had always trailed; they were off about their exploring and their botany lessons of which Father so approved. Science, he had ever flirted with science. And when Miranda had caught up, had joined them ... It was always after for them.

The secret, hidden part had happened already. And the wild barrage of birdcalls that had echoed from the towering branches were mocking, hooting warnings. Miranda, who was all heart and no eyes. Miranda, who believed in what had never been real and true. Book-bound Miranda. Noble Miranda, who would avenge the guilty. Miranda the Restorer. Poor, foolish, stupid Miranda, who knew nothing. Nothing. Muffin, gone for nothing.

Who was she to deny the don his silks or his sins? She caught a sideways glimpse of herself in the gilt-framed slash of mirror that adorned a built-in cupboard. Standing edgeways, like a duelist, Miranda saw herself booted and breeched, a rough linen shirt billowing over her narrow shoulders and a long dagger sticking like a tongue from her belt.

In the lamps, lit by Steele when he'd come for the Spanish Bible, she saw herself as the obverse of Harry, perhaps the Harry of her memories. Oh, she was tired of seeming like. Tired of things that were not as they should be. She slowly pulled the tie from her hair and watched its length swing free upon her shoulders like a curtain. Shuttering something out. Or something in?

She drew her dagger, then tossed it under the fine feather pillow on the broad Spanish bed. She felt weary, more weary than she had ever been before, but she came numbly back to the desk. To the logbook. Her fingers traced its script until her eyes finally focused. Gibberish. She couldn't read the contorted Spanish syllables any longer. It all meant nothing. Miranda abruptly hurled to the door and hung out of it until a sailor passed.

"Send me Captain Steele," she ordered.

The sailor's "Aye, aye" was muffled by the door drawing shut behind her. She sat again at the desk and riffled the logbook until she came to a blank page. A page as white and smooth as silk. She ran her hand across it as if it were a living creature she petted.

Steele's knock hardly interrupted Miranda's reverie. He entered at her command and stood before her. Her downcast eyes were aware of the white of his shirt floating in the cabin's cavelike closeness, the glare of Spanish silk reflecting off her consciousness like some sickly white phosphorescent forest growth.

She brought her eyes from the hypnotic surface to his face, a composed, careful face. An uncommitted face, still sharp from the privations of the rowing decks. And white. Like a page, like a memory. Most memories were pure, blinding white, she decided. Her eyes dropped to the blank logbook.

Chapter Eighteen

"The ship is yours," Miranda said, her face as set as a figurehead's in the rocking lantern light.

"Mine?"

"Yes, take it where you want it. I give it to you, Captain." A thread of mockery still unwound from her voice, but it was a slender filament. "Take it, take my brother, take the whole bloody Spanish armada—!"

"I am not interested in your brother," he reminded her softly.

"Then you're the only bastard on board who isn't!" she burst out in breathless fury. "I should never have come, never have sent the first ship. It's brought nothing but, but—Francisco," she raged. "Your old swordmate, my old tutor. Francisco, who let me handle steel and climb the great cedar trees on Barbados—he, all along, 'twas he who— My brother, I found them . . ."

Her eyes fixed beyond the window on a black and blank sea. Steele said nothing. She turned with real surprise in her voice.

"You," she accused softly, "you *knew*. For how long? Did every able-bodied hand on board have a hand on my brother? And I, rescuing him . . . on the *Merlin*, I would have given myself to them if they'd have had me. I have been paying for the fact that they wouldn't all these months, and it was pointless. My brother is a whore."

She suddenly understood why and in what mood men used the word. One did not need to be a woman to be a whore. "So take the bloody ship. I'll return to my petticoats and petit point."

She leaned back and closed the log, pushing it across the polished wood to him. Steele slowly sat opposite her, paging through the entries written in her well-schooled hand.

"You can't give it up," he said, shutting the book and pushing it back to her. "If you become only a woman, the crew will tear you apart. You've become more than man or woman to them; you've been liberator. That can swing awry as surely as a hangman's rope. I can't take this ship back to England with three hundred brutalized men and a docile female aboard. So keep your claws. And your command."

"Then set me ashore. I'll fend for myself."

"Cádiz, the most vicious port this side of Porto bello? I can't do that."

"Why not? You did before." She spoke with logic, not rebuke. One had to care about oneself to hurl recriminations. At that moment Miranda cared for nothing or no one, not even herself.

"What does it matter?" she asked, impatient with argument. "I'll either take care of myself or I won't. Let me off. I'm sick of this ship. It still carries slaves. It makes me ill."

"Or jealous?" he asked, his eyes bright blue with curiosity and something calculated if she had been alert enough to see it.

She did catch something else in the shifting cabin light—a glance of sympathy. She had thought that pity in his eyes would enrage her; it only tightened the cold hard grip of despair on her throat.

"Jealousy? What has that to do with anything?" she asked dully.

"Francisco. Growing up there wild in Barbados. Was he merely your brother's tutor to you? Oh, you were innocent enough then," he added, "but aren't you perhaps a bit jealous that your brother and not you has been the prize at the end of all this pursuit?"

He was putting everything into the most debased false interpretation, almost deliberately. Slandering the life she had lived on Barbados, her truest feelings, with calculated cruelty. At any other time she would have denied, attacked, defended. At any other time her cheeks would have flamed at such insinuations. Now disillusion with the present gave her no heart to defend the past.

"Perhaps you are right," she said finally, too weary to argue. She spread her fingers wide and looked at her hands as if they were something alien. "All the more reason to release me and take the ship and all it holds away."

"Does madam surrender, then?" he asked, leaning forward to verify her hopelessness in her eyes.

They were hardened pools of guttered green . . . in a face of frozen wax. She shrugged, very slightly, as if speaking were too much of a burden, too human a thing to do.

"Very well, then," he said, suddenly slamming the flat of his hand on the desk.

She only clutched the logbook with a mindless need for contact with something. Steele's eyes leapt to blue flames as if he saw a mirage clearly, yet there was self-mockery in his voice when he announced, "To the victor the spoils!" and swept her into his arms, the log still dangling from her hand.

He carried her to the wide, built-in bed and threw her down on it. He made short work of easing off her shirt, of wrenching her belt untied and pulling the man's trousers from her slender legs.

She lay there passively, like a ship riding out the roiled waves, indifferent, helpless. His own clothing soon joined hers on the floor. Before she could even absorb the quickness of it, his weight was atop her, his hands and mouth were covering her body with swift, driving kisses, touches. She lay like a corpse beneath him, even when his tongue plunged through her teeth and into her unresisting mouth.

No one had ever delved her so intimately before; even he had been impersonally businesslike that first time. Now was a time to protest, now when her person was truly invaded. But the flurry of feeling that engulfed her body washed over it leaving her unmarked, like a beach that has embraced the sea and let it retreat. Even when his hand trickled like water over her breasts, she didn't resist.

His hand edged across her belly, along her thighs, and still she lay quiet. Then it cupped the warmth between her legs. Only then did she turn her head toward him and murmur something. It was either desire or protest and he had not long to find out which.

Her body arched against his, and a sudden dull crash somewhere to the back of his head made him shake his blond mane and rear back with a roar.

Her hand hung below the bunk, still clutching the *Gato de Nueve* logbook with which she had struck him.

"No!" she cried. "Not again."

He wrested the book away, but her resistance, once uncorked, ran over like roughly handled wine. Her free hand snaked under the pillow. It was her bed, and she'd slept with a dagger under her head ever since she'd been on board. She pulled out the blade and, while he still battled for the logbook, raked at him, at his heaviness and his power and his taking. She saw blood blossom on his arm along a thin red slash after her knife had passed.

The phenomenon gave her pause. Steele hissed, then grasped her wrist and twisted until the knife fell between them, the blade shining clean and innocent.

"I thought you still had some spirit in you," he said a bit grimly, "but I didn't think it would be quite this potent."

He rose, collecting the knife loosely in the fingers of his wounded arm. "Where's the rum? I could use a dash."

How entirely casual he was, despite his hurt, like a surgeon who has bled a patient and is well satisfied with his work.

Miranda, trembling, caught the blanket around her shoulders and sat up. He was not behaving like a man whose uncontrollable lust had been rudely interrupted.

"You don't—you did not intend to . . ." she began.

"How long do you think it takes me to learn you're a catamount? I wanted to demonstrate that you still had your claws—and in gratitude you rake me with them."

Steele had tied a piece of linen awkwardly around his arm, but the blood still soaked through.

Miranda rose and stepped toward him. "You *meant* me to resist—? And if I hadn't?"

"Then I'd have had an unexpected but not unwelcome leave from the durance of shipboard life." He grinned. "But as I thought, your father reared you to be a proud and foolish virgin, whether to your loss or not."

"I am not a virgin," she interrupted, her eyes like sullen sails furled under a yardarm of stiff lashes.

Steele flexed his wounded arm, then met her resentful gaze.

"Yes, you are," he said softly, "and I'm the one man in the world who should know." He paused for a moment, then sighed lightly. "I see now that the service I did you the last time we anchored outside Cádiz was—well, deserving of the slash you just gave me. But *you* now must see that it is the nature of the beast to survive, whether it thinks so or not."

Miranda watched Steele dazedly, standing draped in her blanket like a New World Indian princess.

"Hand me my shirt," he requested civilly enough, still tending his arm.

"I am not your cabin boy!" Miranda burst out violently, kicking the clothing at her feet across to him.

She stubbornly kept her eyes on his nakedness as he drew on the breeches. He was lean from the galley still, like a palace greyhound stripped for the races, but his back and shoulders were ridged with the souvenirs of the whip. Old scars, but she had given him a new one. And good enough.

Rage still boiled in her chest like an overhot soup about to sizzle over its kettle rim. It was fury as much at her passivity of moments before, at that other dead-hearted person who had let herself be so handled, as at her handler.

"You must learn to use a knife with a bit more thrust if you plan to seriously discomfit an opponent," Steele lectured as he rummaged through the cabin chest. "Clawing is gratifying, but it only results in scratches."

He withdrew a bottle of crude spirits and clean bandages. His face squeezed shut as the liquor mixed with the blood and burned across his flesh.

"I'll tie a length of linen around to stop the flow; you'll have to help me pull it tight."

Miranda regarded him without moving.

"I haven't two good hands," he went on pointedly. He stared steadfastly at her, but Miranda kept her distance. "Or shall I have Francisco in to help me?"

This threat of a witness to her current state brought her shuffling reluctantly over. She caught up her knife in defiance, but he looked unworried by her gesture. When she lifted her hands to the linen strip he had half worked around his arm, the blanket shifted; Miranda impatiently wrapped it under her arms and caught the end taut. Her hair felt soft falling to her bare shoulders; she was surprised that there was anything soft about her; at that moment she felt as remote and rocky as Gibraltar.

"Pull it tauter," instructed Steele, his tawny head and face burnished golden in the lantern light.

He looked like a lion, lordly and calm. The image confused her, fascinated her. She was afraid of him again—of the masculinity, of the power that rippled under his golden skin. She had been mad to slash at him, there had been no advantage in it, the blow would have been enough.

"Tighter," he ordered, his voice cracking across her consciousness. The order started anger simmering again.

She plied her thumbs to pull the linen so taut her own muscles strained.

"Enough," Steele ordered, wincing. "Now tie it off and cut it."

Miranda obeyed, the knife in her right hand, her striking hand, again. She glanced at his face before she split the fabric. His eyes, a deep, dark blue in the dim cabin, watched her carefully as the linen shredded across the blade with a groaning sound.

It was done. Steele turned away so suddenly that Miranda had her knife at the base of his throat before she even thought about it.

"By God," he said, "you're so eager to slit every passing throat I sometimes think it's a sign of affection with you."

His eyes glittered at hers, seeming to catch some blue fire from the blade poised at his neck. But he kept still, except for his eyes, which probed her steadily, slowly.

She felt barer than she had ever been in her life, like some hidden wild thing whose camouflage had been brutally stripped away. The hand holding the knife began trembling and she dropped it to her side.

A slight smile touched his lips, but Miranda barely noticed it; all her will fought to drag her eyes away from his and she couldn't.

Something was happening, something so strange, so alien that she held her breath without knowing it. Somewhere in the back of her paralyzed mind Barbados' blue-like-eyes waves ruffled across white sand beaches; somewhere abovedecks, pirates reveled and a weary old Dutchman reached out a hand to her head. And Miranda moved away. The hands reached for her always, and always she eluded them.

Now she wasn't moving, now she was impaled on steel-blue spears that pierced her precious privacy.

"What is your name?" His voice came soft from somewhere far away. He reached out to free her long hair, which had been caught to her back by the blanket, and she felt the locks swing against her like a breeze.

Name? Always the same question. "What's in a name?" That was from something of Father's. Were Father here now, would his folios and manuscripts give her some spell to free her from this frozen motion? Father. Father's name.

"Hathaway," she answered hesitantly, as if memory were sluggish.

The blanket shifted from its moorings and she moved a hand to hold it. Christopher Steele reached out to stop her, catching her hand in his. Miranda looked down dully at her softly netted hand; it seemed so small, so dainty a thing in his. She had never thought of herself that way. The blanket uncoiled softly and slid below her breasts, beyond her narrow waist, to pause at the rounded ledge of her hips, then slip to her bare feet. She was like a butterfly emerging from a cocoon and like that delicate creature, Miranda felt too weak, too fresh, to fly.

Steele's eyes had followed the silken revelation of her body lustlessly, as one might watch a sailfish cut the water and leap into pure view for a very brief moment.

"Your brother is more of a woman than you are," he said meditatively, drawing the back of his hand over her cheek and down her shoulder. " 'Tis a pity," he said then, bringing his eyes back to her face, "for it is a body a figurehead-maker dreams of carving."

Miranda was aware of her naked breasts rising and falling with soft quick breaths, like waves from a small pond stirred by a sharp gust of wind. She was melting, dissolving. Almost she could become a still, deep pool for him to dive into. She felt him drawing into her in a nameless way, circling her with his eyes, smoothing her with his hands, naming her, having her.

Steele's Barbados-bay-blue eyes—would she ever be able to separate them now, have her own back?—were growing both sharp and soft, his expression like metal melting as his eyes slipped like the ebbing blanket over the hollows and highlights of her. Now she seemed to be something liquid and languid, that he thirstily drank into himself. She saw him take pleasure in that long, lingering look, she saw it naked in his eyes, more naked than she stood before him.

It was terrifying, it was new power for her, it was balancing a scale, and in a moment it would be hopelessly tipped to one or the other's immortal disadvantage.

Miranda bucked away, stretching to the limits that his holding hand would let her, her wrist writhing in a grip suddenly gone from flesh to iron.

She flailed wildly and the sounds she made were not so much words as moans. Steele stood, still anchoring her wrist as she thrashed away. His eyes reflected only alarm now, the alertness of one who awakens from a midnight dream to find the house on fire. He struck the knife from her flailing hand.

Wordlessly he caught up the blanket and wrapped her in it like a babe, carrying her over to the bed. Miranda struggled against him, she thrashed against the blanket, the bed curtains, but he sat against the corner of the wooden cupboard and held her tightly, remorselessly, against him, hard against his hip and chest, until the beating of his heart under her ear was louder than the wild, savage drumming in her head.

She lunged away and he held her, she twisted and he contained her, until the sobs of an awful grief shook her into rocking mindlessly against him while his hands smoothed her hair and held her close.

She rocked against him as a castaway adheres to a piece of flotsam—the only thing in the whole wide salt ocean left to cling to and it but a perishable thing, too.

"Who do you mourn?" asked Steele when her sobs had finally waned and she was a passive thing—a limp length of blanket, wet cheek and tangled hair against him.

For a long while she didn't answer. As she did, the tears freshened. "Barbados," she said, surprising him. "Barbados."

"Only an island?" he asked. "Barbados is washed by enough water, and salty stuff, too, to forgo your tears. *Who* do you mourn?"

"H-H-Harry." The word came out on a humiliating childish wail, but she couldn't help it. Then all the words came out "Harry, Harry." A boy running across a blazing white beach, driftwood sword in hand. Beside him footprints, matching footprints, hers. She running also. "Father. Francisco." All, all spun away down the corridors of events. Forever gone in some way, forever altered . . . "Muffin."

More tears cascaded down her raw cheeks into the blanket creases around her chin. Sobless tears, the tears that recur but do not release.

"Who more?" demanded Steele intuitively, his arm tightening on her shoulder as both prod and comfort.

One more name teetered on her salty lips, one name she had never mentioned even to herself.

"Richard." The word was out and done clawing at her throat.

It was not such a monster, after all, only a part of herself that should never have been given a chance to exist, a part that could climb possibility as well as rigging, a counterfeit Miranda who still haunted the shrouds of the *Salamander* wherever that brave ship be.

She would have liked to have been Richard longer. Until. Until Christopher Steele had forever wrested Richard away with one tearing motion that still left her reeling. It was not only that he took her as a man takes a woman, whether rightly or wrongly. Her captain had dishonored himself before the silent shadow of Richard who had watched from the cabin shadows that night. Shadows bred shadows. She would have stood with Weatherbee under the long-ago lash to have not seen that.

Miranda's closed lashes fluttered against Steele's bare chest.

She was here, where her loss had begun, as limp and unprotesting as an eel. The thought brought new sobs, sobs of loneliness and rage and desolation. For the moment she clung to whatever human would hold her. But when she was done, she would hold only herself.

Chapter Nineteen

Steele woke.

Immediately his senses strained to verify the first things they did on waking every morning. The ship's even roll, her rhythmic seagoing creaking. All is well.

Next he was conscious of a small aching stiffness in his neck. He remembered then how she had cried and cried against him half the night and how he had finally lain down, still cradling her, and found sleep.

Before Steele even opened his lids he knew that he would not find her still in the cabin, though it was hers. He could have predicted last night that his attempted advances would unstopper her will, her formidable spirit. And he could foretell that she would have evaporated by now, disowning the night's sorrow as something shameful.

He swung his feet over the bed's edge, reluctant for a moment to take his galley-whipped back from the smooth linens that lined the late Spanish captain's bed. Steele pulled on his boots, lying where he had dropped them last night during his mock attack. Or had it been mock, he wondered, pausing in pulling on the Moroccan leather borrowed of Francisco.

Christopher Steele confessed to himself a faint throb of regret. It had been a long while since he had been with a woman, any woman.

Woman? She was hardly that, she was a fey, tropical-forest thing, as mythical as a unicorn in her way. He had so lustlessly taken her maidenhead months before, as one frees an animal from the snare that mistakenly holds it to its death. That had been a mere gesture; he had physically marred her so the world would not prize her innocence so much.

But she would haunt him for it, he realized, unless ... until she accepted her inheritance as woman and went on to other, chosen lovers. But not Christopher Steele, thank you, madam.

No, her brother knew the labyrinths of love better, all the soft satin surrender that warms the flesh, though Steele liked him less for it. He was for himself alone, that boy, and not worth mourning.

Steele stood, catching his skull roundly against the top of the enclosed bed. He cursed softly. Damn the Spaniards, that dwarfish breed. Stiffly he pulled on his abandoned shirt. His arm throbbed in its bandage so tautly pulled. Father confessor was not a role well suited to one's comfort, he reflected. But then, she would not be so supple this day, either.

He decided to ignore the entire incident, play as though the night before had never happened. She could go on from her discovery of Harry's inclinations without having to discuss it further with him. Soon they'd be in England and he would be rid of them both: the entire cargo of stubborn Hathaways. Perhaps his father was right: he was too old for a seagoing, footloose life. Perhaps he would settle in London and toy with the merchant fleet he had dreamed of since his boyhood's first mock man-o'-war sailed Ravenscroft fountain.

Steele's eyes focused on something out of place in the dimly daylit cabin. The log. Unclosed upon the gleaming desk, as white and open to him as a woman. His blue eyes raked the floor at his feet. No wonder his head ached. The vixen had struck him with the log, he remembered now. And the book had fallen while she unsheathed another claw and struck again.

The log should still be lying at his feet with the rest of last night's flotsam.

He spanned the cabin in two steps and spun the open logbook to face him. A fresh entry marked that day's date. "Have this day given Christopher Steele full and fair possession of this ship, *El Gato de Nueve*, taken off Cádiz 4 May 1648." Signed, "M. Hathaway."

Steele's fingertip stroked the script. Quite, quite dry. And not a teardrop upon it. His forefinger paused below the "M." He had always wondered . . . and doubtless always would. He could only think it stood for Magdalen, all tears and waves of corn-silk hair, all rue and very little rosemary.

Steele, aware of an uneasy wave of worry, banged out of the cabin. The sound announced his entrance from a very unconventional door to the deck and its denizens, but any smirks from nearby seamen were forestalled by the lowering line of their captain's brows.

The eyes followed him nevertheless, full of knowing curiosity. He wondered why their assumptions pricked him so when they very well could have been deserved. He found the first mate, Matthews, and hailed him gruffly.

"Aye, aye, Captain."

Matthews stared solemnly beyond his superior while Steele finished drawing his shirt closed and tried to ignore the thoughts writ plainly on the honest sailor's face.

"Matthews, where is the, er, the commander this morning? Our seagoing ladyship," he added impatiently as the man looked dumbly at him.

"Why, she left, sir. I thought you knew. I thought you'd— 'Twas four bells, sir, she took Riversgate and Dirty Dick Richards. Headin' for land they were, sir. You can see the tip of it through the glass. I'm sorry, Captain, if I . . . but seein' what cabin she came from and who was still in it—"

The man's gray eyes sought the boards finally and concentrated on a crack.

Steele glanced downward, too, unsure what to say. "Riversgate, eh? Knows Cádiz."

"Second only to Marlowe, Captain."

"I might have known," snapped Steele, retreating to the cabin he had so abruptly left. He rifled the desk. Any personal effects she might have had were gone. Inspired, he searched and found the Spanish captain's coffers. Almost empty. Damn, she'd take a sizable fortune with her if she went to the bottom of Cádiz Bay. Another chest still here, full of small gold pieces. Of course, the larger doubloons would be easier to carry, more money for less bulk.

The coffer lid slammed shut as gravity tipped its balance, the sound echoing in Steele's cogitating mind. He wheeled, not well pleased with anything or anybody, including himself, and emerged again on deck.

"Where are we, Matthews?" he found himself barking, not troubling to mask his ignorance. Usually Steele knew the ship's every position—by heart.

" 'Tis the Bay of Cádiz, right enough, Captain," offered Matthews with the spyglass, "that pale yellow speck due east. We dare pass no nearer or risk accounting for ourselves."

"Of course." Steele roughly handed back the glass. The man didn't have to explain realities to him as if he were a fool.

He sighed and rubbed his hand across his jaw. Too risky to

fetch them back. Even by longboat. He cast one look about the deck. All moving smoothly under good sail, a galley gliding slowly with her oars tucked up against her sides like a lady's skirts navigating a mud puddle. England was a week's sail northward, given fair winds and a visible pole star to navigate by. He was sick for it—for marshland mists and rolling heaths and crowded London streets alive with the hawkers' cries.

His eyes squinted mastward to check the sheets and flicked across the bowsprit, almost expecting to see a figure there, curled around it like a living figurehead. It was unmounted and bare, pointing bravely for home.

Steele turned away from the pale golden haze of Cádiz and made for Harry Hathaway's cabin. He hoped Francisco, discreet dallier that he was, had long since melted into his own quarters. Steele had no particular feelings about Francisco's tastes in fleshly temptations; he had known too many sailors who'd loved a like lover, but he cared not to witness it, any more than she.

The lad was composing something on parchment when Steele entered the cabin in response to Harry's invitation. Harry was no doubt a beautiful boy. Dressed in black velvet looped and lavishly scrolled with gold braid after the Spanish manner, Harry looked even more porcelain than he had in Don Ricardo's villa that long-ago afternoon. He had that fair complexion that paints pulsating roses of color on each cheek. That annoyed Steele this morning. He had never seen the sister flush—she'd been one alabaster face of ice no matter the case.

"Yes, Captain?" inquired Harry, raising an eyebrow.

Francisco's gesture. The boy had heard, Steele guessed, of the night's sleeping arrangements. Steele's eyes turned to distant blue ice floes floating in a cold white-water sea. Quatrains—the script was formed into quatrains on the paper; the insolent puppy was penning verse.

"If you will wait a moment, Captain, there's a couplet—

> "And if desire be latitude of love
> Then longitude be death by which it prove.

"There, it's been so long since I versified in English ... now what is *your* desire, Captain?"

Steele withdrew further into the arctic regions of his annoyance. A frivolous, foolish creature, well suited for plaything to an overbred aristocrat. So much risked for so little. If not for

Harry, Steele would never have felt his muscles writhe under the lick of Spanish leather. If not for Harry, the milky maiden from the Indies might be dancing at a London masqued ball instead of pursuing fate in Cádiz. If not for Harry, Muffin's whistle and gadfly advice might still be buzzing in his ears . . .

"Your sister's gone," Steele said shortly.

"Again? Dear Captain, you must learn to hang on to her. I thought you had been making progress."

Steele fought the urge to catch the boy by his elegant if old-fashioned doublet and shake him for his complacency. Instead, he snatched up the parchment and walked to the window perusing it. Sentimental verse, gushing with the "blessed sin" and "pure lust" of the poet's conceit. He glanced at the boy, pleased to see Harry's ears redden as Steele's eyes followed his self-revelations across the page.

"May I suggest another couplet for the last?" inquired Steele with velvet in his voice. He intoned in elegant, mocking accents:

> *"And if love's latitude desire be*
> *Then steer thy* sister *soul to propinquity."*

The last word fell from his lips in sharp syllables like ice cracking. Steele watched the boy's face grow scarlet; he'd been faithless to his own loyal sister and well knew it. Satisfied, Steele let the parchment fall upon the bed, where it lay unheeded.

"Will you fetch her back?" Harry asked.

Steele recognized a familiar expression in the boy's eyes: the look his sister had when she asked something to which she was too proud to admit. Perhaps he had been overharsh on the boy. A night on the Dutchman's deck could forge any number of anomalies.

"It's too late," Steele said. "We're all anxious for England. I won't have the men deprived of home after their housing in a galley belly for so many months. Spanish waters are dangerous unless we keep our distance."

The words appeared to satisfy Harry as little as they did him.

"We'll raise the coast in about five days," concluded Steele firmly.

"Very well, Captain. I can't disagree with your decision. She brought it upon herself."

"Did she?" Steele asked levelly. The gray-green eyes regarded him with cool surprise again.

"Perhaps you, too, have lost a 'sister soul,' Captain. Your spirits seem on edge."

Steele didn't bother responding, other than to note, "At any rate, the Hathaways will be surprised enough to see your face. They think you dead." Steele stopped at the door. "And your sister . . . what is her given name?"

"Didn't she tell you? Well, I do not betray my sister's secrets. I know that much of her. She wants her privacy. It is her most precious possession. Now I, I care not if the world know me."

"And half of it does, I'll wager," shot back Steele, leaving the cabin.

Chapter Twenty

She was finally tired from her climb; the air atop these Cádiz hills seemed thinner. Miranda paused, panting, to wipe her abraded palms on her shirt. She felt like something wild and enduring on these rugged crags. She had taken the hard way up, and it had restored something in her that had been shrunk aboard the *Gato de Nueve*.

A dozen pretty painted ships bobbed in the bay below. Seville was mother port to Spain now, but if Cádiz were no longer Spain's gold-bound port, the merchants below her rode at anchor on golden sails, tinted by the sun's setting shimmer over the peerlessly level horizon.

The sky itself was a globe of blue and gold and scarlet. Soon that same sun would slant its last rays across Barbados beach half a world away. Miranda felt transported to her home island again, pain and loss rinsing away with the sunset's rosy glow. Now hunger—not heartache—gnawed her stomach. She turned to the darkening summit and found a high stone wall. She was over it nimbly, as she had once darted into Cádiz bakeshops to steal bread.

Here the soft evening scent of fruit trees drew her on. She felt among the small trees' laden limbs in the twilight. Pears . . . no. She wanted something other. She could be particular now. She was on her own again with none to please but herself. Ah, sweet ripe peaches, delicately furred.

She pulled down two, four—filling her shirttails with the red-gold harvest, so like little suns themselves. Miranda sat under a tree and bit into the voluptuous fruit. Hard. And sour. Green, that was what one got by gathering in the semidark. She hurled it away, hearing the rejected fruit bounce against the hillside to trigger a shower of stones. Another peach, ah, better. Sweet juice ran down her chin.

She ate two down to the pits, which she sucked, enjoying wresting the most from the hard kernel of so soft a fruit. Another shower of stones pattered nearby, but Miranda was absorbed in catching the first faint flicker of starlight. She and Harry had played such games on Barbados. Just when one spied a true star, another faint beam would glimmer elsewhere . . . and another, until the sky was pinpricked with blue fire.

A scuffle again—too loud for the fall of overripe fruit. Miranda rose, peaches cascading from her lap to bruise along the ground. Too late, men were coming—she ran. Not far. Arms caught her; a sour, heavy wine aroma enveloped her. Miranda kicked until her feet were caught up. She dangled in the dark between her captors like a poled wild boar.

"*Madre de Dios!* We've netted a wiry thief. Bring the wretch down—"

The speaker's hand had slipped too close to her face. She bit him tenaciously on the wrist.

"*Ayaaaaaaah!*"

A blow from the darkness snapped her teeth down on her tongue. Her mouth surged with a warm and salty tide, and consciousness drowned in that inland sea . . .

Fire flared someplace beyond her eyelids when Miranda next began to think of waking. She ignored the idea. Her back lay on a surface as cold and level as a blade. The bright fire-shadow beyond her closed lids echoed the pain that tauntened her jaw. She heard the slow, steady advance of boots on stone. Closer, closer—cloth rustled, leather creaked, a joint snapped. A presence hovered over her.

"Open your eyes, thief, and see the dawn in store for you."

The Spanish words were sibilant, soft-spoken. Miranda reluctantly unweighted her eyelids and saw a pitted, rough face buried in black bristles of beard. The man squatted beside her, his dark eyes regarding her narrowly.

"So this is the marauder of the orchards—the one you think is female, eh, Esteban?"

Miranda's sick green glance slid to the other men sprawled around a table.

"*Sí, Capitán,*" said one. "What else bites besides beasts and women?"

Miranda eyed the nearest man again. His mouth split into a full-lipped grin; when he spoke, the smell of garlic and wine flooded her face like a fog.

"She's not for us, *amigos,*" he told himself as much as the others. "Not at any price we would wish to pay. I'll take her"—his dark eyes lifted almost reverentially to the high stone ceiling—"above."

Miranda was dragged with him, up dark stairways and past tapestry hangings, under wrought-iron torches holding sputtering fans of flame. The garden outside had been warm and scented; within, the place was all stone, dark and damp.

The captain finally paused by a broad arched mahogany door, hinged in wrought iron.

"Wait." He hesitated, then turned Miranda into the light of a wall-mounted torch. "So like the lost one," he muttered before vanishing through the dark portal.

After a moment, Miranda swung the heavy door ajar to peer within. The captain reappeared, behind him an even blacker shadow. Shadow—and something sleek and jet edging through the narrow opening like opaque smoke, with a pale face as flat as an eel belly. The lines of that face, framed by a tracery of black beard and moustache, struck her mind like the one page in a seldom-read book that falls open again and again . . .

Miranda was retreating along the wall, her hands pulling her along like a sailor hauling on a cable, a lifeline. The guard whirled, his hands pinning her under the wavering torchlight.

"Ah, that one." The don's tone was too calm for a man seeing an opponent who had wrenched his favorite from him so recently. "Another gilded one."

The don's breath sucked suddenly between his even white teeth as his gaze pooled on Miranda like brown sherry. He crossed his arms on his narrow, gold-braid-latticed chest.

"Occasions of sin throw themselves at my feet, it seems." The don's corrosive gaze scalded Miranda's face. "An eye for an eye. Does not the Holy Book say thusly? What you took from me you must repay. A boy"—an immaculate hand flicked a crushed leaf from Miranda's trousered hip—"for a boy, eh?"

Miranda struggled like a wolverine in the guard's grasp, while the don's soft fingers—somehow cold and warm at the same time—coursed lightly along her neck. She shuddered.

"Faugh!" The don drew back, a cold edge of malice honing itself in his eyes. "I've not forgotten what you've cost me. So you like to pass as boy; then you shall serve as boy. If not— I'll have her below, *Capitán*."

A conspiratorial look passed between master and servant, then they marched Miranda down a nearby flight of spiraling stone steps so quickly that her feet stumbled. Reverse turnings screwed the trio into the damp dark depths of the ancient building. Moss made green velvet of the walls, and torches lit more distant vistas. The earth beneath her feet on a long passage smelled of leeches . . .

The party passed through a heavy-hinged door into a room ablaze with low stone hearths and braziers. Miranda first took it for an armory—iron and steel glistened on every wall. Then she saw that unnatural bed that could only be one thing—the rack, its gears oiled and gleaming black in the hot red light.

"Here," said the don, smiling like a convivial host, "is the heart of my empire, my palace of persuasion. I can contrive an *auto-da-fé* for you, my heathen English masquerader, that would turn all that gold to ash."

He seized Miranda's half-loosened hair and shook her head. Then he paused, and his loathing expression melted upon her face like butter. His fingers softly inched across her face, long, white legs from a bloated centipede. Miranda arched defiantly away. The don blinked his lids slowly shut once, something ophidian about the movement, as if waking from a dream.

He nodded imperceptibly to the guard. Miranda was pushed farther into the rock-walled chamber. Motion made the various metal implements lining the hewn walls glimmer fugitive crimson in the torchlight.

"Ah, the serrated pincers catch your eye—something new from my Moroccan friends. And my poor old rack, not too imaginative, I fear—an inheritance from the last Inquisition, that finally broke after having broken so many, but I salvaged it. I have an affinity for relics."

The don's beringed fingers glittered expansively across the grisly array. "And this, my favorite, my pet."

The captain propelled Miranda to a tall iron casket.

"La Doncella de Hierro," the don intoned with satisfaction. "You English call her 'Iron Maiden,' and like a maiden—if I un-

derstand your word rightly—my lady is also ... virgin." The don's smug gaze rested finally on Miranda.

She wet parched lips before replying, remembering what Steele had said about the perverse value of virginity along the Mediterranean.

"Virgin? I do not doubt your iron lady's virtue, but I am not as she. Perhaps you no longer care to claim me."

"Not? I knew your brother's fate on the pirate ship—he told me readily enough. But you were no meat for those sailors. He told me that as well."

"My brother was marv'lous talkative with his captor," she couldn't help spitting. "Did you bring him here also?"

The don's eyes deepened with savored, secret amusement. "No, Harry never saw this place. Harry was most persuadable without *la dama.*"

Miranda's heart sank at the obvious truth, and her gaze dropped to the Iron Maiden's immobile feet.

"So. To whom do I owe the honor of your initiation? I do not bother railing at what is lost, I am merely—curious."

"On the ship—" Miranda began, loath to be specific. How the don would relish knowing that she was but a relic of his enemy, Christopher Steele! Her pale eyes fastened on his waiting black ones. "The captain—the Dutchman—was not like his crew. I was kept in the cabin with him."

"The Dutchman! That old devil fell off his gloomy metaphysical perch to toy with you? The Dutchman I knew was not wont to let his prizes sail smoothly to port when he was done with them."

"The Dutchman, you know him?" Miranda was as awestruck by the don's casual reference as Christopher Steele had once been by hers.

"Do I know the Devil?" The don laughed. "Ah, yes, I know of the cursed fellow. We Spaniards have dallied in the Netherlands enough to know those thick-tongued Hollanders. There was one Piet Pieterszoon Heyn, a heinous fellow indeed to His Catholic Majesty and any who warm their veins with Spanish blood. 'Twas he who put São Salvador in the New World to flame twice: an upstart admiral who wanted Netherlands burghers to love him for his seamanship when they most loved the Spanish gold he hauled home.

"Twenty years past he took a Seville-bound plate fleet entire—forty-six tons of silver. Some ships sank beyond his cursed greed; the rest he brought back to The Hague in triumph. And though he left few Spanish galleons floating, his home-bound booty floated the entire Dutch economy, which without his meddling would have dragged the damnable country back into the waters from which it rose.

"They say he died soon after, cut in two on the deck by a pirate shot off Dunkirk. They say that his crew, half-mad, threw every survivor on the conquered pirate ship overboard. They say all this . . . they say that wishes flow from wells. I believe it was a ruse. The Dutch knew some Spanish assassin might soon table their seagoing scourge forever. I believe that Heyn still sails, the old freebooter, that he still covets Spanish silver."

The don eyed Miranda. "And mayhap English gold. As do I. *Capitán*," he ordered softly.

The man levered open the Iron Maiden, her hinges screeching as the dark iron cavern of the instrument's vacant interior cracked open like a nut whose fruit has withered to nothingness.

Miranda saw that the metal interior was rounded, as a melon rind after the meat has been carved out, a sarcophagus smithed for the making of death as well as its encompassing. A dozen black spikes bristled from the Maiden's interior lid like giant nails driven through. Miranda memorized their fatal pattern as her eyes scanned each eight-inch blade.

Two, mated at the top—for eyes. A solitaire for the throat. Another singlet, heart. Another and another—spleen, stomach, kidney. And there, at the extremities, a half dozen points scattered merely for torment's sake—points thick as a shark's fin breaking water, ready to ravage skin and bone . . .

"I have till this moment considered my *Doncella de Hierro* the most perfect, most self-contained female I have yet encountered. You encourage me to reconsider. You encourage me to reconsider a great deal—"

The don rhythmically stroked Miranda's hair while she peered, frozen with horror, into the Maiden. The door would creak, cry, scream shut. Inside the Maiden, the space between occupant and blade would slowly dwindle until the first dull prick—the eyes, the eyes gone in an instant and the piercing everywhere and why not the heart in one deep thrust, one final blow?

Miranda's face grew as pale as the Maiden's was black, but she glanced at the don's ebony and ivory countenance and shook her head. Her hair sifted through his hands like wheat eluding the scythe.

"You were right," she said huskily, "to choose your Iron Maiden for the best of company. I choose her also."

The don's face cracked like a brittle mask. He abruptly shoved Miranda inside the body-wide slit.

"Then may you have joy of each other," he said, his voice already distant.

Miranda whirled, her back cradled by the device's curved metal interior, a swath of torchlight striking her body like a shadow from a reversed world. The door creaked and edged inward, and the maiden's barbed points dipped into the bright bar of light, gleaming like faint stars against the black night-sky of iron before her.

Soon those stars would pierce, redden, explode, blaze—and then leave the sky one brief blanketing pall of merciful darkness. Hadn't she seen the darkness begin aboard the *Gato de Nueve*? Hadn't the white-shirted figures of her brother and his tutor formed a mocking constellation in some night sky in her mind? Steele had but drawn her further into that night, blanketing her in humiliation. Then had come the twilight orchard, the blow that had swaddled her in black velvet forgetfulness. If memories were white-hot irons that seared the brain, perhaps forgetfulness came on just such dark lances as yearned toward her now . . .

The door whined louder as the light striping her face narrowed. Something began fluttering in her throat, the same throat toward which the Maiden aimed her now-invisible point. Something faint wanted exit, wanted light as a moth covets it, light to devour even as the light consumes itself. A ponderous black weight suppressed that feeble bleating, then it broke free. Miranda cringed sideways within the Iron Maiden, the pattern of the device's deadly blades inscribed on her memory and her supple body twisting and shifting to avoid each one.

The thing in her throat began whimpering in triumph. Sideways, edgeways. So the Maiden can cut but not kill. Where less lethal? Through the shoulder, across the cheek, in the side? The Maiden had been meant for men. Miranda was slighter than her ordinary prey. There was a chance.

A chance? Miranda mocked the insistent thing in her throat. A chance to let the don use her as he had Harry? A chance to survive the lid's closing scarred and sliced like a stubborn loaf of bread? Miranda's fingers trembled forward in the dark. They touched a cold iron point inches away. Her fingers curled around that barb, as if it were a lifeline. No! No further, no more. It is the nature of the beast to survive, though it know it not. Though it want it not. No.

The waiting black fell rapidly from a faraway sky to envelop her, blanket her, smother her resistance, seize her senses and swoop her to the solitary soundless place from which it had come.

Miranda left behind only the echo of her last scream, rebounding mockingly off the Iron Maiden's empty arms.

Christopher Steele sat alone in the captain's cabin of the *Gato de Nueve*, the Moroccan-bound logbook open before him on the inlaid desk. The twin lanterns above him swayed softly with the galley's easy roll. Night had made the cabin's banks of glazed windows into a mirror, and the lanterns swung in the faceted silver pool behind Steele like myriad fireflies.

The captains' brows were knit and his eyes intent on the pages before him, whose letters squirmed like lice in the shifting light. His quill tip broke. He cast it away, catching up another, trying its point on the flesh of his forefinger and then staring at its long uninked length.

He had set down the facts—the *Gato*'s bearing, how speedily her oarsmen were slicing her homeward. Spain had flowed into her wake like a train. Now she had only to skirt the well-bayed coast of France, beat her way up-Channel, and three hundred sore-tried souls could breathe English air at last.

Steele sighed and rubbed the still-aching muscle at the back of his neck. How to write that other so that My Lords of Admiralty would not shake their curled heads at the tale told by the captured Spanish logbook? He glanced from his serviceable script to the gracefully penned entry above his, her last. Odd enough that this "M. Hathaway" had served as *Gato* log-keeper for a time; odder still to have her vanish into the black waves of writing across the log's wide white waters without a trace.

He would have to say something. What? One female commander lost at sea off Cádiz? Or simply, *Jumped ship, M. Hathaway, P. Riversgate, R. Richards*? Even absent she was an aggravation.

Why had she left him the ship? Perhaps she despised him less than the brother who had broken faith, the tutor who had turned an innocent past into a guilty one. He, Steele, was merely a defender who had turned pragmatic despoiler. And he had done the deed as honorably, as mechanically, as he could, a duty as necessary to him as Weatherbee's whipping on the *Salamander*.

She had not seen that, either. Steele had heard that the people of the Far East believed that if one once saved a life, one was forever responsible for that life. Did the same apply to the taking of maidenheads? She had been his first virgin since he himself had been one. He saw no special nicety in it. Perhaps he had made overquick work of her, but the necessity had repelled him. What he had done, he had done swiftly. He had only wanted to protect her from Mediterranean predators . . . or had he wanted something else, something even he did not quite understand or credit?

Steele shook his lantern-silvered head as if casting off cobwebs and plunged quill into inkwell. *Three crew members have this day left ship to make port at Cádiz. R. Richards, seaman; P. Riversgate, apprentice navigator; and M. Hathaway . . .* —"mystery," he wanted to pen, with a tight smile as to what M'Lords of Admiralty would make of that.

Instead he wrote, "interim recorder." Let them ask if any would tell. Margaret? The "M" still bewitched him, dazzled his eyes in the rocking candlelight. Mary? No. Or Marjory, like his sister, merry Marjory all whipping yellow curls and dimples?

No, more likely Mara; there was a kind of biblical bitterness to her. What would the poets christen her? Something Greek or grandly Roman: Marina, from the sea, like a pearl—something precious and pure with still a grain of sand like a thorn set at its heart, the remote, hidden anger upon which all the rest was erected.

He threw down the quill. Trust her to survive, though he had been forced to reteach her that lesson a trifle harshly but a day ago. By now she undoubtably rocked in the passenger cabin of a Portuguese merchantman bound for Bristol. She had gold enough to carry her back even to Barbados, to take that Atlantic course the Dutchman had so deceptively set for her months before.

A picture of the Cádiz taverns unrolled before his eyes— smoke and guttering candles; sour wine and the greedy white glimmer of Spanish eyes—he put his conscience out like a candle. No, she was too canny now to make shift with that. He was mad to worry, he who bore a bandage round his arm from her latest annoyance.

His eyes roamed to the Spanish bed, low, wide and handsome

across the cabin. He would sleep there more comfortably tonight on those silken sheets. Alone. 'Twas a pleasure to lie tangled with a female only when pleasure had gone before. But she, she was like bedding a briar.

Steele leaned back in the carved captain's chair, stretched his white-sleeved arms wide in the empty cabin, and yawned. His hand slid under the logbook's heavy cover. He levered it shut, the white pages falling closed with a dull clap echoing in the empty cabin like distant thunder.

Chapter Twenty-one

"Ah, Zarifa, she was truly asleep, this one."

"Idiot. It was the sleep of—of faint. That is all. Shahar! Help me."

Miranda heard the voices whisper a long distance above her, as soft as surf. She was climbing a seaweed ladder through a cool green place. Up, ever up. A long way.

"Oh, Zarifa, her limbs are white. Whiter even than the other's. Like goat's milk."

"Rihana, you are the offspring of a camel! Of course she is pale. She is European. Like him. Can't you see by the hair? Goose!"

Giggles punctuated the clumsily spoken Spanish. Miranda felt her body roll lazily, as if tide-caught. Cádiz. The warm, smiling, white-teethed waves of Cádiz had her and Harry, too. Tossing them forever in a gently murderous dream . . .

"Fatma, we must ready her. *He* has called for her."

"Zarifa, surely you dream, why would he—?"

"Your father was a ragpicker and that is what he left you for brains—rags! Now hasten, all of you."

Two sharp claps rang out; bare feet slapped stone amid a fleeing rustle. Miranda felt the throb in her jaw tighten and haul her rapidly to the surface. She must open her eyes quickly, or her dream-speakers would be gone.

Their footsteps died like distant clapping. Miranda finally opened her eyes on an empty room. Room? A shifting sort of place, curtained. Her sky was draped violet silk, her stars a constellation of hanging oil lamps. She drifted on a sea of large silken pillows covered in fantastical designs.

Miranda sat up, noticing only when her hair shifted silkily on her shoulders that she was naked—and free of the cold metal embrace of the don's Iron Maiden. She stood and flailed past the diaphanous hangings that clouded her alcove, until she centered a large room ringed with arched colonnades.

Her breath came deeply, desperately. Yes, free. Wherever she was, it was not there. She laughed shakily, feeling reborn, delivered from an iron womb. She turned around once, her outstretched arms savoring a perimeter of—air, only air.

Giggles echoed off the rainbow-colored tile at her bare feet.

"Fatma, be silent. Rihana, the robe."

A tall, spare woman came flapping toward Miranda from one of the arches, trailing glittery jewelry like a magpie. Miranda retreated before the length of shining Oriental cloth she carried. Muttering exasperated foreign syllables, the woman darted forward to drop the garment over Miranda's bare shoulders like a net.

The rest of the flock—chattering, whispering—fluttered over. Fatma daubed Miranda's cheek with liquid from a brass bowl. A slender one swathed in dark orange cloth knelt to apply jeweled sandals to Miranda's feet. Another sashed her waist to draw the open robe shut.

Zarifa stood watching, her arms folded firmly across flat breasts, an appraising squint in her shrewd carnelian-colored eyes.

Eyes were all the features they had—bright, brown birdlike eyes that darted above the face veils. Miranda had an urge to yank and see if these curious creatures sprouted beaks rather than mouths.

"Rihana. The comb," barked the ringmistress of this Arab circus.

The slight girl at Miranda's feet glanced up with kohl-rimmed, smiling eyes and vanished. A moment later someone was tugging at Miranda's tangled hair from behind.

"What—?" Miranda began in English. "*Porqué—?*"

"Nothing," responded Zarifa hurriedly in Spanish. "*Nada.* No questions. Only the dead ask questions here."

She clapped her hands. The three women surrounding Miranda broke away as one. Miranda glanced behind her where Rihana had been plying the comb and felt a strange sense of abandonment. Empty air was no luxury, after all.

"*Por favor, señora—*"

"Shhhh! Rihana . . . no, Fatma, will conduct you."

A plump figure detached itself from the trio and waddled over to pluck at Miranda's sleeve. Miranda looked at Rihana's languishing dark eyes, at Zarifa's immobile scowl, then followed the anonymous figure across an interior courtyard where vegetation grew to the roofline and revealed stars between its fanned leaves.

The feet ahead of her slapped smartly on the stone; soon they were indoors again. A perfumed lamp led to a huge, fantastically carved double door. Miranda's escort's last tug positioned her charge directly before the great brass rings at the door's center. She bobbled back across the courtyard.

Miranda watched her own pale hand reach out, the alien sleeve falling back from her arm, to grasp an icy ring. She pulled, a motion strong enough to dislodge a sword from stone, from flesh. The door slid by, its carved faces leering in the lamplight.

"Come in," said the don.

More draperies and glowing lamps beckoned, but Miranda saw only the don, a silhouette of backlit danger at the heart of all this unsubstantial, slightly shifting glamour. His hands toyed with something that chattered like frightened teeth.

"My women found this."

She edged into the light to see that he held her purse, which she had tucked into the swell of her shirt. He wore a long flowing robe like hers. It disquieted her to see the don muffled in one great web of cloth. She preferred his velvet-sheathed self, when each limb, each impulse, was revealed. Now he had retracted his claws into one huge, falsely friendly paw.

He elevated a host of coin and tried his teeth upon it. "Quite genuine. *Gato* booty, yes? You and your cursed Captain Steele—running freely over my galley, taking my things. My gold."

He came close enough to rattle the purse before her face. "Even my English gold." He stroked her blond head absently, as one does a pet. "I am fortunate that you did not plunder my Toledo chests," he remarked bitterly, "that your crewmen did not appropriate my fine silken Flemish shirts."

Miranda recalled the don's treasured silk shirts hanging from every back she had ever trusted; for once the Spanish nobleman was right—it was travesty.

"So. Your Captain Steele has the English boy back, after all."

"Yes," Miranda agreed dully.

"Ah, you do not like him, my little yellow English cat? They left you, didn't they, your fine Englishmen? They didn't want you, after all, is that it?"

Miranda raised empty green eyes to the don's avid dark ones. "Precisely, Don—"

"Don Ricardo," he finished courteously.

"They were not as I thought they were, Don Ricardo," she added calmly.

"Of course not. You think I did not know their game? 'Captain' Steele charging me gold enough to buy a bell for the cathedral in Seville, merely for a voyage or two to import my—trinkets—from Africa. Yet on whom else could I rely for secrecy but renegade Englishmen? And all that good Spanish gold soon sent to Holland to buy cannon for your silly King. I knew, but I used him as he used me. Did you see him—after the galley? Did he wax well in the galleys?"

The don's dark eyes had hardened to malicious lumps of coal.

"Exceedingly well, Don Ricardo," Miranda said coldly. "The galleys seemed to suit him."

The don's face stiffened, then stretched into a smile. "I see that I will learn nothing from you, *gata amarilla*. Enough of the past. I have only the future in mind this night."

The don's well-draped arm gestured to a low table. "Sit then, yes, upon the cushions. You must be hungry after your travels. Eat."

Miranda knelt numbly. The trays arrayed on the table held dark, greasy, cold-looking foodstuffs. A metallic clank brought her hand to her hip; she found only a knotted silken cord, no dagger hilt. Her blade lay on the guardroom floor, doubtless, where it would be found and employed to peel a peach or scrape a grimy nail.

The don thrust a silver goblet at her. "Drink. You are my guest."

Miranda stared into the dark liquid that lapped a gilded bowl, her lashes statue-still on her cheek.

"I do not poison guests," he promised softly. "Only the Italians poison—and now the French, since Maria de' Medici has been their Queen."

Miranda's cold white fingers tightened on the goblet. She lifted the dark circle of liquid and saw a star of light reflect on its rippling surface. The ever-fixed polestar, that sailors follow? She rushed the rim to her lips and swallowed the star.

"Excellent," purred the don. "I thought that I—and the Maiden—might make something of you yet."

He swept to a carved chest covered with an Oriental rug and surmounted by a pair of scales, their outline hard and European in the draped Oriental chamber.

"This night," he said, "may be a new dawn to me. You think me an unrepentant villain, no doubt. Villain I may be, but repentant as well. Here, here are the beads of my wickedness."

The don's eyes glittered as brilliantly as the jewels that hung within the velvet-edged lips of the ebony chest he brought to Miranda.

He laughed—a delighted, almost endearing laugh—as she puzzled over his display. Strings of emeralds, sapphires, rubies, diamonds swayed on their hooks, each gem netted in silver wire and strung in odd groups of ten and solitaires. Gold crucifixes pooled at the case's bottom like so many anchors for a gemladen flotilla.

"These are my sins, *inglesa*. The Church tells us that sins are black, but sins shine, little one. At least for the sinner, for a time."

The don's fingers sidled down the glittering ropes, pausing to caress a sapphire here, a pendant emerald there. Their colors refracted like an island rainbow and the swaying lengths radiated a stealthy enchantment. Her body began to circle imperceptibly with them, her eyes fixed upon those little worlds with secrets in their bright, polished depths. A shrill whine of music seemed to move with them. A ringing, buzzing . . .

She held herself immobile, aware then that the sound was in her own head. Everything slid a notch away, as if she had suddenly shrunk. She wanted to lift a hand to still the gems, but found the impulse too heavy. The wine, the diamond-starred wine! She had drunk it and somehow drunk time and distance. The don leaned closer, so close she could mark each hair of his silver-threaded goatee. The silver netted her eye, distracted her. Silver filaments. Like a web. Silver shining, jewels swaying . . .

The don's dark eyes fixed her for a long moment. He replaced the jewel box, talking softly all the while.

"Yes, they are pretty, my sins, but all sins glisten before they are done, else why would we fall so often, no? Perhaps in England, with its heretics these hundred years, they do not find sin so black?"

Miranda answered dreamily. "We, too, walk under a cloak of sin and death. At least 'tis what Father said of our creed."

The buzzing had changed pitch and speed, was thrumming like a guitar string struck and abandoned.

"Ah, death. I do not think on death." The don held a glittering length to the light like wine. "These are unshed sins, *pequita*. And do they blacken when the deed is done, when intention has become consummation? No, they shine as ever, save in someone else's treasure box. I have sinned enough to send twelve good Dominicans to Hispaniola to convert the savages. Enough to forge the Málaga Cathedral bells from pure silver. Such tone. Sin sings with a lovely voice. For each transgression I pluck a petal from my sparkling garlands here and the Church has means enough to do three good deeds to my single bad one.

"I have had to pick many flowers for the likes of your brother. A bitter failing, but now I believe that I can transmute my nature enough to qualify for a lesser degree of culpability. You are—so like. I can advance a stage in my sinning and still believe ... here, for you, this dia—no, this ruby. For you the Credo that links it all together. See, I pluck it off and put it in the scale. When I am done it will weigh in the other dish and balance off whatever ill I did."

The don swept back his sleeve and lay a large unfaceted ruby on one side of the scale. The brass bowl plunged with an awkward clank. Something in Miranda, something remote, plunged also. How hard to concentrate with the hum still swathing her head! Her hands bracketed her temples; when she next looked up, the don was kneeling beside her.

"Too much, golden one? Ah, it matters not. So like," he whispered, his fingers outlining her features. "They breed beauty as well as sugar, those cursed English who stole our bright little Indies island but two decades ago. Ah, you did not know— Barbados was Spanish until your yellow northern pirates wrested it away. I only take back what is mine."

His fingers continued to play lightly over her face, as if testing the strings of a new guitar, tuning her to his purpose. She barely felt the touch, could not blink so much as an eyelash.

"All golden and green, my little English island. I shall drop anchor on you," he murmured, his black eyes canopied by sallow, sunken lids.

She marked again the startling length and lushness of his

lashes, trophies from an island centipede. The buzz that belled her lifted suddenly as she jerked away.

"Pequito lindo," the don murmured, pulling her steadily toward him. *"No, no. Venga con mí ..."*

His lips stung hers, pushing hard against her teeth. Miranda gasped and pulled away, hearing only a steady sort of hiss in her head, seeing only his hooded form and evil, slitted eyes. She began to long for the Iron Maiden.

Miranda's stomach tightened as she broke through the drug that webbed her long enough to thrust the don's slim shoulders away. He looked as waxen as a doll in the oil lamps' light, his eyes the flat black of wrought iron, his dark lips shimmering.

Miranda's disgust reared again, but the spell held; she only stared at him as his hands pushed her facedown into the cushions. She was smothering in silk, her face awash in fabric clouds that threatened to wring her breath out.

"Please—" Miranda murmured into the cushions' paisley ears, trying to push her limp hands into something solid and lever herself to control again.

The buzz intensified and she clapped the drone to her head hoping to trap and expel it. Behind her, above her, the don's ubiquitous hands were turning her like a compass on a drawing board, scribing a circle for his pleasure ...

Down, over the *Merlin*'s side, spinning on some certain dream that ended only in a black bottom where the sand was ground from midnight pearls, and sharks' teeth gleamed amongst it like albino jewels. There, where the Dutchman's face laughed mutely from behind a sunken treasure chest, and there a fallen uncorroded brass mirror—her hand upon it and the face in it, hers ... and Harry's. And ... someone else's.

And then him heavy upon her, putting something out within her that had warmed her like a fire, smothering her into ashes only, weighing her down to drown ...

Miranda wrenched herself violently away from the don, her robe pulling open. She froze, shocked to see him stretched above her like some unhealthy moth, but the shock was mutual. The don stared at the body pooling like milk on the pillows below him—not the long, lean expanse of flesh he was wont to sample. The sight abruptly turned his appetite.

Miranda, sensing the sudden chink in his amorousness, slithered quickly away and gathered her wits.

"I am not your *'pequito lindo,'* Don Ricardo, no matter how

many times you murmur it in my ear or your own. If you would
have me in my brother's stead, you must take me as I am."

The don suddenly lifted a dismissing arm, as if warding off a
bad dream. Miranda clasped her robe together and wove with the
spinning in her head, strong upon her after the hard-won moments of clarity.

"Away!" he said. "I cannot change my taste in flesh no matter
whose face it wears. Your brother came to me as a flower to the
sun, but you are closed to me."

Miranda felt a dim whimper of relief.

The don went to pull twice on a silken rope near the door, then
returned to the pillowed island at the room's center.

"I will find—something other—for you."

He restlessly paced toward the jewel chest and plucked something living and red from the scales, like an overripe peach from
a tree.

"Here, *pequita linda*." He spoke with a ragged, self-mocking
smile, hurling a red arc across the room to Miranda's lap.

She cringed, almost expecting a *Gato* firebomb, but the small
red glow settled harmlessly in the cloth cradle between her legs.
Miranda elevated it wonderingly to the light—a ruby as large as
her thumbnail, throbbing with red life like the egg of some mythical serpent.

"I planned this stone to deck the Virgin's robe during Holy
Week," the don confessed bleakly. "All Seville could have
crowded out unknowing to see the symbol of our union riding on
her snowy shoulders. My first *pequita linda* . . ." He spat out the
feminine endings of the endearment. Pretty little lady.

"We Spanish are dreamers, perhaps even to our hopes of westward empire. I have dreamed in the realm of fleshly kingdoms as
well. Keep that trifle. I cannot tie it to my Virgin's cloak, for I
did not truly earn the sin for which it stands. Nor can I string it
on my beads again, for the intention was there, cannot you testify
to that, *pequita-linda-of-some-other*?

"So, as a leopard cannot change his spots, a la Fontana y
Monteverde cannot change his creed. You are the caretaker of
my virtue as well as yours this night, so keep the bauble. It may
in future remind you of a better time, though now you liked it
not."

Miranda bowed deeply toward her own golden reflection in
the brass bowl. The distorted face before her crumpled as she

retched violently into her own image. Hands held her arms and hair back; Miranda felt suspended over a pit where all her anger and disgust poured in a wrenching torrent. Almost, almost the Maiden would have been better, cleaner.

"*Aaaiiii*, she is a sick one."

"Hush, Rihana, it is always like this after an appointment with him. Remember the other—?"

A hand jerked Miranda's head up by the hair. Her glazed eyes focused on floating lamps and a pair of sharp-faceted eyes like garnets in a leathery face.

"Now, here's a white face for you, Rihana. The don's brew could take the color out of a she-camel's hide. You and Fatma, take her away and clean her."

The twitters that had awakened Miranda were now sympathetic clucks. Miranda felt herded in a cluster of hens as the servingwomen bathed and soothed and tucked her away on a sea of pillows that tossed her as restlessly as had the cabin of the *Gato de Nueve*.

The drug lingered, even as the days flickered bright and dimmed through the pierced windows of her curtained prison. Rihana often urged trays of congealed oddities at her, but every morsel seemed to unleash some lingering wave of distaste left over from the don's dark libation.

Miranda lay quiet upon her pillows and withdrew. When all the lamps had been dimmed and the Arab women's soft breathing in their nearby alcove was the only trace of night wind her ears could catch, she would work the don's ruby from a pocket she had burrowed in a pillow.

Bribe. But whom to bribe? The women were hopeless, helpless, content to serve a master who fed them well and made no masculine demands. And, thus far, Miranda had not been allowed out of the women's quarters.

She crushed the ruby into her palm until her nails left dimpled half-moons on her flesh. That ruby was her one token, her passkey to escape. She squirreled her treasure away. Someday she would find one to take it from her and free her. Someday.

The word had a too-familiar ring.

Chapter Twenty-two

One night a new sound rasped over the tiles, rougher than breathing. It shuffled toward her in the near dark like the Dutchman on his bloody deck, until her own breathing paused to isolate it.

There, a figure there, but an arm's reach away. The don.

She struggled out of the enmeshing pillows, but he waved a calming hand.

"Do not trouble yourself on my account. I have done with you, and perhaps you are fortunate, golden one. You are to be the new odalisque of the Bey of Tunis. I have sold you, at a magnificent price. The bey is a mighty freebooter, lord of the western Mediterranean. Fortunate, indeed. Like your brother, you land on your claws."

"Sold me? You make your Iron Maiden seem merciful, Don Ricardo." Miranda stared at the man's vague shadow. Mercy. Someone, long ago, had taxed her with lack of that noble commodity. Who? Did it matter? The charge had come home truly now.

"First," the don went on, "there are conditions. You are too lean for such a man's taste, and too wind-burned. You will not have to meet your new master for a month. Enjoy your freedom while you may."

"I will have naught to do with any man," Miranda spat into his sallow and mocking face.

"But you will," he promised, whirling like a dervish and melting into the lamp-starred night of the halls.

Miranda thought of freedom, as he advised, but in a sense he never meant, and watched the days dawn in an aura of softer light through the curtains.

One milky afternoon only days later, when the Spanish heat had shouldered its way even into the harem's coldest stone recess, the Arab women came in procession to fetch her.

All giggled remorselessly, though Zarifa's stern face remained unseamed by anything but duty. Miranda's golden hair was veiled before she was wafted through the arches and into the courtyard.

Palm leaves lightly fanned the cloudless sky. A flowering vine crawled to freedom and the sun over the high white stucco walls and there—a crunch of heel on gravel, the flash of a breastplate—a guard. A Spaniard to whom one great single ruby might be prize enough to . . .

She was tugged and pushed into a long, narrow room tiled in a swath of blue like a Barbados bay, blue like . . . Miranda sagged for a moment among her escort. The women buoyed her up and rushed her to—not the oblong of waist-high pool that centered the room—but to a European brass hip-bath near a colonnade of silk-swathed arches.

Chattering, giggling, the women disrobed her. Then Rihana opened a small mosaic box and streamed a column of blue powder into the bathwater.

Together, their hands insistent on her arms, her waist, her hips, the women guided Miranda into the bath. The water warmed her foot and leg, warmed almost to stinging—the women pulled, pushed, laughed, splashed and immersed Miranda to her shoulders.

A fire like a thousand Barbados fire ants rinsed her in one agonizing wave. Her screams joined the women's gay shrieks as their dark eyes twinkled mercilessly above her. Miranda struggled to rise, but their eyes laughed and their wiry brown arms held her down. Miranda clenched her teeth, half-mad with agony, and rose in one huge splash, driving the women away shrieking as water drops soaked their robes.

The burning was so fierce that she leapt from the bath to the tiled floor, where she whirled like a thousand dervishes. The women's faces had fallen finally. Even Zarifa for once stood silent, a worried frown carving itself into her already well-lined face.

Two sharp claps echoed off the tiles. All noise, all motion stopped. The cocoa-colored faces around Miranda turned white, as if someone had poured a quantity of cream into them. She looked across the pool toward the room's other end and then even she stopped her dancing.

He stood there, a figure carved of tiger's-eye and as immobile. A white turban surmounted his finely set features; his bare chest and arms reflected high gold polish in the soft daylight. Full trousers of some rich stuff billowed from his hips to his ankles, an ornamental ivory-handled dagger hung from his glittering belt. Miranda's eyes automatically dropped to the apparition's feet. This time they were not bare and dusty, but slippered in embroidered Moroccan leather.

For a long moment all present regarded one another as if statue-spelled. Then the man, boy, figure moved toward the women huddled around the gleaming tub. He had barely taken a step when Miranda, her gaze still riveted to his impassive face, caught a muslin length to her water-dewed body.

A short sharp giggle escaped Fatma, instantly stilled by a.hiss from Zarifa. The figure advanced, staring steadily into Miranda's unwavering eyes. He fanned his fingers sharply behind him. The Arab women rustled past like leaves buffeted across a courtyard, leaving only swaying fabric as testimony that they had ever been there.

Miranda began shivering, something stinging still whipping the edges of her senses. This was he! The boy from the *Salamander*, the bound prisoner who had exchanged a glance with her once before, on a deck as hot and glaring as this place was cool and hidden.

He advanced until he stood before her, and she had to raise her eyes to continue meeting his. After a long moment, his eyes abruptly dropped—how dark they were, how hidden. He trailed his fingers in the now-calm bathwater, then shook them free an instant later, scattering diamond drops across the air.

Frowning, he hastened Miranda to the quiescent pool. At its staired lip he paused and reached for the muslin drapery clutched to her breasts. Her hands tightened on it. His eyes willed her to relinquish it. Hers defied him, but her color rose until her cheeks felt burnished to a faint red. His expression flowed into disbelief, then into an empty kind of anger that chilled her into shivering again.

He took her hand and, walking alongside the pool edge, escorted her down into the water like the veriest English gentleman leading his lady to a dance. She watched him hypnotically, the muslin slowly dampening on her body like a veil, until she was hip-deep in water which lapped at her like a nagging memory, lapped at her like his gentle dark eyes that never left her face though she was as naked as a wish is to the one who makes it.

He dipped a long-throated ewer into the blue pool and poured its burden over her head, rinsing away the last of the burning. Miranda's eyes closed under the ribbons of water that threaded across her face, down her breasts. Again and again the ewer dipped and rose and tilted to soothe her. When the cool deluge ended, she opened her eyes and watched him through the water weighing on her lashes.

He regarded her gravely and once again led her formally from the pool. Fetching a length of thick cloth, he cloaked her shoulders. Then he turned. And left. Even when the last curtain had trembled shut behind him, something of him lingered, as if his mute presence had been etched on air.

Miranda caught the cloth about her and shivered again. The waters of the pool, the hip-bath, lay mirror-smooth; save for the overturned mosaic box trailing blue powder, no sign showed that anyone, that he, had been there.

A tentative footslap or two, and then Rihana, Shahar, Fatma were peering around a far pillar. They padded over, their dark eyes wonder-rounded but their veils fluttering secretly about their mouths. They escorted Miranda back across the shadow-bathed courtyard to the sleeping quarters, where they unwrapped her and their giggles equally as rapidly, kneeling to dry and dress her and whispering all the while.

"Wait," Miranda implored as they gathered to take flight.

The brown eyes took merry measure of each other, then as a body, the trio descended on Miranda again.

"Ibrahim," announced Fatma, answering Miranda's unasked question, her cheeks plumping into creases around her eyes. "Only Ibrahim."

"*Only* Ibrahim!" Rihana collapsed in gusts of laughter upon the cushions, until Shahar pulled her up to dignity again. "Ibrahim is not 'only' anything—"

"This Ibrahim, who is he?" interrupted Miranda. "I saw him on the ship. I should have known he was bound here, but—"

"Ah, here." Even serious Shahar had edged her voice with laughter. "Yes, here. Like you. Only not like you."

"Oh, white one," lamented Rihana gaily, "if you could have but seen yourself, clutching to that cloth. Before Ibrahim!" She smothered herself against a length of paisley pillow, unable to say more.

"We regret that we burned you," Shahar explained. "We had not been called upon to bleach anyone before and knew not the proportion. Rihana did it—"

"Not I! I would not hurt her—"

"Zarifa must go and wait upon *him* for punishment. I dare not imagine what he will do. What think you, Fatma?"

"Twenty strokes across the sole of the foot," guessed Fatma authoritatively.

"Ooooh, she will not be able to chase us for a week," Rihana predicted, sitting up, her dark face undertoned with laughter's natural rouge. "*Inglesa*, do you not see how amusing it is? You, standing there as if, as if—he is nothing, do you see, this Ibrahim. *Nada*."

Nada. Miranda mentally rolled the word around to view it differently and found only one angle to it.

"Nothing? He was there, Rihana. He—how can you say he is nothing?"

"He is chief eunuch—here to keep us from wandering, to keep any wandering guards from us." Giggles overtook Shahar's sober explanation.

Rihana leaned forward, planted her chin on Miranda's shoulder and poured the tale into Miranda's ear.

"He came, oh, many months ago. He was beautiful, that one, as now. Even Shahar, who was as happy as the camp milk-cow with this Spanish-nunnery life, even she used to peek her long nose round the draperies to see him."

Shahar struck admonishingly at Rihana's knee but bowed her head to a blush. The women settled back on their heels as Rihana drew up her knees and clasped them while her voice softly continued.

"Seven times the don would have him. Always he was back, this Ibrahim. We saw him after, even sicker than you. *Aaaaiii*, it became a crime to cure him and send him back again. He must have resisted still, for the drug came in stronger doses. He almost died, I think."

The other women nodded their sober, veiled heads.

"Then the other white one, like you—he was most unhappy. He paced the halls at night and we, who had never seen him, could hear him stalking like some hyena of the desert."

Miranda shuddered, not at the eerie image Rihana painted, but at the certainty that it was her brother who had prowled the corridors, waiting out his rejection, dreaming not of freedom but of reinstatement. These women must think all northern Europeans looked alike; they accepted her resemblance to "the other" without a thought that they might be blood kin. So Harry had paced and burned. Even then he was beyond her, had she but known it.

"Do not cry, *inglesa*, I have not struck to the heart of my story."

As lengthening courtyard shadows stole into the room, the women huddled closer. Fatma slipped away to fetch a glowing oil lamp, which she set at the center of their circle.

"The last time, I know not what happened," Rihana continued. "Perhaps the white one urged the don to it, but our lord grew furious beyond the lure of flesh. He called his guard, who took Ibrahim and made him what he is now. Nothing. Eunuch. They took his tongue as well. Zarifa said the don wanted to wrest away all the instruments of love, so that none would feast where he had failed."

"Eunuch? Is this as when they geld a bull they wish to keep from fighting with others? On Barbados—"

"He bled. Oh, how he bled, did not we tend him? The drug was still upon him or this time he would have truly perished. Perhaps you are not aware of the harem eunuch; such a one, whose manhood has been rooted out, is set to guard the women as an insult, as we are the least in the house. I think this Ibrahim was made to lie with women only, as I think the don discovered. Now Ibrahim can only lie with whatever self remains, and he must watch us, see us go about our duties. It is a punishment complete upon both body and soul. The don has a facility for that."

"Oh, but, Rihana, tell her, tell her what the don did," Fatma urged. "She is not one of us, she does not know. Besides, I do not think that he had the soldiers *cut* out Ibrahim's tongue. I believe it was pulled out by the root with pincers—"

Miranda hid her face in her hands while hot-tempered Rihana defended her version of the tale.

"No, silly chicken. Cut. As with the other. This is how you make the eunuch, white one, you take not the stem but the root below—I know not the word in this language. This makes a man not a man."

"But sometimes . . ." Fatma's voice was as thin and wavery as she was plump. "Sometimes, something is left. Then the harem eunuch can still . . . salute the women in a certain fashion which . . . suffices, and none the wiser or worse for it." Fatma subsided into giggles as Miranda's brows met in puzzlement.

"This is not the case with Ibrahim," Rihana pronounced.

"How do you know, Rihana?" Shahar's voice was a well-aimed needle.

Rihana's veils tossed until Miranda glimpsed well-set chin.

"I know," she answered levelly, bringing flashing eyes of obsidian back to Miranda's face. "So, you see, we may pity him. We may even fear him, for who but he wields the rod and whip when we are found wanting? But we do not shield ourselves from him. He is nothing, and has been so ever since the night they brought him bleeding to us. He knows he is nothing, for since then a shell has walked like a—a piece of animated humanity. But he is no man. Do not make yourself ridiculous before him, and us, by thinking him so. He is nothing."

Miranda watched the oil lamp flicker at her feet. She hated knowing that she had shared a ship with this doomed creature—what to call him, consider him? As nothing, so they said. No matter how anguished Harry's willing life with the don made her feel, from that moment Miranda knew a shamed relief that it had not been Harry whom the don had carved the soul from.

That night proved to be the Arab women's last opportunity for confidences on any subject. The next day, Zarifa was limping among them while Fatma triumphantly mouthed "Twenty" behind her slightly hunched back. Miranda pitied the seamed old harem nursemaid and turned only amiable looks upon her. Her kindness was wasted on a nature fermented to vinegar.

Zarifa's sour expression brooked no question when she herded Miranda back across the courtyard to the pool the next afternoon. Zarifa's feet skittered gingerly across the sun-warmed paths and Miranda followed, a veil of worry settling over her.

The room was still cool and dim; within it was her—nothing—in attendance. Miranda cast one pleading glance to Zarifa at the curtain. Gone, and only sunlight lancing off the dazzling white walls outside. Miranda tiptoed into the room, as if her own feet had been reproved instead of her escort's.

Ibrahim waited by the brass hip-bath so impassively she finally approached. She feared him now, not as harem disciplinarian, but because he was a black, yawning mystery, something meant to be skirted, like a pit, like the Iron Maiden.

Ibrahim seemed placidly unaware of the horror he raised in Miranda's wary eyes. She came to stand before him because she had no alternative. He took her hand and trailed it in the bathwater. Beyond an invigorating effervescence, no burning sensation. He soaked a muslin strip in the solution and held it before her face like a veil.

She stared across the filmy bridge between them, her green eyes silver-pale in the uncertain light. His eyes were as intent as ever: the bright, unbroken gaze of a hawk just landed on a foreign stretch of rock. That was the look he had named her with three lifetimes ago on the deck of the *Salamander*.

Miranda could not speak; to try would have snapped something that had stretched between them since their first meeting months before. They were balanced somehow, on a violently tipping world. Should either one shift wrongly, they could both be dashed to pieces. Pieces. Was not that what he was now, only pieces? Pieces of a nothing. He is nothing.

Ibrahim's fingers came up in a vee, like a ritual gesture, and pulled Miranda's eyelids shut. Then the cloth webbed her face. Her eyes, mouth, would have fluttered open but Ibrahim's flat palms pushed firmly on her shoulders. Wait, they said as eloquently as any language. She stood there—bewildered, blind, wondering if this was how tonguelessness felt. How nothing began.

After a long silent while, the cloth peeled away and Miranda opened her eyes. Ibrahim's hand made a sudden supple gesture to her midriff. His dark eyes were waiting pits of inexpressiveness. She realized then that he meant her to disrobe; a dim resistance rose with her color.

Nothing, he was nothing. She made fools of both herself and, and—it.

Miranda unclasped the robe. It slithered floorward and she kept her eyes upon it. Ibrahim's hand extended once again. She put her own into it and he helped her enter the bath. She sank beneath the water to her throat, grateful as if it were a garment. She swiftly eyed her attendant; he was busy setting away the mosaic box, not watching her at all.

Nothing, he is nothing. Beneath those strangely figured trousers, behind those well-carved lips there is nothing, only nothing. A well-carved nothing. Her heart began to beat so insistently beneath the water that she wondered that it did not create a small betraying whirlpool.

His well-shaped back and shoulders were turned away, he was a marvelous likeness of a man for being nothing . . . Then he turned and plucked her hand from the brass rim it clutched.

He brought a large yellow sponge to the water, sprinkled blue powder across it and circled it across her hand. Miranda noticed the faint band of darker color that separated her hand from arm. She had indeed been slightly sun-bronzed, her face and hands were not perfectly milky, that was why they had burned her, and now bleached her, in the bathwater. Ibrahim was simply carrying out the don's prescription—himself, because the women had nearly damaged her. And the don's property—with certain notable exceptions, among them the figure before her—could not be damaged.

A gasp of understanding parted Miranda's tense lips. This outré attention, this closeting with some pathetic remnant of the don's previous experiments, was only the preparation of which he had spoken!

Of course Ibrahim was nothing. He was a slave—worse. He was as impersonal a servant to her and to the don's perverse wishes as the Iron Maiden herself.

Chapter Twenty-three

Sir Charles Steele had the face of an elderly spaniel: a fine, faded elegance drooping slightly at the muzzle. His gilded curls, age-polished to a silver patina, fell to his shoulders, forming a kind of halo. Yet the pale blue eyes set into this aristocratic aura were as sharp as sixty summers of survival in a turbulent century could make them.

"By Harry," he vowed, seizing his more massive son by the arms of his royal-blue jacket, "I feared that we would never pry you loose from those cursed Spaniards." Spaniels are a watery breed, and liquid glazed Sir Charles's eyes for the blinking of a lash. "How are you, Christopher?"

His son looked uncomfortable, made so more by surprise at how his father had yellowed and wrinkled in the last months than by his own memories.

"Right enough. And here at Ravenscroft?" Kit's eyes took inventory of the high-ceilinged Tudor house—the great fireplace looming behind his father's narrow shoulder, the heavy carved furnishings his mother had brought with her as a bride.

Sir Charles sighed, letting his hands drop while Kit studied the dappling of liver spots across them. "Right enough, Chris, and wrong enough. 'Tis why I had the Devil's trouble cutting you free of the galleys. I've spent half my time in the ministry halls. I must have sent a hundred packets to the ambassador in Seville. Sit down, boy, you're fresh from the galleys and I'm forgetting."

"I've done sitting enough, thank you, Father."

Kit's irony brought a curve to his father's lips. Christopher was a second son and, unlike most of the breed, not a scapegrace at all. In fact, he was first in his father's affections. For Ben, firstborn and heir to the rolling estates called Ravenscroft, had been reared to be sober, earnest, with a fine head for figures and no head for wine. He had married a girl as stolid and bovine as himself and they promised to found a line of little Steeles that should extend well into the next century.

But Christopher. Christopher was lazy and likable and ambitious and headstrong and clever and impulsive by turn. Of all the Steele sons—there were others at Cambridge, Oxford, and one still in skirts—Chris was the one Sir Charles most hated to imagine sitting the rowing deck of a Spanish galley. And the only one he could see surviving it.

Kit had wandered to the mullioned window, open on a balmy summer day and a cultured expanse of lawn trimmed with the windblown blossoms of women's skirts. He watched them billow on the even green. His only sister, Marjory, just sixteen, playing bowls—he could see the banner of Steele-blond curls trailing her. Then he spied a flash of auburn locks above an emerald gown, his cousin—

"Yes, it's Roxanne," said his father behind him. When Kit turned, surprised, at his prescience, the older man smiled. "We Steeles have a like eye, lad. I'm glad the Spanish haven't dimmed that."

The double doors creaked abruptly open behind them and then the room was silent.

"Katharine." Sir Charles wheeled. "We were about to—"

"Of course you were." The small woman standing there was as still as a startled faun. Her youthful, rosy face was framed by a partially upstanding lace collar. Her hair was as white as the chalky uplands of Dorset, and her eyes bluer than the waters off Weymouth.

"Kit," was all that she said, extending imperious hands, but the dainty fingers trembled until his own enfolded them. She looked at him for one long moment, then withdrew her hands. "Thinner," she noted, shaking her snowy head.

"—and threadbare," complained a girlish voice at the door. Marjory Steele was flushed with conquering three tiers of stairs after word of Kit's arrival had trickled to the lawn. She paused on the threshold like a mischievous pup contemplating a bound at the returning master, then launched herself.

Kit laughed and swung her into the air as he used to, the red ribbons on her shoes fluttering against a white circle of flying petticoats.

"Pity me, Marjoram," he begged shortly, "you've obviously not curtailed your country appetite while I've been away to the wars ... or have you been playing lady and sitting still and growing fat?"

Marjory stamped her fashionable foot as soon as he let her touch ground again. "At least *I* haven't let myself go to seed," she answered, plucking at his borrowed blue sleeve. "Where on earth did you unearth that jacket?"

"At least 'tis of a human origin. I'd vouchsafe that your gown was fashioned nowhere on *terra firma* at all," Kit retorted, eyeing the flat stomacher and reams of silver lace that fountained from her sleeves and shoulders, a pang beneath his pleasantry. The little sister he had left had become a woman, albeit a young and saucy one.

Marjory read his look, for she leaned up to give him a quick kiss. Kit realized again what it was to walk an open, free land, where he was not treading the rim of espionage or sailing uncertain waters. A new stillness in the doorway caught his overwhelmed attention and held it.

"Cousin Roxanne." He advanced belatedly on the vision poised there in perfect composure, one embroidered glove drooping gracefully from her gloved left hand. She extended her bare hand like a white satin streamer from her beribboned sleeve, and he saluted it with the expected bow and kiss.

Roxanne had been a beauty before he left; now she was a sovereign beauty. Marjory's age in years, but never in yearning, she was the rose whose thorns grow stronger with the years so that at her peak she is as able to wound as to dazzle. Kit knew all that; he had been born knowing his cousin Roxanne's toxicity, he sometimes thought. That did not mean that he had developed an antidote to it.

Like his family, like England even, everything was new to eyes recently removed from the shadow of the galley. And, perhaps, he was new to Roxanne's eyes, the odd dark yellow eyes occasionally bestowed on redheads.

Her hand slid slowly from his. She entered the room as if bestowing a blessing. Kit didn't retreat before her progress. Her amber eyes flashed up at him once from under stiff red lashes. Head bent, she circled demurely around him, presenting the creamy nape of her neck for his inspection.

Kit grinned; she'd grown bolder as well as more beautiful. Her coquetries, inborn at birth, had never promised as particularly as they did now.

"Welcome back, cousin," she whispered, passing him to sit upon a clumsy armchair that made her look like Venetian glass balanced upon firewood.

"Where's wee Charlie?" Kit asked then, turning to the family portrait assembled behind him.

They broke their fond ranks at mention of the youngest, the most beloved of the Steeles. Katharine's final baby—a saucer-eyed child with a fat expression and an unclouded face. Sir Charles's lids fluttered across his bland eyes, Marjory's apples fell from her cheeks and her arm dropped from her mother's elbow.

"Fever," said Katharine flatly, standing alone between the passive props on either side. "The fever."

Christopher Steele felt the room reel like the deck of a ship slipping into a trough of wave. His mother's words stung more sharply than Spanish leather, and the blow itself was a mere flick compared to the gnaw such news would have on the spirit.

Fever. He had seen fevers in the *Gato de Nueve*'s belly. Muffin raving for biscuits, Carter burning until he was a dried-out thing they trundled away in a hopsack. He himself had felt the fever's hot heavy hand and the chill admonishment it sent along after. At some time during that season in hell, little Charlie's eyes had burned bright blue, too, and had gone out. Kit remembered the miscarriage that had separated him from Ben. Another Steele who would forever be a mystery, save that wee Charlie had possessed plump pale hands that dropped buttons and other small trinkets, a way of gamboling with the family hounds that made every passerby pause to smile ... Perhaps England was not so much safer, so much more secure, after all.

"Leave us, you women," said Sir Charles, mock-gruff.

They scattered, recognizing the necessity for a new coming together. They had mourned the child and let the earth have him. A new mourner on the scene raked up the little grave and exposed it to eyes that wanted to see only greensward now, only growing.

Kit abstractly nodded the women out. Roxanne was last. As his eyes turned from her to his father, they paused in a slat of mirror to gauge how deeply the inelegant jacket had erred. Passable flashed through his mind before he shook his head, throwing off vanity and melancholy with one toss.

"Perhaps you're right, Father," Kit began formally, following Sir Charles to the tray of decanters flushed by a red liquor.

Without thinking, he cupped his hands around the engraved crystal bowl of one, as if seeking warmth.

"Right? 'Pon my soul, you begin to make me feel old, Chris. About what does my son say I'm right?"

"I'll go no more a-roving. I'm three and twenty. 'Tis time I discovered what I wanted in this world rather than what's beyond the next bay."

"If you don't know, you're not my son." Sir Charles hoisted a goblet and nodded in the direction of the silken exit of Roxanne Wexford.

His son laughed shortly. "Wanting and being willing to ride escort to what one wants are two different things. And if you're not old enough to know that, you're not my father."

"She *is* a beauty, Chris; even your mother couldn't quite touch her at the same age, and Katharine was a handsome girl. Still is, though the last years ... and Charlie. The Warringtons always went white-haired prematurely, though, mayhap why all the men died off and Kate got the estate. You could run Warring Hall if you wished."

The pale blue sliver of question that slid to Kit's face came away unencouraged.

"I'm not a farmer, Father!" Kit said tightly. The subject was an old and sore one. "There are many things I would be; soil-tiller is not one."

"Nay, did I ever say you were? You always lusted for the movable things, not for land. 'Tis why you'd be a fool to let that girl escape you. She'd be a handful, but a woman who wasn't would bore you, Chris, just as Ravenscroft and we Steeles have bored you—oh, don't protest. I'd not know if the same itch hadn't stung me all through my younger days. Now, take Roxanne: the family wants her wed. I can settle Warring Hall upon you to content the Wexfords with a second son. But take her or leave her, till Warring Hall or plow it under, I'm damn glad you're back! My last dispatch must have set the Spanish ambassador quivering in his sable stockings."

Kit eyed his father with the glass halfway to his lips. "They didn't give me leave to go, you know. A Spanish galley rides Gravesend this day that's proof of that."

"Not freed? Then how did you—?"

"English ship, English sailors and . . . English backing. Came to fetch us most elegantly and then we brought the *Gato de Nueve* to England as an exhibit of a kind of Spanish steel seldom seen outside a galley belly—chains."

Sir Charles's face faded into contemplation. He cradled his glass between his hands and paced the room. "Then she did it, as she said—"

"She? Who?"

"Why, that pale girl, dressed sober as a Puritan with a face whiter than her collar. Looked me up in London. 'Tis how I knew, for certain, what had gone wrong with your last voyage, the one of which you wouldn't speak, though there have been many of those."

"When did she come to you? What did she tell you?"

"Why, Kit! Does it matter? Two months past. She said your ship had been taken and the men put into the galleys, that she was telling what families she could find from the crew listing. She said that it was her business and she would have them all back. I didn't believe her. Why believe a reed of a girl when the Admiralty and the ambassadors can't do anything? So she did it, after all! Tell me who she is, where is she from, what people?"

Kit frowned until his bleached brows lost themselves in a parallel furrow between his nose. The very questions his father now posed had picked at his imagination like crows at carrion on the voyage home.

Carrion. That thought became a vision of a ship's boat broken upon the Cádiz shore . . . of something limp and white being washed, washed softly by pale sea foam. No. A better image, more like: a small, set face with bared teeth under the reeking red lantern light of a Cádiz bottlehouse. Fire and water, they were her people, and they would see her through. He looked into his father's waiting expression and shrugged as carelessly as he could.

"I know naught of her, save that she brings more trouble than joy as her baggage. Hathaway's the name. I understood the family to have some wealth. But Puritans—I had not thought she sprung from that ilk."

"Whatever her ilk, she did the Steeles a true service if she cut you adrift again, Chris! If I'm in London, I'll thank her."

"She won't be the Hathaway you'd find there now, I fear," Kit answered shortly, remembering the pale, sullen face that had danced before him like a moth in the *Gato* cabin. Harry would be taking his own back at this very moment, while she—

Kit wheeled to the window, suddenly finding the Great Hall as confining as a ship's cabin. Green lawn unrolled before him like a magic carpet from an Oriental tale. And there—a bright, glistening spot of darker green on the terrace, the emerald gown of his cousin Roxanne.

That one would take work to win—silk jackets to pass court inspection, floral offerings and words as overblown. Despite his family standing and Warring Hall thrown like a bone to her family, he would have to woo the glittering Roxanne as a sail woos the winds. But he could have her; he knew it in the way she had teased past him, bowing her head and bending her heart not an inch. She moved below—a distant, aloof leaf billowing across Ravenscroft lawn. Now was the season to pin her, to cup her in his hands, or risk her blowing down the heath to another collector.

"You'll stay, then?" Sir Charles's soft inquiry demanded an affirmative.

Kit Steele let the heavy brocade drapery drop into place and faced the familiar room.

"No. I'll take a Mediterranean commission next."

"What? Why the sudden change?"

"War debts, Father. I have been reminded of some war debts I must repay." He glanced toward the lawns again and sighed. "See if you can hold off the Wexfords. I should return within two months."

" 'Tis not the Wexfords that need holding off," his father said significantly. "When will you leave?"

"Sooner sent, faster returned."

Steele strode heedlessly through Ravenscroft halls after leaving his father, his spurs jangling. Damn her. Stubborn. He had said so on the *Salamander*, as they had said earlier on Barbados, evidently. Well, he was stubborn as well. He wouldn't have her a question mark forever on his conscience, no matter what the cost.

And if the cost were Roxanne Wexford . . . well, he guessed that men had paid more for dream's ease. But not many.

Chapter Twenty-four

"*O*h, you are so comical, white one; patched, like a goat at shedding season."

Rihana's dark fingers brushed Miranda's cheek, then held a polished circle of brass up to her face. A mottled cream and tan visage greeted Miranda, with the skin flaking off in dark patches.

"The baths must be working," agreed Fatma, her face rising over Miranda's shoulder like a plump brown moon in the mirror. "Else the sight of Ibrahim turns you pale and dark at the same time."

Miranda watched a delicate pink suffuse her particolored cheeks and abruptly lowered the mirror.

"She dislikes talking of him, cannot you silly teases see that?" chided Shahar.

True enough. Although Miranda now presented herself daily for Ibrahim's attentions, she still went nakedly before him as delicately as a fawn. The Arab women would have screeched with laughter if they knew how much she wished for a veil between his eyes and her body.

Nothing. He is nothing.

"When she is as pale as goat's milk, we will see no more of her," announced Rihana. "I, for one, will be sorry. I fear the time comes swiftly." She caught Miranda's hands to pull her to her feet. "Zarifa has come cackling at us to teach you the Rishi."

"The Rishi, not really, Rihana! Then she is destined for a chieftain."

Miranda's head lifted defiantly. "What is this Rishi? Another kind of dish with which you ply me? I tire of this fattening. Soon I will not even fit into the don's Iron Maiden, and what will he hold over my head then?"

The women's faces froze. If Miranda did not like to hear of Ibrahim, they did not care to be reminded of the iron to be mined deep in the don's chambers below.

"The Rishi," Rihana explained, "is nothing to eat, my fine *plump* white goose, and you only now begin to look like a female. Sitting upon pillows suits European women; else you would walk off all your charms and what man would care to pillow himself upon you then?"

Shahar's nimble fingers were fanning through Miranda's hair, expertly twisting it into myriad yellow satin braids.

"I am not your lapdog, ladies, to be pampered, fed, groomed—"

"Are you not?" challenged Rihana. "Remember, it is upon our heads—"

"—or feet," interjected Shahar grimly.

"—if you are not properly prepared. So come. Fatma, fetch the drums and I will teach our English one to fetch more than drums."

Rihana pulled Miranda to the middle of the carpet. The other women settled on crossed legs along one wall, small shallow drums held shoulder-high and their hands poised over the red-patterned ends.

"The Hajir," ordered Rihana. Fatma and Shahar began beating the small drums as Rihana's upper body slithered into sudden motion, her almond-colored face tossing on her slender neck until flying hair and face veil created a tempest around her intent features.

"You see, the Rishi is a dance. We merely give you your own music." Rihana paused to affix golden bells to the ends of Miranda's newly plaited hair. "The toes we worry about later, when you are nimble," she promised.

Miranda did not progress to bells on her toes that afternoon, nor the next. The pulsing, rapid movements that Rihana wore like a second skin she chose to slough came awkwardly to Miranda. She twitched her shoulders and wiggled with a will until her braids whipped her face into a blond blur before the Arab women's eyes. But—

"It's useless," Rihana said finally, settling back on her heels. "You have no heart for this."

"No heart!" Fatma giggled merrily. "Too much heart. She looks like one on the verge of the falling sickness."

"You can jest, Fatma. No one would care to see your rolls of suet in motion—but Zarifa expects her to dance for the don's musicians shortly, to perform The Other. And if she can't do the Rishi, how can she do The Other?"

No answer came to smooth Rihana's furrowed brow.

"I'm late," Miranda said roughly, casting away the bells in an inharmonious jangle. For once she was happy to retreat to the pool and voiceless, unquestioning Ibrahim.

"Oh, it is always late for Ibrahim," intoned Rihana, amusement rather than worry in her dark eyes again.

Miranda rushed away without answer to join Ibrahim in the shadowed room across the courtyard. The sight of flying plaits as she entered the chamber surprised him.

He held one up for silent perusal. Miranda's fingers froze on her sash. His dark eyes considered the braid, then her face. If there had been any question in them, it was gone by the time he glanced at her.

Miranda always found Ibrahim hard to regard. Her eyes were ever tempted to tread the fine-carved bridge of his nose, the proud highroad of his etched cheekbones, the long firm jawline leading . . . His face resembled some wind-carved desert scene, a well-drawn map leading always to the delicate channel between his nose and—mouth. The mouth fascinated her. Not merely for its well-formed beauty—faint, faint purple throbbing beneath the dusky color. No, it was a gate. To something hidden behind. To something as black and empty as the Iron Maiden's endless embrace. She always fancied that one day those immobile lips would move, part, reveal . . .

Her eyes dropped quickly to his bare shoulder, as they always did when tempted to explore his face. The shoulder was neutral ground, with the muscle starting to swell away from it like a golden sand dune and a collarbone cutting horizontal across it. It had shape and substance, Ibrahim's shoulder. She could contemplate it while her fingers unfastened the sash and the robe slipped past her like drifting sand.

She could study it long enough to keep her eyes from wandering downward, past the bronze of chest that tapered to a gilded heavy belt, past the ivory-handled dagger at his hip, its shaft as smoothly molded as its owner's body, down to the other mystery, the other cavern in his being. Two blinding mutilations that forbade speculation. But that, the murder of his masculinity, was not the worst thing for her. From what little she had seen, felt, Miranda did not see much to mourn in its passing. It meant nothing to her.

No, always her eyes returned to his mouth. In secret when he tended her, his head turned away, she meditated on its full, soft profile, on how nearly his lips seemed ready to separate from each other, to curve and part . . . and speak. And never did. To never speak, to never say who he was. To never smile for fear it should send everyone shrieking from the sight of him, the silence of him ...

She had dallied too long at her sash; his elegant fingers were unknotting it. She stepped away even as the knot gave, and moved rapidly into the hip-bath, its warmth rippling up to her neck. Ibrahim leaned forward to drop the bleaching cloth across her face. She closed her eyes to it, glad that she would not have to look at him.

When he stripped the veil away and handed her from the bath, his face was as impassive as ever, and her eyes clung to his shoulder and the muscles sliding under it. Then her foot slipped, came hard against brass. Her fingers dug into the shoulder and he held her up, her wet flesh close to the dry desert expanse of his chest.

She would have pulled away, but their eyes had met during the flurry of her misstep. And to look away would have meant an inevitable journey downward to his terrifying mouth. Miranda kept her eyes fastened to his, even when she felt his shoulders shift beneath her hands and he had picked her up and was walking smoothly to the long blue plunge of pool that lay waiting for them.

Ibrahim paused at the pool's lip, his eyes (mouth) never changing expression. Then he waded slowly into the water, still carrying her until the blue lapped all the way up to his thighs, his hips, his— He lowered her slowly to her feet, the cool water climbing her limbs in agonizing inches of sensation.

He picked up the poolside ewer and began dipping water that ran in rivulets down her hair and face. He still stood as closely as when he had first put her down; the water ran between them both, over them both, like a mutual caress. The sponge with which he usually and impersonally rinsed her was coursing softly down her limbs, breasts, hips, thighs. Soft and rough at the same time, it trickled water and sensation down her body.

He was a statue, some marble fancy constructed to stand forever in a pool, a fountain only. His eyes, his mouth were unmoving. She watched them steadily and they never moved. She never moved. And still the sponge made its circumnavigating exploration of her dimensions. She could have said something, stopped it. One word. Merely to part her lips. But she couldn't. To speak would have been a resounding inequity, would have broken something fragile.

His eyes were pits as black as any other cavern in him. Tender, dark, hopeless, yearning pits that drew her down into them as inexorably as the Iron Maiden had drawn Miranda to herself for a brief embrace.

He is making love to me, Miranda realized dimly. This nothing, this emptiness called Ibrahim. He is nothing. And Nothing was lapping at her senses, touching, lingering. Had any onlooker passed by, she would have seen only the eunuch Ibrahim faithfully, mindlessly washing the don's latest acquisition with a fat yellow Mediterranean sponge. And those watching eyes would have seen as little of the truth as the Arab youth's tongue could tell.

At last Miranda backed away, her eyes never breaking from Ibrahim's. He immediately escorted her from the pool, the water dripping off his trousers to the hard tiled floor. He cloaked her and let her flee back to the harem. Back to Rihana, Shahar and Fatma, who laughed and said that Ibrahim was nothing.

The baths stopped.

Zarifa caught Miranda's narrow but stubbornly set chin in a leathery hand the next morning and pronounced the bleaching complete. Miranda's heart pounded guiltily within her figured robe. Had someone seen, did anybody know? Know what? Even she did not know quite . . . what.

Now they would have her concentrate on the dancing. She hated making herself into a spectacle for some passive watcher, though she never saw anyone beyond the women. The don's Arab musicians, their beating drums and whining music-makers, hid behind a heavily draped alcove, unworthy of watching his prize perform.

The don never came to see her; indeed, there was naught to see. Miranda restlessly mimed the motion for Rihana's sake. They were well embarked upon The Other of which the Arab girl had prattled so mysteriously, this mystery dance that required Miranda to weave her arms and body in an unflagging sinuous circle, to toss her plaited hair until it whipped her shoulders and to circle her resistant hips in an endless motion.

"You are trouble incarnate, you most stubborn of she-camels," Rihana burst out one day, her bare foot stamping the floor until she hurt herself more than she caught Miranda's attention. "Look you!" Rihana fiercely pushed Miranda to the floor until they sat on their ankles. "And go, you two!"

Shahar and Fatma scurried off, the ghost of Zarifa whipping at their quivering robes.

"Listen, white one," began Rihana softly. "This is not a dance for graven images, your Christian statues. It is for the woman to give to the man. It is for your new master."

"And you wonder why I cannot master it when I am to be mastered by it? Rihana, you don't know what it is to be sold, to be—" Miranda's accusations stopped short.

"Yes, I know. Believe me, foolish one, to be sold as prize to some powerful chieftain, to serve his senses, is far the better lot than to wilt of boredom in a manless harem. The road on which you will soon pass from here can be paved with silk. Do you not think a man who has paid well for you will not pamper you, please you?" Rihana shook Miranda's bare shoulders.

"I cannot dance for anyone, Rihana. I cannot dance at all."

"Yes, you can. This is a dance of seduction. There is only the one reason for it. Why else you think the don demands you learn it?"

"Perhaps I can be bought, but I cannot be made to caper for the privilege," Miranda answered stubbornly.

"Look at me, white one, and learn. The way you are bound is hard; you must soften every step of it. This dance can melt the world for you. But you are like rock, you will not bend to anything but wind or water, and we have not time enough to wear you away by such methods."

Rihana bit hard upon her pearly thumbnail. "Listen. Is there not anyone, any man, of whom you can think while you dance, whose flesh has sung upon yours?"

Miranda's eyes were indignant lances perfectly aimed. "I have encountered no man but those who played me out of tune and falsely. This approach will not solve your dilemma, Rihana. Would you have me conjure the don to dance to?"

Rihana shrugged and rose, an Arab expletive curling her lips. "Then we try again, white one. And again. You must learn something from repeating it."

Miranda's failure became the harem talk. Fatma's and Shahar's heads were ever bowed together. Zarifa's dour face only wrinkled more. The flaw became so obvious that Miranda desperately applied herself to the task, fearful her inadequacy would draw the don and sterner methods.

Her figure in the center of the harem floor was a vision of what men would call seductive. Miranda's taut harem bodice, her hip-slung dancing skirt, fulfilled every expectation that a waiting master could wish. She swayed herself from one end of the carpet to the other, accomplished the most arduous bends and contortions with a fencer's grace. And still the spectacle was ugly, soulless, hopeless.

Despite herself, the music began to ring pleasantly in her ears. She thought of Barbados, of some far pacific place where only palm trees swayed, where breezes and not silk caressed her, where she could be herself and free. These thoughts became the visual melody of her movements. Merely blue, bay-blue, washing against her, swaying her softly into the surf. Her homesick eyes tinted the violet tenting above her azure, and made it ruffle in some Indies breeze. When her eyes finally slipped floorward again, they were looking for a stretch of sand, perhaps, a green fan of foliage . . .

There, the lush green curtains across the room, parting like leaves waving in the wind, like lips, and behind it—Miranda's imagined world suddenly supported life: a pair of living dark brown eyes. Her breath stopped, then abandoned her. Ibrahim. Ibrahim watching from some cryptic turning in her secret jungle.

Her cheeks were suddenly fire-rinsed, her feet stumbled and stopped. She paused, and found the distant eyes still regarding her. Like an animal's. Wary. Watching. Why?

Rihana clapped sharply from the sidelines. "Again."

Miranda picked up her motion from where she had dropped it. The swaying started at her feet and circled upward. Watching. He, who had seen her bare, must watch her draped in ludicrousness. No. Her neck extended and then her hips began to swivel more subtly, skillfully, toward the pale green curtain. If she could lure him forward, this watching creature of the wild, could make him step toward her tame and unafraid—her world would then be real, she could walk, sway herself right into it. Into blue and green. And brown.

Miranda's moving arms embraced the richness of her world to caress more air, rock gently in more water. And if her eyes ever fastened on anything, it was a pinpoint flash of brown far away. There, she leaned her hips toward him, her arms entwined the air between them. Come. Closer. They would step together, into another place and he would be—oh, how much better they had been, standing, feet braced, on the *Salamander*'s deck . . . before anyone had made mysteries of them. But she was not afraid now, of the pit behind his lips, the pit guarded by his legs and ivory-handled dagger. She was spinning toward him, faster, nearer, she would make his eyes warm, his lips part—

The music had stopped, save for some sinister ringing in Miranda's head. She halted, disoriented, while the room slowly settled into up, down, right, left. Left also meant ... gone. Alone. From what Miranda thought was her right, Rihana came tripping over.

"O most excellent one. O divinely gifted one. You danced like the wind on the desert at sunfall. It is enough. Rihana's feet are safe. And you," she added, catching Miranda's chin firmly, "you will find a welcome worthy of you at your journey's end." The dark eyes warmed as Rihana's voice dropped. "Minx! There was someone to think of, after all."

"No, Rihana," said Miranda, demurely shaking her skirt folds straight. "I thought of nothing. That is my secret. Only Nothing."

Miranda woke, aware of drifting on her silken pillows, then of the oil lamps' dim shimmer in the hall. This was true midnight, when everything is so still that only a phenomenon as miraculous as the dawn can ever banish darkness again.

A piece of the darkness separated from itself and stood etched against the lamp glow. Someone. There. The don? No, the shadow shape moved in her dark-adjusting eyes. The don had never worn shoulders so broad, a silhouette so fine that it could only be colored in the shade of fresh, foaming mocha. The shadow grew and closed upon her, blotting out all but a halo of light. Her breathing became sharply audible in the still room. She felt the cushions shift at her feet, as if a dream had perched there. Heard the rustle. Her visitor had settled at her feet. Miranda slowly levered herself back down into her pillows. She lay there soundlessly for a long while in the dark, until the tears poured down her face like honey and were as sweet in some unfathomable way. Finally she slept.

If such visitations came other nights, she did not know it. Her troubled sleep abruptly healed itself. As the days passed, she was kept to the women's inmost quarters, where the Arab women appareled her with rare silks. Often she would glance up to see if the curtains had parted to reveal a slice of forest and some wild thing living there. Those draperies always hung sternly shut, as secret as the cloths that veiled the women's mouths.

The day came when Miranda would begin the overland journey to the Mediterranean and her new master.

"You leave me, white one, to rot," Rihana lamented enviously. "Life is so dull here, that I almost wish that the don would call for me as he did once for you. Don't stare so! I am not mad. A pity the handsome Ibrahim has nothing of the man left in him."

Miranda's eyes shifted to the far green curtain and clung there. Nothing. He is nothing. Perhaps now . . . he could become something . . . even for Rihana.

Rihana was gone. Seeing herself finally alone, Miranda started for the courtyard. No clap from Zarifa stopped her, no guarding breastplate gleamed in the hot summer sunlight. She ran for the room that housed the pool, the room she had not seen since that last day.

He was there, part of the cool and the shadow, part of the pool and the very air. He was the same, the same full trousers caught at his ankles, the slippers turned up at the toes, the dagger. His arms, shoulders, face—the same.

Miranda walked quickly to him, a smile on her lips as if she had just seen a green forest curtain parting. He was as brown as a deer, as liquid-eyed, as ready to flee. She stared into his eyes, still afraid her own would wander downward to find his mouth and flee from it.

Then she let her eyes rest boldly on his fine-drawn lips. Only a mouth, only that. She threw her arms around his neck and for a moment they were blended, the warm pressure of his flesh, his arms tight around her, the ivory-handled dagger pushing hard into her hip. Her lips were very near his ear and the shiny fleece of black hair that curled around it. She brought them closer.

"Goodbye, Ibrahim," she whispered. Once. It echoed endlessly, as if some spell had been broken.

When she drew away, his eyes were impassive no longer. She saw anguish spread blackly in them, like dark winter water pooling when the ice is broken. I am nothing, their despair wrote wordlessly. I can say nothing, be nothing. Miranda was frightened.

Whatever glaze had held together the shattered pieces of him she knew as Ibrahim cracked now before her eyes. Behind it was not mystery—nothing so elegant as that—but ordinary human despair. Miranda had never been one to look despair in the face, even her own. Behind her closed lids the thoughts crowded in confusion. She must give him something, even as he had somehow gifted her with—what? Faith in herself again? How odd, how chaotic she felt.

She opened her eyes to find that he had not moved.

Her hands softly bracketed his face, then she tilted her head and brought her lips trembling to his own, to the center of the nothingness the don had wrought.

Blindly Miranda poured all the passion and compassion in her being into that last gateway to Ibrahim, no longer fearful that if his lips should part, she would be sucked into the mysterious vortex within him. His fingers dug into her arms, holding her back as much as holding her. Her lips pressed hard against his, his teeth an ivory wall between them. Then she wrenched herself away and raced swiftly across the tile, never looking back.

I will miss you, Ibrahim, her mind screamed in farewell. I will never forget you. I wish, I wish . . .

She was across the courtyard and in the sleeping quarters, plunging through filmy curtains as if she wanted every layer between herself and the one still standing by the quiet pool—always, would she always see him there?

Rihana found Miranda on her pillows moments later, combing her yellow hair as if bound for a festivity and looking as if all the desert demons had been blowing at her heels.

"Do not worry, white one." Rihana settled awkwardly beside her. "You carry with you to Tunis all the art we three can give you. I should say two, for Fatma is adept at nothing but filling her own stomach." Rihana caught Miranda's restless hands in her own. "Do not despair. You may like where you thought not to like. Ah, but we will miss you. I, Rihana, will miss you most bitterly of all."

"And I you," responded Miranda, bending her face and her fingers to plaiting her hair. "Rihana, I wish you—" Miranda looked up. "I wish you would be kinder to Ibrahim."

The Arab girl's head tossed but her eyes were darkly level. "I *have* been kind to him," she confessed. "It gained me nothing."

"And so you call him 'nothing.' The don's revenge upon Ibrahim for remaining true to himself was to turn us all into blades against him. That is a worse mutilation than any knife can do. We have all stood behind the don in this."

Rihana's eyes fell. "You are right. We travel by many roads to the same marketplace, and Death waits for us all as steadily in one stall as another. Perhaps one should call no man dead until he truly is so. I will remember that."

Rihana clasped Miranda's hand one last time, then Zarifa was scraping into the room on her ancient sandals. Her claps and her commands set Rihana and Fatma and Shahar into fevered motion. Within an hour, Zarifa had shepherded her charges out with Miranda's clothing chests. She motioned for Miranda to follow.

Before she could, Rihana came running back alone.

"*Aaaaaiiiii*, white one, still here? I've forgotten the blue powder! Zarifa said you would darken on the journey without it. Ah, my poor feet, she expects me below this very moment—"

Rihana fluttered about the room, riffling chests and tossing lengths of cloth over her shoulders until she seemed something winged.

"Peace, Rihana," Miranda said. "Go and satisfy Zarifa. I saw the box near the pool; I'll fetch it."

"Ah, you are white because you are angel! Allah be with you." Rihana floated away, blowing Miranda a kiss through her face veil.

Miranda hastily crossed the sunlit courtyard, glad enough to see once more the room where so much had changed for her. She would bid that room and its furnishings a solitary farewell and then . . .

The chamber was still and dim, the blue pool reflecting any light that entered it like a cyclops's all-seeing eye. Miranda moved slowly into the space and the stillness, her bare feet sliding over each grout line. She sensed the room in its entirety, its inner and outer essence. She would like to think, remember, that Ibrahim had been like this room, something secret and untouched within them both. Something . . .

Her eyes fell upon a mocha shadow on the deep blue tile, a cup of cocoa spilled and spreading into a large puddle. She stepped toward it as delicately as a cat. When she saw what it was, her pupils widened suddenly in reaction.

That uncustomary heap of fabric, that odd shadow—all that was left of Ibrahim. She walked closer, seeing now an arm stretched above the head pillowed upon it, the hand trailing in the quiet pool. The ivory-handled dagger floated on the flat blue tile, like something no element would accept. Its shining blade pointed poolward, where the hand drooped as if to pluck a water lily from the glasslike surface. She came near enough to discern a white-edged slash along the inner wrist.

Miranda saw then that the water was infinitesimally muddied, its clarity sullied by some spreading fog that had smothered its sparkle. Ibrahim's tawny skin had grayed as well, emptied like a goatskin of his wine-dark blood.

He had never meant her to know. She would have left, still imagining him pacing the draped and braziered halls, clapping his hands and paralyzing Rihana with a glance. She—Miranda— far away, moving, dreaming, like the water. Somewhere, always an Ibrahim.

Miranda's throat closed. He was as contained in death as in life, save that he no longer contained life. He had let it slither from him like a bad dream and dissolve into an echo. It had not hurt, she thought, at least the actual act had hurt far less than the reason for it.

And she was not his reason, whatever had happened between them. No. Rihana had said that Ibrahim had walked as a dreamer since the don's cruelty. Miranda had merely been the sound that had wakened him, and he saw that it was the middle of the night and no dawn for him. So he set like a red sun on a bright blue pool and woke no more. Miranda stared at Ibrahim one last time, no longer threatened by the emptiness his self was guard upon.

He was beautiful. A pleasure to look upon. Miranda could al- most sympathize with the don's frustration when he saw such symmetry and spirit within his grasp and forever barred.

Gone. Clearly gone. Miranda shook her head; the lash of her braided hair across her shoulders steadied her. Her eyes fastened on the dagger like flies in search of honey. A ruby tied in the corner of her sash, and a dagger. She could do much with both.

Yet she shrank from appropriating Ibrahim's unwitting be- quest. Blood lay upon that dagger's innocent ivory handle. Had she acquired the Arab women's superstition? It was unlucky. No good would come of taking it.

Miranda's feet pivoted on the cool tile and then stubbed against the small mosaic-lidded box lying beside the empty hip- bath. Powder, what avails powder, Don Ricardo Esteban Diego de la Fontana y Monteverde, when your heart's desire will soon be powder as well? May you have joy of him, she thought fiercely, letting one last liquid glance fall upon the body of the eunuch Ibrahim. Nothing, truly nothing now. Ah, how Rihana would weep for him, now lacking an object for her repentance.

Miranda clutched the box and tiptoed away, as if afraid of waking a child from a much-needed nap. In the courtyard, she stopped to stare up at the bright daylight that smarted her eyes with welcome after a long stay in shadowed places. She ran back to the sleeping quarters just in time to be captured by Zarifa. Soon she would be bundled away to the waiting mule train that would cross the inland mountains to the Mediterranean's broad blue shore, to the wrinkling, winking bright blue water where someone brown like cocoa awaited her.

Miranda let the powder spill, a long blue ribbon behind her, as she followed the harried Zarifa out. This for the don! This for the Bey of Tunis! She was done with serving as rowel to their jaded lives. By guile or by battle, she would have the better of them. She could hardly wait to meet the bey.

Chapter Twenty-five

*T*hree days later, Miranda was led, cloaked and veiled, into the oddest ship's cabin she had ever seen. Curtains of swirling, melding colors draped its walls; brass lamps hung from the tented ceiling cast a warm glow upon the drapery folds. A scent spiced the heavy air—languorous jasmine, its origin a brazier glowing cherry against one curtained wall.

Her eyes, so dazzled she almost forgot the sick flutter in her stomach, traveled to the small dais opposite the entrance, an alcove draped with European brocades and lined with figured carpets and the silken pillows that Don Ricardo so fancied.

Startled, Miranda realized that the dim light limned a turbaned figure against the alcove, a seated someone draped in flowing robes that mimicked the background so perfectly that they merged with it. A man, that only could she tell, for the drapery-hung turban shaded his features. A long silence held, lit by lamplight that waxed and waned like guttering candles.

"They say that you can dance," suggested a contemplative voice—perfect English spoken with the trace of a halt, as though the speaker had considered the formation of each word before he uttered it, as though he were casting a spell or were constrained to use a theatrical formality he found unnatural. They had not told her the bey could speak English.

"Yes, they taught me to dance," Miranda admitted.

"Do you like to dance?" The word "dance" seemed to mean more coming from the swathed figure across from her.

"For myself? Well enough. I dance for myself. They thought to make me dance for them, but I took it and made it my own. It is all a prisoner can do."

"Would you dance for me?" The voice was studious, remote;

the request very formal, almost as a man asking himself: will the sun shine today, the wind blow? Will my new slave dance for me?

"If I say no?"

"I will be—disappointed." Again, a flat, emotionless response. "A pity to have a gift and not to share it."

"You have a gift that I would share."

"Name it."

"Freedom." Miranda's heart pounded. Now would come the anger, the whip, the power of master against slave.

Instead, another long pause. Miranda had the odd feeling that the hesitation was not because the man was considering any course of action. He had expected this.

"Dance for me one hour," the voice bargained softly, "and the Bey of Tunis will tend you your freedom. It is promised."

For the first time expression had touched his voice. Irony.

She wanted to fight, or to try for flight; perhaps the weeks in Don Ricardo's harem had softened her, after all. What was outward concession if inwardly she remained free, unshaken?

"I have no music," Miranda objected, nevertheless dropping her cloak and veil to the carpet.

Her gold-threaded brocades and the heavy band around her hips from which the silken skirt fell caught the lamplight and winked in the dim chamber. As she stepped forward, the gold bangles on her arms clanked together, sounding a . . . challenge.

The dancing girl's bodice was purple cut velvet taken from a court lady's gown—a vest with narrow sleeves that scooped to the swell of her breasts and fastened in front with a row of tiny gold baubles that rang together in a light little melody when she moved.

Her body had been bleached to the whiteness of a freshwater pearl. Despite the weight Miranda's languid life had added, her waist was as slim as when it had worn trouser ropes aboard the *Salamander*. The skirt was a circle of sheer violet silk embroidered with gilt thread. Between the velvet vest and the belt's broad gold glitter, Miranda's stomach swelled subtly to her navel, where the don's ruby reposed like a setting sun. Zarifa's last, determined touch.

The man in the turban had not expected all this. She could hear it in the heavy silence. She thought it odd that a Barbary Coast prince buying a European woman for his pleasure should not anticipate that she would be presented to him as seductively as a diamond on black velvet.

"What is your name?" he asked, as if recalling that an interrogation was in progress.

"I have none."

"I must call you something."

"Why, if you free me in an hour?"

"An hour without a name is an hour not worth spending."

Ah, that vague Moslem philosophizing. Miranda began to see a glimmer of personality in this mystery man.

"Call me what you wish."

"Paloma—white dove—I will call you. The Spanish word will remind you of your former guardian and make you but love me more. But will you dance? Some women carry their own music with them. Are you one, Paloma?" Irony, mockery again.

Challenged as if to a different kind of duel, Miranda stepped forward, her bare toes curling into the lush carpet. She raised her ivory arms above her head, tossing her shimmering veil of hair back so matter-of-factly that the motion became part of the dance. She began swaying slightly on her feet, to the music in her head, the music piped from behind the curtain in Don Ricardo's harem. To those invisible musicians—blinded, she'd heard, so they'd hear their sound without distraction—who lured her out of herself with the soft drum and whine and tinkle of their strange melodyless music.

Dangling gold pieces chimed to her rhythm. She liked the sway of the silk washing like water against her, dipping and touching and drifting away, then caressing her ankles. Her hips began the unthinking circle, swaying wider as the dream came back of the phantom lover she envisioned now when she danced; she saw herself, saw him.

As her hips swung, the ruby glowed like claret at the center of her body. She was wine for the air and the music and the invisible lover before her. Her hips arched forward to brush his, her arms uncoiled like twined serpents while the bracelets slid up and down their limber length as if caressing her. She turned in the dance, giving only her back and swaying violet skirt and yellow braids to the man who watched her.

But he, he was always before her—vague, a yearning and unreal thing. She swayed to her knees and began arching back in the most difficult of motions, her body drawn back like a bow, her arms twining gracefully behind her head, her throat extended in a supple curve so her golden hair pooled behind her on the carpet at her feet. Between the taut muscles of her thighs that held her parallel to the floor, her phantom lover lit a flame that licked up to enflame the ruby and travel along her breast and arms and pause upon her slightly parted lips . . .

"Enough."

The mental music ended abruptly, dying at that word from no-where. A harsh word, loud, as if he who uttered it were angry, stopping the music with one resonating drumbeat. Yet she must have imagined the anger, for as she froze in her extended posi-tion, the man in the alcove an inverted mystery in her eyes, his voice continued.

"You dance well." His tone, if anything, was flatter than ever.

Miranda uncoiled and sat on her ankles, feeling drained.

"You must have tired. Come, Paloma; have some wine."

She debated. Could this Paloma, this faceless dancing girl, take wine from him? She wanted wine, that warm tingle running down her throat. She felt dry, thirsty.

Miranda rose and approached the dais, her finery jangling. She hesitated before mounting it, so he poured something scarlet from a brass ewer into a silver goblet that he handed to her. She drank. Sweet wine slightly chill from the metal raced down her throat like a tonic. She took another sip.

"Sit," he said, extending a hand. She mounted the riser to re-cline on the pillows at his left, nevertheless pulling against the pressure of his hand so she sat farther from him than he had in-tended. She heard him laugh softly.

Miranda searched the shadowed face for something she could mark and know. Impossible. His robes tented him. He was an en-igma while she sat unveiled to him. She studied the princely cabin again.

"Paloma." She turned her head, wondering that she should re-spond to an arbitrary name bestowed on her by a man she dreaded and very likely would come to hate with good reason. "Are you virgin?"

Fear unleashed itself to prowl the empty halls of her stomach.

"No." She had never lied to Don Ricardo about that; had he foisted her off as such to this man who had paid dear for her? What would he do?

"And have you known many men?"

"I have known no man," she said harshly, as memory raised its head and stared at her like a predator.

"But—" began that precise English voice, deep-toned in doubt.

"I was—taken. Once. By a—man." What word would describe what Steele had been to her that long-distant day on the *Salamander*—monster? Pragmatic despoiler? Forestaller?

"A man—?" He was requesting explanation, inquiring after the precise circumstances.

"A—man." Miranda's lips closed firmly. Don Ricardo's Iron Maiden couldn't drag any more out of her. The figure in the shadows saw that and moved back.

"So that is why you dance for the angels and no man. Oh, yes, the Koran has its angels—did you think for a moment that I had forgot myself? Azrael, and the white angel of tears. Your guardian perhaps, Paloma? We Moslems say the angels were fired from bright gems—opal. And ruby."

She felt rather than saw his eyes drop to her center.

"Have you not considered that there is a certain peace to letting another master yourself awhile?"

"Peace in slavery? That is what you speak of."

"A peace in not flailing against fate any longer. We are great believers in fate, we Arabs. I am convinced that your fate at this moment is to be with me."

"You mentioned freedom before—"

"Ah, yes. Half your hour is gone, Paloma." A robed arm gestured to a carved wooden stand on which a large hourglass stood, its sand shifting steadily like gold dust in the lamplight.

Bewildered, Miranda searched the face she couldn't see—he had anticipated only detaining her for an hour, could it be?

"How much of yourself do you think you could lose forever in the half hour the glass still holds?"

"I lost half myself in five minutes once," Miranda answered flatly.

He said nothing, though the robes rustled restlessly. "Give yourself to me, as much of yourself as you can, for the next half hour. I will give you yourself back at any moment you ask," he said persuasively, confidently. "You have been taken and hurt by it. Can it do any more harm to give?"

"And in half an hour?"

"In five and twenty minutes, you will be free to go." Humor touched his voice as he assessed the time already elapsed. "I should have named you Scheherazade; you have a way of avoiding the issue."

Miranda couldn't avoid smiling slightly at this allusion to a woman who beguiled her lord with her stories rather than herself.

"A smile to make Allah pause," he noted, slipping down beside her and setting her wine goblet aside. "Do as I say and you will not regret it," he promised.

The sight of his robed figure settling beside her unnerved Miranda again. As she hesitated, he pushed her gently down on the silken pillows, fanning her hair above her head so she shouldn't catch it. The gesture reassured her, but she began to tense again as he removed the turban. No more of his face than before was revealed, for a lamp swinging directly behind him cast its glow upon her, but kept him as much of a mystery as ever.

His fingers began caressing her face, so lightly that she could not resent it. His lips pressed hers—quickly, chastely—then they were gone and his fingers soothed. His lips returned to linger; just when she thought that it was not so terrible, so invasive, he took her chin in his fingers, making her mouth an open door for his tongue and the warm wetness it brought. Miranda arched as against an assault.

"Softly, softly, my Paloma," he murmured against her mouth, and his voice was like silk and she believed in him again.

His mouth dallied on her lips, her face, her throat, kissing her into forgetfulness. Miranda watched him bow over her body, touching it here, there, as if he were a magician who could produce phenomena upon it at will. His hands were silken on her skin and that same hot something that came in her dreams stirred between her legs and snaked up her body to send paradoxical shivers down it.

He knelt over her suddenly, looming so high that the light set behind his broad shoulders. His hands fretted at her bodice lacings and she was glad, her breath came fast as he bowed to her breasts like a sea hawk to something it saw gleaming silver beneath the waves. A storm of sensation engulfed her as his ubiquitous mouth found her navel and sucked the jewel free. She heard the ruby click against his teeth, then he spat it onto the cushions and his hot, clever tongue replaced it.

He raised his shadowed face from her, for a moment reminding her of something wild raising its head from a pool in the forest. What was he to her, this man whose face she had never seen? Then she knew the shape of him—he was the man from the dream, the phantom whose limbs had twined with hers in those strange night visions that had put her beyond an innocence unbroken in her waking life.

She knew him, he knew her, they were sensation-tossed together and that was a stronger bond than formal introductions. She heard a rustle as his form above her shrugged off the voluminous robes like outgrown wings. He dropped down upon her. Her hands ran down his chest, at first shocked by the feel of his smooth firm flesh, like a diver who plunges totally into the water and is for an instant overwhelmed by it.

She ran her hands up his broad back, which seemed to stretch forever in the dark, feeling the hard muscles beneath his skin— was he old, was he ugly, did it matter? She felt the ridge of his spine and climbed it, she felt the slighter ridges along his back and shoulders, ridges that— Some remote part of her memory withdrew from her body and thought it out. Ridges like—scars, scars of the whip. Of course, the Barbary Coast beys and pashas were often much-traveled renegades elected to such posts from the decks of their pirate ships. Outlaws, former galley slaves, even former Christian gentlemen, though most of them were Moslem, and they did not drink wine . . .

Her right hand, possessed by urgency, grasped in the dim light for his left shoulder above her. Such a coincidence was impossible; many men bore the marks of the whip in these warring days. Yet, yet . . . Her fingertips ran down his upper arm, more sensitive than they had ever been, and found the faint three-inch ridge left by Barcelona steel on his arm.

"Kit," she whispered in disbelief even as he joined with her like a sword into a welcoming scabbard, with no pain this time, and it was too late. She arched away, but only because she was a wave slapping a rock, ebbing only for the joy of hurling back upon it. He was reaching, touching something remote and tiny at her very heart and core. A fluttering like a thousand butterfly wings erupted in the eye of her personal storm. Her limbs liquefied as she was rinsed by waves of serenity. She barely felt it when he withdrew to lie beside her, the lamplight finally falling equally upon them.

Christopher Steele, and no doubt, his English face flushed in the light, his gilded hair tousled and falling into his blue eyes, which looked on her with new, warm knowledge and no shame.

"Why?" was all Miranda, breathless with discovery as much

as anything else, could say. She waved her hand around the seraglio environment, but she meant to include herself as well.

"I came to rescue you," he said sheepishly. "I only meant to play the game out for a while; the bey's men would have become suspicious otherwise. But . . ." He eyed her with hot blue eyes and she glanced away, sitting up to refasten her bodice and keeping her head down, veiled by her hair.

"Why?" she asked again, her voice on the edge of breaking.

His voice when he answered was as serious. "Because I gave you an ill welcome to womanhood on the *Salamander.* I didn't want you to remember me that way. Now at least you can remember that I raped you royally." He indicated the brazier and cushions.

"It wasn't rape and you know it," Miranda flared, looking resentfully up from her lacing. "And that will be harder to forgive than the last."

Steele watched Miranda's fingers struggle with the stiff fastenings. He was riding the backwater of satiety and would worry about recriminations later. As she admitted, she had not been unwilling.

His eyes lingered on her. Don Ricardo was enough of a merchant, if no womanizer, to have made the most of her. Where she had been fallow, she was now full; where angular, ample. Her hair, bleached to the color of moonlight to tickle a dark-favored lover's fancy, had caught his imagination, and more, though he was no Moor. Perhaps too much so.

Time to end the masquerade on the Moroccan vessel; the true Bey of Tunis was expected all too soon. His eyes measured the hourglass as he drew on his European smallclothes. She had retrieved the cloak and drawn it over her shoulders like an injured nun, but she still chimed with every motion—credit the cursed Spanish grandee with knowing how to set the music in any man's veins singing. He watched impatiently while she sat on her heels and patted the pillows.

"Looking for this?" Steele extended his hand, fanning the fingers to show the ruby shining as bright and red as revenge in the brazier light. She reached for it, but Steele's fingers closed.

" 'Tis mine," challenged Miranda, her eyes glowing ruby-vivid in the flickering light.

"Perhaps," he said, "but I doubt that you could get it back from me, my dove."

Miranda rose to her knees in fresh indignation, her clenched hands apparently aching to rip the jewel from his grasp.

" 'Tis mine! I paid dearly for it."

"I've no time to haggle with you." He pulled her to her feet and donned the heavy sultan's robes again. "We must wear our Moslem faces until we're clear of this floating wharf they call a galley, and time is running out—"

He glanced to the hourglass. The turban shaded his features again. Miranda watched from the middle of the floor, the fists at her sides still threatening.

"Rescue me!" she taxed him. "You've ruined me by trickery and now want to bring me back to where I would not go—"

Her cries stopped as he dropped the veil over her head, then bent to sling her over his shoulder.

"*Jesu!* You're a heavier bit of baggage than before the don laid hands upon you, or whoever in his retinue taught you to dance so invitingly. Now be quiet unless you wish to perform for the true Bey of Tunis. My spies tell me that he has but one eye, a rotting stomach and a temper that takes no teasing."

Steele smiled as her struggles lapsed into silence. He caught her tighter round the knees, draped the cloth over the sides of his face and lurched onto deck. The bey was also said to be as fond of wine and women as he was annoyed to be interrupted in his pursuance of them both.

A hot lemon Mediterranean sun beat across his robes as he stepped on deck, every muscle taut for any interference—only his own men in borrowed robes, shifting over to him like shadows on the drowsy sun-rinsed deck. The slaves slept gratefully under their tarpaulin.

"Done, Captain?" asked a berobed seaman.

"Aye, well done." He grinned. "We've lulled the crew's curiosity and we've got our cargo."

Miranda kicked a strong foot into his ribs and with some satisfaction heard his breath expel sharply. "Cargo," she hissed over his back. " 'Tis cargo that will sink you to the bottom of the salt sea."

She was bouncing along over his shoulder in comparative shade when the sun suddenly shot up to dangle above her eyes. She lay on her back in a low boat alongside the Moroccan vessel. Steele was boarding behind her. The sailor who'd caught her held her with a none-too-dainty grip.

The moment reminded her inexpressibly of the day off Cádiz when Steele had found her out and had thrown her as ungraciously into the *Salamander*'s boat. She was piercingly homesick for that day, that ship, for Muffin and for the two people she and Christopher Steele had been before that slow row shipward had ended in her hasty ravishment.

Now he had ravished her again; even worse, he had tricked her into accepting it, as if that could cancel the first, forced occasion. True, the lovemaking had been elegant this time, but the deceit was shabby. He believed that paying tribute to her senses should overrule her head and heart.

He knew nothing of such matters, nothing, thought Miranda, tears flowing copiously behind the thick face veil. She could just see through its tight weave, see Christopher Steele but a few feet away in the sunlight. He had removed the turban and his robes fell open, baring the familiar sea-bronze of his chest. His eyes were eagerly directed to the ship ahead; she knew that without having to turn to see the vessel. The sight of him made something secret in her stomach tighten. Miranda bit her lip to divert that tenuous inner twisting, that unwanted aftershock.

Damn! One day she would make him see that if anything was worse than forcing a woman against her will, it was tricking her into doing her will before she knew it.

BOOK THREE:

The Dowsabelle

*"Nor can you more judge woman's thoughts by tears,
Than by her shadow what she wears."*
—John Donne, 1633

Chapter Twenty-six

"Put these on. Some crew members are late of the *Gato de Nueve* and would do you no harm, but I had to fill in with scurvy Mediterranean sea-scum. You'd best keep to the cabin even in that."

"That" was a pile of plain seaman's garb Steele had handed Miranda as soon as he had her aboard and hurried to his cabin's seclusion. She fought the impulse to throw them at him as he withdrew.

Instead, she slipped quickly enough out of the swathing harem silks. Until they lay piled at her feet she had not realized how heavy the gold-hung belt and bodice had weighed. She found it odd to don trousers and shirt again; Miranda's pampered flesh rebelled at the homespun texture. She had dressed quickly and was glad; Steele entered the cabin moments later.

"Better." He flashed her a glance from under eyebrows bleached to silver. She'd never seen him burnished this deep a bronze before; the Mediterranean sun must wax warmer on English complexions than the Atlantic version. He could almost pass for a Morisco—those handsome Eur-Arab hybrids—were his hair not golden, his eyes blue.

"A fine souvenir of your stay with the don," he said as he retrieved the violet cloth and gold trinkets that glimmered at Miranda's bare feet. " 'Tis worth four Arab virgins' bride price, but I've no need to spend sequins where I'm bound."

His fingers snapped the Arab coins dangling from the belt, as his eyes ran over Miranda in her loose-fitting men's clothing. "Yes, better," he said. "More like."

Yet his hand absently stroked along the hard glittering edge of the Rishi dancer's bodice, making Miranda's flesh quiver within her rough-woven shirt. The quiver escalated into rage, so she snatched the finery from his hands.

"If it's mine, then give it to me!"

Steele raised pale eyebrows. "I can see that you'll make a delightful cabinmate."

"Here? With you?"

"I've told you; I'm much safer for you than the crew."

"I doubt that."

"Doubtless you want your old hammock back in the 'tween decks; in this climate not the best idea. You'd be surprised how much more unpleasant it is belowdecks with the sun high and hot above it. No, it's here you'll stay until we make Portsmouth."

He left her then, bracing the cabin door firmly from the outside, for when she tried it, it had no give at all.

Miranda folded away her dancing clothes, then looked around: an uncomplicated, ordinary English cabin—no wide Spanish bed, no tented alcoves; merely a built-in bed, desk and chairs, with swinging lanterns to illuminate all its homeliness.

They swung to a different time now, those lamps. Miranda guessed the ship was filling sail and blowing west toward Gibraltar, past the rocky Pillars of Hercules into the Atlantic. Even Steele wouldn't want to linger with the Bey of Tunis's prize captive aboard.

The lamps had almost burned down before he returned. Miranda, curled in the captain's chair, leapt to her feet.

"Still yearn for mastery, do you? I'd have thought you'd have learned a thing or two about that from Don Ricardo. How did he treat you?"

"Better than you," Miranda retorted.

Steele laughed as he sat in the chair she'd vacated. "Then he has changed his tastes; but you don't seem particularly damaged. The don knew better than to mar his most—polished—possession."

She could feel his eyes burn through the plain clothes he had given her to what she had been but hours before.

"At least *he* did not tarnish me," she rejoined, flouncing away—a difficult accomplishment when wearing trousers and barefoot.

"Come now, you'd have had to pay the piper very soon. I warrant I made your dance more worthwhile than some riches-bloated Moslem freebooter could have."

"You'd be surprised what worth can be gained from Moslems as opposed to 'Christian' gentlemen."

A knock forestalled what was becoming a most satisfactory duel of recriminations. Steele's brusque "Come" brought a lean little cabin boy staggering in under a tray of double proportions.

"I can't offer a banquet to compare with your Moslem paradise, madam"—Steele elaborately gestured her to a desk-side chair—"but 'tis better provision than we had on the Atlantic."

Miranda sat sullenly. She didn't want to eat with him. She

didn't want to sleep with him. She only wanted to talk with him until one of her verbal missiles struck home. So far they'd all rebounded off his easy masculine complacency about making love. Taking love.

Miranda eyed the plain food askance, but followed Steele's example and began thrusting it into her mouth with the dull knife provided. Don Ricardo had taught her to be hungry, among other things, for her plate was half-empty before Steele had more than tackled his.

"Moslem manners," he remarked shortly. "It'll do you good to dwell among restrained folk again." A self-mocking smile cracked the corner of his mouth.

"How long?" Miranda asked between gobbles. The plain fare was suddenly tastier to her than all the stuffed dates and grape leaves and curries of the East.

Steele ruefully eyed the voracious figure across from him. She looked not an hour older than when she had scampered over the *Salamander*'s side and into more of his life than he liked. Impossible to believe that she had proven irresistible to him only hours before. That insidious Spaniard knew only direct avenues to the senses. No wonder her brother had turned pliant so easily. Still, Steele would have sworn that the sister was one to resist enslavement to anything, even her own desires.

Someone had refined those girlish yearnings since last he had seen her, that he'd swear. Not the don, yet surely the don would not let his promised goods be taken by one of his retinue. A puzzle. Yet why did he care what had transpired behind the gilded bars of Don Ricardo's Moslem cage? He should never have . . . whim it was, and heady surroundings. Damn, it'd be good to sail clear of this hot Mediterranean sun; it addled English brains. Both of them had been given proof of that but hours before.

Miranda's eyes, dilated with suspicion, pinned her host to his side of the desk turned dinner table.

"Wine?" asked Steele, interrupting his reverie. She refused the tilted bottle with a fierce headshake. " 'Tis dry stuff without washing down," he warned.

His advice angered her so much that she choked on a piece of leathery meat. He tilted the bottle into her pewter goblet, filling it to the brim. Miranda fanned one hand over its gleaming oval rim too late.

Steele laughed and drew one of his fine enamel-handled daggers, Saracen-work. Miranda shrank against her chair like a cat contemplating a bound. Steele laid the blade on the desk between them.

"There. You've read enough amongst the tomes of your learned Barbados 'clerk,' I'm certain, to know of this practice. I put the sword between us; on my honor, you need not fear for yours from now on."

His voice mocked her, but his eyes were true. He was a man who did not lightly deviate from what he said; she had discovered that on the *Salamander*.

"Now drink your wine," instructed Steele.

She did, though it was not the subtle tongue-teasing stuff the don served but a dry, rugged country vintage.

"How long?" she asked again.

This time he answered, leaning back in the chair until it tilted away from her, like a deck in rough weather.

"Ten days, if we outrun the bey, the Spanish, the French and any spare Hollanders about."

"Where do you take me? Harry?"

"Harry won't have you." Steele was surprised to see pain flicker in her eyes. "He's got the Hathaway fortune well enough without you. You are but a troublesome memory. Harry will be no haven to you now."

Steele watched her lashes flinch with each brutal sentence until he saw acceptance rise in her green eyes and regard him calmly. Green. The color now spoke of Roxanne Wexford, and he didn't like his cousin's silken mental presence mixing with thoughts of rejection—even another's.

Steele rose to pace the small cabin, his hands clasped behind his back and his head lowered against the low-timbered ceiling. He was tall for his time, a mast among men.

He had never looked more like a pirate, Miranda thought as she watched him, with a brace of pistols in his sash and daggers hanging off his belt. The Mediterranean sun had polished him mahogany even to the backs of his hands and the triangle of chest revealed by the open shirt.

She had wondered about the shape and shade of her shadow-masked master aboard the Tunisian vessel; she hadn't considered that her elusive suitor could have been particolored. A smile tweaked her mouth; she wished she had seen him, striped like a zebra. For the first time, Miranda took pride in her carefully tended skin. She at least was now one sovereign shade from her face to the tips of her toes.

"I knew Harry was no longer my brother aboard the *Gato*," she said, returning to realities. "Perhaps it will be harder to be rid of me than you realize."

Kit Steele wheeled on her. She was blossoming forth with irony again, like one who had the whip hand. He had expected a more humbled aspect, but was beginning to learn that was one side of her he would be the last to see—save for the time she had washed against him with grief in the cabin of the *Gato de Nueve*. He wondered briefly if she didn't hold that against him as much as any physical intimacy. She was not one to forgive the pillow into which she wept. Nay, she would blame it for the weeping even.

"To whom do you take me?"

A harsh question, perhaps because there was no soft harbor for her now, with her father dead and her brother dead to her.

"Your lady aunt." Steele saw her face pinch with distaste at the idea of reentering that London lady's circle of influence.

Good tonic for her, he thought. No nonsense. The offices of Helena Hathaway, maiden that she was, would naturally be bent to finding her niece a suitable husband; that was the way of those "unblessed" by matrimony; they were forever urging their fellows into it. Her history was not so sordid that it would not sink beneath the realities of London life. After being brought to bed with a covey of merchant's offspring, she would doubtless forget her seafaring adventures, put on a plain cap and tend to her spinning.

This image so pleased him that he glanced at her, surprised to find her oval face regarding him like a white moon from beneath her tousled golden hair. Even dowerless, it would not be hard to find a man of good family to wed her. Even the perverse don, who had no yen for women, saw beauty in her. Why to him was it always a surprise, like something glimpsed between country hedges as one walked by?

He unrolled a hammock and attached it to hooks above the cabin windows. Miranda watched him suspiciously.

"I give you a choice. Here. Or there." His blindingly blond head gestured to the built-in bunk.

"The hammock," she said coldly.

Steele smiled and in the lantern sheen his teeth matched his hair. He was like some mocking jinn from the don's heathen drawings, Miranda thought. He knew. Somehow Steele always knew. She'd chosen the hammock because it was a solitary resting place, not because it reminded her of Barbados or the *Salamander*. If she had to choose between Steele and steel, she'd trust to the hard-forged point inherent in an enameled handle.

Miranda fetched the dagger from the desk, thrust it into her belt and hurled herself into the hammock with a grace born of practice.

Steele grinned to himself and blew the lanterns out.

Miranda woke, some urgency pulling her consciousness above the tides of sleep. Dark. And rocking, rocking in that lulling teasing way that ships have, especially after three weeks asail. What was wrong?

Oh, now she knew. Pain, searing her belly like a rum-dipped knife across a wound. Her time of the month, she realized—past time. She had been ill with it before, but not this—chill and dizziness and tearing pain. She twisted out of the hammock. The lanterns were devilish hard to snare in the dark, the tinderbox even more elusive. Finally she found and struck flint. Steele was gone, as she'd suspected. He came and went often during the night, called away by nautical matters.

Miranda staggered to the chamber pot, the hot red between her legs heavy, profuse. She sacrificed the shirt, planning to raid the forecastle for a new one in the morning—but, oh, the pain, the cramp of it, harder and longer than any she'd borne before. Had being with him done this, was this the wrath of a mighty God?

Not until she had turned down the lamps and returned to rock in the hammock like a fitful child did she realize that her body was washing away early fruits of that union with Steele in the bey's perfumed cabin. Fear became a pain greater than the worst wrenching of her entrails. Something could have come of that ... that deceit. She could have carried something of him in her body and birthed it. All from that one, confusing coupling. Pleasure—there had been that, more than she cared to consider; pleasure pulled unwilling from her body by guiles no gentleman would use, she was sure—and now, pain. Dear God, it'd been close. Truly ruined and worse, dogged by a homunculus of him, like a court dwarf, anchoring her days ...

When Steele questioned her listlessness in the morning, she shrugged. "Seasickness."

He didn't believe her, it was plain in the way his lips set.

She hated him. Being confined to the cabin drove her mad, particularly when she was feeling this way. The would-be brief voyage home had dragged out for weeks now. She didn't know whether she liked the cabin better when Steele was there and she had to share its silence with him, or when he was away and the silence circled her like a ring, perfectly smithed to imprison her.

In the English Channel, the gale blew up, the cold fast-striking fall gale that had widowed so many coastal women along Dover and Normandy. The storm had no mere fishing boat in its fangs, but the ship rocked nonetheless rudely against wind and waves. Miranda rocked with it in the cabin as the hours passed amid the vessel's desperate creaking, and as a windy howl straight from hell swirled against her harbor.

The chairs hugged the floor to which they were nailed, but the hammock swung wildly, and loose cabin items came hurling at her as if from an unseen catapult—even a quill once, tossed down by Steele when first called to storm watch. The lanterns swung so crazily that she finally blew them out—their motion made every dancing shadow long and lurid.

Miranda took reluctant refuge in the cabin bed, where she could pile the linens against the wall to spare herself from banging brutally, bruisingly into the wood on every pitch.

Hours she spent there alone, with no knowledge of what happened above her. Worse, she could think of no place that she would rather be. That she had always had before, as potent a defense as Barcelona steel, but now she longed not for Spain or Tunis or England. Even Barbados had become an island of cruel irony in her mind, where the calling macaws had been jeering her all the while. She was sick and weary and no haven awaited her anywhere.

The door finally banged against the wall. A cold caskful of wind and driving rain burst open and poured into the cabin, circling the floor and chilling Miranda where she huddled.

Steele came behind it, a black hole of wind and waves smashing behind him. "Light!" he ordered hoarsely.

Miranda danced across the room to relight the lanterns in their wire cages. She turned to him and almost thought herself spirit-visited. His water-soaked cape was stiff, his face a mask of cold-burned red and frostbitten white, the blond mane only a few damp tails. He looked terrible in the awesome sense of the word, like the Hanged Man from a tarot deck.

He slammed the door shut, then stumbled to the desk, finding a green glass bottle and uncorking it clumsily. The goblet he picked up wobbled in his fingers. Miranda, remembering another bottle, another day, watched unmoving. He tilted the bottle neck into the goblet in the still-tossing cabin, glass tapping against pewter like the castanets of Pasquela the Gypsy dancer at La Bicha Roja. His teeth matched that odd percussion.

Before he could pour, Miranda had darted over to wrest cup and bottle from his tenuous grasp. She poured a deep draught, then held the pewter brim up to him. Half spilled between her hand and his, but he threw that red wine between his teeth as if it were blood to revive him.

She watched him straighten, then stagger toward the bed. She trailed him, trying to cut loose the cold, sopping jacket at which his fingers fretted. He paused to let her wrestle it off his shoulders, then stumbled on, throwing himself across the linens, his legs scraping the floor and dangling there as if booted in iron instead of leather.

Miranda tried pulling off his boots, but Steele shook his head and flailed a leg away from her. She realized then that he might be called on deck again and needed to be ready. She caught up the bedclothes from the forlorn pile that had been her nest and wrapped them around him. They absorbed his wet and cold as quickly as Ibrahim's sponge had soaked up bathwater. The memory jolted her mind with an almost physical shock. There all had been warm and soft and simple menace. Here was fury and cold that issued from his very presence, and danger.

"K-Kit—?"

"Four seamen over," he whispered, his voice but a ragged shred of itself after hours of bellowing commands into a gale. "The pumps are holding. We're riding easier now. They'll come again for me soon . . ." His voice faded to a rasp and stopped.

He was asleep from exhaustion. The cold that emanated from him enveloped her in icy dread. On him hung the ship's fate. On him hung sinking or sailing.

She pulled off the damp bedding. He was wet to the skin, his body like the great tapered icicles her father had told her hung from English eaves in the heart of winter. He was half a dead man and the only real navigator the entire crew had. The crew less four.

She darted to the big sea chest to unearth a dry cloak, throwing it over him and sinking into vigil at the bed's foot. His eyes opened once, pale slits through the blond bars of his lashes. He saw her there and smiled.

"You were always a faithful cabin boy, Richard," he said before voice and consciousness drifted away together on the same implacable tide onto some sea only he knew.

Miranda woke, surprised that she had felt secure enough to sleep. The ship wallowed in a soft, steady roll that was either of another world or of passage through the storm. The cloak had been thrown over her and tucked under her chin. She tried to uncoil her legs. That violent tingling that betokens a good ten minutes of subtle torture before the blood unbends and circulates normally began along her feet and calves. She groaned.

"What?"

Amazed, she saw Steele across the cabin at the desk, a chart spread before him. Had it all been a dream?

"What's the matter?" he repeated.

Ah, his voice had cracked into hoarseness just then, and his face seemed stretched, the fine angles of his jaw and cheekbones sharpened somehow. He looked spent.

"My legs, they're cramped."

Steele rose and moved toward her.

"No." His eyes questioned her refusal. "You're half-dead, or should be. I can simply rest awhile."

He came on, scooping her up lightly enough. "I need my bed back and sleep without fear of a dagger through the gullet," he said drily, rolling her into the hammock.

She swung there helplessly, her legs still too weak to trust. She heard him throw himself onto the bed behind her and twisted her head over the hammock's coarse edge.

"We rode it out, didn't we? We're to make land?"

"Yes to both questions and to our mutual satisfaction, madam," he responded lazily. "Go to sleep, my dove. I don't want to deal with ruffled feathers now."

The reminder of intimacy enraged her. She twisted angrily to lie on her back in the hammock, even though her legs tingled like the very Devil. His "dove" had talons, as he should well remember.

Chapter Twenty-seven

*A*s Miranda began her stay on Kit Steele's latest ship, so she ended it. Not many days after the night of the storm they anchored in the Thames, and he came to the cabin with something scarlet shimmering over his arm.

"China silk, madam." He tossed the bundle at her. Two dainty leather shoes with elevated heels followed the gown to lie at her feet. "And a taffeta petticoat." He held up something gaudy and gold. "A bit lively, perhaps, for one just out of the Spanish cloister, but I'm no tailor and at any rate the ship from which we took these was carrying a bevy of French fancy ladies, so doubtless it's all quite the mode.

"Don't stare at me as if my wits were scrambled. I can't cart you to your aunt with a rope around your waist; that good lady would never have you."

Miranda let the voluminous petticoat drift through her hands, soft and rustling. She would never have noticed that before her stay on Spanish soil.

"You needn't remain," she said, her chin rising and her cheeks borrowing the gown's flagrant color.

He bowed elaborately in his weather-beaten clothes and backed out the cabin like a courtier from the presence of a Queen.

Miranda dropped off the coarse seaman's clothing. Standing naked made her feel new, like some elfin visitor. She eyed the cabin. If it were Steele's, it would have the basin she'd ignored until now—yes, there, on the tripod. She untied her hair and washed herself from head to toe, her flesh quivering under icy drops of water. Then she moved around the cabin until the air dried her. She paused before the small shaving mirror above the basin, so like the *Salamander*'s that she touched a fingertip to her reflection.

Not so different, she thought—a fuller face, her hair minted now more silver than gold. She wondered what face she had turned to him in the bey's cabin and wrenched her gaze, ashamed, from the glass.

She confronted the gown left to sink like an incarnadine sun upon the cabin floor. She stepped into the smallclothes and petticoats and tied them around her waist. Next came a limp pair of scarlet stockings and silk garters, then the shoes—confining contrivances that she tottered upon like some sea gull on a line. The gold taffeta wafted over her head, rustling like the curtains in Don Ricardo's chamber.

Steele had been wrong about that. He thought no one would want her, to hear him talk. Her face emerged from the gold like a cold, closed moon. The scarlet silk settled above the full petticoats that swung from her hips. She found she liked that heavy rolling feeling as much as Moslem silk washing her. The bodice had bouffant sleeves tied with black velvet ribbons below the elbow, and great gold-lace ruffles. A gold lace collar, slightly crushed, spread across her shoulders like tarnished wings. The back lacings fought her fingers. She struggled until perspiration dotted her forehead and then, fearful she would stain the gown, paused. She would have to ask Steele to lace her, that was all.

He was back soon enough. He sat on the desk's edge and crossed his arms over his chest to regard her.

"You'll have to finish it off," she instructed ungraciously, turning her loosely laced back to him.

"Scarlet makes madam saucy."

Even with her back to him she could hear the grin in his voice. His fingers attacked the ribbons, pressing into the flesh beneath the bodice for purchase. She stiffened until she felt a sharp pull and the gap grew together, flattening her breasts against the buckram stomacher so that they swelled above the bodice rim.

"There."

His comment spun her around to deter further surreptitious grins. That was when he whisked a wide-brimmed black felt hat from behind his back, its panache of red plumes trembling with vibrant color.

"Oh," said Miranda, enchanted enough to show it. She glided, rustled, swirled to the looking glass to set it upon her head above the hair that hung to her shoulders like unironed sunshine.

This was no sober ensemble of starch and stiffness like the one into which Meg MacTavish had laced her. She smiled at the mirror and saw the plumes on her head nod in agreement. Pretty.

Steele moved behind her, and her countenance became a sheer cliff face. She glimpsed him in the mirror stripping off his grimy shirt and coming to the basin.

In her retreat Miranda noticed that his flesh was white-sand-pale beneath the sun line; like a zebra, she confirmed trium-

phantly, though she'd never seen that beast. Ludicrous. Surely as
ludicrous as herself right now. The conviction comforted her.

She watched him wash, unable to ignore the ebb and flow of
his alien muscles, the paled scars. After much rooting through
the sea chest, he drew out a tawny jacket with an ivory lace collar and ribboned breeches to match. The boots that followed
were doeskin and elegantly made.

"You're not about to . . . that is, I'd rather go—"

"The deck's even less for you now," he interrupted. "Would
madam deny her escort a change of plumage?"

"I would deny you everything," she flared, looking him full in
the eyes: a mistake, facing that fine and fierce expanse of modeled bronze.

His eyes shot bolts of cobalt curiosity at her as though to test
her last assertion: everything? they asked. Everything, her own
arrowed silently back. He calmly unbuckled the leather belt
around his waist. She held his gaze for a defiant moment, then
whirled her back to him in a flashing red circle.

"Preen yourself however you wish. 'Tis no affair of mine."

Miranda strolled to the windows and spent the next minutes
watching what she could spy of the harbor. She saw only an
anonymous mast top bobbing in the same rhythm as their ship,
but she bent her attention upon it as if it were a lifeline.

When his last rustles were done, she turned to find him
dusting off the jacket with doeskin gloves. She recalled a moment in Cádiz when she'd wondered how he would look in court
dress. This raiment was hardly that, but he looked—what was
Mistress MacTavish's word for it?—bonnie, that was it. Blithe
and graceful, as long and supple as a fencing foil, as polished
and reflective. Heart-free, headstrong. Something in him made
her wince interiorly, as if a careless hand had touched a wound
she bore that would not heal.

She was silent and docile when he escorted her down the
boarding ramp off the ship and into a hired coach. In leaving, she
finally saw the vessel's name painted on the bow. The
Dowsabelle had brought her back to England, an inelegant name
for an unlucky errand.

Her aunt's hall was a vaguely familiar painting of which she
felt no part. Kit Steele's eyes had rested on her the more frequently the farther they traveled from the ship. In her aunt's re-

ceiving room, they riffled her like a book he had read once long before and of which he sought to refresh his memory.

In fact, Steele was remembering the *Gato de Nueve* logbook and the uncompromising words she had penned on its final page. She had given him the ship. He recalled the ribboned medal a distracted Admiralty had conferred upon him for the prize, and fished it from among the coins in his purse.

Kit regretted the impulse that had chosen the scarlet for her; there had been more commonplace colors among the pirated gowns. Now she looked like a walking wound, her body cold and contained, quenched in all that gaudiness like water in a flame. Fire and water, they were her people; it opposed nature to leave her to these ashen city relations.

His fingers extended something bright on a blue satin ribbon. Miranda took it wordlessly.

"The gratitude of your country and your Parliament," he explained, "for the *Gato de Nueve*. The lord admiral hung it on me himself with a short speech of thanks and a long harangue about civil disobedience to the gallery. 'Tis yours."

When her palm remained open, he retrieved it and attached it to her hatband. She said nothing, but her eyes were more gray than green under the full black brim and he was glad he was in a civilized house and not somewhere wild and lone, where her nature could unleash its own variety of gale.

Helena Hathaway rustled through the double doors, bringing both visitors pivoting toward her.

"Why—Miranda! It is Miranda!"

Miranda's glance flashed not to her aunt, but to Christopher Steele. Her true name was unrolling syllable by syllable behind his eyes, like the blue satin ribbons of the medal. He knew her now, he could tie her up in his memory like a trophy.

" 'Tis Captain Steele, I believe," Helena chattered on, unheeding. "Had I any notion you were returning my lost niece, I'd have greeted you sooner."

Helena Hathaway turned her plump face upon the young man who stood impatiently before her. "You know that she can't remain here. Harry has the house now—"

Steele nodded, his vivid blue eyes cautioning silence, so—her spirit sinking—Helena glanced to Miranda again: a very stiff figure in fantastic flowing scarlet. Where, oh, where, would she belong now? And to whom?

Helena moved to a heavily carved chair by the great fireplace and sat. An old, old secret began pulsing in her temple, tempting her. They waited on her, these two young people, the gallant captain anxious to be gone and the lovely girl eager for him to be so for some reason. Fifteen years of hoping for a husband had made Helena expert at reading underlying emotions. One underlying emotion she had never divined was love, at least not for herself. Love. It had spawned the girl with the unhappy history before her. And her brother. Helena sighed.

"Miranda—" she began, her course decided now. Both yellow heads rose at that name as if neither cared to claim it. "I am not your sole relation in London. No, not Harry. Your father was a hard-used man. I have never blamed him for what he did." She sighed. "Your mother lives, Miranda. I could take you to her."

Miranda's heart beat achingly beneath the stiff stomacher. That and a pulse at her throat were the only things moving within her. Otherwise, she stood like a pillar of salt.

Steele stepped forward into the silence. "Her mother lives, mistress? Are you certain?"

"Too certain. I have at the bottom of my painted India box a letter that tells it better than I could. I'll fetch it."

She bustled away, evoking no answering rustle from the girl's silk-swathed figure. It was unnatural, that stillness. It was inhuman to pause so on the threshold of revelation.

Kit moved to her, to Miranda. Even the plumes on her hat seemed frozen into carved coral. His breath stirred them as he stood behind her. The voyage was ended and conscience had come to safe harbor. What better place to leave her than with her long-lost mother?

"It seems you have an unexpected future," he told that immobile head and back beneath the glance of his eyes. "I'll not wait, then. I've business about the ship—"

She was cut to the heart, Kit knew that, but he was no surgeon for her. He had a way of lacerating her wounds. He lifted off her wide-brimmed hat, exposing a fair head bared as if for the executioner, crowned with a circle of sheen reflecting daylight from the windows. He held the hat before her face so that she could see the medal in its band.

"Keep your medal, madam; you earned it. Mayhap someday you will grow ambitious for another."

"Mayhap."

Her voice was clear but faint; he could hear the reins upon it. He caught her to him suddenly, an arm around her shoulders, her face forced sideways against his tawny jacket. Tightly he held her, as if he wanted her to learn what it meant to be strong in one harsh embrace.

"Farewell," he said, releasing her as suddenly.

Miranda stood unmoving while his boots clicked across the tiled floor, then silenced over carpet and rang again on hallway stone.

The silence stretched to minutes. Her fingers stiffly stroked the gold lace collar his embrace had ruffled into place, like a cat tidying itself from an unwelcome petting.

She saw the window, wide and high and a room away. She could have walked to it, to gaze upon the street or courtyard below, to watch him go or someone else come. She could have turned to see the back of him or to await her aunt with her parchment mystery. She could have moved, breathed, something. But it was all too heavy, too far. Even Father had his secrets. She was merely somebody's secret and imagined thing . . . had always been so.

Miranda was still numb, dumb, when her aunt returned, the rustle of aged paper added to her normal feminine flutterings.

"Oh, Captain Steele gone?"

"Yes, Aunt, gone."

"Without farewells?"

"I think he felt us embarked upon family matters."

"And so we are. Sit down, child, your face is white as snow, and you've doubtless never even seen that substance. 'Tis good your father made certain I read; this is a missive I'd prefer not to have another read to me."

Helena Hathaway's kind eyes fell upon the girl seated in the great tapestried chair, her gay hat upon her knees, her face waiting, as her aunt started to read:

"My dear Helena,

"I know you will not take this leave-taking with any peace of mind, so I will make it brief. I have taken the children and embark for the New World. England wearies me. I think you know that the actions of she whom I call my wife are most wearisome of all. She insists upon this unseemly self-expression, though she bring the jeers of the court upon my head. I know she has not yet cuckolded me—forgive my bluntness, sister, yet even a maiden can comprehend certain realities—but she will if she continues on her present course.

"I hope to make a new life in a balmier world, where breezes do not blow so sharp through the heart. I know her; she will not miss the children, her mind is all for that pomp and elusive admiration. I pity her; she was beautiful. I trust you will not find it necessary to trouble my exile.

"If aught should befall me, I will see that Harry and Miranda return to England and their inheritance. Until then, leave us to ourselves.

"Your most affectionate and aggrieved brother, James."

Helena looked up, rattling the parchment to mask the clearing of her throat. Her niece sat unmoving, only the plumes of her hat trembling a little now in the waning London light.

"What course did he mean, that my—mother—had embarked upon?"

"The stage. She was as enamored as he with it, save that she was not content to play audience, but needs must—act—upon it."

"Father always said none but men played even the women's parts in the stage plays he had. He was most particular about that."

" 'Tis true, save for these court interludes and masques by Sir William Davenant and the rest, when the more daring improvisers invited certain women to partake in their fancies . . . even the Queen before the troubles came. Your mother was ever the most beautiful. She defied your father. They all came to see her, to talk of her. He could not live with the whispers, and so he left. All I ever knew of him or you or Harry was the annual income sent back from the tobacco, and later sugar, plantations on Barbados."

"And did my . . . our mother mourn us?"

Helena folded the letter into quarters once more. "No, Miranda, she was not made for mourning. I doubt she even knows that James is dead now, or that you and Harry live. But she is still in high position, she could protect you here, particularly with the peace so uncertain. A very powerful man has been her . . . protector . . . these last ten years. I do not trouble her unless necessary. Perhaps it is time that she took some trouble for your birth."

"I am naught but trouble of late," Miranda said softly, turning the hat upon her lap.

"Come then; you're no trouble to me. You can refresh yourself first, then I'll settle you at an inn and tomorrow we'll find your mother." Helena reached to take the headgear from her niece's frozen hands.

"No, 'tis mine, I'll keep it with me."

Chapter Twenty-eight

"*H*elena, Helena, Helena! 'Tis ages. Your message was most intriguing. What surprise have you?"

Sylvia fluttered across the receiving room, her fine white fingertips extended to brush those of her onetime sister-in-law.

Sylvia was a fair-haired, furbelowed beauty in her ripe thirties. Save for the fine lines about her gray eyes, the Great Geographer had carved the continent of her face as firm and clean as quartz. She had a certain brilliance—that well-cut profile, the cameo complexion—and she turned it next upon the dark-clothed presence behind Helena.

Miranda raised her eyes to the glittering figure who rustled more extravagantly, billowed more clouds of subtle scent, than any Moslem odalisque. She understood why her Aunt Helena had taken away the royal-red gown to attire her that day in plain, almost subservient maroon stuff. Too vivid a reflection would not please this shimmering, self-absorbed creature.

Miranda felt a pang for her father who had seen his love make a profession of it.

"Well, what is it? And who is your sweet companion?"

"Your daughter, Sylvia."

"My daughter?" Sylvia's well-arched eyebrows rounded even more, her face turning into the mask of a merry cherub.

How astoundingly young she looked! Miranda began to feel drab, drained, wrung out by comparison. Light gray eyes considered Miranda, the thoughts transparent behind that unlined forehead. Surprise. Slight distaste. The dawn of an idea—a dramatic announcement of a long-lost daughter ... She advanced slowly on Miranda.

"Why, yes ... Millicent. I was so young and you were so—little."

"Millicent?" Miranda's eyes darted to her aunt's in panicked supplication.

"Your father renamed you, Miranda, in the New World, to his

fancy. I know not why. Your mother is right. That much of you she remembers. You were christened Millicent."

"You injure me, Helena, I remember more than that. Millicent! So this is what you've become fifteen, nay, sixteen years hence. You make me feel—older than I thought to be. How old are you? Precisely?"

"Eighteen, madam."

" 'Madam,' how delightful. Of course you must be terrified of me! You would be a pretty child, were you not so frightened, would she not, Helena? But why bring her to me?"

Miranda deafened herself to Helena's explanations, fraught as they were with reminders of Miranda's many unsuspected desertions: her brother, won to the camp of Francisco, and now his inheritance; her father, ransomed by death; even Christopher Steele, leaving her in his wake like an island upon which he had been marooned for a time and wished well behind him. Now her aunt passed her along again, to this careless, gay creature that nature said was her mother and that Miranda's heart said was mother only to her own moods.

"I can hardly introduce her as my own," Sylvia fretted. "Who would believe it? As a niece perhaps ... Of course, My Lord Desmond wouldn't tolerate her living under my wing— Oh, I have just the solution. Carmina! Carmina would be far better guardian to my ... niece ... than I. Naturally, I shall launch her with whatever investment is required, until she finds herself a husband, if that be her aim, or someone other. Don't frown, Helena, 'tis terribly aging. If you had listened to me you would have more to warm your bed than hot bricks, my dear."

Miranda had never been so humiliated, not even when the don had told her that he'd "sold" her. But Miranda's incredulous gaze was lost in the self-confident clouds of indifference her mother emanated like scent.

"Come, my flower, surely one as widely traveled as you knows more of life than she lets on! Do not simper so, Helena, it always did drive me distracted. My little Millicent ... but Carmina must play duenna, eh? My Lord Desmond is not to be trusted with so fresh a bloom within his garden—I am not unaware of that. Now go, Helena; your drab Puritan face reminds me overmuch of someone else. Return to your fancywork and respectable circles. Leave the—my child—with me."

A series of short, sparkling waves from those bejeweled fingers drove Helena Hathaway to the door. "Miranda," she began, her bewildered eyes turning cowlike for conscience-ease from her niece.

"Millicent," interrupted Sylvia impatiently. "She shall be Millicent now."

"And will you return to being plain Kitty now also?" asked Helena with a defiant flash.

Sylvia flushed, a phenomenon that swept her with a tide of becoming rose color from bodice to brow. This was perhaps the one peculiarity that still endeared her to admirers—an ability to blush like a bride for her seventh husband. Sylvia sighed, her milky bosom heaving against the silken stomacher and her large eyes suddenly wounded.

"You have never understood me, Helena. Neither you nor your brother. You brought my daughter to me. To me. Now leave her to me."

Helena nodded and retreated.

Once again Miranda stood solitary in the center of a room for another's inspection. Helena had not been able to discard the brashly feathered hat. Miranda turned it mindlessly in her hands until a flash of gold caught her eye. The King's medal. England still had its King, though he be embattled, and its besieged court of sorts. Now she was here in London, wondering why she had expected it to be any different from the court of the one-eyed Bey of Tunis.

Her eyes, pale green in the bright, light-painted room, watched the woman who was her mother through an insubstantial screen of lashes. Miranda saw nothing of herself, or Harry, in the woman. She was pretty, this Sylvia, pretty like a lavishly iced cake; only the icing cracked a bit here and there if the eye lingered too long on the trimmings.

"Ah. I thought so." Sylvia concluded a slow circle of her daughter and touched the flaxen hair that broke upon the plain gown's shoulders. "Bleached. Where did you learn that trick, my little one? Spectacular, but I think we will forgo that deception here."

She shook her own luxurious yellow curls. "Time enough for that when there's a reason to it. You can't go to Harry, I suppose. Yes, I've heard he's taken your father's inheritance—and the eye of our most adoring gallants. That is what comes of wresting a boy from his mother so young. I would have stayed with you both, I would have been a mother to you, but James wanted me to live as if in a nunnery—without the color, the gaiety, the free-

dom God grants the lowliest sparrow. Turn around, Millicent.
And don't start every time I call you that! 'Tis your name. You
are in my care now. You'll love it better than with sour Helena.
So smile for me, niece; but not overmuch. My Lord Desmond
might come in."

Sylvia saw her "niece," née daughter, out of the way long before His Grace should chance upon the new bloom on his doorstep. Miranda rattled silently alongside her mother in the
leather-lined coach. Every cobblestone jolt was a goad nagging
her to some kind of action, or reaction. Now she knew how
Harry had felt—a hopeless, helpless thing buffeted by forces not
worth resisting. Now it was Carmina to whom she was passed
along. What was Carmina? If Sylvia was not Sylvia but Kitty, if
Miranda was not Miranda but Millicent—who was to say Carmina was Carmina?

Miranda's head ached—that dull, sick headthrob that comes
from heartbreak. Her fingertips smoothed the bit of gold in her
hatband. Cold metal soothed, drew out the fever in her emotions.

She remembered the rhythmic clash of the *Winning Way* and
the Spanish galley, the black magic puffs of powder that had
seemed a suitable mask for death by cannonball; the *Winning
Way*'s horrible heel at the moment the galley severed her rudder.
And Muffin.

Odd, but Muffin's face came to her more often now that he
was farther than tide and time could bring back. She mourned
Muffin. She was proud that she, that her ship, had set him free
at the end. How glorious it had been—that certainty that the day
was hers. Now she was a wanderer through other people's days
and she didn't like it. Better to be playwright than puppet.

Miranda's first meeting with Carmina made her feel only more
of a puppet. A buxom woman of fifty-some years with a complexion as yellow as tallow and tumbling black curls frankly
streaked with gray, Carmina's deep brown eyes peered over the
bridge of a formidable Roman nose.

"Sylvia! No! Your very own girl? *Si*, she is . . . *bella*.
Millibella. Of course I play nursemaid. I have little other to do
these days. We may not have long to lady it over our garden. I
may have to return to Venezia sooner than I think. Well, why
not? These foggy English winters turn my skin to wax. But for
now, I can shepherd your daughter. Retirement leaves one idle to
perform good works, no? I would even say a prayer for her at

this English society, save that my Romanish entreaties would not sit well upon your Protestant hearts. You look tired, *bella*. Come with Carmina. You will see your 'aunt' again soon."

"I don't mind if I never see her again," Miranda remarked dully as Carmina led her commandingly down a strange corridor.

The woman stopped.

"For shame. She is your mother. Only a mother knows what she could have suffered. I do not say that she did, only that she might have. That 'might' must earn your respect. You are strange, cold people, you northerners. You do not forgive easily. If you would confess your sins like good Christians and bad Catholics, perhaps they would lie easier upon you. Now, shhhh. You are tired, I have never seen a child so tired, and you say what you do not mean."

Carmina saw Miranda bedded, although it was midafternoon and seemed slothful, and left her floating on a wide mattress that was strangely still compared to her accustomed hammock.

She slept. All the faces of the last few hours—Sylvia's, Carmina's, Helena's, Christopher Steele's—slid behind her like land from an embarking ship. Steele's flamboyant hat and Helena's frugal gown kept mismatched company on the chest.

Sylvia's long-lost daughter dreamed odd, swirling visions of sinking in a bright scarlet sea until a hand in a black Spanish-leather gauntlet reached out to her and then she sank deep, deep into the Red Sea waters until she found she could breathe them.

She bobbed to the surface again, aware of daylight still pushing at the drawn curtains, of distant servant voices chattering softly out of sight. Perhaps they were discussing her. The thought drew no alarm. She drifted on the rim of consciousness. Here she was Miranda still. Her lids were so heavy she was loath to open them. Some great weight pinned her to that white linen expanse. It was neutral territory. Finally. Whatever, whoever, Carmina was, she was a neutral party. There was nothing between them, no blood or belief to link them.

Miranda opened her eyes to the brocaded canopy hanging stiffly above her. She heard Carmina rustle into the room, the hushed servant voices reporting. Sleeping. Not really. But why tell them? Dinner? Why not? There came the heavy rustle of Carmina's Italian brocade and then her boisterous voice.

"It's been hours, *bella*! Come sup, and then we talk, eh?"

Miranda pulled herself up, hampered by the billowing silk nightshirt into which she had been thrust like a doll. She impatiently yanked the full sleeves with their fingertip ruffles above her elbows. She'd been used to collapsing in a hammock in the men's clothes upon her back. The world of women was composed of many filmy webs with which to enmesh them.

Carmina laughed, a low contralto rumble that made Miranda smile.

"You *gattina*! You like some stray yellow kitten who has many tale to tell and only her secret yellow—no, *verde*—eyes with which to do it. Here, under the chin with the napkin. Cook has made a plateful of pasta and I do not wish you dribbling over my Venetian linens."

Miranda allowed Carmina to lay a tray across her lap, then assist her in eating the strange but richly seasoned dish. The bizarre noodles slipped off the knife like fish eluding a net, despite Carmina's tutoring.

" 'Tis plain my Italy have not been among your ports of call," said Carmina finally, removing the noodle-strewn napkin and plumping the pillows behind her guest. "Now a little wine and much talk. We Italians love talk as much as *eau-de-vie*. So talk with me, Millicent."

A frown creased Miranda's pale brow on hearing that new name. Carmina settled closer, taking Miranda's chilled white hands in her own, rather graceless, square ones.

"Come, a little confession between friends is a comfort. And I will be your friend. I have naught left in life but to play friend to those without them. Let me meddle; it occupy me. I was a princess once, you know. Oh, yes. All your princesses are not slender moonlike things from bloodless lines. Italy has grown her princesses broad for generations.

"When I was sixteen, I was taken off a Neapolitan galley by a Barbary pirate. A corsair. You know the breed, eh? Then I was sold to the sultan at Constantinople. Ah, that interest you, such a tale? 'Twas there, where what transpired you do not require to know, that I fell across a so-amusing man, an English Cavalier. He contrived to free me. Now, honorable families do not reclaim dishonored princesses, so I come to England and here have lived nigh on twenty-five years. So you see, I have no family, nor none that truly count as such. And still I survive. So squeak up, little mouse, and tell me of yourself."

Miranda began with Barbados. With sea and sand and plantation, with armadillo and ant and candlewood tree. She had meant only to sketch the barest details, to justify the geography of her wanderings. Yet soon such words as "Father" and "Francisco" crept in unwilling. And "Harry."

Carmina dipped absentmindedly into Miranda's abandoned pasta while the travel tales unraveled, but the sympathetic brown eyes never left Miranda's face, though not a noodle slithered off her broad knife blade.

"Ah, *cara*." Carmina sighed, dotting her lips with the napkin and settling back against the padded roll that held out her skirts as a grandmother leans into the curve of her rocking chair. " 'Tis a sad story but not new to me. Your brother Harry. I saw much boys turned to such use by the sultan's court in Constantinople. Those in the East live on another side of the globe and they seem to find another side to everything. Of course your brother disown you! Your Hollander pirate captain was right; none of our weaknesses bear witnesses. But how got you to England after?"

"Ship," said Miranda shortly.

"Which? Few make harbor now with the times so changeable."

"The *Dowsabelle*."

"Ah, Captain Steele's new vessel. Yes, I know this one. Captain! I knew his father when he was but a pup himself. Yes, I did. Before Charles wed that pretty Katharine and settled down to breeding a whole flight of stairs of English children—all lookalikes, you say, no?—little yellow heads like butter cakes so." Carmina's hand pantomimed a series of rising levels as if patting heads spun out of only sunshine.

"Pretty children. All pretty, all look like the rest. The Steele hallmark, one cannot fail to trace it. Now yours, yours would be—not Ben, no . . . Christopher, yes? A handsome boy, though they all are, but something in him— How unjust that your chill northern air breeds more warm-headed children than all the siroccos blowing from the African coast on Italy. You are a gilded race, you English, I begin to think. Look; you could be cousin to half your countrymen."

Carmina's fingers sifted through Miranda's soft-spun yellow hair. "You could be yet another Steele—"

"I am naught like him!" Miranda challenged, wrenching her hair from the fingers that combed it.

The plate upon Carmina's lap shifted disastrously. She caught it just before the scarlet sauce spilled across the coverlet.

"Softly, my little guest. I'll not have you play Vesuvius across my Venetian linens. Love-apple juice is not a lava that wash out easily. Why take such exception to my harmless chatter?"

"I am not anything like him! He is a terrible man. You haven't seen them for years, have you, your pretty Steele children? You do not know what has been made of them."

"Tell me, then." Carmina calmly set the tray aside as prelude to what promised to be a stormy tale.

Miranda's eyes darted to her hands, folded tightly on the coverlet's embroidered border. Splendid work, she noticed, well worth Carmina's care. Miranda folded the worked portion under, as if it were too exquisite to witness her telling.

"I meant never to speak of this, but I would not have you believe better of 'Captain Steele' than I know to be true. He did not merely convey me to England. He—he—ravished—me."

"Aaaahhh." Carmina sank back again against her skirts. "*That* is the wrong that rides you! I see it from the first. Like a thorn, broken off—one views that dark slim invasion but find no way of reaching it to withdraw it. Just that much below the surface. I saw the thorn in you, but would have blamed Sylvia, I think, had you not told me this. Raped you. Ah, *cara*, and how did most of us get to be women in these days if not by some rape or the other? Worse things walk the world, that we call by longer names, but it takes years to find them out."

"Nothing worse," said Miranda stubbornly. "Nothing."

"Only the very young speak in such extremes as 'nothing,' or 'everything.' If this man, this boy that I remember, robbed you of your maidenhead, I imagine there was worse that could have happened had he set a mind to it. How many times did he so abuse you?"

Miranda's conscience did a rapid toting-up. Once. On the *Salamander*. And again whenever she thought of that occasion. And the last, less-certain time. Deceiving her that he was her inevitable future, making her overcommit herself as to a chess opponent who dissolves into an empty space across the board ...

"Once," said Miranda, inflexibly honest. "Once."

Carmina's dark eyes flashed in her sallow face, the beginnings of a smile peeling from her lips like a rind from an orange. "Only once?" Carmina mocked gently. "No wonder you hate him so!"

Miranda's hand flashed an arc across Carmina's waxy face. She saw it fill suddenly with surprise, like a sail puffed by a vagrant gust of wind.

"Once is a thousand times," Miranda said passionately. "With all your travels and tribulations, you have not learned that. You live in a world where women accept such things as a natural hazard. You see it no more than he did. I once thought that I had to extract revenge—which is not a hard thing to do—to get my own back. But 'tis more difficult than that. I . . . I must make you, make him, understand what a crime it was against me. Yet that is one thing a person cannot make another do. Understand. I could make him feel regret, feel sorry, ashamed—perhaps I have; but it is not enough."

Carmina was unused to such spirited debates. She was tempted to take her hand from her reddened cheek and shake the girl's shoulders. Something stopped her.

"I do not understand," she admitted. "I will believe that what I say was dishonorable to you. But do not ever slap me again. I have more pleasant ways to redden my cheeks."

Chapter Twenty-nine

The thin silver blade hung above Miranda like a dream stiletto, then lunged for her. She screamed and wriggled out of its reach until her back was brought up on hanging cages of brocade.

"Millicent." Carmina stood there, hands on well-bolstered hips, her dark brows one lowering thundercloud line. "Your screeches drive my poor Flammetta to shake. How do you expect to have pierce your ears unless you stop all this fluttering?"

"I don't wish my ears pierced. 'Tis barbaric."

"Oh, my Millicent, come from under the bed curtains and talk with Carmina. Yes, I keep away Flammetta. Here, silly goose, give me the needle! And you, come here, child."

Miranda reluctantly scrambled forward to inspect an empty, sunlit room. Carmina had settled at the bed's foot and sat watching her with shaking head and sighing breast.

"Millicent. 'Tis a great festivity to which I take you this night. London has not had many of late. Why think you I spend so many time closeted with the best French Huguenot dressmaker sovereigns can buy? Silly folk, these French, to drive out their finest seamstresses for reasons of religion merely! Millicent. Why have I had you curled and scented and gowned for a fortnight if not for this, your first masque, your first London ball? But. Without earrings you set not so much as a satin toe outside this chamber. 'Tis unbelievable that you expect to live through life without the means to stud an ear with a pearl. You will be no lady until your ears are most fashionably ringed. Now hold silent and Carmina shall accomplish it."

Miranda tried to eel away but the Italian woman had her firmly by the earlobe.

"Millicent! I break patience. You who tell of traveling half a world, of living on a ship like man, and from this so tiny needle you are afraid? Be still, foolish one, and it will be *fini* in an instant."

Miranda squealed as something stung her earlobe.

"Be still if you cannot be quiet," ordered Carmina, commandeering the other ear.

In a moment Miranda had both hands clapped over her injured lobes, while her eyes silently accused Carmina of atrocity.

"Hush, child." Carmina saturated a handkerchief with cologne and brought the astringent to Miranda's ears. "Look. Pretty pearl drops from the topaz stones. You will see, my reluctant savage, how well you like them." Carmina expertly strung the gold wires through her protégé's freshly punctured ears and sat back. "Yes. 'Twill complement the gown of coral you wear tonight."

"It hurts," Miranda insisted stubbornly.

"—and will stop hurting soon. You will have other things to think on ... to remember the proper curtsy, and to see your mother, Sylvia, again."

"She will be there?"

"Of a certainty. They begin the evening with a very fine masque with music by Signor Lully and poetry by Sir William Davenant: a tribute to the union of Venus and Vulcan, I understand. A union not made in heaven, but in Vulcan's own nether kingdom, as the myths would have it. Your mo—Sylvia, of course, will play Venus. I cannot quite imagine her as Vulcan, the underworld lord. It amuse me much how you English worship the gods of my ancestors, but have no great regard for nowaday Romans.

"Ah, who is to understand the workings of history? Better now, yes? Come, we up and dress, and by the time the lights of Bridgeport House reflect on those"—here Carmina gave the dangling pearls a tap—"you will have forgotten completely that you paid any price at all to have them."

Carmina underestimated her protégé's capacity to remember slights. The ravished earlobes still throbbed slightly when Miranda stood beside Carmina that evening while all the gallants left in London, and their ladies, paraded at Bridgeport House.

Each one, Miranda felt, bent an unbelieving gaze precisely on her earlobes. That was unlikely, for Carmina had groomed her West Indies visitor with far more guile than Miranda could appreciate. Carmina had forgone thick white face paint, had forsworn patches and rouge and all of polite society's fripperies, merely pitting Miranda's flawless complexion against a glimmering coral satin gown and simple pearl choker.

Miranda's fingers worried at those pearls from time to time; they seemed like to throttle her. Or was it merely that her neck was stiff, unaccustomed to bearing the elaborate knot and twin crescendos of curls tumbling from her head? Inside her heavy circle of embroidered satin skirts, her feet teetered in delicate shoes that stalked along on high jeweled heels. *Diablo!* An ankle twisted beneath her skirt, the entire superstructure twitched and Miranda's arm clutched Carmina's.

"*Piano, piano,* my Millicent. We soon seat ourselves for the masque. You had better master your shoes, or you will not remain mistress of yourself this evening."

Miranda minced obediently to a tapestried chair as a tuneful prelude by a string quartet heralded the masque's beginning. Then lute tones prevailed, and the curtain rose on a lavishly painted stage. Servants solemnly lit tiers of onstage candelabra as a magnificently attired gentleman stepped before them.

He began declaiming long sonorous lines of poetry more remarkable for the complexity of their metaphor than for their meaning. Miranda had never seen a play performed, much less a London masque. So this was how her father's folios came to life! She forgot the pinch in her ears and let her eyes rule her senses.

"These masques are not what they were," Carmina whispered, leaning so close that their earrings swung together. "Not as when the so-great Ben Jonson put quill to foolscap. In those days even dour King Charles would consent to speak a verse or two, and his Queen wore such gowns that Inigo Jones concoct—such *décolleté,* as the French would say—that every court lady ached to partake in the masques the better to dazzle her admirers with her anatomy. But this is before these civil wars began . . . Ah, here is our Sylvia."

Miranda watched a clamshell chariot grind forward from some

invisible mechanism. It trembled to a stop, then the lustrous shell lips parted slowly to reveal a rider. Onto the stage emerged a creature all in silver lace, trailing a tunic than parted halfway up the thighs. Her bare shoulders and arms gleamed with silver powder as she posed deftly on the stage, her draperies flowing in ever more inventive disarray.

Shame swelled Miranda's throat until she thought the pearl necklace would burst. She would have risen to leave, but horror sat heavy upon her shoulders and held her fixed. The softly glittering creature onstage assumed an attitude and froze. Instantly a sudden shower of fireworks parted to reveal a blackened, hunched figure that limped to center stage and declaimed elegant couplets whose meaning completely lanced past Miranda.

A chorus materialized about the pair and began a pure-voiced song to accompanying instruments. The candles onstage were bright and hot; Sylvia's neck and forehead glistened in the glare. Miranda looked around: each surrounding profile was directed intently stageward. Every eye was setting as faithfully as a sun upon the glittering figure of Sylvia Hathaway . . . no wonder Father had taken ship halfway around the globe!

She saw no art in her mother's part in this, only spectacle for the senses. Miranda dropped her eyes until the last syllable of song had echoed off the high, coffered ceiling. When she raised them again, the candles were being snuffed one by one and all the actors were gone.

"You like to see her?" inquired Carmina.

"I have," Miranda replied grimly.

"Ah, I mean in closet, privately."

"No."

"No? Very well. I go alone. Stay here for me."

Carmina glided into the crowds fanning out of the masque end of the room. Dancing—Carmina had said there would be dancing. Miranda did not care to think of it, but only moments later, a shadow loomed over her. She brought her eyes from her gleaming satin lap to a face inclined to hers.

"Charming mistress," intoned the face's owner. "Perhaps you would care to tread a measure?" He had a long face, slightly pox-marked; his nearness made the pocks seem pits. "Sebastian Banebridge, if I may present myself. Would the lady be so gracious as to present me with either her name or her hand?"

His long white palm tapered toward her from a froth of silver lace. She let herself be drawn up and regretted it a moment later as she teetered on the treacherous heels. The man's amber brocade arms snapped shut upon her instantly.

"A hand was all I requested," he murmured with a satisfied smirk.

Miranda shook herself loose and planted her heels hard on the thick Oriental carpet.

"My name, sir," she said icily, "is Millicent Hathaway." For once she appreciated her recent rechristening. Letting this man's rose-gray lips mouth her real name would have been odious. "You may return my hand," she added.

Instead he led her to a shoulder-high chimneypiece. They were now isolated in the room. A figure who had observed that fact detached itself from a circle of gleaming shoulders and came to stand unobtrusively behind Miranda. Something in Sebastian Banebridge's long face grew longer.

"Would Mistress Hathaway care to dance?" His fingers found and twined in hers again. She unwound them.

"I think not," she said, not bothering to mask her distaste.

Sebastian Banebridge's face set for three blinks of his furred lashes. He inclined his head so his well-curled black hair hung sharply against his amber-colored jacket. When his face surfaced again, it was paler than the powder made it, and his dark pupils were overtaking the yellow of his eyes, so he was one black, unforgiving look.

"Perhaps the lady would prefer to dance in our masques," he suggested. "A charming"—his eyes carelessly tripped through the maze of her person—"Diana, the moon goddess. Goddess of the hunt. And the hunted."

Sebastian Banebridge's lips split into a particularly repellent smile. "I see her as a young, chaste Diana, eh, Farnsworth?" he said to the man who had joined them. "Wearing only her quiver and a bit of gauze—there. We must improvise something for our fair young visitor, Oliver and I. I will have to talk to Oliver."

As he spoke, Sebastian's yellow eyes watched hers, while his forefinger traced an intimate path across the small naked bronze figure of a nymph on a German mantel clock. Miranda felt her eyes drawn to that slowly moving finger, felt herself shrink into that defenseless figure—she tore her eyes away and turned to the man behind her addressed as Farnsworth.

"Nay, gentlemen," she said levelly, "one actress in the family is sufficient. I will leave theatrics to my—Aunt Sylvia. I have no talent for it."

"Theatrics require no talent, my dear." Sebastian's finger left the bronze to play airly at the farthest reach of her curls, so she could hardly accuse him of laying hands upon her.

"Then I have no taste for them."

"Tastes can be acquired," Sebastian went on, his tongue—fat and rose-colored—pausing obscenely between his yellowish teeth. "I for one," he confided to Farnsworth, "have been known to change my tastes at the drop of—a knee breech."

"Pay no attention to this gallant, mistress," Farnsworth cautioned firmly. "You are too new a chick to London to languish in a corner with such old game as we."

He led Miranda away, his hand stiff upon her elbow, and stayed beside her until Sebastian Banebridge's tall form eased like a snake's through some narrow opening and escaped the room.

To Miranda's relief, after Farnsworth had left her she drew a faded gallant in search of an audience to whom to chatter while he punctuated his remarks with airy waves of a lacy handkerchief.

He was, he said, a costumer for the masques, had in fact festooned the lovely lady, "your aunt," who had played Venus to such a turn this night. A shipment of rich Orient stuffs was to inspire the next such theatrical.

Across the room, Sebastian Banebridge's highly curled head surfaced again. It turned slowly left and right amongst the other heads. Miranda knew in her corset bones that it was she he sought. Her effete escort babbled on about his tissues of gold, his well-worked brocades and India cloth as light as cobwebs.

"I've only now unpacked it. Trunks of the stuff. Perhaps you'd care to see—?"

"Yes, yes!" Miranda said breathlessly, her eyes fixed on the nearing head of her sinister admirer. The unnamed gentleman guided her into an empty corridor. "I am most anxious to see your wares, sir; where are they?"

"This way."

The unnamed gentleman led Miranda up a flight of ill-lit stairs and down a dark upper passage. He opened a door on a room ringed with draperies and candle stands.

For a moment, Miranda thought that she had returned to the bey's cabin. Her heart began beating with a certain terror. But the gentleman in lemon silk was eyeing the position of a face patch in a small mirror atop a China chest; Miranda guessed that she had no fears there.

An open trunk stood in the room's center. Such a small, cozy room. Strange that such an imposing house should contain so curtained an alcove.

"Here, Mistress Millicent—taffetas and silks to delight a sultan. Feel of them. You've not touched stuffs so fine in your life."

Miranda plunged her arms into the cloudy cargo from the Orient. They felt like dry water, waves of emerald and ruby and crystal blue that wafted over her bare forearms. One length tangled around her wrist—in a moment her arm was jerked upward and secured to a hook hung from the tented ceiling.

"Sir!" Miranda protested, uncertain what phenomenon had pinioned her.

The light-footed gentleman darted to loop another silken tie around her free wrist. The silk was soft, but Miranda was as neatly bound as a tame bear leashed to its master. She fought the fabric, but her thrashing only tightened the knots.

"Sir!" Miranda still sheathed her confusion in courtesy.

His faded face turned to her, an expression of triumph changing it from a foolish to a rapacious one. He minced around the room like a ballet master, drawing each curtain back with a metallic hiss along its rod. A Miranda leapt into view on each wall of the octagon, a mirrored Miranda who beat her gauzy wings against capture, like a dragonfly.

Her white face flashed into each mirror and then moved on to confront the next panel—still the same, still outré and awful. Her treasured first court gown ripped at the arm seams as she bucked against the filmy bonds. She paused and tried reasoning with the creature.

"Surely you know that hundreds are but paces away. My screams—"

"Shall enthrall me," said the aging gallant, supporting his long chin on an elegant hand. He cradled his elbow on his palm and leaned his weight on the heel of a beaded satin shoe. "Do scream . . . this room echoes most delightfully. And the glass will not let exit the smallest scrap of sound."

Miranda pursed her lips; if he wanted screams, she should not oblige him.

"Ah, stubborn. This shall be most rewarding."

He pace slowly around his captive as her head twisted to follow him. He finally ducked to the still-open trunk and fished among its gauzy contents. Miranda searched for the exit which seemed to have vanished into the glazed octagon that reflected her.

"Yes, you will sing for me, little bird," he was prattling, "but little birds must have feathers . . ."

"You must release me. You must regain your senses, you—"

"Ah, but I am regaining my senses, you have no idea how much."

A hinge creaked and he paused, alert.

"What is this tumult?" The man who stepped from shadow into the blazing light of mirrors reflecting rows of torchéres was Sebastian Banebridge.

Miranda drew in a breath of despair at her fate in finding a rescuer as odious as her ravisher. Her tormenter hung back in silence, seeming suddenly to shrink.

"My poor girl!" Sebastian Banebridge's eyes lingered on Miranda for so long that she wondered if he would bother freeing her. "Such an introduction to London's wicked ways."

He shook his bewigged head and clucked his fat pink tongue most distressfully. Finally he walked over to her, his eyes bent on her bodice front most forthrightly, and began to untie one of her wrists.

"Poor child," he said.

Just as the silk loosened, he caught her fiercely around the waist, so fiercely that her breath came in a great gasp and then she couldn't catch it. While Sebastian held her in a clawlike grip, the other man scurried forward, twittering and pursing his painted lips.

"Now, Oliver, patience," began Sebastian. Miranda's angry eyes rested on the yellow silk dandy's face. Oliver? This was the Oliver of whom Sebastian had spoken in the ballroom; from their like looks, they must be brothers!

"I want to see what our web has netted us this night."

Miranda anticipated them. When they reached to free her other wrist, she struck out so forcefully that her nail swept a red line across Oliver's encroaching face.

"Oh!" He pressed his lace handkerchief to the scratch. "Look, Sebastian, she's quite ruined me for a week. Nasty child."

Oliver pouted in the chest-top mirror and dabbed at his hurt, leaving his brother to master Miranda alone.

Hampered as she was by her heavy court gown, Miranda gave him as good a fight as any got on board the *Gato de Nueve*, but at last Sebastian managed to bind her wrist again with the silken tie attached to ceiling hook. Miranda paced and raged to the end of her leash, but could not tear it.

Panting, Sebastian drew back to regard her. "Oliver? Stop that foolish fussing. I need help."

Oliver still patted into place the new patch he had found to cover the mark she had made.

"Diana, as I said, no?" A slow smile crawled across Sebastian's face until he licked it away with the bloated tip of his tongue. Miranda was beginning to hate the sight of that appendage.

"Phidias could have carved her," agreed Oliver, something like daring in his loose-lidded eyes.

"Or per-Phidias," Sebastian sneered then. "You should have deigned to dance with me, Mistress Millicent. You would have found me a less-demanding partner than the pair of us."

Oliver leaned his lemon-silk-swathed arm on his brother's amber brocade shoulder. "When may I begin, Basty? I'm simply dying to begin."

Miranda clenched her teeth and stood silent; her struggles only fueled the fires in their sulphurous eyes. Sebastian abruptly nodded to his brother and Oliver darted out of sight again. Sebastian began slowly to unfasten his jacket, his eyes torn between her person and her reflections in the mirror.

"Oliver is the more—inventive. I shall let Oliver be first, but you will remember me longer, I promise you that." He stepped forward to run his fingernail along precisely the course it had traced across the bronze nymph but minutes before.

Miranda shuddered but said nothing. A disturbance at her feet drew her gaze down. Oliver had returned and was crouched at her skirts, crisscrossing her ankles with red silk ribbons. He glanced up, his lank brown locks brushing her calf; Miranda recoiled with distaste. He looked like some drooling spaniel.

"Like Diana, you said, Basty. I shall dress a Diana that will delight you." Oliver giggled and crawled away, more doglike than ever.

"Most amusing, is he not?" Sebastian dropped his jacket and began undoing his silk shirt. Oliver bustled back, ropes of pearls twisted in his hands. He drew them slowly over her bare shoulders. They were cold and left a trail of gooseflesh.

"Ah, see!" exclaimed Oliver in delight. "That you don't get with marble. The real ones are so much superior."

Oliver draped an airy cage of pearls over Miranda's bodice. Sebastian advanced then, his long fingernails softly prodding the lengths into better position, his fingers picking at her here, there, touching bare skin now and again.

Miranda was ready to scream enough to shatter every mirror around her, but Sebastian yanked back his brother's leering face back by the hair, like a recalcitrant spaniel's.

"Not yet," he ordered between clenched teeth. "Later," Sebastian said more calmly. "You haven't finished the costuming."

Oliver nodded eagerly and scurried away. When he was gone, Sebastian smiled. His eyes purposefully met hers. She gave him a wall of green smolder, but that only seemed to warm him further. Miranda turned her face against her arm and refused to look at him.

Oliver was gone for a long while; when he came back his face was very flushed. A length of white silk wavered from his fingers. Oliver bent to fasten this across Miranda's torso, like an insubstantial quiver.

"There, Basty. There is your Diana. Look on her and then . . . Can I watch?"

"No," Sebastian said sharply.

Miranda was certain her moment of greatest humiliation had come, but after a long look, Sebastian turned and vanished behind the same screen that had hidden Oliver's exits.

Oliver remained, grinning foolishly. He darted an occasional feverish gaze in the direction Sebastian had gone; twice he seemed tempted to follow, but each time he returned and looked at Miranda again.

She began to conceive that these odd men had no intention of misusing her in the usual way. Contemplating what variations they might invent unnerved her.

"Oliver," she said tentatively. He looked at her, startled, then giggled. "Since I'm to be a Diana, why do I have no bow, no arrow? That isn't correct, is it, Oliver?"

"True, all the classical representations of Diana have real bows and quivers, of course, slung over the shoulder." His fingers drew a line along the gauzy bandolier.

Miranda forestalled the shiver such touches gave her even through her clothes, and went on. "Oh, I don't need all that, but an—arrow, perhaps, would be just the right touch."

Oliver's long face puckered into consideration, like a shrinking length of flat pink fabric.

"A Cupid's arrow, Oliver. Is that not a nice conceit? Would not Basty like it when he returns?"

Oliver's face smoothed into a certain lewd anticipation. Then he pouted, daubing his new patch. "I have no arrows here. Not a one. I'm no huntsman, you know."

"But you are inventive. Even Basty said so. You could fashion an arrow, from something long and sharp . . . You must have the wherewithal for one arrow."

Oliver eyed her with a secret grin. From his side he plucked a dress dagger that gleamed like a giant pin in the light.

"Yes! Perfect. I will hold it in my hand for Sebastian when he returns."

Miranda's bound wrist twisted toward him and she fanned her fingers for the handle. Oliver waved it toward her, then withdrew it.

"No! It has no feather. All arrows must have a feather. I know!"

"Be quick about it," urged Miranda. "Any feather'll do."

Oliver returned in a moment from delving in the trunk, a cock feather incongruously wired around his dagger handle. The blade itself was but a plaything, brittle steel meant for show and not service.

But when Oliver put it into Miranda's waiting palm, it was strong and sharp enough to slice through silk in one swift stroke. Her wrist was free before Oliver had even blinked. One hand tore the enmeshing pearls from her bodice.

"My pearls," he wailed. "My precious pearls, you naughty child! You've ruined my pearls." He plunged to the floor to pluck them up with his thumb and forefinger.

Miranda caught up her billowing skirts and ran to the conclave of mirrors. Her reflection beat against herself for entry as she strove for exit, searching for the panel that had admitted her. Some catch, some trigger mechanism—her fingers traced the bevels while her eyes ensured that Oliver remained bent on scooping up pearls, that Sebastian had not returned.

A click. One mirror slid sideways into a sliver of light until the fantastic scene of which she was part spun away. The passage was dark after such reflected light, which had been like being inside a silver goblet. She plunged into that undemanding shadow.

Her elegantly shod feet clattered down the hardwood floor and the red ribbons round her legs fluttered behind her.

At the staircase balcony, she paused and glanced over her shoulder. The dim passage arrowed away into dark wood wainscoting and echoed no pursuing footsteps. From below, murmuring voices and a candlelit glow wafted up. Miranda bent to undo the shepherdess's ribbons at her ankles. Oliver's pretty party blade she clenched in her teeth while both hands struggled to remove the ribbons.

The taste of steel reminded her of something—something distant and quite different from this scene in Bridgeport House. The precise memory eluded her, just as the laces slipped through her overanxious fingers. How dare they! To pinion her like an unruly falcon— She was angrier than she had ever been, ready to return to her glazed prison and do a thorough job of carving Oliver's pasty face ...

The snap of a door frame down that dim passage paralyzed her vengeful thoughts. Coming for her. She fluttered down the steep hardwood stairs, her dainty heels catching in a trailing band of red ribbon.

A trip, and her feet were stuttering down the steps too fast, her hand sliding helplessly along a slick walnut handrail too broad to cling to. Miranda kept balance until a shoe spun off her foot.

The hard paved floor at the foot of her descent awaited her collapse upon it. Then a body loomed around the massive newel-post. Miranda was enveloped in dove-gray velvet that staggered back with her weight but ultimately braked her fall.

Chapter Thirty

"*Sacré bleu! Mademoiselle, vous êtes une comète. D'tombez-vous?*"

Miranda balanced against her rescuer on one shod foot.

Though young, he was dressed with a richness to have done his elders credit. He cocked his head, the glossy brown locks he wore Cavalier-style slipping sideways on a faultless white lace falling band. His eyes punctuated his astonished French phrases by darting to the dagger she still clasped so tightly that her hand was whiter than the collar upon which it rested.

"*Pardonnez moi*, I have lately been in the domain of our

French cousin, Louis, and am inclined to forget which tongue to wear." He looked mischievous. "Does the mysterious airborne lady speak any tongue at all, or is she merely a mute vision that has dropped from this so beautifully painted ceiling?"

"Do not be ludicrous, sir," snapped Miranda, casting one quick glance to the painted hall ceiling and the sinister barred railing near it. "And you need not clutch me in this oversolitious fashion. I am quite capable of standing on my own."

"Not merely a tongue, but a well-honed one." The young man released her obediently.

Miranda tottered until her unshod foot rested on cold flagstones. The young man shook his brown satin head and bent to retrieve her lost slipper. He led a limping Miranda to a bench and seated her.

"Ah, *mademoi*—mistress. In France a delightful folktale charms even the court with the tale of a lovely lady and a certain slipper of fur that she loses at a great ball."

He paused in his recital to kneel and extract Miranda's shoeless foot from beneath her frothy petticoats.

"She loses this rather improbable piece of footwear—yours is so sensible, I see, merely brocade and pearls, no fur. The slipper is found by a gallant prince who returns it to her dainty foot, so. She becomes his bride. *Cendrillon,* they call her. The lady of the ashes. Perhaps you are another."

He had performed the intimate service of shoeing her with an impersonal dignity that stunned her into silence. "Is there any other service I can perform for *mademoi*—for you?"

The French manner draped his Englishness like a cloak that flaps around its wearer in a high wind and hampers as much as shelters. He would be Royalist to have spent so much time in Paris. Miranda stared into his frank eyes and felt a simmer of embarrassment.

Anger surged to her every extremity; she had to lace her fingers shut on her lap to keep them from trembling, and still felt a violent, utter need for someone, something.

"Do you know Sylvia Hathaway?" she asked before she could stop herself. Sylvia, why Sylvia? Sylvia was nothing to her but a glittering, vacant doll.

"The lovely Venus of our masque? You wish me to find her? You must speak, lovely mute, if you would direct me." When Miranda didn't reply, he rose. "I will find Sylvia."

"No." Miranda clutched his gray velvet sleeve so tightly that her fingertips left white ovals on the nap. "Carmina." His brown eyes regarded her expectantly. "The Italian. Take me to Carmina."

He bowed and offered his hand. "I must introduce myself, *Cendrillon*. I am Justin Waverleigh and no prince, I confess. I hope your heart is not set on princes."

Miranda gave his gallantry a distracted smile, but she was glad enough to have him by her side, a flesh-and-blood wall against any pursuit.

"Ah," he said suddenly. "Not fur, feathers." He abstracted the dress dagger from her tightly curled hand. "This plaything is an odd ornament for you, mistress, and may encourage questions you would not answer. I should don it."

He tore the feather from its handle and impaled the dagger in the gold-worked baldric that lay diagonally from his shoulder to hip.

Her hand in his was icy, but Miranda was lost exploring a fiery inner turmoil as her guide led her back to Carmina's side on a well-carved settle in the Great Hall. The world instantly became noisy, crowded and real again when Miranda met a face she could trust.

"Take me home, Carmina," she implored in a low voice, her request producing deep brown question marks in the Italian woman's eyes.

"Millicent, what has happened?"

"Millicent—?"

The tiresome gallant was still there, still making pleasantries and seeking now her name. Miranda shot him an angry iron gaze that only intensified the inquiry in his eyes.

"Allow me to ask *mademoi*—your name, mistress."

"Hathaway," she finally said between her teeth. The anger was spreading now, threatening to scald everyone. "Home, Carmina, now!"

Carmina shrugged. "I'll have the coach brought round."

"Allow me, madam. Justin Waverleigh of Oxfordshire, Paris and no great address but some small sufficiency to be of assistance, I trust."

Carmina measured the young man with a sweep of her midnight lashes, then nodded regal assent.

"Millicent, what has happened?" she asked as Justin's boots diminished into soft slaps on the hard floors. "You're white with fury, yet so pretty a companion you have conjured. Young, perhaps, but such a fine gentleman he will polish into."

"Hush, Carmina. I will tell you when we are alone."

"Surely nothing is so secret that it cannot share the space that surrounds us now, *Cara*? Did the young man do anything untoward?"

"No! But I must leave before— Now, take me home now."

Young Waverleigh soon returned to escort both women to the torch-bracketed door where Carmina's coach waited on the shining cobblestones.

It had rained while the guests were romping at their masque. The night's shiny freshness made both Waverleigh and Carmina pause to appreciate it. Miranda was oblivious, even when Justin handed her into the carriage and kissed her white-knuckled fingers.

"Adieu, *Cendrillon*. I will keep both eyes open for any lost slippers of yours."

The coach rumbled away over the gleaming cobblestones, tossing its occupants about its lumbering interior.

"*Basta!*" cried Carmina as jolt followed jolt. "A chair would have been smoother, though these chairmen are ofttimes foxed. Oh, for the canals of Venezia. Now." She frowned at Miranda huddled in the leather seat. "Now what?"

" 'Tis those awful, those—bloody—Banebridge brothers." Miranda spoke in tones so intense that Carmina had to lean into the dark to hear. "Those dogs of the meanest gutter, those whoreson—"

"*Basta!*" Carmina implored, a laugh trembling in her tones. " 'Tis clear you're a well-traveled minx. I've not heard such fervor from my coachman— Oh, but I begin to guess, little spitfire. Of course. I should have warn you, but they seldom tease the petticoats. So the Banebridges have caught you in one of their inventive pieces of drollery. Such a shame!"

"You know of them?" The voice from the dark was even more intense. "Drollery! I cannot bring myself to tell you."

"No need. All Whitehall has guessed at the Banebridges' disportments. Young Lord Foxblood must be dispatched to the Continent for a tour last year, and wasn't his dear mama upset? The brothers were nearly exported themselves. Most know their inclinations, and know enough to sail well round them. I'm sorry, my little manicotti, but don't fret your noodle-brain about it. They cannot—they have no inclination—to actually dishonor a woman, you see."

"Your notions of honor are miraculous flexible, Carmina," said the voice from the dark with an even darker undertone. "They have dishonored me and I shall not endure it. They can go to the Devil and I will be happy to set out the stone for their first step hellward!"

"*Cara, cara, cara.* Hush," Carmina instructed as the coach rocked to a stop.

The pair clattered into Carmina's Italianate town house and up the wide interior stairs. The Italian woman pursued a striding Miranda all the way to the bedchamber, murmuring soothing Italian phrases like a lullaby to a troubled child.

Miranda whirled on Carmina when the last servant was out of earshot, her dark cloak spinning away from the glitter of her gown, which set the bedchamber alight as if she were a blazing human chandelier at full fire.

"*Basta, cara, basta,*" implored Carmina.

"Enough? 'Twill never be enough until I am avenged. Until my honor has been redeemed." Miranda paced, dragging the heavy cloak behind her like flapping raven wings.

"Honor. How you English prattle of it. I thought, my little innocent, that you counted your precious honor taken previously."

Miranda raked Carmina's face with a bright green glance as sharp as a fingernail. Then she unclasped her cloak, letting it puddle around her feet like a rejected bit of the black evening outside.

"With that, too, I have not finished. This is different, this happened only an hour ago, when I was in their hands—" She broke off in disgust.

"Be practical, then, if you cannot be forgiving. What can you do, other than announce your indignity to the world and hope a champion will step forward to avenge you? A heavy price, *cara*, for some trifling—no, don't burn at me so, I know to you is not trifling. To you, nothing is a trifle."

"I do not seek a champion, Carmina. I merely want to see those two—weasels—with their vicious ears well boxed. Look at my gown, look at it! Torn, ruined. I never wish to see it again, not even if 'tis ripped into cleaning rags!"

"Millicent. Calm. Stay still and let me unlace you. Tomorrow all will seem a dream. If you still want satisfaction then, I wager you can persuade young Waverleigh to be your champion, eh?"

"Waverleigh?" Miranda's green eyes, smoldering gray like still-smoking ashes, fixed in astonishment on the Italian woman.

"The young gallant who escorted us coachward." Carmina balled up the elegant gown and bustled it out of sight.

"Waverleigh . . . I'd forgotten."

Mention of the man's name snuffed Miranda's high dudgeon. She stood puzzling for a moment, the half-removed white petticoat foaming around her shoulders like sea spray around a figurehead.

Carmina paused, remembering then that her charge's startling beauty had lured the Banebridges from their normal prey. She was indeed beautiful. *Now*, Carmina added, taking credit for the curled golden hair, the gems—for everything, the entire polish, if one were to be honest . . .

For what had the child been but an appealing castaway when she had arrived? A good complexion, yes, that jewel beyond price in times of pox, and that pastel almond-pastry coloring that turns so many men's heads. Yet the style, the sparkle, that was her, Carmina's, doing. The older woman's smile put crow's-feet at the corners of her eyes, but also banished her sallow skin and the pale spiderwebs woven through her dark hair.

"You'd forgotten," she said in affectionate rebuke. "Forgotten. I'll venture young Waverleigh has not forgotten."

Miranda thrust her head into a voluminous tent of nightdress. When her face emerged, it was still set. "There are some things I do not forget, Carmina, and the Banebridge brothers are two of them."

"Yes, and your Captain Steele is another. *Dolce Gesu*, by the time you are twenty, you will have to engage an army to avenge your wrongs. You also forget that you're pretty enough to draw more of these attentions."

"*He* did not seem to think I was pretty and it didn't stop him," Miranda growled, hurling bedward.

Carmina threw up her expressive hands, then let them flutter across the slightly disheveled curls that framed her protégé's face like softly spun sunshine.

"Sleep, as you did when you come to Carmina. You were not happy with your hapless mother then, remember? And you forgave her."

"Did I?"

"At least you forgot her. Sleep. Think on what the future may bring, not what is past."

Miranda sat up in her wide empty bed for a long while after Carmina had pulled the heavy carved door shut. Yes, she would need an army to right the wrongs that pierced her like so many nettles. Christopher Steele. The don. Now this. Carmina was right, what could she do?

Helpless anguish propelled Miranda out of bed. The wood floor chilled her feet; its remorseless polish reflected back her own despair. This was all so different, *she* was so different now. To what had it come? To fleeing down a staircase with her petticoats dipping in surrender. To throwing herself upon a mere boy for protection. To listening to Carmina's compromising cluckings.

Miranda paced to the tall Italian wardrobe in which resided all the silk and satin gowns Carmina had ordered for her. She opened the wide doors and stared at the softly shimmering skirts and bodices hung inside, like so many empty other selves, all waiting to be donned: the demure Millicent, all ribbons and white lace. The beauteous Millicent, in yards of sea-green satin bowed in violet velvet. The workaday Millicent, something plain in peach-colored cut velvet with a frosty lace collar . . . where was Miranda in all this? Was there no Miranda to avenge any longer, no Miranda to care?

Something sparkled in the light of the last bedside candle left burning. High on a shelf. Miranda stretched to her toes and knocked it down with her fingertips. It lay across her hands, heavy and soft to stroke—a hat, a fine, broad-brimmed beaver hat with a rich red plume and a medal pinned to its crown, a small gold something that glimmered like a conscience.

She remembered when Christopher Steele had produced that hat like a magician flourishing a dove in the cabin of the *Dowsabelle*. How the royal-red plume had bowed to her and trembled. A smile tiptoed around the corners of Miranda's mouth. It had caught her instantly, that hat, had bewitched her somehow. It still took up a lion's share of shelf space, though she'd never worn it since that first day.

He had said once that she hadn't the slightest idea . . . that was what he had said when she'd taxed him for taking her virtue. He had been speaking of men like the Banebridges, Miranda realized, who took no pride in their work, only perversity. Pride. Miranda drew the plume through her palm slowly, until the sensation verged on some other memory.

Pride had made Christopher Steele seduce her—there, that

word was out—on the Bey of Tunis's barge. Pride had made Miranda so inflexible to the don's blandishments, so unable to forgive anything. Pride made her half-mad with fury now.

Steele, the don, they'd both been given as good as they gave, in some way. But now. Now she was in a civilized city that would vie with Paris for urbanity. Now she wore silken petticoats and dainty pearl chokers tied with ribbons and bejeweled slippers to teeter upon, skirts to snare her, hats to hide her eyes. She was all those, those—things—piled upon her, weighing Miranda down, far below the waves. And when she asked the question—was there nothing, nothing she could do?—the answer came in her own voice. No, Millicent, there is nothing you can do. Nothing.

Miranda fingered the cold gold medal one last time. No more medals for her. She was safely netted now, as firmly pinioned by the world she had entered and its customs as she had been by Oliver's silken ties. Miranda leaned up and replaced the hat upon the shelf, its feather dipping to caress her hand one last time before it settled again into stillness.

She closed the heavy wardrobe doors, one by one, her hands high upon the carved wood. She hung there for a moment, as she'd hung from the broad Barbados cedars at the last instant of descent before dropping back to earth again.

Then her arms dropped to her sides; she pattered back to bed on icy feet and leapt in. She leaned toward her one flickering candle and formed her lips into a kiss to blow the flame out.

Miranda huddled into the covers in the utter dark. Before she shortly slid into restless sleep, her arm swung over the bed's edge to the floor. Her curled fingers brushed softly against something rough and smooth beneath her hand.

It was a shoe.

Chapter Thirty-one

Other London festivities were held that fall of 1648. Within the week, in fact. No one answering to the name of Millicent Hathaway was among the powdered faces and shoulders, the billowing and bowing gowns that paraded under the candle-crowned hanging lights.

Carmina had tried; she had cajoled, pleaded, recited various saints' names until even she could produce no more.

"By Holy Petronilla, Millicent, by all the common sense in Sardinia, for me—for me, *cara*. You must not let this contretemps make you hermit. Come with me tonight."

Miranda kept her eyes firmly on the swinging sapphires in Carmina's ears. "No."

Carmina's shoulders shrugged so violently they threatened to unseat those flashing blue stones, but she whisked away in a great circle of plum silk.

"Very well. When one behave as child, one will be treated so. Do not expect me to deliver any fascinating reports of Master Waverleigh."

Carmina's penetrating eyes sentried Miranda's reaction to this last thrust. The girl sat on her bed, as unruffled as her plain daygown. Carmina sighed enough to set her own bodice ribbons fluttering and wafted away.

Her charge's behavior still weighed on Carmina's mind as she sat contemplatively by a drawing-room fire that evening and re-arranged those very ribbons endlessly.

"Madam." The hand extending her a glass of sherry was pale and smooth and so was the face that bowed above it.

"Why, Master Waverleigh, late of Oxfordshire and Paris. How am I so honored?"

"Nay, I am honored that you recall me. I venture 'tis more than others of your acquaintance do." He sat wistfully beside her, leaning a saffron silk arm along the settle's carved back and softly beating his palm with yellow kid gloves.

"What, young sir, you confess to a lady that someone other than herself is on your mind! Indeed, it cannot be long you spend in Paris, for Maria de' Medici has ruled there and I believe she makes strong medicine for rude young men." Carmina swiftly pantomimed tapping a ring into her sherry glass.

"Forgive me." Justin produced a pale smile at her raillery. " 'Tis my nature to pick thistles instead of amaryllis. Any sane man would seek no further than present company."

"A somewhat pretty speech, but no heart under it. Ask your questions, then, Inquisitor, and be done with it, so I can move on to more receptive prey." Carmina's fan tap on his arm was both playful blow and prod.

"She is not here," Justin stated abruptly, a frown plowing between his brows. Carmina only fanned her hands while her mouth took a downward plunge. "Is it I, madam? Was it that silly French tale I told her? Did—"

"Alas, my young swain, I must tell you the tiresome news that she do not even remember enough of you to be offended. Ah! Now you truly resemble these water spaniels with your ears drooping so. Do not take unkindly of it. Other matters occupy her. Is nothing to do with you."

Carmina shot his attractive figure a passing glance. "I would it were," she told herself under her breath. This is what her most difficult Millicent needed, one her own age to scatter bouquets and compliments before her feet, to set her dancing on a lighter path than she had trod.

The two settled into companionable silence, dwelling on the same subject from different perspectives.

"Come, Master Justin Waverleigh," Carmina said abruptly, captive gaiety under her tone. "Surely a gallant who has spend so many time in Paris has drolleries to unfold. I've heard the ladies there paint their lips green now—do not the French gentlemen find these fruits too unripe to pluck?"

Justin laughed. *"Mais oui, madame. Vraiment."* So fast had he forgotten the source of his disappointment that his tongue had instantly retreated to a gayer language. " 'Tis true—and not merely green but black, so one must think a plague has fallen upon them."

"I trust our fair English ladies will not look to Frenchifying their features, young master; think you not the same?"

Justin's brown eyes were still bent upon his gloves. "Of course," he said softly.

Carmina shrugged her bare shoulders. Foolish girl. If she had wanted to turn her new acquaintance into a moping puppy, her absence was surety.

"Do you know what the women in France do now?" Justin asked abruptly. "The brunette is all the fashion, so even the most delicate of blondes powder their hair with a black like soot to acquire this—*cette magie noire. Cette magie noire folle!* Black magic indeed; they all resemble witches!"

Justin's earnest look glanced off his companion's startled face, framed in quite natural dark hair once considered its glory. By more seasoned gallants than he, Carmina reminded herself. Sylvia had been no fool to palm off her daughter. Budding roses had a way of making even blooms in their prime look overblown. Carmina's lips tightened into a suppressed smile.

"Tell me more, young Justin, of these foolish, nay, even mad you say, French ladies. My young ward may want to ape some of their fancies."

"Nay, I think not, madam," continued Justin, Carmina's irony slipping past him like air.

"Truly, young Englishman, you are faithful to your kind. I shall not wonder if you do not throw out your King and let the burghers govern you. Though he is a dull enough fellow with his unimaginative fidelity to his sallow Henrietta Maria and his flair for fashion going no further than his sharply pointed Dutch chin hairs. For this you should arrest him."

"Madam, you speak lightly of subjects that are most serious to my family. The Waverleigh plate has long since melted into cannon. Our hearts are as set upon supporting His Majesty as you seem to be upon mocking him. King Charles is our God-appointed sovereign. 'Tis blasphemy to speak of dethroning him, though all of London's merchants and half of Parliament and yon 'Brewer' from The Fens try to tie his royal hands. The day that the likes of Cromwell sits above Charles Stuart shall be one all England shall rue and that I shall not live to see."

"At least your Oliver Cromwell appreciates the sweetness which ferments, which is more than some of your sobersided Puritans nowadays. Forgive me, Master Waverleigh. I am foreign to your politics and religions—the twin bookends to every Englishman's life, it strikes me, and oft likely to crush them in between. Let us speak of something other."

Carmina's eager eyes paged the growing crowd for some diversion and fastened on a newcomer to such festivities. Her hand crushed the saffron silk at her companion's elbow.

"By the Virgin, 'tis a better chance than we knew our little Millicent withdrew this night. I'll be sworn that is a Dorsetshire Steele among us. The breed is as finely stamped upon the features as a royal profile is upon gold coin."

Justin followed the arrow of Carmina's look to ground at a young Cavalier in obviously new-tailored buff silk with butterfly buckles upon his boots of such size that they threatened to flap both themselves and their wearer ceilingward.

"Steele? I knew a Steele or two at Oxford, and knew of more, Sir Charles's sons—now, there's a loyal Royalist! Good old Sir Charles! I must offer guidance to this fresh-hatched chick; I swear he's only of an age to have come directly down from Oxford."

Since Master Waverleigh had preceded the newcomer in this state but a year before, Carmina pressed her lips and eyelids together for a moment after her young companion had shouldered through the expanding crowds to alight at the newcomer's exquisitely tailored side.

That the new young man was freshly festooned for London socializing was too apparent.

His shoulder-length blond hair was lightly curled and separated before each ear into a ribboned lovelock. A tentative set on his broad shoulders betrayed his nervousness, no matter how smoothly the wheat-colored silk sheathed them. His hand clung to the pommel of his prettily scabbarded dress sword, and his steps in the lavish butterfly-buckled kid boots were wont to be of an overlong and firm bravado.

"Wait there," Justin hailed as his prey appeared to wheel and move away at his approach. "Perhaps I am impertinent," he told the cool sea-colored eyes that regarded him, "but I spied you from yonder and thought—are you not a Steele? A Steele of Ravenscroft in Dorset?"

The youth's mouth dropped in ill-concealed surprise. Justin rushed on, realizing his approach could be construed as rude.

"So few I know remain in London nowadays," he explained. "I knew your brother Sydney at Oxford, but he was off in Cornwall fighting for the King, while I was sent to France to do my duty. Are you Philip? The younger Steele that I never met?"

"Your inquiries overwhelm me, sir," responded the young gallant with a challenging tone that belied his apparent foppery. "May I be so bold as to inquire *your* identity?"

"Forgive me. A familiar face—and you wear the look of the Steeles like one born to it, say what you will—at any rate, I am Justin Waverleigh. I assure you, I am not so often flummoxed at introductions. Though I've reason to be off stride tonight," he added gloomily.

"Oh?" The young man raised pale eyebrows, regarded Justin for a piercing moment, then spoke with sudden resolve. "You are quite correct, sir: I am a Steele, though in these times to confess so too loudly may be more foolhardiness than courtesy."

"Then you are indeed Philip?"

"No." The Steele youth appeared bemused. "I am—James. I fear I am the infant of the lot," he added, a flush rising to his unpowdered cheeks.

" 'Tis no shame," consoled Justin. "I, too, would be as unworldly as you had I not sojourned in France. There I met your elder brother as well, so I now am like to know the entire family."

"Elder? Which elder?" inquired the Steele youth vigilantly.

"Why, Christopher, of course. No man slips the Channel between Calais and Gravesend as neatly as he, with never a scent of a Roundhead ship upon his stern. And Ben is captain in the King's own. You must be proud of such a clan. I am the sole Waverleigh of my generation."

"Yes, they are a devilish well-traveled lot," the youth remarked drily. "I, alas, have seen only my mother's knee and a bit of Oxford town."

Justin reflected that brothers, and well-known, accomplished brothers, could be a heavier burden than no brothers at all. He smiled warmly and clapped the youth upon the shoulder, a gesture that brought the lad's fingers once more to his sword pommel, though Justin, hard upon his good-natured advice, did not notice that.

"Come to me if you seek aid and comfort for your London stay," Justin advised, "although I fear my company would not be what you crave for your introduction to London gaiety. I am in mourning."

"Mourning?" Young Steele's eyes impolitely dropped to the magnificence of Justin's colorful attire.

Justin nodded solemnly, his fingers curling into his new friend's shoulder, his voice a reverent hush. "For the absence of a lady."

"By your leave, sir, is there a death amongst your relations, then?"

"So you might say, but only in my heart," sighed Justin.

The youth's mouth dropped, then a comprehending twinkle lighted his pale eyes. "In Faith, sir, I thought such fine manner of expression was reserved for first folios distributed amongst one's friends."

"Oh, yes, 'tis all metaphor to you," remarked Justin bitterly, "but it's honest melancholy to me. You have much to learn here, young sir. I trust you will manage without my escort." Justin's brown eyes gleamed in self-mockery. "At least until I recover from my disappointment—or put it to paper before I lose my melancholy."

Young Steele laughed and bowed. " 'Tis a pleasure to have

made your acquaintance, sir. I hope the lady may someday feel the same sentiments."

Justin shrugged and melted back to Carmina to report what he had learned.

"A pretty youth," Carmina judged from afar. "Had he another year or two upon him—like yourself, Master Waverleigh . . ."

Carmina's mock flirtation availed nothing. Justin was mooning at the embroidery on his pale gloves, as if an augury were written there.

"Perhaps if you would call," suggested Carmina. "I do not see how she can object to that."

He nodded morosely; Carmina finally left him on the settle, watching the crowded drawing room with bored brown eyes.

Justin did not notice James Steele again, although another pair of eyes in the same room even then followed the light-colored figure with something dark behind their yellow irises.

The watcher ventured into a passage, where he found another observer safely installed behind a tapestry.

"Forget this lurking, brother," he instructed a lanky man in lavender satin with a purple patch upon one well-rouged cheek.

"Basty, you said yourself that I must be wary tonight, after last week's folly."

"Now I say forget that. I have found fresh prey." Sebastian's shapeless mouth made itself into an eel's maw on the word "fresh." Oliver's dull eyes lit up.

"Dare we? After that foolish girl? Who knows whom she told? Even you fear we might someday be called out by an indignant relation. Remember Foxblood."

"I remember Foxblood. Better than you. I tell you we have fair, fresh game inside. Were we not defrauded last week? Did you not let our captive spring the trap? You will fetch him. A slender lad in buff silk. He is new to our circle."

"But, Basty, he may have friends, relations. Do we know who he is, if we dare—?"

"Be quiet, Oliver, or I shall have to reduce your role in our little private masques. Would you like that? I thought not. Now find and lead him to our mirrored nest. I will do the rest."

So it was that young James Steele—raw from Oxford, alone amongst London's most practiced ways—found himself backing into a sudden wall of lavender satin only moments later.

"Your pardon, sir. 'Twas most clumsy of me."

The lavishly gleaming figure was surmounted by a long, pale

face that now folded into perfect dismay. It produced a fine white lace handkerchief like an affronted magician and began daubing at its green-and-gold-embroidered jacket skirt.

"Most clumsy, young sir, 'tis fresh"—the yellow-hazel eyes looked up directly on that word—"from Paris, this work, and now 'tis claret-colored. Here, hold my glass."

The youth accepted the long-stemmed vessel thrust into his hand while the gentleman bemoaned his ruined jacket further.

"I must find a steward to wash it. Well, don't merely stand there, you might prove wall for another unfortunate like myself. Come along while I fetch some assistance."

Dazed, young Steele glanced around the room, then meekly followed the outraged dandy, doubtless cursing his loutish debut into London circles.

The stranger quickly threaded the crowd and cut through a knot of chattering matrons without a backward glance, although the youth in tow bowed apologetically all round as he trailed the man through. They neared the room's double-doored exit when the man turned on his heel.

"Set the silly glass down, my dear boy," he instructed, gesturing to a mantel. "We will find a better vintage once this mess has been cleaned." His eyes, fresh from perusing his jacket skirt, came to the lad's face. "You are a clumsy fellow," he added, his voice rough with something that was not reproof.

"Why, sir—"

"Oliver," the man insisted, stepping toward the figure poised in setting a glass on the mantel. The crowd was thin here; the pair might have been perfectly alone. "The name is Oliver," he repeated softly. "What is yours?"

The young man knit his brow, as if to puzzle out London ways. "Why, Steele, sir. James Steele."

"Set down the glass, James, and then you may come and—assist me. With my jacket."

The Steele youth toyed fitfully with the buff kid gloves thrust through his baldric. He looked up with guarded pale eyes to find the stranger who insisted on being called Oliver but a foot away and eyeing at him oddly.

"I trust, sir, that you have taken no great offense at my clumsiness."

"No, no . . . my dear boy," breathed Oliver, edging nearer.

" 'Tis most kind of you—"

"No, *you* will be kind," murmured Oliver, drunk on his brother's absence, lured by a seemingly innocent compliance he had not encountered before.

Steele. The name rung unpleasantly off his memory. Did the Steeles sport an offshoot who would play avenger? What matter? Perhaps another continental tour would suffice. The Banebridge purse could withstand it. This one, this one he could have without Basty—he knew it.

Oliver edged closer, until the lace foaming at his knees verged on the young man's, until the extremest edges of their clothing brushed and their faces hung but inches apart.

"My dear boy," he began, "trust to it that this was a most happy accident." His thin powdered hand slid between the silky golden hair that bracketed the boy's cheeks. How smooth, how warm, the neck—

"Oliver!" A furious hiss at his shoulder, and then Basty was there, his face livid and his taut lips purple. "Not here, fool."

Something stung Oliver's rouged cheek, reddening it further and cutting loose a tear to unseat the heart-shaped purple patch beneath his cheekbone. Injured hazel eyes rolled to Sebastian, but his brother's face was as shocked as his own. Sebastian's yellow eyes stared beyond Oliver to . . .

Oliver wheeled. The Steele youth stood three paces back, utter triumphant anger turning all his soft features to adamant.

"You have insulted me beyond endurance, sir, with your most unnatural attentions. You and this man. I call you both to account, and set this good company as my witnesses."

The lad's blond head gestured around the circle of avid faces that had gathered at the echo of his gloved slap to Oliver's face. That face blushed redder until the glove marks were lost in matching shame. Sebastian merely whitened under his leaded face paint. His fist pounded once upon his sword pommel.

"Very well," he said icily. "On the field of honor. Let it not be said that the Banebridges shirk anything—even a challenge from a callow youth eager to construct insults from trifles so that he may exercise his sword or pistol. Pistol I choose. Be warned that I will not refrain from aiming true, young cockscomb."

"I welcome it."

"But, Basty," Oliver objected, still shaken. "I do not wish to fight. I . . . my pistol aim is—I cannot."

"Then choose another weapon, fool," Sebastian urged softly between his yellow teeth. "It is your choice. Choose the sword and let your silly wig be sliced off. Or more to the point, your brains."

Oliver cringed against the mantel while the crowd twittered. "Swords," he finally croaked.

"Perhaps Master Waverleigh and another will serve as my seconds, since I am a stranger to the city," young Steele suggested calmly, folding his elegant gloves through the baldric once more and glancing up to isolate his new acquaintance in the crowd. "My brothers are not immediately available."

Justin stepped forward briskly. "It seems, my Oxfordian friend, that I underestimated your capacity for making yourself at home. I shall be quite willing, and—able," he directed fiercely at Sebastian, "to assist you in this delicate matter."

"And I," offered an older gentleman, stepping forward to fix the Banebridges with a contemptuous glance.

"That is very fine of you, Farnsworth," said young James Steele, settling his sword firmly into place at his cream-colored side.

"Have we met?" the second volunteer asked sharply, eyeing the youth. "I do not recall it."

"Long ago, perhaps?" James shrugged. "I was very young but my memory is as long as your good nature, sir, so I do not wonder that you do not recall it." He turned to the Banebridges.

"Five days hence should be sufficient for you to practice with your sword, sir," he told Oliver. To Sebastian he was more blunt. "You, sir, should practice to meet your Maker, for my pistol knows as few reins as yours."

He pivoted to his seconds. "My servant, sirs, will call upon you so we may settle upon a place and time acceptable to these most—unacceptable—gentlemen. My compliments." He bowed and walked quickly from the room.

Carmina edged toward Justin and cocked an interrogatory head.

"*Sacré bleu!*" The young Englishman breathed the old French curse, his brown eyes still examining the air where his fierce new friend had stood. "It seems I am a marv'lous poor judge of temperament. Perhaps I should set that young man to guide *me* through this tangled world."

"If he does not catapult himself into another soon."

Carmina's finger sketched a significant phantom fencing feint in the air.

* * *

"Ah, Millicent! Not the pale satin with this ocher velvet. Where is the black kid?" Carmina flipped up her skirts and dove deep into the cupboard interior.

"How matters it, Carmina, what shoes I wear when Justin Waverleigh comes to call?" Miranda queried the twitching skirts that were all that remained visible of the Italian woman. "He shall hardly be peering 'neath my hem."

"Ah! One is never sure what these English Cavalier will do." Carmina's muffled evaluation of the extant English gentleman only caused Miranda to shrug her lace-frosted shoulders and sit on a tapestried bench.

Carmina emerged triumphant with two black shoes rimmed in gold braid and applied them none too gently to her protégé's feet.

"I wish, silly · sardine, that you recover of the decline into which our roguish English brothers have send you. Young Master Waverleigh was most courteous the other evening—and melancholy at your absence. Shed your thorns and give him a warmer welcome than is your current nature, eh?" Carmina set the pearls swinging in Miranda's ears. "You do not like these at first and now you hardly know they are there, no?"

Miranda nodded glumly.

"Mayhap Master Waverleigh will grow upon you as nicely."

Nonetheless, Miranda insisted on having a tapestry screen at her side when her suitor called, lest conversation flag.

Carmina's thick eyebrows exploded heavenward like soot. "I think, *cara*, that Master Waverleigh is capable of entertaining you quite smartly. The young man is soon to take part in a duel."

"A duel? How tiresome. 'Tis all too easy to fall into useless affairs of honor. It cheapens honor itself, this constant pistoling and fencing." Miranda yawned pointedly.

Although Carmina had resolved not to mention the youngest Steele's spectacular entrance on the London scene for fear of roiling old wounds, she was anxious to lance the ill-humor that had veiled her ward since the humiliating affair at Bridgeport House. So she leaned forward, her dark eyes piercing Miranda's tapestry as expertly as the girl's needle.

"Master Waverleigh is not to duel himself. He is merely to be second . . . to Master Steele."

Miranda's needle paused, withdrew, then plunged deeply into the fabric. Fortunately, Carmina's lids were lowered to inspect the design; Miranda's hot green glance almost burned through them.

"Well?" she demanded, iron in her voice.

"Well—you wish to know more of Master Waverleigh's affairs? I thought you utterly bored by them, and him also."

"Carmina, do not vex me. I've done as you wished. It has earned me little but the dubious joy of traipsing about in dangles and laces, luring insults and worse for it. You know what I wish to know, so tell me."

Carmina shrugged. "If you insist, Millicent. 'Tis merely that this new lad to our circles—a James Steele—was put upon by our—by *your* brothers Banebridge. He challenged them both to duel and called upon Justin Waverleigh to second him."

"So those weasels will be called to account? This . . . James. He is of the family, then?"

"I did not ask," Carmina began. Miranda's sharp glance needled her as if Carmina had been rotten tapestry to disintegrate at a probe. "Of course he is of the breed, *cara*! He looks—so like; that burnished northern fairness, though not so polished as our young Justin."

"You're certain that 'tis not *he*?" Miranda managed to demand a moment before Master Waverleigh was announced.

Carmina shrugged. "Why not interrogate Master Waverleigh? 'Tis certain *he* will regard such racking an honor."

Miranda turned impatiently to the figure advancing across the gleaming wood floor. Waverleigh looked jaunty in Lincoln green sparked with a well-starched white falling band and crimson ribbons at his knees. His gilded spurs rang merrily with each bucket-booted step; even Miranda felt a certain softening behind her stomacher. She went so far as to offer him a hand.

"Master Waverleigh, you honor us. Carmina had said you would call."

"I would more than call, *Mademoiselle Cendrillon*." He bowed to present a bouquet hidden by his well-plumed beaver. "Lady's slipper," he offered with a smile and a hopeful raise of his well-shaped brows.

Miranda stared at him, then laughed and accepted the bouquet. "Indeed, Master Waverleigh, I am very well slippered by now, for Carmina has seen me most appropriately shod but an hour past."

Miranda kicked her hem into a froth of petticoat lace to reveal her black kid footwear, while Carmina shot her a told-you-so glance.

Justin seated himself. " 'Tis a pity my brief duties as dresser have been superseded, though Madam Carmina has a taste for fashion that doubtless makes her invaluable. However, flowers are clothing for the soul, Mistress Millicent, and I would gladly relinquish any claim I had upon your person for the merest touching of your soul."

Miranda stared at him for one blank moment, wondering why he made her despised true name sound real for the first time, and why she had no ready answer for his gallantry.

"Millicent will be pleased to wear your offering." Carmina pushed the stems into Miranda's silk-sashed waist so the flowers bloomed against the amber velvet.

" 'Tis kind of you, sir," responded Miranda tardily. "I fear you will require all our kindness. Are you not embarked upon an affair of honor?"

"Embarked, but not the captain of this venture, mistress. I serve as mere second mate to a country lad who tangled himself in city-bred gallantry. I cannot say more. The French have ways of saying these things but—" Justin waved an apologetic hand, the trail of his sapphire ring sparkling across the air like a comet.

"I understand." Miranda exchanged a glance with Carmina. "This challenger, you know of him?"

"Not precisely. He is a gentleman and a King's man, be assured. Of the Dorsetshire Steeles, a fine old family and most busy in the King's cause, from all I've heard. A somewhat simple lad to city ways, if I be frank, but likable, most likable." Justin leaned back in his winged chair. "Then, all the Steeles are."

"Yes," Miranda agreed faintly, until she saw Waverleigh's brown eyes questioning her as mutely as a spaniel's. "I have heard, that is, of the Steele devotion to His Majesty. You could not do other than support the young Steele. When is it to occur, this set-to?"

"Ah, but there are better things to talk upon on such a vibrant day. We will not have much sun left to us this season, mistress. I trust that Madam Carmina will allow me to escort you through the mystery of her climbing azaleas, which are the wonder of all London."

A pair of pleading brown eyes and threatening green ones

turned significantly on the placid Italian. Carmina spread her square hands wide and beamed upon them both.

"What can I say, my dear Master Waverleigh? It is, of course, the choice of our little Millicent."

Miranda aimed a hot spark of reproof at Carmina before nodding assent. Young Waverleigh handed her up and out of the garden doors as smoothly as to a dance floor.

The fall sunshine was already fading as the pair began their ramble along the formal alleyways.

"I must hear more of your duel, Master Waverleigh," Miranda said after sailing alongside him in velvet grandeur for a while.

"Is it possible that you have some small concern for my well-being?" he asked, half mockingly, and half so eagerly that Miranda found herself unnerved.

"I fear for the well-being of all gallant young gentlemen, as every young lady should," she answered, taking refuge in a primness that would have delighted the late Mistress MacTavish to her Calvinistic soul.

"You are not 'every young lady,' " Justin said earnestly. "I apprehended that the moment I saw you. You are Indies-bred, Carmina tells me, and there is something as fresh and exotic about you as in any cargo of cinnamon or sugar—I fear you've given me some foreign fever. I swear I was not wont to play such a stricken swain, not even in my Oxford days."

Justin had caught her hands during his last fit of verbal enthusiasm and now he cast them away as dramatically. Miranda felt amusement twitch the corners of her mouth.

"My dear sir, 'tis clear you have contracted some malady, for you seem not to know which course you prefer. One moment you are forward and the next you seem unable to be rid of me soon enough."

Justin sighed, clapped his hands to his green-breeched sides, turned his hat around once, then swept it expansively at the sky as if seeking answer there.

"You are right, Mistress Millicent. I am a most muddled suitor, but suitor I am, and I beg you not to smile. This cursed civil strife keeps young Englishmen from practicing their gallantries at Whitehall long enough to become silken in their service. Forgive my roughness; it does not mean my cloth is not cut as true as any other man's."

Miranda felt plummeted far deeper into the matter of Justin

Waverleigh than she wished. She fought her way to surface sentiments.

"Heavens, sir, you conspire to turn my head and 'tis heavy enough with Carmina's headdressing upon it to be spared more exercise. I think you have visited sufficiently. Must you not prepare for this fierce encounter—when, did you say, and where?"

"Two days hence, at the Commons at dawn. Can I believe your thoughts will be with me then?"

"Master Waverleigh," responded Miranda a bit breathlessly, "you may rest assured that you shall not be far from my mind then. Come and tell me of it when the thing is done."

Justin bowed assent and led Miranda back to the drawing room, where Carmina calmly plied her ward's abandoned needle.

"And?" she inquired inexorably once Justin had bowed his way out.

Miranda clothed her face in the nosegay for a moment. "You are quite right, Carmina. He has not forgotten me."

"The Waverleighs have only this young Justin to carry all their fine estates. They've lost much with their support of this so-foolish Charles, but they have much to spare. He is very, very rich, *cara*. One could wed worse."

"Wed? You sound like old MacMutton when she bundled me off to England. I do not wish to marry for the sake of it. Justin Waverleigh will have to do more than ply me with flowers or flowery phrases to convince me."

It seemed that Waverleigh was intent upon just that course. The following day a servant delivered a stiffly rolled parchment beribboned in green satin that Miranda accepted as formally.

"Are you not to open it?" Carmina teased. "Perhaps I should withdraw. This is clearly a most private epistle. I cannot imagine—nor I suppose can you—who send it."

"Stay," ordered Miranda, unrolling it like a list for the dressmaker and scanning the elegantly penned words.

She confronted, it transpired, the first sonnet dedicated to herself she had ever read:

My Indies treasure fleet there rides the tide,
A bow upon her to whom kings might bend.
What's sweet without is sweeter still inside;
The lanterns of her eyes all storms forfend,
Her arms like gilded oars of ivory
But match the whiteness of her breast and cleave

The waves of Love; an emperor's argosy
Harbors where I'll anchor without leave.
She is seaborne ransome worth twelve London townes,
And in the glories of her ruffling stern
Her keel doth curve so smoothly 'neath her gown
That a Troy topples and proud Carthage burns.
So on the burning pyres of my desire,
I quench my ardent self; and ask more fire.

"Well?" Carmina's curiosity was bottomless.

" 'Tis a . . . a piece of poetry."

"Ah."

"A sonnet merely."

"Indeed."

"To me."

"But of course, *cara.*"

"A sonnet after Master Shakespeare, if you must know the form."

"How versatile."

"And prettily done. If one care for the subject matter."

"It appears that young Waverleigh does."

A blush that Miranda had been forestalling finally rose like a winter sun on her snowy cheeks.

"Truly, Carmina, you are ridiculous! I cannot think why—my mother—should have given me into your care. You are quite, quite . . . frivolous."

With this last charge, Miranda gathered up her skirts, and her parchment, to retreat upstairs, where she read the verse more leisurely at her window and blushed far more freely.

She let the paper suddenly flutter to the window seat. It lay there like a page torn from the *Gato* logbook. Miranda leaned her troubled forehead against the fine, unclouded glass some long-ago lover had bestowed the means to install upon Carmina. It cooled her, the glass, just as the simple piece of paper had flushed her.

How dreadfully easy to become a mere fluttering excuse for gallantries in London town, Miranda concluded. Far simpler to fret about iambic pentameter addressed to one's person than such insubstantial issues as revenge, integrity, honor. The Dutchman had been right. Honor was as transitory as air, and air was ever the most whimsical of elements.

Give her fire, water. Give her duels and pistol and sword. Give her right or wrong. Harry rescued or lost. Steele taking or leaving. There was a paradox for the poets. Give her love or hate. Passion or disdain. Not this muddy, gray wavering tug-of-war on the emotions, this tide of indecision ebbing and flowing in her veins and turning all to a matter of degree, a mere question of more or less.

This, this was the world of Justin and Carmina and Sylvia. And Harry. That was what she had condemned most in her brother, not the road he had followed, but that he been pushed upon it by some other! How did one keep others from pushing, pulling at one? How did one hold to self as a helmsman holds a ship on course?

Miranda held Justin's sonnet up to the dimming daylight, watching the letters wriggle across the page as if eager to escape. He made her uneasy, this Justin Waverleigh.

He saw her as he wished to see her and perhaps . . . perhaps . . . Miranda—Millicent—was weary enough to become precisely that.

Chapter Thirty-two

*T*he Thames River fog slithered across the gunmetal water and wreathed the swans' necks arched under their wings.

It crawled up the damp river steps onto streets empty of all but one still-uncollected carouser. It flowed against half-timbered second stories and fanned noiseless fingers across closed shutters. Twisting inland, it spiraled up like smoke and made each sputtering torchlight a solitary silhouette in the early dawn.

As it escaped from Thameside, it expanded, took a deep, wraithlike breath and billowed over the Commons' gemstone-green sward, frosted here and there with white now. The fog elbowed softly through the leaf-bare trees and left them stark monuments to remembered greenery. It circled through alleyways between oaks and beeches before settling on an open space.

The swirling fog curled up like Graymalkin and gave its plumy tail one last twitch until it pointed like a finger at a small conclave of figures beneath a brawny, leaf-stripped oak.

Justin Waverleigh clapped his hands upon his upper arms, then clasped the gesture to himself. He paced impatiently, spurs ringing, finally addressing a taller man who stood guard with the massive oak.

"The cold, Farnsworth, makes one's blood run thick. 'Twill slow our contest, and such river fog is bad for the humors. I like it not. This young rapscallion from Dorset will be mincemeat for the Banebridges."

"Perhaps, Waverleigh. Mayhap he will have thought better of it and decline the meeting."

"Did you see his face when he challenged them? He would have carved them into kidney pie then and there had not courtesy forbidden it. Nor are they ones to forgo it," Justin muttered, darting a tart brown glance at four figures sheltered under the dubious grace of an opposite tree.

"No," Farnsworth agreed. "They dare not renege, else their game is over forever. Yet I think our dainty Oliver chatters with more than morning chill. 'Twill be pretty to see him dance to the tune of steel instead of stealth."

"Perhaps our overeager lad has called off, after all," offered Justin, pacing until his musical spurs rang like a clock tolling the hour.

A hollow thud drifted through the eerie fog-hung landscape—the dull, undeniable clop of horses' hooves. Something dark thrust through shreds of fog, then lumbered forward into the clarity of a hired coach. A dark-clothed youth in forest green sprang from it before the horses had slowed to their last, tentative steps.

"Well met, gentlemen. Is this not a day for it? I trust you're ready to play witnesses. I am well prepared for a little warming—" Young Steele sketched a fencing tierce until the wrist lace fluttered foglike around his hand.

"You meet Oliver first," Farnsworth said soberly, "with sword. He has been practicing mightily, so do not mistake him for a reed."

Justin watched the young man's eyes narrow. "I well know, gentlemen, the seriousness of what I undertake. If I happen to require an undertaker," he added blithely, "yon carriage will suit to draw the body home."

Young James drew his sword and sliced off a chunk of fog. " 'Tis thick enough to butcher, this fog. The long-faced Banebridge will need every shred of it between himself and my blade. I see our pair of buzzards have surrounded themselves with seconds as dark-browed as ravens. Mayhap it will be Banebridge bones those carrion shall pick and cart away."

"Wait!" Justin's lighthearted features were heavy. "Should you . . . perish—you are alone in London, sir; we bear a responsibility to your kin. If someone should come along to avenge anything untoward—?"

"If I should die?" the youth inquired bluntly. "I do not anticipate that, good Master Waverleigh. I did not invite you and Farnsworth to be my pallbearers."

"But if I should see Sydney again and he should want—"

"Ah, I understand. I assure you, should the youngest of the Dorsetshire Steeles perish on this rather clammy ground"—the young man raked his blade tip across the grass in an arc—"then I guarantee a host of Steeles will arise to revenge it. In that case, my most confident Justin, I will rely upon you to present them my final compliments."

The lad bowed mockingly, as if he were more sophisticated in these matters than the anxious Justin, and strode toward the open dueling ground. The fog closed behind him so quickly that Justin followed only the sound of ringing spurs.

Once each party's seconds had conferred, both principals converged on the clearing's center. Oliver was long-faced but held his shoulders straight. When he slid his Sheffield blade from its embroidered scabbard, it hissed as if hot, while the fog swirled around the two duelists like steam.

The Steele youth unsheathed a length of fresh Spanish steel. Both men bowed, the plumes on their black felt hats afflicted with a kind of palsy in the uncertain air.

"Slippery grass," hissed Farnsworth worrisomely to Justin as the duelists' blades slid off the intervening sword of Oliver's second.

The seconds hung back at the clearing's natural edge, like blackbirds lined upon a fence, as the duelists advanced, their spurs jangling to their movements like castanets to the heel-and-toe work of a Spanish dancer.

"Banebridge has by far the longer reach—a good foot of steel more," Waverleigh said. "Curse it, Farnsworth, I fear I'm to witness an execu—"

The blades rang together, then spun off, circled, darted, dove and fell away again. Fog swirled around the two darting figures like magic smoke manufactured by their flashing silver wands. The duelists circled.

Suddenly the slighter figure was lancing inward on a rapid flutter of rapier strokes. A last slash and the full ostrich plume in

Oliver's beaver hung half-severed, like a listless pennant on a mast.

"Well done," Farnsworth cheered from the sidelines with new optimism. Justin clapped him on the back and grinned.

Oliver's face set petulantly under his amputated panache and he angrily beat forward. Young James Steele was forced toward the ring of trees, finally finding his left shoulder against bark. He lunged forward and struck a high blow. Oliver wheeled to meet the steel, but his blade slid off and upward. Young Steele sliced opportunely and slit Banebridge's jacket where the arm joined.

Oliver lowered his sword arm, uncertain whether he was hurt.

The young man danced around him, teasing the faded face with his blade while Oliver stood dumbly there, his features puckered into almost infantile distress.

"Engage him, you fool!" urged Sebastian from the surrounding fog.

Oliver straightened and struck forward, his blade as listless as his plume. In a moment Oliver's halfhearted defense brought his swordless arm still higher. Another able lunge and Oliver's jacket materialized another slit, this time at the other armhole.

Oliver's face and sword drooped together. The Steele youth advanced and retreated like fog seeking a chink in an unimaginative but stubborn wall. Oliver dropped back with no pretense to swordsmanship. The oncoming edge of Spanish steel was cutting the fog into ribbons in front of him, tying his hands somehow, choking him.

Oliver needed a glass of Madeira. A warm and firelit bedchamber. His adored lapdogs. Not this . . . A whimper surged to his throat. Then, as surrendering words teetered on his enraged lips—something happened. The figure before him lunged again and lunged too far. A heel caught on a slick section of grass and overcommitted, pulling its possessor into helpless range.

Oliver's face brightened with instant triumph. His drooping sword straightened and slashed viciously at the nearing figure.

The lad wheeled with whatever balance was left to him.

Oliver's Sheffield seared by with a light, tearing sound, leaving a long slash in the youth's left jacket arm. The cloth only . . . ? Red seeped slowly to the fabric's severed edges and swelled to limn a maroon line across the forest green like a slash of crimson silk drawn through.

Both contestants paused to watch the scarlet spread. Justin

strode involuntarily forward until Farnsworth's gauntleted hand restrained him.

The duelists paused still. Then young Steele retreated to the clearing's center, where he pointed his sword earthward and waited. After a moment Oliver followed, jabbing quickly at the still figure in the fog's center, then etching bolder strokes as he watched the red swelling against the dark cloth.

The Steele youth waited, waited until Oliver was quite openly baiting him, until Oliver's lips curled over his teeth in a smile, until his opponent's triumphant hazel eyes flashed to the dark, fogbound figure of his brother, Sebastian.

Young Steele suddenly forged forward on a purposeful glitter of dancing steel. Oliver's eyes returned to his prey too late. He saw only the glare of something cold and gray slicing past him like an old sin remembered. Then the heat of that steel meteor followed and a sheet of liquid oozed like a red velvet curtain down Oliver's long painted cheek. He was slit from nose to cheekbone, in a graceful arc that drained whatever color remained in his face into that crimson sheet and washed it onto his immaculate white Brussels falling band.

Oliver dropped his blade and brought both hands to his face. "Basty, oh, Basty! See what we've done. It will be my ruination."

Young Steele sheathed his weapon with a steady rasp that hastened Oliver's retreating steps. Then the young man returned to Waverleigh and Farnsworth, materializing through the veiling fog like a spirit.

"Well done, lad." Farnsworth raised a hand to clap it on the returning youth's left shoulder and then stopped. "By God, that sniveling fool pinked you! On the slip, was it?"

Young Steele nodded and gingerly clasped his arm.

"If Sydney or Philip could see you now, James, they'd not call you the babe of the family," swore Justin. "Let the other go. You're wounded now, why give Banebridge the advantage?"

"I am not grievously hurt, 'tis not even my pistol arm."

Sebastian's seconds had walked silently to the clearing's center, where they loomed more like pillars than men. The light was sifting through the fog when Farnsworth and Waverleigh jangled over to inspect the weapons. They lifted, weighed, sniffed powder for dampness—turning as much suspicion upon the Banebridge-supplied weapons as their generous natures allowed.

"All seems well," reported Waverleigh glumly when he returned. "I can find not a lock or bit of powder awry, but I warrant there's some trick in it."

"It's a heavy stock the ill-born fop has chosen," cautioned Farnsworth. "You'll need a steady arm and eye, and once it's cocked, no tripping or 'tis yourself you'll bowl a ball into."

Young Steele nodded, his yellow hair pooling briefly on a collar as snowy as his face was becoming. Yet he walked to the circle's center steadily enough, converging on the boxed pistols with Sebastian Banebridge.

"Your choice, young sir," Sebastian said coldly, "but whatever choice you make shall be to your regret."

"Ah, we often regret our deeds, do we not? I learned such pithy philosophy at Oxford, where I learned also that what you practice was studied at no university any gentleman would claim. Now that I have rekindled your affronted honor, sir, perhaps we can step off the length of our enmity."

The Steele youth bowed until his broad-brimmed hat obscured his features. Sebastian cast one sulphurous look at his young adversary and curled back his rose-colored lips.

"You mistake me, puppy. Because I play with my prey you take me for a toothless old hound. I will not aim to graze your impudent hide. I advise you to do likewise, my pretty Cavalier."

"Very well." Young Steele saluted with his long-barreled pistol. "I dedicate this affair, then, to—Diana, goddess of the hunt. And the hunted."

Sebastian's narrow face crinkled into a facial exclamation point as the youth's last words pricked his memory like a spur teasing the side of a reluctant mount. A familiar phrase, something like a refrain about it . . . Damn him, the cub sought to confuse him.

Sebastian raised the long muzzle to his pearl-pierced ear and faced away from his slight opponent. He had a longer reach, but in a pistol contest that would count for naught. Trueness of aim and instrument only would decide the matter. And that once.

The duelists strode away on the first of the agreed-upon ten counts. Each step was punctuated by a mutual chime of spurs, as though their hatred had joined them with invisible shackles.

The fog was lifting, dissipating upward to the forked branches like a curtain rising on the first act of a drama. They stepped away across the dew-drenched grass, their faces set and the last of the fog curling away from their upheld gun barrels like some last, ghostly breath exhaling into the warming day.

"Four . . ." intoned the faceless counter.

The number drifted over to the young Cavalier and drilled insistently into an excited brain. Four. Four Marys had Mary, Queen of Scots, to serve her. An old song. *There was Mary Bea-ton and Mary Sea-ton and Mary Car-mich-ael and me* . . . The Marys-in-waiting. Dead. All four Marys. And—

"Five . . ."

And five dead. To count the first. Mary the Queen. Mary Stuart. Grandmother to Charles. Fateful. These Stuarts were fateful. *Full fathom five thy father lies and those are pearls that were his eyes* . . . Five. No—six passed and not missed.

"Seven . . ."

Stepping onto fractured frost, like crystal pearls, that icy dew. Scattering them. Seven Ways of the Cross. Times two. The road to fatality. Where was revenge for that?

"Eight . . ."

Eight steps. Only sixteen strides between muzzle and muzzle. *'Tis now dead midnight, and by eight to-mor-row / Thou must be made immortal* . . . Eight. Master Shakespeare again, a tiresomely apt versifier. From *Measure for Measure*. And step for step. The only way to be made immortal is by being made mortal in the first place. *Look, here's the warrant, Claudio, for thy death. And by eight to-morrow* . . . Eight.

And where is the nine? *Were there not ten cleansed? But where are the nine?* Luke, St. Luke, from the King James Bible. James. Son of Mary. Son of four. Father of Charles. Did King James bring the nine? *A woman hath nine lives like a cat.* Now, that was a phrase to hold to, from Heywood's *Proverbs* and still wise enough to credit a hundred years after.

. . . *nine lives like a cat. A woman hath nine lives like a cat.* And a duelist? How many lives—? Nine, where was the nine?

"Nine . . ."

A stitch in time . . . and a crack, a mortal ominous crack—no cracks called for here, only the rhythmic ring of spurs. Now a sharp fanning—loud, unusually loud, like a grouse startled from the underbrush, beating upward for freedom, spiraling away from some congealed piece of lead hurtling toward it . . . Turn! Now! Now or not one life or nine shall matter—!

Waverleigh and Farnsworth watched like spectators at a grisly masque. They saw how Sebastian had set his bootheel like a compass point on the moist grass and spun smoothly to face his enemy's back, how his dark jacket skirt had scribed a circle in the air. How something—a stick—had cracked then, and a flash of feathered brown had come fluttering out of the underbrush.

Nine, the counter had said. Only nine. Was there not ten called for? Yet here was Sebastian leveling his extended pistol arm toward the back eighteen paces away, his eye drawn upward momentarily by the fleeing bird as if torn between which prey to shoot.

Young Steele whirled then, his eyes only on Sebastian's gun barrel yearning toward him like a spyglass seeking to end vision instead of to aid it. He sprang sideways, lowering his upheld pistol like a fencing piece.

Something snapped hard in the stillness. A cloud of powder mushroomed around Banebridge's hand in an explosive burst of sound. Silverworked. The stock tracery and barrel were silver, dull silver. A moment hung there long enough to stretch silence on the rack.

And nothing. Nothing happened. Sebastian had fired but his bullet had been as untrue as his intentions. Both duelists stood frozen.

"Ten," concluded the counter lamely.

The young man from Dorset set his face remorselessly and pulled on the tapered curve of metal under his forefinger. Trigger homed against the stock. Again nothing. He pulled until his knuckles showed white. Nothing at all.

Sebastian Banebridge stared at the small distant circle of black frowning toward him and shook his head, setting the pearl in his left ear swinging.

Young Steele held his firing position as if somehow time would overtake his motion. Then his pistol exploded into tardy life, spitting up smoke and shaking his arm as if it bucked to unseat him.

Sebastian paled even as the morning light grew stronger. His eyes twisted once toward young Steele's seconds as if expecting them to explain something—the universe, man's humors, the ways of pistols that misfire . . . that delay speaking their fatal message—

Sebastian's hands enfolded his face while his pistol clanked leadenly to the ground. Once again Banebridge blood flowed copiously down Banebridge cheek. In the grass, a pearl shone white under a sheen of red.

Oliver, his own face wound stanched, gingerly trod over, setting his feet sideways on the grass as if expecting another ball from nowhere. He pulled his brother's wrists away from the distorted face and leaned a timorously inquiring look to the wound.

"His ear! You've taken his ear. *Quel*—barbarian!" he complained to the motionless figure that still held the spent pistol parallel to the ground.

The Banebridges, enveloped by their seconds, turned and hobbled off to where horses nickered behind a screen of trees. The remaining duelist let out a long breath that collected on the brisk air like the last of the fog, released. It disappeared even as Waverleigh and Farnsworth came forward.

"Where," said young Steele, his voice shaking on the word just as his arm had shaken at the pistol shot, "did Banebridge's mysterious ball go?"

"I—I cannot conceive," answered Justin. "Are you certain that it was not into you? His aim seemed true enough."

"And treacherous enough!" barked Farnsworth. "By God, I feel like calling them both out again, and their seconds, for this pretty piece of villainy. You've got ears as well as eyes, lad, else we'd be carrying you home by the heels."

"I'll not shoot any feathered game again, that I vow," agreed the youth, dropping his pistol arm as if it suddenly had grown too heavy. "Take this undecided thing, Waverleigh. It seems the Banebridges are content to forfeit it and I do not require it."

" 'Twas lucky that you held your aim after Bainbridge's seemingly undelivered shot. If you could not shoot the dog dead, at least you scarred him," said Justin, escorting his champion from the field.

"A pity that you could not turn time back and lower your aim by a foot," grumbled Farnsworth. "Then Banebridge should have paid for his treachery with his life instead of his vanity."

"A penny's worth of vengeance is worth more than a pound of flesh, Farnsworth. I never intended to aim better."

"You wished merely to pierce the fop's ear?" Farnsworth was incredulous.

Young Steele levered himself into the high, hired carriage, groaning as he sat, but he instantly thrust an impudent face out the window.

"Aye, Farnsworth. They are twins, are they not, in blood as in vice? 'Twould be a shame to ruin such a set. Besides, the tale of their wicked ways will be told whenever a fresh eye falls upon their faces." He winced and fell back into the coach interior as Justin bounded inside.

"I'll take our duelist home," he promised Farnsworth.

" 'Twill be a day or two before he's abroad again."

"No, no," protested the young victor. " 'Tis a mere slice. I require no company but my own."

Justin was pulling his buff kid gloves off with his teeth and ignoring his patient's protests. As his fingers reached to work the jacket away, his prey subsided farther into the corner.

"No, I tell you," young Steele enunciated through set teeth. "Away with you! I'd have stayed in the nursery had I wanted such tenderness."

Justin's fingers ebbed away while their owner regarded young Steele, puzzlement contending with suspicion in his quicksilver face.

"Rest easy on it, my dear sir," implored his patient more softly. " 'Tis only a scratch and hardly worth exposing to this dank river fog. Who knows but that might set some poison boiling in the blood?"

"Ah, poison. Yes, some ill-humor might set in—" Justin sat back on the stiff leather and let his victim rearrange his blood-soaked sleeve in peace. " 'Twas a valiant duel, the best I ever saw. Of course, I have seen no other. Though I've heard of many."

He fixed his listener with a fierce frown. "In France they do this sort of thing all the time. I expect that you shall do quite right at it as you get older. I myself would have done more than pinned the dog's ears back, but then had I escaped an early ball only by its falling wide—I wonder where it spent itself? I heard it land not."

Justin buried his smooth-shaven face in his ungloved hand and meditated until the conveyance stopped. He was suddenly aware of the ebb and flow of morning voices beyond the carriage windows.

"I took the liberty of seeing *you* home," explained the pale youth beside him with as pale a smile. "Thus I guarantee myself some peace. Protest not. You've been a valiant second, sir. 'Tis merely that I need to—compose—myself after this morning's set-to. Adieu—a phrase, I think, they use in France to imply that we shall meet again."

Young Steele had opened the opposing door, nudged Justin out and had leaned out the window to address his parting words to the bemused figure on the pavement even as the hired coach clopped away.

"By God, sir," called Justin dazedly after the departing coach. "You are no gentleman!"

The ghost of a laugh drifted back to him like fog.

The hired carriage ground its way from Justin's home on Cheapside to fashionable Fleet Street. It lumbered through by-ways clogged with early morning bustle until it turned inexorably riverward.

By the time it reached the Three Cranes in the Vintry Tavern on Thames Street, the river fog had reasserted itself and threaded through the wooden wheels as if to slow the heavy coach. The sign of the Three Cranes swung protestingly in the damp air, a sound that matched carriage springs creaking to a halt before it.

The passenger lurched out and stood alone on the street. In the fog, watermen could be heard calling back and forth from their invisible wherries and barges. The swans that adorned that length of sluggish yellow water were still shore-packed, even their whitest feathers looking dingy in the murky light.

The young Cavalier shivered and pulled a crimson-lined slash of cloak over his shoulder more tightly. He entered the tavern, empty save for the simpleton who even now scrubbed the stones in an ineffectual sweep. The Cavalier's boots nailed the flimsy tavern stairs more firmly into place as he swiftly mounted to a chamber at the establishment's rear.

Tonight the place would be thronged with iambic pentameter and song and the lusty romping of unemployed actors, artists and poets at their evening ease. By day, by morning, the Three Cranes was as torpid as the Thames outside its still-shuttered windows.

Yet had one of the lazy, rocking swans on the river's foaming edge happened to stretch a sinuous neck upward, it would have observed an oddity to give even an uncurious swan pause.

For the heavy coach remained poised on the cobblestones, its driver dipping his chin into his cloak for warmth in swanlike surrender. The street was quiet save for the slap of water against the embankment or the distant tread of solitary feet now and again.

Then a figure emerged from the Three Cranes. A figure cloaked from head to toe, hooded, masked. A dark pumpkin of full-cut skirts swayed softly toward the waiting carriage.

The coachman snorted in surprise. Then a crafty grin dissected his unshaven jaw. He nodded his new passenger into his conveyance and threw a knowing glance to the shuttered windows above. He slapped the reins heavily on the horses' broad buttocks. The entire mechanism creaked down Thames Street.

The swan's sable-tipped head followed the sound, then burrowed wingward again. It slept. The carriage plodded on to join the trickles of humanity coverging on London streets. Such sights did not seem to interest the passenger; the coach windows remained curtained.

The coach was slowly passing through wider streets as the fog reluctantly untied itself from the axles and slipped behind. Hawkers were out already, volunteering chestnuts, fish and oranges to the morning air. The carriage plowed through them like a ship ignoring the supply boats.

It finally anchored on Old Broad Street at the deserted gate of a fine cut-stone house bezeled by a wall. The passenger materialized on the ground, cast a shower of sovereigns at the coachman and swirled through the gate.

The carriage's departing creak drifted after the hurrying figure, but soon dwindled. The figure brushed along the house's cut-stone side to a rear door, where it sagged a moment against the hip-high head of an ornamental stone lion. Then key scraped in tumbler, the door sucked silently inward and the shadow vanished into the dark that still swallowed all but the residence's faintly lit kitchen.

The visitor swished rapidly up the rear stairs, flattening along the wall as a burst of kitchen admonitions wafted upward. But no one came, and the cloak glided unimpeded up another flight, down a dim passage, around a corner, down another hall, in another door and then—silence.

The figure turned from securing the heavy door to face a room dimly tented with a great testered bed and peopled with furniture limbs protruding from the shuttered darkness like the arms of drowning persons from the water.

The cloaked figure swam surely through the dimness and drew the window shutter back so the pale morning light fell inward. It dropped its hood and the newly minted light fell on a shimmer of hair as golden as the coins awarded the coachman. It sat suddenly on the window bench and untied a black velvet mask which peeled softly to its lap.

Miranda put a hand to her forehead, dewed with more than river damp. Her fingers trembled as she began sloughing off the heavy cloak. Her laces were only half-done; she pulled them out ruthlessly. The bodice slipped off her shoulders as she rotated her arm into the faint light. She sighed. Good. Bleeding stopped. The tavern-improvised bandage had done its work. She slipped totally out of her gown now, wrenching the petticoats to the floor, then caught all her clothing up in the cloak and thrust it to the back of a wardrobe.

She lurched for the bed and collapsed there before reluctantly thrusting herself into the nightdress marooned on the coverlet. Her bandaged arm broke through the sleeve on a hiss of pain, but she burrowed under the covers and lay there, her open eyes glistening in the semidark. The shutter! Her eyes almost willed the errant barrier shut—now, there would be something to question. She debated rising to close them, then let her head loll back on the pillow. Too much. She was tired. And hurt. And cold. She would have to plead flux and keep to her bed all day. She would—

Miranda sat up violently, her face a mask of concern. She pulled the nightdress down her wounded arm and stared at the ribbon of red-tinted linen wrapping it. Well below the shoulder. Only a pink. No, it should not be visible beneath even her most bare-shouldered gown.

There would be a scar, of course, just as *they* bore her scar. Even as *he* did. A small price to pay for triumph. Miranda sighed again. She worked her face, cold frosting even her cheeks a pinched white, deep under the swansdown pillow, and slept.

Chapter Thirty-three

"*P*rithee why so pale and wan? Ah, I dare say no more, but prithee why so pale?" Justin Waverleigh inserted his inquisitive face between Miranda and the space into which she had been staring for some moments.

"You are not an unpleasant sight, Master Waverleigh, but you make a better shutter than a window."

Justin retreated while Miranda bent her eyes to her abandoned tapestry and took a series of industrious stitches, her first that afternoon.

"I do not need a window to see that you wax as white as my Great-aunt Philomena, and she has been passed from us since James's time."

" 'Tis nothing. A mere touch of—something. Pray tell me of

your infamous duel. Carmina says that neither Banebridge has shown his face these past three days."

"True enough. 'Twas a duel of scratches rather than of mortal blows, though I think poor Oliver has taken his scarring rather to heart."

"Poor Oliver! Did you not tell me the last time we met how wicked these Banebridges were? Have you changed sides, Master Second?"

"Of course not. My young man did tolerably well, and paid for it, for he pinked himself—right there." Justin flicked a line across Miranda's lavender silk sleeve.

She drew away, but he did not notice.

"An odd fellow," he went on. " 'Twas as if he were playing a trick upon us all, from sober Farnsworth to witless Oliver. Oh, but they are a vile lot. Completely treacherous. Sebastian turned to shoot a count before agreed; had not his ball gone wide, we would have had to call him out, Farnsworth and I, in retribution. Then such dancing there would be, for who could count upon it that he wouldn't turn on 'eight' in his next engagement? At his pace, he could as well fire at 'one.' "

"I thought 'firing at one' was what duels were all about," Miranda noted primly.

"I thought my figures of speech were lost upon you," returned Justin in tribute to her pun. "In Faith, I believe you are far less interested in this skirmish's outcome than you were its outset. Come for a turn in Madam Carmina's garden. The air will bring a blush to your cheek, my wilting English rose."

"What the air will do is doubtful, but I think your flattery will accomplish it speedily enough," returned Miranda, allowing herself to be escorted into the garden teeming with carnations, though the chill had taken a victim here and there.

"The roses last the longest," said Justin, pausing to cradle a yellow bloom in his fingers.

"Perhaps because they have thorns."

"You think so? Or that no one dares pick them?"

"It strikes me that roses are no rarity—whether vased in Venetian glass at Somerset House or climbing a whitewashed cottage in Cornwall."

"Cornwall? What do you know of Cornwall, Indies Princess?"

"Only that Mistress Carmarthen's suet pudding must be a powerful dish," responded Miranda ruefully, recalling blunt Captain Pentreath.

"I beg your pardon?"

"And so you should, Master Waverleigh. You wonder what turns my color pale and yet you cannot recognize a perfectly healthy case of melancholy. I thought you held yourself some sort of master of the art, sir."

"Why should you be melancholy? But 'tis obvious. You have been close-kept too long. You must come to the next masque—ball, then, if masques disaffect you."

"Speak to Carmina of it." Miranda trailed to a carved Italian bench and settled upon it like a lavender-winged butterfly. Justin perched on the narrow swath of stone Miranda's voluminous skirts had not claimed.

" 'Tis not Carmina I would lead through the lively cebell, or even bring the pillow in the cushion dance."

"Do you think, Master Waverleigh, that because I am a poor foreigner I am unaware that more tokens than mere pillows are exchanged in these decadencies?" Miranda retorted. "Ask Carmina; I care not."

"Now it is I who am melancholy," complained Justin, rising and catching up Miranda's hand. "If I cannot be certain that you will bring me the pillow in the cushion dance, I must make the best of other opportunities." He smiled, bowed and kissed her pale fingers.

Miranda let her glance fall upon these evidently desirable extremities after he had gone to seek Carmina. She saw no fascination in herself. Bored, she was mortally bored. She sighed and wandered back to the rosebush that had caught Justin's attention. The frost-touched blossoms drooped on their stems, as if hanging their golden heads at their coming demise.

Miranda stroked the chill velvet petals. Only a day or two earlier they had been strong, vital. Only a day or two earlier she had been facing the Banebridges in glorious combat, teasing them, hurting them, having her revenge. Now she was bored.

Whatever the exhilaration of the duel, it had wilted like a last unnatural burst of energy, that escapade: the final bitter beat of her wings upon the windows before she drooped her head, like a rose, and waited.

Justin's silks were rustling down the path toward her, sounding brittle as a leaf buffeted by the fall wind. She turned before he approached her.

"I'm sorry, Justin, if I was unkind. I fear I am—homesick."

"This is your home, Millicent—nay, don't flinch when I speak but the truth. How can you care for some wild island oceans away? *This* is our island, this England we stand upon, and I sometimes swear she is sinking. Yet you will stay afloat for me; I know it. I shall depend upon it."

He had caught her hands again and his look was so earnest that she dared not pull away. His arms encircled her. He was so attractive, hurt and hope sharing the warmth in his brown eyes . . . such a handsome, glossy creature, a fine-tempered colt kicking his heels up for the first time; she didn't want to unshoe him.

So Miranda hung in his arms for a moment, like a guest welcomed by a particularly exuberant puppy who doesn't want it to jump upon her skirts but is too taken, too flattered, to repulse it.

He mistook her pause for assent; in a moment her fingertips were to his lips and he was covering them with kisses and amorous nonsense.

"Ah, my Indies Innocent, cease pining for that fathomless wilderness. In Barbados could you find a gentleman to frame a sonnet upon your smallest fingernail? 'Here, where the lambent moon of her crescent nail / But meets the extremity of all her outer being, / I cast my inner soul and there impale / The dullest of my hopes, my sharpest seeing . . .' Or upon your ear, perhaps, though I should have to seek further than the oft-used 'shell.' What? I have it! 'As the oyster broods upon its pearl / Not so my Millicent safeguards her jewels / But lets the oyster's prize openly unfurl / From ears whiter than pearls pursued by fools.' The rhythm's off, but then 'tis impromtu."

Justin shrugged. His fingers moved from toying with her pearl earring to stroking lightly down her neck.

Confusion, laughter and a certain lingering pleasure kept Miranda netted in her suitor's arms. How pleasant to be petted like a kitten, pleasant and somehow—harmless! Justin masked his seriousness in a winning exaggeration. For Miranda, it was the first time in months that someone's embrace felt natural and lulling. So she and Harry had fallen into each other's arms in half-play, half-unspoken affection as children on Barbados—had that time ever been?

She could not recall a human touch for months that had not carried threat for cargo. Her mother's careless cheek-brush, all the while her gray eyes alert lest her lord happen by; the don's abortive advances; Fat Juana prodding her from table to table in La Bicha Roja . . . No, only Ibrahim's half-choked caress. That had been the only honest touch. That, and Steele, spasmodically gripping her as a captain leaves a soldier bound for a fatal mission, when he had said farewell—a sexless sort of contact, that somehow gave Miranda her due, but she had been hollow by then, and beyond touch.

Now Justin danced upon her emotions, played glissandos across her heartstrings when she'd thought herself out of tune forever. It paralyzed her, this ardent storming, so she bowed to it as a willow does to water.

"You are delicious," he said, realizing her surrender, and brushing his lips across hers. They were silky, dry. He was all smoothness, no roughness to him, no mystery.

"I could linger my life away with you, like this." Justin turned her to escort her down a farther path. His arm still circled her waist and his lips were but an inch from the ear he had celebrated in verse but moments before.

"Listen, my *Cendrillon*. I was drawn to you the moment you came hurtling down those dark stairs like some falling star to my feet."

"Falling stars are said to be unlucky," Miranda hedged, but he ignored her.

"My future hangs within the power of your lips to say aye or nay, as that pearl swings from your earlobe, on which I could say more, but I fear you find it tedious. 'Had we but world enough and time,' I could dedicate an entire sonnet sequence to every particle of you."

"Yes, you favor the form."

"Though you would frown, and laugh and sigh, you would come to like being my muse. But there is no time. Every Kingsman is in danger of losing all he has, including his life. Yet I would rather have you and lose you, than let you slip from me altogether."

"You seem to have settled the matter, Master Waverleigh. Why trouble me with your conclusions?"

"Because even the most confident suitor must have assent from the lady herself. I want us to marry."

"Marry!" Miranda broke away. "You are too young," she said severely.

"No younger than you."

"So you think. You cannot simply marry me without seeking your family's permission—"

Justin laughed and pulled her to a stop. "Am I to go scurrying across Roundhead lines, then, to my besieged family seat, to demand that they stop fighting to consider the state of my affections? Millicent, Millicent, I am old enough to know the old forms mean nothing in such times as these."

She regarded him for a moment, strangely, like one who has been playing with a kitten and suddenly finds it a cat. "I have no family to speak of. I have no dower," she said finally, walking away.

Justin followed. "Dower? I am glad that you have none, for if you did, my family should only melt it into metal for cannon or coins to pay the Scots for some last rescue attempt. The Waverleighs may once have been a mighty clan, with pride enough to put any wench who would marry into their ranks through a noble grilling, but I am the last of my line, and a mortal frail link, I promise you." He smiled. "What I do no longer matters to any but myself. And, I would hope, to you."

Miranda sat again on the Italian bench. She ran her hand over the cold marble, then pulled her skirts aside so Justin could join her.

"What you say may be true, Justin, but I cannot wed you. I cannot marry any honorable man of good faith—you do not know how I got to England, at what price."

Justin's quick fingers fanned across her lips. "Hush, *Cendrillon*. Even in folktales, one does not need to confess that one's coach was once a pumpkin! Carmina had said something of your travels. I care to know no more. I will be a refuge to you, that is all I ask."

He caught her to him and pressed her face into his gray silk shoulder. To Miranda, he was like fog, smoke, mist. His affection was nothing she could box, shape or name. She could not call it friendship or lust—it was oddly different from any emotion she had known.

She found a pair of hot tears welling behind her closed lashes, and so she paused in Justin's arms like a gull on an ocean-long journey who lands on an unlikely island for only a moment and then—stays. She pulled away, feeling oddly smothered, her heart beating for release as a bird's wings fight the air for flight.

"Justin. Justin, you are very dear, but—"

"But? Is that the proper word to trip off those pretty lips?"

"You are impossible. I shall say what words I wish. My lips are not so pretty, nor my ear so white, nor my eye so bright to merit your versification. I begin to think these Puritans are right; Cavaliers are very excessive fellows."

"I speak my truth in my own manner," he said seriously. "The beauty I see in you is truer than any hyperbole I could give tongue to."

Miranda finally fell victim to the blush she had been eluding all afternoon. " 'Tis certain you are altogether too accustomed to having your way. On this I must say no."

"No?" Justin sat back, his face as gray as his garb.

"Yes," Miranda said quietly.

Justin paused, then stood. "At least you'll not deny me your hand for the walk back."

For a moment, it appeared that Miranda would. Every gesture with him took on a significance which somehow committed her further. What was a hand? Miranda placed hers in his. He brightened and led her back up the walk, past the sober carnations nodding sleepily on their stems, past the roses drooping on their lattice like soldiers sleeping on guard duty.

"This is the last we shall see of Carmina's famous garden this year, I fancy." Justin turned to view it one last time.

"Yes," agreed Miranda, reclaiming her hand.

She was not so agreeable when he had left and she was foolish enough to tell Carmina of his desire to marry her.

"And you refuse, you refuse, my so annoying little English duck! Waverleigh! *Santa Maria!* But why?"

"I don't know, Carmina, no more than I would know why I should accept him. I thought for a moment that I had recaptured something—but it was only a game. I feel like a piece on somebody else's chessboard. I don't know what is expected of me, what I am to do with myself."

"Do with yourself? You marry, that is what you do with yourself, silly Millicent."

"There. You call me 'Millicent,' but in my own mind I'm 'Miranda' still, what my father called me. Still my father's daughter and this is not what he intended for me." Her hands circled the elaborate room like a Gypsy's encompassing a crystal ball.

Carmina settled back into her skirts. "This Justin, he is very—*simpatico*, no? I have told him he may escort you to next ball. Why not let him dance attendance upon you some more; perhaps you will come to like the tune?"

"Oh, I like the tune," Miranda said, spinning away in a circle of lavender silk. "That is entirely the pity of it."

Yet she was meek enough a few nights later when Carmina cajoled her into the sea-foam-green gown that lapped her shoulders in a wave of snowflake-patterned lace. The pale green and white made honey of her hair and turned her eyes to peridot in a pearly setting. Carmina sighed once for her lost youth.

"Tonight, my Millicent, you could bargain for the moon and win it as an earring. How wise of me to keep you from the paintpots—the young do not need it and some say overuse eats us from the inside out. But I do not appear too ravaged, no?"

"You look splendid, Carmina. Why don't *you* take young Waverleigh and be done with it?"

"Too young, *cara*. I like my meat well seasoned, though there is precious little food for romance in London of late, save Roundheads with spindly shank and somber dress. God save us, I may turn to young Justin yet; veal will suit when beef is scarce for even the most jaded palate—"

"You are a wicked old woman, Carmina," interrupted Miranda, tapping the Italian's arm with her ostrich-feathered fan. "You need not think that I do not comprehend your metaphor."

"There is more than metaphor I could tell you would you but listen. Forget the past, forget whatever you thought you were! That is as plain as I can say it. These are my last words of motherly advice for you, yellow chick, so heed my clucking."

Miranda drew the white feathers of her fan through her hand, until their fullness stretched thin before they fanned out again beyond her fingers. She brought the fan abruptly to attention and fluttered it before her face so the golden tendrils kissing the edges of her features took sudden flight.

"Have I not heeded you all too well? I can hardly walk for tripping upon my Brussels lace or nod my head for dislodging a lovelock. Very well, I will have Master Waverleigh practice his courtship one more time, and decide tonight whether I will have him or no. He would be some relief from your constant prattle, even if he must deliver his sentiments in poetry rather than good English prose."

Very little poetry passed Justin's lips that evening when he collected Miranda from Carmina's side and led her into the first of many stately dances across the wooden parquet floor.

"*Cendrillon, Cendrillon*, you are lovely beyond the work of fairies this night," he began above the tuneful strum of lute and harpsichord.

His brown eyes were admiring over the arch of their raised

hands, but Miranda treaded her pattern demurely and watched him slide to the side.

"Not fairies, but Carmina," she responded when they faced one another again. "Why must I always be the object of your praises? You, too, are magnificently outfitted this night, and such knee ruffles, sir. I swear you may very well vanish from below the knees and give yourself over totally to boots."

Justin gave a very Gallic shrug at his magnificently bucket-topped boots. " 'Tis fashion, mistress, makes shoe trees of us all. In France this is the fashion, although their new King has taken to going bootless."

"Bootless?" Miranda laughed and made a stately circle away from her partner. "A bootless King does not bode well for France," she tossed over her milky shoulder. "That is worse, perhaps, than a crownless King."

"Hush," entreated Justin as their hands joined once more and their faces glided parallel again. "Even here there might be those who—but you mention the King. I may be called upon to do him some service soon. I would be gladder of the task if my domestic circumstances were settled."

"Then get yourself a cook, sir," retorted Miranda.

"O cruel beauty. It strikes me you are marv'lous quick at carving a man, if not a roast. I would gladly submit to your knifeplay if you would call my hearthside home."

"Knifeplay?" Now Miranda's hand and face fell. "What do you know of my knifeplay?" His face was innocent. "These days I take up naught but my fan or dropped stitches," she added more lightly. "Surely you would not want so useless a creature in your employ?"

They stepped together, the green hem of Miranda's swaying skirt lapping momentarily at the toes of Justin's pale kid boots. His fingers held hers and his eyes as well caught hers, clutched them somehow in an expression as bottomless as quicksand that pulled her down into his seriousness.

She laughed suddenly, but not successfully. "So tell me more of your bootless French King. I am mortal intrigued by the French. I never saw so many Englishmen as have sojourned on that Papist shore. Why would their King go bootless?"

" 'Tis said he has a turn of leg so excellent that it is a crime to sheath it—and he aspires to his majority, to the heights. He is but a boy, after all. So young Louis wears satin shoes like a lady over silken hose. I have seen some Englishmen try the style, though it takes a straight leg and a certain French crookedness of vanity, if I be judge. But, look, such a one is merely down the line."

Miranda's eyes swept sideways and floorward until her gilt lashes grazed her cheeks. Indeed, a very handsome pair of legs—if one regarded French-blue silk stockings from knee laces to shoetop the proper province of a gentleman—and dark blue velvet shoes of most exquisite beadwork all mounted on a set of high red heels that advanced and retreated on the polished wood like fireflies. The possessor of the red heels retreated behind a row of swishing skirts.

"How annoying. I was just comprehending the fashion—are those crimson heels also the mode for men in France?"

"Most assuredly. 'Tis a pity our man is so far down the line, but our pattern will bring him nearer. Does it strike your fancy?"

Miranda strained her neck toward where the sleek legs and shining heels had last surfaced. Nothing. Then suddenly—a flash of red like a tongue stuck out at the world. She followed the remnants of the figure upward. Red Heels did not appear to require the elevating services of his crimson stilts; his curled fair head—if indeed that was he—emerged a good half foot above the rest.

"I cannot certify who he is," Miranda complained. "Can you tell his partner?"

Justin frowned. "I would rather look at *you*, my Millicent, but very well. She must be that redhead—see, *La Rouge* in Lincoln green. 'Tis too florid a combination for me."

"Yet she is very pretty, Justin—such mahogany hair. She matches our elegant swain, Master Red Heels, and looks a lady who would like French fashions. I predict within the week all our men shall dance on crimson stilts."

"Not I," swore Justin. "I could not bear to be removed a particle more from you."

Miranda blushed as crimson as the heels in question. She sighed and kept her eyes to the floor as if puzzling out the steps, but really to evade Justin's earnest brown besiegement.

Her speculation returned to Red Heels. She could see little of him, though the dance was drawing the couples closer . . . merely a set of blue silk shoulders here, a sheen of golden hair moving there. Now—a hand, half-hidden in silver lace, with a vibrant spiraling flash of red upon it—a ring. A red ring, like his heels.

Odd, once before she had erected a man upon the look of his

footwear. At La Bicha Roja. The Red Snake. Red again. A shiver circled through Miranda and coiled somewhere near her heart.

Justin's head shone like satin across from her. Red Heels's partner's curls gleamed like polished wood. The candlelight reflected from a dozen intervening pates and settled softly on the tall blond head weaving in and out of line, closer now. Much closer.

She caught a sudden flash of profile, the rim of cheekbone, chin . . .

He was most elegant, this gentleman. Too elegant to slouch behind a thick glass of Jerez de la Frontera in a smoky Cádiz tavern. He had abjured Wide Boots, this Red Heels. He was nothing like. And yet, and yet . . . had not the slice of face reflected in the light worn too burnished a cast for an ordinary London gentleman? Had there been a bronzing to him—sea bronze?

Her imagination was peopling this London hall with ghosts. Perhaps she did need Justin. Miranda shut her eyes, her fingers tightening upon his.

"*Ma petite?*" She looked into brown eyes as foreign as his words . . . warm but alien, almost as unreachable as his, as Ibrahim's. Was Justin mystery, after all, when she had thought him so open? Yet he was open, to her; he was as open as a book when one wants to read to forget, as open as a gate when the wolves are after one . . .

They spun, in the dance, it seemed. At least Miranda's head swam. Their hands broke and she paced a circle on the floor, afraid to make the full turn, afraid that when she came back to her original position Justin would not be there . . . and who would be? A tall and remorseless shaft of watered silver silk and French blue, silvered, gilded, sun-bronzed—

She turned and faced her partner like a duelist, her hands raised as much for combat as rejoining. Her eyes swept upward from the floor. No Red Heels, only softest pale English kid, only Justin, as safe and solid as any mortal flesh could be. Her eyes surfaced on his. She smiled and watched the flare it lit in his eyes. Why worry about a sliver of a man twenty paces away?

Justin was here, and he would protect her. Her eyes slid remorselessly leftward, over the fence of shining starched lace collar guarding her bare white shoulder. Closer. In pursuit. Devious. Like a pirate ship that anchors in a harbor and at first seems only to be swaying amongst the other ships, docile as a lamb. Shift-

ing, swaying closer ... then it is among its prey broadside—
nudging bows, twining bowlines, sending boarding parties to
storm the decks.

Miranda's hands slipped from Justin's; she held them tighter
as their motion converged. His eyes crinkled warmly, she fastened to them, stepped away, looked sideways.

Closer. And she swaying and bobbing in the water, armor
gone, naught but starched lace between her and—what name did
that trespassing bow wear?—something sinuous and serpentine?
Something ironic? Something familiar? A salamander burned in
her imagination like a figure from a tarot deck. The stars were
bad now, the astrologers said, for old enterprises. Bad for Stuarts.
Ill for Hathaways from half a world away. The figures rocked
closer, oblivious.

Red Heels advanced and retreated until she thought the man
was fencing and not dancing. Close enough for a glimpse of face
beyond the intervening heads and shoulders. There, his motion
brought him to the side, there—the eyes. Ice-blue and looking
only at his mahogany-tressed partner.

Miranda spun out of the line, whirling Justin with her. The
couples merged to fill their vacancy, and behind her Red Heels
advanced and retreated without a pause.

"My dear Millicent, whatever is the matter? Your snowy falling band blushes in comparison to your face. Come, *ma blanche*,
to the fire."

Justin guided her to the high Tudor chimneypiece. He settled
her in a wing chair and half knelt before her. "Millicent, what
has affrighted you? I'd swear some careless foot had trod upon
your grave."

"Nothing," she said hollowly. "Nothing."

She watched his hands swallow her lily-pale fingers. It was
like watching a gate closing, a gate she'd always known was
there, waiting to be of service. Something good and solid to
swing behind one, to keep the world out.

"My Millicent. Smile a bit, that's better. Better still would be
to say you'll wed me. We needn't make a fuss, just some established preacher still allowed to keep his Book of Common
Prayer. You must let me protect you, Millicent; it is not good for
you to be alone."

She looked deep into his eyes and found only concern there,
no speculation, no question. How good to move behind a gate of
sweet concern, to hear it creak shut behind her and end the sound

of careless passersby, advancing and retreating on high red heels in the street.

"Yes, Justin. I will marry you. You may regret it but—"

"I? Regret it?" His fingers crushed hers to well-protected passivity. "Never."

Miranda believed him. That was the only thought in her mind when she betrothed herself to Justin Waverleigh in the light of a flickering fire under the dark shadow of the Tudor chimneypiece. That and one other thought.

She believed Justin, and she still did not know for certain who Red Heels was.

Chapter Thirty-four

A cold November rain slashed itself to pieces on the mullioned windows, almost driving through the cloudy glass like icicles. It struck, then melted into spittle and coursed down the panes in weary little rivulets.

A pair of tears etched the same meandering course down Millicent Waverleigh's cheeks as she sat on the window seat in her white silk nightdress and watched the rain try to reach her. She almost wished it might batter its way in, that rain, might soak her to her soul and tear away the warm, lulling fog that bound her.

She pulled her knees closer and stared to the street, nearly black, its few ungutered torches winking feebly. The night was dark and painted the interior of the room in which she sat an unremitting black. Still, she knew its nighttime shapes well enough. Knew where the cupboard waited to entice her toe into a stub, where the farthingale chair crouched to trip her. The embers in the great stone fireplace still glowed pale red; their flicker penetrated the bed and its dark tapestried hangings to flutter on the white of Belgian linen like a moth.

She brought her eyes back to the rain-pierced night outside. Millicent was glad of toes tucked up under lace-trimmed ruffles. Miranda, who was almost a memory, would have bolted for the street and danced into the storm as if it were salvation . . .

She sighed and clasped one wrist tight within another, so she served as her own jailer. Her back was strained against the hard walnut paneling, but better honest hardwood than the sinking swansdown treachery of the great bed looming into the room's dark like a darker chamber within it.

Three weeks had she been Justin Waverleigh's wife. Three weeks since she had forsaken Carmina's hardheaded marble villa for the well-timbered Waverleigh town house on fashionable Cheapside Street. Three weeks. Tomorrow would begin the fourth.

Tomorrow. And tomorrow he would take her down Threadneedle Street and Three Needles Street to Silk Street where the slippery foreign tongues of the French Protestant refugee silk-makers would extol their paradise-colored fabrics. There would be mountains of silks for gowns, for garters, for lining cloaks as wide as any London thoroughfare . . . hats and laces, gold-threaded gloves, shoes . . . even high red heels, if she wished. That seemed to be the fashion now . . .

Shoes. And where and when had she lost that one lone shoe of hers, tumbling down the stairs and into Justin like a singlet die well-cast? Not so long ago. *Cendrillon*. A bitter-ashes *Cendrillon*.

For this night it had happened as it had always happened each night since the furtive Anglican minister had bound them both in holy wedlock with a Book of Common Prayer and omission of the wedding rings the Puritans despised and forbade. Justin and Millicent.

And home to a dark-paneled Tudor horror that welcomed her as harshly as her aunt's hunch-shouldered house behind the Strand. Where . . . where Harry now lived. She'd not thought of Harry in a long while—no, she'd kept him well out of any mental niches, chinks. Harry was driving into her mind now, just as the rain drilled the windowpanes. She had heard that he had found a fine young set of Cavaliers to entertain him, most royally, if that word had any meaning with the King under arrest in Westminster until he bowed to Parliament's wishes.

Her hand choked tighter on her wrist. Perhaps it was the Hathaway inheritance, this obsession. Hers as well as his. For the thoughts that drummed her temples faster than the rain beat watery fists upon the mullions were unwelcome, unworthy. What had she to complain of? Justin had lavished trinkets upon her, led her like a doll from dressmaker to cobbler to jeweler. The days since their marriage had been a parade of luxuries, ladled out with a loving hand.

And the nights . . . the nights had unraveled themselves in

dying embers and sweetly whispered words, soft kisses, an arm lying affectionately along her hip, heavy upon her, and the words, the wishes, dying like the embers, turning gray, ashy. Sleep. And she lying there, thinking what she did not wish to think—that there should be more, that she required more.

Her fists ran aground on her temples, her eyes squeezed shut against her inner rain and the world's outer deluge. Surely it would reach her; any instant something long and thin and cold would strike her cheek, wake her from this sleepless dream.

He was like a puppy, her husband, all loving, lapping tongue. All wag and wiggle. Who was she to push him away at each on-coming wave of limpid, anxious affection? And yet, he always fell—quite exhaustedly, quite peacefully—away from her at last, curling up beside her and settling into sleep without warning.

And she lay there, waiting. Every muscle tense. Tonight. It must come tonight. He would swivel suddenly, reach out, begin with her what many others had tried, what Ibrahim would have given his eyes for, what her brother did with his don, the lowest of the Dutchman's venal pirates with his latest portmate. What her mock Bey of Tunis had extended with her freedom under a gaily striped awning on a Mediterranean galley . . . No, it was hateful! Justin, Justin would have made it all come right, could have soothed the raw edges of her previous experiences and carved his own message into her mind and body.

And he simply lay there. Night after night, while she waited for what must surely come and never did. He did not even seem to think it odd, nor expect that she would. All the poetry, all the nibbling and petting, only play. He had only been playing at manhood. Had he thought her, fresh from uncivilized shores with reason, perhaps, to dislike the sensual saraband that led so many a merry chase, had he thought her beyond it all? Beyond feeling?

Shouldn't she be? What was the matter with her? She had married respectably without paying the cavort between the sheets that sealed the bargain. Justin was attentive, engaging; he clearly worshipped her, submerged her in his nightly endearments. She was mad, that was it. No reason to mention her distress to Carmina, as she sometimes thought, no reason to do anything but live her life as it had been dealt to her.

And simply lie there. Night after night. Waiting for the hunter to come and spring the trap, to collect his catch. The thought made her heart pound louder than the rain, so she ran back to the bed and slithered in. Sleep. This time I will sleep, she promised herself, pleating the linens neatly under her chin.

Yet the whites of her eyes still shone in the faint firelight. Her fingertips still clenched the bedclothes. Sleep, when it came, as it always did, toward morning, brought the subtle insinuating hiss of an Arab melody, brought unremembered undulations and dark brown pools in the sandy center of her memory, melting like chocolate and wrapping her entirely in something warm, velvet and wet, like a lizard's tongue drawing deep under the waters of sensation.

Now it was a snake of tiger's-eye, sizzling across the hot dry sand toward her, trellising her limbs like some shining climbing vine, entangling her until its flat gold-touched head rose to face her own paralyzed one. It slid back its golden lids and ran its long forked tongue out at her. A red tongue. The eyes were sapphires.

"Love? You cannot lie the day away abed. Overmuch sleep will rob our time together. Up, then, I've such a surprise for you—"

Miranda blinked into Justin's lukewarm brown eyes smiling into hers. He always woke with wrinkles pressed into his youthful face, as if he worried while he slept.

"Surprise?"

"Yes, my love. I shall collect you after you breakfast, but don't dress for town. This surprise waits in our own parlor."

Justin slid away, leaving a triangle of pale bed linen exposed. She quickly drew the covers closed, so her bed was an undisturbed expanse of brocaded coverlet. She was lost upon its generous surface and, once Justin was gone, edged herself into as narrow a strip of it as possible.

The ample breakfast the equally ample Betty brought remained mostly in the porringer and under its pewter lids.

"Mistress be a trifle pale of late. Be it like—?" A country giggle. But the bodices into which Miranda's French Huguenot Hortense laced her drew closer sooner these days.

"*Mais non*, Bettee. Madame ees too sleek for zis fatness that vanish in nine months, eh?"

Hortense tautened the laces while doubting Betty exited and her mistress thought she was being drawn into one slender filament that should waft away in the slightest breeze.

"Ah, you are so perfect in apple green, my Millicent," said

Justin when he came to collect her under the Frenchwoman's approving gaze.

He was so a loving 'usband, Monsieur Wav-erleee. Though zat go ze way of the wind soon enough, *non*? And she so *gentille*, so *très belle* ... The maid hoarded a smile at the corner of her sharp little mouth and tended to the wardrobe.

"What have you for me, Justin?" Miranda asked as he installed her formally in the tapestry-hung downstairs sitting room. A ring of woven Venuses and Atlantas in unveiled beauty held off a circle of equally unclothed suitors in the tapestries' storied surfaces.

Miranda found her eyes drawn to this classical disportment with a morbid curiosity. Had Eurydice found her Orpheus more intent on fetching her back from Hades than finding her fetching before she was gone? Did Venus wish more ardor from her fiery consort Vulcan and seek her mortal lovers then? Miranda's thoughts flushed her cheeks, so she warmed her hands against them until Justin pulled them imperiously away.

"Now look. These foolish tapestries have hung there all my life, but these, these are yours ..."

He flourished open a well-buckled chest. A brittle army of color stormed Miranda's eyes. She gasped. The don—no, only Justin's overeager eyes expecting gratification from her. She donned her most overjoyed face—it was becoming a mask—and glanced at the box's glittering entrails again.

"The family jewels," explained Justin. "So out of fashion these last thirty years, with no lady amongst the younger generation to claim them, that they've survived even our civil troubles. Look—such a pity, these emeralds would become you so. You'll not wear them now; I cannot require my bride to play the laughingstock of London for traipsing about in antiques—but they are yours. Perhaps they will suit again and then will you make Gloriana, our old Queen, look paltry indeed, despite her penchant for gems. There are some pearls—here, a black baroque— perhaps large for you, sweet. I want no black for you. Black is mourning. You shall not mourn for me."

He kissed her fingers, dropping the jewels he had dredged up back into their harbor. They clicked together like hard pendant raindrops, the first foreboders of the storm.

"Justin. You muddle me. Why show me these?"

"This is their resting place, behind a secret turning of the chimneystone. Come here, my pet, and see how they retreat into the dust that has veiled them well. Sit here with me."

He sat upon a great flame-stitched wing chair whose flaring shoulders kept off draft and listening ears equally. Miranda allowed him to pull her upon his lap despite her recent unease whenever his affection became physical. She sat quietly enough while his fingers toyed with her curls, the yellow ribbons in her sleeves, her laces.

"I do not know how to tell you this, and most of it I cannot tell at all. I must leave. The thing I feared is upon us. For the King's sake, it is now or not at all. A few of us hazard upon this scheme. I am sworn to partake. Ah, I must surprise you more frequently, your eyes grow paler green with every question in them. Plans are afoot; that is all I can say. All England hangs by a hair, and it a royal one. Trust me. Forget me not. If I can, I'll send some message. When I will return, I cannot say. Carmina will look after you, *Cendrillon*. Should anything untoward befall, I have left you keys enough to unlock any door there—in your fireplace. So apt a cache for my *Cendrillon*. Do not languish in the ashes for me, sweet. I wager that the day will be King Charles's—and ours—yet."

He stood so quickly that she slid to her feet before she knew it. His motion set his spurs ringing; only then did she notice that he was too sturdily attired for a day guiding his bride about London town.

"Justin, I must say something before you leave, I must—"

His hands netted hers. "Yes—I? And you. And you and I. 'Tis a shame to separate such felicity of phrase as 'you and I.' But 'I could not love thee, dear, so much / Lov'd I not honor more.' Do not frown for the source. 'Tis a modern London versifier, and a good Kingsman. One Lovelace. 'Tis his words, but my heart. Goodbye. I'll not prolong it."

Miranda was alone in the dark wainscoted room, under the honeycomb of white plasterwork. She stepped fireward and stopped at the sound of her own footfall on uncarpeted hardwood.

Jewels. He had left her jewels worth a king's ransom, perhaps Charles's ransom, and had gone—where? To do what? He had left her. She would be alone now on the great bed, with its linen like canvas and its foot and headboards carved like the sides of a lavish ship.

She had sailed far in that bed these last weeks—a long, inward voyage that had left her certain only of more undiscovered territory within her. Carmina. She would see Carmina. Cling to Carmina. Do whatever Carmina said. Listen to Carmina. And never tell her.

Never, never tell Carmina what had—not—happened.

Chapter Thirty-five

Carmina drew Miranda back into her world, into the taper-lit brilliance of marble foyer and Palladian design, personally, leaving footmen scattered and maidservants scandalized.

"*Cara mia, cara·mia*, come in. I be true old woman now. I have miss you. How lovely you come early to my ball to be with me. I have not yet finish my gowning, come above. Drop your cloak, my pet, you shall stay awhile, after all, eh? Ah, how exquisite. All gold tissue over a pink like pearls—you must help me choose my trinkets. What you think? This amber earring, or shall it be the pearls again?"

Carmina's face nodded to itself in the looking glass atop her dressing chest. Her plump hand patted a nearby fringed stool. "Sit, if you can bend your currency of dress. Such gold. How did I never think of you in this rose color? Where did you find such fabric?"

"At the Pawn. Justin took me there nearly every day, to stroll and buy until I would have bought myself free of it. I should wear the pearl, Carmina."

"Ah! Such what the French say—blazeee? You pine for your young husband. So natural, you know? Worry not. Here, I have fashion straight from Venezia for your serious face. Give me your chin—"

Carmina had plucked a small glittering gold star from a China porcelain box and held it wetted to her fingertip. That single celestial body hovered judiciously above Miranda's unpainted face.

"Here, at the eye, so you will seem always to wink? No. The forehead? You have an unlined one, *cara*, a thing worth thanking one's stars for . . . Where, my Millicent? Ah, here! At the corner of your mouth. To remind you to smile! It is a ball I hold; not a wake. Christmas is soon upon us, no?"

"The Puritans would not have us celebrate that joyous season, do you not know that, Carmina?"

The Italian woman's rouged lips contemptuously kissed the air as she defiantly pierced her fleshy lobes with amber pendants.

"I tire of you English. So—conservative, so close. Walking only the road some other has laid out before you. We Romans laid out many of the routes your countrymen still tread. So. You do not wish to twinkle, like the so-clever star I give you. So, do not. I wash my hands of you."

Carmina shook her powder puff so vigorously it clouded both their faces.

"Pity, Carmina. Your battle powder seems more lethal than any pistol's. Very well. I will come and smile at your guests, but I shall not dance." Miranda elevated a gilded mask surmounted by brilliants and gold lace.

"*Cara*. Put that down. You look most mysterious behind it, but rather frightening as well. Why the mask? you wonder. Are there not faces behind some of those masks whose owners would merit Tower lodging were their features known? I care not for these things, and neither should you. You must move the roses from your gown to your cheeks. Look at your moth—at Sylvia. Her lord is in daily peril of the Tower and yet she dances and smiles as daintily as any court lady in Europe."

"That is *her* failing." Miranda swirled to the window in a cloud of rustling silk.

Her bodice was deep rose velvet diamond-patterned with gold thread and pinned at each gilded crossroad with a pearl. To Carmina, the girl's back looked as impervious as mail. Carmina clucked to herself, then shrugged, so the white lace falling band settled lower on her ample shoulders.

"She is not here this evening?" Miranda's voice was remote.

"No, *cara*. She can no longer move in any circle she wishes. Some—scheme is up. I feel it, a pall of black fog rising from your ever-chilled river. It will come soon to swallow us all. All. I must go to France." Carmina's tortoise comb snapped down on the dressing table.

"Carmina, you are gloomy. 'Tis good I came along to relieve your spirits with my own high ones." Miranda's mouth turned up in an ironic smile and so did the star at its corner.

She laughed and pulled Carmina from the room, leaving the candles still shimmering within the chamber's beautifully hung perimeters and her hostess's mask abandoned on the tapestried stool.

Below, the high-ceilinged rooms brimmed with beeswax tapers. Chandeliers dripped light down upon polished marble floors, on gleaming wood turnings of cupboards laid with Venetian pastries as translucent as the glass for which that city-state was famous. Goblets glittered like frozen soap bubbles. Great silver punch bowls winked warmly from various corners of the rooms bracketing Carmina's stately entrance hall.

That hall was tiled in alternating squares of black and white marble, like a chessboard. A white marble circle of Roman deities gazed down from their arched niches as the first guests stepped into the light and warmth, the night outlining their splendor like a black velvet curtain behind a jewel.

They stepped into Carmina's hospitality, these silk-swathed Cavaliers and their pastel-petticoated ladies. Their well-made boots and dainty shoes minced lightly across the enduring marble. They stepped unknowingly from square to square, no king at their back to defend, their queen in exile, their bishops banished by the Puritans, their knights hard-pressed since the battle of Marston Moor, their rooks besieged, their pawns wooden and worthless upon the board.

Still, bright and rare colors festooned their persons as well as their spirits. They yet paused to curl their hair, perfume their otherwise-untended bodies, to tuck a great white plume like a boast into their beavers . . . to wear their swords in richly braided scabbards on a night such as this, Carmina's last London festivity.

Miranda skimmed among the growing crowd, expertly avoiding scabbard and goblet-equipped arm. She paced the limits of the downstairs chambers like a family dog unleashed to do his rounds. No Oliver trailing pearls or Sebastian oozing venom. No—Sylvia.

She sighed and caught a sliver of herself in a piece of Venetian looking glass. Something creamy and rose, gilded everywhere, with a special golden gleam near its unsmiling mouth. A little yellow patch that winked at her and laughed . . .

She spun away. Carmina found her later, sitting upon a fireside stool, looking as unmoved and rosy as a porcelain figure.

"Ah. I feel like St. Lawrence on his gridiron. These fragile ices of Henri do not cool. Are you not hot, Millicent, by the fire?"

"No, I feel a chill."

"So do half the gallants in this chamber. I see you turn an entire parade away. I must ask you to move your position occasionally, so traffic will not remain in only one corner of the chamber."

"I told you that I did not wish to dance this evening, Carmina. I will only watch these courtiers come and go. I never saw such—"

Carmina's inquiring dark eyes saw Miranda's face freeze to alabaster, the green eyes glaze suddenly into glass.

"My Millicent?" She leaned nearer, brushed the clasped hands with the rough edge of her fan. The girl did not move.

When she finally did, it was to snatch the fan from Carmina's hand and unfurl it before her face, her green eyes rising over its pleated horizon like moons in some unnatural other world.

Those eyes still focused far away, across the room, where candlelight fell equally on every head. Yet one, one blazed as brightly, as solitarily, in the sparkling scene as if it stood alone.

"There."

Carmina never saw the hidden lips move, heard only that low word. She frowned over her powdered shoulder to the point that transfixed her guest.

"There," repeated her amazing Millicent, as if hissing a state secret.

Carmina paged through the faces—some masked, some bare— that wafted leisurely through her festive rooms. No Sylvia, surely, no Banebridge had darkened her classical pediment . . . Her sharp eyes fluttered past groups of guests, then stopped and retraced their path.

Something—familiar—had flashed by; something, someone without a name, but with a memory for her. She glanced once more at the rock-crystal face beside her, shuddered slightly and read the features across the room again.

For some reason her eyes settled as insistently as a fly on one figure—something distant in sky-blue satin of a very fine cut, even from this vantage. A fair young man, in every sense these English mean the word. Blond, as only Englishmen and Norsemen can be. They all look alike, these English that fall into that type, all—like—one—another. Like steps, the long-ago Steele children, with hair of melting butter. She had not seen Sir Charles and his brood in years, save for young James's cometlike appearance on her horizon. Strange, no one had heard of him again . . . and this was not he, not James.

This man was tall, assured enough to don pale blue hose and buckled shoes instead of doeskin boots. A courtier—or one who would appear as such, a bold pose in such times. Carmina turned abruptly to all she could still see of her protégé, the intent eyes hardening some unknowing victim to pure marble.

"So this is your Steele?" Carmina inquired calmly.

"I—I cannot conceive why *he* would be here . . ."

Carmina measured the distant figure of a woman whose emerald silk gown was crowned with a cameo of creamy shoulders and face, and a fall of curls that even from here glowed deeply red, like claret. This apparition nudged silks with the man in blue.

"*I* can imagine why he comes here, *cara*."

Carmina's meaning was lost on her bench partner.

"It must be he, although . . . he looks so, so—"

"So—yes?" Carmina's dark eyes were twin challenges.

"So . . . fine."

Carmina laughed. "Child, is no duplicity in you. I am happy to see that no matter how you loathe a monster, you can still discern if his scales glitter, no? That, I warrant, is an exceptionally handsome monster."

Miranda watched the older woman's eyes fasten again on faraway blue silk. "Carmina. If the hand that strike you be gloved in satin, does it make the blow any lighter?"

The Italian shrugged, sending her falling band plummeting dangerously low upon an already awesome cleavage. "The father was a well-miened fellow and not known for rapine. I do not see how this one should require to stoop to such to pluck whatever flower he wish. Look how our rarest blooms flutter around him, eh? Though I fancy he is bent on picking that thorny English rose—I know her now—Roxanne Wexford."

Miranda let Carmina eye the distant scene alone. "I would rather be willing consort to a leper than victim to a god," she stated coldly.

"Ah, Millicent, I have upset you. I am old woman now and know nothing but the joy of watching others cavort upon the board. Do not fret; your queen is safe with me, and I will not make off with the knight."

Miranda opened her mouth to retort into Carmina's latest array of veiled nothings that made Rihana seem plain-spoken by comparison. Instead, she shut her lips firmly. She shot one last arsenic glance to the man in blue. Bonnie, Meg MacTavish would have said, she thought icily. Her eyes pooled on the painted silken scene decorating her commandeered fan.

'Twas not right that *he* should sally lighthearted into London salons while she— No, she would not look again! Ah, closer, coming closer, and with something purposeful in his step, an unbooted step. The latest fashion from France, and wasn't her first duty aboard the *Salamander* unbooting him—my God!

Carmina found the fan thrust rudely into her hand and watched a blaze of rose-gold silk flutter away across the crowded room.

A moment later a sound scuffed on the uncarpeted floor beside her. She glanced down to a waiting pair of ivory satin rosettes on ice-blue shoes, up a well-proportioned leg extended for a bow, beyond the froth of knee laces and ribbons, beyond a delicately embroidered expanse of blue silk as fully well cut as her expectation, past the clean-shaven face—a mistake, that, for a would-be courtier. Or courter. Beyond the sweep of sun-gilded hair, curled just enough to pass London muster . . . to eyes of vivid blue, glittering with a certain suppressed amusement.

"Madam Carmina, if I do not mistake?"

She nodded as he straightened slowly.

"Christopher Steele, madam. I believe you—knew—my father, Sir Charles."

"Oh, do you believe it? And where were you, sir, when all this acquaintanceship was a-brewing?"

"A mere mote glimmering in the future, madam, but I seem to recall a foray to London after my mother was brought to bed with my sister Marjory, and my father's pilgrimage with all of us boys in tow to this house."

"All!" Carmina's eyes melted. "All indeed, an entire flight of young Steeles. 'Twas the last time I saw your father. How fares he?"

"Older. Wiser. Well." Steele swept his dark blue velvet dress scabbard aside and sat beside Carmina. "I fear I flushed your benchmate, speaking of flights."

"Surely, *I* was the only attraction that drew you hither? Or are you your father's son, young Christopher?" Carmina's fan settled flirtatiously across her décolletage. Steele laughed and leaned back, crossing his arms with the air of one who had been on guard and now relaxed it.

"By the Cross, I would have seen you lead my dignified sire on a chase in the old days, madam. I warrant you have not lost a one of your winning ways."

"No," conceded Carmina. "So. Do I satisfy your so odious curiosity? There is nothing more disconcerting than to serve as a monument worthy of visitation by the young. May I suggest the genuine Roman ruins for your next excursion, if you tire of this one?" The fan fluttered in mock anger.

"Pray table your weapon, madam," pled Steele. "I only paused to give the greetings my father would were he here—and to pass some conversation with the only face present that looked as if it could unbend into something human." His eyes ranged restlessly over the well-dressed rainbow of saffron, violet and green arching the room.

Carmina studied his slightly sea-bronzed profile. A wicked speculation took root in her mind, then put forth a tentative stalk, propelling her tongue somehow into motion.

"Yet, young Christopher, I thought you a much too purposeful young man to dwaddle amongst what the Puritans would call this iniquity—without a reason."

"Aye, our poor Queen Henrietta Maria named them rightly, those Roundheads. All blunt about the brain and long about the face. Maypole-burners and theater-demolishers. There's room enough in my world for what I dislike as well as what I favor. Our poor Queen-in-exile, forced to charity at her cousin's Paris court, and the niggardly French faulting her every sou—I'm bound there again tomorrow. If enough Englishmen saw their Queen in such straits they'd settle affairs here soon enough, even your sour Puritans."

"You avoid my point. You're far too devoted a fellow to languish in a salon when there are Queens to serve. I suspect you are spy."

The fan suddenly pricked the embroidered baldric which slashed diagonally across his blue silk chest. Steele's guard instantly clanged shut, like a portcullis falling across his face.

"Nay, madam. I do not wear such colors but those that may be flaunted. In England, at least. Can you not tell my mission?" he asked with a laugh, gesturing to his magnificence of person. "I come a-courting, madam, and find it a tiring pursuit."

"Only when the game is red fox, young Christopher," Carmina retorted. "Be warned: you shall run your race well before you win it with that one."

"You have marked the prey?" He cast a startled glance to a slash of flashing green engaged in the lively steps of a galliard across the room.

"I have marked the prey," said Carmina gravely, her eyes fixed upon him, "and I am looking at it."

She saw the lines draw taut around the ice-blue eyes.

"I do not fancy myself any man's prey. Nor any woman's."

Carmina shrugged. Steele dispassionately watched the broad lace collar shift shamelessly upon her shoulders. He did not speak for a moment. When he did, his eyes glittered remotely.

"Perhaps I keep Madam from conversations more welcome. I must not become a monopolist, though King Charles was happy to create quite a few while his royal quill still carried some weight."

"Oh, no, indeed. I was merely enjoying an idle chat with my *amica piccola*—the child in rose and gold you saw fluttering away."

"Child?" His eyebrows rose.

"So one of my years think. Perhaps you know her husband."

"Husband?" Steele's face formed a façade of polite attention.

"Yes. One Waverleigh, a good Royalist like yourself. Off he go and leave his poor Millicent to pine. She will not dance, and must spend her evenings talking only to old women." Carmina's face grew as doleful as a statue of Our Lady of the Sorrows.

"No wonder, then, that she did not linger to speak with you," Steele said lightly, extending an inclination of his head with his gallantry. He stood and bowed silently.

Carmina watched his straight figure vanish amongst the crowd. "So that is your monster, my Millicent . . . ah, what glitter."

She suddenly rested her mouth on her furled fan, as if to stop an inopportune word from escaping. Her lips curved into a smile against the stiffened silk, then whispered, "Very well, I shall," to the fan and the empty air around her. She snapped the fan open and began wafting it across her face.

So she was when Miranda returned, the gilded mask a mystery across her eyes.

"Well?" Miranda hovered by the bench, as if expecting certain manifestations and ready for flight again.

"You need not have retreated to the mask, *cara*. I doubt he remembers you well enough."

"Then it *was* he?" Miranda's hands manacled Carmina's wrists.

"*Piano*, softly. As I say, he has forgot you well enough to show interest in you as if you were some other. I believe he seeks a small diversion to teach his *La Rossa* a lesson."

"He would not do that," returned Miranda hastily.

"Ah, no?"

"I mean that his villainy is above that sort of trifling."

"So women have believe of men since Eve. They are wrong."

Miranda turned her masked profile to the dance floor while Carmina thought how well the stiffened fabric matched her protégé's interior spirit. The same smile that had twisted her lips before reprised briefly.

"Listen, my Millicent. You were different then, no? Younger. Not so splendid. Not a married lady. How should he know you now? Do you delude yourself that what is between you shall name you to each other forever?"

Mockery threaded Carmina's voice. Miranda's eyes lanced the tapestry of her discourse like a needle, but the Italian woman's face stayed as blank as muslin.

Then Carmina leaned forward, her slightly sallow neck and shoulders looking somehow serpentine in the soft candlelight. Her lips moved softly near the pearl in Miranda's ear, so that any moment it seemed her words would set it in motion.

"Such revenge you could have upon him, my sweet. A woman's revenge for a man's misstep. He does not know you, I tell you. It would not take much, I warrant, and he would patter after you like a puppy, no?"

The phrase made Miranda's bare shoulders stiffen, but she listened still.

"Then, when he was fawning, at your mercy—'twould take only pushing him away with one small finger—so!"

Miranda watched Carmina's forefinger brush contemptuously at air.

"You think that would not sting, *cara*? When he is hunting other game and takes a side path—and that path ends in briars and brambles?"

Miranda took a deep breath and drew a passing gallant's admiring eye. Her voice was low and serious. "He would not be lured upon such a path."

"Ah, so noble is he."

"No! But he is—not easily deceived. And proud in that."

"I congratulate you on knowing so well your enemy."

"Besides, that is not the way of my vengeance—trickery and mockery. I would have it clean, final, unforgettable."

"Then leave it to God," Carmina said shortly.

Chapter Thirty-six

God did not intervene, but Farnsworth did.

Miranda had remained marooned upon the bench after Carmina had flounced away. For one island-reared, she found herself disliking the emotional isolation that now lapped at her shores. So when Farnsworth's gentle shadow fell across her lap of shimmering sand-gold silk, she glanced up with more relief than surprise.

"Mistress Millicent, I have not seen you since the last masque, or your marriage. Come and tread a measure with an old gallant who will not turn your absent Justin's eyes green."

Miranda hesitated, her face a mystery behind the gilded mask. "I cannot deceive you, sir. I would welcome a turn about the room. As for Justin's jealousy, he urged me to occupy myself, though not till now have I had an offer worth the accepting."

Farnsworth led her gingerly upon the floor to join the couples awaiting the first scrape of bow on strings.

"Alas, mistress," he noted with a nervous look up and down the row, "I fear I've picked our measure badly. These striplings are arranged to step the cushion dance."

Miranda analyzed the formation with a dismay equal to that of her elderly partner. The cushion dance, a boisterous romp up and down the room that would tax an older set of joints, was also a kissing exercise. Miranda reluctantly let her hands fall from Farnsworth's as the facing rows of men and women stepped apart.

A last darting glance down the line showed a sliver of pale blue across the way. She craned her neck for green, but had to step decorously back as a young gallant bearing a lavender silk cushion danced impishly along the lines.

He made a great fuss about eyeing the ladies, plucking pompously at the tuft of hair adorning his young chin and cocking his brows into almost acrobatic contortions. He turned and strolled back up the line before spinning suddenly on his new red heels and coming smartly to rest before Miranda.

Her imploring look to Farnsworth sank like a sun over her new admirer's shoulder. The musicians struck up the tune and the ritual began.

"Then this dance it will no further go," sang the young man limpidly to Miranda.

She stared for a moment at him, at the plump lavender growth on his hands, at the floor, and then recalled the necessary response. She remembered because it so mirrored her current emotions.

"I pray you, sir! Why say you so?"

"She must come whether she will or no!" he retorted with as much emphasis of which a tenor is capable. He bowed to lay the cushion at her feet and Miranda sank to her knees and her fate upon the pillow. He bent to kiss her.

Then they were up and circling in the dance. The measure ended, he bowed and vanished back into line, leaving her in mid-floor with the guilty cushion somehow materialized upon her open palms.

She automatically danced down the line. She would make a single circuit and return to Farnsworth—dear Farnsworth, safe Farnsworth . . . annoying Farnsworth! If he had wished to dance, he should have made certain of the tune. How excruciating to hop ceaselessly down the line, her curls bobbing and her eyes circumspectly studying possible partners.

The women all seemed to eye her coldly, but, then, she had been first-chosen. One set of yellow eyes rested on Miranda's forehead more venomously than the rest. Here the gallant had first paused. Miranda absorbed the well-piled mahogany hair, the long arrogant face as white and thick as country milk. The yellow look pooled upon her innocent passing face like bile.

Miranda glanced over her shoulder and spied the reason for this enmity from her left. On her right, Christopher Steele stood watching her, or rather some point in the vicinity of her bare shoulder.

Perhaps he was a particular admirer of Venetian lace. She retarded her steps long enough to see his blue eyes traverse the route of her arms and the long trailing splendors of her gown before they returned to her face.

Their eyes crossed for a fractured second; before his expression could acknowledge that mutual glance, she had glided on, leaving only the rose-beribboned nape of her neck and the straight, noncommittal slope of her shoulders in her wake.

Ahead of her, the candles glimmered against Carmina's brocaded Mantuan draperies. Swaths of silk and satin slid by in a meaningless blur. A pulse was pounding in double time to the violins against the pearl circlet embracing her throat. That baleful yellow stare had decided her. That, and a brief graze of blue across her face. Her glance fell on a silvered expanse of mirror between the distant windows. Her glance fell upon herself, dancing demurely into the reflection.

She was totally other now. Father, even Francisco or Harry, would not know her. If some supernatural agency were to swoop her up to the rigging of the *Salamander*'s mainmast now, the waiting sailors below would swear she was some glittering heavenly apparition, or some hell-sent hallucination. They would never see the simple cabin boy in her now. Nor would he.

She turned and tripped implacably forward until she had retraced her dancing steps. With no hesitation she swept into a deep curtsy before the man in blue.

"Then this dance it will no further go," she sang, raising her eyes slowly to his. Her heart was drumming as madly as if she had just issued a challenge—a challenge to duel to the death, with velvet glove instead of iron; with Steele, not steel.

Christopher Steele glanced with some dismay to the billow of shimmering fabric at his unbooted feet. Usually one chose partners from among one's acquaintances, and he did not know her—save as London's eternal feminine, laced and lovelocked into an almost epicurean display of charms. Her subservient posture but deepened the abundance of her breasts overflowing the low-cut neckline—Steele felt a momentary pity for the Puritans in their doomed attempt to banish fashion as well as frivolity. Her curls, her slightly flushed cheeks, the level light gaze from a face that masked some unfathomable emotion—it was an invitation no man, no sailor worth his salt, could refuse.

Steele bowed to mouth the next line—"I pray you, lady! Why say you so?" meaning it more than convention intended.

"He must come whether he will or no," she trilled sweetly, the star-shaped golden patch near her mouth winking wickedly.

Steele surrendered, bowing to exchange the ritual salutation. He brushed her lips with the better part of valor. He brushed by in a brotherly sort of public manner, as if it were important somehow to do so, and found his intentions overruled by the soft cling of her lips halfway through the infinitesimally fractured moment.

The exchange seemed to have pressed her smile to the edges of the mocking star. They rose and danced their measure gracefully. When he left her to find his next partner, her hands melted from his like spring snow.

Steele was instantly aware of a burning saffron malevolence in the vicinity of the back of his eyes. He advanced a step or two to find the fair Roxanne livid. He could hardly be held liable for every bewitching creature who chose to play footstool in a dance! He did not relish passing on this intelligence to the fair Roxanne. Sir Charles had always warned him of the Wexford temper.

And Steele was beginning to feel a certain irritation—he had not wedded the wench yet, who was she to knit her brows into fences for his fancy?

Steele glanced once more at the beauty in rose and gold who'd led him astray so skillfully—her eyes were slipping away down the line, where had they rested last? He took a lengthy turn down the facing rows and then paused abruptly to present the little lavender cushion to a lady as lofty as a mountain, and as snow-capped.

The Dowager Duchess of Livermore raised her scanty eyebrows toward a hairline as diminished. Her thin lips crescented suddenly as she responded to Steele's sung declaration in a wispy soprano.

The unlikely pair finished their round by dancing robustly up the floor, where the duchess, out of some perversity, relinquished Steele back into line opposite his mysterious partner. 'Twas but natural as the set ended to find himself near her.

"We have not met," he declared.

"Have we not? Are you a gentleman to kiss a lady and then tell her that does not constitute a meeting? Shame, sir!"

"You know my meaning. I do not believe that we have met."

"Yet—?" She smiled mysteriously.

"Yet," he conceded, "I do not think you are a stranger."

"And yet and yet. Riddles, sir, bore me. You must have some purpose in trailing me more closely than my train. Pray speak it."

Steele paused ruefully as she settled into slower motion. He shrugged. "Your name, mistress."

"Name, name, name. 'What's in a name?' Never mind. My name is Millicent Waverleigh. Do those few syllables settle your questions?"

"Nay, I think not. It strikes me, Mistress Millicent, that you seek some wordplay, a partner with whom to slice through a simile or two to earn a smile. I have been too long from London to accommodate you with the skill which you require."

He bowed to withdraw.

"No, wait! You are right, sir, I have been marv'lous enigmatic. Come sit with me, sir, and tell me your name and where you have traveled that so dulls your wits that you dislike exercising them."

A barbed invitation, but Steele sailed the wake of her trembling silk skirts, aware that basilisk stares from a certain quarter would be deserved from this instant on.

They settled near the overbearing chimneypiece, sending Madam Carmina fluttering away with a significant raise of her eyebrows to Steele—or was it to the girl? He sat beside her and watched the nearby fire-flicker ebb and flow over the creamy curve of her pearls, in the mirrored brightness of her eyes, uncertainly colored in this light and with the mask. Hazel, he thought.

She leaned back into the settle's high wooden embrace. He felt a brief prick of unease as she studied him.

"I have loaned you my name, sir; can you not repay me in kind?"

"Christopher Steele, late of His Majesty's fleet and more late of less-favored ventures elsewhere."

"Ah. A mariner. A—captain, mayhap?"

He inclined his fire-burnished hair, so that the shoulder-length curls dipped forward and then retreated as he briefly shook the mane back. Miranda's very unhazel eyes widened in the dim light. The firelight had ricocheted off a pearl stud in his briefly exposed earlobe—only one, like a pirate. Ah, he was well domesticated now, Master Christopher Steele, curled and powdered and pearled and shod to make a Frenchman envious . . .

"You smile, Mistress Waverleigh, does my name amuse you?"

"All names are a source of amusement to me, sir, particularly 'Mistress Waverleigh.' Can you not contrive to call me something other? Master Christopher."

She said his name with a certain precision, her lips kissing the air with each syllable . . . he found himself suddenly aware of the fire beating upon his silken back and another slow flame rising invisibly between them.

He would be mad to dally with a London matron when his long-sought Roxanne was fanning herself into fury across the room. That was the prize he sought, not some trifling episode with a bored London lady whose Cavalier husband was off risking all, and more successfully than he knew, for King Charles.

She carried no fan. Her hands lay placidly in her lap, the wrists delicately circled with pearls. They suited her, pearls; he had forgotten what flattery that popular gem played across a complexion that truly foiled them.

"Lady, I could clearly coin a king's ransom of names for you on parchment, but 'twould be a waste of both my time and yours."

"How so?" She seemed surprised.

"Because you have but one name and that is—Beauty."

"Nicely done, Captain. I tax you for lack of gallantry and you deliver your shot where aimed. We have exchanged fire long enough. Your lady—and I do not know what you call her, very like it is 'Beauty'—appears somewhat vexed. I have been watching her, if you have not. I suggest that you weigh anchor and engage upon a peacemaking mission. Perhaps we shall share harbor again."

Steele bowed and retreated. His place was shortly taken by a breathless Carmina.

"*Mamma mia!* My Millicent, you beard the lion. My little cub, you use your claws well—I have not seen a gentleman's attention so excruciatingly engaged in some while. Now I think you have but to lead him some small ways yet and you shall have him. Take him far enough so that retreat is impossible, then abandon him—so!"

Carmina's fan slapped smartly across her palm. Miranda flinched. "No?—you do not like to see him slapped down—so?"

"Yes, I wish it, but what must I do now?"

Carmina smiled like a tigress. "Simply thus. I feel a chill, ah, these old Italian bones. I wish a shawl. Something bright and Persian from my cupboard. You fetch for me, eh? You fetch and dally. I will have to send another messenger, some gallant who cannot refuse a personal errand for a lady. For a poor, old, chilled Italian lady . . ."

"Carmina. Old! Chilled! I believe only that you are Italian, and you are worthy of the Borgias."

Miranda danced away, up the wide marble steps to Carmina's chamber. The second on the left and still well lit.

Chapter Thirty-seven

*T*he second chamber on the left. Christopher Steele took those same steps two at a time minutes later. The exercise forestalled boredom and at that moment he did not feel inclined to do anything in the way he was wont. Roxanne had given him naught but a snowy shoulder on his dutiful return to her envious green side. He did not like that calculated kind of punishment; he wouldn't hold still for it.

Damnation. His father could keep Warring Hall—if the Puritans let him—and the Wexfords could bloody well keep their precious . . .

The chamber door stood ajar. Steele paused. Madam Carmina could have easily sent a servant for her shawl. He was suddenly uneasy about crossing a strange threshold, but he stepped into the room, his flimsy shoes soundless on the hard floor.

The place was populated with tapestries of life-sized figures cavorting on a ground of greenery, with flickering candlelight and glowering pieces of dark furniture guarding the room's rim. A figure moved in the shifting light, there in a tapestry. It stepped forward and was in the room with him. It was she, the masked lady.

"Oh. Captain Steele."

"Do not call me that," he said quickly, advancing to meet her. " 'Tis too formal. Besides, we are on land, where such titles, I find, are more liberally used by an enemy than a friend."

"You sound like a man who has many enemies."

"And many friends."

"Perhaps they are the same persons."

He watched her sway softly across the Turkish carpets toward a looming cupboard.

"I came for Carmina's shawl," she explained, swinging wide a heavy door, "but I fear the wretched thing is on the highest shelf. Perhaps you could—?"

He stood uncommitted for a moment, then crossed the carpet to reach easily to the top shelf, where her straining fingertips had surrendered. He pulled down a shower of silky fringe and chaotic color. It fell over and between them somehow, and she surfaced, sputtering fringe like one drowning.

"My word, dear Captain ... Christopher—there, is that address better, or ... do they call you Kit?"

He was seldom called that on land. The sound of it from her mouth riveted him for a moment, the itch of memory vague in his mind.

"At any rate," she was mocking him, "I would be loath to sail on your ship if you can come so close to drowning one on land. Here, I'll take the trifle—"

She spun the shawl around her like a great rainbow wing that settled on her shoulders, and adjusted it precisely, so it rode the low straight line of her bodice, underlining her bare shoulders. How tantalizing was the leisurely way she pulled the silk across her skin and held it taut. Her soft white shoulders and sweet swell of breast rose from that rolled rim as if that shawl were all that stood between her and utter revelation.

She trailed to the door, the fringe undulating over her skirts. Steele followed, pondering. He was not one to be led along by sirens, seagoing or otherwise. He did not even share Ulysses's urge to hear them sing. Yet she pulled him, this one, in some magnetic subterranean way. She was undertow, he swimmer. Like most men of his time, he did not know how to swim.

She paused by the door to glance over her shoulder. Despite the mask, he saw uncertainty on her face and a small, troubled twist to the corner of her mouth. Her amusing little star seemed to have lost a bit of shine.

He would escort her down, kiss her hand, deliver the shawl to Carmina, collect his renegade Roxanne, go home, marry Roxanne, cultivate Warring Hall, stop sailing, cease wearing Royalist ribbons, sire a new flock of Steeles, grow old in some fragrant corner of England, die ... He would do all that.

And then the shawl shifted, slipped off her shoulder—he reached for it, his ring tangled in it, the ruby flashing through the fringe as if netted. She reached for it. They were tangled in fringe, shawl, sleeves, each other's arms, lips, lashes brushing, twining, swirling in mad colors, soft and silkily slipping ...

Steele surrendered and caught her to him, her solidity that seemed to elude him, so that he had to pull her closer and closer, absorb somehow the silks, the flesh, the hair, the smoothness and the softness. His pursuit of some physical possession of her had brought them both up against the door and swung it slowly shut.

The click of the latch momentarily parted them, like guilty children in a pantry. He saw her masked face, so near, so calm, a stranger's face—it seemed impossible that he had been storming it but seconds before. Remote, that was it. He saw the shawl lying pooled at their feet. Strange, he had felt it drifting over him all the while.

"Your ring," she said, her voice husky with surprise.

"What?"

"Your ring is caught in my sleeve."

He felt suddenly sheepish, as though he had danced to her tune and she now disowned the melody.

He untangled his ring from the lace at her elbow.

" 'Tis a radiant stone." Her eyes moved to his face with a glow as warm as the ruby's.

"An Orient ruby," he answered, "a keepsake. I had it faceted in France—a new method of gem-cutting. Sharply—for fire."

He waved his small finger by way of example, before her face. The ruby streaked across her vision like a fiery comet.

"Ah. Faceted. I see. All the better to tangle in a lady's finery. Or heart. Have you finished explaining the lapidary's art to me, Captain? Perhaps there is some other learned subject upon which you would discourse. . . ."

A small click ended her sentence as firmly as a period.

Steele's eyes fell upon her arm half-bent behind her and knew the lock had turned . . . She was smiling up at him with those (gray-green, they looked now in the shadow of the mask) eyes as bright and brittle as her asterisked mouth.

He had never seen a plainer invitation, nay, not even along narrow Stew Lane or under the lanterns of Dark House Street. Nor one more polished, like a blow from a blade so shining it is more like fire than metal. Something other than what it seems. . . .

He caught her to him until her silks crackled. "There is one subject that takes no learning, Lady Millicent, though I warrant that you have mastered it."

"Have I?"

Both their voices had lowered, as if they were no longer alone. His fingers brushed an errant lock from her cheek.

"Aye. A thousand times a hundred have you studied that subject, Mistress Millicent, and taught such dullards as I their sums beforetimes, I vouchsafe."

He was still holding her at fingers' length, forestalling the moment of what—capitulation? Capture? They measured each other, like duelists caught hilt to hilt and eye to eye.

Then she smiled slightly, and hid her thoughts behind the mask.

She had him. She had him paying court to her, dangling pleasantries before her like a hook before a fish. Thus he was truly caught, snared by his own ordinary desires. She would let him commit a few more liberties, unfurl a farthing's worth more of flowery compliments and then—adieu. Off. I do not want you. Go. Lick your wounded vanity, saliva your pride, Sir Lion-who-has-met-his-thorn. Console yourself with your shrewish fellow predator—if she'll have you. Men! They were children.

Miranda began laughing softly, deep in her chest. It was not an amusing sound. Steele suddenly kissed her to silence it. His lips paid court to hers, then wandered lightly across the remote planes of her face.

"What is your game, I wonder?" he asked himself more than her. "It matters not. You are as inevitable as the tide, pretty Millicent. And you ebb and flow as enchantingly."

His words were whispers, his kisses fell as softly as feathers upon her face. So this was how he would court a European woman, Miranda thought, with murmurs, mouthings and only the glimpse of blue between his lowered lashes. He was imbibing her, consuming her and lost in the intoxification of it.

Now, when he was most absorbed in her, she had but to withdraw the draught, slap him away like an erring child ... and—she'd—won!

She would have truly deceived him in herself, for which he had once unjustly faulted her. She had earned her revenge, she would show him that playing the fool was something more than mistaking the cut of a cabin boy's sail. Ah, poor little Miranda, there in the *Salamander* cabin corner. Poor little soul ... just wait, child, and I will step between you and the shadow. I will strike back for you ...

She had bowed and bent to his lovemaking while these contrary thoughts seethed in her brain. Once again she was conscious of the sheer persuasion of his touch, of his total immersion in a maelstrom of the senses. Now! Her shoulders stiffened, ready to wrench away.

"Millicent, do not abandon the game yet," he insisted softly, plying her with kisses that traced a crescent from her temple to her chin. "My pretty golden one, my lovely, lost Miranda ..."

His lips were insistently reconnoitering the other side of her face, but he could have been storming the dark side of the moon.

She didn't feel it. He. He was the victim, the prey. She had him off guard, revealed, and she must live with what lay behind it—herself.

Miranda drew away in unfeigned horror, intent on breaking free, but his fingers dug into her arms, like a sea anchor dragging until it takes root.

"Pretty one, have you taken a hurt?"

Miranda looked dazed to where her gown had slipped off her shoulder to reveal the thin white slash of Oliver's—or had it been Sebastian's?—sword.

"An injury. From childhood," she said into the melting eyes that seemed to require knowledge of every flaw, every facet of her.

She was sinking into nightmare, and only his fingers held her to the surface. He bent to kiss the scar, then his finger traced an exploratory path along the neckline of her gown—over plain, mountain, crevice. Miranda shuddered as if she'd been cut.

"Are you cold?" he asked, his hands warm about her throat as he bent her face back to kiss her more deeply.

He kissed her in the fashion of a lover, a courter no longer. He was quite right; it was how she wanted to kiss, to be kissed. No more light flutterings about the edges of her senses, no more lips upon her fingertips, no more poetry standing in for passion.

She twined her arms in his and pushed desperately toward what was as predictable of him as it was of the Pillars of Hercules guarding the Mediterranean's mouth: an unalterable rockface of resolve toward the world, an invincible, masculine composition, an element suddenly as necessary to her as air.

She had no mask to drop. She had thought herself like the ruby cabochon, one smooth surface molded by events and true to that shape alone. But there were other ways to treat a ruby. One could slice it sharply with a blade, until its fracturing was new brilliance. This Millicent of hers who had lured the English captain upon the rocks of her femininity was not a mask for the Miranda of another day, but merely another facet of her. As the cabin boy on the *Salamander* had been.

No broken trail of shattered selves remained behind her to wink accusingly at anyone. They all met and melted into the full-cut present. And he was as faceted as she, as fugitive, as precious. And hard. There's an attribute that flesh is heir to. A hard man. One said that as criticism, yet life with Justin had taught her that softness had little virtue. A softness like some Sargasso Sea, becalming her. Stagnant, a surface sort of condition.

She did not want surfaces now. Now she wanted to sink below sight, touch, all the specifics of the senses—and something more, something as chimerical to pinion as firelight. He. He had it, somewhere, concealed. He had always contained it, always.

She wound herself into his arms, trying to blend herself with something of Christopher Steele that was beyond looks, names, appearances. She required it, like food, air. Her mouth sought it as mindlessly as a babe's, brushing the slight roughness of his shaven face, the secret satin places of his ear and neck, the overriding, penetrating warmth of his lips, tongue . . . No wonder the don had so maimed Ibrahim long ago, robbed him of that which could speak best when it was most silent.

Miranda abandoned herself on Christopher Steele, her fingers slipping off his jacket, her mouth deliciously stung from the slight human salt of him. As on that day she had washed ashore near Cádiz, she was driving blindly onto him, a beaching that every particle of her required.

His fingers came between them to cut loose the pearls that drew her bodice together. She was anxious to slough her silken shell; it seemed to hamper her. Her own hands slid under the blue silk guard of his jacket to probe the shift of flesh beneath her fingers through his shirt. He was a paradox of soft and hard, a pleasure to be dredged only from her fingertips. Her extremities explored his center, found and climbed mountain, valley, shoulder blade, the small hard ridges of the galley . . . she felt she healed as she passed.

Her bodice washed adrift on her hips, pulling her hands into fabric manacles at her sides. His hands warmed themselves at her body's inner fire, polished her like a jewel, burnished her like gold. He knelt to drink from her breasts, but she could not tolerate even that much unequal distance between them. She sank into her skirts, their faces joining once again, her fingers teasing at the dozen silver buttons holding his jacket shut. He had shrugged out of it in a moment, casting it aside like some forlorn puddle.

She instantly knew how to tease and slowly pulled the shirt from its breeches' harbor so an attenuated silken thread should unravel his senses. He caught her hands; she laughed. He kissed her quite roundly. She surrendered until he was distracted, then slipped the shirt from his shoulders, until he let it join the jacket.

Her hands etched in the geography of the flesh she'd freed. A forefinger found a scar welt on his arm and swung back and forth along it, like a gentle pendulum.

His hands combed suddenly into the hair at her temples, pulling her face away from his with almost a will of their own. He stared at her with a frown between his brows for a long moment.

"They're *green*!" he said, removing the mask and tossing it aside. "Sorceress." He laughed softly in placid recognition. "You always masquerade for me—loblolly boy, odalisque. What spell were you casting this time?"

She stared at him, stunned by this sudden withdrawal of her intoxicant. When she didn't answer he drew her face forgivingly closer and plied her equally with kisses and questions.

"What was your game this time?" His lips interrogated the corner of her mouth so she could still answer.

"You," she admitted grudgingly.

"I? How?"

"I am leading you on," she confessed huskily. "You are making a fool of yourself. Carmina said it will teach you a lesson."

"Indeed." His mouth centered on hers again and she was drowning in sensation.

"Ki-it." She broke away, using his name for the first time since the *Salamander*.

His eyes blurred tender. Or hers. She wanted to cry. Instead she laughed, shakily. "I am to lure you into utter frenzy . . ."

"You have." He was kissing her again and she never wanted him to stop.

"—and I'm going to repulse you brutally."

"I am crushed," he said, demonstrating by crushing her to him.

His arms circled her waist and she felt a clutch of excitement, anxiety, as the ties at her back pulled and gave. His fingers nimbly unanchored each of her petticoats that clung to her like onion skins, transparent and stubborn. Her heart began reverberating like the *Gato de Nueve*'s galley drum—loud, disconcerting thumps.

She buried her face upon his chest for shelter from that pounding and found the thunder of his heart there, beating the pulse of their desires in double time. The drumming enamored her further, her blood danced to it, as her body had danced to the Arabian drums of the don's harem musicians. The sound under her ear tripled as he lifted her up by the elbows and deftly pulled her sideways. The skirts slipped behind her like a ruffle of white water. Steele deposited her gently prone on the Persian carpet.

"Infidel rugs seem to be our fated bedding, madam," he observed, his long and naked back bowed away while he stripped off his breeches. Then the lean warm length of him lay upon her like a tidal wave of love. They had mutually settled into a lazy lover's pace, into a pattern of twining their limbs and glances into inseparable entities. They basked in the luxury of chaste little kisses, in drawing each other's hair against their faces and fingers. They secretly examined each square inch of the other's flesh with a shy and swelling curiosity.

"Kit . . ."

He brushed her lips as if to seal his name there. His hand outlined the length of her leg and caught her satin-shod instep in his palm. He pulled the slipper off and ran his fingers teasingly up to her gartered knee.

"Kit!" She kicked lightly, freeing her leg. Somehow having her shoes and stockings off would be too indecorous. She blushed. He laughed and lay beside her again, delineating the curves of her body with his hands until she felt entirely encompassed by him. In a moment, he drew back and scooped her up, just as he had in the *Salamander*'s cabin. Save that now . . .

"Kit—what?"

His face was strange, molded with the seriousness of passion. He only nodded over his naked shoulder to the wide, curtain-hung bed looming behind him like a tapestried ghost.

The bed. Tapestried, as was Justin's. Where all those frozen frolicking medieval beasts embroidered above her had looked down so many nights . . . had peered round the bed curtain folds and had watched her lying there, waiting. Waiting to be loved. The stares she had exchanged with them those nights. The bed curtains' rustle as herds of those embroidered beasts scampered across mythic plains and whinnied at her predicament.

No. She wanted no bed. Kit was solid, the floor had been hard against her back, like a shield. She wanted to be wedged between him, his hardness, and her own stony resolve. Beds were soft, downy-throated betrayers, beds were . . . Her arms tightened around his neck and his taut shoulder muscles.

She pulled his mouth demandingly to hers and pressed him with her will, her willingness. "No—here. Now."

Like a wave he flattened her to the floor and took her breath away. He pulled her hand, clutched into a fist behind his neck, before his eyes and slid something bright and crimson onto her second finger.

" 'Tis yours. It was always yours."

"You have had it all this time, keep it," she entreated with a lover's fondness for bestowing. He shut her fingers on the token.

"I have better rings for my fingers," he promised. She gasped with the slow, sweet shock of his engagement, remembering the dark invasion of another day, another place, another person really. As he joined with her she became a ring for him: a seamless golden presence smithed since time began to contain him. They moved together in the instinctive ebb and flow of lovers that hammers body and spirit into one bright alloy. New metal, bright metal, a rough tenderness that melted all one's senses.

Miranda clung to her Kit, the center somehow of the strange force that rode them both. Then his hardness pounded her flesh like surf, her island self began shattering, sifting into a hundred spinning fragments. She was lost, lost in the wind, whirling away in sensation, falling and she mustn't let go, some thread still held her connected to the *Merlin*'s gunwale, she mustn't fall ... but he was waiting on wings to catch her, as he had always been. She felt herself totally rinsed away, a sword of fire spiraling deliciously into all of her nerves. She screamed with the delight of it and splintered into stars ...

"Shhhh, my love." Kit caught her close. His lips whispered against her ear like sea foam hissing against shore.

A spasm of warm waves exhausted themselves on the furthest reaches of her mind, body, heart. She clutched him, gratitude clothing her emotions. She still wanted to recapture it, that split moment of absolute, disembodied unity. It was gone. They were only Kit and Miranda, naked in each other's arms and clothed in their separateness.

His eyes were summer blue and fastened to her face. All that and there was still so much she didn't know of him. Fear began nibbling at her heart.

"Miranda." He said her name as if he were used to saying it.

He gently disentangled himself and donned his breeches. She lay languid upon the jewel-toned carpet, among the Orient designs. She lay there like a pool of warm milk when he turned to pull her to her knees. He shook out her petticoats and pulled them one by one over her head, like a nursemaid dressing a docile child.

All sensuality had washed away, save for its backwash in their eyes. He methodically tied on her skirts, pushed her listless, lazy arms into her shimmering bodice and caught the fastenings tight. She watched him float his shirt over his still-bronzed frame like a cloud. He tucked it into his breeches at just the fashionable level of fullness and pulled on his silken jacket.

She gravely watched him button each silver fastening wrong, then silently redid the process, knowing that his eyes rested on her agile fingers, her gleaming hair, her lowered lashes. When she was done he touched the gilded star near her mouth briefly before he spoke.

"You had better return first." His voice was everyday, sensible. The ring upon her finger slipped sideways. It was a shade too large. She warmed it in her palm as he helped her to her feet.

He found and arranged his embroidered sash, reinstalled his scabbarded sword at his hip. She watched him, memorizing each motion from some dreamy precipice of her own. He stepped to a long looking glass and shook out his lace, straightened his hair. She watched him preen, loving each phase of it.

Kit noticed her passivity and pulled her mirrorward. He patted her curls into place and smoothed her lace, finally catching her glance in the glass. A frown settled near one eyebrow and took up permanent residence. She adored it.

"I'm bound to sail. Tomorrow. To France. I should return in three, four weeks. A mission for the King." She hated the King.

He led her to the door, opened it, remained discreetly behind. She was gliding down the stairs, into a room overflowing with strangers, a shawl trailing from her hands. He must have given her it at the last moment. Carmina . . .

She was by the Italian woman's side, the shawl spewing from her hands into Carmina's lap. It slid over the ruby on her finger, leaving her hands naked.

"I've—the headache. I'm calling a chair." She wished to share herself with no one other than him.

Miranda glided away, leaving Carmina only a glimpse of something red twinkling in her wake.

Chapter Thirty-eight

*A*bove Carmina, in her still-occupied bedchamber, Kit Steele paced in his soft-soled shoes, drawn finally to a crimson twinkle from a decanter. He poured a stream of burgundy into a glass and went to sit upon the testered bed.

He would dally for a few minutes to quiet speculation of a mutual absence . . . sence. Senses. He must have been out of his senses. God's Blood, but he had muddied the waters. What did he think, that she was some fripperied courtesan with whom to trifle? He had truly ruined her this time, indeed. Husband. The word stepped from behind an arras in his mind, like a footpad. He'd forgotten in the heat of the moment, many moments. Husband. One Waverleigh.

Steele found his teeth clenched upon the glass rim and pulled the wine away. His knuckles were white on the stem. He relaxed the pressure. It would not do to leave shattered Venetian glass behind in Madam Carmina's bower. Shattered intentions, perhaps, but no physical evidence of an all-too-physical encounter. He took a deep swallow and leaned back on his elbow, looking at his well-tended hand in its uncustomary wrist laces, holding an unaccustomed draught of French wine.

And he, thinking unintended thoughts of dunes of pale skin and distant green grottoes, lapping already at the limits of his memory like some heady poison.

Why? Why had she done it? She had laughed about deceiving him, besting him. Yet—had she? Had it all been contrived? That passion, he could have buried himself in it, that was something fresh from her. She'd always been reserved from him, something of herself locked away like a prize Benedictine brew.

Now she had unfurled herself for him—where had she learned such, such—? Husband. Always it came back to that. He was not one to meddle with wedded women. Now he had forsaken his intended bride, slipped away from a merrymaking like the loosest Cavalier despised by the Puritans, to frolic with some other man's wife.

The thought made him squirm. She had won, by God—

ruthless. Steele stood, setting down his glass on a bedside table for Carmina to wonder at three hours later.

He walked to the mirror and fussed about the edges of his attire, seeing nothing but the green of her eyes rising and setting in his very bones. Husband. No wonder the sudden passion. The man had been gone. Alone. Bereft. She had amused herself with him to quiet her pulses until her precious Cavalier returned.

That was why she would have nothing of the bed. She would not betray the marital bed, no, she would have him on the floor like a groom . . . He viciously set his sword into place at his hip and stalked to the door. That only could explain it. She did not contain such passion, not even on the bey's barge when he had teased her into compliance with his—pride. He had tricked her out of pride and now she'd truly tricked him in return.

He would forget her. Utterly. As she would forget him now that she was certain of her revenge. Steele cringed interiorly. He had been a bloody fool. Almost a kind of cuckold . . . why did he feel that she was unfaithful to him because she had a husband? Who was this Waverleigh? Was he young, old, bonnie, bold? Steele's mind seethed in circles. Hadn't his brothers mentioned some Waverleigh or other? What matter, the dilemma was solved. He would forget her.

Never—touch—her again. Never see her again. And if he did, well, he would not roll over quietly and play prey to her huntress. Not he. Steele took a last, long glance around the room— the tapers flickering invitingly, the silent watching furniture, darkly foreboding, the shrouded bed. He shut the door sharply and strode downstairs, through the crowds to Madam Carmina's side.

"I bid you good night, madam," he said formally.

"I wish you good night, too, young Christopher." Carmina smiled intently.

Steele watched her shoulders shift within the shawl, something in him wanting to snatch it off her. He made a fist upon his sword pommel instead and bowed a trifle stiffly.

"Wait, Captain Steele. Are you not going to bid the fair Roxanne adieu?"

He looked reluctantly to the verdant spot Carmina indicated across the floor, then shook his head slowly.

"I've early sailing on the morrow, madam," he answered brusquely. "No time for farewells."

"She will not like it," Carmina sang warningly.

"Then be damned to her!" spat out Steele, pivoting so swiftly his soft sole scraped on the marble.

He was gone and Carmina had the fringed shawl edge cupped to her mouth, laughing, laughing until her tears spilled and mingled with the fringe.

BOOK FOUR:

The Derelict

Lament, lament, old abbeys,
The fairies lost command;
They did but change priests' babies,
But some have changed your land.

And all your children stolen from thence
Are now grown Puritans;
Who live as changelings ever since,
For love of your demesnes.
—Richard Corbet, 1647

Chapter Thirty-nine

"What of Justin?" Carmina asked for the first but not the last time.

Christopher Steele had been gone for a fortnight, but Miranda still glowed as exuberantly as the new ruby blossoming on her finger like a wound that will not heal.

"My Millicent, you do not listen. What of young Justin?"

"He is gone, Carmina, to the wars." Miranda wandered to the window seat to fan her fingers on the leaden crossroads between the panes, as if she made a mental journey even while she talked to Carmina.

"Gone, yes, but not dead. Had I known what is the end of it, I would have never—"

"Never what, Carmina?"

"—never let you play Columbine to that particular Harlequin. You have forgot all seemliness. How can you betray Justin so?"

"You were willing enough for me to betray him the night of your ball."

"Ah. One toss of the dies do not make a game. I thought you would learn that all of life do not fall on one side of a line or another. I did not think you would overcross that line."

"Perhaps the line has crossed over me . . . enough complexities. 'Tis very simple. I am truly come to anchor at my home; and that is myself. What I was, am, will be. I do not need Barbados, or my brother or old faiths, but him I do require."

Miranda brought her steepled fingers to her mouth. The ruby sparkled reminiscently in Carmina's dubious eye.

"You are worse than your mother!" she charged in exasperation. "Head-powerful—oh, what is this word? Stubborn. Your mother at least would have make pretense of it."

"My father would have naught of lies and neither will I. I'll speak to Justin when he returns." Miranda paced to the window again. "A fortnight gone, and danger waits out there. In the dark, on the water . . ."

"Justin also courts danger, *cara*."

"Justin? Oh, Carmina, you know nothing of what you speak. I vow he's bound to France and has forgotten me, with King

Charles to be put to trial. Who would have thought it? Parliament putting the King to trial?"

"More like your young Justin is thick within some curdled plot to free your foolish King," snapped Carmina. "He has too much feather in his hat brim to fade into exile at such a time."

"Yes, Justin is all flourish and little . . . but he must be quite safe, Carmina, or I should have heard. Don't glower so. You swear yourself my Kit has a marv'lous glitter to him."

Carmina watched the girl polish the dark wood window frame as if it were a cage side. Girl! She was wedded to one man and had taken another as a lover. Perhaps these Puritans were right: mayhap the times were scandalous loose.

Carmina felt old, hardened like tallow. She could not shift with changes as she had in the old days. It frightened her, this English girl who cast all at one throw. What if her Steele died? Or her Justin? She did not think of that, Sylvia's iron-willed daughter, she thought only of a man who made her veins run molten and that 'twas an effect that could as well be gained from a good fire . . .

Carmina sat straighter, realizing that she herself preferred a well-warmed brick between her nightly linens to any configuration of flesh and bone. A sobering insight. She had better hie to a warmer climate. Roundhead Fever lapped at even her. She shrugged and said no more. Her silence was no more heeded than her speech.

For Miranda lived like a homunculus in an apothecary jar during those days. Like a sealed-off passenger in some bottle tossed upon restless seas, she saw the turmoil around her, but did not feel it.

So when, in the cold final days of that January of 1649, a winter gust blew a vagrant broadside to her windowpane, the contents of that ill-printed paper almost wafted past. It was only one of a dozen blowing down Cheapside that day, like ghostly leaves from a fall long past. The street was deserted—and why not? She had heard the servants clucking that the Thames might freeze for the first time in a generation since Good Queen Bess's Golden Days.

Idle and curious, Miranda told a lackey to fetch one of the fluttering messages from London's wagging private presses.

"Nay, mistress. Ye want none o' that," grumbled Thorpe. " 'Tis likely treason to hang on to. It only tells 'ow Charles the

Martyr met 'is be'eadin' and makes bad readin' for them what done it."

"What? King Charles dead? Beheaded? You must be—daft."

"Aye, mistress, but that's what be upon that paper ye crave. 'Twas yesterday at the banqueting 'all. Whitehall, it was. They had 'im swinging by 'is long royal 'airs after."

"Fetch me a broadside. Instantly." Miranda's eyes quickened into commanding green for the first time in weeks. She sensed a crack in her bottle; the wind that blew through was mortal cold. Kit, it hissed. Where was he? Kit. They'd killed his King. What of Kingsmen now?

The cold-stiff sheet Thorpe brought crackled warning in her very hands. It was a Royalist documentary of the foul and hideous crime against God and the nation when Cromwell's Rump Parliament had condemned King Charles to die. She had heard none of it, had not seen even Carmina in a fortnight.

Miranda sank upon the settle and read the smeared letters by fire-flicker, finally dropping the sheet to the tiled floor. The waiting Thorpe kicked it casually into the grate where it caught flame in a protesting curl that finally coiled into ashes.

"They be arrestin' lordly folk up one side of Old Broad to t'other, mistress. Lucky Master be not at 'ome. Mayhap the Ironsides'll be ridin' for 'im, too."

"Cromwell's cavalry? Here in London?"

"Aye, the counties be all 'is now. I don't read them papers, but I 'ave those as tells me. Don't worry yerself, mistress, likely Master's far off enough to be safe. I'd not be in 'is boots if 'e were London-bound right now."

Thorpe shuffled away, a sudden gleam in his eye as he pivoted back to Miranda motionless on the hard wooden seat.

"I'll be takin' meself to church regular now, as the Law says. We'll all be churchgoers now, mistress. No Maypoles, or it'll go hard for us. Best mind yerself, mistress. Or get yerself where Master is."

The door swung shut on his advice. Miranda leaned toward the fire's warmth. The King truly dead. England had not killed a reigning monarch in all her recorded history. A King or two had been deposed and marched to meet his Maker, but never had one been brought to bow before the axe while the crown still rested on his hapless head.

All his men would fall with him. All the Steeles, like a flight of steps. Tumbling down. Old Steeles, young Steeles. Steeles that faded, Steeles that glittered ... Kit was due, when? In a week. A week and he would sail unknowing up the Thames, if the ice didn't stop him. Then he would blunder on, into a world in upheaval, with no shield to meet it.

She was out of the room, cloaked and instructing the reluctant Thorpe to find her a chair, a wagon if need be, anything.

The sedan chair Thorpe dredged up from Cheapside's deserted byways was well-worn, more chipped than painted in its heraldic colors, with two weary-muscled men to trudge her between stoop and gutter. The curtains kept out the snow's weak little flutters. The previous afternoon's installment lay like a pall on the cobblestoned streets and gabled rooftops, an albino pall, somehow sinister. White was ever unlucky for Stuarts. And for Steeles?

The Duke of Desmond's town house was as blank-windowed as when Helena had first coaxed Miranda from the family coach into that palace's forbidding environs. Built of stone, like Carmina's, but thoroughly Anglicized, it was all importance and no charm.

The afternoon was late, evening descending like a drape across a window. Few lights glowed within the well-veined marble lids of M'Lord Desmond's house. Miranda passed through the portal, feeling as though she had been swallowed.

No servant came to bar her way, or to conduct her. She wandered up the double staircase, its white marble steps set as adamantly as teeth. She found more light but no more habitation upstairs, and peered unchallenged into deserted chambers where dead or dying fires rattled like idiot tongues in the hearths' vacant, black mouths. Pulling off her kid gloves, she cupped the ruby in her palm. To warm it. Or herself.

"Mignonette! *Vous êtes impossible! Venez ici, cet instant!*"

Something white fluttered out a further doorway, peering avidly down the passage to Miranda. "Well, come then, you infuriating lump of La Rochelle milkmaid. *Venez!* Dolt."

Miranda moved into the pale rectangle of light sliding hallward like a ghostly coffin.

"My God! 'Tis you. Daughter. Millicent. Or has Cromwell unleashed ghosts upon us as well as cavalry? Are you real? Yes. How cold your hand is—ah, hide the gemstone. Are you mad, the very servants could strip us and who would help us?"

Sylvia was gowned in dove gray for traveling. Her pale curls washed against a stiff white collar, breaking into drooping tendrils. Her face was paler than even paint could whitewash it, and its fine incised wrinkles were as simple for her daughter to read as the broadside's heavy lines had been.

"Mignonette must have fled, the silly. They would not harm her. Help me with my cloak; I must not tarry. Have you passage, a ship? I must go with you!" Sylvia's hands throttled Miranda's, who shook them loose.

"A ship? I'm not bound anywhere—"

"You must go! Even Carmina has left. All of us must go. My Lord Desmond must go—has gone—to the Tower. This morning. His neck will not be the first to feed the headman's axe. A royal precedent has been set. Do you suppose that axe runs blue now?"

Sylvia laughed, her teeth splitting into a circlet of pointed pearls in a dark and mirthless mouth.

"I need your help. There is a man due on next week's tide, a Royalist—"

"There *was* a man, my dear, if he be Royalist. Send him to the Tower to cradle M'Lord Desmond's head. Help? By all the saints, I'll be lucky to come through myself without my back being whip-shredded from Newgate to the Commons. You come to a Cavalier's mistress for help? My dear, you *are* your father's daughter."

Sylvia darted down the hall, her figure lost in darkness for a moment.

"Mignonette! Curse her for a featherbrain—these French, never trust them. Leave me, daughter, or unearthly visitor, or whatever you be. I claim no kin but my wits. They may come for me. So leave, be gone, vanish as you appeared, like an old dream forbidding sleep."

Sylvia pushed her daughter down the dark passage in rough little shoves. Miranda went alone down the white marble stairs; it was like transversing a grinning mouth. A death's-head still toothed . . .

Sylvia hung above, the shadow haloing her paleness. "If it's Hathaway aid you seek, try your brother."

"Harry?" Miranda stared upward.

"Aye, Harry. He consorts with Roundheads now, does James Hathaway's fine, unnatural son. He's bound for blessedness, from what a confirmed sinner like myself has heard of it. Go consult St. Harry, daughter, and leave me be."

The figure swirled away into the echoing dark, a faint candle winking out. Pain circled Miranda like a cloak. She knew the antidote for that crushing emotion, but he was still far away.

Harry. She did not ever want to see Harry again. He was acid-etched on the cameo of her mind, a treacherous blur of white Flemish silk against a dark and primeval forest. But Christopher Steele had burned himself into her heart and body more deeply than Harry Hathaway had scarred her mind.

Outside, she found the chair deserted, and dredged the bearers from the Golden Bottle at the corner. This was a well-bred tavern for such as they, one that had once rung with Cavalier spurs and spirits. The tables were empty of those lighthearted ghosts; instead the oxen lowered their heavy heads to drink from the same trough the thoroughbreds had used. She was fortunate these men still served her for the coppers she gave them.

She wore plain hunter green and bore a huge, warming muff, but her wide black beaver wore a crimson plume. Its flagrancy challenged the City's post-execution mood, and the feather still trembled as delicately as it had when Steele had produced it from behind his back in the *Dowsabelle*'s cabin.

They carried her meekly enough, ale settling any doubts. Old Broad Street still thronged with remnants of the day's commerce drifting home. Silas answered her knock, ignored her nod of recognition and conducted her grimly up the tortured wooden stairs to her father's library. There she had planned the rescue of Harry Hathaway, with Christopher Steele first, then with Francisco de Salazar and Captain Pentreath.

Dear, dead Captain Pentreath, hadn't she sacrificed enough captains, couldn't the Fates, the stars, the winds, leave her but one? Merely one, who glittered . . . but Harry would help her salvage his onetime rescuer. What reason had he to not? She was the one who had been deceived—undone, betrayed. Of course he would help her, eagerly.

She stood the supplicant's side of the oaken draw-table now, the same surface that had borne the weight of her long-ago purse thrown on it like a gauntlet, the scratch of Kit's signature on the *Forced Man*'s Articles of Sail.

Her brother let his goose quill peck and scratch across a half yard of white parchment. His bowed head was the same pooling honey color as her own, but when he finally raised his face, the hair fell into a close-cropped bowl whose barbered edges rode roughly over sharpened cheekbones.

"Harry? You, a Roundhead now?"

She would have sworn irony was shaping itself to curl from his lips. Instead he frowned. "And you, a Cavalier's lady, so I hear." The Spanish origins of the word "Cavalier" seemed suddenly overbearing. "I am writing a description of the City's sentiments in view of yesterday's great occurrence. I labor in prose these days," Harry explained, methodically setting aside quill and ink, "but I have time to discourse with you. Pray sit yourself."

Miranda sank onto a chair. The slight farthingale was gone, and she felt instantly surrounded by the ample wooden frame of its successor. But it gave her arms to cling to.

"I thank you, Harry, for what time you may spare me." His expression remained politely attentive, as if he took her words at face value, ignoring the mask of irony she had set before them. "Our—mother—flees London."

"That, too, had I heard."

"Have you ever seen her?"

"I? No. There was no necessity."

"She said that you wore your clothes with a Puritan cut nowadays; I did not think such conversion would go to your head." Miranda wondered what Don Ricardo would think of his prize now, shorn like a sheep for some heavenly pasture.

"Cast what witticisms my way that you wish, Miranda. I will be no net for them." Harry's eyes raked her with a hint of scorn. He had been boy and brother when she'd last seen him; now he'd stepped even farther behind their shared past to emerge a man and a stranger.

" 'Tis true?" she said. "You have moved into the Puritan camp, you have influence there?"

"A measure."

"Measure enough? I require a pass. Some paper, I imagine, that will see the bearer through any lines, any barrier."

"For yourself?"

"I? Who would want to send me to the Tower?"

"Then for she who bore us?"

"Our mother has made her own arrangements to flee. No. I want this pass for . . . you remember, the man who tried to take the *Gato* and regain you. For Christopher Steele."

"Aaahhh." Harry sank back into the shield-backed chair. "For Christopher Steele. The man who—"

"—who brought you back to England, yes."

"The man who did *not* bring you back. You left that ship." Harry's forefinger tapped the table abruptly. "Are you not wed now, sister? To some Cavalier called Waverleigh? Yes. Yet you come for a pass for Christopher Steele." Harry stared at her intently, then leaned forward. "I am not unfeeling, though those of us who embrace the more demanding faith are oft accused of it. In the name of my conversion, I will write your pass."

He scraped the inkwell over to the paper and selected a fresh quill with an irritating precision.

Miranda watched the pen scratch across the empty page, trailing lifesaving letters in a thick black stroke. He signed it, plainly, with no flourish, and passed it to her.

She scanned the paper eagerly until a certain alphabetical configuration brought her eyes over its ragged edge.

"This pass is written for Waverleigh! For Justin Waverleigh."

"Is he not your husband?" Harry had leaned farther forward, his eyes inquisitorially green. She felt she gazed into an accusing mirror.

"Y-yes, but—"

"Is he not a Royalist, too, as much in danger as any vagabond seafarer?"

"Perhaps, but—"

"I give you a pass for your husband in the eyes of God and state. That is all you should ask of a brother, all you should ask of an honest Christian."

"Harry!" She was standing, her voice and the parchment in her hand both shaking. "Kit risked his life, slaved in the galleys to retrieve you. Has not your newfound God no breadth to encompass simple gratitude?"

"Perhaps. But He does not encompass what you practice, mistress."

Miranda could only bite her lip, just as she had on the *Merlin* when Harry had told her she had no right to think of battle-watching when she wore woman's garb. Now he told her she had no right to love where her heart led. It occurred to her that Harry had always thought she had no right to anything.

"I saw it brewing," he added gloomily, like any convert pressing an opportunity to sermonize, "on the *Gato*. You think I did not learn to sense that sort of thing, on the roads where I have walked? Sit ye down, sister, and think. Think on what you propose. To leave England, is it not true, with your Christopher Steele? To forsake your wedded husband? To act the jade as your mother before you."

"She did naught before our father left her," Miranda flared. "He thought the worst would come of it, and who's to say it did not happen because he thought it? I have done nothing I cannot shut my eyes upon at night. Nothing. Harry, how can you, who led a life beyond my ken for so many years, how can you fault me for following my heart?"

"I have prayed many nights for the faults of my—other life. You make me recall a name, Miranda, that I have attempted on my knees to mutter into oblivion. Francisco."

"Yes, what became of our faithful tutor? Where did he go when you came to England and found your faith and turned faithless to him? There cannot be many rookeries for birds of his feather."

Harry lanced through his sister's bitter words with a look. "He did not have to seek far to find a nest. Francisco always was a blade that 'twould cut both ways."

"Cut both ways? What do you mean?"

"It is to you I owe my penitence now, Miranda. Had you not existed, I would never have served as any man's bed."

"I?"

"He always preferred you, as Father did. Always, save his chivalry precluded despoiling you. I watched your womanhood swelling and his fancy for you with it. But he, like Brutus, was an 'honorable' man, and an inventive one. To love a woman, one always risks the body's betrayal. To rob our father of his daughter's honor would ever be despicable. My body would not bear the consequences of any sin. I was safe harbor for his lust."

Harry sat, heavily, his face corroded into bitterness. Miranda sat as well, her hands holding tightly to the carved chair arms, her fingertips caressing them, the channels like wounds in the wood.

She tried to remember. Francisco's reticence when she had fumed over Harry's loss of innocence at the don's hands. His willingness to fly into the face of the don's galley to retrieve Harry. And Kit. Kit's mock accusation in the *Gato* cabin about her growing up wild on Barbados and finding more in Francisco than elder brother. But she never had, never.

That was the farthest thing from her mind, and so she never saw it; never saw him turn to the mirror image of her brother. An island like Barbados, with few women, would encourage innovation. Francisco had doubtlessly sliced life on the diagonal before, as Harry said. He had traveled widely, had a rogue's willingness to slake himself where he could . . .

Once again Harry hung in the balance of her fault. She was responsible. Always. She folded the pass into knife-sharp creases and tucked it into the lining of her muff. She patted the beaver, sheared like velvet, as if it were a living thing in need of consolation.

"I thank you for your intervention, Harry. I doubt if we will see one another again. Remember me to your new gods, Cromwell and the Letter of the Law. I have judged you harshly in the past, I see, and now you repay me in kind: a hard currency for brother and sister to exchange, but perhaps our only medium now."

With his head bowed back to his paper, the foreshortened lines of his face seemed hostile. Nothing of the Hathaway elegance showed in it now. His taut face looked as if it had been pressed into an alien mold. On that thought, Miranda drew the heavy chamber door shut and stared for a moment at the blank oaken surface. She saw herself.

"Father's favorite," Harry had said, and Francisco's as well. The Spaniard's visage shaped itself from the swarthy wood she studied, like the carving of a faun coming to life. She saw a dozen sliding glances, a hundred glancing touches skitter round the edges of her memory. Yet he had always been on guard with her—dancing somewhere behind an arm's length of restraint. An honorable man. Honorable to the letter, not the meaning, of the law. Like Harry. And who was Harry to judge her? Harry knew nothing of the façade her marriage with Justin Waverleigh had erected. Nor did Carmina. Nor even Kit, for that matter . . .

Kit, that was her center. He was returning soon to an England that considered him an outlaw now—and all his kin, all the pretty Steele children in a row. Dorset. The family seat was in Dorset. She had a week—seven days—to fetch them, intercept Kit in London and persuade them all to flee. As she herself would. She wanted nothing of this island climate with its suffocating fogs and chill onslaughts of damp, this cold that penetrated deep enough to stiffen a royal neck for the block.

Her feet beat a tattoo of determination down the well-worn Hathaway stairs. To Dorset with her! To the Steeles and a quick evacuation before the Puritans could gather to bring the widespread Royalist families down.

She would hire a carriage and hie herself westward to Ravenscroft. She remembered the name well from her initial inquiries about the Steele family. And Sir Charles! She had forgotten him—that calm aristocratic composure—he would tell her how to save Kit. Inconceivable to think of that sagacious silvered head bowing to circumstances, to a mere change of politics. Perhaps they would all be safe in Dorset, perhaps all that was required was to spirit Kit there and retire in rural obscurity . . .

She was on the thoroughfare and running lightly down Old Broad Street. Her chair-bearers watched their erstwhile passenger fly by on foot, heedless of cobblestone filth, and dropped their mouths in mutual amazement. Both were slouching toward the nearest tavern before Miranda had even vanished around the corner.

Above, behind a loosely drawn shutter, Harry Hathaway was busy in his father's library scraping quill across paper, molding prose into a record of the week's cataclysmic events.

. . . and many Royalists panic at the death of their murderous King. They flee even to the women and children. For the stiff-necked Stuart went to the block without bowing his obstinacy by so much as a hair. Yet his heretical spawn, infected with the rank disease of Popery, survive their sire to rage across France and the Netherlands. And Charles Stuart's supporters also, men who have hazarded fortune and family on the triumph of their sovereign, even now scatter from the City and the shadow of the Tower. A cheerless road will meet them. And those that love them . . .

Chapter Forty

The road was a rough sea of frozen wheel ruts. It meandered through Dorset's chalky uplands, then down to the meadows and a sea like a cold white mirror. What the sea mirrored was only overcast sky as chalky as the earth it arched.

Miranda surveyed the sweep of countryside, empty save for scattered knots of sheep grazing on snow-dusted furze. Another day's jolting over rumpled country roads would undo the springs of her hired conveyance as well as her endurance. She studied the bleak landscape once more from her perch on the brow of a long, slow slope.

"Move on."

The coachman grunted as his horses picked up their feathered feet and plunged down the incline. Within the coach interior,

Miranda bounced about the tufted leather like a die in its casting box. An unconscionable jolt made Miranda thrust her hatted head out of the window. From a dark grove of winter-stripped trees in the west a wave of small black specks wafted upward like cinders from a chimney. Ravens!

Miranda's fingers wrung the windowsill. Ravenscroft was not far, merely miles this side of Poole. She would soon be there, where Kit had been born' and bred, perhaps taking some of the chalky soil into his very bones. No matter how one roved, one never utterly dusted one's heels free of native soil.

Even the chill winter air bore a distant salt taste and a certain faraway warmth, the lure of roving, to tickle the lungs and inebriate the brain with wanderlust. Who would want to tarry in this desolate landscape—grazing land, suitable for sheep and cattle and other spiritless breeds? Not designed for free men. Or honest women. No, she no longer thought salvation lay in country-bred anonymity.

The coach was lumbering under a row of leafless trees, and road had become alley, leading to a hulking house that sprawled across her vision, an E-shaped edifice that seemed to spread its dark stone wings wide to welcome her. Miranda was on the pavement before the coach had seesawed to a stop.

"Wait!" she tossed behind her like a farthing to the coachman. She was up the shallow steps and pounding the knocker roundly on the heavy double door. The wood withstood the vibration of iron on iron as if it were made of even sterner stuff—good English oak, four hundred years aged. Odd that no dogs came hallooing round the wings to bark alarm, that no servant poked a curious head out of the casements . . . Miranda turned to the coachman sunk into his cloak upon the box. The horses, too, bowed weary heads and drowsed in the way of things wont to wait.

Miranda was no such creature. She darted across the yard to a service entrance. That, too, was deaf to her pounding. She rambled back to the house's Norman façade—one towering battlement still looming against its modern additions like a stone finger admonishing the sky.

She paused before the wide, well-seamed door again, hearing a restless hoof strike ground behind her, the distant croaks of another raven wave. When the pondcrous knocker fell once more into silence, she strode to the low glazed windows near the central hall. Among the closed shutters, she found one unsecured

.and swung it open. Behind the unveiled glass was only interior darkness that lapped against the daylight like a midnight fog. The wood strips lacing the glass together gave easily to Miranda's rattling. She drew herself up on the ledge, her heavy skirts and cloak dragging across the stone, and finally fell into the room beyond, exhausted.

It was no warmer within. A dimly visible chimneypiece hooded a yawning, fireless hole. Miranda stood; a small windowside table tipped to smash upon the planking as her cloak unseated it. Something fine and porcelain spattered into shards of white. Yet no one came at the sound. Miranda moved slowly, seeking the room's shape and function.

A door cracked open, distinctly open. A door somewhere, there! Ahead, but no light beyond it. And now before it, a murky figure.

"Who are you?" the apparition inquired.

Ah. A girlish voice, quavering with more than cold. Only that. Miranda stepped forward, her cloak hissing confidently across the uncarpeted floor.

"What do you want?" the voice continued. "They are gone. All. All gone. And shutter the light. Do you wish them to see us any sooner than they must? They must, you know. Return. They'll come and press us to their iron bosoms, to their thorny hearts ... 'Tis cold. C-close the shutter, I pray you. The daylight cuts me, and I have little left to bleed. Who are you? Who?"

Miranda swung the shutters tight on the ebb and flow of hysteria lapping at her from the person opposite. In the deeper dark, she sensed a relaxation as the next words came.

"If it's Steeles you've come to collect, few of us remain to swell your sins. Or Ben? Is that you, Ben? I've heard your step, above me, in the upper passage. You *did* escape, you were not so easy for them as Father—!"

The figure had advanced on tremulous puffs of speech, as if buffeted by some interior tide. Miranda felt cold hands close upon her own, and warm breath whisper toward her in the dark. She caught the reaching hands in a grip that would tolerate no escape.

"Come," she said. "This room is empty of anything you seek."

She escorted her captive into the outer hall, where the light from high unshuttered tower windows fell on a white, frowning face bordered by cold satin lengths of yellow hair. The frown deepened.

"Who are you, who?"

"My name is ... Miranda Hathaway. I am—friend—to your brother, I think. Christopher."

"Kit?"

Miranda turned, expecting that one optimistic syllable to evoke him. No, she saw only the girl, her face unfolded into expectancy, stepping forward with sudden faith, hope and charity.

"Kit, you say? Oh, yes, Kit. You know him! He will help us. With Ben—oh, Kit will make them dance for it now! Won't he ... Miranda, you say? Surely Kit has mentioned his sister Marjory? He had promised me red-heeled shoes from Paris this trip. Have you got them? I want to see them! 'Tis not fair. They'd not keep my shoes, my Kit, from me, too."

Miranda ignored the girl's pleading. "He's not here yet, Marjory. We must make do without him. Have you no firewood?"

"Firewood?" Marjory's gray eyes considered the beautifully carved Tudor chairs lining the hall as if they were fit candidates for kindling. "The servants always see to the fires, though I've kept one upstairs burning. Mother always liked a fire."

Miranda vanished behind a low door, returning with an armful of hardwood. " 'Twas only in the servants' hall," she explained over her cloaked shoulder. "And here's flint—"

A spark leapt between her hands, then a slow crackle of flame popped amongst the logs on the grate. Marjory's eyes clung to that burst of red. She slowly shuffled over, extending her candle-white fingers to it as if she meant to catch fire.

Miranda gently pushed her a pace backward. She untied her cloak and set down the fat beaver muff that hung still from her neck, like an anchor. Marjory watched the outer layers peel off her guest with a vacant curiosity.

"Now, Marjory, sit on this stool, and tell me what has happened."

They crouched together near the growing heat and listened to the hollow flap the flames made as they fluttered up the chimney liked darting red birds. The mobile tongues of fire etched kinder lines in Marjory's face—she was a pretty girl, Miranda realized with a startled glance—golden and rosy, like a chandelier cherub. The firelight burnished Marjory's fear until her ordinary, unshrinking self shone through again.

"Miranda—?"

"—Hathaway. Yes, a friend. Of Kit's. He'll be with us soon. So tell me, Marjory, what has—"

Beyond the snap of log came another sound: some regular, almost metallic clicking, like an army of pistols cocking. A clumsy shadow lurched into the wan circle of light ringing the hearth. Marjory's fire-dappled hand pulled it to her feet: an ancient water spaniel, his muzzle age-frosted, and his elegantly curled ears framing a pair of mournfully weary eyes. Marjory twisted her fingers in his thick crimped fur and looked at Miranda.

"Tell me, Marjory."

"Yes, I should like to tell someone. Then it would not happen over and over in my head. They came, you see, before any of us could anticipate it. They came as they had never dared before, because they had killed the King. I should have known when Ben came back by night. He talked to Father endlessly in the Long Gallery, pacing back and forth, both of them. Mother bade me stay below, but I heard them, their steps. I think they talked to the portraits, I do," she confided with a child's dramatic hush, "but it was too late.

"The next morning, before the fires had been laid, he came, the major-general, with an entire company of horsemen milling in the yard. He came for Father and was taking him away when Ben came clattering down the stairs—those stairs . . ."

Marjory's pale head bowed to a broad stone flight against the farther wall. "Ben came. He fought here with them all, until they took him away, but I think even then he had taken his mortal blow. When she heard, the next day, that Ben was dead, she said nothing, but she fetched a pail and scrubbed the stones. Of course the servants were gone. They had run away, so there was no one but us to scrub the stones. Yet there was nothing on them; I saw, Miranda, nothing! Yet Mother scrubbed and scrubbed and wouldn't say a word."

"When did this happen, Marjory?"

"Yesterday? Last week? I know not for certain. That was not the worst. Barely had they buried Ben, on our ground at least . . . dear Ben, he was a husbandman through and through, 'twas why Father loved him. Ben was our roots, of the earth and now in it. Then came other Kingsmen, fleeing to the chalk caves to hide, they said, till sanity and Stuarts should rule in England once more.

"But do you know, Miranda—?" Marjory tugged insistently on Miranda's silk sleeve, her pale face looming like a vapid full moon. "I think sanity shall never reign in England again. They've killed the King, and what they did to Father ... The Cavaliers explained it to me. They would not tell Mother. I had to tell her."

Marjory knelt, putting her hands so near the fire that Miranda bit her lip, but refrained from pulling her back. Marjory wove slowly on her knees, the light dancing on her skirt folds like a caress.

"Treason," Marjory said in a hard voice. "They convicted Father of treason. He was of noble birth, so it would have been the axe, no rope for him, but if he died as a convicted traitor, all his lands should revert to Them: Cromwell and his scavengers! Picking bones that still wear their flesh. So Father—oh, listen, Miranda, to what Father did."

Marjory rustled nearer to trap Miranda's wrists in her corded hands. Despite their recent closeness to the flames, her fingers were still icy.

"Father chose the pressing. No food, no water, no quick sudden slice from above. Only all that heavy iron—each day they added more. So slow, the pressing. His friends—those who were not suspect themselves—stood watch with him for one, two, three days, I think. As long as Our Saviour was in the crypt, save no one came to roll that stone away from Father. They begged him, said Jarvis and Hervey—good friends both—no water, you see, no food and all that weight crushing bone and blood. And whom was there to save Ravenscroft for? Ben dead, Sydney and Philip fled with Prince Charles, though they would not be recognized as heir. And Kit—where? And Ben, did I mention Ben? Yes, Ben gone. All gone ...

"And Father. Not gone soon enough. At the end, they added their weight to his burden. Good friends, Jarvis and Hervey. 'Twas quicker that way. They stood upon Father and he finally sank beneath all that weight like a stone. And They'll claim Ravenscroft anyway. 'Twas what Hervey said before he left us the last time. They buried Father. With Ben. But with no inscription, who was there to carve the names, the date? And Ravenscroft will be Theirs, because all Steeles are outlaws now. Traitors. If they find one, they kill him. If not, they declare him traitor in absentia ... yes, a barrister's word. They have many barrister's words. Women they do not kill. We are fortunate we count for naught. We escape a great deal that way, do we not?"

Marjory's gray eyes glimmered on Miranda's with terrible, mad logic.

The fire sighed up the chimney as the old spaniel lay back on his side with a wheeze.

"What of your mother, Marjory?" Miranda asked after a long moment.

"Oh, Mother's quite right, quite warm. I've put her to bed. She became ill, sometime when Father was—leaving us. I've kept a fire going just as the servants left it. You need not have made this great blaze here, Miranda."

"You had better take me to your mother, Marjory."

The girl rose docilely and rustled across the dim hall. She paused at the stair foot, her head cocked and her yellow curls swinging past her face like twin pendulums.

"A step? Do you hear a step? I swear Ben has walked ever since the day he left. We'll have to pass through the Long Gallery. Take my hand, Miranda, please."

They stepped up the long staircase together to the house's portrait gallery, a place well lit by rows of candlesticked torchères.

"I saved all the tapers for here," Marjory explained. "I wanted to see these painted faces when I passed through. I'm glad you've come, Miranda. My wax was burning low."

Miranda studied the gilt-framed lines of formal faces standing at eternal attention on either side of the sixty-foot-long corridor. The Long Gallery was ideal for childish forays down its polished length. Had these stone walls echoed to the laughter of all those steplike young Steeles Carmina recalled so fondly? Had Marjory played hide-and-seek behind the tapestries; had flaxen-haired boys sought her out, their mock-hunters' footsteps loud in the hollow room? Had those composed Steele eyes—those lordly men and serious women in their ruffs and farthingales—bent their poses long enough to wink down upon such doings?

Kit. She had hoped to find more of him than she knew within this house. Instead, the Steele ancestral halls immured him into walls lined with his forebears, so she lost sight of what or who he was, and why he was so specifically rare to her.

They were behind her, those unchanging guardians, and she was in a chamber bright with daylight and warm from a thriving fire. All the vitality left in Ravenscroft had boiled down into this one room. The life and light ran like mercury and pooled into something snowy adrift on the creamy Belgian linens lining the room's great bed.

"See, Mother, I've brought a friend. A friend of Kit's."

Marjory led Miranda over, her voice supple for the first time.

Miranda bowed over the figure lost in the linens. A blue bolt of memory struck her head-on—so this was where Kit had mined his precious eyes. The shade was truly startling in a parchment face capped with strands of cloud-white hair.

"A friend." The woman's voice was low, vibrant. "We can use a friend. Dare you be our friend?" She smiled. While half her face lifted, the other side remained unmoving. Her face was like a mask of comedy and tragedy spliced into one visage.

"I have been ill," she confessed, "though not so ill as some of my kin. My wee Marjory has had a heavy burden for a lass of sixteen—" The hand she lifted to her daughter's bowed head fell back. Bright blue eyes turned slowly to Miranda. "A friend."

Miranda saw no need to delay. "I'm taking you with me. To London." She saw fear rise from them as palpably as steam. "To—Kit. He's due soon. We'll warn him and all leave England together."

"Leave together, yes." The woman considered for a moment behind closed lids. "I suspect—good child, good friend—that Katharine Steele has more leave-taking to make than you mean. Yes, we must leave. Child. My Marjory. Fetch my cloak—the warm woolen one of wine color—now! Fetch it."

Her eyes pierced Miranda once Marjory had left the room. "See she wears and keeps it well. I made it ready long ago for such a day."

Marjory, returning, draped the cloak across the coverlet so carelessly that Miranda had to catch it to keep it from sliding to the floor. She saw then why such a simple length of cloth was precious to a woman who had lost so much; the falling weight resisted her. More than wool would warm its wearer; jewels likely, sewn into the lining.

Miranda met the woman's eyes. "Is there anything other you require?"

"Take care of Marjory." Katharine's lips barely moved, but her eyes slid to the window where her daughter's figure hovered.

"Is Marjory—? She seems distraught."

Katharine shook her head slightly. "No. Nothing wrong there that a better world won't cure ... but, listen—your name?"

"Miranda."

"Listen, Miranda. You seem a spirited sort; see my Marjory away. All my children away, that still live."

"They come again." Marjory's plaintive monotone from the window barely brushed across Miranda's concentration.

It brought a flash of alarm to the still-lively blue eyes in Katharine's immobile face. Her limp white hand weakly clasped Miranda's. "See to that. Quickly."

Miranda skimmed to the window to peer over Marjory's drooping shoulders. A party of horsemen circled her waiting coach below.

"They've come for us all," Marjory intoned listlessly.

Miranda pressed close to the imperfect glass, seeking and finding the slash of yellow in the men's garb. Cromwell's kind. Puritans, ready to purge again ... Miranda swirled swiftly to the passage, where her eyes had grazed a wall-mounted circle of Spanish pistols earlier. Flintlocks, thank God! She ravished the cupboard below them for a silver-scrolled powder horn and—where, dear Lord?—her hand clawed the dark until she withdrew a ramrod.

"Miranda! What are you doing? I told you they'd return. 'Tis useless to clatter so, that won't stop them."

Marjory hovered above Miranda like the faint voice of doom, causing her hasty hands to slip, the powder to spill, the shot to roll across the cupboard top like dice ...

"Diablo!" Miranda hissed appropriately to the Spanish pistols resisting her attentions. Ah, both primed—truly she hoped. She darted down the Long Gallery while Steele faces careened past her and one pale contemporary edition haunted her footsteps.

"Miranda, wait! Don't leave me here."

A gasping Marjory trailed her all the way to the broad staircase and halfway down it. Miranda froze as the last turning brought the chessboard-floored hall into view. Marjory fell into her and silence at the same instant.

A sigh rustled through the room below, like a spirit breathing itself inside out. A faint clock ticked somewhere. Marjory breathed heavily behind her.

There, the sound, the sigh, again. Only the old spaniel, wheezing by the cold fireplace and dreaming of long-ago chases, of hunts for grouse and quail.

A pounding split the silence. The great double doors gave not a quiver in recognition of any exterior buffeting, but Miranda saw that most of its interior latches were as undone as a strumpet's corset lacings.

Knocking and shouting continued without, like an old head-

ache returned to pound the house's doughty skull for entry. The
doors finally groaned open and spit in a stream of strangers—
men sashed and sworded, booted and spurred. For riding. For
hunting. The old dog lifted his head, a curled ear falling ludicrously across his grizzled muzzle. He sank back into a wheeze.

They paced below, their faces hidden beneath their broad hat
brims, their bodies foreshortened by Miranda's high vantage
point. They looked to be little men from her perch, seven perhaps in all, armed. And hunting.

"Our Royalist vixens must have fled with the sheep who
served them," noted one, returning from a hasty tour of the lower
floor. "I'll stroll upstairs, Major-General—"

He swung himself jauntily around the newel-post and froze as
the two women hugging the tapestried wall came into his view.

"Major General!"

A man stepped forward to mount the first two steps.

"Mistress Marjory—?" He squinted at Miranda's golden hair.

"So you know the family, sir," said Miranda. "The more
shame to you for pillaging it."

The word brought him up straight. He swept away the obscuring beaver to bare a smooth, inflexible face bracketed by lengths
of graying shoulder-length hair.

"Major-General Eustace Hatch, mistress. Of the county, as you
guessed." He eyed her with some wonder. "Do they grow new
Steeles now, to burst forth fully mature, like Minerva from the
brain of Zeus?"

"I be not that wise, Major-General," she said firmly, "and
am but mortal, besides. As are you." She raised a Spanish pistol barrel.

Major-General Hatch backstepped so quickly he almost sacrificed balance.

" 'Tis not loaded," he challenged.

"Oh, I think so. I primed it myself."

"Since when do"—his glance traveled her gown—"London ladies carry primed pistols?"

"Since English gentlemen cut off their King's head and press
their fellows into Ironsides' service."

"A Royalist!" trumpeted the first soldier.

Major-General Hatch merely nodded, his eyes never leaving
Miranda.

"Perhaps." Her shrug allowed a sinister flash of light to reflect off the long steel barrel. "I know worse epithets than that, sirs. Murderer. Despoiler. I mention but a few."

Boots scraped menacingly on the far-below stone. For a moment Miranda thought she clung to a mast top, and that a hostile circle of faces waited her momentary plunge to an iron-gray sea. Her thumb stretched to cock the pistol.

"Mistress! You are mad. We are Colonel Cromwell's designated agents in this county. You cannot impede us."

"What do you want, Major-General Hatch?" inquired Miranda unimpassionedly.

"To take possession, as is our right and duty. No male heir remains to Ravenscroft—at least, no one living who is not also an outlaw. Leave, and take the chit with you, with our blessings."

He pointed behind her. Miranda glanced at Marjory, sitting on the stairs like a child peering down at some forbidden festivity. Miranda's trigger finger caressed the cold metal curve.

"I care not for the results of your blessings, Major-General, and we cannot leave. A woman is dying up yonder . . ." She felt a clutch from behind, but ignored it. " 'Tis said you march into battle singing psalms and bearing prayer books as well as pistols and sword. A New Model Army, indeed. 'Tis an old model of soldiering to come terrifying women and children, the old and the ill and the weak. I have no liking for you, Major-General Hatch, nor does the ball in this Spanish pistol, I warrant."

"And what likelihood have you of sending a ball home, mistress?" he mocked, advancing a boot up another step, so the spur rang like the very Mass bells his new religion would stamp out.

"I am Barbados-reared, sir, and what I can do with a pistol might surprise you for the blinking of a lash. You would have eternity to reflect upon it after."

He leaned forward until his arm rested on his elevated knee. His eyes were narrowed missives aimed to leap the space that separated them. "Bravely spoken, but when I am safe within my Maker's bosom, what shall you do concerning Coldsgate here? Or Fielding?"

Miranda raised the second pistol, hidden by her skirt folds, in answer.

"And then? How would you do for the rest, Mistress Invention?"

Miranda's eyes flashed up to an ornamental pair of crossed rapiers on the wall. "The rest, why I would cut them and make them bleed, sir."

Major-General Hatch turned and suddenly swept his arms wide in an almost theatrical appeal to his men.

"You heard her, my lads; there is no converting this heathen. We'll ride on to Poole. But I warn you, mistress." He spun back to her. "Begone, with your children and ill and old and your Spanish pistols and your Barbados obduracy and your damned English pride"—he was grinning a hard, bitter grin—"for I'll be back and do my duty though the Devil himself materialize to stop me. And I'm not sure the demon hasn't."

He left, drawing his men into a knot behind him, first pausing at the breached double door. "Begone by evening, Kingswoman, or Beelzebub's own breath won't serve to warm you."

The doors did not swing quite shut behind the party, as if forever unsprung by the forced entry. The spaniel beside the ashy hearth wheezed again. Miranda's sigh echoed him as she let the pistols droop.

"Dying . . . you said dying!" came an accusing voice.

"Marjory. Here, stand up."

"You told him that my mother was dying!"

Miranda saw that Marjory's face mimicked the weaving behind her—sickly yellow tones underlined with a vein of doleful blue.

"Come, we must leave."

Marjory's arm resisted her. "No! Can't you hear? That sigh. It's Ben above. I don't want to see him again, not now, all bloody, mortal bloody! I won't go up again." Marjory huddled to her knees.

"You must. Don't be addlepated." Miranda whipped both eyes and ears upward to interpret something new—a sound, a sort of shuffle in the Long Gallery above them.

"You see! Ghosts, Miranda. Philip and Sydney always said so. Kit said they were only making merry with me, but where are they now? Where's Ben? And Kit? Ghosts, all only ghosts, I tell you. All gone."

Gooseflesh tracked Miranda's spine, slithering beneath her gown to take residence at the nape of her neck. A definite ghostly shuffle rasped above—in that vast, dim gallery filled with long-dead faces.

"Nonsense." The word was an afterthought, thrown like a crumb to Marjory as Miranda mounted the steps to the Long Gallery entrance. Infinity echoed before her. Painted faces with eyes that followed one. Portraits of butter-haired children, their locks melting in the daylight's last shafts. Kit trapped here—where? Kit powerless to step forth from a former self and change so much as the course of a dust mote caught in a bar of light.

Miranda watched a flurry of such motes congregate in the pillar of light cast by the setting sun through a narrow window. A form almost seemed to quiver there, a manifestation of something golden that shifted—Marjory's ghostly Ben?

Miranda stood motionless, her arms pistol-weighted to her sides, her imagination just as helplessly anchored to the Long Gallery's spell. Ben. Had his too, too solid flesh melted, dissolved into dust motes? Her throat was dry from swallowing Marjory's dire verbal potions—a mix of ancient children's tales and all-too-recent adult horrors.

Then she realized that for even dust motes to become whirlwinds, something, someone, must have moved in the Long Gallery recently. Her eyes pasted the portrait faces to their canvases. All there. None walking ... Miranda's glance fell to the shadowed floor, there—beyond the still-swirling light shaft to a puddled drapery near the window. She ran to it, letting the pistols fall to the floor like footsteps.

"Marjory! Help me with your mother."

Marjory materialized at the Long Gallery entrance and hung there.

" 'Tis not Ben, nor any other ghost," Miranda called. "She must have come to aid us. Help me bring her back to bed."

Together they half dragged the unconscious Katharine to her chamber. The woman seemed to have been peeled off a family portrait—a pigmented puppet of herself lay quietly among the linens, her blue eyes open but unseeing.

That was how Katharine Steele finally died, slowly, silently. One moment Miranda was anxiously watching her and the next she knew the woman was only a forsaken shell.

Miranda's veed fingers slid the pale lids shut on their mockingly vivid contents. She was reminded of Ibrahim and shuddered to think how close his gesture had been to death's everyday ritual. She felt a certain foreboding with the gesture, as if she were locking Kit away, too, confining him someplace remote where she could not reach.

She had come to Ravenscroft, in part, to chart more of him in the place of his birth. With each inexorable blow to his family, she felt him retreat farther behind a mask of tragedy she had no right to penetrate.

Miranda sighed deeply and came to herself with that inadequate epitaph to Katharine Steele's earthly existence.

"Marjory—there you are, at the window again. Here, take your cloak. 'Tis heavy." Miranda slipped the wine wool over Marjory's stooped shoulders. The girl cast a sideways glance to the bed.

"Gone, too? Yes. Ben came for her. I heard him." She let Miranda lead her to the chamber door. "No! We must have the proper ceremony. The bishop to preside and all the family—the Wexfords and de Normans and the boys back from university. And Ben, Ben back from the wars, and Kit from the sea. We must bury her."

"We can't, Marjory." Miranda peeled the girl's hands from her arms and held them tightly. "We cannot. The major-general will see to it, as he did with your father and Ben. The Puritans at least will do that."

"No! 'Tis no proper burial without the Book of Common Prayer, and They would not use it. Why do the Puritans not let us have our words as our fathers did? I remember them, what was said for wee Charlie. I read them again and again in Mother's prayer book at the place where the blue satin ribbon always rested. The words for the dead. They are hers."

Marjory had fetched a venerable prayer book and held it out to Miranda like a weapon case. It fell open in her hands to the services for the dead.

Miranda read through them aloud, through the grim section from the Book of Job and the melancholy ninetieth psalm. To the Book of Jonah she had gone for Muffin; the Book of Job and the view of the psalmist spoke not so gently of mortality.

> *"For a thousand years in Thy sight are but as yesterday;*
> *seeing that is past as a watch in the night.*
> *As soon as Thou scatterest them they are even as asleep;*
> *and fade away suddenly like the grass.*
> *In the morning it is green and groweth up;*
> *but in the evening it is cut down, dried up, and*
> *withered . . ."*

Miranda let the book close. "Now we must go, Marjory, and Major-General Hatch must bury her, and he will. These Puritans even took King Charles's body into respectful custody finally, from what I read in the broadsheets. They will do no less for your mother."

Marjory let herself be led out, even through the Long Gallery, without a whimper. Miranda was inwardly reluctant to leave Ravenscroft, even though the house stood still and chill like some graveyard monument already.

She had learned nothing more of Kit from her pilgrimage, she thought. The Steele family faces were ghosts indeed as they slid past her during her last traverse of the Long Gallery. She could not hear the echo of Kit's boots on the wide, well-worn staircase.

She tried to conjure him in the stone-paved hall below— playing chess with his toy soldiers on the even squares, clattering in from a day in the fields with his dogs, coming home after months at sea to laughter . . . She could cast him in none of these roles here.

If he were wise, he would never see this place again. She looked around one last time, then collected her cloak. She had retrieved the pistols from the Long Gallery floor, reprimed them, and thrust them barrel-first into each side of her ample muff.

"Is there nothing here, Marjory, some fond memory for your brother, that we could carry away with us?"

Marjory regarded Miranda incredulously. "For Ben? Ben is gone."

"For Kit, Marjory. We will see him soon."

Marjory's eyes surveyed the hall, pausing on the Turkey carpet covering a table, the chairs' fringed cushions, the rapiers mounted high on the walls, the Dutch still life over the service table, the settle by the empty fireplace.

". . . only old Trojan."

"Old Trojan? Oh, I see. The dog."

" 'Tis Kit's. He would hunt with that foolish old dog even though he came back without so much as a feather. When Trojan got the stiffness and even summer waters were too cold for him, Kit never marked a new pup out for himself. He was gone so much; Trojan stayed by the fire and grew gray waiting for Kit to come home."

"We can't take a dog, Marjory! An old dog. 'Tis trouble enough we'll have with ourselves."

"You asked me, Miranda, and I told you. That is what Kit would want. That."

Marjory pointed stubbornly to the venerable spaniel reclining on the cold hearthstone from habit, the only creature left living in Ravenscroft.

Who would feed him now? Major-General Hatch? No, they would leave him or loose him upon the countryside to die in elderly inches. A wave of anger washed to Miranda's throat. The old dog's plight seemed the last and most vicious blow to be loosed upon the Steeles.

"Go to the coach, Marjory. I will be a moment longer."

"What will you do?" asked Marjory, reacting to the iron in Miranda's voice.

"Nothing, Marjory. Close the house, set it in order, that is all."

Marjory hissed away in her floor-length cloak like a skater. As Miranda looked down on old Trojan, the dog wheezed and raised his head.

She knelt to pat his shallow silky skull, ran her fingers through his crimped brown and white ears. The white feathering on his legs was muddy and tangled, his deep brown eyes red-rimmed. He resembled a crotchety old courtier settled by some hearty blaze and wondering why it no longer warmed him.

"Good Trojan. You have waited a long while, haven't you? Yes. We all must wait at times. You don't want to wait any longer, do you?"

The dog deeply sniffed her caressing hand, then lay back with a sigh. He cast his eyes straight ahead, no longer looking at her, as if he had scented her purpose.

Miranda stood and pulled one smooth cold silver pistol butt from within the warm fortress of her muff. She moved back several paces, stretched out her arm and aimed the long barrel at the floor and the dog lying patiently upon it. There. Midway between eye and ear, both age-dimmed, both beyond seeing, hearing, the shot journey past them. One clean shot, let it be, her aim truer than thought. For Kit, for herself, for all things that see their world wrenched away—one quick merciful shot.

Her eyes squeezed shut to the discharge and recoil, but she saw the form on the stones give one spasmodic twitch. When she looked again through a thinning haze of smoke, the dog was as still and serene as ever. She forced herself to locate the small dark circle in Trojan's temple, a new marking on his dappled coat. Then she ransacked the first floor until she found another powder horn and supply of shot, reloading the pistol.

She took a last look around the undisturbed hall. A perfect study for a Dutch still life painter: the faithful old spaniel lying by the hearth, the stones waiting endlessly for the echo of a familiar foot.

Major-General Hatch had been righter than he knew. The Devil had materialized here on Ravenscroft stones. He had whistled through generations of one family's careful erecting and had converted every stone and board of the place into a private adjunct of hell, into his personal game preserve. May the Puritans find him as obdurate to unseat as their King.

Chapter Forty-one

Miranda never looked back as the coach rolled down the tree-lined alley past waterless fountains and unblooming gardens.

Neither did Marjory, who sat silent next to Miranda on the journey eastward to London, who docilely mounted rough inn steps and lay sleepless on country mattress-ticks under restless roofs that welcomed the winds for nightly games of hide-and-seek.

Marjory was beyond questioning her course any longer; in an odd way, withdrawal strengthened her. She no longer started at the turn of a coach wheel over a stone, a too-loud voice from the inn's hearthside. Marjory took a long inner journey around the limits of her sanity and found the fences holding. She walked back to her center and exited through the door of her inner self into a world that corresponded to most other people's view of it.

"You said we would find and warn Kit. Is he in London?"

This was the first time that Marjory had spoken in the three days they'd been on the road to London. The question's very normalcy wrenched Miranda from her own introspection. Kit. For an instant the name didn't warm her memory. She panicked briefly.

"He's not in London yet, I pray, but due soon. We must persuade him to leave. England is no home port to him now."

Marjory nodded and said no more, not even when the coach finally lurched onto Thames Street. London bustle flowed past their curtained windows with an almost profane ordinariness. The coachman headed directly for the Three Cranes in the Vintry Tavern as ordered.

Miranda peered out to see the high clumsy silhouette of the

cranes that named the tavern. Here the ships' bellyfuls of ruby
Bordeaux wine were slung ashore; here the French merchantmen
anchored in the Thames's murky bottom.

The tavern, former haunt of artists and actors, would be quiet
now that the Puritans who abhorred all aping of life on the stage,
all adornment of person or pulpit, ruled London. Miranda remembered driving by the burned husk of the New Fortune The-
atre even in better days. She would not have been surprised to
find the Three Cranes a smoking ruin. Yet it stood as solidly as
ever beside the river steps, its sharp gables looking anxious
against an unreadable overcast February sky.

Miranda shepherded Marjory into the Three Cranes and to a
chamber under one of the sharpest gables overlooking the river.

"Let no one in, Marjory. I've an errand on Cheapside. If you
like, watch the river. It's here Kit will drop anchor. His ship's the
Dowsabelle, can you remember that? It means 'sweet and
pretty'—*douce et belle* in French. Another word for 'Ladylove'
in ours."

"Dowsabelle. Of course I can remember," Marjory said accusingly. " 'Tis what he called me as a child. If there is a Kit in yonder river to be seen, I will see him, Miranda."

"God willing we both shall see him again soon," rejoined
Miranda, whirling from the room with her cloak and muff.

"God willing." The phrase ringed Miranda's mind like iron
bars the next few hours.

God willing she would find a perspective glass for ship-
watching in the street market at which she bade the coachman
stop on the way to Cheapside. That much God found willing—a
tarnished brass spyglass that took most of her remaining gold but
rested securely beside her the rest of the way. 'Twould give
Marjory something to do these last days. Watching and waiting.

God willing that no inquiring party of London guard should
stop her coach to demand her identity and mission. But London
was calmly busy as usual, its people—more Parliamentarian than
Royalist by nature—caught up in their rough daily routine.

And, God willing, she would find the Waverleigh house secure
against confiscation, with no waiting Puritan delegation to welcome her back into those high, half-timbered environs.

Miranda's green-kid-gloved hands wrung the carriage windowsill as they had once belabored a similar carriage sill in Plymouth. Now a house—not a ship—caught her attention, and the
heavy freight of revenge no longer interested her, but the treasure

that rode in a secret hold behind the house's warm-throated chimney.

Her eyes played hide-and-seek with the many chimneys looming into the cold afternoon air. One led from her treasure trove; she hoped Thorpe's diligence had not built the fires too high. But those chimneys were smokeless, lifeless. Her knuckles tightened on the wood, then she swung the coach door open and spilled out. The hired coachman waited as stolidly as he had during her mission to Dorset and back.

After a last glance, she swirled to the door, rang the elaborate bellpull, waited, paced, worried, pushed on the broad timbers. Inward they swung on silent hinges. Thorpe was ever scrupulous about such matters—and about keeping the doors barred.

Thorpe was gone. She knew that the moment both feet were within the narrow entry hall. She was alone in the house. Even the below-surface ticking of the Waverleigh clocks was stilled. All had run down, as had the Royalist cause.

She rustled into the parlor, its dark wainscoting an expressionless witness to her new stealth in what had briefly been her home—an unhappy home, if she would grapple honestly with her memories.

The shadows seemed more bitterly etched into the plastered ceiling above, like a smile that hardship sets into a once-blithe face. Miranda's mouth echoed the ceiling's grim lines as she fought the keystone to the fireplace niche. Justin had showed her the mechanism, but she had no facility for it. She paused in her labor when a triangle of charred white amidst the hearthstone ashes caught her glance.

"... unto death." The words rang familiar, like an unheeded omen. Yes, of course—a fragment of last week's broadside, kicked by the now-absent Thorpe into the fire for ready destruction, though the fire had expired before the last of the message. "—and the minions of Parliament hath done good King Charles unto death." That had been the phrase.

She had forgotten this was a city that had killed its King. Had not the Romans a name for it? Regicide. Father would smile at how his rudimentary Latin served her now. And Harry, how Harry would laugh, to see her scraping fingertips on stone trying to squeeze a king's ransom from it. Damna—open!

At last here was the box—secure, brimful with cold gemstone fire. Emeralds, out-of-fashion diamonds, ransom enough to spirit three Royalists out of London ...

Miranda cradled the chest and swung the stone door shut on emptiness. The closing scrape was echoed by the sudden shift of a boot across the planked flooring. She froze and turned a stricken face behind her.

Nothing to see but the tapestries wafting in the cheerless winter drafts. The figures within them wavered, like the dust motes in Ravenscroft's Long Gallery. Other than the tapestry figures softly struggling against their woven prisons, no one was in the room. Nothing. No Ben to frighten Marjory. No stalking memory to hunt down Miranda—but there, a motion at the great flame-stitched wing chair sitting with its broad back to her.

A hand flailed softly across the slightly worn arm. Miranda stood, the chest held shield-wise before her. The hand was pale and well shaped. Its linen cuff was yellowed, wilted. The fingers lifted and fell again as if signaling some ritual to begin.

"You have returned to your ashes, *Cendrillon*."

"Justin!"

Miranda darted around the chair to confront the speaker like an audience member testing the reality of a stage illusion. He was slouched deep in the familiar flame-stitching, his face moonstone-white against the relentlessly cheery pattern. He was shrunken and limp, his feet in bucket-topped boots turned out at the ankles and lying listlessly on the boards.

"Justin, I didn't see you. How long have you been here, how did you come through to London? How—?"

"Shhhh." He shut his eyes and brought one bloodless finger to his lips. "I am upon the very edge of being taken. They almost had me in Old Broad Street, but I gave them the flat of my sword and its edge as well—" His hand rummaged vaguely at his side. "Lost, though, somewhere . . . good sword, too. Meant to slice King Charles out of Westminster but a fortnight ago."

Justin laughed softly. " 'Twas a scheme to make the angels weep. We had not a bishop's prayer of success in it, we four who swore to free the King. They heard of it and hunted us ever since. The others are Calais-bound in empty wine casks. A rough ride they'll have of it, but I—I had to ensure that you . . ."

The hand fluttered toward her and Miranda scraped back a step. Justin paused to examine his hand. His glance fell to his side, then inventoried the room in confusion.

"I—frighten you. Did the stain—? But, no, I wiped it well." He put his hand to his side again. When he took it away the palm was drenched in red. "Ah, *quel massacre. Nom de Dieu.* I fear

I shall not see Paris again." He smiled. " 'Tis odd how the pain runs down. And the will. *Je regrette rien, Cendrillon.* No, stay back; you are quite, quite right. Not a wholesome sight."

Justin spread his hands again and studied first the unsullied palm, then the bloody one.

"A trifling blow, really, not enough to keep me from over-leaping a turnip cart and two chestnut-sellers' stands and losing them all in Pater Noster Alley. Will you say a Pater Noster for my soul, Miranda? I fear I did you a wrong, but you cannot even guess at its nature. How should you when I cannot myself?"

His deprecating laugh faded into a cough.

"I would have written sonnets for you," Justin said, smiling. "In Spenserian style. In French. Or the late King's English. See, my mind runs fast, only the blood moves slowly now. For you—'My love is like the wings of victory / That thrust above the ordinary earth . . .' Not a bad start, no? 'She beats her heart against mortality / And makes of death a richer form of birth.'

"Ah, not gay enough for you? My thoughts grow morbid. But you are safe. Yes, take the jewels and survive. I returned to tell you that. I would not flee abroad without you, without you safe." He smiled again as his head lolled against the upholstery.

"I am content. But chilled." Justin frowned. " 'Tis cold, is it not? Ah, our gallant King, in the January cold to make his bed upon the block. He wore two shirts, they say, so that none might see him shiver and lay it to cowardice. I am a poor servant to such a King. I have my shirt and my good heavy satin jacket and still I feel a-tremble.

"No! Come no closer. I have always felt apart. Even from you. I am slipping, Millicent; I need no mortal anchor. Leave England, go with Carmina, if she has not gone already. Oh, *Cendrillon*, I fear you have married a fool. The only redemption in it is that he is wise enough to make you quickly a widow . . ."

He laughed again, then his head jerked sideways to his shoulder.

Miranda knelt by the chair, its flame-stitching vibrating through the tears that windowed her eyes.

"Justin." His lashes opened on lifeless brown pupils. His hand—a cold, dry hand—lay limply in hers. The little spark left in his regard was dimming rapidly, shooting away into the limitless dark at the back of his eyes.

"Justin, you are no fool. 'Tis I, I who have—" His hand was

slipping through hers, gently, gracefully. She caught the last glimmer from his eyes and fixed upon it. "Justin, I—"

He shook his head almost imperceptibly, then his shuttering eyelids closed her out. She saw him gather himself. A breath sifted through his blue lips on a rough, indrawn sigh. It was almost like watching someone leap a chasm.

Miranda let his limp hand continue its agonizingly slow withdrawal from her own. She sat unmoving for long minutes, unmarked by any chatter from a household clock. Her tears gathered at the lip of her lids and remained there—a thick bitter sheet that distorted her vision. They would not fall.

She stood at last and blindly gathered up the chest. Her hands were as cold as Justin's had been; she thrust them gloveless into the muff with its burden of firearms. Something sharp stung her finger.

She pulled out a white piece of parchment, still stiffly folded. Harry's pass. For one Justin Waverleigh. She had forgotten it. Had she not gone storming off to Dorset, had she remained in London, or even left the pass with an associate of Justin's, it would have found him and have made an encounter in Pater Noster Alley no occasion for a skirmish. She ought to have known he would not have ever left London, and her. She had left him. She was not what he had thought her. She had not even thought to toss him a thread in her mad rush to weave lifelines for Christopher Steele.

She watched the spreading thin line of blood the parchment edge had drawn on her blanched finger. It corresponded to a deeper self-inflicted injury on her soul. How willing she had been to love Justin once, eager to shelter in his undemanding devotion! She had been so sure of him that she could forget him, as Kit had forgotten the faithful spaniel that grew old at Ravenscroft.

Miranda sucked the rising blood from her finger, desperate to erase any reminder of her faithlessness. 'Twas not so great a fault. Justin had ever been prone to dramatize himself. All his devotions had been askew—to the muse for whom he composed his facile iambic pentameter, to the King he could not rescue, to her—the wife he could not love in any real sense.

And she had ridden on that vulnerability, Miranda saw that now. Wounded herself, she had gratefully taken passage on so willing a conveyance as Justin. Never seeing, nor caring, that her burdens would only strain the vehicle to its limits.

For a moment, she thought that she could not endure the clarity of her insight, as if someone had unveiled a Medusa to her in a mirror and even that indirect image was enough to shatter her. She brought the muff to her face and buried her mouth in it, as if to smother a scream.

Her eyes etched the limp figure of Justin into her brain: his muddy drooping boots, the rumpled satin suit and flimsy lace about his wrists and neck. The silky brown satin locks framing his dormant face. At any moment she expected him to raise that face, look up at her, sigh, say—

Miranda left the room, still clutching what she had come for—the chest—and something she had never expected to carry away from the Waverleigh house on Cheapside. A heavy conscience.

Chapter Forty-two

"*I*t *is* the *Dowsabelle*. It is!"

"Let me see the glass. Are you certain it isn't the *Dor-chester*, the *Deuce*-something?"

" 'Tis Kit, I tell you, Miranda! This waiting has so wearied you that you would doubt the Second Coming were Gabriel to appear before you blowing his trumpet. Give me the glass again."

Marjory applied the secondhand brass tube to her eye and eagerly leaned out the open inn window into the cold winter air.

This was the third day of their vigil and Kit was overdue. Three days' waiting at the Three Cranes. Perhaps that was an omen. Perhaps the clear winter stars were watching over them and applying some celestial harmony to their circumstances.

The weather had warmed just enough to sizzle great banks of steam from the Thames's surface. The river was a vast misty witches' cauldron that late afternoon, a forest of uncanvased masts protruding from it like dead twigs. The westering sun tainted the river's gunmetal water with unwholesome coppery greens and salmons, and the fog shifted across that corroded surface like a veil over the limbs of a leprous Rishi dancer.

"Miranda! You simply stand and stare—I vow, you seem sorry to be seeing Kit again."

"Sorry? No, I was merely thinking what we should do next." Miranda made her gaze focus on Marjory, then recovered the spyglass. "If it be the Dowsabelle, one of the boats is putting ashore. Make haste with your cloak. We must intercept them. Who knows what Kit might blunder into on land if he's not warned?"

Before the Dowsabelle's small boat had rowed halfway to the embankment, two shrouded figures were waiting, as immobile as carved caryatids, at the top of the shallow steps leading from the landing. No one was about, though one of the three cranes creaked burdensomely through the fog and a distant clatter spoke of a last upswing in wharf activity before dark would end it.

The cloaked and hooded women waited, shoulder-to-shoulder, while the Thames lapped at the steps. Their own heartbeats outpaced the river's pulse.

"Marjory."

"Yes, Miranda? I see the masts still, the furled sails, but the fog is thicker at the waterline. What if they row to another stair, what if—?"

"Marjory. You must say nothing to your brother of how Sir Charles died. Nothing of the pressing."

"Of course I must tell him of Father! However horrible, he must know."

"No." Miranda caught Marjory's cloaked arm and held it in her own iron grip. "Do you want Kit thundering back to Dorset to put that major-general in his own press and likely die himself on some Parliamentary sword? No, tell him your father died like Ben. One final noble attempt for the King's sake. Kit must leave England instantly, can't you see? Carrying such tales would only anchor him here."

Marjory eyed the short span of murky water to the fog separating her from whoever rode the Dowsabelle's little boat. "Keep it from him? You ask me to bear a heavy burden, Miranda."

"I will wear its weight as well," Miranda insisted. "Will you do it? If you will not, I would sooner see you dead and drifting below us with those swans than standing hale and whole here to lure your brother on a venture as fatal as ever the King's was."

Marjory glanced down to the huddled swans buffeting against the wall that sheltered them from the chill. She put her hand to her throat and stepped away from Miranda.

"I—I will try to keep it from him, but I am not adept at manufacturing falsehoods. Perhaps you can aid me," she finished bitterly.

"Hush. The boat comes. Hear the oars?"

A triangle of bow nosed through the mist, then the boat and the shrouded figures it carried soon nudged the steps. One figure sprang up them, almost brushing by the fog-draped watchers.

"K-Kit!" Marjory stepped forward to impede what might only be a disappointing fog wraith.

"My God! Marjory!" His voice breathed certainty into both figures; they imperceptively softened with relief in the mellowing light.

"Oh, Kit." Marjory was clinging to his neck, pulling his head down with the weight of her excitement and grief. "He's dead, dead—"

"Dead? Who? Marjory, why are you here?"

Marjory exchanged a glance with the unheeded figure a few paces behind her and recalled her vow.

"Dead . . . Who? Why—why, the King, Kit. Beheaded. All England has gone over to Parliament, and who to stop it? Not Father, not—Ben. They are dead, too. And the boys gone over the water; I think they're safe. And Mother. Gone, all gone. But not you, not you." Marjory buried herself in his arms until he pushed her away to stare into her eyes.

"Gone, you say? Father and Ben dead? Killed in battle?"

Marjory nodded until her hood slipped to her shaking shoulders.

"And—Mother?"

"Only days ago. She had the sickness that drains the motion from one, as Uncle Warring had, Kit. She could not speak at the last and then she—she simply died. That was what it was. She died. If Miranda hadn't have come, I would have—"

"Miranda? You are mad, Marjory!" He shook her fiercely. "None of this is true. You are dreaming. You know no Miranda—"

" 'Tis true." Miranda stepped forward from the fog and her presence was suddenly obvious, like an unwelcome word on a page.

Kit stepped toward her, his hands reaching as if to encompass her reality. He froze halfway through the gesture. Miranda didn't move to complete it. The bitterness of his last thoughts of her had stopped him as effectively as a chasm. Miranda saw that gulf between them, though she didn't understand why he had excavated it.

When she had last seen him, they had built bridges together that she had believed still held, for her to cross over upon—but these spans were shattered. In an instant she had examined the depth of that ravine in his eyes. She did not know why it was there, but for her part, Justin Waverleigh lay at its bottom, quite peacefully dead but living still in the barrier he put on her heart.

Miranda's hands had instinctively moved toward Kit's. Now she altered the gesture to bury them in the muff weighing around her neck.

"Marjory speaks true, Kit. When the King was beheaded by Parliament, I went to Dorset. She was all that I could salvage. Only Marjory. Your mother died quietly. We read from the Book for her, Marjory and I. Cromwell's men took the estate. Nothing remains there for you now, and nothing here. We must leave."

"Yes, Kit." Marjory came to weigh upon his arm again, as if to pull him down into the depths of her grief. "Let us leave this vicious land that can kill us all. They've taken Ravenscroft and there is no longer anything for us here."

He slowly shook his pale head. Miranda nearly drowned in pity for him.

"Father, Ben killed? And Mother dead? Philip and Sydney fled . . . Ravenscroft lost. Yes, we'll away. But first, there must be something we can save—what of the Wexfords? What of . . . Roxanne?"

"Roxanne, cousin Roxanne?" Marjory sounded puzzled. "Still in London, Kit, that I know. Roxanne may have been your intended wife, but no Wexford stood by Father at—at the last. They wax safe behind their doors in Dorset. 'Twas Hervey helped. And Jarvis."

"Of what do you babble, Marjory? Roxanne is our cousin. I must see her safely away. There is something yet to retrieve. Let go—"

Marjory's hands clung but tighter. "Kit! We risk everything with each breath we draw on English soil. Miranda said so, and she is right, I see now. We must go—take us away, please!"

"Of course, of course, sweet." He patted her clutching hands. "First I have a simple errand to run on Tudor Street. Miranda will see you aboard—"

He was slipping her grasp, edging into the fog, leaving her. "Miranda! Stop him, 'tis dangerous, you said. You said London's very stones would kill him."

"Kit, wait!" He paused for her, unwillingly. Her hand escaped the encompassing muff, bearing a long-barreled pistol. "You may need more persuasion than your sailor's tongue to extract this Roxanne Wexford from a Parliamentary city."

Marjory whimpered in despair, but they were oblivious to her. He came forward to cradle the pistol in his hand, to eye the mother-of-pearl-inlaid hunt scene. Miranda realized that she had inadvertently salvaged him a Ravenscroft souvenir.

Kit almost smiled as he lifted the familiar firearm to sniff the chamber.

" 'Tis primed," she assured him. "I did it myself."

Her words fell like salt on some invisible wound he bore.

"I'd not deprive you of your protection," he said stiffly.

Miranda wordlessly slid her other hand from the muff long enough to reveal the butt of the matching pistol.

Kit laughed hollowly. "I should have known Madam better."

Her glance fell to the pistol he still weighed in his hand. He finally nodded and thrust it into his sword baldric.

"And this—you may find it helpful, too," she said.

The parchment snapped as he unfolded its virgin crispness. In the fog-shrouded light he bent his head to read it, his blond hair falling forward on his shoulders. Miranda almost felt the motion, as if some spirit of herself pressed close upon the man a yard away and drank in his every particle. She stepped back to put reins on her imagination.

"This is for Justin Waverleigh!" The first steady look he had allowed her brought the blue of his eyes against her like a wave dashing a rock. The rock gasped and the wave splintered and trickled back to the page unheeding.

"Yes," Miranda said. "For Justin Waverleigh. He has no need of it. He is dead."

"Dead?" His look was as sharp and slicing as a parchment edge grazing her finger.

"Three days past."

"I am sorry." His eyes still anchored the page.

She was certain for a moment that he would refuse the pass. Then he recreased it and thrust it inside his jacket.

" 'Tis not a time to refuse any man's aid, even if he be dead," he remarked bitterly. "Nor any woman's."

Christopher Steele was only a fading figure in the fog and the brisk click of mournful spurs dying into a distant chime.

"Miranda! How could you let him go! Kit—oh, I do not wish to hear Kit walking in my dreams ..."

"He does what he must, Marjory. And so do we."

Miranda gathered up the Waverleigh jewel box from its post at her feet and pulled Marjory toward the waiting boat. "Put your cloak about your throat, child, you'll catch the cough. Gentle sailors, you'll row us shipward. No pretty sights unfold in London nowadays; you chose the better part when you signed up to sleep on Mother Ocean's bosom."

The seamen, strangers all, laughed and helped them aboard. They liked a landlubber who credited their way of life. Miranda sat in the bow; Marjory, beside her, gazed shoreward.

Miranda peered intently ahead, waiting to glimpse the *Dowsabelle*'s wooden belly through the rolling mist. She was suddenly as eager for a ship as she once had been for Barbados. And not so strange; a ship was an island, wasn't it, and she was island-reared? Island stock. For herself alone, as Francisco had once said, of both her and himself.

Perhaps she had proven so to Justin; perhaps she deserved to be back-to-back with Kit Steele now, pacing off from him as if in a duel, knowing him to be cannonading toward Roxanne Wexford at this very instant. The thought twisted and drove deep. She caught the Waverleigh box tightly on her lap and stared more single-mindedly forward. The ship. She remembered her first row toward the *Salamander* in Cádiz's unconcealing daylight, how the Spanish galleys had prophetically loomed over that day and sickened her with their evil stench. She had sent him into the galleys.

Now, with one instinctive response to a world turned inside out, he had set her rowing eternally on a land-locked lake of inner agony. To Roxanne Wexford he had gone. If that was what he wished, then she should not stand in his way. She would never force him against his will again, though she die for it. The tears fell swiftly, encrusting the sturdy box lid with out-of-fashion diamonds to match its inner fire. But the fog was discreet, keeping this between itself and Miranda.

Later, Miranda rocked for hours in the much-misnamed Great Cabin of the *Dowsabelle*. She and Marjory had been immediately escorted there, and there had remained, each steadfastly watching the other, neither speaking the thought that roweled them both.

An hour surely. And where was he? Two, certainly. And Kit? Kit, where, dear God? Dark dropped like a cloak over the narrow cabin windows. Miranda and Marjory sat woodenly on their opposite bunks, their cloaks still about their shoulders, their eyes on a collision course.

Three hours, veritably, for the love of God. Too long, another minute would be an eternity not to be endured ...

Miranda rose abruptly, set down the box and left the cabin.

Marjory rolled stricken eyes after her, but sat silent.

Moments later Miranda was back, something limp fluttering over her arm. Marjory watched speechlessly as Miranda methodically stripped off her cloak, bodice, skirt, petticoats—down to her shift. She donned a pair of breeches and a shirt, tying the whole together with a ludicrously gay silk sash. She pulled on a dilapidated set of boots, taking a sloppy step or two and making her only comment thus far.

"Forecastle flotsam."

She slid a knife into one boot before withdrawing the remaining pistol from its furry vault and thrusting it into her improvised belt. She resumed her cloak only after tying back her long yellow hair with a ribbon filched from her bodice sleeve.

"Tudor Street, he said. Hawkers should be about who know the house. I'm going to fetch Kit. Don't worry."

Marjory was beyond worry; her mouth hung at half-mast and her eyes were Delft saucers. Miranda smiled and shut Marjory's mouth with a chuck on the chin.

"Watch my jewel box. Who's to know what manner of scurvy wharf rats your brother has sailing for him this time?"

The cloaked Miranda who materialized on deck was not so different from the lady escorted aboard short hours before.

"Perhaps your captain is detained ashore," she told the first mate, a man of middle years named Bacon. "I will lead to where he was bound, but I believe it will take some persuasion on your part to induce his hosts to part with him. I warrant the captain will be most grateful for your efforts. I already have a token he tended me."

Miranda held up a pendant emerald and found an answering gleam in Bacon's beady eye. Captains came and went, but a sailor's loyalty was ever to a certain far-off glimmer over the next horizon. A chimera called adventure, and sometimes greed.

Bacon rounded up a shore party and armed them to the incisors with no further prodding. They were ashore as stealthily as any smuggling party and moving through semideserted byways. Now that the Puritans were London's abiding influence, decent citizens had less reason than ever to be abroad of a night. No gaming, bull-baiting, cockfighting, masqueing, maying, wenching, singing, swilling or—to sum it up—sinning were permitted, so none but such villains as would practice all of the above vices were about.

Miranda glided down the fog-damp streets secure, a treasure galleon amidst an escort fleet of sturdy seamen. The party found the Wexford house on the first throw by rousting an unreformed drunkard from the pavement where he wallowed.

"There, lads," he drawled, pointing an unsteady finger to the shuttered façade of a house bracketed by its darkened neighbors.

"There, gentlemen," said Miranda. "I warrant we need not knock."

It took some doing—some noisy doing—to entreat entry at the rear courtyard door. A porter, for instance, required a bit of admonishment on the pate before his reedy objections subsided. The house remained still and the sailors fanned through the premises in search of odd sweetmeats for their trouble, swiftly subduing who they must.

Miranda directly sought the upper stories, after borrowing a rapier from a startled sailor whose arms were too full of Wexford silver to object.

The hall candle still burned brightly. Miranda appropriated it and swept through the first bedchamber door. The candle threw long drapery shadows across the bed and brought to the surface a fine, furred catch of auburn hair, attached to an indignant personage in a Lowlands linen nightdress.

"My God, sir, you trespass!" breathed Roxanne Wexford in contralto indignation.

"You are wrong on both counts, mistress." Miranda set her candle down on a nearby table and herself at the foot of the damsel's bed. "Though perhaps your entreaty to the Deity is not ill-advised."

Miranda's sword point delicately replaced the ebbing nightdress on Roxanne's creamy shoulder. Her Dignity squealed.

"I have come, dear lady, with no intention of disturbing your slumbers, but for Christopher Steele." Miranda's eyes hardened. She found a certain humiliation in being forced to utter his name before Roxanne Wexford; it was like standing naked before an enemy. "I cannot say truthfully that I had hoped to find him here"—Miranda glanced around the bedchamber—"but I was mortal set on finding him. Perhaps you can assist me."

The slender silver blade flicked an auburn curl back from Roxanne's face. Roxanne shuddered and clutched the bedcovers to her throat.

"Such modesty," Miranda noted. "You should affect it more often. But come, tell me where I may find him."

"B-below."

"A captain installed below? How inhospitable, mistress. Get up."

Roxanne obeyed after some tender urging by Miranda's rapier and stood barefoot, her fingers twisting in her gown. Miranda turned her roughly away, wrenching a satin cord from the bed draperies, and bound Roxanne's white hands behind her.

"What were your intentions toward Captain Steele?" she asked, spinning Roxanne around so swiftly that the blazing hair almost became a gag.

"H-he . . . he is an enemy of the state. I merely held him for Parliament. My servants apprehended him—good Lord, it was burglary, you should see the state in which he left my dining chamber before they pinioned him! I can't imagine why he would storm this house at midnight, unless . . . unless his intentions were even more dishonorable than I first guessed. A . . . a lady like yourself cannot be but sympathetic to her sister under siege."

"I should like to see Truth besiege you, mistress. I vow you would give it a bitter fight of it. You meant to betray him to Parliament because it would set the Wexfords down on the Cromwell side of the ledger ever after, isn't that true? Marjory Steele said that your family was not to be found when they brought Sir Charles down. In the morning you would have tended your intended husband into the same hands that saw his father and brother dead. You are an elegant credit to our sex, sister, and to your country. Now take me 'below.' "

Roxanne lifted a lacy hem to display an unprotected foot.

Miranda merely collected the candle and propelled her prisoner out the door and down the turning steps, past isolated sailors on a rampage, who favored Roxanne with lusty grins throughout her descent.

"Ooooh, you're pulling my hair! Turn here, through the kitchen and down . . . but I won't descend further. Rats live down there!"

Miranda let loose of Roxanne and drew back. "Rats? Rats, you say?"

Roxanne nodded her lavish red head and shook a dainty bare foot again.

"Why, you are right, mistress. 'Tis brutal to force a well-bred—and shoeless—London lady into such a hole as that. Get down."

Miranda prodded a whimpering Roxanne down narrow and splintered treads into the deep below-kitchen cellar.

The candle flickered in the damp, but revealed an enclave of wine tuns, barrels and piled foodstuffs, as well as rows of pork and beef sides hanging from great iron hooks on the massive ceiling beams. The place was low and seemed small. For a moment Miranda feared her charge had betrayed her. Then she saw the girl's glance angle anxiously around a pile of casks.

Kit was there, looking mortal discomfited, his head and shoulders bowed to a broad beam like Atlas holding up the world and his wrists roped to a hook just above his bent neck. The candle glimmer showed the facts of his predicament; it did not illuminate any surprise, or relief, at Miranda's arrival.

"You appear to love London too well to leave it, Captain Steele," she noted, making light of his embarrassing quandary. "This lady, too, appears to desire your company."

She shoved Roxanne forward, aware of how the flame danced over the abundant red hair, of how white and refined the Wexford features were even in such a place.

"I should not tarry in freeing you."

Miranda lowered her eyes while pulling the short dagger from her boot. His hands were imprisoned directly behind his neck. She had to lean close along the length of his side, had to peer narrowly over his shoulder to find the knot and bring her blade to it. She was too near to deny herself a glance at his face.

His own eyes ambushed her there, so her blade stopped its sawing at the rope even as her breath halted its rhythm in her chest.

"You are most considerate," he said softly, seriously. "Madam."

This time the word was not reproof, but tribute. Miranda was startled enough to let her face question him. Suddenly his arms dropped around her.

"I fear I have anticipated you."

The ropes hung in shreds from the hook above him. Kit brought his abraded wrists to rest on her shoulders. "It is a mistake to tie a man to that which can untie him."

She saw the hook's barbed point and how he must have painstakingly used it to saw his bonds. She also saw how close they stood and that the chasm between them had somehow narrowed in the last hours into mere inches.

Miranda broke backward, bending to replace her knife in her boot and wishing her hair were loose to veil her face. She stood with a flush quite attributable to her recent efforts and turned to the awestruck Roxanne, pulling her forward by the hair.

"What of this bauble?" she inquired with elaborate indifference. "Do you wish her for cargo?"

"There's no market for deceit," he said quickly enough. "Leave her to her kind." He started up the stairs.

Miranda and Roxanne exchanged a mutually venomous look.

Roxanne's prominent chin lifted and a certain smugness dawned in her odd yellow eyes. Miranda shoved her roughly over to the hook just vacated by Kit. She caught Roxanne's trailing red hair into two thick tails and tied them into a double knot on the metal.

Roxanne panicked and pulled, caught fast like another betrayer, named Absalom.

"Witch!" she hissed through clenched teeth.

"Whore," rejoined Miranda with unruffled visual alliteration.

Kit paused in his ascent to marvel at the meetness of Miranda's revenge. "They will have to make a Roundhead of her to cut her down."

"Aye," said Miranda. She passed him on the steep stair, like a lady trailing through a portal before her escort. "Mayhap a trimming will improve her looks."

Their departing laughter played bitter counterpoint to Roxanne weeping for her doomed lovelocks and rat-bait bare feet below.

Chapter Forty-three

*T*he shore party of the good ship *Dowsabelle* clanked back to Queenhithe Dock, Kit and Miranda trailing them in mutual amusement.

Fortunately the London through which they strode was dormant for the night. It was debatable whether the able seamen's boots or booty made the greater commotion in the cobblestoned streets.

Kit and Miranda's joint adventure had almost restored the camaraderie of *Salamander* days; he let her clamber up the

Dowsabelle's fog-draped side with no gentlemanly aid, and she felt no need to inquisition his recent actions. She now understood that it was not for Roxanne Wexford's self alone, nor her crimson hair, that Kit had risked a return to London. Otherwise, he would have taken his cousin along despite her treachery.

Marjory was overjoyed to have Kit back. And what of Roxanne?

"A slight—misapprehension—on both parts," Miranda explained in the cabin. "It seems your cousin was content to remain and your brother well content to let her. Kit will see you as soon as he has set the ship to rights."

Marjory dropped her cloak off her shoulders, finally convinced that all was well. " 'Tis heavy," she said, stroking the ebbing wool, "as is everything we carried away from Ravenscroft. Including memories."

"Hush. Kit will ask you more of the last days. Remember your promise: not a word about the pressing. Kit would not accept your father's selfless choice. He could not. It makes him heir."

"Heir?" Marjory's face tautened bitterly. "They have taken Ravenscroft—or all we valued there—what is there to inherit?"

"What your father shrewdly foresaw when he chose the pressing. The major-generals and Cromwell may ride roughshod over the law in these tumultuous days. The law and the land will outlast them, as they always have tyrants, even New Model tyrants."

"But they have taken everything, Miranda! The Puritans canted that they had no need for the luxuries of office, the frills of decoration or beauty beyond nature. Yet the innkeeper's wife told me that seventeen cartloads of Whitehall booty have passed into storage at the Three Cranes since the King's death, all overflowing with riches marked out by Cromwell's lady wife. They are still stored there, but a row from where we sit now, she said so."

"And Cromwell had sworn to auction off the Titians and Rembrandts, the porcelains and jewels from the King's collection—with the proceeds to be given to the people of England. That much I believed of him. Like Major-General Hatch, he seemed a stern and scrupulous man, though not much merciful."

"Aye, and is not Mistress Cromwell a 'people of England'? They will be hanging portraits of Steele ancestors in their halls, setting Steele plate in their dining chambers and claiming them for their own since the Crusades. They will take it all, as they have ever done. Religion will have naught to do with it."

"You surprise me, Marjory. I had no inkling you were so

politic-minded; but do not trouble Kit with this. You have seen this England ebbing away for weeks and are stronger for it; he had lost his ground in one great gulp."

Perhaps Marjory heeded Miranda, for she returned from a long closeting with her brother subdued but undistraught. "He wishes to see you."

Miranda almost did not return the sentiment. She had been living on the afterglow of one intoxicating hour weeks ago, thinking Kit shared in her emotional repast. He had evidently been drinking bitter wine at another trestle and did not want her for a tablemate.

The deck bustled with sailors doing what they could in the dark to prepare for departure. Miranda mounted to the *Dowsabelle*'s captain's cabin, which she had shared with Kit on her sullen return to England but a spring ago. A better season.

He sat at his small slanted desk, his jacket flung across a chest, his rapier and pistol carelessly afloat on the built-in bed. The cabin's solitary lantern cast shadows across his face. It was not that the interview with Marjory had not been highly charged—only that she had not been permitted to feel the burden of it.

"Sit down. Please." He gestured wearily to the space in front of him without glancing up. Miranda, finding the customary stool missing, sat finally at the edge of the bed.

"I'm taking you home," Kit announced finally.

Home? She sat up straight. He could only mean Barbados. Where else could she apply that one-syllable word with any accuracy?

"Holland and France make poor residences for unfrocked Englishmen, I've seen that. You know your island, and loved it once, I think?" Miranda nodded. "I have a yen to see it. I have a yearning to sail as far from this forsaken slice of earth as I can."

He pulled a long-throated bottle from a chest and set it firmly on the chart atop his desk, like a seal.

"I have a chart that will take us there, Neptune willing. I think I had better trust to the old gods. Those defined by the late King and Cromwell seem barbaric by comparison."

He uncorked a thick stream of red wine and poured it into two crystal goblets he unearthed from a leather chest. "I have acquired a better table service since you last sailed with me," he noted ruefully. "From a French trader off Brest with whom I had a small discussion on my return voyage. May I offer you a toast to our departure?"

Miranda rose to accept the proffered goblet.

"I talked to Marjory." Kit drained his glass in one draught and refilled it to the brim.

Miranda felt immeasurably weary. She returned to the bed and leaned back into the rough wood as she wet her lips with the bittersweet wine.

"French wine," Kit said suddenly, watching her face pucker slightly.

She was surprised that he had observed her so closely and slouched deeper into the bed's shadows.

"Marjory told me of all you did. She is quite awed by you, almost afraid." He leaned back in his chair and let the creak punctuate his sentence. "She could hardly stutter her tale of what happened at Ravenscroft without invoking your name every other sentence. 'Miranda said we must leave, Miranda told the major-general to go to the Devil, Miranda said ghosts don't walk.' "

"The major-general told *me* to go to the Devil," Miranda noted. "I vow Marjory remembers little of those days. She was quite crushed by it all."

"No, Marjory is perhaps not the best witness." He leaned forward heavily. "You tell me what occurred, Miranda."

So she did, speaking slowly, but her mind racing ahead to delete the worst details, the entire sorry tale of Sir Charles's manner of death. She would not lie to Kit, merely smooth a few unnecessary wrinkles of inconvenient truth cut from whole cloth. It still made a grim recital. Kit set the few drops left in his glass swirling round and round as she told it, watching the whirlpool of wine until his concentration made her dizzy. Miranda ended with her encounter with Major-General Hatch.

"And old Trojan? Marjory skittered around something to do with that."

"Oh, yes. The dog. The old dog. I shot him, Kit. Cleanly. There was no other way."

"Yes." His waving hand flattened her apologies. " 'Twas well done. Some things, some matters, reach a state beyond retrieval, no matter how much one would wish it."

Miranda quavered under his steady blue stare. He was speaking veiledly, like a sybil. He poured another glassful of wine.

Miranda drank hers in one swallow to keep pace with him on the dangerous road he had taken, this time a mental one.

"Beyond retrieval." He tapped the nearly empty wine bottle on the chart. "There she sits. The cursed Bermudes. The New World. By God, be that place ridden with vermin, pestilence, famine and piracy, 'tis bound to be a better world than the one we leave!"

He looked up, his eyes ragged ensigns of grief. She ought to have known that he had taken it too well. She ought to have been ready for this sudden slap of agony across her face.

"Kit, it—" He waved her silent.

"We leave on the morrow's tide. Fade away. Leave them the spoils to weigh down their immortal souls, though I'd like to burden their mortality with my sword." He glanced to the unsheathed rapier lying like a long needle across the bed. "What use be swords in such times, what use be any of us?"

"I still have your pistol." Miranda drew it from her sash to distract him from his melancholy.

He came over for it, weighing it in his hand like an ingot. "Spanish stock. Taken by some Steele or other during a siege of Cádiz in 1625, when King Charles was a lad eager to wed their wide-skirted Infanta. Nothing came of that, either. Keep it. You may need a pistol yet."

He looked down at her, wavering slightly on his feet, more from wine than the ship's rocking. "How did your husband die?"

Miranda dropped her glance to the glass and brought the rim tight against her teeth. "Of the sword," she said after a swallow.

He hung over her for a moment, as if he would say, do, something more. Instead, he lurched back to the desk, tilting the wine bottle and letting its last drops slide slowly forth into his fine French crystal.

"And what will the widow Waverleigh do now?"

Miranda flinched. He was not himself; she would not unleash any anger at this wounded shadow. "My father's friends still reside on Barbados. I have the Waverleigh jewels, as Marjory has her mother's. I will buy a house, perhaps our old house, if Harry will allow it."

"Harry. What, still living? Harry signed your cursed paper, yes, I recall." He dredged his jacket from the chest and patted it until an answering crackle came. He held the folded rectangle up to the lantern light, and her, like a toast.

"Are you an omen, I wonder? Even the Dutchman dares not

touch you, kill you. Death seems to trail you like a train, Mistress Miranda, whether you bother to wear skirts or not. Muffin dead, Waverleigh dead, but not Harry. Harry turned Puritan, else his signature would have no weight—amusing, is it not? Do you remember how we found Harry, dallying in the don's silk-swathed cabin? Harry, turned Puritan! These times have a sense of irony."

He overturned the sluggish bottle. Its last drop plummeted like a liquid ruby to the ivory chart to make another Indies island there.

Miranda clutched the faceted ruby astride her finger. She had forgotten it. Kit saw the gesture and came over again to catch up her hand and study the ruby with the lantern light swaying softly across its contours.

She fought the impulse to snatch away her hand. He was not drunk, not as drunk as the Dutchman even had been, but his emotions were inebriated with too much disaster swallowed too quickly.

His brittle blue glance rested on her face; he studied her for a moment as sharply as he had scanned the ruby: as if he had just remembered them both; as if he had remembered under what circumstances he had acquired them both. Miranda's eyes were frozen to his face, fresh-shaven for his heart-free jaunt ashore that very afternoon.

The lantern behind him softened the weariness, the pain, and gilded him with some of the old glitter. Yet she knew his surface reflection hid an intemperate zone of aimless emotion, a compassless center where love and hate jousted, where past and present, indifference and desire, contested. No, not indifference. Disdain.

"Where did you get those?" His glance had dropped quixotically to her borrowed boots with the swift turn of logic wine accomplishes.

"The forecastle."

"And that?" He pulled lightly at her silken sash. It gave so readily that he peeled its entire length off her waist in one motion.

Miranda remembered a rope that had been as treacherous a belt as that silk. She looked up to find him laying the length across his spread hands, like a dead thing.

"You found this in my sea chest with those—" He pointed at her breeches and shirt. "But do you know where I got this? By

Harry"—he smiled ironically—"it was a token from Roxanne Wexford."

By invoking the names that had betrayed them both, he brought a measure of sobriety to the cabin. Their eyes met and he let the emerald silk slide to the floor. He sat beside her, rummaging deeply in her eyes, as if she were a chest with some hidden contents to give up. He had gone to spirits for comfort and found them wanting; now he sought surcease in the flesh.

He pulled deliberately on her shirt's neckline tie. Then he flicked the fabric back like a surgeon to unveil a triangle of skin from her collarbone to where her breasts broke from their deepest crevasse. His eyes had abandoned her face since the sash had fallen and Miranda was glad.

Despite the weeks, the days, nights, she had yearned for him in every respect, including the most physical, she did not require or desire him now. It did not mean she loved him less, only that the physical pull of her love had ebbed under the tow of his deeper agony. She was startled to find that emotion so arbitrary. No wonder the inconstant moon was the lovers' celestial token.

Kit's eyes were desire-darkened, given over to that unimpeded selfishness that brands passion. He wanted to beach himself upon her body; drive onto, into her, wearing all the anguish that burdened him. He wanted to come away rinsed, soothed, satiated. And she would be willing to serve as sand to absorb his sorrow, she would be as open to him as an island to a shipwrecked sailor. That was all he required, no more at this moment. She could have been insensate, mindless, as dead as the Dutchman's reputed lovers, and she would have served . . .

He was suddenly standing with her in his arms. One of the overlarge boots fell to the cabin floor. He bent with her to retrieve it and tossed it into the cradle of her airborne lap. He was at the cabin door, kicking it open, clattering down the narrow stairs to the lower deck. He bent with her again to shoulder through the Great Cabin door and deposit her swiftly on the bed opposite Marjory's.

"Kit, Miranda, what—?"

"Hush, Marjory. Miranda is very tired. I'll see you in the morning."

Miranda lay quietly after he had left, her heart finally beating the fandango it should have begun minutes earlier. Relief and worry washed over her in alternate waves of warmth and chill.

She was proud that he had chosen to wrestle with his demons alone. And frantic that they would overpower him.

Above her, she heard his cabin door muffle shut, heard the pacing that began. And stopped. And began again. After a long while, she pulled the boot that still drooped across her body away and laid it softly on the floor, so as not to wake Marjory. And she cried softly, so as not to wake Marjory. She cried for a very long time, until the backwash of her tears made her feel ill. She cried until the pacing stopped. And then she slept.

Miranda awoke alone in the Great Cabin, to blotchy squares of daylight lying across its shadows like fresh scars. A wave of illness overcame her and she felt for, found, the slop pail and vomited into it. When she rose, she took off Kit's breeches and shirt and worked herself back into her abandoned corsets and gown. She went out onto deck.

Sunshine struck with winter dazzle. She bent her glance to the deck and began dusting her bedraggled skirt.

"Miranda! Come over, we're asail."

Marjory stood at the gunwale with her brother. Miranda walked over shakily. Odd, her sea-bred feet seemed to have forsaken her. The supply loys were pulling away from the *Dowsabelle* in a spirited little flock. Fresh water and victuals must line her swollen hold already.

Miranda squinted into the sun and cast a shy glance at Kit. Ah, better. The torment of the night before had drained away. His face was emptied of something. Perhaps it was youth, for Miranda saw a faint ribbing across his forehead that she had never noticed before, a certain slight grimace as if even a bright day might bring a blow.

His eyes flicked over her restored garb with the indifference of the observant. "I have something you left in my cabin," he said, striding away.

Miranda waited beside Marjory, fearful that he might return bearing something long and green like a snake. Instead, it was a pistol he carried.

"Keep this with you and Marjory in the cabin. One never knows what may befall."

It felt heavy, awkward in her grip. She had no place to stow it on her gown. So she glided back to the cabin and put it by the men's clothing. Once sitting upon her bed, she was uneager to leave it. Ah, she was tired. Bone-tired. Why should she not be?

But they were bound away. To Barbados. To her beloved Barbados. With her beloved at the helm. It would be better there. It would have to be better there.

Miranda found it hard to hold to that happy thought. Each morning brought her awake with a backwash of nausea that smothered her like a bad dream. Marjory hovered over her, but Miranda ordered her out. Once Kit came to inquire and she drove him away as harshly.

Miranda hugged her homely wooden bucket between bouts and thought grimly that this was punishment for her past faults. For Justin. She had lost her seaworthiness. *She*, beset by seasickness while landslady Marjory flitted abovedecks with Kit, turning nicely golden-skinned under her faint freckles while Miranda grew green below!

Miranda's isolation made her lurch to her feet and try for deck, but always weakness drove her back to the bunk if she tried before noon. So Miranda grew to rock in misery all morning by custom, nursing a new understanding for Meg MacTavish.

All was not fair winds and high hearts abovedecks, as Miranda imagined. True, the breezes blew the *Dowsabelle* sturdily down the Thames and out the river's generous mouth, where Kit steered the ship smoothly through the treacherous Downs and southward along the Channel.

He and Marjory had reprised their happiest days at Ravenscroft when she had been old enough to speak intelligently to him, just before he had left on his various voyages.

Marjory was almost as delighted as he to find herself seasuitable. She lolled for hours by the gunwale; Kit frequently broke his duties by edging over and discoursing on the thousand natural questions she had of this and that.

Yet the silences would fall and their eyes would edge away from their inestimable bereavements. What would Marjory know of Kit's older-brother sense of responsibility, his manhood's unebbing rage at his powerlessness to prevent, avenge, the destruction of his family? What would Kit know of Marjory's gallant, broken struggle to hold what little remained of the Steeles together, even it were only her own mind, until an older, stronger hand should come to help? So they turned their talk to surface matters and steered their affection onto a smooth shallow plane.

"I should have taken you to sea a decade ago, Mistress Marjoram," he teased one day when another of those silences had burrowed between them. "You seem another Steele born to it, as I was."

"Weren't you ever seasick, ever? Oh, Kit, I recall Uncle Warring taking you for a sail off Poole that turned you green as copper."

"Never! And only once."

"You couldn't have taken me to sea anyway; your sailors would have never countenanced a female. But I am quite seagoing, aren't I? Not retching myself green below like Miranda."

Kit frowned. "She has held her own on board a ship enough to require no scornful words from novices." His voice held enough admonition to make Marjory rise to her remark's defense.

"I was merely teasing, Kit. 'Tis clear 'tis not seasickness that ails Miranda!"

"Not seasickness? True, she never was prone to the malady, but she has been ill this past week; perhaps something should be done." His palms struck the gunwale. "I would we had a surgeon aboard, but the last one lingered in France—wisely, it turns out—and I had no time to secure another."

Marjory regarded him with alternately amused and anxious eyes. "Kit, a surgeon will do naught for her. What ails her is not an—ailment."

"What do you mean?"

"Oh, Kit." An appealing wash of color tinted Marjory's sunrinsed features. He was seven years her senior, after all, and they had never talked of certain matters plainly before . . .

"Marjory. I am responsible for all who sail on this vessel, and for her especially—tell me."

" 'Tis nothing to fuss over, Kit. She is only with child; such sickness is the first sign."

His hands had frozen on her arms and his face was as blank as if it were masked. "With child?" His voice had instinctively sunk to a whisper, as if that could change the circumstances. "How can you know? A girl of sixteen?"

"Wasn't I there when Mother was brought to bed with—with wee Charlie? While you were gone? And Sydney and Philip, don't you remember, Kit? How ill she was with them both at the outset? She had no time for me; I ought to remember, though I was but a child myself. Why are you staring so? Miranda had a wedded husband—he who died but a fortnight past. 'Tis not so strange as some begettings in Scriptures."

"No," agreed Kit, letting his hands finally slide from Marjory's arms. He leaned his elbows on the gunwale and contemplated a monotonous distance of sea and sky. "She will be well?"

"Well again? I suppose so. Mother, after all, survived. That. I know little of it, Kit. Don't ask me such questions."

"If she is—to bear a child, can she survive this voyage? She must barely be eating enough to keep alive."

"Perhaps the morning sickness is worsened by our being at sea, but we are here, aboard ship; what else can we do? Besides, 'twill take more than that to stop Miranda."

Kit brought a dubious blue glance to Marjory's face. "She is not indestructible, Marjory, but mortal like you and I. I would not have you think more of her than she is; 'tis bad for you both."

"Mother regarded the sickness as merely something unavoidable, and she survived. Though wee Charlie did not. Now she is gone as well, and Father, Ben . . . I try not to think of it, Kit, but sometimes it comes upon me by stealth and I think I surely must scream and scream and never stop."

"Marjory, Marjory." He caught her in his arms, a slender harvest of three centuries' worth of Steele breeding, held together now by nerves as fine-spun as the hairs on her golden head.

Marjory welcomed the embrace, but broke from it. Kit had been staring over the top of her head to the horizon, his eyes a sleepwalker's. Marjory turned to the empty sea.

"Off Oporto by now," he muttered. "With luck we might find a Frenchman Bristol-bound from Cádiz."

His mind was back on seafaring matters, Marjory saw, relieved. She may not understand things nautical, but he was clearly out of his depth when it came to aught to do with children beyond the begetting of them, as with most men. Marjory basked in her feminine superiority for a moment. Truly, men were children.

Miranda had not the luxury of meditating on such matters. She kept to the cabin, accepting the sickness as but one more catastrophe ladled out from the hand of an angry God. Yet one agonizing morning two days later, Miranda rocked to more than misery in her narrow bed.

My Lord! A cannon discharge below her. The ship wallowed back and forth with the recoil as if demented. Miranda stood.

Another board-vibrating boom knocked her back into the bed linens. A moment later a white-faced Marjory rushed into the cabin.

"Miranda! He's gone mad, utterly mad! 'Twas merely a merchantman gliding idly by and Kit sending up the flag to salute her most courteously and then—he's mad. Quite mad. 'Tis the Warring streak come out. He's attacking it! Like a pirate! And the poor, peaceful thing but a hundred yards off our starboard. No, larboard. Oh, I can't remember the cant. It's to our left and he's loosing our guns at her as if she were a Spanish galley."

Another jolt catapulted both women together on the bed. Marjory hid herself in Miranda's arms, bringing her head up only for one pertinent inquiry. "You're not going to be sick again, are you?"

"Of course not." Miranda rose and found herself steadier than she had been in days. "I'm going on deck."

Marjory trailed meekly after.

The deck was quiet now. And why not? A white flag of surrender fluttered from the *Joie de Calais*'s tattered mainmast. There was no joy in Calais three days later when the French ship limped in with her timbers shivered by an Englisher.

At the moment, Christopher Steele, mad or not, was no longer aboard the *Dowsabelle*. Bacon reported that the captain had boarded the defeated merchant to negotiate terms. Shortly after, the *Dowsabelle*'s quarter boat struck away from the *Joie*. Kit climbed over the *Dowsabelle*'s side and into a waiting committee of two concerned faces under equally matching yellow hair. He appeared pleased with himself.

"My terms were magnanimous," he volunteered. "We parted company quite amicably. In fact, we may regard the contents of yonder boat as a token of Captain Fanchon's esteem rather than as anything so vulgar as—booty."

Miranda and Marjory leaned as one over the gunwale to watch the boat row toward them. Four seamen, pulling valiantly. One burly Frenchman with a droopy black moustache that gave his fleshy face a mournful cast, and a crate of hens, three pigs, four sheep . . . and a goose! Miranda and Marjory exchanged glances of pure wonder diluted with worry.

"I was tiring of watching my dinner walk away," Kit explained, referring to the weevils and vermin that spiced most shipboard menus. "I have sought to embellish our hasty and humble larder and hope to accomplish wonders with the aid of

. . . this gentleman. *Bonjour, monsieur, venez, audessus le plat-
bord.*"

The mournful moustache rose over the gunwale as invited and
then the remainder of the man—a fleshy mountain that vibrated
like a blancmange—oozed onto deck.

"Monsieur de Rognon," Kit introduced him. "The finest
French ship's cook with a yen to see the Indies within bowshot,
I assure you, ladies. Monsieur, *vôtre royaume.*" Kit waved a
courtly hand below and the new crewman, with a rosary decade's
worth of *mercis*, rolled below. "We dine at eight, mistresses, in
my cabin."

Miranda was laughing for the first time in weeks as Kit strode
away.

"*Mon Dieu*, Marjory, as no doubt yon Captain Fanchon is
muttering into his weevils at this moment. Now, that is the Kit
I remember!"

"When precisely did you know Kit, Miranda? I've never heard
the story."

"And shan't, for there is none. We met—when he had come to
port. Now we all leave home port for another home. That is all."

The three sat down to a cramped table that evening. Kit's elbows nearly scraped the little cabin's perimeters as he poured the
wine, but the previously commandeered silver plate had never
borne food that matched its magnificence so well—at least not
on the *Dowsabelle*. The ship's former, hastily drafted cook was
happy to serve or stand and wait. They dined on chicken stewed
with Monsieur de Rognon's voluble apologies, but well sauced
with ingredients from the mysterious barrels that had accompanied him aboard.

Miranda and Marjory glowed in the small circle of lantern
light. Out of daylight, their falling bands and cuffs looked immaculate again. Marjory's heart-shaped face grew plump at the
cheeks, lifted by smiles. Miranda's eyes waxed green again, as if
siphoning the deep forest color from her gown.

They talked of Barbados in glowing terms. Miranda spoke of
its perfect bays, its sand as fine and white as a great lady's face
powder. She lit verbal vigil lamps to the island's candlewood
trees, its broad cedars and dozens of flaming-faced flowers. She
toasted its green sea turtles and boasted of the soup made from
therein so shamelessly that Monsieur de Rognon was called in
and interrogated as to whether he could prepare such a beast
when they neared the island.

By unspoken decree, all dinners in the captain's cabin that fortunately smooth voyage were forward-looking. Miranda served as Kit and Marjory's figurehead, the only one of the three who knew how to draw them forward.

She told them of El Dorado, the fabled Indian city erected from sheer gold deep within the Orinoco River jungle. El Dorado, for which Sir Walter Raleigh had stalked through miles of steamy, uncharted jungle a generation ago, which fruitless search was to cost the great English explorer and courtier his head.

She made Barbados, the entire Indies, live in their minds' eyes, until they were as eager for it as she. It was her home, she believed in it again. Harry and Francisco were gone, but her father's bones bleached there, white as the island's silver sand. Her mother was merely a European afterthought before her time. This was where the future lay, in what the poets apostrophized as "the cursed Bermudes." What did poets know of it?

One night of such talk saw Marjory retire early to dream of giant shelled snakes that waddled into cauldrons and stewed themselves. Kit and Miranda lingered on deck together, alone again for the first time since they had left England. The *Dowsabelle* had wafted westward for a week now, without a storm between them and their small island goal. They had spied no other ship since the Frenchman who had so paid for the privilege off Oporto.

Now night was ringing down on the empty horizon circling them. A few stars twinkled far away while a full-faced moon hung like a great silver coin low over the water. Silence hung as heavily over the two on deck.

" 'Tis like a ladder," said Miranda finally, gesturing to a stretch of whitecaps catching moonlight like rungs to the horizon.

Kit nodded. "The moon is a sailor's light o' love, but 'tis the stars his life hangs upon. Some philosophers say the souls of men live on after death in the stars. I would like to think I once knew the glimmer that guides us."

Miranda dropped her glance from the heavens. She knew of what souls he thought, and she had enough of her own with which to people the skies—Father, Meg MacTavish, Captain Coyle, Captain Pentreath, Ibrahim . . . Muffin. The thought brought her glance to Kit and intercepted his own. He looked up again.

"Those same stars shine on Ravenscroft," he said abruptly.

"On the roofs, chimneys, courtyard stones, the garden greens, the rolling fields around, the grazing cattle. On meadow and monument equally."

"But they do shine, Kit, no matter what happens. It is we who lose our brilliance, our glamour."

He turned from the gunwale as if momentarily renouncing the sea.

"I hated Ravenscroft. Hated it from a boy. I was never so high-hearted as when I was leaving it. Now it's no longer there for me to leave and I could"—he hesitated over the word, then stood by it—"weep . . . for it."

Miranda kept silent, her hands tight around the wooden gunwale.

"Do the stars care whether Royalist or Puritan keep sway over what they shine upon?" he went on. "My father was only a paper Royalist. A few hundred pounds to the Scots when they seemed to be allies; Ben to fight across the Midlands. I, I went my own way, and saying I earned gold to fuel the King's need for ordinance is as good a way as any of saying I had a wanderlust and an excuse to indulge it. I never cared enough for either King or Parliament to more than feint at the edges of their quarrel. I never thought 'twould come to slaughter. War, yes—though what's the difference if Ben and Father take their wounds at Marston Moor or on their own lands?"

"A great difference, Kit. We like to think we go forth to battle, not that it comes home to us. A home should be a sacred place, our own, with none to sully it but ourselves."

He laughed ruefully. "You were such an optimist when I found you. You seemed to think the milk of human kindness ran in rivers from the ground. The Dutchman, even, you would have pardoned. Have you learned yet? I was your first schoolmaster, I think, and it was a hard lesson I taught you."

"Yes," said Miranda.

"So we are left with the stars, you say." He looked up again. "That way lies England, Ravenscroft, Cromwell's head upon a Whitehall pillow likely. I feel it, as if it tugged at me still. Ravenscroft. As if the skies were a pivot and Ravenscroft and I but two points upon its overarching surface. Do you recall John Donne's poem of the drawing compass? The one fixed foot, that 'makes no show to move, but doth, if th' other do'?"

Miranda smiled and recited the next verse.

> *"And though it in the center sit,*
> *Yet when the other far doth roam,*
> *It leans and harkens after it*
> *And grows erect, as that comes home . . .*

"See, Kit, 'home' again. 'Tis natural to yearn for it, to weep for it."

He didn't answer for long seconds and when he did, it was with the last verse of the late poet's poem.

> *"Such wilt thou be to me, who must*
> *Like the other foot, obliquely run;*
> *Thy firmness makes my circle just,*
> *And makes me end where I begun."*

Miranda was afraid to speak. He had somehow juggled mental metaphors; it was no longer Ravenscroft of which he spoke.

"Such wilt thou be to me . . ." Her mind clutched at the intimacy of those words as at a charm. He was telling her something, but what? He, who must "obliquely run," and she, who must "in the center sit"? Like an island, and he the currents that wash past it? She was too weary for riddles and spoke only to the obvious.

" 'In my end is my beginning.' 'Twas Mary Stuart's motto, Kit. Does her grandson King Charles spy down on us from a yonder star, do you think? Does he begin elsewhere?"

"I know not." Kit's voice sounded as remote as the stars.

Miranda would have given the moon to hear it vibrate as it had a moment before when he had spoken John Donne's words. But the moment had fallen into the sea, like an unlucky falling star, and Miranda no longer believed that she could catch a falling star.

Chapter Forty-four

"Soon, Miranda, soon. Kit says 'twill be but days ere we see this marvelous island of yours."

"It had better be soon, for I fear Monsieur de Rognon's galley magic will make me as wide as a sea turtle. Help me with my bodice laces, Marjory."

Marjory lanced Miranda with a veiled look from under bleached lashes.

"What ails you, Marjory? I trust I shall not lace you with laughter when Monsieur de Rognon's culinary conspiracy sets *you* thick about the middle."

Miranda put her arms akimbo at her delinquent waist and stared stonily at her swelling bosom while Marjory accomplished the lacing.

"Oh, Miranda. You're as thick-headed as you are waisted. 'Tis not the food. Surely, you of all people must know—"

"Know what?"

" 'Tis the child swells you out, that's made you morning-ill these weeks."

"The—child?" Miranda spun around so swiftly that her untied laces abraded Marjory's hands.

" 'Tis obvious. I thought you knew. 'Tis fitting. Just as I brought Mother's jewels away from Ravenscroft, you carried something of your late husband away within your body. Such a pity, he must have died young. Yet even as Kit remains heir to Ravenscroft, your husband has an heir."

"Of course, so appropriate . . . but—don't tell your brother of this."

Miranda had caught one of Marjory's hands for emphasis. The girl winced as the grip bore down on lacerated skin, but a spark of independence flew into her gray eyes.

"Not tell Kit, as we did with Father? You find much unsuitable to Kit. Very well, I promise that from this moment forth, my lips shall be sealed like a Spaniard's chest upon the subject. Now loose my hand."

"I would not burden him with—matters best left to women. He would fret and fuss and doubtless blow us right by Barbados, all for the sake of something that is no mystery to us," said Miranda lightly.

Marjory plied the laces in guilty silence. She had already told her brother and he had reacted with just that degree of out-of-character fussiness that Miranda predicted. Even his mad escapade with the French merchant ship had been a transparent attempt to tease Miranda's sea-tormented palate, though she seemed unaware of it.

Marjory drew the last lace taut and made a thoughtful bow of it. "I'm sorry, Miranda, if I've said aught to displease you."

"Of course, you haven't. 'Tis only that I'm tired and cross

from all this sequestering below. Run up to deck for your sunshine while you may, Marjory, or you'll be rocking company to me; as you can see, I'm not suited for it."

Marjory nodded at Miranda's too-pale face and left the shadowed cabin. Miranda slowly sat upon the bed, as if she doubted it was there, then leaned against the cabin side, her arms cradled tightly across her stiff bodice front.

She had no doubt whatsoever that Marjory spoke the truth. With child, of course. With child these more than two months past, since she had brought the lavender cushion to Christopher Steele and he had later brought her to bed on Carmina's well-carpeted marble . . . She had a sudden longing for the figured shawl that had been the pivot of all those quick-swirling events. She was chilled, she would have wrapped it round her.

Just as that shawl had served as lure that night, another and more permanent lure for Christopher Steele was within her grasp all too literally, Miranda realized. She had but to repair quietly to his cabin, lay out the cards of her condition and sweep him off the table with the stakes.

That she could even consider such a course struck her with a wave of shame. All it would require would be stripping the veil from Justin Waverleigh's memory, a few disparaging but true remarks about his manhood, a long silence or two. All it would require would be taking Kit's good nature in hand and turning it back upon itself. And why would she do it? Only because the revelation of her condition had left her shaken, lonely and what—a trifle possessive?

She had secreted a piece of him away, after all—she felt a tender surge of warmth for the burgeoning memory within her. It was his, as she was his, heart and soul. To that she would cling through all the sickness and fear. She required no more of him than that. 'Twas clear he required no more of her, else he would not be content to watch her from across the chasm of his creation she had sensed between them since he had stepped from the *Dowsabelle*'s quarter boat and into more Thames fog than he knew.

Miranda moaned softly to herself, feeling she had begun already the agonizing delivery of an ignoble thought. It washed from her with her tears, the rejected firstborn of her union with Kit. Possession. The kind of love-child that truly earns its bar sinister. Passion's bastard, a grappling hook of the flesh . . . No, one could not anchor a person, as one did an insensate thing. He must ride his own wind and waves.

And if some inner tide brought him ashore on her again, she would be there, always waiting, an undiscovered island on his sea charts, that which "in the center sit." And waits. Ah, John Donne, did you know of waiting, late Dean of St. Paul's, late poet? Early man of passion and late man of God? Perhaps the two were incompatible, after all. Perhaps one could not love well and be good. Miranda's fingers slid mechanically down the smooth silken bodice of her gown. Flat still, but thicker surely. Beginning to grow. Oh, she wished him with her! But she could never, never force him, not even with the truth.

Above her, Christopher Steele sat with the Indies charts spread across his slanted desk. His eyes traveled the convoluted Central American coastline, the lacy undulations of ink that indicated New Andalusia on the northern coast of South America—a place future generations would know as Venezuela.

To Christopher Steele the chart spoke not of the future, but of the present. He was sailing to this New World to escape an old one grown curdled. Santo Domingo, Hispaniola—the New World names for islands and cities all spoke with a Spanish accent. He sailed for the Spanish Main, into the very heart of what the grandees of Seville and Cádiz regarded as their inalienable right from the Deity. Any ship not a Spaniard was fair game for sinking and looting. Any man or woman not Iberian-born faced torture and death for piracy.

And yet—there, that wart of an island at the easternmost point on a string of similarly impertinent islands challenging the Atlantic's uninterrupted fury—that was Barbados. Where he was bound. Where a band of English as impertinent as their ladle-shaped island chose to spit in the Spanish eye. No wonder the Barbados-reared one the *Dowsabelle* bore back to that defiant little speck was as tough-hided as a native pineapple. One did not awake every day facing into a thousand miles of arbitrary ocean and a nest of hostile Spaniards for naught.

He was suddenly minded to seek her out and peel her like an island fruit, strip away that hard-edged outer self that always held him at bay. Not always. He had peeled beneath the surface once and found her softness even more wounding than her outer guard. Perhaps it was always that way between the sexes. What did he know of women, at any rate? No more than he knew of

Ravenscroft cattle, a coarse analogy but apt. He had desired the one product of his native Dorset and familial ties that was utterly rotten, the overripe Roxanne. He admitted to an almost relief to find her faithless, as if somewhere he had already sickened of his own hunger.

Miranda. She was foreign, he had always thought that. Yet he yearned for her as Raleigh for his golden, glimmering distant El Dorado. And what had Raleigh earned for it? His own fair head upon the block. Such was recompense for visionaries. Visionaries who coveted another man's gold. Or another man's wife, another man's widow, another man's child like a foreign island within her.

Sin and death. 'Twas what the preachers said was the totality of man's earthly lot. Christopher Steele had done his share of one and seen his fill of the other. Why should he expect any omniscient generosity to hand him a slice of paradise? Yet he would claim it all, settle upon her like an unwanted guest and drive her native claimants out. An unworthy ambition; this time at least he would leave her to herself, as he should have in the *Salamander* cabin, in the Bey of Tunis's borrowed tented pleasure dome, in Carmina's now-deserted London chamber.

He now saw his deepest inclinations as his basest. He had ever been an opportunist, and now he had her within the palm of his opportunity—alone, child-heavy, bereft of brother, husband (and him she must have loved, if she could love in that man's absence a man who had so injured her as Christopher Steele). Fit torment for his sins that she should never be so near as now, and so remote—a mere shape from some other's map that he must stare at upon the page and never claim . . .

He memorized the Barbados configuration, looking past the fancifully finned fish the chartmaker had drawn onto the paper. There. He would take her there, where the Dutchman had aimed her a deceitful year ago. Then he would make a pilgrimage back to what he knew and no longer needed. To France. And Holland. To find his brothers, gather the scattered Steeles together for his dead parents' sake. He, who had begun by finding her brother, now sent to search for his own. Irony. And honor. They ever ran a parallel course, like two coach wheels upon a road never meant for such a conveyance.

Irony and honor. And Miranda.

* * *

"We'll make your island by the next day or two," he told her abruptly at dinner that evening.

" 'Tis not my island," she objected mildly, "but that of any who care to live there."

"Yours and Marjory's, then," he answered brusquely.

Marjory looked up from Monsieur de Rognon's latest innovation with goose liver. Her brother's eyes were riveted to Miranda's knife-work on the plate, as if he studied how she sliced her meat. Miranda's lashes remained serenely anchored on her cheeks.

"You do not remain on Barbados, then?" she asked calmly, bringing a knifeful of meat to her mouth.

"No."

Miranda set the morsel down, as if she had just noticed it and found it oddly foreign. "Where will you go?" Her fingers toyed with her goblet's spun-glass stem.

"To wherever something of England remains. That will doubtless be France and Holland. I must find Sydney and Philip."

"Your brothers." Miranda intoned the words to her glass and then tilted her head back to take a long sip.

"Oh, Kit, you will find them!" Marjory was overjoyed.

"I will try."

"And bring them back?"

"Only if they wish it, Marjory. They are nearly men grown now, they have fought for the King. They may wish to persist in that battle." He, too, took a long draught of wine.

"Are we to wait there on Barbados, not knowing if we shall ever see any of you again?" Marjory began to comprehend what his decision would mean.

"I can send word." He smiled faintly. "Word and—a pair of red-heeled slippers from France."

"Kit—don't." Marjory's tears salted her food in sudden drops.

"Don't fret, Marjory mine. Miranda will care for you." Marjory's tears streamed unheeding. "And you will care for Miranda."

An order underlay his voice that brought Marjory's drooping head to attention. She met her brother's eyes and honed herself on the edge in them.

"Yes. I shall take care of Miranda, and she of me. We will do quite well on our own."

He nodded and every head bent back to its plate. It was as if a pact had been signed there in the small captain's cabin. A pause was broken only by the scrape of knife on plate. Miranda hoisted her goblet at the same moment that Kit raised his. Their eyes met over their respective brims, then they both quaffed the last of their cups.

He reached for the bottle and she thrust her goblet forth so quickly that her ruby ring rang on the green glass, like a ship's bell tolling a change in watch. He poured a rich vein of red into her goblet, the rim chattering nervously against the bottle.

Marjory thrust her empty goblet forward, gazing at each of them in turn. Kit finally turned the flow into her vacant goblet. Miranda drank hers hastily, like water, and rose so rapidly her skirts nearly overturned her stool.

"I'm going on deck."

Each sway of the lantern after her exit lit up a different emotion in Kit's face. Marjory studied them all and could name not one. He, too, was standing and excusing himself. Marjory sighed and helped herself to the last of the wine. They were obviously fretting over matters too deep for her, the sort of things with which those said to be truly grown-up concern themselves. For herself, there were times when it was helpful to not see the full meaning of things.

Miranda had stationed herself at the larboard gunwale, the vessel's Barbados-facing side. Kit came up behind her, as she had hoped he would ... and would not. The stars, luminous and large as saucers, were unmistakably southern now, not the brittle northern points of light under which they had talked but a fortnight before.

He stood behind her, his body swaying as harmoniously with the *Dowsabelle*'s roll as her own.

"Look," said Miranda finally, the first to concede his presence. "How odd, the very wave crests appear to shine."

He stepped forward; she could feel the press against the back of her full skirts. His hand materialized on the gunwale next to her own.

"Yes, very odd. 'Tis more than moonlight. See, it's a veritable patch of shimmer and we're riding into it."

Each distant wave crested into the night in glittering silver spray now and the phenomenon seeped across the horizon as the *Dowsabelle* plowed sturdily forward. In minutes the very waves they had seen from afar were lapping at the ship's plain wooden sides with silvery licks until a ring of phosphorescence circled her along the waterline.

"Kit, what is it? Have you ever—?"

"No, never."

He called a crewman to fetch a bucket and they delved into the water below. Kit impatiently hauled the line up himself and lofted a bucket brimful with glowing silver.

"By the Cross, a Spanish plate fleet must have sunk here and this is her soul floating to the surface. Such glimmer would light a cabin—take it below, Rendall, and try my theory."

He shook his hands free of the water. They shone faintly silver in the moonlight.

"Kit—don't touch it. It may be Devil's Fire; we are in strange seas. Leave it!"

He laughed. "I've sailed enough seas to know Milady Ocean has more surprises in her belly than Leviathan. You're not afraid?"

"Yes, 'tis something odd about this sea . . . I feel a strange pull—don't laugh. I think you're right: a flotilla sank here once. I can feel the draw of her rusted chains, hear the call of her ghostly crew. Her plate is a magnet for us, all her spilled silver on the bottom."

" 'Tis some New World phenomenon, that's all. A will-o'-the-wisp of the deep to guide us our last part of the journey."

"No! These seas do not offer kindly tokens. They are ever treacherous."

He had hemmed her in at the gunwale, his hands bracketing her between himself and the wood. The phosphorescence reflected off the white of her collar, the bones of her face and sheets of pale hair. His own hands on either side of her still shone silver, as if mailed in seawater.

"How can such beauty be treacherous?" he asked, his voice as liquid as the element upon which they sailed.

She wheeled, aware of a rarer phenomenon at her back than any that worried her over the water. The moonlight and the sea magic that matched it made him ghostly. Their mutual resolves were suddenly beaten thin, perhaps because they had always been a false façade, like sheet metal over lead. Like silver plating.

It was a moment for melting; she ran into his instantly encircling arms like molten metal. He tilted up her moon-white face and burnished it with his lips. The phosphorescence painted her silver-cool, but her flesh was paradoxically warm, like his own, and he reminted her features to the shape of his mouth as he traced a lover's infinite variety of routes across them.

It was cool passion they forged between them, it would dissipate in soft pressings, and lingering kisses that did not demand satisfaction, it would lock words within lips and fold hearts away in secret velvet boxes. It would be a phenomenon as easy to deny in daylight as the silver sea.

Miranda suddenly slid away from him. "Kit, listen," she breathed. There was no endearment, no intimacy on her mind. "Mortal danger awaits out there. Heed it."

By morning the seas were ordinary blue. Yet they were sluggish, heaving long rolls of wave toward the *Dowsabelle* to thunder upon her hull and dissipate. No beads of mercury danced upon their crests, no sheen burnished their motion.

A mossy smell tinged the air. The sky was washing gray, misty, a faint fog was stealing over the horizon. They saw their first sail in a month asea—a lone speck on the horizon, instantly large enough for the naked eye to see.

The winds fell, as if weighed down by the spiritless sky. The *Dowsabelle*'s canvas was teased this way and that to catch the most fugitive breeze, but eventually hung heavy and had to be furled into lumpy gray lengths against the masts. A three-masted sailing ship with her canvas furled on an empty sea looked like Calvary from the deck below.

Something more stole across the planking, a lassitude almost as tangible as fog, that saw the sailors gathering in the forecastle to coil hemp and whistle eerily into the still air.

In the distance something thick and green coiled like an endless serpent and stretched out long feathered tentacles to the merry little *Dowsabelle* buffeting softly toward it on an almost waveless sea.

" 'Tis unnatural." Kit's fists against the gunwale almost pushed the ship forward. Beside him, Bacon, the first mate, shook his head, Miranda's pendant emerald glittering from his pierced ear.

"More than unnatural, sir. Devilish. It be Satan's work."

"Nonsense, man!"

Kit had no more than that to say and returned to his cabin, where he pored over the charts for the third time that morning. Finally his finger fell on the spot he had avoided since dawn—

the serpentine letters above the Windward Islands of which Barbados was the southernmost. His finger traced the tortured script until he surrendered and voiced its message. "The Sargasso Sea."

If he were off course, over-far north, then he could have very well blown into the heart of it: a murky, weed-choked patch of hellish water where the sturdiest ship was helpless. Where lost flotillas were said to slowly swirl until nothing but flotsam remained of their timbers.

Their true course was due west. Were he north of the Windwards in the Sargasso Sea, their compass's painted seven-pointed star should show the error as truly as any celestial pinpoint.

He clattered to the helmsman's station at the whipstaff, just forward of the Great Cabin. The man at the staff regarded his captain with unspoken amazement as Kit wrenched the golden circle into the brighter light of the latticed hatchway above.

There, where the gilded fleur-de-lis represented true north, there the needle hung—no, it was *moving*, spinning leisurely on the decorated dial called a compass rose. Now northeast . . . impossible, now east . . . now—Kit watched the slender needle flirt past each compass point, like a lady making her silken rounds in the cushion dance. The needle ended where it had begun, stopped, swung backward and recommenced its circle at a faster rate.

"Watkins! How long has the compass been so fickle?"

The helmsman leaned an attentive face away from his whipstaff, but his hand remained sure upon the wood.

"Why, Captain, I'd not noticed . . . M'God, sir, it be spinnin' like a loblolly boy's 'ead after 'is first ration o' rum! I never seen such madness."

Kit cradled the brass bowl in his hands until he warmed it. Still the needle accelerated; now it spun almost merrily around the dial divided into the world's four corners by fine-drawn lines.

So where was beginning, end? North, south. Southwest they should be steering. "In my end is my beginning . . ." The lines of Donne he had recited but a fortnight earlier came to haunt him. In his beginning was his end? Was every Steele drawn to disaster like a compass needle to true north?

He clattered to deck again to find Miranda and his sister at the gunwale and himself annoyed that they should witness his befuddlement. He joined them to stare grimly at the creeping tangle of rotting green wafting toward them. A few far-flung tentacles were plucking greasily at the *Dowsabelle*'s decent wooden hull already.

"The Sargasso," said Miranda.

He nodded, bitter that the lips he had kissed the previous night should mouth his failure. He had brought them straight for the slimy heart of the Sargasso Sea. Last evening's silver had been the whited sepulcher that leads to it and she had warned him.

Becalmed in the Sargasso Sea. No wonder the air hung sulphurously heavy on the masts, that the sun dimmed behind a spreading pall of mist.

"That other ship seems to move well enough, and she stands in the center of it." Miranda sounded matter-of-fact.

"At least we have a partner in our peril," noted Kit, calling for the perspective glass. "A high-pooped breed, likely some Dutch merchant homeward bound from Curaçao. Aye, the bastard is moving! Bacon, can we tease enough wind from above to float nearer that Hollander?"

The *Dowsabelle* creaked gallantly with effort, but her canvas hung as hollow as an empty wineskin.

"Damn. I'd give my soul to know how that foreigner sets his vessel against a wind that doesn't exist. Look at him skitter like a water bug. Bound away, I warrant. We shall be alone with our misery." Kit thrust the glass into Bacon's waiting hand and paced a narrow length of deck.

The day wore on, like a chain around a capstan. An inexorable sludge of gulf weed slithered around the *Dowsabelle* and embraced her. It tangled in her wooden rudder and left a moss-green scum on her unpainted sides. It resembled thick green glass, a substance that must be shattered before the seawater would float them free.

At three bells, Kit stripped off his limp linen shirt. "I'm going overboard to see how thick it is."

"You cannot swim," Miranda objected.

"In that, it does not matter." He threw a bucket over the side and pointed to it floating on the encroaching thick green tide.

Marjory and Miranda hung silently over the gunwale while he climbed down into the seaborne jungle, blanching as the green strands sucked over him like quicksand. He worked his way around to the rudder and finally returned, dripping slick green grasses like graveyard cerements.

"A foot thick, and woven round our rudder like a skin," he

said, shaking his wet head while dripping weed and water to the boards. He looked up, then focused on the horizon.

"By God, there's our fellow ship again. And moving still! The glass, Bacon. What colors does she carry?"

He looked through the glass for a long time. When he lowered it, his voice was wary. "No colors. Yet she's moving . . . toward us."

The putrid green marsh sucked softly at the *Dowsabelle*'s sides, kissed her slimily. The ship's motion had stilled so much that she felt as solid and safe as land. The *Dowsabelle*'s crew and passengers had ceased to fret at the carpet of weed that clogged her progress. They watched instead the dirty gray sail that skimmed the Sargasso like a gull, dancing here and there, on the horizon, in and out of shrouds of mist. Yet coming closer, always closer, across the still and weed-wrapped sea.

Kit called for the glass again and stared through its unreliable eye, until the eyepiece left a weary circle impressed to his face.

"I can see her cabins, her masts—but no crew. There, at the gunwale, I see her captain, with a glass glued to his eye like my own, like a damned teasing reflection."

"Kit. Let me see it."

He handed Miranda the glass, for there was iron in her voice that he had not heard since they had shared passage to England, and little else, on the *Gato de Nueve*.

Miranda wet her lips and raised the glass to her eye. She was frozen for a long moment, then she tore the perspective glass away from her face as if it burned her.

"What? What do you see?"

" 'Tis a flaw within your glass," she answered breathlessly.

"No flaw," Kit returned. "I peered through it but moments ago."

"It must be a flaw. A flaw! I see *him*, the ship's captain, but Kit, he's upside down in the glass!"

Kit appropriated the tube and trained it on the nearing vessel. "No. The mists roll a bit before my eyes, but he stands there still, as do I. Feet deckward, head skyward."

Miranda held out a hand and brought the eyepiece to her face again after one small pause. "Nay, he rides upside down, reversed like a Hanged Man in a tarot deck, I tell you. But right side up or Devil side down, I would know him. It is the Dutchman."

He ripped the glass from her grip, but did not raise it to his eye again. "Are you certain?"

"My memory is very good, Captain, I assure you." Her eyes were as green and inescapable as the weed around them.

He nodded. The ship's bells began to toll evening watch, but the sea and sky were still milky and veiled. A subtle sort of sheen reared up from the weeds and vibrated on the horizon. The mist hissed slowly shut around them, like a bed curtain.

The ship before them wavered for a moment, then vanished behind a wall of oncoming fog. In an instant that fog had blanketed them, until they were only ghostly voices on the deck.

"The Dutchman," Kit repeated.

"Yes, I swear it."

With the mist had come sudden, greedy dark. The ship's lanterns were rapidly lit by the crew and as rapidly dimmed to faint points in the fog, tiny stars in a moonless sky.

"Take Marjory below," Kit instructed Miranda.

She complied, but surfaced through the mist at his side moments later.

"Stay below," he ordered. " 'Tis my fault we steered into this hellish place."

" 'Tis my Dutchman," returned Miranda.

"Do you know what you say? What he would be if he hangs out there beyond the mist? We may freeze for eternity upon this brackish water, with ever your Dutchman to wink an immortal eye at us."

"You said he was evil and would in time be destroyed."

"I thought him but a mortal man then, not one who—listen!"

They concentrated intently in the dark, hearing the ragged edge of their own breathing, the scuffle of crewmen across the fog-obscured deck, then . . . a quiet sucking, slurping sound followed by a distant creaking.

They also heard the rhythmic screech that wood and rope and canvas make when they waft across the water. A ship was lurching toward them in the misty dark, across the weeds as thick as lawn.

A sudden whip of wind hissed boldly across the Dowsabelle's deck, wind enough to whip the sheets against the masts, to tear the furled sails from their mountings, to set the masts swaying and falling. Miranda waited for her hair to stream across her face, for her skirts to billow like sails. She was ready to shout her words across to Kit wind-rippling but two feet from her.

Nothing moved.

The howl accelerated, piping like forgotten notes from a simple whistle, from the whistle dropped to the *Salamander*'s deck months and months before. Muffin's whistle, dear dead Muffin.

"Muffin," she called into the shriek. "Muffin!" A creak from starboard overrode the howling wind. A ship was hard upon them, driving to rub hull-to-hull, to slam broadside into the *Dowsabelle*.

Kit caught Miranda in his arms, as if that would stop the wind's wail, the invisible ship's creak—there, three points of St. Elmo's fire burning lavender through the mast-top fog like ghostly ship's lanterns.

The flames glided forward, vanished, and the *Dowsabelle* lurched slightly in the seaweed, as if some leviathan had slithered by to pull her into its wake. Ahead of them came a steady clank of chains.

"You see, Kit," whispered Miranda into his nearby ear. "Long-ago-sunk galleons, come to claim us. A fleet of silver sank here; look, even the mist shimmers with it now."

He caught her hand and pulled her forward, where one unearthly flame still flickered and a silver phosphorescence spilled over the bows like rain.

"Sweet Jesus," said Kit, invoking as well as swearing. The ectoplasmic ship creaked unabated before them, driven by the invisible wind that screeched in their ears but left the *Dowsabelle*'s deck unruffled by so much as a hair.

Then something whistled sharply through the heavy air like a cannonball winging wide of the mark. Came a rending, a tearing of wood from wood so near that Kit and Miranda stepped back as one.

Before them, beneath the dim glow of the ship's forward lantern, the wood of the bow peeled back as if a great iron claw had clutched it. The grain splintered before their eyes, whatever attacked it biting deep. Another arching whistle sounded and the larboard-side wood cracked away from itself in one slow, rending motion.

Ahead of them, the hollow clank of chain being drawn taut circled methodically.

Then slightly, ever so slowly, with a motion more thought than reality, the *Dowsabelle* glided into a sail-less movement. Kit and Miranda felt a faint breeze across their faces, felt their hair waft back as if stroked by an unseen hand. The chains ahead rattled rhythmically.

"We're moving." Kit sounded grim. "By saint or Devil, I know not which to invoke, but we're moving through this unholy muck. Without wind, without sail ... without direction."

He caught Miranda's hand so hard the ruby grazed him and then he pulled her below to the helmsman's station.

Watkins was the only one of the *Dowsabelle*'s crew not huddled in the forecastle murmuring forgotten prayers. Perhaps he remained on duty because he had not heard the malevolent wind abovedecks, or seen the seaweed's myriad mouths sucking, or the evil mist that shrouded the stripped masts like phantom sails.

Kit searched frantically for a lantern to illuminate the compass in its box, struggling with flint while he looked.

"Kit, wait! You'll not need your ordinary light." Miranda's hand upon his arm stopped him; they stared at the compass set within its fine-carved box.

The needle wallowed still within its circumscribed limits, floating slowly, toying with direction. A ghastly ring of St. Elmo's fire irradiated from it, lighting every waver of the needle.

Kit cupped his hands around the glowing brass, then drew them back as if fire-scorched. The unearthly lavender-pink color lit their hovering faces. Kit looked at Miranda and thought of rose velvet lapping at her like a jewel-box lining at a pearl. Her eyes were only on the ornate compass rose, as if she saw her future written in it.

"Look, Kit, the needle slows. It's bearing us south. South-*west!*"

"Southwest?" He looked again, unbelieving. The needle nodded softly at the elongated script of "SW" and then clung precisely on the point.

"Is not southwest our proper bearing? Kit, does it not take us homeward? To Barbados?"

"Yes, if the needle does not lie." He brought his eyes, almost deep purple in the reflected rose-glow, to hers. "Did not your Dutchman set a southwest course for you a year ago? A course from which you veered? I believe he rides out there, and he would drag us all on his own immortal course. Southwest lies the Devil's domain, and all our destruction."

Miranda cupped her hands around the compass for answer. The St. Elmo's glow faded with her touch, but the needle kept its bearing—southwest.

"No. I think we take the Dutchman's course—I shall believe it till I die—but we are not destruction-bent. He is drawing me home, I know it. So he set me a year ago and so he shall see me now. He is not as evil as you say, Kit; nor as greedy as the don would have had me believe. He let me go a year ago—"

"Setting your course for certain destruction."

"He let me go, Kit. And so he has again."

Kit took the compass from her. It was cool to the touch, but damp, as a brow after the fever has broken. He restored it to its place.

They walked on deck together. The wind's roar had shriveled away, the mist had withdrawn. No unseen chains ground their links in the dark beyond the bow.

The *Dowsabelle* rocked softly, aimlessly, upon a sea that no longer stuck to her like lethal mud. Clear dark simple starlit night fell beyond the bright burning of the ship's great lanterns. Furled sails flapped slightly in the fresh wind that shook them.

"Loose the sails," Kit called to the still-quavering crew. "We've a fresh, fair wind to blow us Barbados way, and the polestar to guide us there."

The crew scurried to their stations, suddenly not men at the brink of death but mere seamen duty-derelict.

"Aye, it blows above," Kit said quietly to Miranda. "And I care not whether it be Beelzebub's cheeks himself that puff us on our course; 'tis a good wind and I'll ride it. Yet I pray it blows your Dutchman far from our path by morning."

BOOK FIVE:

The Ladylove

And that this place may thoroughly be thought
True paradise, I have the serpent brought....
                    —John Donne, 1633

Chapter Forty-five

*B*y morning the mist had risen as effectively as a curtain, revealing a world glazed blue with sea and sky. Not a cloud drifted in the overarching blue; not a spot of sail teased at the horizon's edge.

Sometime in the dark, the Dutchman had drawn up his ghostly chains and clanked away into someone else's nightmares. The *Dowsabelle*'s compass needle pointed unerringly southwest and her prow dipped deeply into the Atlantic waters to plow just such a course.

A new shower of silver greeted the sea-weary sailors as they neared their voyage's conclusion—not unearthly phosphorescence now, but bright shifting rainbows of flying fish, arching out of the waves.

"Miranda! 'Tis like some court astrologer's vision of the sign Pisces. What fish are these? Or birds?"

"Nay, those are birds," Miranda told Marjory, pointing to a trio of tropical fowl above them, their ribald patches of color jesterlike in the sunshine.

Kit joined them at the gunwale. "We should sight land soon, if my charts don't lie and the Dutchman's compass works as well on earth as in hell."

"Hush, Kit, you'll frighten Marjory if you talk so."

They both glanced to the girl hanging over the rail with her honey curls sticking to the breeze, her eyes dancing to follow the leaping squadrons of airborne fish.

"I'll frighten myself if I talk so," he confessed wryly.

A shout from the crow's nest made him bring the perspective glass he carried to his eye. He smiled and offered it to Miranda, but she shook her head, instead leaning forward to wait for the promised land to swell in the sea in front of her.

It did, suddenly growing from a rough stretch of steady green to the high gray cliffs laced with white sand at the waterline that was Barbados' face to the arriving European. Even Miranda had never seen it so; it quite took her breath away. A dense tropical growth twined over the cliff face, so the whole was as darkly green as an emerald in a dim room. The brilliant white beach slashed the prominence foot like a scar as the Atlantic waters roiled gently on the sand in shifting shades of aquamarine. A great sail-backed fish leapt suddenly into the sunlight, a chartmaker's symbol brought to life.

"Ah, Brave New World," mused Kit, leaning his elbows along the gunwale, "that has such creatures in it." His glance finally rested on Miranda. " 'Tis your world and only serves to remind me that mine is an Old World indeed, with old sins for which to atone, old causes for which to fight and old crimes to avenge. No wonder Raleigh was so enamored of his quest for El Dorado. Raleigh's folly. That is what you can name your Barbados plantation, Mistress Miranda, if such christening amuse you. Raleigh's Folly."

"If I were to name it after any who had lost his head, I'd be more likely to choose the late King," answered Miranda stoutly. "I'll call it Hathaway House."

"You hath a way of returning always to your roots, no matter who pays the fare. 'Tis a quality much to be desired."

"Is it better than mercy?"

"I think mercy is merely another name for forgetfulness. We both have a deal to forget; I wish us well in it."

Marjory's tug on both their sleeves ended their discussion, though what lay beneath it gave Miranda a new stirring of unease, almost as if an internal seasickness now had her in its grip.

The ship was working its way along the island's leeward side and bringing the clear scythe of Carlisle Bay and Bridgetown's terraced streets into view.

"You mustn't overshoot the island, else you will have a Devil's time of it beating back," warned Miranda, repeating by rote what she'd heard muttered by all new-landed seafarers.

"I can read me a chart," responded Kit testily, striding away nevertheless to shorten sail. Marjory had inherited the glass and ran to larboard as the ship circled into the bay.

" 'Tis a bigger town than I thought and, look, the houses have two and three stories! I feared they might be hovels. The growing things look quite like a, an ordinary Dorset garden."

"Aye." Miranda came slowly to the gunwale. " 'Tis changed. The great trees have been—cut. They grew closer to the water when I left, the candlewoods and cedars."

" 'Tis glorious, Miranda. I shan't be frightened here at all. Oh, but what's that? Is that a black man, there by the wharf? And another? We shall not have to worry with Kit leaving. We shall have a great quantity of black men to work for us."

Miranda caught the spyglass rudely away and trained it on a shoreline familiar, but overpainted with strange additions. The church spires were there still, but the English gabled roofs had multiplied, as had the cane fields in well-matched rows spreading round the settlement. The familiar forest had rolled back much farther along the terraces leading to the island's level central plateau. The jungle was retreating in formation, the island balding like a dotard's pate until only a fringe of original growth should cling to its prominent center.

And there, the flash of many brown and black bodies in the fields, at the wharves—nearly naked, it was impossible not to see them. African slaves had been imported to work the cane in her father's time, a few, but bondsmen in hopes of earning ten unsullied acres with an equal years' worth of labor, and transported Irish and Scots had provided the backs to build Barbados' sugar and tobacco enterprises before. Now mostly black bodies labored there, sweat-shiny in the sun, looking from this distance like the native ants that built busily across the soil and bit when bothered.

And where was her father's plantation, so visible always with its sugar refinery, one of the island's first? Now the smoke of such enterprises blotched the landscape at every turn. She could not mark the Hathaway holdings from among them.

Miranda let Marjory reclaim the glass; she was as loath to overlook her island as she had been to see the Dutchman's weary face floating upside down in the very same glass. She could almost hear his hollow laugh again, drifting across the *Dowsabelle*'s deck like a shadow on a cloudless day. Southwest he had sent her, southwest she was brought to home port and a sorry welcome she had of it.

So it was Marjory, not Miranda, who rushed into the island's open arms; Marjory who yearned ashore to gawk at the pineapple and pomagranate bushes growing like hedges in the gardens. Miranda led Kit and his suddenly spirited sister directly to the Gideon Bell house.

Bell was a loyal Royalist who had been her father's friend. That gentleman welcomed the party with open hammocks, with bowls of green turtle soup and roast wild pig hot from the spit, with sweet strong rum fresh from the fermenting.

"A house, is it, lass? In truth, I thought this island'd see you and your brother again. Gets in yer blood, like these damn merrywings!" Bell swatted one of the small biting insects that had strayed past the circling smoke fires into his sturdy-built house.

"Where be Harry now, the young whelp? Can't you stay on the Hathaway plantation?"

"No," answered Miranda, the Waverleigh jewel box on her knees as if she might be called upon at any moment to pay for something. "Harry and I have fallen on different sides. 'Tis the matter of—the late King."

"The late King? I've heard naught of that. By God, you've a tale to tell and had better begin. More rum for ye, Captain Steele; ye look like ye can handle it. And a touch for Mirandy—I've seen you swallow your share at yer father's elbow. No more for the young lass, she's an English rose, by St. George, and requires a sweeter watering."

They glanced to Marjory, flushed and nodding in her chair, and then turned to Gideon Bell to spill the story of the past two months' events.

"King-killers, the lot of 'em," he pronounced when their voices sank silent. "Harry's among 'em, you say. Puritans! Well, it won't suit for you to go knocking on his overseer's door, that's certain. You say you've the means, lass." Bell cocked his grizzled head toward the chest on Miranda's lap. "Your father was not one to rear a scatterbrain. I can find you a house and sixty acres of sweet cane that 'twill do for you three."

"Not I," said Kit quickly. "I sail as soon as they're settled."

"Sail, Captain Steele, with two English lasses to live on alone? I don't know—"

"I'd find it safer to swing my head to sleep in a Barbados hammock than to lay it on some Parliamentary block in London," noted Miranda.

"True, true, but we have our honest English beds now, all mos-quee-to-netted to keep the bleedin' little beggers out. 'Tis become a mighty enterprise, this sugar-growing, ever since the oversea merchants found our tobacco bitter. The great owners are consolidating the plantations, but we can find a proper little one to serve your needs."

"Must we trouble ourselves with a plantation—perhaps merely a house in Bridgetown?" Miranda suggested.

"Daft are you? Too much traffic through Bridgetown nowadays. No proper place for ladies to stay, mark my words. No, you want a place with a sturdy bar to the door and a hamletful of blacks outside to raise a cry should anything untoward occur. These blacks are a noisy breed, Captain, ready to warble as if the Second Coming were upon us at the drop of a boot."

Kit was absorbed in his island rum; he nodded absently and said nothing. Miranda had much to say but held her tongue. So Marjory kept the conversational fuel replenished, despite her flush, so well that Gideon Bell ended the evening by regaling her with tales of renegade flesh-eating Caribs that landed on the island from time to time still.

Perhaps he oversold island terrors, for three days later when he escorted the party to a strong stone house overlooking Carlisle Bay, Marjory spent her time looking over her shoulder and up the terraced landscape to the plateau brow.

"There are no Caribs there now, Marjory," Miranda finally reassured her. She glanced to Kit. He was focusing moodily on the *Dowsabelle* below, a furled ship drifting like a painting on the bay-blue water.

Miranda anchored on his countenance, watching it slip from her as certainly as a vessel blowing out to sea. Neither she nor Marjory paid much attention to a quick tour of the furnished premises.

"Well, now, lasses, the innards are yours as well as the outards, for the erstwhile owner succumbed but a fortnight ago to Barbados distemper. We've not got the thievish malaria on our island, Mistress Marjory, but breed our own brand of fever. So the lot is yours, Mirandy, for the outlay of gems in yer casket there. And forty strong-backed blacks to go with, as well as Easy Nellie to do in the house until her bond expire. A slattern and Irish atop, but women is hard to come by in these islands. I keep my old eye peeled for a fetching one, by God, but the Old World breezes blow only old whores here. 'Tis why I bachelor it still."

Bell tucked his hands behind his back and rocked back and forth on his rotting bootheels.

"Blacks?" inquired Miranda. "Slaves? Could I not have bondsmen instead? I do not relish having—"

"Ah, fret not. True, you're used to bond servants, but they make a reluctant field worker, no matter how you beat 'em. If it's a caretaker you're fretted about, I've found a fine fellow below in town, who sojourned on the island hitherto. A foreigner, true, but I have a pound upon it that you'll be proper pleased to employ him as overseer."

Bell winked broadly at a mystified Kit on the last prophesy. Miranda appeared unimpressed.

"No games, Master Bell. My father said never to buy Barbados tobacco unsniffed nor Madeira sugar untasted, so I must know what you propose to install upon us before we subscribe."

Bell leaned toward her, his cloved breath bearing news he thought would rest as sweetly on her ears. "A surprise and you have defrauded me of it. 'Tis an old acquaintance of yours I found drifting through the Green Bottle. A Spaniard with a long narrow sword and a nose to match. Your brother's old tutor, Francisco—the de Salazar your father depended upon so."

"Francisco!" Miranda's eyes glittered so hotly green that Steele had her by the arm and away from Bell in a moment. "Francisco?" she demanded of the very air, her hand going to her waist for weapon and finding only a pelmet.

"Hush. It may not be such an evil coincidence."

"You know how he betrayed my father with my—"

"I was on the *Gato de Nueve* as well as you, but Harry is a Puritan now, with no need of a partner in sin. So the Spaniard has drifted here again. 'Tis opportune. I would sail away easier if I knew a canny swordsman like Francisco shared your circumstances."

"Kit, you know what kind of man he is. You would leave us here with him?"

"I have known his kind of man long before I knew him. There is no outright evil in the fellow, I'll be sworn. If you deny him your old regard because of what he was to Harry—well, the balance weighs equal in that he is the perfect guardian for you and Marjory, as is a toothless cat upon a mouse."

Miranda stewed. Kit was attempting to placate her with a hasty, hushed explanation of his logic. Logic, it was, but then Christopher Steele did not know what longings may reside within even a eunuch's breast, had not heard Harry accuse Miranda of causing Francisco's original sin. Englishmen found Barbados' untreed terraces hot. Kit Steele was flushed, impatient; he looked a stripling aching to be off playing with his fountain full of ships rather than debating domestic arrangements.

Then let him go as he obviously longed to, she thought. She would not weigh him down with any ballast, be it the whisper of Francisco's true temptations or a shout of her own circumstances, which even now stirred within her.

"Very well. He'll have to make shift with Bridgetown lodgings; I won't share the house with him."

Kit urged her back to Marjory and Master Bell, like a reluctant sail he would put fresh wind to.

Miranda looked about the garden Justin's jewels had bought. She glanced over the distant, straight rows of cane stalks to the clot of grass-thatched huts beyond. Below her, gabled roofs rose in dark tiled waves to meet the glittering waves of the bay. Farther below her, Kit Steele's *Dowsabelle* rode prettily at anchor. And somewhere shadowed likely, Francisco lounged in a bayside bottlehouse. Both men would have back what they wanted most: a place in a world that welcomed them, that they trusted to. Save she. A fitting price for Justin Waverleigh's head lying askew upon the flame-stitching.

Like the Dutchman's eerie vessel, Miranda was launched on her own lonely journey. She would blow heavy with sail, glide through fogs that confounded mortal man into that vague, feminine world of generation. She feared the voyage, feeling compassless. Yet she was as utterly bound to her physical fate as the Dutchman to his spiritual one, and she would drag no reluctant crewman along on her destiny. No matter how he glittered.

Miranda reminded herself of her resolve two days later when she and Marjory stood with Kit outside the house again. This occasion for farewells told her more than ever that she was truly embarked; she could feel the tug of tide within her. And "first mate" would not be too ironic a berth for Christopher Steele. All she need do was whisper the truth—she could picture his eyes paling with shock, could see the sudden wrinkles crease his bronzed face as if acid had been thrown into it. He would stay, yes, swear devotion, pamper her with repentance until they both grew sick upon it ... The vision was so awful she turned away from it with renewed conviction.

"Bell was right," he told her. "You'll need the income from the cane to keep yourself here. Prices seem to rise even as one looks upon the goods."

Kit turned his plumed hat around in his hands. He was booted and sashed for a formal occasion. They could have been in some English garden with linnets over the next hedge. Indeed, Miranda had the oddest feeling that the stone house behind her—though cedar and not oak sketched out its limits—was a proper English dwelling, with proper English service within, for Kit had pressed his shipboard plate and glass upon her, as though he could not bear to have them lack for anything within his power to grant them. Except himself.

" 'Tis your native island, Miranda, as England is to me. You shall thrive here, like one of your exotic fruits. Best you forget what transpired over half a world of ocean. Those loved ones you . . . lost there."

He spoke of Justin Waverleigh, the Justin Waverleigh who prowled his mind, a mighty figure who wielded the fact of his marriage to Miranda and subsequent tragic death before him like a broadsword.

She thought Kit spoke of Harry, Harry among his shadowed tomes. And Muffin in his eternal whale's belly.

Neither questioned the other's reference point.

"Miranda . . ." He leaned toward her then, the hat fixed in his hands for the first time, his eyes fixed full upon her for the last time. "Miranda, take care of—" A call from within the house, a flash of flying locks at the door. " . . . of—of Marjory."

She was there, his sister, her eyes raw from secret weeping, her hands locked around his fresh white falling band, crushing it.

"Don't weep, Marjory," he urged lightly. "I'll be riding enough salt water soon." He kissed his sister's wet cheeks and turned again to Miranda.

Surprised, he saw the European stiffness was slipping off her already; her throat-high collar was unbuttoned against the heat, her skirts swelled with a Barbados breeze, as darkly green as the darker side of the island.

Continental Europeans were scandalized that Englishwomen were so free with their kisses to friends and guests and even strangers. Greeting or going, an English lady was quicker to offer her lips than her hand. So it was not uncustomary that Christopher Steele should catch Miranda Hathaway lightly in his arms and brush his lips across her cheek, her mouth. Not quite her mouth, but at a place near the corner of it where a certain star had once glimmered . . . Nor was it odd that Miranda Hathaway's fingers should briefly anchor on the cloth of his jacket, and slip slowly off his arms during the flurry of farewell.

Marjory looked on, her own sobs held behind her mouth by her palm. But she was smiling when Kit embraced her one last time and turned to follow the well-worn path down to Bridgetown.

Before he reached the last dip in the verdant green, he turned back to wave his plumed hat. Miranda and Marjory watched him swallowed from sight as if by a great green mouth. They returned sluggishly to the house, where Marjory pleated linens and Miranda supervised the lackadaisical Nell, Irish Nell, at her cooking.

Afternoon came, and Miranda materialized from the upper story wearing the breeches, boots and shirt of her last errand into London.

"Dear Lord, I thought you an intruder for a moment! I was primed to scream for aid from the fields," sighed Marjory. "What are you up to now?"

"I'm off to look over my island." Miranda thrust the Steele family pistol into her belt. She wound a length of mosquito netting onto her hat crown without removing the crimson plume. The effect was somewhere among that of a veiled London lady, a beekeeper and a Cavalier.

"A walk?" demanded Marjory, trailing Miranda to the kitchen. "You mustn't. 'Tis not proper when you're—" Marjory caught Irish Nell's gimlet eye and hushed herself until they were in the front rooms again. "Miranda, you mustn't strain yourself when you're breeding. I've heard it said a hundred times."

"Indeed. 'Tis no strain to walk up yonder ridge to overlook the island," replied Miranda, assembling her kitchen lantern and flint. Marjory followed her out the well-timbered door.

"Miranda! Kit would be furious at your doing this, and him not yet sailed. He told me I must watch over you, so that you, your—state—not go awry."

"Kit?" Miranda stopped, puzzled. "What does he know? You swore you would not tell him."

"I didn't. Not then. He . . . knew. And he found a Bridgetown physician, one Dr. MacDougal, to tend you. Later. Surely Dr. MacDougal would not recommend walks about the island—the insects, the beasts, the Caribs over the hill!"

"Quiet yourself, Marjory," began Miranda, her attention drawn over the girl's shoulder to a lounging shadow under the nearby candlewood tree.

Marjory turned to see what had captured Miranda's attention and recognized a potential ally.

"Sěnor de Salazar! Persuade her. She would walk out alone."

Francisco hung at a distance, finally raising one eyebrow and spreading his hands in a shrug. Miranda waited only long enough to see his gesture admit that he had no hold over her.

"I'll return by sunfall, Marjory. I know this island as you know Ravenscroft garden paths; don't fret."

Miranda strode away without a last glance at Marjory; she was afraid her face would shatter if someone else regarded it one more instant.

The path led upward, above one of the hillside cemeteries already well populated by twenty years' grueling settlement on a New World island. Sharply upward it climbed, like the uneven route to Don Ricardo's Cádiz villa.

'Twas odd how time turned one round in circles, as if one's entire life were a game of blindman's buff. Once before Miranda had fled and overlooked a ship Christopher Steele captained, had fled up a hill and into hazard. The landscape blurred beyond Miranda's mosquito netting, or her tears. She had intended merely a pilgrimage to see the *Dowsabelle* set sail from a prominence but two miles beyond the Hathaway plantation. Now Marjory's most recent words had ensured that more than fond memory drifted out with the tide.

He knew! Had always known. Knew that her body led her along on a lonely leash of time and he had left her to run it out alone. It was one thing to stand nobly silent while one who made the sun rise with his eyes put back to her and wafted a world away. She had been so certain that he must not know because then he would remain: she would not root him with necessity, with any obligation, no. Now Miranda savored the bitter fact that Kit knew her state and still had left her. Why had she deluded herself that she must protect him from himself?

She was climbing higher in almost direct proportion to the downward plunge of her thoughts. The trees fringed the horizon on her right, one-hundred-foot-tall signposts to the island's inner barbarity.

Miranda was high on its coral-based plateau, her face set toward the bay and something minor that moved upon it. A ship. No perspective glass was near to aid her searching eye. She would not have used one had she had it; her world was turned upside down enough without it. The sun glowed gold like a Spanish doubloon and spun brightly on the horizon. Sinking here but rising elsewhere. Setting on the sky, but rising in the sea?

The entire world was a mirror, she realized, a great watery reflective expanse that winked illusion back at the sky . . . as did the Dutchman. No wonder he had laughed at her. And let her go. She was a more potent destructive force toward herself than any other.

How could she blame Kit? He had done as she intended, and more, had kissed her at his leave-taking. Miranda rubbed her knuckles past her face, as if to polish the path his lips had taken but—what?—hours ago? Somehow her clenched fist ended against her teeth, where it dueled with the rage she always sought to quell. This time the grief and anger won, pouring in a mighty herd of sobs from her mouth, drinking greedily from the hot fountains of her eyes.

Miranda sank to her knees on Barbados earth. Always when great sorrow caught and shook one, somehow the earth was always the answer. Cool earth, seething with life.

Through her tear-starred lashes she saw the wiggle and squirm of it past her face. All she knew of Barbados insect life—the bugs that bit and stung and sucked—told her she should not lie listlessly there, an island of flesh in a sea of forest and fit meat for a half dozen pests. Miranda could not move. She hugged the ground, called it hers, beat her grief flat between it and her body. Always it seeped out to strangle her, like some smothering jungle snake. Her cries were cast downward, just as the calling birds threw theirs to the sky.

His child, she bore his child. And he had left her. As she wished him to, but longing knows no logic. Her hands made fists to beat the unyielding Barbados rock, built up from Mother Ocean over eons of patient effort. Miranda had no time for that, she required quenching now. Her sobs finally abated, like a storm that exhausts itself and retreats to store up more fury.

She lay on her back to watch the dimming blue dome above her and ran her palms along the slight swell of her midriff. His child? No, hers. It was she it anchored in, rode in, sheltered in. The thought suddenly calmed her. Yes, hers. How strange. She had not requested such a harborer, no more than she should invite the bite of a passing mosquito. Now the burden grew in her and she felt a certain pride of possession. Hers.

Once she ceased to regard it as his doing, his affair, she felt an incipient union with that within her. They were in conspiracy, they two. They were mated, as surely as a sail and the wind that fills it. It was fitting, proper, right. Her fingers fell to her sides and Miranda washed back and forth on the even pull of her body's own breathing until it calmed her.

She rolled over onto her stomach—how long would she be able to do that? she wondered—and stared down at Carlisle Bay. The setting sun was gory now and so it dyed the bay. The *Dowsabelle* was already beyond the half-circle of turquoise water and onto deep, open blue that evening dimmed to black. Her lanterns were even now flashing into tiny points on a darkening sky.

Goodbye, thought Miranda. Farewell. God be with you and fare thee well. Those little winking lights above draw you safe to land, to your home, to what you seek.

She was suddenly as warmly drawn to him as she had been racked with loss on his leaving. She felt like a great beneficent goddess on her plateau, as if her hand could dip into Carlisle Bay to fashion waves to float him home, her cheeks puff winds into the *Dowsabelle*'s departing sails. As if it didn't matter how far he roamed, as if every southwest-blowing breeze brought a particle of him back on it.

What had he talked of? The pull between one's self and a loved one as like two compass legs, each drawn in a different direction but inevitably circling back to one another. Joined by a pivot at their center.

Each human born was a pivot of two unique and sometimes warring forces, she realized. She was the pivot between the late James Hathaway and the fled Sylvia, though a rusty one. The babe within her was the thread that spun itself fine through space and through time, but still knotted her to Christopher Steele.

She tugged once firmly on her emotions—no, the tie still held. That day's last tears coursed slowly down her cheeks as she stood and dusted herself off. She licked them off her lips as they rolled by with a certain savoring. Even tears greased the mechanism, kept the pivot operational.

She struck flint to light her lantern, only then feeling the rash of stinging, burning, that was her penalty for wallowing like a lovesick sheep on Barbados' well-populated breast. Well, there she had made her bed, and so she would lie in it. Miranda had made her pact with the past and future in one sweep. Now there was only the present to get through.

Chapter Forty-six

"Miranda, you're looking so liverish. 'Tis surely time to call for Dr. MacDougal."

Miranda tried to rise in the hammock hung between two towering candlewood trees and surrendered as her swelling body weighed her back down. Marjory smothered a giggle in the loose locks wafting past her face.

"That long-faced young turnip," complained Miranda. "He'd

have me still in corsets for the birthing and have leeched all the blood out of me by now if I'd followed his prescription. No wonder he's the only physician within three days' sail; his practice is so wrongheaded that all others fear to come near it lest they be contaminated. Have you seen the tools he carries? He has more the look of a carpenter than a midwife."

"Kit said that he was truly certified."

"Truly certified for a poor excuse of a healer. How he comes simpering to pat my gown and tell me my bread is rising well, though any who weren't a blind man could see as much and not expect a handful of coins for it. And his potions and possets—oh, I'd rather bear my babe under a candlewood tree than in some bed he plays footboard to."

"Miranda. I've a mind to send Francisco for the doctor anyway. This irritation is not like yourself."

Miranda finally turned herself out of the mosquito-netted hammock by a dexterous sort of twist that deposited her on the ground like an overturned turtle. Marjory was racked between concern and laughter so equally that Miranda lurched upward on her own power.

"In Faith," she admitted, smoothing her swelling skirts, " 'tis something to be said for the Papist manner of offering a maid but three choices in life—spinsterhood, wivery and the veil. In this instance, the middle course has its hazards—but stay, Marjory. Swear you'll not send for that pudding-faced fool from Edinburgh yet. Irritable I may be; I'm not mad. This heaviness unravels all my edges."

Miranda patted back her damp hair. It fell forward again as if sprung, in slender tendrils that gave her the look of a Renaissance madonna.

She retrieved the broad leaf fan that constantly companioned her nowadays and glided slowly houseward. Her London gown was bedraggled; she'd had neither time nor opportunity to replace it. The bodice laces down her back stretched wide toward the bottom, like a mountain base. Save for that telltale trace, one would never guess her condition from the rear.

This Marjory mused upon as she trailed Miranda through the garden, dutifully attendant. Perhaps widows only naturally wore a more shadowed face during their time with child; Miranda's spirits had come and gone these last six months in abrupt turnabouts. Some days she seemed as serene as a Dutch housewife;

at others, her eyes were wild and dark, like a Gypsy's caught stealing.

Marjory's own mother had not been like that, despite the sickness that had played prologue to every delivery. Marjory watched Miranda move ponderously to face the bay and turned her own head to the fields behind them, where even now the slaves made their obeisances to the stalks they tended.

"Ingots that grow"—so Master Bell had termed the cane. As good as Spanish gold. Barbados' sweet export was rival only to the products of the Canaries, Madeira and Morocco. And no one refined the cane into piles as dazzlingly white as Barbados planters.

No wonder buying this plantation had gobbled up all the gems in Miranda's heavy little box. This very earth was grist for sudden new spears of gold. In time, money would flow back and then Barbados' sugar aristocracy could import even more gems and silks, spices, European beds and Virginia tobacco to make their durance pleasant.

Even now it grew better; Marjory could have never slept in a swaying hammock as Miranda had. She still couldn't imagine a time when all table legs had to be anchored in water cups or when foodstuff shelves were hung from tarred ropes to keep the insects away.

Master Bell delighted in telling Marjory these tales of the island's immediate past almost as much as he enjoyed trotting out Carib atrocities as an after-dinner conversational condiment.

Miranda had been too listless of late to support Marjory's polite horror with admonitions that Master Bell bridle his sadistic streak, as she used to. On such occasions lately, Miranda had even tolerated the presence of the Spanish overseer, Francisco, at table, although her eyes always watched his olive fingers toy with Kit's Venetian glass with a certain hooded distrust.

Kit. Ah, only one letter. Sydney found in France in the new King's retinue; Charles II he would be when they rethroned him. Of Philip no word. Nor word of what Kit did there these six months past. Marjory had tried confiding her worries to Miranda once.

"What does he there? In France, Marjory? Oh, do not fret. I'll be sworn he dances at the French court, side by side with the boy-king Louis, on his high red heels. He eats peacock pie and bows only to the loveliest of the Parisian ladies. That is what he does in France, Marjory. I would wager my good green gown upon it."

And she had laughed ruefully, pulling at the fabric of her swelling skirt.

So Marjory had asked Miranda's opinion no longer. No, Francisco de Salazar was the only civil person about of late, Marjory thought, watching his dark-garbed form advancing from the fields. He always wore dark clothing, despite the heat, dark clothing that seemed to mirror a certain secret mourning in the man. Marjory felt that; what he carried was kin to her own mourning, the sort of thing of which Miranda or Kit would never speak.

It demeaned a man with Francisco's arched spirit to labor on a plantation for a wage to keep roof over head and food on plate like some transported bondsman, some criminal. Yet Francisco bowed gracefully to his position, as if he were working out some Papist form of penance.

Penance: odd that Marjory had thought the word. She knew nothing of such elaborately balanced scales of the conscience. Yet Francisco always seemed to her a man who bore a burden exactly so askew, weighted all on one side. And not another.

"Good day to you, Mistress Marjory."

His tone held that teasing sort of courtesy that made her feel a girl of thirteen instead of a lady grown. Marjory noticed the pearls of sweat strung along his olive forehead; like everything else about the man, they were neatly laid out.

"How is our lady?" he inquired more softly, nodding at Miranda's sea-gazing back.

"As right as any this near to her time, I suppose," said Marjory, blushing. It still unnerved her that this barbarous land made it necessary to share such tender matters with the opposite sex, but Irish Nell was worthless for shared responsibility.

Francisco's dark lashes swept Marjory's face, marking her reticence. He stepped back a silent pace, offered her his arm and drew her away from Miranda's vicinity.

"She misses the sea, I sometimes think," said Marjory suddenly. "She is like Kit. She has no use for land." Marjory looked for the Spaniard's reaction to her insight and saw him regarding her more attentively than her remarks deserved, one eyebrow elegantly arched.

"And you?" he inquired politely. "What does Mistress Marjory have use for in this life?"

"Why, whatever is to be, I would suppose. At Ravenscroft 'twas understood I should wed some suitable Royalist when times were smoother. Then—Ravenscroft was gone. They were all gone."

Marjory looked at Francisco, faltering. He had a way of asking careless, polite questions that somehow dug deep.

"I—I must tend Miranda, help her with the babe when it is born." Marjory glanced down and removed her hand from Francisco's black-silk-clad arm. He stopped with her.

"When is that to be?"

"Soon, I think. I urged her to send for the doctor from Bridgetown. MacDougal. But she will not."

"She will have to. Shall I fetch him now? I've a pestilent matter with Master Bell, but I could delay it."

"Now? No, she might be angry with us. What is the matter?"

Now the Spaniard's eyes avoided hers, sliding to the forestation around them. His fingers smoothed his sharp beard into a finer point.

"Oh, 'tis a small thing . . . one of our men has got Bell's black Dido with child. She's a house servant so the offense is greater. Poor old Pompey will pay for his pleasure."

Marjory blushed scarlet in the clear Barbados air. Such subjects would be the death of her sensibilities, but her natural softheartedness spurred a hard question.

"What will they do with Pompey?"

Francisco searched the ground again for answer. Finally he brought his dark eyes fully on her still-flushed face. "His flesh will pay for it," he said frankly. "The brand or the whip. Perhaps they'll merely split his nose as it's a first offense. I doubt they'll go to . . . harsher . . . methods. Bell is friendly to us."

Marjory quivered under his words as if her own extremities were endangered. When she had first arrived on the island, it had seemed the most natural thing in the New World that Irish Nell should sell a decade of her life to labor for them, that the remote blacks should worship the nearby cane six days out of seven from sunrise to sundown. Servants were as air and water to her, and she did not question what drove them to their servitude.

Yet here she had finally seen that Irish Nell was merely a transported prostitute, too old and too profession-pitted to wed a plantation owner and rise with him, as her more astute sisters had done. Here she had seen that the black slaves were not a plodding sea of beings as impersonal as cattle, but human creatures who looked as if currycombed by cockroach bites, whose dark bodies beneath their scanty clothing bore the bites of vermin and their master's vengeance. She had heard of a black lackey or two in London—something clever like a court monkey in a gold-braided jacket. Here there was no gingerbread on their lot and Marjory found the reality hard to digest.

"Your worries weigh upon you, Mistress Marjory," said Francisco softly. "Clear your overcast eyes. We will see Miranda through her birthing and ourselves through whatever befalls."

His consolation cheered her; God knew she got none from Miranda. And his eyes were kind. Marjory smiled and returned to Miranda.

Francisco watched her slight form sway away. When he turned to resume his errand, his mouth was grim.

Within days, Francisco was sent upon an errand less grim but more urgent. Marjory had come running into the cane that morning, heedlessly brushing by the blacks that normally distressed her by their very existence. Francisco slapped at his cane-dusted doublet as she came, sending powdery clouds aloft.

"What is it?" he asked, catching her arm to steady her.

" 'Tis Miranda's time! I had to leave her with Irish Nell—oh, Francisco, that woman's so helpless! But I had to fetch you; come quickly."

Francisco followed the onrushing Marjory back to the house and into its upstairs bedchamber. Irish Nell rocked by the west-facing window, muttering helpless wails and Hail Marys by the dozen. Francisco summed up the scene in one quick glance, almost as if he were surveying a battlefield.

Miranda lay marooned in the heavily hung bed. She looked ghost-pale. Her face contorted even as he watched, but her teeth caught her lip and no sound came. When the pain had passed, she regarded him with the same unspoken hostility that had been her measure of him since their paths had crossed again. She was still well in hand of herself, he saw, and he divined that his presence at such a moment must be bitter. Even in agony her eyes held him at sword's point.

Francisco wheeled, pulling Marjory into the hall.

"I'll fetch the physician, belike he's analyzing the efficacy of island rum at the Green Bottle."

"No! Is the man not reliable?"

"Time will tell us, but I'll not deceive you. What manner of man rots his life aimlessly away on a foreign strand?" A smile twitched at the corner of the Spaniard's mouth. "A man like me, no? Well, perhaps our surgeon has seen better days as well and can call upon them. Tend her as best you can, and make your house slut help you. I'll return in an hour or two."

"An hour? No, Francisco!" Marjory convulsively caught his jacket sleeve. "Who knows what turns she might take in an hour? In an hour once Ben—I can't . . . Don't leave. But I must have the physician; you must go. Oh, but you'll not come back, like Ben, like them all. Like Kit. Please, Francisco . . ."

He caught her plucking hands and pinioned the pale, fluttering glance with his own dark one. His resolve seemed to forge her scattering wits into one even gray focused look again. Marjory sighed wearily, as if expelling exhausted demons.

"I'm quite right now. I'll watch over her and you go."

Francisco's gaze softened. "Fret not, Marjorita." He brought up a hand to smooth her yellow hair. "Womankind has had a way of bringing babes into the world without aid of magic or medicine since Eden was lost. 'Twill be all right."

He tilted up her grimly set chin and kissed her softly on the mouth before he set her away and clattered down the dim stairs.

Marjory stood staring into the shadowed hall, her breath bottled within her. Only a quick, careless comforting kiss, God knew, but Marjory had received the lips of no man but kin. A flush that no eye could see stole over her there in the semidark. The quick close of his arms about her, the pressure of his lips on hers—Marjory knew that she could never see Francisco again without that memory looming in her mind, without her studying the set of his lips, wondering that they had touched hers. She would have to dredge up the mystery of that moment and toy with it again and again. And perhaps never solve it . . .

A clenched-teeth moan from the bedchamber exorcised her thoughts. Trust Miranda not to scream. She would fight the pain within her even as the babe bore down for escape. Marjory sighed and returned to the bedside. Miranda's hand slid out from under the netting and wrung Marjory's.

"He's gone—?" Miranda's breath came in hard pants. "He's gone? The Spaniard?"

"Yes, but not for long." Marjory's words did not seem to reassure Miranda as she had hoped. "He'll fetch the doctor."

Miranda shook her head, the golden hair lying damp on the pillows. "I'd rather have you, Marjory."

Marjory watched the light green eyes fasten on her own with an expression of dogged trust that added another brick to the wall of self-reliance building within her. Miranda needed *her* now! She was not a mere comma to the sentence of Miranda's life, trailing after helplessly. Marjory was a parentheses to the laboring woman, she saw, someone who joined Old and New Worlds in her person and promised safety of a sort.

Her hand tightened on Miranda's. Dear Miranda, it must be hard to be so strong. Better to bend a little with the blows, as she herself did.

"Nell!" The woman wailed on despite Marjory's sharp address. "Nell, stop your caterwauling; one would think *you* were to give birth and to more than your misery. Fetch me some balmed water. Then get to Master Bell's and fetch his Bessie, that's to wet-nurse the babe."

The woman shuffled out under the rowel of Marjory's instructions, returning promptly enough with the requested bowl of sweet water. Marjory dabbed it on Miranda's face while Irish Nell leaned her grizzled red head under the mosquito netting and shook it direly, like a mournful mop.

"By the Virgin Mary an' all the saints, she has the look o' labor that'll end in the grave for 'em both together . . . There was those on Darkhouse Street unlucky enough to get with child and when the pains came before the water, 'twas always an Irishman's time of it."

"The pains came before the water? She said nothing of it. Oh, for once I long for that foolish MacDougal! Quick, get yourself to Master Bell's; we may need the wet nurse soon."

Irish Nell's tangled head shook again. "Nay. That babe'll come out as hard as a cork from a bottle o' Dutchman's brew. It has the look o' it."

Irish Nell's diagnosis was matched by her fellow Celt's more learned but no less dour opinion. Dr. MacDougal was a lanky young man with a scanty ale-colored beard. He pulled upon this insignificant sprouting with slightly shaking hands as Francisco escorted him to Miranda's bedside the promised hour later.

"How long has the lass been laborin'?"

Marjory's shyness at discussing such indelicacies had vanished with the sight of Miranda writhing on the imported linens. "Nell reports she had the pains before the water came, so 'tis at least a day, though impossible to tell, for Miranda's not one to say."

The Scotsman bowed under the netting and moved to feel the

limits of Miranda's swollen stomach. The venomous green glance that welcomed him made the freckled hands freeze in their approach. He prodded gingerly at her body, withdrawing as Miranda twisted under the spur of another delivery pain. A line of sweat started up on his pimpled forehead and marched slowly down his face.

"What is it?" Marjory had read enough tragedy in the faces around her to need no translation now.

"I fear—dinna ye clutch so at me, lass—I fear the babe be a trifle awry. 'Tis hard to be certain; the mother twists like a vixen in a trap, but I believe the birth will be a breech."

Breech. The word fell like an executioner's axe among the small company. Irish Nell and Master Bell's cook, Bessie, had entered the room in time to hear it. Irish Nell whimpered and Bessie drew the babe in her arms closer to her milk-swelled breasts. Francisco's dark shoulders heaved once and heavily.

Marjory looked first to Miranda and around to the others.

"A breech birth? But Dr. MacDougal, isn't that when the babe comes—"

"Upside doon," the Scotsman said flatly. "Feet first, as one would think a man should enter the worrrld. 'Tis the head first that gives us hope of an easy time o' it. I dinna wish to frighten ye, lass, but—" He shrugged, the ill-fitting jacket shifting off his shoulders like a forlorn hope drifting away.

"Is there naught you can do?"

"Aye. Try to pull the puir thing out, but I'm liable to break every bone in his wee body. An' hers beside. Best let the Lord midwive 'em both."

He turned to reclaim his surgical box from Francisco.

The Spaniard pulled it away like a piece of bait from a fish. "So you'd abandon her to writhe her own way out of it. Why do you think we called upon you if you can offer us no more advice than that? You'll not leave us so lightly."

Francisco had caught the physician by his jacket front. The rotten material rent like a soft scream as the sweat poured in a sheet down the man's pale brow.

"I found you swilling in yonder bottlehouse," the Spaniard went on, "dousing yourself in ale like an English lord in his village. You've taken our pay all these months and now you want to slither back to your burrow and—"

"I—I've a powder I could leave for ye to gie her. In my box if you'd hand me it."

Francisco's enraged look pierced the man's slack-lidded eyes. Then the Spaniard shook the Scotsman off, like a dog relinquishing a bone he found too lean to chew upon.

"Take yourself and your powders away," Francisco said in raw contempt. "We will fare better without them."

The Scotsman left, so shakenly the steel instruments in his chest rattled together like loose bones.

"We're better done with him." Francisco put a hand on Marjory's shoulder.

She looked up at him with even gray eyes. "Yes, but you'd better withdraw. Miranda would feel freer with only women about."

Francisco cast a troubled glance to the figure on the bed. For an instant he seemed ready to lean toward it, to say something. Instead he shrugged his elegant shrug and faded away into the downstairs parlor, where he poured Barbados rum into a glass and then sat warming it with his hands.

Above him, Miranda drifted on her bed. The mosquito netting veiled all the hovering faces, so she was pleasantly alone in her travail ... only when those blotched and raw-knuckled hands had broken through to paw her—the thought made her grimace as much with distaste as with pain.

And then the crest of pain built, like a wave that caught fire and tightened and rode up the summit of her swollen stomach and crashed in a sheet of agony on her spine, leaving a backwash that twisted slowly through her entrails until she felt she was being drawn and quartered.

It was terrible, the pain. No woman would willingly wish it upon herself. No man would lie with a woman if he knew the torture of its outcome. And yet, and yet—her body strained, even in the pain, to push forth that which still anchored in her. Ah, another mountain of anguish rearing up—Miranda whipped her head sideways and saw Marjory leaning toward her through the gauze.

Marjory, was it Marjory's hand she grasped so tightly? Miranda smiled as her blurring eyes slid over the girl's face. Marjory was growing up, she looked so serious, so—Steele-stern. Like one to be relied upon although it kill her. How good to hold Steele flesh in her own. Another kind of compass touch. A pivot tightened.

Miranda felt the pain coming to take her again. Even the Maiden could not promise such exquisite unending agony. She turned her head away and felt her fingers tighten on something warm and soft and human in its grasp.

"Kit," she cried softly. "Kit." And then the Other came and caught her in his cruel arms and made her run molten into rivers of suffering.

"What?" asked Marjory, leaning nearer. "Miranda, what did you say?" Marjory sat back on her hard little stool unanswered, her hand wrung until her fingers were compressed into tingling stalks of pain. But she would not withdraw her hand, nor would she let Bessie take her place.

They all kept vigil there, as the day darkened and Irish Nell, contrite to efficiency, lit the lamps. Only the fussing of Bessie's babe disturbed the silence. That and an occasional strangled scream from Miranda that set Francisco lurching out of his chair below. It ended, as always, and they were left to watch silently.

Finally Bessie rose and handed her babe grimly to Irish Nell and beckoned Marjory. In the dark hall, Bessie's hands tightened on Marjory's arms.

"Mistress. I fear for her. 'Twill only go on until the burden exhausts her. 'Tis naught we can do. Listen, she cries again. The screams, the pity of it—"

Marjory listened to the ironic squalling of Bessie's temporarily abandoned infant and Miranda's uncontrolled cries rising to a counterpointing pitch. Miranda would never allow herself such sounds were any will left in her.

"They'll be hearin' her down in Bridgetown," said Bessie, a break in her voice. "An' I was lookin' forward to another."

One more scream of drawn-out torment came from the bedchamber.

"Is there nothing I can do?" The low question came from the darkened head of the stairs. Francisco drawn unwilling above.

"Nothing," said Marjory.

"Save put yer sword through her, sir, and end her misery."

"Bessie! Miranda has not asked for that, and never will."

"But she be thinkin' it," said Bessie grimly. "Even the sweetest labor brings that thought sometime."

Marjory turned back to the room, waving Francisco below again. She sank to her knees by the swathed bed and prayed desperately. Anglican prayers. Perhaps the Puritans were right, perhaps God only heard the right denomination of entreaty and hers were ineffectual. Still, they were the only ritual she knew and her mind tolled them again and again, Miranda's hand caught be-

tween her own, the only remnant of her that remained attached
to an ordinary world still.

A shadow drifted across the darkness of Marjory's thoughts.

A true shadow, of this world and not another. The lamps threw
it long and lean across the pale bedclothes until it seemed to
swallow the figure there. Marjory looked up. A black woman
stood at the bed's foot.

"Here there," began Irish Nell, stirring at this invasion. Her
protestations faded as the visitor stared calmly ahead at the bed,
like a dark angel of death.

" 'Tis Black Doll from the cane fields," whispered Bessie over
the slumbering babe's head on her breast. "I've heard of her."

Marjory's puzzled eyes returned to the Negro woman. She was
ageless, but held herself with an easy flexibility. She seemed tall,
but perhaps that was merely the shadows lengthening her. Lamplight flickered over the lean proportions of her scantily clad
body—the long neck and arms, the strange configuration of
beads upon her half-naked breast.

The ebony head swiveled slowly to Marjory. "I hear her all the
way to the huts," she said. "For long time. We all hear."

As the woman's eyes turned to her, Marjory was startled to see
them glimmer blue, like pools of water in obsidian.

"I will help." Black Doll stretched forth a hand, a bag of
strange shape rattling as she wielded it.

"Pagan magic! Witchery," wailed Irish Nell, crossing herself
in triple time.

Bessie clutched her infant tighter, her hand shaping a bonnet
for its unprotected head.

Marjory stared suspiciously at the black woman. "How did
you come past Francisco?"

The blue eyes slid obliquely to her. "He sleep."

Francisco sleep at such a time? Marjory doubted it, then felt
contrite. Was Francisco not human? Had not even the disciples
slept?

Miranda's screams had ebbed to moans, even more terrible in
their weakness. Black Doll shook her amulet bag and raised another from her side.

"Brew this."

She held it stiffly toward Irish Nell, as if she knew each person's household duties without being told. Bleary eyes wide,
Irish Nell edged over and snatched away the bag, like an urchin on a raid.

"No." Marjory stood. "How am I to know what you have in that concoction? Even the Bridgetown doctor wouldn't touch her—"

"Doctor is fool. Sit."

Marjory sat, muttering protestations like prayers.

"Ask her." As the black woman pointed, Marjory turned to find Miranda's blinking gaze upon her.

"What is it?" Miranda asked weakly. "I fear . . . I feel—"

" 'Tis a, a black woman from the fields. She has some heathen potion she would give you. I will have Francisco take her away."

Miranda's pain-blotted eyes struggled through what seemed to be oceans of filmy netting to a silhouette etched at her bed's foot. She saw past the linen-draped mound of her belly to a certain unrippled calmness gathered there. That and two astonishing blue eyes in a midnight face.

"Doll, they call her, from the fields," Marjory explained.

"My name is Lusati," the woman said implacably. "I will help."

"Yes," said Miranda, lilting away on a swell of pain. Her closing lashes saw the distant blue glimmer leaning closer, and her consciousness fell into the deep unwavering color.

"But—" began Marjory, supplicating the pale face slipping from her.

"Yes," hissed Miranda.

Irish Nell tiptoed into the room, a pewter cup full of something aromatic in her shivering fingers. The black woman took it.

"All go," she instructed. The two servant women scuttled away gladly. "All." Marjory finally rustled to the door, defeated.

She went downstairs to find Francisco truly sleeping in his wide-winged chair, an untouched portion of rum beside him. Marjory drank the rum in one long dose, then sank onto the nearby settle to watch the Spaniard sleep. Her ears were aimed upward.

And there the black woman who called herself Lusati, though the planters called her the mock-fond name of Doll as if she were a London doxy, brought her mysterious brew to Miranda's raw lips.

"Drink, lady. It will loose the knot within you and we draw the little one out like a cane stalk from the earth. Straight and easy. Lusati has the gift."

She lifted Miranda's head off the sopping pillow long enough to loop the amulet bag around her neck. An aroma like earth drifted into Miranda's nostrils. Like earth and air and like water. The pain-fog slipped away and Miranda suddenly saw clearly.

"She said your name was—" Miranda again searched the remarkable azure eyes before her.

"Lusati. I am Lusati. Lusati have the gift. You must lay your life in my hand."

The woman's open palm was a mocha plain rutted by dark, almost runic lines. How odd, Miranda thought, that one's hand could be so dark above, so light below, how odd that one could feel pain coursing through one like a razor sharpening itself on one's nerves and still feel ready for the onslaught, as she did now. Miranda had time to nod once at Lusati before the agony bit into her and she was clutching the woman's hand even more tightly than she had Marjory's.

To Miranda's pain-racked mind, it was as if Lusati were the inner part of the don's Iron Maiden, that which had been carved out to create the instrument of death. Everything had both a good and an evil side; this ebony shadow was the warmer part of darkness. Miranda could surrender herself to it, she believed that, could fall upon it as she had fallen upon the dark-soiled earth of her island in her moment of deepest mourning.

There was an endurance in them both that prevailed against the despoilment of mankind. In all women, really, endurance. Miranda gave herself over into the blessed dimness that veiled her. Just as the Iron Maiden's daggers would have plumbed her, Lusati's narrow fingers delved within Miranda for the trouble's source. Miranda heard her distant commands to push with her body, and gave herself over to tumbling off some mental cliff that was a barrier to what she desired, to what must be done. The pain came with a new, industrious hardness that carried the promise of success.

She felt a corkscrewing through time, a breaking beyond retrieval, a . . .

"A daughter for you, lady."

Lusati was elevating something squalling and wriggling, a shadow as dark as she. Miranda was suddenly washed back into the reality of her weakened, sopping self. Lusati lay the shadow across the diminished linen mound of Miranda's body. An oblong of dark red and squirming flesh—Miranda laughed, though it hurt her. She laughed breathlessly at the apartness of the little creature. Hers? No, how mad to think it so. It was its own, strange self. Neither hers nor his, but of itself alone. How wondrous.

She caught it to her breast; the babe's tiny lips immediately sipped there, with a tenacious pull that brought an answering spasm from her empty belly. That long, slow swell below was as purposeful as a wand of pleasure drawing through to erase the agony there. It was a shadow of the pleasure she had felt upon the babe's conception. It seemed she still had enough blood left in her to blush at feeling that intimate piercing with two strangers in the room—one small and red, one tall and black.

Lusati still bustled between her legs; Miranda was oddly removed from all that. The blue eyes arrowed to her face once.

"We let baby drink from you now. Then we call the woman you have chosen."

It was unnecessary to call.

The bedchamber's contented silence filled the room with Irish Nell, Bessie and Marjory, shutting out Lusati's face. They all made odd grimaces at the babe, and Bessie's raw-knuckled hands obviously itched to take the child.

Miranda was wrung out enough to feel a slight relief as the burden slipped off her chest and into a fine-spun wrapping Bessie flourished like a spiderweb. Marjory was smiling, her face a moon of delight. Even Irish Nell looked dewy through the mosquito netting. Miranda smiled idiotically with them, as if they were all foreigners to each other with no other way of expressing their feelings.

"Have you needle and thread, lady?" Lusati's impassive tone plummeted through their self-congratulation. Irish Nell rustled away to return with a precious slice of German steel in her fingers.

Lusati took it, then nodded to the door. All three women fled, bearing the babe with them. Miranda lifted an anxious head.

"You see plenty enough of baby later," said Lusati dryly.

Miranda's yellow head set on the linens like an exhausted sun. "What are you doing?" she asked, appalled at more tuggings below. She was suddenly alert, anxious to talk, even laugh.

"Sew lady up. Make lady tight for baby's father." That practical earthiness of Lusati's would have made Miranda blush had not a slice of a different kind of pain come between her and her recent accomplishment.

"The babe's father is dead," Miranda said flatly.

The bright blue eyes glanced up impassively from their task.

"Make lady ready for baby's father. All things come again to their beginning. Lusati has the gift."

Miranda said nothing; Lusati tolerated no contradiction. Besides, the woman's eyes were blue and one tended to believe blue eyes . . .

"How—oh, that pinched! How did you come here, Lusati?"

"I born here."

"Born here! There were so few . . . slaves . . . on Barbados when you must have been born."

"You born here, lady?"

"No, but I came to Barbados as a child."

The woman worked in silence. When she looked up again, her light eyes were hazy, memory-filmed. "Lusati's mother come here as girl on ship with irons. My father was a freedman. White man. He die. Mother die. She name me first. You must name your baby. Child runs better with a name as a walking stick."

"Didn't I hear before that you were called something other?"

"Do you answer to every name another give you? No, lady. I am Lusati. I bear the white man's mark upon my body," she said fiercely, jabbing a long finger at her unwinking eyes. "Even as my mother bore me. My name is my own. They may spit as I pass, white or black. I have the gift."

The woman stood and sighed. It seemed too ordinary a gesture to come from her.

"Lusati return later. They"—she gestured contemptuously beyond the door—"will wish to make much of lady. And baby. I come later."

She shifted through the door and was gone. For the first time in a very long while, Miranda was alone. For the first time in a very long while, she was content.

Chapter Forty-seven

Miranda's body rebounded swiftly; she was not yet twenty. As soon as she felt well enough to sit up in her linens, she asked for Lusati.

In untormented broad daylight, the black woman assumed a more ordinary appearance. Miranda marked how the island vermin had burrowed into Lusati's skin, fond as they were of the Negro quarters. Their pink bite tracks clung to Lusati's ebony flesh like barnacles to a ship hull. She wore them as proudly as tribal tattoos.

Miranda offered her freedom.

"Freedom, lady? Lusati have freedom. But not from here. Where would I go?"

Miranda had no answer, so she sighed and plucked at the coverlet, recalling the forlorn European who had succumbed to Barbados distemper but months before under its auspices. "Then I would like you to move to the house. We will find you a gown."

"I will move to the house," said Lusati after a pause.

The gown was never mentioned again. In truth, few paid attention to Lusati's semi-bareness. Well-traveled Francisco gave it merely a passing glance. Nell and Bessie expected nakedness to be a slave's only clothing, though when Master Bell came to dine, his eyes circled in his head like cruising sharks whenever Lusati's polished breasts skimmed into view. Such visions were small pay for the sacrifice of his cook, Bessie, to Miranda as wet nurse. Yet the canny islander fared not badly; within a fortnight he had snapped up Kit's Monsieur de Rognon, and the inhabitants of Hathaway House were frequent dinner guests at Bell's more rambling stone residence.

Lusati's addition to the household instantly established an unspoken hierarchy. Irish Nell took to serving solely as housemaid, though her cleaning was ever of the lick-and-promise variety, often literally. Bessie brought forth a tastier fare from the fragrant kitchen and played nursemaid with a will, almost reluctantly surrendering the new babe to her mother's arm.

Lusati served from the first as head housekeeper and even Irish Nell dared not dispute her. Nor did anyone ever call the slave woman "Black Doll" again. Miranda had asked once of her real name's significance.

"Father—die—shortly before Lusati born," she said only.

"And your mother named you Lusati for that reason?"

"Among my people across the water, such a one as I is like a stalk of maize that stands alone in a harvested field. After all others pass, it stand still."

Miranda nodded. Like Lusati, she, too, stood alone. Neither this nor that. Neither New World nor Old World. Neither wife nor maid. As Lusati was neither black nor white.

"Have you trouble, Lusati?" Miranda paused, embarrassed.

Daylight had showed her savior to be no more than twenty

years, and yet so skilled at women's matters. "Do not the men of the huts or the town—?"

"No one touch Lusati. Lusati have the gift."

Miranda inquired no more.

The expanded domestic arrangements left Marjory finally free to collapse from the strain of attending Miranda. She began by drifting in restorative sleep, her newfound strength finally ebbing. It was Marjory's withdrawal that brought Francisco de Salazar to Miranda's bedchamber one late afternoon when the babe slumbered in its cradle.

Miranda was sitting up in bed, her yellow hair limp across her shoulders, swathed in a fine China shawl from Master Bell.

"Marjory still sleeps," he said by way of explanation, and apology, for his presence.

He handed her the posset of rum that eased any lingering discomfort and strolled to the window to look down upon the infant within its wooden cradle.

"What will you name her?" he asked abruptly.

"Name? I had not thought it," lied Miranda over the silver ellipse of pewter at her lips. "Katharine, I think."

"Katharine." He gave the name a Castillian twist. His eyebrows shot together in a question. "Was that not the name of Marjory's mother?" His look was Inquisitional, though his voice was velvet.

"I—perhaps it was. 'Tis a good English name," she added severely.

Francisco tilted his dark Spanish head to regard the babe. His eyes slid over his shoulder. "You were ever fond of things English," he said slowly, "quite proper in an Englishwoman."

He leaned down and plucked up the infant, cradling it with a vigor no woman would use. Miranda sat forward in alarm, but Francisco smiled and tilted the blanketed bundle so she could view its placid face. The child liked his rough rocking. Miranda sank grudgingly back into her linens.

"Katharine," crooned Francisco meditatively into the flat circle of face at his crooked elbow. He deposited his burden gently back in the cradle.

"How do you know what name Marjory's mother bore?" asked Miranda after a moment.

"I have spoken somewhat with Marjory, of how you left England."

"She told you of that? Our last days there?"

"Confession is good for the soul of Anglican as well as a Papist. Or do you not believe that?"

"I do not know. And have you confessed?"

Francisco stepped toward her. "The New World is no place to nurse old wounds, Mirandita. Can we not be ... peaceful ... with each other again?"

Miranda looked at him for a long moment. She had liked, admired him even, once. He had done her no direct wrong—had been loyal to Harry to the point of reclaiming him, had come to serve meekly for her here.

Her eyes were still veiled as they delved his dark ones. She was startled by the depth of feeling in Francisco's eyes even when guarded; she had always thought him sleek, elusive to life's injuries, like marble. Now she saw a below-surface fissure, a weak spot it would be easy to press upon and bring the whole man tumbling down. He needed her regard; he was contrite. She dropped her glance to the coverlet. When she spoke, her voice was lightly matter-of-fact.

"Bring my Kate to me, Francisco," she asked, holding out her arms.

He brought her the child eagerly, as if to prove his worthiness, and presented it to her waiting arms like a court porcelain. They gravely inspected the tiny, still-folded face together. Miranda recalled how Francisco had never by so much as a glance questioned her approaching motherhood, how discreetly he had skirted the amazing fact of her ballooning pregnancy. He was a man of the rapier, as subtle as a surgeon, she thought. That did not mean he had no heart.

Their eyes met, Francisco's fresh with her forgiveness in them. It was divine to forgive, she realized, feeling suddenly sick at heart that she had learned this lesson so late ... too late. Her fingers tightened on the child in her arms until it mewled.

"Gently, gently, Mirandita," said Francisco, rising to leave. " 'Tis yours, you needn't hug it to death."

He was gone and Miranda rocked the babe to quiet it. Poor fatherless thing. Poor Kate. Poor Miranda. The tears caissoned down her cheeks and made it unnecessary to mention the third name on her mind.

Miranda became as obstinate a mother as she had been a child herself. Bessie and Marjory prepared a sheltered, closed nook for the baby under a gable. Miranda insisted on keeping Kate in her own chamber near the window that was often open and doubtless admitted a dozen foulnesses and pestilences.

Nor did Miranda relinquish her Katharine to Bessie's utter care, but often lingered when Bessie nursed the child or changed the foul linens herself. Eyebrows raised at these departures from conventional wisdom, but nothing was said. While little Kate was the apple of every eye within sight, Lusati was curiously aloof from this, the object of her intervention. She seemed to have attached herself to Miranda instead and often accompanied her wordlessly about the house.

More eyebrows elevated, but Miranda was as blithely unaware of them as she had always been. There was only one person whose lilt of expression might give her pause and he was far away.

Good Bessie and Marjory and Irish Nell would have been even more appalled if they knew how Miranda would take the babe to the open shutters and stand for long minutes watching the bay twinkle in the sunlight and the local sloops come and go. The air was hot and humid now; little Kate blossomed in agonizing rashes along every crease in her small body. She squalled the nights away and Miranda often rose to rock her to intermittent silences by the night-cool windows.

This was hardly better. July in Barbados bred great stinging squadrons of mosquitoes and other airborne biters. Kate's small face and arms already had borne their share of inflamed marks. On other West Indies islands, mosquitoes were deadly carriers of malaria. One bite could have swallowed Kate whole into the time's yawning infant-mortality rate. Neither physician nor savant knew the cause of such feverish scourges.

But Barbados was a fortunate isle; malaria never dropped anchor on her shores. Nor did the cannibal Caribs who still fought a guerrilla action on other islands with tooth and nail quite literally, a last sullen rebellion against the conquering European. Even the fearful fer-de-lance, the lithe snake whose bite is the world's most deadly, forbore to slither through Miranda's island garden.

Yet her paradise, her Brave New World, had its ageless evils. Like all Barbados houses of the time, Miranda's was blind on its eastern side, windowless, because of the great tropical storms that often slashed in from that very direction. The east was also the side from which the cane fields stretched in rows of horizontal precision. At the end of their limits festered the meager, thatched-roof scab of slave huts. Miranda instinctively knew that the trade in human flesh that peopled her island now to the tune of ten thousand naked, sweating souls was a planting sowed to reap the wind: the raging, raw *Hurri-cano* of which Indies natives talked, when walls of wind and water pounded the earth for entry.

She could not even gaze on her distant bay nowadays without seeing fresh shiploads of Africans snaking ashore. It was a great trial that she could see no way to live with, or without, this fact. Freedom could not be tended like a belated present, she'd seen that with Lusati. Lusati. Already bred between two worlds and rooted into the same island Miranda loved.

Miranda's melancholy in the weeks following her delivery was only the predictability of new parenthood. She rocked Kate and hoped for a finer world for her and cast distant eyes on the world that contained them now. This was a very natural phase and no one troubled her retreat, but all went on about their business most naturally. A bit too naturally on one steamy, subtropical morning.

Bessie had just fed Kate and left. The cradle still swayed slightly, but Kate slept. So did Miranda, in that dreamy, indolent half-state in which it is so pleasant to linger. She rocked herself, in the new silk nightdress Marjory had procured somewhere, an impractical fabric in this humidity that rotted threads and rusted steel. Steel. And Steele and Steele light all our days to dusty death. And breath. Her own breath hushing in and out. The light pushing gently at her closed lids but unable to beat down the bar of her lashes. And the shhhh-hushhhh of the sea. And voices. Voices there in the water, gurgling upward in round silver bubbles. Ah, a sharp word, the bubble breaks—voices?

Miranda thrust herself to her elbows in the softly lit room. Yes, voices deep below her, downstairs. Urgent voices, drifting upward like a cold draft of warning. Miranda cocked her head. No, no bangings from the kitchen since midday. Bessie must be about errands outdoors. Someone was talking feverishly below. Rapidly. And dwindling the words to whispers. There was a quality to that sound . . .

Miranda slid her bare feet to the floor, mindless of any stray crawling things. She moved as silently as through sand out into the dark interior passage, down the stairs. The voices grew no louder, no more distinct, than when she had first discerned them. Then they stopped. Two voices, yes, definitely. Both hushed.

Miranda rounded the cramped turn of the stair and came into the front room, a place shuttered against the Barbados heat like the don's villa had been against a Spanish sizzle long ago.

Something started within the shadows. A beast raised its head and revealed itself to be two. Miranda's gasp struck the quiet like a clock chime. Once before she had seen something dark bowing over something golden. A head. Francisco broke away from Marjory Steele, still holding her in his shadowed arms.

"Miranda?" Marjory's voice was slow to come to lips that had been occupied in other than speaking. The girl's fair head glowed like a moon against the treacherous night sky of the Spaniard's doublet.

Miranda strode across the room and cracked a shutter open upon them. Francisco held Marjory still, his dark eyes meeting Miranda's over the pale head between them. Miranda swooped like an avenging ghost to the tall chest in the corner.

"Leave us, Marjory," she said carelessly over her shoulder, metal in her tone. There was no obedient rustle; Miranda turned slowly. She held one of the Steeles' twin pistols in her hand. The bright sliver of daylight hissed across its silvered butt like water dancing on a hot stove.

"Miranda!" Marjory only clung more tightly to the Spaniard's doublet, her face lengthened with alarm.

"Leave us, I said."

"N-no . . . no!"

The man beside her slowly ungrappled Marjory's fingers. "Do as she says. Rest easy, 'tis no great stir." His lips pressed once into the rippling hair at her temple. "Go now."

Marjory whispered away while Francisco went to pull open the other pair of shutters, so both sunlight and an irritating buzzing flooded into the room.

"I would not wish to hamper your aim," he noted, returning to sit on the broad side-table opposite the windows. The light etched in every dark fold of his garments, every line in his face. He crossed his arms over his chest and waited, unblinking as a cat.

"You deny nothing . . . what I saw?"

"I deny nothing that is natural to me, you should know that, Mirandita."

"Natural to you? Perfidy is your nature, Spaniard. Had I dreamed—'tis my fault for allowing you to stay."

"Your fault, your fault," he mocked. "So much is 'your fault.' Can you not leave us poor mortals even our sins?"

Miranda shifted the pistol and caught the ebbing shawl to her shoulders. Francisco remained immobile, as if he had expected—even welcomed—this moment.

"Have you no shame?" Miranda asked.

She saw Francisco retreat within himself to page through a sheaf of emotions. His glance returned to her empty.

"No. No shame. Is there not some other attribute I could produce in its place? No . . . you never were one to accept substitutes. As I was."

He was calm for a man who had been apprehended in a dishonorable act and now stood before one who had reason to hate him and bore a pistol with which to make that hatred tangible.

"But—but I had forgiven you!" said Miranda, blood finally flowing from this, her latest wound. "Now you betray me again."

The Spaniard swept his arms wide. "This, there is nothing for you to forgive in this."

"You mean that you intended nothing toward Marjory Steele?"

"Nothing more than everything, and that honorably. To wed her—"

"Wed her? Worse and worse. After what you had been to Harry and he to you? She is but a babe in such matters, and you would sweep her away with your false face, but then, you were wont to prey upon babes, if I recall. Harry—"

"Harry. Always we come back to Harry. Your forgiveness, it seems, runs as deep as my honor."

"There is a simple solution. You will leave here, vow never to see Marjory again."

"Admirably simple, save that I cannot, will not, promise it."

"But I can promise you a ball between the eyes should you ever set bootheel on Hathaway land again."

"Then keep your pistol cocked," advised Francisco, standing to face her off.

Miranda studied him for a moment, truly puzzled. "But why? Why, Francisco? Surely there is enough of what diversion you seek in the Green Bottle each night. Can you not even go that far for your debaucheries, must you always foul your own nest?"

Francisco's face hardened until his expression armed him as surely as the pistol weaponed her. "You have become a bully, my Miranda. You hide behind your pistol and your skirts to say things no man would without willingness to take up sword."

" 'Tis my house, Francisco, and I have found you, like a householder who discovers a thief engaged in an act of burglary, though it be an intangible prize you seek. I am entitled to shoot you down like the lowest footpad or cutpurse or—"

"Yes, you would like to think the worst of me; it suits you in thinking better of yourself. Do you suppose I have no aspirations, no soul, Mirandita, because I am a Spaniard and wear a dark exterior? Do you suppose I have no good intentions toward Marjory, that I do not love her?"

"How could you love her? She is nothing like you. She would not even comprehend were I to tell her how you wear reversible colors."

"She would understand better than you, Mirandita," said Francisco softly, warningly.

"Then tell me as you would tell her." Miranda's challenge was mirrored by a lift of her chin and a corresponding elevation of the gun barrel in her hand.

Francisco turned to pace the room, the light and dark from the windowed wall falling across his somber form like shadows from invisible bars.

"Did it never occur to you, Mirandita," he began, still walking so his voice was a thing that fell across her from several sides, a sort of verbal whip. "Did it never occur to you to wonder that a man who speaks two brands of the same tongue must have reason for it? No. You learned the Castillian 'esses' lisped to you and Harry as unquestioningly as you prattled the patois that would suffice in the meanest gutter. That Spanish served you well in Cádiz, no?"

He raised a characteristic eyebrow and Miranda found herself uncharacteristically shaken by the knowing gesture.

"You always thought me a gentleman of parts, fallen upon lean times, as did your unworldly wise father. Did you never think that one to the velvet born does not learn to weave homespun? That no Castillian learns to mouth street cant? Yes, adventurer, even a dishonorable one, is a role to which I have *elevated* myself. So it amuses me, to see how little you think of my improved self."

Francisco paused to sit at the table edge again, wearily, as if tired of his own story.

"I was born, though I doubt you would call it that, in the streets of Cádiz. She who bore me was likely of the streets and to the streets she left me. I remember little of my early years, save the battles with packs of curs for what little bread fell to the stones.

"I was a liar before I could speak and a thief before I could walk. The first thing I remember clearly is a vision—a chariot of gold, its wheels flashing like fire, and grinding through the offal for which I and my fellow urchins contested. 'Twas merely some grandee's coach, but I thought it a celestial vehicle and vowed to ride on one before I died . . ."

Miranda's pistol barrel had sagged lower the longer Francisco spoke. His raised eyebrow noted the fact; he caught her glance and held it.

"You know what it is to live in the streets, Miranda? Not on some balmy island, but close-packed with your fellows until you would throttle them for the air in their lungs or the bread in their stomachs?"

"I saw—some—of that in Cádiz myself," she conceded.

"Some. And when such a life is the sum of all your days, weeks, years . . . I reached an age—not a very old age, but it sufficed. Some in the streets could earn their bread by a more refined kind of larceny. That of the senses. Those who came to barter in that commodity, some wore scents and gold braid. Those I found, as they found me. When they whispered whatever endearments it suited them in their intimacies, I studied the cast of their speech and mastered it even as they thought they mastered me. They tutored me in their manners even as they spun me the coin after, or lavished some frivolous piece of clothing upon me. I apprenticed them, those well-bred dons and wealthy merchants; as they delved on the lower sides of life, I used them as a ladder to the higher. Then I cut myself free.

"I was, by all accounts, thirteen years old. I had gathered together a fine suit of pilfered and proffered clothing, a sword. When I set foot from Cádiz, I spoke only Castillian unless I chose otherwise. After some roiling about in the world, I came here, to this English island in a Spanish sea. I had learned a bit in my travels, your father taught me more. I was content. And then—"

"And then you began with Harry!"

"No. Then Harry began with me."

"Be careful, Spaniard, Harry has told me something of how that began, do not lie."

"Harry? Had told you? What?" Francisco walked toward her until the pistol levered up again. "What would Harry tell you?"

His fingers smoothed the tuft of dark hair beneath his lower lip until Miranda found her eyes fixed by the gesture.

Francisco laughed harshly. "You have become distractable, Mirandita. Come, up with your guard."

She raised both pistol and eyes at that, the eyes brimful with resentment, the pistol barrel noncommittal. Francisco leaned forward, speaking with an intensity that made her draw forward also.

"Harry told you . . . ," he guessed, "that I, I had a certain interest in you once."

She waited, breathless, for his denial.

" 'Tis true."

Miranda jumped back at his admission, like a hound who finds itself facing off a mountain cat. Francisco laughed—richly, warmly, unashamedly.

"And why not? I was a very young man. I had toyed a bit at the edges of such yens even while earning my way out of Cádiz. I was—enchanted—by the courtly aspects of such things, by that with an innocence able to cleanse my own experience. You were a fetching girl, Miranda, strong and soft and yellow as the sun—I had a bitter battle of it. The wenches in Bridgetown saw more of the rafters than they would have, had it not been for you."

His words had become as potent a weapon as the metal-fashioned one she wielded. Francisco was fencing her with his story, the truth in it was lancing at her on sharp steel barbs. He was adept at touching her there with a pinprick of reality, twisting it into a fact not worth facing and slipping back to his position unscratched. He was confessing to her, the object of his sins, and it was a terrifying experience.

"So." He crossed his arms and she saw the graceful strength of his fingers etched sharply against the dark doublet. "We have Francisco, battling to maintain his newfound honor, his aspiration as a gentleman, if you will. We have Mirandita, pale yellow Mirandita, blowing like a butterfly down the beaches unaware the net hangs like lust above her. And we have Harry.

"Did you ever know your brother, Miranda? You knew the laugh of him, the look of him. But did you see him, Mirandita, when you leaned forward to take the sip of rum from your father's cup first? Or when your fencing foil slipped past his guard and paused good-naturedly? Or when I turned from watching you and found him watching me, until I felt impaled between two looking glasses.

"I saw all this. I even saw when Harry began to turn his Miranda-green eyes on me. He was younger then. He was a beautiful boy, Harry. It was easy to slip into the old ways. I became fond of him, but I always knew him for what he was. I cannot excuse myself. I have regretted it since and even during. That which had been between myself and Harry ended with your father's death.

"He no longer needed me and I knew how expertly he had imprisoned me in my own weakness, your own remoteness. It is over, gone over with Harry to the Puritans. He was made for them. He only measures love, he does not dispense it. I told you once we had no use for any other, you and I. I was wrong about you, and that which proves it slumbers above us. I was also wrong about myself. Now there is for me only Marjory. I love Marjory, as I have never loved anyone or anything else. I will never willingly give her up."

He stopped speaking. Miranda stared at him until she understood that he had said all he would. She sat then, in the low chair at her back, that she had always known was there. The man across from her looked tall and mighty; she felt a child, sitting there in her nightdress and bare feet, holding a metallic toy she'd brought from bed . . .

He looked older, wiser than she, as he always had. Impossible to imagine that he had aspired to be her lover, he was so alien to her mind in that respect. Harry had only been a common betrayal of the flesh, after all, that is what he had been telling her, Francisco.

Miranda forced her eyes to run remorselessly over the Spaniard, recasting him as a lover, if not hers, then some other woman's. He was lithe and grave, a panther sunning on a rock. Some bitterness gathered in the dregs at the back of his dark eyes. When she had been younger, she had called it cynicism, a long and difficult word. Now she would call it pain.

She was older now. He was older as well, but not so old as she thought, not so much older than—Kit. Ah, they were contemporaries, had fenced at friendship at Thibault's Antwerp academy.

Francisco was a young man still, though he had led an old life. Now he had found a new reason for the living of any life at all. Marjory. Was it so odd? Marjory needed a shield-arm against the world, as Miranda had never had. Marjory was the real Miranda of those long-ago days, something innocent that he would treasure for the balm it brought his bitter eyes. Perhaps no man would love Marjory more gratefully than Francisco.

What would Kit say? 'Twas his sister, his friend—if Francisco could be called that by any man. And why not? Miranda stood, the pistol still caught against her waist, as if she who had so recently delivered life was still as willing to give birth to death. She cocked the pistol and its click was her answer.

Francisco stood, alert and unbelieving.

"Mirandita—" he rebuked her.

"No. I cannot tolerate it. You will never see Marjory again. I will tell her that I have ordered this, though not why, so she may blame me and not you. That is the best that I can do."

His hands beseeched the air; even this hopeless gesture had a grace that made her stomach writhe with unwanted pity. In a moment she should be calling the parson—

"Go, Francisco, and be certain that I shall surely shoot you if you come near either of us again."

He was gone so swiftly that she searched the shadows of the room, expecting him to have secreted himself there. He would always be there, Miranda realized. When a self-confessed perjurer refuses the escape of an easy lie, a breakable promise, he becomes a dangerous man. It was far from over.

She next called in Marjory and adopted a sternly fair parental tone, forbidding her sight of Francisco at least until her brother should return and judge the matter.

"But why, Miranda?"

"He is not suitable, Marjory, that is all that I can say."

Marjory stared at her for a moment with limpid, resentful eyes. Then she bowed her head with a stubborn inner resourcefulness Miranda recognized from herself. It was new to Marjory.

That troubled Miranda as much as the vision of Francisco declaring his love for the English girl as if he were the world's most welcome suitor. Miranda wandered to the west-facing window in the silence, the pistol barrel rapping silently across her palm. She was in time to see Francisco's dark form crest the ridge leading to Bridgetown below.

Something in her posture alerted Marjory, for the girl rustled over to stand mutely alongside Miranda. Their shoulders nearly brushed as both watched Francisco sink out of sight in a green wave of Barbados grasses.

Miranda turned from the window, leaving Marjory sentry

there. She brought the pistol back to the cupboard, laid it within, paused, extracted it again and finally brought it upstairs to the bedchamber, where little Kate still slept.

Miranda paused by the still cradle, her hand petting the supple covers. She was torn: were there two sides to everything? Was she always to be balanced between a nature that could deal death as well as life? Judgment as well as love? And Francisco: was he merely a man whom life had forced to drink deep from two alien brews pressed from the same grape? Right and wrong. Love and hate. Death and life. Desire and disdain. Soft and hard. No, there was no extreme between soft and hard; one's choices were always hard.

Francisco's banishment may have been hard on Marjory—it was difficult to discern how much, for she screwed into herself resentfully and refused to share her distress.

It was harder still on Miranda, for purely practical reasons. Churlish Francisco, trust the man's absence to make clear how valuable he had been! In from the fields drifted a thousand petty concerns like stinging merrywings, all falling at Miranda's feet eventually. Each one must be picked up, dusted off, placed thoughtfully in its proper place, disposed of. Luckily, Lusati welded herself to Miranda in those days, an able interpreter between two worlds that previously only the men of Barbados had bridged in any daily manner.

" 'Tis not proper," stewed Irish Nell over her kettles, "to let that black devilwoman be makin' servants of us all while she slips 'twixt house and fields like the Queen o' the Cane. So she witched the babe from the mistress—'tis no reason to be lettin' her run free like a white woman born."

Bessie sighed and clucked and sympathized and brought baby Kate over her shoulder for an expert burp. "Mistress'll have Master Francisco back, just you see; dark-favored he may be, but he knows his duties. It's no place for a woman to lord it alone, this plantation, and 'tis clear the pestiness of it already eats her."

Once again, Miranda's native stubbornness had been underestimated all round. Francisco knew of it, nursing his exile in the Green Bottle's most shaded corner and emptying a good many of its namesakes into a bitter bottomless circle of pewter between his fingers.

He, too, was torn. He swore that his love for Marjory Steele was a new moon minted from the night sky of his previous existence. He knew, too, as a dog whipped from the doorstep knows it, that he sought the scraps of love across the threshold of a house not his.

Sweet Marjory—her face flickered in the ebb of every taper, he fished it unawares from the silver-clear bay's mirrored surface. She was light, he knew that, and he would only serve to shelter her glow from any vagrant gust that might blow. He would not be wind to her, but wick. The more Francisco knew this of himself for a certainty, the more he knew that Miranda would never believe it.

He drained one last flask of hot-cold rum and left a Spanish coin upon the Green Bottle's rough-timbered table. The next sloop bound for Porto Bello carried a slender dark figure at its gunwale.

He promised nothing; save that if he stayed in Barbados, some moonless night he would storm that well-shuttered house and bring some dark ruin upon them all ... Better to sail away while sanity maintained a steady grip on one's arm. Better to leave before Miranda's pistol played period to the passive tense of his life.

Chapter Forty-eight

*F*rancisco had been gone for a week. Miranda missed him, as one misses a bad habit upon which one may pile all one's mistemper.

Francisco made an ideal scapegoat; no matter what course the man took, something in it was bound to smack of betrayal. Had he, for instance, been found dallying with Irish Nell, or Master Bell's boyish clerk, he would have been equally culpable. Miranda pondered the corner into which she had painted her conception of the man and began to wonder if it was her brush strokes and not his nature that was at fault.

Such introspection may have been humbling, but it was not allowed to last. Once again Lusati's shadow loomed over Miranda while she wrestled with a matter of life and death.

"What is it?" Only Miranda in all the household was not discomfited by Lusati's silent standing at attention *for* attention. To her the woman—girl—was a seamless presence, woven smooth without an edge of demand.

"Lady, the clouds come."

Miranda pushed away the ledger—she could make nothing of Francisco's Spanish scrawl, at any rate—and ran a hand over the back of her neck. It came away damp and grimy.

"Clouds, Lusati—what of it? I wish some clouds would come and cover my accounting, 'tis so badly botched."

"Clouds, lady, shaped like the tails of those beasts of burden that come to the island on the ships. You see, clouds come."

Miranda pulled herself up and out to the front garden.

Another steamy September day, when the island verdure was heat-polished to emerald glitter and the bay danced like water drops on hot iron. Miranda looked down to Bridgetown, inventorying the familiar. Lusati's fluid hand flowed onto her shoulder and spun her to face inland. To the east.

Rows of curved cloud wisps scaled the even blue. A huge azure fish seemed to be leaping out of the sky to overshadow the island. Miranda felt like a dishrag in Lusati's firm grip. She was tired and hot and disheartened and most likely wrong about everything she had ever thought was right. Now she stood outside like an obedient puppet and stared at a meaningless sky awash in as pointless rows of mares'-tail clouds.

"The clouds . . . mares'-tails! Lusati, have you seen a tempest come before?"

The black woman nodded. "Seven year gone by. Great wind come from demon's house at the navel of the world and blow"—Lusati's narrow arms encompassed the calm sky in a gesture—"blow all world away. Like that."

She huffed onto the humid air, her hands shaping the breath. For a moment Miranda would have sworn she saw a mist like London fog licking at the tropical humidity. A mist like the Dutchman's precursor.

"Mares'-tail clouds have come before without the tempest riding their heels, Lusati, why this time?"

Marjory had swirled out of the house to join them, concern carved into her face, as it had been ever since Francisco had left.

"Miranda! Are we under fire? Is it Spaniards, or pirates? I heard—"

"Heard?"

Miranda focused her ears on a distant drumming, a reverberation like a cannon shot, behind her. She whirled back to Carlisle Bay. Empty, save for the ordinary sprinkle of sloops and merchant ships. And then—a booming again, like a great missive hurled to the sand hundreds of yards below her feet.

As she looked, she saw that the waves rolled on Carlisle Bay in long, slow swells—like some huge underwater denizen stretching its supple spine. Each lazy curdle rolled inexorably to the foot of the town and crashed on the batteries. Somewhere, far away south in the fiendishly calm Doldrums, a monster was stirring, shaking its sea-weeded mane and stretching northwest to the Indies.

"The storm shutters, quickly! Lusati, warn the huts and Master Bell. Look below, people are already swarming upward," she told Marjory. "Thank God we settled high enough to see the demon storm if it comes and low enough to have the plateau to our back."

A sudden gust whipped Miranda's skirts elbow-high; she pushed them down and herded Marjory inside.

"What is it?" Marjory implored, following Miranda from chamber to chamber. Miranda roughly slammed shutter after shutter closed, each clap seeming to echo the deep-throated boom from the bay.

"A tempest, Marjory, a tempest to shake the gables off our houses and the heads off our shoulders. Kate . . . I'd best have Bessie keep her close, for I've much to do—rope, where would the rope be?"

"Where would Francisco have stored it?" asked Marjory, silent criticism adding timbre to her voice.

"Francisco . . . yes, probably by the huts. I'll go down."

"Alone? Miranda, you mustn't go down there alone, with the storm upon us, who is to say what they might do?"

"The slaves, you mean? They'll do what we masters will do— save our skins if we can. Let go, Marjory, I haven't time to mete out explanations. Besides, Lusati is there."

"I don't know why you trust her and not Francisco! If you hadn't sent him away we wouldn't be alone now, facing this, this—"

"*Hurri-cano*, the Indians call it, and they have lived longer with it than we. The *Hurri-cano* beast. Stay here with Nell. And look after your—tend Kate, I implore you. We may ride out the winds safe in our houses"—a blast shook roughly at the closed shutter—"but the slave huts will never stand; I must get them rope."

Miranda ran outside to read the sky. Day was dimming; she didn't even know if it was the sun's natural time to ring down on the world. The mares'-tails had galloped westward. On their heels came a thicker gray wave of cloud, colored copper along its rising edge. All of it wavered behind a misty veil of lower clouds.

Something impelled her to turn bayward—Carlisle Bay was the center of her island. She looked to it always for Kit's coming, for a bright blue orientation that never forsook her.

The monster of the Doldrums had breathed fire under the water—the two elements warred as the threatening red spread and bubbled under the bay's crystal surface. Above the water, the sun burned crimson like a blood-soaked ruby and oozed toward the horizon. The western sky flared into a fiery aurora and seemed to pulse with a sentient rhythm. Miranda shivered in the unrelenting heat and raced down to the slave huts sitting like thatched mushrooms in a natural clearing.

Lusati was there, dispensing hempen coils to darting figures that seized them and scrambled up to the forest line.

"Did you find Master Bell?" Miranda shouted into a buffet of wind that threatened to ram her words back down her throat.

"Yes, lady."

"Does he wish to join us? We're newer-built, more stones at our foundation."

"No, lady, but he wish Lusati to stay with him." The cobalt eyes glimmered with the first refraction of humor Miranda had observed. "Lusati not fear the *Hurri-cano*. Lusati wise enough to know where to fear. There are more big winds that blow from small mouths."

Three black children pulled as many loops of hemp from Lusati's wiry arms and skittered away. She was like some beneficent goddess, standing anchored in the village and dispersing rounds of lifesaving rope.

Miranda caught up a heavy armful of hemp. "We may need these ourselves. Will Master Bell ride out the tempest?"

"He say he tie himself in his hammock, as he has done before, and swing himself to sleep on the storm."

"He'll be rung like a Bell verily then, Lusati!" Miranda laughed as the wind whistled past them. "Come, we must make ourselves fast in the house."

Rain fell in sharp drops as if in agreement.

Miranda glanced up to the towering candlewood trees at the plateau's brow. Around each base a black body had blossomed, tied there in hope of rooting itself to a storm survivor. It was to the trees that Barbados' earliest white settlers had trusted when they found the island subject to the fall tempests; now they had stone-built houses to shelter them and the great trees were felled memories, save for the tangle at the island's top.

Before she and Lusati sheltered in the storm-blinded house, Miranda looked down once again on the bay. The sun had set utterly, but a crimson corona soaked upward from its deathbed. A reflected red ripple edged the crests of the slow swells that rushed shoreward.

Above, the dim and hazy sky spilled small daggers of water and slapped them suddenly with rough winds that blew first from one side, then another. The hurricane bar of dark cloud was spreading like something spilling and running against probability, against gravity upward on the dome of the heavens. Red ringed the horizon like molten metal ready to harden into something inexorable. It tightened on the world around her and drove Miranda inside to as tight a ring of worried eyes.

She avoided the glances gathered in the house's eastern room and went to pluck a slumbering Kate from Bessie's arms.

"M—Master Bell—?"

"Fret not, Bess. I'll warrant Master Bell will swing sweeter in the teeth of the storm than we huddled away from all knowledge of what happens without."

Rain drummed the stones in an audible tapping that belied her words. Then the howling began, a throaty screeching that hissed through every chink in roof or wall and kept up a wild thing's wail until they all slumped together in a corner and ignored it, staring past each other into nothing.

"I'll cradle Kate if you tire," offered Marjory finally. Miranda's arms seemed perpetually bent into a crook. She really didn't want to surrender the comforting weight, but she bowed to Marjory's contrite offer.

How easy it was to use a child as a palliative, she thought, remembering how Kate had been go-between for herself and Francisco before their latest falling-out. Francisco. Miranda glanced at Marjory's bowed head. Baby Kate reached up one of her increasingly clever hands to capture a lock of Marjory's yellow hair; the tiny hand tugged the lock down until Marjory's face was hidden. Even Miranda had to admit that she would have felt safer with Francisco still at hand.

Hours they spent there, their only sense of an outer world emanating from a wet-earth smell that seeped through the stones.

The high winds rattled the shutters so vigorously that shafts of intermittent light fell into the room like lightning bolts.

They were silent; even Kate suspended her infant gurgles. What was there to say in the dim prison their home had become? They stared at the floor, at their fingers laced upon their laps, as the oxen that pull the plough look only to the unfurrowed earth before them. After a long while, Miranda raised her head.

"It's stopping."

Lusati unwound herself—a joint creak making everyone start as if at a thunderbolt—and edged to a shutter. She pulled it open. A brilliant but diffuse light made slits of every eye in the room. Kate bawled.

They wandered wordlessly outside into a stillness so overwhelming they eyed each other to ensure that they were all belled in the same quietude. Every tree, grass blade, wave, seemed suspended in mid-motion. Only the rain moved, in gentle sheets of drizzle welcome on their sensation-starved faces.

Below in Bridgetown, the harborside buildings lay tumbled and broken. Ships piled against the shore in a kind of inebriated logic.

"Great Wave come," observed Lusati.

Miranda walked to the terrace overlooking Carlisle Bay. The eerie, half-smothered light glanced off an unlikely brassy gleam halfway up the hill: a cannon floated free of its shoreside emplacement. Below, other bemused Barbadians were scrambling to lower ground to assess the damage.

Miranda strolled along the prominence's lip, her eyes on the remote chaos below. Along here she had paced with Kate within her—waiting, waiting for Kit perhaps. Certainly waiting for Kate, and wearing all the while a path so familiar that her feet alone knew every dip and stone of it.

A foot came up hard against an unexpected obstacle. Miranda glanced down, absorbed the configuration at her toes, whirled to face the sea, paled, and finally turned woodenly to the women thirty yards behind her.

She moved toward them, her eyes glued upon them as if an instant's look away would find them vanished through the ground, what she had seen before her on that ground whirling queasily in her mind. Her eyes looked backward even as she rushed forward, and dwelt appallingly on the sunken, worm-pitted features, the thrust of bone through moldering flesh . . .

Miranda caught her arms around her waist to contain her revulsion. She knew what she had seen, knew instantly. The cemetery with its humble monuments so picturesque against the plateau's profile, the cemetery that served Bridgetown below, that she often ambled through on her way to the town.

It had regurgitated its dead in the great wash of water that had swept inland. Islands of human vomit were left stranded in various stages of decomposition. It was not enough for the *Hurricano* to make fresh dead, it must unearth the old . . .

"Inside, we must go inside!" she ordered Marjory.

"But Miranda, Lusati said 'tis likely to be calm for another hour yet. I'm weary of the dark and that endless din. I long for fresh air."

"In! Pestilence is abroad, Marjory. More die of the agues and poxes that trail a tempest than perish in its wind and water. In, all of you!"

They returned sullenly, but not too soon. Within minutes a crash came like a drumroll on the taut sky and then the storm was up all around them instantly, shrieking, gnashing, trembling, tearing, pouring, driving . . .

Miranda felt the floor flutter below her body, as if the earth itself were shivering. The earth—no, the house! She looked up to find the walls wavering stone against stone, the shutters leaning conspiratorially inward as if to whisper the news, "The house is falllling."

She clutched any odd arms about her, pulling their owners to their feet. "The house! Outside, we must get out!"

They hung back for an instant, each one appalled at moving into the caterwauling fury around them. The north wall wiggled more crazily, then slid into a heap of stone in one graceful motion, like a lady's skirt pooling on the floor as she curtsies. The most awful part of the performance was that the wind wailed so raucously that no sound was heard from that collapse of rock from rock.

Miranda paused only to press Bessie's arms more firmly around baby Kate, then herd her flock outdoors, Lusati silently at the rear, coils of hemp trailing from her limber arms like medieval sleeves.

They fought their way into a howling that made speech useless toward the nearby pair of candlewood trees. The force of the others' bodies drove Bessie, her arms clamped about the baby, into the broad trunk. Irish Nell, for once sensible, sandwiched Bessie and the infant between her muscular body and the trunk, Marjory on the other side. The tree sheltered them somewhat from the wind's most fearsome blasts but the sound and the rain oozed around it.

Lusati and Miranda beat opposite ways forward around the tree, the hemp in their hands wet and raw. They inched into the windward side and flattened against the bark, gradually passing each other to shoot suddenly around the side and into the tree's lee as the wind aided them momentarily.

Again they made the interminable round until with exhausted eyes they met again behind the three women, and the baby, all tied now by two loops to the trunk.

Miranda struggled to knot the heavy rope, almost sobbing with weakness as even that much effort seemed insupportable. What use was it to dance around a candlewood tree as if it were a Maypole against ninety miles' velocity of ill-tempered wind if the knot should not hold at the last? She twisted the rope blindly; her hair had become permanently blown into her eyes with the rain.

Finally an awkward lump of hemp held when she pulled all her weight against it. Miranda looked again to Lusati's vivid blue eyes; she idiotically envied the black woman her naturally crimped hair that resisted the wind as stubbornly as tree bark. Miranda swept her sopping strands away and held out her hand to Lusati.

The two stepped out of the candlewood's leeward shelter. The wind immediately drove them backward against their goal—the second candlewood but ten feet away.

They were thrust up against it as if knocked there by a giant fist. Together they made their infinitely weary way around to the leeward side and panted in rest a few moments. While Miranda anchored the rope, Lusati began anew her macabre Maypole dance, inching around the trunk and appearing after what seemed minutes on the other side.

She cannoned into Miranda, but her eyes glimmered triumphantly before she lifted the rope over her shoulder and circled the tree again. Miranda, left alone to embrace the soggy bark with an almost sisterly fondness for its solidity, found the steps of their survival dance reminded her of something else . . . sailors trudging round a capstan to weigh anchor—only now it was anchorage they sought.

Once Lusati finished her round and Miranda fashioned another

knot, all six of them should be safely trussed until the storm's
fury dwindled to the showers that always ended such an uproar.

Miranda's mind etched Kate into mental place in Bessie's
sturdy arms. Yes, the ropes should hold, and Kate, nestled between Bessie's cushioning breast and tree, should survive with
only a bruise or two, pray the Lord. Miranda saw the edge of
Lusati's returning shoulder and felt a surge of triumph. House
may fall, wind may blow, but—they—would—survive.

Lusati's wet obsidian limbs suddenly jerked, an unnecessary
motion. Miranda saw her mouth make a surprised circle to match
her widened eyes as a hammer of wind knocked her sideways,
off her feet, blowing her beyond the candlewood trunk.

Miranda thrust out the hand not cleaving to hemp and snagged
a stalk of arm, an elbow slipping through, a bony wrist—hold,
hold to that . . .

The wind usually gusted, now it stuttered stubbornly, never al-
laying its force. If only Lusati could drift behind the tree, behind
Miranda, not sideways, as the wind pulled her—she would be
out of it. Miranda's eyes communicated this urgent information
to the perfect circles of blue awash in white panic clinging to
her.

Lusati's dilated eyes suddenly squeezed shut and Miranda saw,
felt, the slippery flesh slide joint by narrowing joint from her
own hand. The nails raked by in parallel precision. Someone was
shrieking, but it couldn't be Miranda, though her mouth was
open for some reason and rainwater drilled into it like liquid
teeth. Lusati—!

Miranda watched the woman spin backward fifteen feet into
the rubble of what Miranda had always intended to name
Hathaway House and never had. The house was heaped like an
anthill now, even the door gone. Lusati—standing like a black
marble pillar on the gauzy other side of pain. Then peace, then
something soft and wondrous and miraculously there . . . Kate.
Lusati. Slave. Black Doll. Kate. Lusati.

The black woman was suddenly scrambling to her feet, rising
from the rubble as the wind weakened. Lusati would rise, beat
forward, join Miranda at the rope, survive—no, another gust, another sickening loss of ground, backward, to where the earth fell
away on the bayward plunge. Where the half-dead lay with their
rotting eyes watching the skies for some bull's-eye of optimistic
blue . . .

Lusati. Miranda had tried, had held 'til her own hand seemed to break from her body. 'Twas merely fate. People do die. Had died. And what could she have done for Meg MacTavish? Nothing, of course; nothing. And Kate, she had Kate to tend, she was meant to be with Kate . . . Lusati. She who came through pain. What pain would there be if Lusati never came again?

Miranda screamed in surrender. She didn't hear her own cry, but this time she knew it for hers, she felt it racking her body.

She hurled herself around the candlewood trunk into the full savage wind to unwind the rope that secured her. Now, too late, committed. She turned—over and over against the bark until she was to its outer edge, stepped once more, was scooped up by the wind, pushed toward the fallen house, the falling-away land, toward Lusati.

Her fist clenched so hard on the unwound rope that trailed her like an umbilical cord that she wondered dully if she still held it. She was tempted to open her hand to see. Stumbling, blowing forward, ankles against stone. Pain. Hair in eyes. Blind. Ah, flesh, wet and chill, but with still the pulse of warmth to it.

The wind and the rain blindfolded her; it seemed Miranda had fastened onto a forearm. She dug in her feet to slow the steady ebb westward where only gradual plummeting space and finally buckets of blue water waited them. The effort brought her to her knees with Lusati and they rolled backward, dolls a careless child had left out in the rain and soon never to be seen again . . .

Miranda forced her eyes open. Lusati's face lolled before her, a rich rivulet of blood welling from her temple, instantly diluting in the rain that lashed her face, and springing up ever-fresh as instantly. She was semiconscious and as heavy as an anchor. Miranda's skirts swelled up with a wind gust, blocked this disconcerting vision, blinded her again. The pair rolled another five feet westward, to where the sun had last taken its daily ablution, to where earth dropped sharply away to water.

Why had she untied herself when the hemp held as safely to the candlewood trunk as the hair to her head? Nothing remained to tie themselves to—no trees, no house. No hope. Once before Miranda had drifted without hope and found herself washed upon a shore she had never expected to see. Cádiz. Shimmering distant Cádiz. The vision was as sweet and clinging as honey. This was pure vinegar, pure gall: driving wind and wetness, chill and fury, smolder and slash.

Miranda's stomach overturned; together she and Lusati rolled over the terrace edge and down, beyond wind now, caught by an everyday invisible force—sheer gravity, them both caught, turning, turning, bruising, dying . . .

Miranda felt her hair circle her face like a winding sheet. Good, better not to see. The earth's smell seeped into her skin. She and Lusati would soon dissolve into such mortal fragrance. They spun together, all direction muted, up and down melded into one terrifying vortex. Time, relationships, expanded and shrank.

The feel of Lusati in Miranda's arms became suddenly and eerily similar to Kate's smaller but constant weight. No, thank God, Kate was tied to a stalk of salvation on the hill above. This was merely she and Lusati, corkscrewing into oblivion while the winds howled accompaniment. And somewhere, somewhere, did the Dutchman stand bowed over a compass rose and watch the living needle whirl endlessly? Did he laugh each time it passed the gilded letters reading "southwest"?

Miranda's hair rolled away from her eyes by a vagary of motion. She saw the sky clouded and arched above them, Lusati's head bouncing against her sopping shoulder like a coconut. Ah, a pity. Her falling band was ragged, dirty. Quite beyond redemption. She'd not need a new one now . . .

A glimmer of gold struck her senses like a trumpet. Another tumble over while earth and sky were all she saw, then that disembodied flash of something glittering and solid. The cannon. Another piece of Barbados flotsam. The bayside cannon tossed halfway up the terrace like a toy, and she and Lusati but two more playthings rolling toward it. Odd how one's senses worked.

Miranda remembered clutching the rope that was to have tied them both to the long-surrendered candlewood trunk. She could not feel that rope through her still-clenched palm, had not thought of it for years, it seemed. Yet, something told her against all probability that her battered fist still sprouted a tail of rope.

The cannon's heavy wheeled base rolled up on her left like a ball across a green that seeks to shatter the pins. Miranda cast out with her hand, swirling the phantom rope at the looming golden bulk just even with them. They rolled into the armament's lee, the lack of wind slowing them slightly.

A pale fer-de-lance of hemp reared its frayed head above her, looping over the cannon barrel like a spray of sand. Miranda clutched at that ellipsing strand.

A new and shocking stillness gripped her. She lay on her stomach on the ground, half over Lusati, her hands stretched up the terrace, now fisting upon two rope tails. They had stopped. On either side the wind streamed past with visible fury. Behind the cannon's metal hulk, they were snug in the tempest's pocket, her rope providentially looped around the massive cannon wheels.

A burning on her palms reminded Miranda that once again her own flesh had stemmed a precipitous descent; once again the ropes of her mortality had held. The needle clung to the southwest no matter who laughed.

She began to believe she survived for a purpose, and one that had more to do than with Lusati, or Kate, or even Kit, for whom she waited. It had to do with herself. An odd thing, a self, but Miranda had never had a firmer grasp upon that four-letter concept than she did lying in the lee of the great harbor cannon, an instrument of death her anchor—and in a moment a more intensive gust could unseat it, send that looming metal crashing down, the wheels rolling them both into a sort of human pastry.

No. It would not happen. The tempest would end. The cannon would hold to its new niche, just as Miranda always held to whatever thread the Fates wove for her.

Above her, the noncommittal sky cleared its throat in a roll from east to west. The Doldrums' monster shuddered and scampered to the west. Thunder. Thunder that should set the beast baying away to other islands. When the thunder spoke, the tempests always rolled over and away like a lapdog.

Once again the Iron Maiden was forced to clang shut on vacuum, to thrust her daggers into emptiness. Life always had its choices, its inner and outer teeth to mark one. The Maiden was only more obvious about it. But flesh was a kind of iron, too; mortality a variety of weapon. Trial only forged the mortal metal stronger. Time merely tempered those who would not, will not, shatter.

The Miranda who pulled herself to her feet against the cannon's golden muzzle to overlook a passive land whipped into destruction knew more about both sides of everything, including herself. Loss is but the other face of love and an inescapable coinage. Whether early or late, it will someday spin across the counter toward one, a piece of change well earned.

She had merely paid before the dance and had missed its most complicated steps. She had not spared the man she loved the drag of a generational anchor out of regard for him, but from respect for herself. It had been what she wished, always. For one's wishes one did not need revenge.

She looked to her hands in the oddly vibrant light. Blood blossomed on them, and the ruby still, not looking that much more precious than the common cabochons of red mined from her body's rich and secret veins. If mercy were only a variety of forgetfulness, perhaps love was only a mask for memory . . .

And memories were probably enough.

Memory. Few other than Miranda would have meditated on such matters in the days following the tempest.

Most were fortunate; the winds had swept away any specifics that would haunt them. A party of hardier Barbadians scoured the terraces seeking unearthed bodies to restore to their ravished earth. Sentiment moved them; few knew that the diseases that clung like lint to the *Hurri-cano*'s skirts were brought on by the putrefaction death left in its wake.

Food, fresh water, a swatch of something over their heads concerned the survivors. The slaves erected their simple huts from ravaged cane remnants with embarrassing rapidity. The masters tried to reconstruct stone on fallen stone, disdaining residence in cane product castles.

The first thing Miranda did, after finding and freeing the foursome still tied to the venerable candlewood, after seeing that Irish Nell tended Lusati's abraded brow and that little Kate occupied a cradle on Bessie's lap, was to go to the fallen house and move heavy stone from stone.

"Miranda! Master Bell has sent for us; his house still stands. Leave it. 'Tis no more use to us than Ravenscroft is to Father or Ben," Marjory urged.

Miranda paused in lifting a bread-shaped block. "Your cloak. Your warm woolen cloak of wine color. I must find it."

"My cloak? Are you mad? We've enough to worry about; 'tis the hottest season of the year, Master Bell said. We'll not need that cloak."

"We will, if we're to eat or ever erect a roof over our heads. Or feed *them*." Miranda jerked her serious and quite sane face toward the fields before bending back to her task.

Marjory looked over her shoulder toward the newly sprouted huts like the pursued in a game of seek-and-find. The blacks' very adaptability unnerved her. If only Francisco . . . for a moment some strong emotion rushed at Miranda's back, something very like hatred. Marjory swallowed its backwash and rubbed the dirty hair from her eyes like a child scrubbing away tears.

"Miranda. We must go to Master Bell's. What good is a cloak when we've no roof for our heads?"

"That particular cloak is broad enough to serve as bed and board and a good deal more. Your mother sewed the family gemstones into it."

Marjory regarded her incredulously, then stooped to set one stone aside, and another. Moments later, Lusati, her head swathed in a band of scavenged petticoat, joined them. Bit by bit, blacks came silently from the huts to help. Marjory turned with her back bowed under a stone's weight and rubbed shoulders with a bare ebony limb. She froze, looked around the silent methodical company, then bent to her pile again. She had exchanged one unsettling glance with the blue-eyed Lusati and had marked a calm assertion in that unnatural eye that buttressed her suddenly, like stone, like European stone.

By the time they had moved stone from weary stone, sifted through collapsed floorboards converted to splinters and excavated the remains of Marjory's wardrobe, it was a dusty piece of scarlet wool that Miranda fished from the ruins.

She sat instantly on the ground and began to butcher out hem stitches with a dagger point. Marjory stood behind her so the slaves would not see the jewels ... A sapphire from an onyx face winked amusedly in her direction. Lusati shepherded the blacks away.

"Powder." Miranda's voice was flat, her palm dusted with a few grains of green. "Emerald dust." They stared helplessly at the palm, still raw from its struggles with the rope. Marjory felt contrition wash across her and the salt of it pool in her eyes. Miranda's finger probed viciously in the material. She abruptly plucked forth a bent but gem-set necklace that flashed red and white in the daylight.

"Emeralds are the softest, I've heard. Perhaps more rubies have survived."

Miranda lurched to her knees to mine the bedraggled cloth until it yielded a rubble of gold, sapphires, rubies, diamonds even, as well as more powder, more broken remnants.

"This was my Grandmother Warring's!" cried Marjory, elevating a dusty headpiece. "Surely we shan't sell them?"

"What else are they worth to us now?" asked Miranda. "I'll have to sail for Porto Bello. The Spaniards will pay Peruvian plate for such trinkets; not a great deal, but perhaps enough." She stood, her foot catching in her forest-green hem and punching one more rent.

"Master Bell will get me passage. I'll go as soon as I can."

Marjory caught up the jewelry in the cloak corners and carried it herself down the path to Bell's still-solid house. She said no more about preserving the jewels, not even when Miranda, brushed and mended in her green gown, hatted in one of Master Bell's out-of-fashion London beavers, collared in something plain and rather pathetic from Bessie's simple stock, took up the chest and bade her goodbye the next day.

" 'Tis for this they were intended, Marjory. I'd not sell your heritage had I any other way. Look after Kate. I'll return before a fortnight is past."

Marjory nodded, the bitterness of her loss making it easy to overlook the fact that Miranda was venturing alone onto the Caribbean waters, to Porto Bello, where the Spaniards retired after their forays against the Dutch and English.

She didn't even stop to think that the reason the jewel chest weighed so low in Miranda's grasp was something else salvaged from the Steeles'—a well-primed pistol riding atop the box's precious cargo.

Miranda looked back at her island as she wafted out of Carlisle Bay on a trim little sloop. The ravaged terraces looked like heavy-lidded eyes. The shoreline settlement had fallen into the drooping dishevelment of an unhappy mouth. Her island was a fever victim who had survived the malady and now must face the world weakened, shorn, forever marked. Miranda felt much the same. The calling birds that circled the mast tops sounded even more mocking than before.

Miranda clutched her chest and went below, to the small guest cabin, where she rocked quietly with the box on her knees.

It was a bright blue and yellow day; the sloop *Victorine* fed her canvas to the breeze and rolled speedily out to sea. She'd been fresh careened and painted and was a pretty sight, her prow bucking the waves like a princeling's pony out for a romp.

So she appeared in the perspective glass to the mariner's eye that followed her for a moment as she slipped onto rolling ocean. A pretty sloop, that made one think three decks as lumbering as an elephant and a towering poop the palanquin atop it.

The watching eye swiveled to shore, to Bridgetown and all it

held. There was a bareness to the slopes, an overglaze of mudd
brown and surely a spire or two less among the rooftops? An
there, that glint halfway up the terrace below Master Bell
plantation—by God and King Charles, no battle on earth force
a forty-pounder to retreat half a mile up an incline . . . unless
be a battle of earth and the elements.

The perspective glass lowered from the spectator's features
unveil a troubled face and worried blue eyes. It revealed Chris
topher Steele Barbados-bound and not sure he would like wha
he found.

The commands he called back to Bacon echoed in only ha
his mind. The other half barked warningly at the future and di
no more to repel it than the family dog does an invited guest

Chapter Forty-nine

M iranda had gone to the *Victorine*'s gunwale and instantly re
gretted it. The sailors marked the chest she carried, an
their shrewd eyes peered under the hat brim to assess her fac
her figure.

She tried the box latch to see if it opened quickly and held he
place. The sun moved high over the masts and turned the pitc
between the boards to acrid-smelling obsidian pools. It was to
hot below anyway.

A crown of perspiration gathered under the hatband and mean
dered down her face, stinging like fire ants. She moved to la
board, looking ahead as always. Empty ocean. And two nervou
nights in the tiny cabin below, nodding over her chest with pistc
in hand, before she would be on land again. Spanish land. Port
Bello on the Central American neck. Porto Bello. Famed for i
fleshpots and bottlehouses, for wealth and sin.

Francisco. Had he gone there? Much there would welcom
him, more beyond a common tongue. She almost wished sh
could find Francisco, rely upon him to help her in a foreign city
Never. She had depended upon him once and found him a blad
that bends. Never.

A sailor shouted at the rim of her consciousness, then anothe
The *Victorine* lurched suddenly, as if her helmsman steered he
against the waves, then a sort of flying fish catapulted the bow
and splashed into spray in the waters beyond.

A nine-pounder behind Miranda belched on the open deck, spilling a powder smell that a rough hand spun her to face. She looked into the tension-folded features of the *Victorine*'s master.

"Below," he said with a jerk of his head, and spun away.

Behind him she saw a three-masted ship in full sail bearing closer, her cannon barrels glinting in the sun with each toss she took on the waves. Another cannonball leapfrogged the *Victorine*'s bow, universal seaman's language for surrender. The sloop's crew merely plied their canvas more frantically. One stopped for no vessel in these waters, unless one liked the scent of match powder under one's nails or impressment into a pirate crew.

In Captain Pentreath's memory, Miranda obeyed the *Victorine*'s nameless commander and ducked below. She found the minuscule cabin hot and pitching, but if Brothers of the Coast pursued them, 'twould be best to make a stand. She unboxed her pistol, sat on the chest and held the pistol butt braced against her breastbone. Her eye nailed the door's inner latch into place, though she saw it to be flimsy wood, brittle, breakable . . .

A long time she buffeted there, so long that she removed the heavy hat and set it beside her, its wavering plumes ever after giving the uncanny impression that there was something else in the cabin just beyond her vision.

The *Victorine* shuddered intermittently from the recoil of her few mobile cannon and evidently desperate maneuvers that almost brought her broach to the waves. The pistol butt slammed into Miranda's diaphragm on each of the sloop's sudden shifts, but always Miranda brought it back to center and aimed it chest-high at the door.

It had been some time, she realized with a desiccated throat, since the *Victorine* had lurched any way in particular. In fact, she seemed to be standing off in the waves, rocking as passively as an oarless rowboat. Miranda ran her finger down the cold trigger curve; it had the same symmetry as the line of a cat's throat.

Killing was a sort of disembodied petting, if one wished to think that way. One stroke on the gleaming metal, one throttle, and death . . .

A clatter, a booted clatter outside her door and pounding, such pounding, without, within.

She wanted to put her hands to her ears, but she held the pistol and that was the most important thing. Shouts, laughter without, silence within. The door, exhaling, inhaling with the force of fists upon it, as ready as Ravenscroft's portal to breach inward and spill in, spill in . . .

Her name, yes, in the confusion, her own name spit faintly back at her, like a reproach or like, like welcome . . .

She stood, the door before her wavered as if viewed through the heat and then shattered open. Ah, sash and sword, boots and baldric, danger, mankind always its own worst danger, and flashing steel, teeth, blue brighter than memory, older than pain and someone dancing toward her across deck, across marble, across crossed swords, crossed purposes . . .

She knew who he was but something in her was far away and could not catch up to the moment. He, too, was stunned, for he had stepped into the cramped cabin spilling vitality, triumph, but his eyes had somehow remained shocked and six feet behind him.

They stared at each other for a long minute, learning nothing.

He finally spoke first. "My pistol—or yours now. I pray you surrender it. 'Tis new Bruges-woven silk, my jacket, and has buttonholes enough already."

So close was the cabin that his outstretched palm brushed the barrel that sprouted from Miranda's midriff like an Iron Maiden spike growing outward.

She lay the silvered butt sideways in his hand, her head cocking slowly with it, so she regarded him askew. No, that did no help. He set the pistol aside hastily, like the corpse of a dead thing it was best to hide.

"Miranda," he said, not so much as a greeting but as a question.

Oh, yes, she was she, there was no doubt about that. But he . . . he was different, nearly half a year different. She stepped sideways twice and shot him another look. Bruges weave, yes . . . elegant. The French dressed their bodies as they did their food, with light and subtle glazes, with sheen and a certain after-Eden decadence. Ah. The face. Not as bronzed as it had been and so the eyes seemed less vivid. And the trimmed sweep of a light moustache across his upper lip, the neat inverted triangle of a Van Dyck below. In Paris he had been, all right. Different. A stranger. That the pistol barrel had known more surely than she.

"Miranda." He stepped forward to shake her by the arm as if accosting a sleepwalker.

She coiled into herself and said nothing.

Kit stared at her. The milky skin had gone tawny. Her hair was nearly as silvered as it had been at the don's hands. And her eyes, her eyes were light, watery green, fathoms below vision. He was shocked at how tawdry she looked, the gown sagging, the collar plain as a Puritan's. He had never ever thought her beautiful, though he had recognized when she had appeared so; now he saw her like a precious porcelain figure that had drawn dust on some forgotten shelf and finally crackled its glaze.

"How ... how did you find me?" She took advantage of the question to swing away and brush back a damp strand of hair. She finished her circle looking slightly less disheveled.

"Why, Barbados. I sailed into Carlisle Bay as you left it. When I found Marjory and—I came after, of course, for your mission is no longer necessary."

"Of course." She stooped as gracefully as she had to the lavender cushion once and rose bearing the little chest. "You came to recover these."

She thrust the box at his chest as impertinently as she would a pistol muzzle, as if with one gesture she redeemed an old debt that he owed.

Kit looked bewildered; even through his new facial adornments she could read that.

He thrust the chest on the bunk so roughly its lid unhinged and the jewelry within spilled out until the lid snapped shut on it in mid-stream.

Her eyes accused him of treating brutally what she had struggled to salvage.

He unleashed a faint, exasperated sigh; in the confined space it heaved like a tempest blast. "I've brought money enough to keep us all in food and fashion. Money and bright new gowns and red-heeled shoes, ribbons as green as a jungle vine. I've brought an entire crew willing to sail into the New World for adventure and Spanish plate. We'll turn about now that I've convinced this sullen captain to let us board, we'll put about for Barbados."

"And will you ... stay?"

"Of course, stay. I found Sydney and Philip; they are a new breed in an old world, they are Kingsmen, new Kingsmen. I am an old one. I shall serve myself. There's much here for any man who commands a half-acre's worth of canvas and a crew to make it blow favorably. I can ferry 'tween our English outposts, dicker a bit with the Dutch, admonish a Spaniard or two and call myself an honest man. What more could a sailor ask?"

Miranda didn't answer, save with another of those disconcerting sideways glances. "Marjory would have been overjoyed to hear that," she said finally.

"She was, though I didn't linger long to elaborate. I had to catch your agile sloop before she blew into some Spaniard's net."

"What did you think, seeing Marjory again?"

"Of Marjory? Why . . . she is stronger. And sadder."

"Francisco," Miranda intoned ominously.

A long pause. "She said a bit of that. It seems my choice of guardians for you both was uncommonly misplaced. Francisco . . . I have traveled too far in too many ways to think on it now. And the surgeon—if I find the scamp lurking about Bridgetown I'll deliver him of his coward's breath."

"It was no matter. I found another—"

"Yes." Kit grinned suddenly. "Your midnight Amazon. Lusati, she said. Like has a way of calling to like. I left Marjory behind without a tremor, though I can already guess that I should fear for Master Bell—"

"And . . . my daughter, you saw her as well?"

"Yes, she is . . . safe, believe me, in Bessie's charge, if that worry you, your little—"

"Kate, yes. I call her Kate."

"Is that all you call her?"

"All? Of course, my own name as well. Hathaway. I wish to see Hathaways on this island still."

One long step brought him awash on her. "Miranda."

His hands reached for her arms, she spun, fluttered and was away despite the narrow space that caged them together.

"Miranda. I've come back for you, don't you see that? Not for Marjory, or the family gemstones or Spanish plate or even a glimpse of my daughter—"

"*Your* daughter?" It was as if he had said something unthinkable. "She's mine. My Kate. I bore her. She's naught to do with any but me."

He swept off his hat and instantly looked more familiar, meltingly familiar.

"Do you always intend to limp along on one leg, like a broken compass, Miranda? Yours. You are well aware of that. Your brother. Your honor. Your child. 'Tis a pity you cannot stretch such firm conviction to include another in your calculations."

This time the thrust penetrated bodice, bone, being. Miranda's hands came up to either side of her face and fisted. She could not believe he was saying, could say, what he had just expressed.

"And when I say 'mine' is it not always yours?" she cried in frustration. "Always, always, always. Twined through me and woven within me until 'tis like trying to follow but one strand of a braid."

His hat sliced the air to land unnoticed but neatly atop the discarded jewel case. He caught her into his arms, kissed her squarely on the first throw, a miracle of precision in so crowded environs on such a tossing surface.

She gave up her body to his claims, but the tears gathered behind her closed lids and ran glassily down her cheeks until even he could taste them and withdrew. She brushed them away openly and went to sit on her narrow bunk under the sloping cabin side.

" 'Tis no use. We've stretched our pivot to its breaking point. If some gentlemanly fancy makes you think that claiming Kate will solve anything—"

"God's Blood, Miranda!"

He stepped forward so impassionedly that he forgot to lower his head against the sloping ceiling. He knocked it roundly and backed off, his face squeezed into almost comical pain.

A certain concern brought Miranda to her feet before she thought.

Her own head came up sharply on the cabin's lowest point.

"Ohhhh!" The tears flowed fresher and then laughter spilled out as they stood watching each other rub their subdued skulls.

"Perhaps this ceiling is sense," said Kit, rapping it with his fist, "and it has knocked some into us." He ducked and drew her from her lowly retreat. "Come here, my prickly pear, and let me taste a sweeter fruit."

Miranda couldn't help herself. He was so insistent. He required a physical access to her as desperately as a tenant farmer requires passage to a stream. She was no landlord to deny him. His arms wound round her, his mouth made sweet incursions onto all her rightful property within plain view. Man was a perpetual trespasser. Ever since Eden. She broke away.

"About my daughter . . ." she began more gently.

"Miranda. I sojourned in France, where the Cavaliers linger over their bitters and dream young men's dreams about the old days. 'Tis not for me, such a life. And they are indolent, these unemployed swordsmen and gentlemen.

"They compose ballads, in every style and rhyme scheme. Some are quite rousing, others ribald. Some would break your heart, others would merely break every mandolin string within miles. Others are jocular, and being jocular, often cruel. They even composed one of Justin Waverleigh."

"Justin?" She broke away, but he only let her lean back enough to see his face more clearly.

"Yes, Justin. Justin Waverleigh. They sing rhymes in praise of his swordsmanship, his gallantry and, God save us all, his poetry. They have memorialized his duel in Pater Noster Alley in a quatrain. And they sing, in such elegantly shaded meanings, that their hero was a beast with his sword amongst the men ... and a babe amongst the women."

"No." She was genuinely shocked. "They call themselves his friends? Friends in no cause but their own cruelty. Poor Justin. How did they know when even I only guessed?"

"The tomcats on the rear courtyard wall always know more than the hearthstone tabby; it has ever been so. I'm surprised that wily Italian leopard Carmina had not discerned it."

"She was absorbed in cares of her own."

"So." He caught her closer, his voice ruffled against the grain, as if he were impatient to dispense with talking. "Let us bury young Justin together; he can have no better mourners, I think. You who loved him for the wrong reasons and I who feared him for them."

He tilted his face to kiss her but she interjected her hand between them. The new moustache tickled her palm in an oddly agreeable way.

"And your new daughter, sir, what did you think of her?" Her tone was limpid, but it was the pivotal question of the catechism she had been administering him since he had burst back into her life.

"I confess," began Kit cautiously, torn between a twinkle and paternal chagrin, "she seems a somewhat insignificant little person, quite like unrolled dough—though I discernibly see an incipient Steele forehead there, and a stubborn Hathaway will behind it. Such hands ... I imagine the Spanish would not twist off one's fingers with such unbridled glee."

They laughed together, but Miranda was still unsatisfied. "And you would not have preferred a—son?"

Kit's face smoothed into seriousness. "I have enough trouble with this big self of mine than to fret about spawning numerous small selves to mold."

"But you have some natural feelings of a father, of possession—"

"I accept but I do not possess. You're afraid that without her I should not want you and that with her I want you only because of her. This small stranger who could have been seeded elsewhere, like as not . . . Miranda, to me, the child is evidence, not motive. My motives are simpler than you think. I wish to take you back aboard the *Dowsabelle* and delve into the best of my three clothing-filled trunks. I will find you a more becoming bodice, a collar starched in the freshest French blue, ribbons—"

He was undoing all the buttons of her frayed bodice, pulling the plain collar aside, his fingers strumming on all her deeper-toned strings. She resisted slightly even as her body vibrated to his tuning. He pulled down onto the bed, rapping his head again, and while she was distracted with his injury he made further inroads on the long trail of fastenings from waist to neck.

"Kit, 'tis not the place, one knows not who may enter—"

"The Devil take them! And me as well; I have enough of paradise."

She giggled. His moustache and beard tickled abominably, but she didn't have the heart to tell him.

"I think that you do not love me," she teased. " 'Tis clear from your last words that you only aspire to be my dressmaker."

"Ah, no, that is not the height of my aspirations." His hand slipped under her skirts and climbed her bare legs with the assurance of a longtime lover's. "As soon as we return to your island, I shall seek whatever spire is left standing and plight my troth most politely before the parson." His hand began such delightfully unparsonly probing beneath her gown that she blushed to think of spires.

"Unloose me. You have become even more of a Cavalier now that your cause is dead." She slipped away, nimbly redoing her bodice until he gave up his pursuit and let her reassemble both her exterior and interior selves.

"The *Dowsabelle*," Miranda mused. "Yes, I'd like to sail on her again. Back to Barbados, then; but I agree to no more than that. I still cannot see any way for us to . . . to be both what we are and yet make a marriage of it. Forget not your hat, sir, and the chest, if you would be so good; a lady for whom you have sailed a thousand leagues for should not be expected to carry more than her own weight."

He weighed the chest upon her arms in answer, and gathering up his hat and the abandoned pistol, followed her out on deck. Bacon relieved her of the chest and burdened her with a disconcerting wink. Miranda hated to think how much could be heard leaking through the *Victorine*'s somewhat splintered timbers.

The *Victorine*'s chagrined crew regarded Miranda suspiciously and the chest she tended Bacon more avariciously than ever. Surely this sheaf of a girl in a patched gown was not worth the waste of good shot over an island sloop's bows ... the prize yonder three-master had sought must reside within that well-hinged wood now vanished over the side in the first mate's custodial hands.

Their greed helped them overlook the guarding aura with which the visiting captain escorted their erstwhile passenger to the gunwale.

Clambering over the side of even a sloop in full petticoat was not easy. Miranda had to drop off three feet above the *Dowsabelle*'s boat and collapse into the four seamen rowing her.

"A bit more nicety with your captain's intended bride," advised Kit, jumping aboard and extracting her from the clumsy assistance of his crewmen. "You'd think she was China porcelain meant for ballast, the way you pitch her around."

" 'Intended' is the word, gentlemen," Miranda amended hastily. "For myself, I am happy of a safe landing, no matter how lumpy the ground."

Kit sat her carefully on the rough wood and dusted off her hopeless skirt with his hat, an exchange of favors that saw his fine beaver the worse for the encounter.

"My dear Captain," she demurred. "I'd not have come with you if I knew I was to be dusted thrice weekly like your China porcelain. Leave it be."

The crew cast off at his nod, their eyes down from the domestic discussion that swirled at the center of their cramped little boat.

"You must get used to it," Kit told her. "I have every intention of developing into a doting husband." He smiled so engagingly that some of his good humor seeped into her face.

" 'Twill never do," she warned softly.

"Of course it will," he boomed back so vociferously that his hat plumes and his crewmen's ears trembled jointly.

"I have not the temperament of a sailor's wife," she said finally, turning her sea-green eyes to the waters that matched their troubled surface. "I am not one to sit shorebound. I am not one to wait."

"Wait? Of course you shall not, you shall sail with me."

"With you? What of the plantation, who will tend it?"

"The Devil may have it and make of it what he will. You are no farmer and neither am I, whatever island we call our home. 'Tis a marv'lous new world we have here to toy with, Miranda, we can do with it what we will. Owning a few acres of immobile land and the souls of those who tend it is not my way. My crew can desert, stay ashore, sign on at their will. They knew I was Indies-bound and sailed with me of their own desire and for a share of the profits. 'Tis all the allegiance, all the ownership, I ask, and the terms are the same for you."

"But the house—"

Kit laughed. "That heap of stones, you mean? We'll see another built, well lee of the wind-path; even a gull likes a cliffside rookery to nest in."

"But your sister—"

"Ah, Marjory . . . She may live as she likes where she likes. I do not know how long I can hold her if Francisco returns. And I care not. She must find her own way of things and I bear the Spaniard no grudge, as you do."

"Then you ought," said Miranda, with a look that forged itself to his face. The look remained adamant, but something behind it softened. "And Kate? Where, O doting one, have you made provision for Kate?"

His blue eyes glittered with almost overweening triumph. "You've your Ethiope nursemaid to watch her ashore . . . and asea, well, if my ship's cooper can sail with a raucous odiferous fowl and foul-tongued as well, I'll be sworn the captain can be allowed his own flesh, even if it be somewhat inarticulate at the moment."

" 'Tis unheard-of!"

"Aye." Kit nodded. "So were those but a century ago." He pointed to a flying-fish squadron which conveniently broke water and rainbowed across the air like an arching good omen.

" 'Tis unheard-of," repeated Miranda, looking to the seamen for support.

Those diligent oarsmen had slowed their efforts, and the more their eyes were cast dutifully downward, the more their ears yearned toward the intense debate before them.

"Is it not?" Miranda demanded of them directly.

Their captain was most annoyingly silent as they exchanged glances. Another devil-and-deep-blue-sea situation, as sailors face often enough. Their captain was no ogre, but he demanded discipline.

"Why, yes, mistress, 'tis out of common practice," began one rower after glancing nervously to the diplomatically silent Bacon. No one joined him, and once embarked, he splashed verbally on. "Not common. Babes aboard. But a wee one might—"

The blue eyes across from him were aggravatingly noncommittal, the green ones growing as ominous as a North Sea gale . . . The seaman plunged. "—might make our slack times merry and give us reason to steer well away from gales."

" 'Tis none of your affair," snapped Miranda.

Kit crossed his arms and smiled beatifically on the crushed seaman, like a schoolmaster well pleased with a habitually dull pupil who for once gives the right answer.

"This is insanity, Kit," Miranda said more softly. "You said yourself once that sailors would not sail with a female. And female I am—"

"Who am I to deny my blessings?" he said, laughing. "But you've more argument in you than a Dutchman over his cups— and I've the cure for that malady."

He plucked off her overshadowing hat and spun it backward, where it came up square on the rear rower's chest. The reluctant recipient paused to clutch it over his heart like a token, there being little else he could do with it, and his eyes were hypnotized, at any rate, on the pair in the boat's center, the captain kissing his lady as if they were marooned alone for eternity and it not long enough by half.

" 'At's the way," growled his oar partner under his breath, exchanging an approving nod with the bemused hat-bearer.

All oars had surrendered; if Kit and Miranda felt that the world had stopped, certainly their small mobile portion of it had.

Bacon in the bow looked back like a playgoer treated to an especially riveting bit of upstage action. A pretty picture, the captain with his timbers all tidied with fancy French wearables and hadn't he been an hour in his cabin selecting the garb before they even saw the curve of Carlisle Bay?

And she was a handsomer thing than one thought at first, her hair shining like a slick deck and her neat little profile dovetailing into his at a heart-tugging tilt. Shore-leave had been a while and the Indies were said to host a whole new breed of lasses, exotic raven-haired maids . . .

More than one Adam's apple bobbed in a stringy throat. Even a ramble down Stew Lane would be welcome, or a look at the ladies on Old Broad Street. Why, even the crisp white cap of a Puritan maid would be a vision worth sailing far for . . .

Miranda pushed off the alien feel of Kit's new clothes and the foreign feel of his moustache across her lips. She wanted to blush into the three pair of intently observing eyes that faced her—and the two that certainly burned into her back.

Kit ducked his head to bob for more love apples from the surface of her gently shifting expression, but the emotion now ascendant in it was caution.

"Hadn't you rather convince me at your leisure, Captain?" she asked lightly enough to stop him; it was one thing for him to throw privacy to the waves before his men; it was another for her to begin wrapping him around her small finger in plain view.

He broke away and glowered at his rowers, in direct contrast to the sheepishness he felt. "Well, get on with it. I've no desire to spend my day dallying between two ships," he growled, present words blithely contradicting past actions.

The oars hit the water in unison with guilty vigor. Conversation at the middle bench quieted by mutual accord, though Miranda dished up Kit amused sidelong-sliced glances at irregular intervals. She was, she decided, falling in love with him all over again. Perhaps she always would.

When she made her small gestures to keep him at a distance, it was herself she really looped the leash over. She didn't care how many seamen witnessed her joy. She was so perilously close to capitulation that it made her slightly delirious. Bacon knew that, regarding her as stoically as a cat over the jewel chest on his knees. The backs of the rowing pair of seamen in front of her knew it. The inner Miranda knew it and wrapped herself around it like a cat its tail around its paws.

And Kit, Kit almost knew it, else he wouldn't warm her with his eyes so deliciously. Yet it was always hard for the outer Miranda to concede anything, even her own heart. She combed her loose curls with her fingers and strained forward to see the familiar bowed sides of the *Dowsabelle*.

The entire crew, it seemed, was lined up along the gunwale, an audience for their mid-ocean drama. An audience lined up and leaning half over, laughing. As the little boat nudged its mother hull and the oars saluted into inaction, it became apparent what drew the crew to this mass desertion of their posts. Two of their company scrambled back over the gunwale from the ropes that held them near the prow where the ship's name rode.

The *Dowsabelle* was dead, *vive le* ... Miranda and Kit squinted into the shiny new letters still wet-wiggly in the sunlight. Long live the ... the *Ladylove*!

Miranda stood so quickly the little boat rocked and the seamen grabbed for the sides as Kit grabbed for her elbow.

" 'Tis their idea, not mine," he swore.

"What did you tell them?"

"Only my errand. But I like it. 'Tis a good English word for a love of a ship. Now that she's named after you, you are duty-bound to sail upon her."

"What's in a name? Not substance certainly, Master Romeo. Your crew may wear a lady's colors, but they will not rub elbows with her."

"I'll put it to them," Kit offered. "What say you men, if the lady be more than our figurehead? I've a mind to sign her on."

The laughs grew louder and more unbelieving, then a bold voice shouted down.

"What be her previous berths, Captain?"

"Loblolly boy," Kit answered promptly, "on the good ship *Salamander* out of Plymouth. I've seen her serve as bowsprit lookout and scale a rigging like the cooper's parrot. She can prime a pistol in a minute flat and, what's more than most of you, discharge it where 'tis aimed. She's as nimble with a rapier as with any needle ... and has as much love for the Spaniards as a Dutchman—"

"Enough," yelled a sailor.

"I vow we should elect the lass captain," a bold one from the back proposed.

"And—" added Bacon from halfway up the side, his eye twinkling as much as the emerald in his ear he fingered reminiscently. "And, me lads, she leads a most profitable shore party."

"Aye, you'd know about that, wouldn't 'ee, Bacon?"

"And, beyond all that," interjected Kit, quieting the peals of glee ringing down from the gunwale, "she makes the captain happy."

"Why, then, sir, 'tis done!"

"Aye, content the ship that carries eight stone of such a cargo better than two tuns of rum."

"I'm for that."

"And I!"

"But she'll have to take a new man's share to begin."

Miranda stared up into the varnished, nodding faces, tilting her head toward the sun. Such a fine mettlesome row of seamed and sympathetic faces ... why, there, for certain, 'twas Black Ned nodding under a disreputable scarf. It was! She looked quickly to Kit.

He was still less bronzed, less seamed than they, but he was smiling and nodding as well. "Aye, Ned signed on again ... and some others of the *Salamander*. Many men leave England these days. You'll recognize more faces if you'll take yourself aboard, madam." His hands at her waist lifted her toward the ropes.

She caught hold and clung for a moment, looking up, although the sunlight rinsed her eyes with a welcome sort of mist. She looked up and down the long, long row of seamen. Black Ned and yes, Smeach—could she have ever known she'd be glad to see his crafty face again? And strangers, but smiling and nodding strangers, as if they were on holiday lined up to see the Queen pass ... save England had no Queen now.

Such a fine line of sailors, all friends already, welcoming, accepting. She finally believed that she could find a place between two worlds, that she had earned it. She was proud to be one of them, to be of them, no matter how separate. This was the moment for which she had apprenticed on the *Salamander*—and it had only taken two years, a mended heart and half a world's distance to achieve.

Tears glazed her vision but she was no more ashamed of them than she would have been of a smile. The strange faces floated on the sea of emotion that buoyed her—and there between Smeach and another sailor, surely not, yes! Meg MacTavish crowding to the gunwale. *You'll tear your fine gown, girl, with such antics, let be ...*

And Captain Pentreath, shouldering into line, his sole good eye winking at her absurdly ...

And Muffin. 'Twas Muffin drawing the wooden whistle from his lips for a moment to smile and vanish like an elf behind a burly Welshman ... Wait, Muffin, wait! Her hands tightened on the ropes; she pulled one, almost expecting it to ring like a bell hung over them all.

And there, there and no mistake, a faint foggy face, not nodding and smiling like the others—could ever a face that weary reverse course to a smile? Oh, but there, very clearly there against the mast rising like a cross behind him: the Dutchman. Not smiling, not nodding. But right side up.

She saw him, she did! Had seen him, for he vanished as her eyes gave a last waver and then stilled, two tears seasoning the salt water below. No new ones came to take their place.

Miranda tightened her hands on the ropes and began climbing.

SF AND FANTASY BY
CAROLE NELSON DOUGLAS

☐ 53587-1 PROBE — $3.50
Canada $4.50

☐ 53596-0 COUNTERPROBE — $3.95
Canada $4.95

☐ 51248-0 CUP OF CLAY — $4.99
Canada $5.99

☐ 53594-4 KEEPERS OF EDANVANT: — $3.95
SWORD AND CIRCLET I — Canada $4.95

☐ 50046-6 HEIR OF RENGARTH — $4.50
SWORD AND CIRCLET II — Canada $5.50

☐ 50324-4 SEVEN OF SWORDS: — $4.95
SWORD AND CIRCLET III — Canada $5.95